THE ADVENTURES OF LAFOREST-DOMBOURG

VOLUME ONE

THE ADVENTURES OF LAFOREST-DOMBOURG

VOLUME ONE

ERIC GAUTIER

Translated from the French by Roger D. Taylor

F

THE FITZROY PRESS

Cover illustration: Eric Gautier
First published as *Garde-Marine* by Editions Pen-Gan 2012
Re-published in two volumes as *Le Bagne de Brest* and *De Saint-Malo à Savannah* by Editions Pen-Gan 2017
First published in English by The FitzRoy Press 2023

F
The FitzRoy Press
9 Regent Gate
Waltham Cross
Herts EN8 7AF

ISBN 978 1739214 227

ebook ISBN 978 1739214 234

A catalogue record for this book is available from the British Library

Publishing management by Troubador Publishing Ltd, Leicestershire, UK

Contents

AUTHOR'S FOREWORD

I have always loved maritime literature, particularly historical works about the Navy, but to enjoy my preferred books I had to read in English, as they were written by the likes of O'Brian and Forester (to name but the best, as there is a whole army of such writers across the Channel). Opposing them there is little more than Melville, for the Americans, and our own dear old Garneray. At least, for the latter, the French were not playing the role of stooge for an ever heroic and victorious Royal Navy. I would have liked to reverse the roles, but the truth is that neither the wars of the Empire nor of the Republic were especially happy ones for the French Navy.

It was the memoirs of the Chevalier de Cotignon, a Marine Guard prior to the Revolution, which sowed the seeds of this book, and which led me to embark on a voyage into the Navy of Louis XVI. This became a voyage through time which took me much further than anticipated. Like all accounts of voyages, it is well garnished with descriptions – too many, I admit, for it to be a simple 'thriller'. This was, I believe, necessary, to recreate the character of the prints and paintings of Vernet, Ozanne, Van Blarenberghe and their students, as well as the maps from the national archives. I also chose to write the story in the first person, the better to identify with my narrator, a callow young sailor somewhat in the mould of *Treasure Island's* Jim Hawkins.

Our ancestors, on the eve of the Revolution, inhabited a universe that is hard for us to imagine. We know, as we were told at school, that it was the Age of Enlightenment without electricity, but try to imagine the rest: they used objects which today would be considered useless; they manoeuvred in port without engines; they fought duels over trifles; doctors bled you for your own good and surgeons cut off your limbs; you could find moorland and proper Lower Bretons everywhere in Brittany; you had to go to the post house to collect your mail; public services, the metric system and political correctness had yet to be invented. This was the *ancien régime*!

Welcome aboard!

Eric Gautier
St Lyphard, Brittany
October 2023

TRANSLATOR'S FOREWORD

In 2013 I had the honour of being invited to Concarneau, in Brittany, to the *Festival Livre et Mer*, one of my books having been awarded the principal literary prize of the festival, the Prix Henri Queffélec. It was there that I first met Eric Gautier and was introduced to his extraordinary novels about the young eighteenth-century French Naval officer, Pierre-Marie Laforest-Dombourg. Having read them, and reread them, I knew that, however long it took, I would translate them and so make them available to an Anglophone readership. This was not with any commercial intent in mind; I simply viewed it as something that had to be done. Even now, as I write this foreword after five years' of mainly winter work and nearly half a million words of translation, I am just as astonished at Eric Gautier's achievement as I was at outset. Despite the years of repetitive toil and the endless round of editing and reworking of my original drafts, I can still read passages and feel moved; still wonder at the depth of the author's historical knowledge and exactitude, and at his ability to recreate a thoroughly convincing and vivid picture of the times; still marvel at the sureness with which he has constructed such a complex and compelling story; still admire the skill with which he has interwoven his fictional characters into the fabric of the real history and people of the day. Our hero, at outset a fifteen-year-old orphan, unsure of his genealogy (a not unimportant matter under the *ancien régime)* rapidly finds himself involved in serious affairs of state, and over the first few years of his Naval service, is thrust, often unwillingly, into direct personal contact with some of the great names of French maritime history: d'Estaing, Lapérouse, Lamotte-Picquet, de Suffren and so on.

The enemy is of course the Royal Navy, and it is refreshing to have a different perspective on the great naval actions of the pre-Napoleonic era. There is nothing rose-tinted about this perspective; the author's rigorous historical sense, backed up by painstaking research of contemporary documentation, tells it just as it was. Nothing is distorted or glorified for cheap effect. The overall impact of the writing is so much the greater because of this.

The work of translation was riddled with challenges, conundrums and dilemmas, some of which are still not resolved and perhaps never will be. There were many French institutional concepts of the time for which there are no real English equivalents; the French Naval ranking system under the *ancien régime* bore only a passing equivalence to that of the Royal Navy; the author deliberately used many now obsolete French words which are difficult to render with an appropriate eighteenth-century feel; and, of course, there are a myriad arcane technical words related to ship parts and ship handling which had to be deciphered. For that I was greatly helped by the wonderful 1848 *Dictionnaire de la Marine à Voile,* by Captain Pierre-Marie-Joseph de Bonnefoux, who had used his time in a Thames prison hulk during the Napoleonic Wars to create a lexicon of English naval terminology, which he used to good effect in his magisterial French work. Despite help from Bonnefoux, and the author himself, it is almost certain that there remain some technical errors within the translation, for which I am solely responsible.

Names and titles were problematic too, as the original French can move fluidly from, for example, *Chevalier* to *Monsieur* to *Monsieur le Chevalier* and so on. Given that the Anglophone reader already has a lot to cope with regarding the sometimes long and complex French names, let alone their variations, I have in general stuck with a single form of address for each character. On the other hand, I have tried to retain a sense of *Frenchness* by retaining French words that ought to cause no problem for the reader. So, for example, the *rue de Siam* stays as the 'rue de Siam', rather than becoming 'Siam Street'. Perhaps more importantly, I have, after much agonising and many changes of mind, retained the French definite article in the naming of ships. The cutter *le Moucheron* stays as *le Moucheron* rather than becoming 'the *Moucheron*'. I finally opted for this system as the *le* or *la* or *l'*, although uncapitalised, is really an integral part of the name and is used unfailingly in the historical documents, even in lists of ship names. A combination of the English definite article and the French ship's name sat uncomfortably on my eyes and ears. Others may take a different view.

I have not in any way changed or added material, except for explanatory footnotes here and there, but with the author's forbearance I have excised a certain amount of the original, to make it more digestible for the Anglophone reader. The excisions relate mainly to background political information that a French reader, more familiar with the names and the history, may find easier to assimilate. I have been very careful to ensure that nothing taken out in any way impacts on the narrative.

Finally, a word of thanks to my two 'readers', Annie Hill and Richard Rogers, to whom, with great trepidation, I entrusted my final drafts for reaction and comments. Their enthusiastic and positive response, along with a series of perceptive and pertinent suggestions, were of immense help, both technically and in giving me the confidence to present the finished product to a wider readership.

Roger D. Taylor
Ardaneaskan, Wester Ross
October 2023

PART ONE

FIRE AND THE DEVIL

1

My name is Pierre-Marie Laforest-Dombourg.

I was born on 20th May 1761 in an old house backing onto the ramparts of Port-Louis, beside the south passage giving access to the harbour of the same name. It was a former shipowner's house which my parents had acquired just after their marriage. For the first eleven years of my life, I lived there. During the winter evenings I would fall asleep to the sound of the swell breaking on the reefs which bounded the two entrances to the harbour and the channel into the port of L'Orient. Perhaps that is why I have always been attracted to the sea.

My father would stay with us for several months at a time, between long voyages to the far ends of the earth. He was good to me and I think that he loved me, but he was always guarded about his life and his past. I knew only that he was born in the French colony in North America, that he was an officer in the King's Navy, that he was a Chevalier of the Order of Saint-Louis, and that he had temporarily left the Navy to serve as a captain in the India Company, until 1771. My parents passed away without having the time to convey to me certain secrets which only they knew. They died one after the other within two years, my father in a winter storm in the Bay of Biscay, aboard his ship, my mother in strange circumstances, the victim of unknown criminals who stole her body.

As for myself, it seems that my own adventure, which I am now going to recount to you, truly began on an afternoon in June 1776, the 15th to be precise; the day when I learned that I had been accepted as a Cadet in the Brest Marine Guards. I had finally overcome the grief caused by the loss of my parents. My future in the Navy seemed all mapped out. I believed, like many youngsters, that my life from here on depended only on myself and, to a lesser extent, on chance. I did not know that someone else had already decided otherwise four years earlier, following events closely linked to the premature and unforeseen death of my father and the tragic disappearance of my mother. This man, of whose existence I was completely unaware, was a perverse and evil man, *like a demon vomited from hell*, who had started to take an interest in me from the beginning of 1773.

This is why, before starting my story, I must go back to the winter of 1772-3, during which misfortune fell on my family. I was then eleven years old.

2

On a cold and rainy morning in December 1772 an officer of the Port of L'Orient brought us a letter signed by the Superintendent of the Navy at Brest. I have kept this document, in which it is written that: '*...following a despatch from the Minister, the order has been given to terminate the campaign, after ten months, of the King's corvette la Fouine, under the command of Monsieur Laforest-Dombourg, Ship's Lieutenant, there being no reason to doubt the total loss of the ship and its complement on the coast of the Americas...*' My father left a widow and two orphans, my little sister having been born on 24th November 1765. It was my mother's wish to call her Anne.

Our bearer of ill tidings had arrived soaked and numb from his crossing of the harbour. He accepted without too much hesitation the glass of ratafia offered to him by Lénaïc de Lomalo, our governess. If my memory is correct, he seemed most relieved by the dignity and restraint of my mother. In fact, the poor woman had known for at least six months that there was no basis for any hope. We had learned in June that there had been no news of my father's ship since she had been separated from her division during a bad storm just after her departure from Brest in November 1771. If the authorities had taken so long to advise us of this, it was because the Commissioners of the Navy had, out of charity, delayed things to enable the crew of *la Fouine* to complete nine months of their campaign, thereby qualifying for a bigger indemnity. The families would certainly have been happy to benefit from this, if the Navy had the means to make the payments immediately, but at that time the Ministry could no longer settle its debts on time. As regards my dear mother, who was not in a needy situation, she felt that she had had to wait too long for this notification, the delay stopping her from mourning her husband in a way she thought appropriate. She now had to leave immediately for the bedside of her mother, the Baroness de Kermean, who had fallen ill several months previously, and whose state of health had deteriorated alarmingly. As the weather had turned pleasant, my mother sought passage for us aboard the first coaster leaving Port-Louis for the river Vilaine. Old Lénaïc stayed to look after the house. I was about to leave for ever the roof under which I had been born, although I did not know it.

Our passage was quick: just one day with a fresh and biting north-westerly under an icy blue sky. Once we had set off my mother seemed worried. That morning I had caught her taking off her pendant to add to its chain a strange little key of brown metal, whose design had piqued my interest. The ring of the key resembled a tiny cartwheel, reproduced with meticulous precision. It was the work of a master craftsman, such as I had never seen before. My mother wore little jewellery, and her pendant was a plain Medallion of Saint Anne d'Auray, one of those cheap souvenirs in pewter that are sold at the religious fairs in Brittany for a half-penny, but she was very attached to it.

The tender of our little boat put us ashore at sunset on the right bank of the Vilaine estuary, not far from the Abbey de Prières where we were to stop for the night. My uncle François, the younger brother of my mother, had just been named, at twenty-eight years of age, the Father in charge of Guests, at this rich Cistercian abbey. He told us that the Baroness de Kermean had passed away the previous evening. He had organised transport and had been awaiting our arrival to go to the family manor with us.

The next day we left at dawn in a light carriage drawn by four horses belonging to the Abbey. A barge took us over the Vilaine at a spot called la Vieille Roche, in the parish of Arzal, and at the Pont d'Armes we joined the salt workers' track that took us, via Saint-Molf and the Guérande road, to the edge of the Kermean estates. My mother told my uncle, within my hearing, that she had decided to take up permanent residence at Kermean and sell the Port-Louis house. She then said nothing during the rest of the journey. My little sister only dared speak to me in a whisper. The weather had grown milder. The sky was completely grey. I remember that there was not a single tree on the banks of the Vilaine, nothing but moorland as far as the eye could see. The tracks were muddy, as the ground had not yet frozen, but thanks to the good draft horses loaned to us by the rich monks of the Abbey of Prières, we reached our destination just before the Angelus.

I had always loved Kermean. The manor house was huge but plainly laid out. On the ground floor, to the left looking at the front of the house, there was a kitchen and pantry with earthen floors, in the centre of the building a huge hall with a brick floor throughout its whole length, called the 'barons' room' on account of the ancestral portraits which adorned it; and, at the other end, a room which served as a library, with a parquet floor and shelves up to the ceiling laden with books. The sleeping areas were all on the first floor. There were also huge outbuildings. Seen from the outside the property gave off an air of old-fashioned elegance, with its walls as thick as those of a fortress, its steep slate roof over the windowless attic, and its old-style windows split vertically by thick granite mullions. The house stood on the rounded summit of a crest which gently dominated the area, and was bordered by two streams flowing towards the salt marshes between Mesquer and Quimiac. In olden times, the lords of Kermean had been able to survey the whole coast across the moorland from the top of their stronghold, but since the end of the religious wars their descendants had not stopped planting chestnut and oak trees around the house. These trees now formed a dense wood crossed by a pretty avenue leading to the entrance steps of the main building.

The manor house was constructed on land of the parish of Mesquer, almost astride the boundary between Mesquer and Piriac, and half a mile north of the northern boundary of the parish of Guérande. The land was rich and well cultivated for moorland, with fields of wheat, hemp and even flax, with good pastures, two woods, saltworks between Quimiac and Mesquer, vineyards towards Piriac, and with, above all, its good folk: clay diggers and salt workers, rough, obstinate and stubborn men who, all the while balking and grumbling, had nonetheless contributed, through good years and bad, generation after generation, to the establishment of their lords' wealth.

In 1772 the estate was administered, with the greatest attention to the least detail, by its legitimate owner, the Baron de Kermean, my maternal grandfather. He did not call himself the 'owner', however, but the 'tenant by right of birth'. He was keenly interested in agriculture and had a passion for breeding horses for riding. He had acquired a Barbary stallion from the Pompadour stud farm and was attempting to cross it with local mares from Savenay and Faou. He spent most of his energy, however, battling the heathland, which took over again as soon as a field was left uncultivated. In his study he had amassed a number of practical works on agriculture and horses. In December 1772 he was still energetic, although he seemed to me to be old, perhaps because of his bald pate and the long white hair flowing freely over his shoulders.

It was on this occasion that I got to know my mother's elder brother, my uncle Jean-Baptiste, although he was always called the Chevalier de Kermean, to distinguish him from his father the Baron and his brother the monk. He was a Musketeer in the King's Household, as had been his father before him, but I only saw him in his beautiful scarlet uniform on the day of my grandmother's funeral. The officers of the Army, unlike those of the Navy, rarely wore their uniforms outside of service. At that time, he was thirty-seven years old. He was a tall, rather handsome man, blue-eyed, good company, but still unmarried. Like my father when he was alive, he always wore the flame-coloured ribbon of the Cross of Saint-Louis pinned to his jacket. That was without doubt partly why I very quickly developed an almost filial affection for him, an affection which I had not been able to keep solely for a father who had died too early.

The Baroness de Kermean was buried the day after our arrival. The lords of the estate had been inhumed for many centuries in the Manor chapel, whose paving stones were covered with inscriptions, many of them half worn away. They had nonetheless found a place for the Baroness not far from the porch, where a large flagstone was lifted and an over-sized space created for the fragile frame of the deceased. Despite her tiredness from the journey, my mother insisted on maintaining a vigil all night in the chapel, where she remained alone even during the darkest hours. At the house, everyone expressed admiration at her conduct. Nevertheless, the next morning, she seemed to me to be surprisingly fresh and reinvigorated, her face relaxed for the first time since we had left Port-Louis, as if she had been relieved of a weighty burden. Three days later, however, on the Sunday evening, she suddenly became worried again and had me called to her rooms.

'Pierre-Marie!' she said. 'I must go away for a few days. Should anything happen to me, for one never knows, I would like to be buried besides the Baroness de Kermean, in the grave that they have just dug for her. Neither she nor I are big and we will both fit in there. I have spoken about it to the Baron de Kermean. Swear that you will remind him, should I die before him...Do you swear?'

I wanted to cry. 'You think you will die while you are away?'

'No, of course not, my little soldier, I am only going to Port-Louis to collect our furniture so that the house can be put up for sale. That's all. And besides, Lénaïc will come back with me to live here with us.'

'But why are you talking about dying?'

'Just to be prudent. I'm following the example of your father who took a similar precaution. We are in the hands of the Lord. If you ever have to bury me before I have been able to talk to you about certain things, you will understand why I am asking this of you. Above all remember this: I must without fail be placed next to my mother. It is very important. Well then – do you swear?'

I swore an oath.

'Good! Your father never had a grave. You know nothing of his life, although it is worth telling about. A son must be proud of his father. I will need to tell you about one of his friends to whom he had made promises that he could not fulfil before his death. I have no news of this friend. I wrote to him before leaving our house and I hope to find his answer at the Port-Louis post. That's also why I must go there. I will explain all this when I come back. You are big enough now to understand certain things...and to help me carry this burden which so weighs me down.'

She spoke these last words in such a low voice that I was not sure whether I had heard her correctly. I would realise later that I had. I have for a long time believed that my mother had an extraordinary intuition about the tragedy of which she would be the innocent victim just a few days later, and that would mark my mind even more deeply. However, the reason for these confidences had nothing of the supernatural about them, as I would discover from my uncle, the Chevalier of Kermean, inadvertently, on a June afternoon of 1776. But I am getting ahead of myself.

I cannot help feeling a painful sadness when I recall the end of the year 1772. The festivities were restrained: it was necessary to respect the mourning for the Baroness de Kermean. However, the Baron had not been together with his three children for a long time, and they were all glad to see each other again, even if their joy was tinged with solemnity.

During the week of Christmas, the domestic servants kept a fire going every day in the great hearth of the 'barons' room'. This beautiful hall was the place we withdrew to. On the evening of 24th December, a log was burned, prettily decorated by our chamber maids with a design inspired by the one on the ceiling of the Manor chapel: a moon and golden stars on a field of azure. This log was big enough to last through to the end of the religious rites. During those long winter evenings, my grandfather and my uncle regaled me with memories of their youth and their military adventures. I listened attentively to their stories as, like any boy, I was excited by tales of this type. I will have occasion to come back in more detail to their campaigns, which had enabled them to establish close ties with people of the highest rank; this would have useful consequences later on, both for my uncle...and for me.

My mother set off on Monday 4th January, together with her two brothers, who had to return to their respective duties, the Musketeer to Paris and the monk to the Abbey de Prières where he had to be back for Epiphany. My grandfather had provided them with horses from his stables that a valet would bring back to the Manor. They would travel together until the Vilaine crossing and spend a last evening together at the Abbey. From there the Chevalier and my mother would go to Muzillac, where she would take the stagecoach to L'Orient and then the harbour pinnace to Port-Louis. As for the Chevalier, he intended to hire post horses for the return to Paris. After his years of army service in Germany, he was not afraid of three or four days in the saddle.

We rose early on that Monday to accompany the travellers to the end of the Kermean avenue. It had snowed the previous evening and the whole night. A radiant sun lit up the countryside. The air was sharp, the moors were white, and hoarfrost had made curtains of the fine lacework of the gorse and dead ferns which bordered the paths. The first part of the journey was like a pleasure outing. My mother still seemed so young and so full of life despite the sadness of her recent losses. The children of the Baron de Kermean were like their father: a clear look, a solid frame, energetic, resistant to pain, but naturally inclined to optimism.

My father had been very different: more fluid and slender in his general appearance. He was also more contained, never losing his composure. I remember his smooth face, his dark hair, his narrow almond eyes that made him look, all at the same time, sombre, impenetrable and gentle. I have always been told that I am like him, whereas my sister Anne is blonde like a true Kermean.

Our mother told us that she would not be away for long – a week, or two at the most. She wanted to sort out her business as soon as possible and relieve Lénaïc de Lomalo, who had remained alone at the house. Our old governess had nothing to keep her at Port-Louis and would come and join us at the Manor once everything had been arranged. That filled little Anne with joy, as she loved Lénaïc most dearly. While kissing me, my mother reminded me several times to be good during her absence. I protested, as usual. I have never understood why I was always thus called to order, as I had always been obedient and respectful of the advice that was continually handed out to me by members of my family and, later on, my superiors. My dear mother and her brothers said that I was a good lad at heart, that they knew I meant well, but that I was too inclined to act hurriedly and without due reflection.

Before departing, my mother asked whether, on her return, it would be possible to have a funeral service in memory of my father in the chapel of the Manor. The Baron gave his consent. He promised to have an engraved plaque made, by way of a memorial, in the name of Ship's Lieutenant Jean-François Laforest-Dombourg, Chevalier of the Royal and Military Order of Saint-Louis. My father had no family in France besides us. He was from Louisbourg, on the far side of the Atlantic and had lost all his close relatives there during the war. The name Louisbourg made me daydream. I had been told that it was an important port of the colony of New France, situated on an island, called the Isle Royale, to the south of the Gulf of Saint Lawrence. In that country the sea is covered by ice every winter. I had difficulty imagining it. I had also been told that the English had captured the town after a long and difficult siege, during which my father had fought bravely.

I had heard many times the stories of the campaigns of the Chevalier and the Baron de Kermean, and I think I knew them by heart, but I knew nothing of those of my father, as my parents had never talked about them in front of me. Later, on recalling the revelations made to me by my mother before her departure for Port-Louis, I began to think that this was not forgetfulness on their part, and that they had good reason to keep quiet. Unfortunately, I could not guess those reasons.

Two days after my mother and uncles left, it started snowing again. My sister and I spent our days in the warmth by the kitchen fire. At night, fires were not lit in the bedrooms. The servants warmed our beds, which was pleasant enough, but getting up in the morning was hard. The country folk of the estate stayed at home with their animals, behind the carefully sealed doors of their cottages. We lived in slow motion. Nobody came to visit.

It had been agreed that my mother would send us her news as soon as she could. She had to give her packets to coasting skippers who intended to call at Le Croisic. She addressed her letters to a clerk that my father maintained each year at the port to supervise the loading of the produce from his saltworks.

We received a letter on Friday 15th January. It was dated Wednesday 13th. All was going well. My mother had arranged for a Le Croisic brig to bring her back, along with her furniture. The boat was called *le Cerf-volant.* The loading of the furniture was set for Sunday 17th January during the afternoon, at low tide. The brig would be ready to sail on Monday 18th on the midday tide. Her skipper intended to call at Belle-Île for the Monday night, arriving at Le Croisic on the afternoon of Tuesday 19th at high water. My grandfather ordered his steward to hire two bullock carts and a carriage, and sent a groom from the stables to Le Croisic to alert his clerk.

Tuesday 19th January passed. There was no sign of *le Cerf-volant.* The weather was good despite the cold, but the wind had fallen away. On Wednesday morning the weather changed. I remember that my grandfather alluded to this in a loud voice when he saw me watching from the windows; proof, if it were needed, that he shared my concerns. It was so dark in the kitchen that the flames of the fire still lit the room completely, well after nine o'clock. During the night the wind had turned to a fresh south-westerly. Outside, the grey clouds brushed the tops of the bare trees, as if the sky was about to collapse on our heads. And it started to snow again on an already white countryside.

Towards ten in the morning a boy from the stables told us that archers from the Mounted Police were coming up the avenue on horseback.

There were three of them: a sergeant, a corporal and a private, mounted on dark bay mares. They were wearing blue serge uniforms trimmed with a red scarcely brighter than that of their frozen noses. Their necks were sunk up to their ears in their collars and their caps pulled down to their eyes against the wind. The Baron de Kermean ordered his groom, Nicolas Ottmeyer, to give the horses shelter. He brought his unexpected visitors into the kitchen – the only heated room in the Manor house. Having greeted the Baron, the sergeant asked to speak with him alone. The Baron de Kermean took him immediately to his private quarters on the other side of the barons' room, at the far end of the house, well away from the prying ears of the servants. The corporal and the private stayed with us in the kitchen. I remember that for soldiers I found them very ill at ease. Instead of trying to get close to the fire they kept well away in a corner of the room, standing, with their hands on the pommels of their sabres. Melanie, the cook, had twice to offer them a glass of cider before they deigned to come close to the fireplace. The corporal then told us that they were from the La Roche-Bernard brigade, but that the sergeant came from the Vannes command.

After half an hour my grandfather came back with the sergeant. He told Melanie to serve up a quick meal for the soldiers and had his groom Ottmeyer called, along with Squire Pierre-Jean Henry, the steward and tax-collector of Kermean, who lived with his family in a small house beside the entrance to the domain's avenue. The Baron asked Henry to assemble all the workforce of the manor in the barons' room and ordered his groom to saddle his horse and prepare a travel bag, adding that he would leave within the hour for Vannes, together with the Mounted Police archers.

I can still picture my grandfather as he was at that moment: seated in his usual place at the end of the table, behind him the vast hearth, on ordinary days cold and fireless, of the great heraldic chimneypiece of the barons' room. With his left elbow leaning on the edge of the table, his right hand on his knees, his shoulders relaxed, his head high, his neck straight, he watched intently as the chambermaids and the kitchen maids, the laundrywomen, the stable lads, the coachmen and the labourers, all the servants employed by the manor, lined up behind Squire Henry. They arrived one by one, the men with cap in hand, and ordered themselves in silence, exchanging questioning looks. A maid brought a chandelier and placed it gently on the table beside the Master.

It was altogether too dark on this snowy morning. The glow of the candles lit the face of my grandfather and on seeing his expression I guessed that something serious had happened.

My little sister came close to me without a word and shyly put her hand in mine. She was just seven years old. Monsieur de Kermean wanted to talk to her first.

'Mademoiselle Laforest-Dombourg...'

But he could not continue, his voice suddenly strangled, his shoulders shaking with a pain that he could not contain, trying vainly to hold back his tears in front of his people, every one of them gripped by his emotion, without yet knowing the cause. In a manor like Kermean, living to the rhythm of country work, the relationship between the servants, the tenant farmers and the Master were based on a kind of brutal frankness which did not stop the naturally stubborn and loud-mouthed Bretons from complaining, but which in the end rested on a form of mutual respect. There was no hypocrisy in their dealings with each other. It was quite different from what I saw later in certain grand and refined houses in Paris or Versailles. Melanie, who had left the archers at their meal while she came to listen at the half-open door of the pantry, had the presence of mind to bring my grandfather a glass of brandy that he emptied in one draught before continuing.

'Your mother will not be coming home today, my child. She has been...delayed...I don't know for how long. Go with Jeanne Gregoire, she will make you a glass of hot milk in the kitchen. I'll come in a moment to say goodbye as I've got to go and find your mother with the soldiers who came this morning.'

After my little Anne had left the room, in the company of the girl who was to be her new governess, as we would soon discover, the Baron de Kermean told us what the sergeant had just revealed to him.

On the morning of 18th January, a messenger sent by the superintendent of the Vannes Admiralty at Hennebont had presented himself to the Lieutenant-General of the Admiralty at Vannes itself. He carried a message saying that our house at Port-Louis had been attacked by unknown villains, that the interior of the house showed signs of violence, that old Lénaïc had been savagely murdered, and that her body had been found but not that of my mother. The enquiry into these tragic events was the responsibility of the Vannes Admiralty, as they had occurred at a port where it had an office and where there was a military garrison, and because my mother was the widow of an officer of the King's Navy. The Vannes Admiralty had responsibility for investigating all the crimes and transgressions committed within the maritime sector from the mouth of the Laïta to the Vilaine. Monsieur de l'Espinay, the Lieutenant-General of this Admiralty, had entrusted the enquiry to his deputy in charge of criminal investigations and had ordered the Vannes Mounted Police to inform the Baron de Kermean, who was known and respected throughout the province.

My grandfather announced that he was leaving for Vannes with the horsemen from the Mounted Police. He would stay there for a while to follow as closely as possible the enquiry undertaken by the Admiralty. He also wanted to deal with the funeral arrangements for poor Lénaïc and see the notary who handled my parents' assets. He appointed Squire Pierre-Jean Henry to act for him in his absence and to represent him on the Parish of Mesquer Council. He would send him instructions by the Abbey de Prières' mail. His son, the monk, would send on his letters to Kermean. He then spent a while in his library with his right-hand man to give him detailed instructions on the management of the estate during his absence, whose length he could not predict in advance. Then, still shaken by what he had just learned, he mounted his horse and left immediately, dragging in his wake the sergeant and his two horsemen.

I too felt unspeakable grief on learning that my mother had been kidnapped and poor Lénaïc murdered. The news of these terrible events hit us while we had scarcely begun to overcome the consecutive pains of the loss of my father and the death of my grandmother. Moreover, these last two events, although infinitely sad, were no more than part of the natural order of things: shipwreck for a mariner, sickness for an old person, and could not be considered totally unpredictable. But as far as my mother was concerned, she had disappeared in the murkiest of circumstances. It was, to be sure, more difficult to accept than if we had been told of her death.

I could not eat or sleep after the departure of the Baron de Kermean. I would soon have fainted with exhaustion, were it not for the energy and action of our groom Ottmeyer. When leaving, my grandfather had told him to have me riding without delay, and the good Ottmeyer stuck to his task. He had me woken at dawn and after a light breakfast sent me to saddle and bridle my horse. Then, whatever the weather, he had me circling the meadow opposite the entrance to the stables, from where he could keep an eye on me while getting on with his work. The Ottmeyer method was very simple: one hour at a walk, one hour at a trot, half an hour at a canter, then back to a walk before returning the horse in its head collar to the stable where I rubbed it down myself. In the afternoon I started again with a new horse. With this regime my thighs were soon bloody, but my appetite came back and I was dropping off to sleep by the evening. Ottmeyer was not a Breton but from Alsace, as his name indicated. In his youth he had served in the Dauphin's Cavalry. He had been wounded at the Battle of Lutzelberg in 1758, in Germany, at the same time as my uncle, who had then taken him into his service. After the war the Chevalier had placed him at Kermean, where the Baron soon came to appreciate his reliability and his knowledge of military horses.

At the end of January, a letter from Vannes arrived via the Abbey de Prières. Baron de Kermean had addressed it to his steward who then passed it on to me as it contained instructions for me. The Baron had decided that it was high time for me to start serious study. He had discussed this with the Abbot de Meaux, Father Superior at the Abbey, and following a strong recommendation, it had been agreed that the Father Superior of the College of Saint-Yves in Vannes would accept me as a pupil in his establishment. My grandfather arranged for me to meet him at the Abbey de Prières on Saturday 13th February. Ottmeyer would accompany me and bring back my horse. I would not need much baggage, just a simple holdall would suffice, as I would be fitted out once I got there.

That is how I found myself a student at the College of Saint-Yves. I did not become a boarder straight away, as I was living at first with my grandfather. He had installed himself on the first floor of an inn in a square that the people of Vannes called the Manlière Square. This square is overhung by corbels projecting out over the uneven flagstones. From here it is impossible to see the roofs of the cathedral, as the houses are so crowded together. The cathedral is nonetheless very close and moreover, when my grandfather opened the windows during the day, you could hear the hammering and singing of the workmen still engaged in the refurbishment of the Choir of Saint-Pierre. During the three years I spent at Vannes, from February 1773 to June 1776, there was always work going on at the cathedral.

3

The Vannes Admiralty made remarkable progress in unravelling the mystery of the disappearance of my mother and the murder of Lénaïc: by the end of March all had been explained. Monsieur de l'Espinay, Lieutenant-General of the Vannes Admiralty, went so far as to provide the Baron de Kermean with a copy of the memorandum concerning the enquiry. This document, which I have managed to keep, is made of three different files on three different cases which at first sight had no obvious connection between them. At first the enquiries had stalled on account of this. Then suddenly, in March, the discovery of a new element enabled all the established facts to be tied together and the enquiry brought to a firm conclusion.

The principal document was composed of a verbal witness statement made at Port-Louis to the deputy criminal investigator of the Admiralty. This statement, given on 20th January, made it possible to establish that our house had been attacked six days earlier, during the afternoon of Thursday 14th January, by persons unknown who had come to the house in a carriage and had left the same evening. The sentinels at the town entrance reported that there were three men, two inside the coach, whom they had not seen, and a coachman in a green overcoat driving a sturdy chestnut horse with a pale mane and tail. The travellers had said that they were going to see Squire Murphy, which was later revealed as false. The apparent motive for the crime was the theft of an object of value hidden somewhere. The body of poor Lénaïc had been retrieved from our well and the surgeon who had examined her had established that her neck was broken. The body of my mother had not been found and it was assumed that she had been taken away by the assailants. Nonetheless, the traces of blood in the house suggested that there had been a double murder, even if only one victim had been found. I will just give here the deposition of the under-officer of the Port-Louis garrison who had been the first to arrive at the scene of the crime:

> *...has appeared before us Pierre Guimar, sergeant of the Condé infantry, age thirty-four years, garrisoned at the Port-Louis citadel at the time of the events. Who, after having raised his hand and sworn to tell the truth, stated that he was on guard at the postern of the Citadel with twelve riflemen of which three were sentinels on Sunday the seventeenth of January. Towards a quarter after three he saw arriving Squire Caro, carter, who told him that he had gone to an appointment at the house of Madame de Kermean, widow of the Ship's Lieutenant Laforest-Dombourg, to load up her furniture, but nobody had answered. Guimar had ordered the infantryman Kermel to take an axe and follow him. He first knocked on the door of the Murphy house, the only house close by in that part of the town, where the servants told him that they had not seen or heard anything at Madame de Kermean's house since at least Thursday, and that she had not been at Mass that morning. He then ordered Kermel to open the gate with his axe. He saw nobody in the courtyard. Snow covered everything and there were no signs of footprints apart from his own and those of his infantryman. On the floor inside the stable were horse droppings at least two days' old and an empty fodder sack. He saw that the door to the house was open and he went in. In the hallway, a display cabinet had had its glass smashed and there were many blood stains on the stone floor. Planks had been torn up from the landing of the main staircase to disclose something apparently hidden there by the owners of the house. This hiding place was empty. All the fireplaces were cold. In the bedrooms the beds had been shifted and the flooring torn up in places. He heard Kermel call him and he went back down into the courtyard. The infantryman was*

leaning over the well and showed him the body of a woman on the surface of the water at the bottom. He left the infantryman to guard the door, returned to his guard post and ordered his corporal to send two armed infantrymen as sentinels to relieve Kermel and to organise a guard rota. He had then gone to report to his captain.

This present deposition having been read to him by our assistant, he said that it was the truth, that nothing needed to be added or taken out, and that he held by it...

The other statements, notably those of the soldiers on duty at the gates of the town, established without doubt that the alleged assassins could be no others than the three strangers who visited on Thursday 14th in the coach driven by a coachman in a green overcoat. The detailed descriptions of this band, contained in these depositions, was later found to be very useful.

The discovery of an empty hiding place indicated the motive for the crime. I knew of the existence of this hiding place. My father had constructed it himself during the first week of September 1771, just after his final return from India. The old oak staircase leading to the first floor of our house at Port-Louis was wide and was composed of two flights turning at a right angle by following the walls. There was already a cupboard under the landing between the two flights. My father had installed a false ceiling inside this cupboard, thus creating a space that was accessible only by lifting the planks of the landing above it. He had done that himself, without the help of a carpenter, and I had helped him, as far as a child of ten years of age can help an adult in this kind of work. Once finished, this hiding place was completely invisible to anyone who did not know of its existence. As I was already showing some talent for drawing, my father had asked me to make a sketch of his work. I made it using graphite, and to show that I well knew how to write, I signed it by copying my name. My father did not tell me what he intended to do with my drawing. My parents of course told me never to say anything about this hiding place, but I did not know what it was for. When I told all this to my grandfather, at Vannes, he took me straight away to the criminal investigator of the Admiralty, who took down my deposition and asked me to reproduce the sketch which I had given to my father, which I did without difficulty. These two documents were added to the original file of the enquiry, at the

Admiralty office. The investigators presumed that my father had put together some savings during his long voyages to the Indies, and that the criminals had got wind of it.

The second part of the dossier consisted of a statement signed on Friday 15th January at Port-Louis by the Admiralty superintendent of that port: that is to say, two days before the discovery of the attack on our house and five days before the hearing conducted on the spot by the criminal investigator of the Admiralty. At first sight there was nothing to suggest a link between the two incidents.

Some fishermen had pulled out from the harbour a body which was being carried off by the ebb tide. At that stage, the Port-Louis office had no reason to ask the King's Prosecutor to draw up an action, or even to start an enquiry. The superintendent had simply questioned the witnesses informally and had the body examined by the chief surgeon of the garrison, whose findings he had reported, along with some comments:

> *We had the body examined by Jean-Marie Lahaye, chief surgeon of the Condé Infantry at the Citadel of Port-Louis, who declared the following:*
>
> *Firstly: that the victim had had his throat cut very cleanly, evidently by a well-sharpened knife blade, that there were slight wounds to the head, that the body was still somewhat stiff despite its time in the water, from which it can be deduced that death was at some time during the night between Thursday and Friday.*
>
> *Secondly: that the victim was a man of five feet in height, well-built but rather thin, a full round face, an average nose flattened at the base, pale beard and short hair, seemingly light-coloured eyes; a scar on the right side of his forehead. Probably about thirty years old.*
>
> *Thirdly: having undressed him we found the letters GAL[1] branded by hot iron on his right shoulder. Following that we examined his ankles and found clear signs of lesions caused by the manacles worn by convicts.*
>
> *Other observations and conclusions, made by us etc.…*
>
> *The individual was wearing chamois-coloured breeches, soft boots*

1 Translator's note: *GAL*: indicates *Galérien* – a convict sentenced to 'the galleys' – i.e. hard labour.

of black leather, a chamois-coloured bodice, a grey serge jacket. All these clothes new and of good quality. The jacket pockets were empty. However, there were found in an inside pocket of the bodice three écus and a certificate of which the printed parts were still intact but the parts hand-written in ink were illegible because of the time spent in the water. To wit: a "Release of a convict from the Superintendent and Controller of the Navy at the port of (illegible) certifying to whomever it may concern that on the order of the King dated (illegible) that the here-named (illegible) has been released from the chain and given full and entire liberty."

We interviewed local experts, who by analysing the tides concluded that the body had been thrown into the water more than four miles up the River Ponscorf or the River Hennebont. In conclusion it seems we have before us the body of a recently released convict who was killed on the night of the fourteenth to the fifteenth of January, upstream in one of these rivers by the afore-mentioned distance.

We have sent a copy of this report to Monsieur the King's Councillor, Lieutenant-General of the Admiralty in Brest, entreating him to kindly make enquiry of Monsieur the Superintendent of the Brest Prison as to whether the above description matches that of a prisoner recently released at the end of his sentence, and have sent another copy to Monsieur the Superintendent of the Hennebont Admiralty for his information...

The Port-Louis superintendent had finished by asking the Admiralty investigator at Vannes for permission to bury the unidentified body in a common grave without further delay; this was in fact why the report had been produced quickly.

The third part of the enquiry dossier came from Hennebont. It had not at first been meant to go to the Vannes Admiralty, or even the King's local investigator. It was a straightforward case following a complaint made by a private individual who hired out carriages. The complaint was against a Nicolas Dugoin, who had hired a carriage and a Breton post-horse, a chestnut with a light-coloured mane, saying that he was a carter by profession, that he was enlisting as a volunteer in the expedition being mounted by Baron de Benyowski at L'Orient, and that the hire was for gentlemen of his retinue. Dugoin had paid a deposit, but he had not returned the carriage within the allotted time.

The client had not been found, but the carriage had been found the same day at a mill south of Hennebont, where it had been abandoned. Archers from the Mounted Police, told of this the same evening, had brought it back into town on Saturday morning.

According to the Mounted Police sergeant's statement, the carriage had been found by a certain Jules le Mauf, a tenant farmer. It was about three in the afternoon and had been snowing heavily since the morning. Le Mauf had left the road to follow the track to Parco when he had heard a neighing coming from an abandoned mill on a stream down to his left and had found there a chestnut draft horse still harnessed to its carriage. He had gone the next morning to tell the Hennebont Mounted Police and had brought the sergeant back to show him the place. The latter had been able to confirm that there were no footprints apart from those of the farmer, showing that the horse and carriage had already been abandoned for some time. Searching the interior of the carriage he had found a bottle green overcoat which Quéric, the hirer of the carriage, later recognised as the same as the one worn by his client. A worrying detail, however, was that this overcoat was soaked in blood. The sergeant had also discovered in the stable relatively fresh hoof prints, indicating that at least one, if not two, horses had stayed there recently.

The carriage hirer Quéric having persisted in his complaint against this Dugoin, a search warrant was issued to the Mounted Police, with a copy made for the Vannes Admiralty at Hennebont. The preparation of this copy had taken a little while, so it had not been sent until the following Tuesday. The prosecutor had sent this on to Vannes during the next week. At that time, the criminal investigator of the Admiralty had already begun his enquiries into the disappearance of my mother and the murder of Lénaïc. A link between the Hennebont and the Port-Louis incidents was only made a while later, as we shall soon see.

The enquiry was concluded at the beginning of March, thanks to the arrival at the Admiralty of a key piece of information. It concerned the reply from the Brest Admiralty in response to the request for information about the body of an unknown ex-convict carrying on him a pass showing that he had been released at the end of his sentence. Brest had taken some time to reply. The document had arrived after some delay at the office of the Vannes Admiralty and had been filed without any follow-up. However, the superintendent of the Vannes

Admiralty at Hennebont had seen it come through his office and had himself read it. The name of the freed convict reminded him of the file sent to him regarding the complaint of the carriage hirer Quéric. He had subsequently sent another memorandum to Vannes making the appropriate connections between these elements, along with his personal comments.

This last communication had greatly pleased the Lieutenant-General of the Vannes Admiralty, and even more so his criminal investigator. Amongst the convicts unchained in January 1773, there was one who corresponded exactly to the description given by the Port-Louis office, and whose name was in the Hennebont report: Nicolas Dugoin, groom by profession, number 2223, age thirty-six years, height five feet, round face, flattened nose, blue eyes, blond hair and beard, scar on the right side of his forehead, branded GAL, native of Guingamp in the bishopric of Tréguier, sentenced at Rennes by an order of Parliament dated 31st March 1757 for '*theft of a horse*' to '*fifteen years' hard labour*'. He had been listed as a convict due for liberation on 1st October 1772, his release had been registered and signed on 31st December 1772 and he had been definitively unchained on 5th January 1773. At his request, he had been authorised to join the corps of volunteers of Baron de Benyowski, an Austro-Hungarian aristocrat who was preparing an expedition to start a colony on the island of Madagascar. His description had been sent to the Mounted Police at L'Orient, where he was required to be checked when he arrived there. He had presented himself at L'Orient on 8th January, and at the office of the Baron de Benyowski's representative, where he had been entered onto the roll for the expedition the same day. He had been given advance pay of eighteen pounds with which to equip himself and been given a week's leave prior to embarkation. He had not been declared a deserter until February. This delay was due mainly to the total lack of organisation of the Benyowski expedition.

According to the Admiralty, the ex-convict had probably met, at L'Orient, two scoundrels, without doubt former sailors of the India Company, who had learned, by one means or another, that a captain of the Company had saved a nice little nest-egg which his widow kept hidden at her house where she lived with an aged servant. Dugoin, a hardened criminal, had organised the robbery and hired the carriage in which the three had gone to Port-Louis. They had killed Lénaïc and forced my mother to reveal the hiding place of the money. Once the job was done, they had abandoned the carriage to make their getaway on horseback. They had quarrelled and the two scoundrels had got rid of Dugoin. The investigators thought it possible that these two criminals were also volunteers of the Benyowski expedition. Unfortunately, the Baron de Benyowski had sailed, and his ships were now well out of reach somewhere between the coast of Brazil and the Indian Ocean. A despatch was to be sent to the Île-de-France[2] so that enquiries could be made. But by the looks of it that would take time, months if not years. The perpetrators could desert in the meantime or even catch one of the fatal diseases found in the Tropics.

The matter was clear. It was a case of a vile crime, carried out by seamen, in a port, against the widow of a Naval officer. It was therefore totally within the jurisdiction of the Admiralty. There were still some grey areas: the body of my mother had not been found. The traces of blood in the hallway showed there was little doubt that she was dead. This, to a certain extent, was a relief to my grandfather and me after the months of sadness and uncertainty we had lived through. I could apply myself seriously to my studies and think about my future, while the Baron could return to look after his estate, knowing that he had done his duty.

---

2 Translator's note: *Île-de-France:* the old name for what is now the Île Maurice – Mauritius.

4

We now return to 15th June 1776, the day that I finished my studies at the Saint-Yves College at Vannes. I had been there for three years and four months, following the worst misfortune that could strike a twelve-year old. This venerable establishment had been founded during the time of Henri III and had become famous thanks to the Jesuits who had taught there prior to their expulsion during the reign of the late Louis XV. The priests who succeeded them were able to maintain the college's reputation for excellence. Originally the subjects taught were French, Latin and some aspects of rhetoric and philosophy. This education was directed at pupils destined for the seminaries or the law schools, but the Good Fathers had also wanted to do holy work by accepting orphans, sons of mariners like myself, and so they had added, over and above the subjects put in place by their illustrious predecessors, classes in history, geography and mathematics. I studied this last subject under the iron hand of Father Deniel, and I have on more than one occasion blessed my luck, for this excellent man knew how to teach me the basics of this difficult science and was even patient enough to allow me to develop a taste for it.

*

Vannes, Saturday 15th June, towards four o'clock in the afternoon.

I learn that a letter has arrived for me at the Post and I go to fetch it. I find that my package was sent from Versailles by the Chevalier de Kermean and has taken five days to get here. When I come out of the Post office with my uncle's letter in my pocket, I am in such a hurry to discover its contents that I sit down immediately on a stone bench beside the street, in order to find out.

First, the Chevalier writes that the machinations he has undertaken to have me proposed as a cadet in the Marine Guards have been successful. This news, far from making me happy, makes me shudder. The extravagant idea of having me pass through the Marine Guards, at any price, so that I can then enter directly the Grand Corps of officers for the King's ships, does not please me at all. It is an initiative of my uncle, who maintains quite stubbornly that it is the most convenient and quickest way to obtain a sea-going commission. But Father Deniel, whom I have long been asking about this problem, has told me that you must prove a noble blood line of at least three-quarters in order to enter the Marine Guards. My father was not a Guard, but that did not stop him from achieving a most honourable career, since he rose purely on his own merits to the rank of Ship's Lieutenant. I could easily obtain all the required recommendations to be accepted as a Volunteer, and then try to follow my father's example without danger of embarrassment. I had said this to the Chevalier, and I thought that his letter was going to tell me exactly that, whereas here, on the contrary, in asking me to join the Marine Guards, I am almost certain, given my origins, that not only will I suffer a publicly humiliating rejection, but I will also waste my time to no account. I have said this several times to my uncle, but it seems that he has not paid any attention.

The Chevalier's letter continues in the same vein. He tells me that Monsieur de Sartine has told him that he is working on the next set of nominations for the Marine Guard Cadets and '*nothing will be more urgent than to propose that the King includes Monsieur Laforest-Dombourg.*' I read that there are now only two conditions that need to be met to complete my future acceptance at Brest. First, I must have an income of six hundred pounds, which sum corresponds to the annual cost of lodging a Cadet Guard, and second, I must not forget to provide my proof of nobility. Has my uncle gone mad? We can leave aside the six hundred pounds; I have no doubt that between the small inheritance from my father and the relative wealth of the Baron de Kermean, that sum can be put together without too much difficulty...but the proof of nobility? In principle, it is no more than providing the original titles of nobility for my great-grandfather, my grandfather and my father. My fingers start to tremble and I curse the unthinking zeal of my uncle. For him it is no more than a formality: his ancestors fought in the Crusades! But he ought to have thought that it is not the same for everyone!

Fortunately, the rest of the Chevalier de Kermean's letter is more reassuring. I learn, as I read, that my uncle has seemingly been manoeuvring with great skill and patience and a self-assurance that leaves me dumbfounded. While searching through the Navy archives, he has dug up old documents showing that my forbear, Jean-Baptiste Laforest-Dombourg, had obtained a commission as captain in the Louisbourg militia in 1730, and that he was the object of a glowing report for his role in the defence of the town during the War of the Austrian Succession. My paternal grandfather had also received several despatches from the Lord of the French Admiralty instructing him to arm his own vessels. Finally, a report certifies that he had served for almost thirty years as a captain of the militia when he was killed by an English mortar bomb in 1758 during the second siege of Louisbourg. I knew nothing about all this, obviously, as my parents had never talked about their relatives.

In conclusion, my father having been lost at sea along with the corvette that he commanded, I can lay claim to two ancestors, renowned officers, both killed in the King's service and of which one, my father, was a Chevalier de Saint-Louis. According to my uncle, I perfectly meet the conditions of a royal edict of 1750, on the 'military nobility'. This specifies that '*Any officer born in legitimate wedlock, whose father and grandfather were exempt from the Taille Royale* [3] *in fulfilling the articles hereunder* – articles referring to the status of officers in general and Chevaliers de Saint-Louis in particular – *will be considered noble as of right.*'

All the same, I know that this is still not enough for entry into the Guards, as I must prove too that my great-grandfather was noble. It is here that the Chevalier has really shown great resourcefulness and

3 Translator's note: *Taille Royale*: a tax levied to pay for the Army and Navy. Noblemen and military men were exempted from it.

expediency. He has managed to persuade the King's Genealogist to draw up a certificate declaring that all the documents concerning my ancestors were destroyed in a fire at Louisbourg because of the wars with the English. Based on this I am authorised to present as proof of nobility an attestation in the correct form, that my uncle has had signed by eight gentlemen, all of them, like him, Chevaliers de Saint-Louis, and which has been countersigned by the Secretary of State for War himself, the Comte de Saint-Germain.

*

I was at last totally reassured and happy that I would be able to present myself at Brest with my head held high. Nonetheless, I remained realistic. I had suddenly found myself holding a certificate of nobility that was as unhoped for as it was unexpected, but I did not allow myself to forget that it had stretched things to the limit and that its sole object was to have me accepted as a Cadet in the Marine Guards. For the rest, I was no more or less noble than before.

I was nevertheless surprised by the connections displayed by my uncle in this affair. How had he managed to persuade the King's Genealogist so easily? I knew that the Corps of Musketeers had recently been disbanded and that the Chevalier had joined the Court. But what was his position to have so much influence? He told me in his letter, without any more details, that he had left his old unit in June 1775. Since then, he had occupied the post of Special Adviser to the Ministry of War, close to the Maréchal du Muy who had appointed him. He added that after the sudden death of the Maréchal, a few months later, he had 'quite naturally' retained his place as Special Adviser to his successor, the Comte de Saint-Germain. The King, Louis XVI, was particularly well disposed towards the Chevalier, remembering the friendship shown by his father, the late Dauphin Louis de France, towards the Baron de Kermean; something which, my uncle explained, always impressed those at Court. In discovering all these explanations, I realised that the names Comte du Muy, Comte de Saint-Germain, and even the Dauphin Louis, were by no means unfamiliar to me: I had already heard them when listening to the tales of the younger days and campaigns of my grandfather and of my uncle.

5

My maternal grandfather was fifteen years old when he became a Page at the Grand Stable of Versailles. For a boy to be accepted as a Page at the stables, it was necessary for the family putting him forward to be able to provide an annual maintenance of six hundred pounds, the same as for a Cadet at the Marine Guards. The comparison only went so far, however: to become a Page at Versailles it was required to show at least two hundred years of unbroken nobility. This was not a problem for the Kermean family, as their ancestors had fought in the Crusades, as I have already said. They are one of these families which go back so far that no genealogist has ever been able to find any document relating to their nobility. I have never dared allow myself to smile about it in front of my maternal grandfather, but I cannot help pointing out that the ultimate for a noble family is to have no written trace of its origins, proving without doubt that its nobility predates the creation of nobles. For myself, I think that the finest indication of the nobility of my mother's family is to be found on a stained-glass window in the little chapel at Mesquer, to which are attached the Kermean coat of arms and the blazon of the Knight Templars. In the twelfth century there was a Templar Lodge nearby, and the soldier-monks joined with the Barons of Kermean to finance the building of a parish church for the people of Mesquer.

After spending four years at the Grand Stable, the Pages who graduated had the right to become a sub-lieutenant in an army corps. It was my grandfather's preference, in line with the family tradition, to join the First Company of Musketeers, in which he served for eleven years. The Musketeers were all noblemen, and even a simple horseman amongst them held the rank of sub-lieutenant in the regular army. He had left the army when his father died, to take over the management of the Kermean estates. He was then thirty years old and had participated in the Battle of Fontenoy where, although not winning the Cross of Saint-Louis, he did win the friendship and personal esteem of the Dauphin Louis of France. This would subsequently be of great help to the career of his son. As a result of his education in the King's Household, as a Page and as a Musketeer, the Baron had maintained a great predilection for the equestrian arts in general and the breeding of cavalry horses in particular. My grandfather used to say that it was very difficult to find good horses for the army in France, where they tended to breed draft horses. This forced us to buy expensive horses from abroad and except for the King's Household Cavalry, the French cavalry had the worst mounts in the world. 'In France,' he would always say in conclusion, 'apart from the Limousine breed, we have never been able to raise anything except nags!'

My uncle Jean-Baptiste, like his father, was first a Page at the Grand Stable, and then a Musketeer. When the Seven Years' War started, the Musketeers were not sent out on campaign, but thanks to the connections of the Baron of Kermean, his son the Chevalier was allowed provisional leave to act as the aide-de-camp of the Comte de Saint-Germain. It was in this capacity, while still wearing the uniform of his original Company, that he took part in the campaigns of 1757 in Saxony, and 1758 with the army of the Lower Rhine.

The Chevalier de Kermean had sought permission to leave the headquarters of the Comte de Saint-Germain, to join the Dauphin's Cavalry Brigade. The Dauphin, like his father Louis XV[4], had remained at Versailles, but he had freely granted this request. It was thus that my uncle was finally able to realise his dream, by participating in a charge,

---

4 Translator's note: *Louis XV, the Dauphin Louis and Louis XVI*: Louis XV's son, the Dauphin (Prince), died before he could take the throne, and so Louis XV was succeeded by his grandson Louis XVI, the son of the Dauphin.

on 10th October 1758, at the Battle of Lutzelberg, in his Musketeer's uniform, in the first rank of the Dauphin's Cavalry. He took several sabre blows and a pistol bullet through the chest, but he would never regret this wound as it stopped him returning to the Lower Rhine army, which was a major determinant of his future career.

At the end of his convalescence, my uncle had the luck to be taken on as aide-de-camp at the headquarters of the Duc de Broglie who was considered by the whole army to be France's best military commander. The following year the Chevalier de Kermean made the acquaintance of the Comte de Broglie, the Field-Marshall's younger brother, who had come to serve as adjutant to his elder brother, now Commander-in-Chief in Germany. From that moment on the Chevalier kept close contact with the Comte.

My uncle had a final opportunity to shine at the beginning of the following year, at Cassel, within a little garrison commanded by the Comte de Broglie. The Duke of Brunswick, commander of the Prussian army, had decided to remove this place quickly by attacking it with all force before the beginning of the campaign. The unexpected resistance at Cassel enabled Field-Marshall de Broglie to gather up the French army with remarkable speed and to swoop onto the rear of Brunswick, who was not expecting it. Our troops won a great victory and the Chevalier de Kermean was finally awarded his Cross of Saint-Louis. The aftermath of the campaign was unfortunately tainted by accusations made against Field-Marshall de Broglie and his brother, who were certainly less able in the field of intrigue than on the field of battle. They both fell out of favour at Versailles, just like the Comte de Saint-Germain the previous year. The Chevalier de Kermean, tired and disgusted at the sight of courtiers continually reducing the efforts of real soldiers to nothing, asked to re-join his Company of Musketeers. His war stopped there.

6

Vannes, Monday 17th June 1776, six o'clock in the morning.

In his letter my uncle has confirmed that he will set out for Brittany the next day. He expects to arrive at Kermean on Saturday 15th or Sunday 16th and will send Ottmeyer to wait at the Abbey de Prières with a horse for me.

I have found passage on one of the inshore coasters that are so numerous on our coasts. This one has just unloaded fresh sardines and leaves for Redon to pick up a cargo of barrels of white wine. Her skipper has agreed to put me ashore at the mouth of the Vilaine. We are due to sail at ten this morning, just before high tide.

It is already light when I say farewell to Father Deniel. He accompanies me to the gate of the College to give me his blessing. I am moved: I owe him so much and do not know if we will see each other again. All the same, I am not totally overcome with sadness. I am young. I am leaving for a new life which I imagine, rightly or wrongly, will have its attractions.

*

So it was that I set out alone, towards six in the morning, hands in pockets and spirit light, my travelling chest having been put on board the previous evening. I entered the empty town by the old half-ruined Solomon Gate and went down towards the Place des Lices, leaving the dark mass of the cathedral to my left. Seeing the cathedral made me think that there was still nobody around at this early hour, and that nobody could follow me without my knowing. In fact, during my time at Vannes, I had several times had the impression of being watched. At first, I thought it was no more than my imagination, and I kept it to myself. However, one Sunday, when I had gone to High Mass, at the cathedral of Saint-Pierre itself, when coming out of the porch, I once again felt observed and I turned around quickly. My eyes, just for a moment, had locked on those of a fellow of average height, wrapped in a grey overcoat, with a hat of the same colour that he quickly put on his head while turning away. I had time to register piercing black eyes, very handsome, and a straight and elegant nose, worthy of a statue of antiquity. The man was swarthy, had a small moustache, a carefully trimmed beard and long black hair tied behind. I rushed towards him, banging rather brutally into a high-born lady who had just that moment come out and whom I had not seen. I apologised as I passed, rather cursorily I admit, but the lady's husband was not impressed. He grabbed me by the collar and made me apologise more politely. Once I had regained my freedom, the unknown man had disappeared and I did not see him again. I wondered if I had been mistaken. Was it perhaps no more than coincidence?

However, there was, on the square behind the cathedral, a woman who sold fresh fish with whom I chatted from time to time in order to practise my Vannes' Breton. Her husband was master of a barque and her sons had all gone to sea at an early age. She missed them, hence her fondness for me. I always went to say hello to her, as she gave me fresh sardines or raw mackerel fillets spread on well-buttered black bread, which I loved. This good woman told me that a stranger had asked her about me: whether she knew how long I would be at the College...and whether I had told her what I would be doing afterwards...that kind of thing. She had not answered, firstly because she found the questions indiscreet, and also because she spoke French badly. When I asked her what the stranger looked like, her description matched the man I had seen in the porch of the cathedral.

*

Vannes, Monday 17th June 1776, towards half past six on the morning.

I had hoped to have fine weather for my passage, but I can now see reddish clouds over the roofs of the city. The rising sun is completely veiled when I arrive at the port. The air is warm, however, and my rapid walking has made me perspire. I see my coasting lugger at the end of the Quay de la Rabine, on my right. High tide is close: tomorrow will see the new moon for June. The flood tide has started to mix with the mud of the moats under the bridge, sending up dull and sickening smells. Birds are chirping in the branches of the trees that line the promenade beside the port.

*

The skipper was waiting for me. As soon as I was on board, the lugger pulled out under oars into the channel that leads to the Morbihan, where we were quickly carried out by the ebb tide. I thought that I had escaped for good the curiosity of the unknown man at the Cathedral of Saint-Pierre.

Coming out of the Morbihan we were met by a fresh breeze, sometimes strong in the squalls, and a big swell from the south-west. The sky was entirely hidden by cloud, the horizon dark. Our little craft had to stay hard on the wind to weather the Grand Mont headland. This part of the coast looks austere from seawards. Bordered by steep cliffs, it is completely bare except for a wood whose upper branches can be seen behind the summit of the Grand Mont. During this part of the voyage, we were constantly buffeted and soaked. I had been used to these crossings since an early age and took a keen interest in the performance of our lugger. These little ships were originally conceived for collecting the catch of sardine sloops at sea, but their qualities made them ideal for coasting. They also served as the model for Navy luggers. Ours had a hull forty-five feet long and a beam of fourteen feet. She had two masts and a thirty-foot bowsprit, more or less horizontal. On that day the usual mainsail had been replaced by a smaller sail with a shortened luff. We had reefed the mizzen and carried a small jib. Despite this reduced sail, our craft heeled heavily in the gusts. Once we had enough sea room, the skipper put us on a shy reach to run along the coast then, after the Penvins Point, on a broad reach. No longer having to confront the waves of the big swell, our lugger, as if relieved, began to slide down the wave faces and our speed increased, so much so that we made the entrance to the river Vilaine just at the start of the flood tide.

*

Mouth of the Vilaine, Monday 17th June 1776, towards half past eleven in the morning.

It is raining. The lugger now ploughs its way on a square reach between two banks covered in flowering gorse, through waters which have suddenly quietened down. I see passing, behind the top of a lone orchard on the moorland, about half a mile away on our left, the rooftops and dome of the Abbey de Prières. Their tiles, running with rain, seem to shine under the showers driving in at an angle. The mouth of the Vilaine has a bad reputation. I have sometimes heard it said that its banks are 'terrible'. This is no doubt due to the desolate and uninhabited aspect of the shores of the estuary, with their reddish cliffs and muddy waters. It is true that in a good sea, at half-tide, the entrance is usually cut by a breaking bar which even the most experienced mariners never cross without misgivings. The skipper of the lugger would happily push on to La Roche-Bernard without stopping, but I have paid my passage and told him that I am expected at the Abbey. He has no choice but to anchor briefly and launch the ship's boat just for me. He stops his craft near to the left bank, in five fathoms, just opposite a hamlet on the other shore.

The flood has been running for three quarters of an hour. The sailors ground the bow of the ship's boat on a beach of rough sand, on the right bank, where I can jump out without taking off my shoes and stockings. They unload my chest and head back to their ship. I find myself ashore, soaked through, alone with my baggage in the rain. Some dirty, snotty-nosed urchins have come down from the hamlet to watch proceedings from a respectful distance. I give them a shout, and with the help of a few coppers, get them to help me pull my chest above the high-water mark. I want to ask them where I can get a cart, but they have already gone off, counting their money, and I get no answer. I hear the Angelus tolling in the distance. I must be about three miles from the Abbey. Gulls circle overhead with raucous cries. It is still raining, but some blue patches appear in the sky. I think that I will have to get someone to look after my chest while I go on foot, when I see a light carriage drawn by two horses coming down the track.

*

From a distance, the coachman had a familiar look. The carriage stopped between the cottages, and I saw a monk in white and a gentleman get down. They soon waved to me and I recognised my uncles, the Chevalier and the Abbot of Kermean. As for the coachman, it was none other than dear old Ottmeyer.

My joy was matched by my surprise, firstly at seeing my uncle Jean-Baptiste when I thought he was already at Kermean, and secondly that he had come to collect me so quickly, when I had not had the time to write to tell them of my arrival.

'My journey was quicker than expected,' said the Chevalier, 'and so I decided to come and wait here. It was the Abbot who told me that a boat had arrived at the river entrance and that you were bound to be on board.'

'We don't have much time,' said Father François de Kermean. 'It will soon be dinner time.'

'Ah, yes!' said the Chevalier. 'There is more discipline in the monastery than in the army! After dinner, the two of us will go and walk in the garden. I have something to show you.'

I had never dined in the grand refectory with all the monks. When I had passed through Prières with my poor mother and my little sister, we had taken our meals in the private apartments of the Father Superior. Imagine a huge hall, with rows of tables holding one hundred and thirty diners, monks and lay brothers combined. I went first, as is proper, to greet the Father Superior, who was seated alone at a small table, before taking my place with the Chevalier at the visitors' table. The rule at the Abbey is to abstain from meat for the whole year, and so our meal was composed of green bean soup, some fish, two soft-boiled eggs, turnips, and cheese for dessert, along with red wine and cider. Simple though it was, the meal seemed to me to be interminable. I wanted to know what the Chevalier had to say to me and could easily have left the table before grace was said. When we finally went out from the refectory, the wind had veered to the north-west and freshened. Rounded clouds raced high across the blue sky. My uncle led me through the gardens to find a sheltered spot. He invited me to sit beside him on a bench at the end of the vegetable garden, against a south-facing wall. Before beginning he stayed silent for a while, pensively tapping the pocket of his jacket.

*

Abbey de Prières, Monday 17th June 1776, towards three in the afternoon.

I wait patiently. We are in an island of calm, warmed by the June sun, protected from the gusts rustling the branches of the trees of the orchard above our heads. The Chevalier takes out a yellowed piece of paper that he unfolds on his knee.

'This letter was sent to me by your father and is undoubtedly the last letter that he wrote before setting sail on his last voyage, five years ago. When you know of its contents you will understand why I have kept it for so long.'

So that was it! A letter from my father! I take the paper with emotion, my chest tight. I want to cry. My father, Ship's Lieutenant Jean-François Laforest-Dombourg! His writing is neat, the words formed carefully and easy to read.

> *Brest Harbour, aboard la Fouine, this 8th November 1771…*
>
> *You will no doubt be surprised to learn, my dear Chevalier, that I am once again in service on the King's ships. When we parted in September, I was looking forward to some peaceful days with your sister and our children following the decommissioning of my last ship at L'Orient in August. But the Ministry decided otherwise. I had to replace at short notice the commander of a corvette which is part of the division making the next relief of our Saint-Domingue*[5] *station. I would certainly have welcomed a longer rest after a year and a half of difficult campaigning, but I am very proud that they called on me. Breaks of service to sail with the India Company are not always well regarded by the Navy, and my designation for active service as a commander of a King's corvette was a most flattering honour. The opportunities to command at sea are so rare that I could not refuse,*

5 Translator's note: *Saint-Domingue:* French colony on the Caribbean island of Hispaniola, roughly in the area of modern-day Haiti.

despite certain commitments I had made which must now await my return.

Alas! My time at Brest has been nothing but misery. The port and the arsenals are short of everything. The seamen have not been paid for months. Would you believe that I have had to dip into my personal funds to supply my sailors with the necessary kit to enable them to withstand the rigours of winter? The powers that be objected that they were going to be campaigning in a warm climate. That I understand, but first they must face winter storms in the Bay of Biscay. Moreover, it is not simply a matter of supplies; morale is low too. When I took temporary leave from the Navy, ten years ago, we had certainly been beaten in combat, but we thought only of redeeming ourselves, while today it's as if everyone sets sail already defeated.

But I am not writing to you to speak of all that. The life of a mariner is full of hazards; we are in the hands of the Lord on the wide ocean, even without the fact that, despite all my efforts, my corvette will never be as well prepared as I would like. In short, I am not afraid to confront my fate, but if God wills that I do not return from this campaign, I would be most distressed to leave as an inheritance to my wife a burden which is far too heavy for her to carry on her own. So much so that I have agreed to undertake a very special command once I return. Also, if you should learn that I am no more of this world, go and see your sister, show her this letter, tell her to reflect well, and if ever she feels that she is not strong enough to keep on her own the promise that we made to my former comrade of the old Formidable and of India, I release her from the secret that ties us so that she may confide in you. In the meantime, keep this letter to yourself. Do not speak of it to anyone, and if I return, as I hope, I will ask you to return it to me without me having to explain why. I am well aware that this strange request may seem insulting and hurtful, but please understand that this is not my intention and that this is not in my control. I am sure you will excuse me when I will finally be able to explain the reasons which force me to act in this way.

I have the honour to be, my dear Chevalier, your devoted and humble servant…

The letter, so surprising in itself, continued at the bottom of the page with an even more surprising post-script…

'What do you think? It's strange, isn't it? I don't mean the beginning, of course.'

I do not reply. Certainly, the beginning is moving, but it is the ending that strikes me the most. It makes me think of my last conversation with my mother.

'Did you ever show this letter to my mother?'

'Yes, of course, but she only said that she would think about it seriously. It was just before her death. Sadly, we never had occasion to discuss it again.'

My uncle has said 'Just before her death'. That seems to confirm what I am thinking.

'Was she shocked by its contents?'

'No. She was obviously a little surprised and she shed a few tears. She certainly did not expect to be reminded of your father in this way after all that time. No! She knew what it was all about, of that I am certain. The way she answered proves it. Besides, when I wanted to leave the letter with her, she begged me to keep it, saying you never know what might happen. I think she knew that it contained a sort of message that would be more useful to me than to her.'

'When did this happen?'

'When did I show her the letter? Well, it was at our house, at the chateau, four years ago, when we were all gathered for the funeral of the Baroness de Kermean.'

'Can you remember the exact day?'

'The exact date? Is it of any importance?'

'It might well be,' I say, thinking about it.

'Well then. Wait...I remember that it was a Sunday. We were returning from the High Mass. Yes, that's it. It was the first Sunday after the burial of the Baroness.'

My maternal grandmother had been buried the day after my arrival, a Thursday. And three days later, on the Sunday evening, my dear mother had called me to her room to tell me that she wanted to be buried next to her mother. I remember that she had been very serious that day, while she had seemed surprisingly calm after the burial of her mother. I did not know how the interment of the Baroness could have been a relief to my mother, but I now understood why she had become worried three days later. Without doubt, reading this letter had been the cause. Besides, had not my dear mother said, as I well remember: '*I am following the example of your father, who took a similar precaution*'? I am about to speak about this, but a something holds me back.

'There is also this puzzling phrase as a post-script. Does it remind you of anything?'

'Absolutely nothing,' I say. 'What about you?'

'Well...I think that therein lies the message contained in this letter, and that that is the reason why your mother wanted me to keep it, since the rest is reasonably explicit. But it is apparently a coded message, surprising as that may seem. I have shown it to Monsieur the Abbot de Meaux, who is very knowledgeable. In all confidence, of course.'

'And what did he say about it?'

'Nothing precise. He thought that it must be some sort of oriental saying, pagan probably, but he was unable to grasp its meaning. After a long hesitation he advised me to show the letter to the rector of Mesquer who, according to him, is very erudite in this area. All the same, he tried to warn me by saying that the rector was a man of strange behaviour and to remain on my guard with him. He told me that the rector had tried to rehabilitate the memory of the Templar heretics, and what an awful thing that was. That made me smile and I replied that the rector of Mesquer has been our family pastor for a long while and in short, we like him as he is, even with his little obsessions. I even told him that he had baptised my younger brother François, which he did not know. I suggest that you go and see our rector as soon as you can. I can't come with you, unfortunately, as I must go off to Nantes as soon as we get back to the Manor. I have to do something for the Baron de Kermean that I can't get out of. But I will come back as quickly as possible, be sure of that. Also, I must train you in the use of arms before you leave for Brest.'

'The use of arms?'

At first, I do not quite understand what he means.

'But of course! Even as a simple Cadet you must carry an epee. What will people think if you don't know how to use it?'

'But won't I have fencing lessons at the Company of Guards?'

'Of course, but if someone provokes you as soon as you arrive at Brest, how will you manage? You don't want to be killed, or be taken for a coward, I presume?'

'Aren't duels forbidden?'

'In theory yes, but you won't be left alone until you have proved yourself, believe me. I know all about these things. We'll talk about it again later.'

My uncle picked up the letter and read it again.

'This letter suggests some kind of secret. Your parents must have had a secret. Were you ever aware of that?'

'Not really, but it is true that they never talked about important things in front of me. I knew nothing of my father's past, for example. I think they thought I was too young to be told and that they were waiting for me to grow up before talking about it. A comment made to me by my mother before she left for L'Orient makes me think this. If that is the case, then it could well mean that they were hiding a secret sufficiently serious not to disclose to an indiscreet child. But what sort of secret? And, if it still exists, how is it linked to my father's past? You yourself, who were his friend, perhaps know more about this than me.'

'We were friends, that is true...and I was very close to my sister too. At least that is what I thought. Do you think that her death is linked to all of this?'

'I don't think so. According to the Vannes Admiralty, our house was attacked by an ex-convict and two seamen who wanted to steal the money my father had saved during his voyages. My parents kept it hidden under the stair landing. That suggests that my father was making money on the side. That really disappointed me! But all the commanders of the India Company are at it, it seems. In any case, this doesn't seem to have any link with this letter which talks about an old comrade of my father.'

'You can't say that your father was making money on the side! Nobody knows exactly what happened! But let's come back to the letter. Your father speaks there of the old *Formidable* and of India. The *Formidable* is, I suppose, the name of a ship, but India would seem to be the country. He is talking then about a friend with whom he served aboard a ship named *le Formidable* in India. But why has he not given his name? He has nonetheless underlined this passage, if you look closely, which shows that it is important. In any case it seems that your parents were in his debt.'

That reminded me that my mother had spoken of 'obligations' that my father had towards a 'friend'.

'Have you noticed that the post-script is also underlined?'

'Perhaps,' replied my uncle, 'this suggests that once de-coded, the post-script will allow us to identify this 'comrade of the old *Formidable* and of India'.

'We have to start by trying to find his name. Do you know of any friends of my father who served with him in the Navy?'

'I only knew one,' replied my uncle, 'but he could be the one this letter is referring to. He was a Captain of the India Company that your father presented to me using the name Macé. I had been to visit your parents at L'Orient when I came back from the war. This Macé had got to know your father not far from here, just a little way up the river. They were together on the vessels of the Maréchal de Conflans' squadron, which had escaped from the Quiberon Bay disaster, at the end of 1759, by taking refuge in the river Vilaine. I know that your father won the Cross of Saint-Louis during that battle. He was wounded, and the English put him ashore at Le Croisic. He was released on parole[6] by the English and looked after at the house of the Marquis de Becdelièvre. It was there that he met your mother. Once his convalescence was over, he re-joined the ships which were near here. Your parents were married at Mesquer the following year, and when they introduced their friend Macé to me, they said that he had been a witness to their marriage, along with two other Naval officers from the ships in the Vilaine. At the time of their wedding, I had been in Cassel, in Germany, with the Comte de Broglie. It was then that your father had a problem: the English did not want to exchange him, saying he had been released by mistake. As a result, Macé suggested that your father come with him as First Mate aboard a ship of the India Company of which he was about to take command. There were agreements between the Navy and the India Company, with the officers of the King allowed to serve on ships of the Company without losing their seniority on the Navy list. Your father agreed, as it was the only way he could go to sea during wartime without breaking his parole. He left before your birth and only came back in 1764, to L'Orient. I had gone to visit my sister, whom I had not seen since my return to France, and I was there when their ship arrived.

6 Translator's note: *released on parole:* released on condition that he would not take part in any military activity until 'exchanged' for an English prisoner of war of similar rank.

It was then that I got to know your father and that I met this Macé, one evening, at their home.'

'What was the name of the ship?'

'Well, it wasn't *le Formidable*, otherwise I would already have said. No, I remember it well, it was *le Comte d'Argenson.* I liked your father immediately. He talked about this first voyage to the Mascarene Islands, which I found extraordinary, but it was nothing compared to what he told me later, when I saw him again after his second voyage: Chandernagore, Bengal, elephants, tigers, temples that the worshippers call pagodas, snake charmers! The extremes of penitence of the Hindu religion! The spells of their magicians!'

'He was as talkative as that, then? Did he talk to you about Louisbourg or the Battle of Quiberon Bay?'

'No, you are right! These are subjects he never broached. That always surprised me. As far as Louisbourg is concerned, all things considered, I can understand it. The Seven Years' War had affected him deeply with the loss of his whole family over there. But Quiberon Bay...Hell's teeth! He had won the Cross of Saint-Louis. And before me, too!'

'I wonder about one thing, since you say that both my father and this Captain Macé were serving aboard the ships which took refuge in the Vilaine. Could the Abbot de Meaux possibly give us a list of these ships? If *le Formidable* is among them, we would know from this that this Macé is the friend mentioned by my father. We could also look for the names of the Naval officers who were witnesses at my parents' marriage. Have you asked the Baron de Kermean about this?'

'Not yet. I didn't want to do anything before talking to you. I think that the answers we are looking for are to be found in your father's past, either at Louisbourg or at Quiberon Bay. That's where you have to look. You must try to find these officers that your father knew, starting with this Captain Macé. But this must not stop you from working hard at your studies. Your parents are dead, which is sad, but nothing can be done about that. The best way for you to honour their memory is first and foremost to become an officer of the King's Navy.'

I agree with my uncle, of course, but I also think that if my parents had 'obligations' towards this Macé, then it is my duty at least to try to find him. What could my parents owe him, apart from the fact that he took on my father as First Mate when his career risked interruption on account of this strange refusal to exchange him? It is a pity that my parents have made such a mystery of it. It complicates my task at the same time as I have so many new things to learn at Brest in order to become a Naval officer.

*

When we enquired of the Father Superior, he told us that he had come to the Abbey de Prières seven years after the Battle of Quiberon Bay. However, he had one of the oldest Brothers called, who remembered some things about this time, and told us that about ten ships took refuge in the Vilaine, 'mainly big ones, but as for their names...' The ships had gone higher up the river, to the bend after La Vieille Roche in the parish of Arzal, at least six miles from the Abbey. They stayed there for about two years. Some had even sunk there, with the bones of their hulls still visible in the mud opposite Arzal. A group of ships had managed to escape in the fog in January 1761, and two others later on, in November. That could not have been easy, for at that time the English were holding permanent station outside and had even taken possession of Belle-Île. The then Father Superior, Abbot de la Fruglaye, had not taken kindly to having such a big collection of soldiers and sailors on his doorstep – 'nothing but bandits' according to him. He had forbidden the monks to go to Arzal for as long as the ships remained in the Vilaine. Only officers were admitted to the Abbey, as their commanding officer was a gentleman, a certain Chevalier de Ternay. He had left in November 1761 with the last two ships which had managed to be repaired.

My uncle had two other letters for me which he had left at Kermean. The first was my summons to the Company of Marine Guards of Brest, where I was required to present myself by the beginning of October at the latest, together with my proofs of nobility. The other contained these much-touted proofs. I would take them with me when I left for Brest at the end of the summer.

I asked my uncle François, the Father, about the officers who had been present at my parents' wedding. He had been there himself, but he was only fourteen years old, and could not remember their names. He advised me to ask the rector of Mesquer to let me have a look at the parish marriage register.

The next day was fine when we set out for Kermean. My uncle

and Ottmeyer had come on horseback and brought a mount for me. The Abbey loaned us a mule for my baggage which Ottmeyer led on a long rein. We were going to take a ferry across the Vilaine at La Vieille Roche crossing, as we always did. The sky was clear, with a few sparse white clouds. The west wind coming in from the sea had dried the mud of the tracks and stopped us getting too warm. We crossed the du Mes marshes. Salt workers wearing smocks were making great piles of salt which sparkled in the sun. After we left the crossing, the land started to rise imperceptibly and we were once again on a plateau covered with gorse and brush and dotted with depressions filled with water. In this kind of countryside it is easier to travel on horseback than with a carriage. We had to wait until we had reached Kermean before encountering cultivated land. The estate started on the left bank of a boggy stream that marked the division between the parishes of Saint-Molf and Mesquer. From there on we used a metalled track across fields bordered with spikey hedges of gorse. This led to a crest topped with an oak wood that was called the Bois de la Justice, as it had been planted at the spot where the lords of the manor used to have their gallows. This name was a reminder that in former times the lords had the right of life and death over their subjects. It showed too that when these oaks were young, French was already starting to replace the Breton language, which at one time was spoken by all the inhabitants of the land, including the Barons of Kermean themselves.

We arrived at the manor well before dinner time. The Baron de Kermean had gone to inspect his pastures beside the sea to prepare for haymaking. We were welcomed by my little sister. The Baron de Kermean had become very attached to her and had decided to educate her himself. Fortunately, Jeanne Grégoire, her governess since the death of poor Lénaïc, well knew how to keep the Baron in check, otherwise my poor little Anne would very quickly have had her head stuffed full of rural philosophy, accounting and agriculture. Jeanne Grégoire was the widow of a fisherman lost at sea, who had left her with a little son who lived with us at the Manor. She was a pretty country girl, full of life and good health, as well as good sense, who had received some education from the Ursuline Sisters at Guérande. She had never remarried, and I often wondered whether her self-confidence in the presence of the widowed Baron stemmed from a relationship somewhat deeper than that of simple governess.

*

Kermean Manor, parish of Mesquer, Tuesday 18th June, in the afternoon.

When I have the Baron de Kermean read my father's letter, he seems moved, but he cannot tell whether or not my father ever talked to him about a ship called *le Formidable.* This hardly surprises me, knowing my father as I do. What does surprise me is that the name Captain Macé means absolutely nothing to him. It is the first time I have ever asked my grandfather about my parents' past. He tells me that our officers taken prisoner were released on parole a few days after the Battle of Quiberon Bay and that they had disembarked in Pénerf harbour. My father had been released on parole too since he could still stand. He would normally have been released at Pénerf at the same time as the others, but he had lost so much blood that he passed out on the deck of his ship and the English, taking pity, had decided to put him ashore immediately, at Le Croisic. It was thought that he would die. As a result, he was not taken to Vannes with the other injured. The Marquis de Becdelièvre had offered to look after him, along with some other officers in a similar bad state, at his chateau near Quimiac. Of course, the Baron de Kermean had only found out all this later, through his daughter. My future mother had wanted to nurse these convalescing heroes and her parents had willingly agreed; they could not refuse her anything as they had lost two daughters at an early age before the birth of my mother. That was how my parents met. If I am calculating correctly, my father was twenty-seven years old and my mother scarcely seventeen. My father regained his health after two months. The request for a nominal exchange had been sent to the English, and in anticipation of its acceptance, he had been listed as crew on one of the ships blockaded at Arzal. He had waited until the spring of 1760 before summoning up the courage to ask the Baron de Kermean for his daughter's hand in marriage. The Marquis de Becdelièvre had acted as go-between.

The Baron de Kermean admits that this initial interview with the Marquis de Becdelièvre was somewhat stormy. He had grown angry, swearing that, out of respect for his ancestors and the honour of his name, he could never accept such a poor match, even if it was only for a daughter, and certainly not with a sailor!

*

Kermean Manor, Tuesday 18th June, in the afternoon.

The Baron de Kermean admits to me that he even thought of arranging a *lettre de cachet*[7] for my father, so that he could be imprisoned without trial. His reach was long after the Battle of Fontenoy, and I believe my parents had a lucky escape. They were saved, in the end, by the Chevalier de Ternay, whom the old monk had told us about when we had talked to him in the presence of the Abbot de Meaux, at Prières. The Chevalier de Ternay had presented himself as my father's commanding officer. Not content simply to come and plead his case, he had also accepted the role of principal witness at my father's wedding. It seems that this officer had completely won over the Baron de Kermean. My grandfather describes him to me as a real gentleman, disciplined and respectful of traditional values. The Chevalier de Ternay had told the Baron that he perfectly understood his reaction and that in principle he agreed with it, but, in the case of Ship's Ensign Laforest-Dombourg, he could make an exception without fear of contravening his values. My father had recently served with distinction under his command, and previously under another Captain who had particularly appreciated him, who was ready to act as a guarantor for him, and whom the Chevalier de Ternay had praised so fulsomely that my grandfather still remembers his name: Taffanel de la Jonquière. This Captain, according to the Chevalier de Ternay, had personally known my paternal grandfather, Jean-Baptiste Laforest-Dombourg, and had always talked about him as an honourable man who had rapidly fitted out his own ships as privateers, at his own expense, at Louisbourg, during the last two wars. Finally, the Chevalier de Ternay had swayed the decision by talking about my father's Cross of Saint-Louis and explaining that he had become a full officer of the King's ships. I note in passing that the Chevalier de Ternay, having been my father's superior, could never have been referred to as 'my old comrade', even in a letter written many years later.

My parents' marriage was celebrated in the Kermean chapel by the rector of Mesquer on 26th September 1760. By the end of that year my father had still not received a reply for his exchange, unlike the other officers

---

7 Translator's note: *lettre de cachet*: a letter signed by the King authorising someone's imprisonment without trial.

who had been liberated on parole at the same time as him. This seemed to surprise everybody, except my father himself. The Baron de Kermean well remembers having heard his son-in-law say that this was certainly because the English Admiral, Boscawen, would have intervened to ensure that his friend, the government minister Pitt, blocked the exchange. My father said that he was lucky that the English fleet at Quiberon Bay was commanded by Hawke and not Boscawen, otherwise he would never have been released, even if badly wounded. When my grandfather asked him what the English Admiral had against him, my father simply replied that it had been like that since the siege of Louisbourg. The Baron advises me to ask the old Marquis de Becdelièvre when we see him soon, as perhaps he knows more about this mystery than us. We have to visit the Marquis out of courtesy before I leave for Brest, for he is my godfather following a request from my parents, and in this regard, he had proposed to my grandfather to provide the six hundred pounds a year required for the Marine Guards, which my grandfather has accepted. But, for the moment, he is not at his estate in Brittany.

In any event, whether Admiral Boscawen was the cause or not, it was essentially because of this problem of exchange that my father decided to enter the service of the India Company. He told the Baron de Kermean that one of his comrades was a Captain in this shipping company and had offered to take him as First Mate for a voyage to India. I tell my grandfather that this comrade was called Macé and that he is certainly the one mentioned in the posthumous letter from Brest. But the Baron tells me once again that he is quite certain that he has never heard this name before.

*

We had arrived at Kermean on a Tuesday. I waited until the following Sunday before going to see the rector of Mesquer. It was the eve of the Feast of Saint-Jean. I went to Mass with my grandfather and little sister. The three of us were lined up on the Baron's pew up to the right of the nave. The Baron de Kermean's allotted place was besides the central aisle. The Marquis of Becdelièvre's pew was on the same row, but on the other side of the aisle, so that they could be offered the blessed bread at the same time. However, the Marquis was not at Mesquer on that day and his place was empty.

*

Parish of Mesquer, Sunday 23rd June, towards eleven o'clock in the morning.

During Mass I several times have the feeling that someone is staring intently at my back, just as at the cathedral at Vannes. Going out, while passing through the horseshoe-shaped door, I look all around the village square but can only see salt workers in their fine white costumes, tenant farmers dressed in dark serge, women in bonnets and their children shouting and running everywhere. I push aside my uneasiness while waiting for the rector, who is supervising the tidying up of the sacristy. His two vergers are not too good at controlling the boisterous children of the choir. When he joins me there is nobody left in front of the church, except for a lively group playing quoits alongside the cemetery wall, on the other side of the square. Having presented myself, I ask if he will allow me to look at my parents' marriage document, in order to find the list of my father's witnesses. He replies that the old parish registers are at the vicarage and that he will be happy to see me there. I mention too my father's letter and its strange post-script. I add that I have been advised to consult him because of his wide knowledge. He makes no comment and very politely invites me to visit him tomorrow after vespers. Don't be late, he says, as he has a number of duties to fulfil during the evening. There will be Mass, prayers, singing, and he himself will light the first fire of the Feast of Saint-Jean on the square, between the church and the cemetery. After that, the night will be dotted with the red flowers of braziers burning almost everywhere across the countryside. The young will dance around the flames to bring luck for their future marriages.

My uncle has not come with me as he left on horseback, this morning, for Nantes, at the request of the Baron de Kermean. My grandfather has been corresponding for a while with a gentleman from Nantes who is seeking a husband for his daughter. The Baron is still surprisingly youthful, despite his sixty-two years, but he is nonetheless starting to worry about his blood line, seeing that his elder son still has no thoughts of settling down, even though he has turned forty. He has therefore decided to take the matter in hand himself. He must have been pleasantly surprised, I think, at the lack of opposition from the Chevalier. True, I have heard that the prospective bride does not lack for certain charms: not only does the young girl bring a dowry of one hundred and sixty thousand pounds, including a lifetime annuity of one thousand pounds, but she is also said to be pretty. I start to imagine the Chevalier leaping over the Saint-Jean flames with his promised one.

The rector has inspired confidence in me. Before taking leave of him I give a brief description of the man at the Vannes cathedral and tell him that I would like to know whether someone of his description was seen at his church during Mass. Once again, he does not ask any questions, but promises to let me know.

*

The rector's manse is situated outside the village, below the church. I walked up to an elegant and imposing building, rectangular in shape. Its courtyard was protected by a granite wall. The gate of forged iron had nine-foot high posts. The rector of Mesquer was the youngest son of a grand family of the Breton nobility. He had had this vicarage built thirty years earlier as a smaller version of his parents' manor house. If, at first, wicked tongues had wagged at the amount spent, they had long since fallen silent. Since then, the parishioners had unfortunately had many an occasion to appreciate the devotion of their spiritual shepherd, along with the rightness of his reasoning in difficult times. Storms, droughts, famines, epidemics! It does not take much, when you consider that a single violent thunderstorm can flatten, in several minutes, the work of a whole season and the well-being of a whole year.

*

Mesquer, Monday 24th June, during the afternoon.

While showing me to his study, the rector tells me that he has enquired of his vergers with the description I gave him, and one of them told him that a bearded individual, a stranger to the parish, had refused to contribute money to the collection plate. The verger had immediately told him to either pay or leave, at which the stranger had left without further ado. According to the rector, who obviously found this story amusing, his verger had above all been dismayed by the departure of this unknown man without making a scene, as well as without making an offering.

The rector has already got out the marriage register for 1760 and has opened it on the table at 26th September. I can immediately see who my father's witnesses were.

There are three, but no Macé.

Monsieur Charles-Henry-Louis d'Arsac, Chevalier de Ternay, Ship's Lieutenant

Monsieur Marc-Joseph Marion, Squire Dufresne, Frigate's Lieutenant

Monsieur Jean-François du Galaup de Lapérouse, Marine Guard

The rector of Mesquer is in his sixty-seventh year. He is a small man, modestly dressed, restrained in gesture but not in word, in no way stout, which is unusual in his calling, and surprisingly lively. He puts on glasses to read my father's letter, which makes him look inoffensive and deceptively candid. The rector reads it carefully and without hurry. At last, he puts down his spectacles and looks at me.

'Yesterday you asked me if I could make any sense of this letter's post-script. Before beginning, I would like to know who gave you the idea of asking me.'

'It was my uncle, the Chevalier de Kermean, but it was not his idea originally. It was in fact the Abbot de Meaux who told him that you are very knowledgeable about religions. He actually said 'pagan religions'. Please forgive me.'

The rector laughed loudly.

'The Abbot de Meaux, that worthy professor of theology! Did you know that he was for a long time a professor of theology before being appointed at Prières? And a professor of philosophy too! But, between the two of us, he is too strict. Outside of the Holy Scriptures, no salvation! I am a priest and I have the Faith, and I in no way contest the supremacy of the Holy Evangelists. Otherwise, I would be a heretic. But I think that nowadays, with our enlightened philosophers constantly banging our ears about the Supreme Being and roundly despising the Church, it is useful to study the ancient religions and the world to which they freely refer. But I'm sorry, I am digressing. Let us come back to this post-script.'

He puts on his glasses in order to read again my father's letter, then places them once more on the table.

'At first sight what we have here could be a definition of the principle of Karma...but that would be surprising, knowing your father.'

'You knew my father then?'

'It was I who officiated at his marriage, after all! After that we only met on few occasions, unfortunately. But we passed some pleasant times together, discussing things, right here. He had a very open mind, like most sailors, I suppose, but perhaps even more so. He was very responsive to anything concerning primitive religions, particularly those of the natives of Canada. He told me too about the things he had seen during his voyages. I told him about my own reading and together we tried to make sense of the history of the world. In our own modest way, of course.'

'He talked to you about Canada! Did he tell you about his campaigns at the siege of Louisbourg?'

'Not at all. We only talked about the customs and religion of the Canadian Indians, about which he seemed to know a lot, but we never talk about military matters. It is true that I never thought of asking him about that.'

'And what is this Karma?'

'Oh! It's an old Sanskrit word.'

'Samkit?'

'Sanskrit! A very old language. It is the origin of most of the dialects spoken today in the vast continent of India, which your father also talked to me about. It is still the holy language of the Hindus, which is the biggest religion in that distant country. Like Latin and Greek for us, it is always used by their wise men priests, called brahmas, but it is much older. It was without doubt spoken thousands of years before Our Lord Jesus Christ. Its writing is very strange. It is a little bit like Greek. I can show you some as I have a Sanskrit dictionary.'

The rector gets up and goes to find on the shelves behind him a huge quarto volume, bound in leather with a gold blazon on the spine. He puts it on his desk, opens it and turns it towards me. It is in manuscript. I can see elegant signs, with curves, dashes and strokes. These characters have been written in black ink, in one hand, for sure, with perfectly geometrical downstrokes and upstrokes. The letters are joined with horizontal strokes, no doubt to create complete words.

'It looks like a musical score,' I say.

'You are right. I have even copied these characters onto a roll of paper that I put in the hand of one of the Wise Men at the Christmas nativity scene at Mesquer. Do you know how I came by this book? It will surprise you...it was your father who gave it to me. I had told him in passing, more than ten years ago, in 1765, that I was interested in Sanskrit. He had left for India at the start of the next year and asked a Jesuit father at Chandernagore to compile this for me. He came back to France in between times but never said anything about it. It was on his return from his second voyage, in 1771, that he had this volume brought to me by his First Mate, Captain Muterse, from Guérande. Six years had passed, and I had completely forgotten about it. Imagine my surprise! What is more, your father had the thoughtfulness to have it bound with my family coat of arms. And to think that I never saw him again to thank him.'

1771! That was the year of my father's last return from India. He had arrived at L'Orient right at the end of August. Three months later he had left us to return to Brest and we never saw him again. The next year it was my mother's turn to die. Four years later, the memory of these dreadful events is just as painful. But, this time, my grief is to an extent eased by the interesting aspect of what the good rector has just told me.

'An old First Mate of my father's lives at Guérande, then?'

'Yes, and I would advise you to go quickly if you want to see him, as he leaves on a new voyage soon, this time as Captain. But let us return to the principal of Karma, about which we were talking. It is a difficult theory to explain in just a few words. I would say that it is founded on the belief in reincarnation, the transmigration of souls from body to body. The Hindus think that the acts committed in our previous lives have a direct influence on our present life. It is also an original way of dealing with the role of fate in our existence. I don't know if you follow me…'

'I think so,' I say. 'But your explanation seems quite different from the definition given in the post-script to my father's letter.'

'Exactly! And that is what troubles me. I discussed the principle of Karma often enough with your father to know that he was perfectly capable of presenting it in a coherent and intelligible way. However, if you will pardon me, the sentence he has left you does not really mean anything. It is pure gobbledegook.'

The rector puts on his glasses once more and reads in a loud voice: 'Karma enjoins reasoned sentiment and lucidity amidst unending night'.

'This makes no sense and that is why I don't think that your father had the least intention of giving a definition when he wrote this. He must have been trying to pass on a message that he did not want to write in full and for that, he will have used some sort of code. Do you know whether he ever had occasion to use a code or a cipher?'

'Not as far as I am aware, no, but this seems to be the case and the Chevalier de Kermean said exactly the same thing.'

The rector leans back in his chair, joins his hands in front of his face and closes his eyes for a moment before speaking again.

'In that case, it seems likely that your father thought that whomever he was addressing would not have the key to decipher it. Logically, he would therefore have used a very simple method. I am going to copy down this sentence, with your permission, so that I can think about it from my point of view. The rest of the letter is clear enough and presents you with no problem.'

*

Before taking my leave, I explained that I was looking for a Captain Macé and a ship called *le Formidable* on which my father had apparently served. The rector once more advised me to try to get to see Captain Muterse. He told me that he lived just outside the centre of Guérande, but that is all he knew. Before I left, he copied the post-script on a plain sheet of paper that he put away between the pages of his Sanskrit dictionary.

On the way home I thought about the bearded man chased out of the church by the verger, and stopped often to look behind me and listen. I was sure that there was nobody following me. It could just have been a coincidence, this time.

I went to Guérande the next Thursday morning. Captain Muterse lived in a new house just outside the town. He welcomed me warmly when I had explained who I was, and invited me to a terrace at the back of the house from where one could enjoy a superb view over the Guérande saltings and, in the distant countryside, the twin bell towers of the towns of Batz and Le Croisic. Captain Muterse had all the time in the world, contrary to what the rector had told me. He was not leaving until the following year as Captain of a ship bound for Bengal. Since the winding-up of the India Company he had worked for independent ship-owners. In fact, he had not been First Mate to my father, but Second Mate, aboard *le Marquis de Castries,* which set sail from L'Orient for

Bengal in January 1766, returning to L'Orient in October 1767. He was First Mate on his next voyage, but not with my father this time. He had left L'Orient on the 20 March 1770 as First Mate, aboard *le Massiac*, bound for Pondicherry. My father had left the day before as Captain of *le Triton*, again for Bengal. They only saw each other again back at L'Orient, the following year. *Le Massiac*, which had arrived two weeks previously, was finishing its unloading when *le Triton* reached port. On learning that Muterse was going home on leave at Guérande, my father had given him the parcel to deliver to the rector of Mesquer. My father therefore made three voyages in the pay of the India Company, one as First Mate and the next two as Captain.

I asked Captain Muterse whether he could tell me anything about a Captain Macé, with whom my father had made his first voyage to the Indies. He told me that he was one and the same person as Monsieur Marion Dufresne, the Frigate's Lieutenant, who was the second witness at my father's marriage. Macé was simply a nickname used at the time amongst friends. This explained why the Baron de Kermean had never heard of him. I then asked where I might possibly find this Marion Dufresne, and if there was any chance I might get to meet him when I went to Brest at the end of the summer. The Captain replied that unfortunately I had no chance of meeting him as he had been dead since 1772. What was more, he had never been buried anywhere, since, incredible as it may seem, he had been eaten by cannibals[8] in the Pacific Ocean. Captain Muterse had seen him for the last time at Port-Louis, on the Île-de-France, in 1770. Captain Macé had been given the command of a voyage of exploration in the Pacific islands, as escort to the Aoutourou.

'Aoutourou – you have certainly heard of him? He was the famous native from the island of Tahiti, whom Bougainville brought back from his voyage around the world and presented in person to King Louis XV, at Versailles.'

I just nodded politely. I did not know much about Monsieur de Bougainville. I had heard at Vannes that he had led a voyage around the world, that he had published an account of this voyage and that the book

8 Translator's Note: *eaten by cannibals:* Dufresne and 26 of his crew were killed and possibly cannibalised by Maoris in the Bay of Islands, New Zealand, on 12th June 1772.

had been a great success. That had piqued my interest, but unfortunately for me the book had been withdrawn from the library of the Saint-Yves College by the Good Fathers, just after my arrival at Vannes, because, they said, of a series of scandalous articles inspired by the *Voyage of Bougainville* and published in the periodical *Correspondance Littéraire.*

My father's letter was dated November 1771, and he must have died a few days later. At that time, his friend Macé was still alive, and so he could well have referred to him in his last letter to his brother-in-law. If this Macé, or rather Marion Dufresne, was the comrade that my father was alluding to, his death without trace at the other end of the world released me from any obligations towards him. However, to satisfy my conscience I still needed to check the name of the ship he had served aboard with my father.

'Have you ever heard of a ship called *le Formidable*?' I asked.

'*Le Formidable*? As far as I know she was a King's ship. She was part of the wretched fleet commanded by the Maréchal de Conflans which was defeated at the Battle of Quiberon Bay. She was captured by the English during the battle. But she had had such a rough time and was in such a poor state that they could never have got her sailing again and so they scuttled her. What do you want to know exactly?'

'My father was an officer aboard *le Formidable* and I simply wanted to verify whether Captain Marion Dufresne had been on this ship at the same time as him.'

'I don't think so. But I can't say for certain. I know that in March 1759, at L'Orient, Captain Dufresne had unloaded a frigate which belonged to the India Company, but which had been provisionally armed with 32 cannons. He brought her back from the Île-de-France. *La Diligente* – I remember her well. Then he joined the King's Navy with the rank of Frigate's Lieutenant. But I don't think he was at the Battle of Quiberon Bay. He only joined the ships in the Vilaine later. He was assigned to *le Robuste*, a ship of the line, commanded by the Chevalier de Ternay. However, I don't think that he and the Chevalier got on well together, to the extent that Marion Dufresne soon re-joined the India Company. I am only repeating what I have been told, as I myself was at the Île-de-France during this time. However, I do know someone who can help you. At Le Croisic there is a former bosun's mate from *le Formidable*. He lost a leg in the Battle of Quiberon Bay and so was put ashore at Le Croisic. In the end he stayed there. He married the daughter of a port shopkeeper, a ships' chandler and sailmaker. Nowadays he manages the whole business, I think. His name is Le Touze. His shop is easy to find, on the quay in the middle of town. I don't think you even need an introduction from me. As soon as you tell him your name, he will welcome you with open arms. The seamen and petty officers always loved your father. He was a good captain.'

This Battle of Quiberon Bay had certainly created a lot of marriages!

*

Guérande, Thursday 27th June 1776, during the morning.

I have one more question to ask Captain Muterse before leaving. It is a painful question, but I have to ask it to try to lighten my heart.

'Did you know my father well?'

'I lived with him in the confined space of a ship for a whole expedition to India and back. Two years! I don't know of a better way to really get to know somebody.'

'Did you ever see him get involved in making money on the side, a 'private stash'?'

'Good Lord no! Who told you that?'

'It's a rumour coming from the offices of the Admiralty in Vannes.'

'The Admiralty! They don't know what they are talking about! They would be better to keep quiet! For a start, making a bit on the side was tolerated, by the Company, within certain limits. Each member of the crew had the right to 'get involved', as you say. It was perfectly legal as long as the limits were respected relative to each crew member's rank. It was called a 'port-permission' and it was kept track of. It was of course tempting to go over the limit, a lot of people did so, and without exaggerating too much, the Company usually turned a blind eye. However, certain Captains got into trouble with the Company management on account of this. Marion Dufresne, for example, was known as a big trader. But to come back to your father, he never did it. He even refused to take advantage of his 'port-permission'. He said he was an officer of the King and it was incompatible with his position. I heard him quote his father-in-law, the Baron de Kermean, whom he greatly admired. If your father is to be believed, the Baron had told him that it would be a total dishonour to make even a penny in the service of the King.'

*

When I returned to the chateau from Guérande my uncle was there. His visit to Nantes had apparently gone well and the Baron de Kermean was delighted by this.

The Chevalier once more brought up the matter of duelling.

'But uncle,' I said, 'Why do you so want me to fight a duel? I don't want to.'

'I know, Pierre-Marie, I know, but I know you too well. With the best will in the world, wherever you go you have the ability to get yourself into impossible situations. And in any case, if the Marine Guards are anything like the Pages, you just won't cut it.'

He gave me one of his old epees, a service arm from 1767, on the blade of which, in its central groove, he had had engraved the motto of his Company: *quo ruit et lethum*[9]. This detail apart, it was identical to the one I would be issued with in Brest, as all the officers' epees were the same, in both the Navy and the Army. I would doubtless be offered one, but in my uncle's opinion it was vital that I start to familiarise myself with this sword straight away, if only to get used to carrying it all the time, on foot and on horseback, without getting the sheath caught between my legs. He undertook to teach me the art of fencing and began by explaining that a battle and a duel were totally different. He had experience of both and knew what he was talking about.

'In battle, one often strikes blindly, with the point, using the momentum of the horse, or else with the blade, from side to side. You have to strike quickly, without looking too much at your opponents, and without thinking too much either. In any case, you don't usually have the time. The best weapon for that is, I think, the cavalry sabre. It can be used like a club, without too much finesse. Any woodsman can do it. However, you need a strong wrist. That is perhaps the only thing in common with fencing. The art of the epee is quite different. It demands finesse, a good eye, and skill that cannot be acquired without careful practice. But it is not enough to be skilful and well-practised in order to win. A duel is prepared for with both head and heart. The result of a fight is decided almost always at the first clash of steel. The whole of you must therefore be like a living blade, from the soles of your feet

9 Where one falls, there is death

to the point of your epee. It is your will which decides the victory, or the defeat, or perhaps your death. I can tell you that I have fought many times, perhaps too often, but you do not joke about matters of honour. I want to teach you everything I know and educate you in the art of the epee as best I can. But before beginning I want to give you two pieces of advice that you must never forget. The first is to avoid duels with pistols. They leave too much to chance and if you are not killed on the spot, the wounds take a long time to heal. Often a bullet has to be extracted, with a greater risk of infection. It is nothing like a clean sword wound. My second piece of advice is this: when you know that you must respond to a challenge on a particular day, empty your head completely when you wake in the morning; forget everything, even why you are fighting. Think of nothing but your fencing. Use every free moment to prepare for the first clash of the blade. When the moment arrives, enter the combat with a cool head. Look your opponent straight in the eye, without animosity, with both complete detachment and keen attention. You must not be angry. Keep a cool head and a lively mind: that is most important!'

'Duelling! I didn't think it still existed. I didn't know my father well, but I could not imagine that he was capable of risking his life so lightly.'

'It is true that I never heard your father speak about duels. He was not talkative about that kind of thing. In any case, he was not a man to seek out a quarrel. And I doubt anyone would have wanted to seek one with him. Despite his calm and friendly character, one could sometimes sense in him something strange...and wild...yes, wild is the right word. This was not noticeable except in extreme circumstances, but I did have occasion to witness this at least once. It was at L'Orient. We had been accosted in the street by some drunken, aggressive individuals. All they had to do was to get close to him to feel exactly what I just told you. I had goose pimples just watching. In the end they left; we didn't even have to draw sword. But then, what with his campaigns in the Seven Years' War and his voyages to India, he would not have had much opportunity for duelling. As for me, I only remember having to draw sword once in Germany. But in Paris and Versailles it was a different matter. At the Pages, we used stolen foils in the fencing hall. We took the protection off the points and sharpened the blades. They had a square section, which made wounds very dangerous. That is the main trouble with duels. Although one would be very unlucky to be killed, one is often wounded and stuck in bed for some time. It is always annoying. That is why it is frowned on to fight during a campaign. No, believe me, when you arrive at the Marine Guards they will sure as anything pick a fight with you, and the sooner the better! If you don't want to be fighting the whole time you are there, I can only see one solution: be an outstanding swordsman from the start. They will respect you and leave you in peace.'

From then on, I was allowed several lessons a day. And, when I was not fencing with my uncle, I had to strengthen my wrists. The Chevalier gave me a heavy lead bar and prescribed exercises in which I had to hold it in one hand with my arm outstretched. He taught me too how to handle a pistol. He was an excellent teacher, and I took his lessons seriously. I wanted to go to sea and had no desire to waste time in hospital over silly questions of honour.

7

I had decided to go to Le Croisic the following Saturday as it would be high tide towards two in the afternoon. The most convenient route was across the Traict sands using a ford at low water. By leaving early in the morning I could make my visit and be back by the same route before nightfall. I left on horseback at dawn. The fording route across the Grand Traict in fog can be dangerous for those who do not know it well, and so Ottmeyer made sure someone went with me. My guide was called Leguen and was about the same age as me. He was the younger son of a salt worker. His father had placed him at Kermean as an apprentice groom in the hope that he would learn to look after his mules. Leguen had been well trained by Ottmeyer, who had passed on his love and knowledge of horses and had taught him to ride. But the veteran of the Dauphin's Cavalry had also talked about his campaigns, while embellishing them somewhat, to the extent that the boy now thought of nothing but joining the cavalry, much to his father's disappointment.

On leaving the manor we headed due south, across woods and moors, as far as the village of Trescalan. There we took a path which winds down between dunes and cliffs then crosses the saltings. Leguen put us into a gallop across the wet sand of the Traict at low water. Noisy seabirds wheeled up in front of us. To the east, a little to our left, the view was lost in the flat stretches of the Guérande saltings. To our right, in the extension of an arm of sand and moorland, several anchored barques rocked gently in a depression still filled with water after the retreat of the tide. The bigger boats in the port were aground behind the *jonchères*, with only their masts visible from the Traict. These *jonchères* are embankments forming walls in front of the quay at Le Croisic, which create docks in which the boats are sheltered from the choppy waves at high tide. They have been built up over the course of centuries from the stone ballast thrown out by the boats which have come to load salt. I left my guide with the horses in front of the town cross, at the eastern entrance. He would wait for me at the house of my grandfather's clerk.

Old Le Touze's shop was on the quay beside the biggest of the docks, in the middle of a row of opulent houses belonging to the merchants and leading figures of Le Croisic. His establishment was indicated by a beautiful sign in painted wood fixed flat against the front of the building. It showed a King's ship of the line under full sail. The door of the shop was open. After going up a step I entered a huge dark and cluttered room with a wooden floor like the deck of a ship. The place was weakly lit by two little windows facing the quay. After the sharp brightness outside, I had to wait a few moments before being able to distinguish the objects which surrounded me in the half-light. Quantities of diverse merchandise, crammed together and piled up everywhere from the floor to the ceiling, created a sort of confused maze in which at first I thought I was alone. You could find anything at Old Le Touze's: tan sailcloth, drums of chain, ropes and cordage of all sizes, every sort of block, signal lamps and glass lanterns, shipwright's tools and caulking tools, steering compasses and spare compasses in their boxes, propellers and floats for ships' logs, barrels for salting, bails of twine, lobster pots, nets, fishing spears, porpoise harpoons, buckets made of boiled leather. Hanging at head height from the low ceiling were clog shoes and painted waterproof bonnets in heavy cloth whose strong smell merged with that of the hemp of the ropes and sails, with the perfumed odour of the vegetable resins of the tarred cables and the less pleasant stink of the pots of fish oil for the lamps.

*

Le Croisic, Saturday 29th June, towards eleven o'clock in the morning.

Someone comes across this Ali Baba's Cave to meet me. Even before seeing him, I know that it is Old Le Touze, from the unmistakeable sound of his wooden leg on the oak floorboards. He gets around remarkably easily despite his infirmity, without a stick or a crutch, leaning from time to time, as he goes, on the furniture and objects within reach, simply to keep his balance, and without stopping. He stops a few paces from me in the light from a window. Of average height and rather corpulent, he has a length of wood below the knee of his right leg. He is wearing a blue and white striped waistcoat over a linen shirt, open at the neck, and the sleeves rolled up to reveal hairy forearms. He has blue eyes and only slightly greying black hair, pulled back and held by a length of twine which serves as a ribbon.

'Well, m'lad, you lookin' for sommat?'

'Good day to you, Master Le Touze. My name is Pierre-Marie Laforest-Dombourg. I have come because I was told that you knew my father.'

'The son of Lieutenant Dombourg, are you? Well, me Gentle, you look like him too, not half! I heard about your father and Madame your mother too. What a terrible thing it is! What can I be doing for you? Here, look at this, it's a little achromatic telescope made by them Saxons in London like them of their Mister Dollond. Just the job for a future Navy officer like you.'

'It is magnificent but I'm afraid it is far too expensive for my means, Master Le Touze. Who told you I was joining the Navy?'

'What you talking about? You're the son of Monsieur Dombourg, with the sea in your blood, just like 'im. 'Fraid o' nothing, black eyes, calm as he was. We saw all that right enough in that damned battle.'

'Well, I didn't come to buy a telescope, or anything else for that matter. I would like to find the names of friends of my father who served on *le Formidable* at the same time as him. Can you help me?'

'*Le Formidable*? My last ship, was that! Eighty-four guns! It's her I had painted on the sign outside. Did you see it? Them Saxon bastards wanted to take her home as a trophy, but they come unstuck there. Holed everywhere she were, wi' more than a thousand balls planted in her woodwork. Got it both sides she did, but mainly to starb'd. What a bloody mess, b'Jeezus! Forget that? Never will long as I live. And them's as weren't there'll never know how it was.'

'Did you know an officer called Macé, or rather Marion Dufresne, aboard *le Formidable*?'

'Never 'eard that name. What rank would he be, then?'

'Frigate's Lieutenant.'

'Like your dad then. Can you say them names again, me lad?'

'Macé, or Marion Dufresne.'

'Oh aye! Well, there weren't nobody of that name on *le Formidable.*'

'You're sure?'

'Certain.'

I am somewhat disappointed, I admit. The discovery of the death of Captain Marion Dufresne had seemed to sort things out, as it released me from any obligations towards him. But here I am back at square one without any resolution to my problem. Old Le Touze seems to have a good memory and will certainly have known this 'old comrade' of my father. I have to get him talking and encourage him to search in his memories. However, I realise that it would be very impolite of me to question him there, while he is stood up and balancing on his wooden leg.

'It will soon be dinner time, Master Le Touze,' I say. 'If it is no trouble to you, I would very much like you to tell me about the last moments of *le Formidable*. May I invite you to an eating house in the port?'

'You won't be payin' for me, my oath! That's for me! Long as a future officer like you ain't ashamed to be treated by an old bosun. Just you wait a moment, I'll go and tell the mistress.'

He reappears not long afterwards, wearing a dark blue serge coat and a little round hat in black velvet. He closes the door of the shop as we leave and leads towards a square I crossed while coming. He walks using a strange stick. When I ask about it, he tells me that it is from his native district. It's called a *penn-baz*, and as we walk he explains that it can also be used as a defensive weapon. The country folk of Cornouaille never go anywhere without one, just as noblemen always carry their swords. The tavern that he leads me to is on a projection of the quay between the Grand Dock and the Little Dock. Le Touze is well known and has his own table beside a window from which one can see part of the Grand Dock.

The old bosun of *le Formidable* orders a bottle of young Nantais wine and a plate of fish cooked in wine and onions which is served to us on hollowed-out wooden bowls.

'Well then, here we are. How'd you like me to begin? Should I talk about your father, or the battle an' what happened?'

'Whatever you like, Master.'

'Well, I'll start at the beginning. It was towards the end of 1759. Weren't many ships left in du Ponants' fleet. The war was still going but we'd lost too many. Those what were left were sheltering at Brest, behind the batteries at the mouth of the harbour. Against these Saxons, or these *Angliches* if you prefer, we was no longer up to it. You can't teach topmen how to manoeuvre a ship of the line by going round and round between Roscanvel and the Horseshoe. Aye, listen well to what I'm saying, what we lacked for, more'n ships, was enough trained sailors for our vessels.'

'So there were not enough Bretons left on the coast to man the King's ships?'

Old Le Touze pointed with his hand, through the open window, to the coasters now floating at the level of the quay.

'Look at our port of Le Croisic. What d'you see? Smacks, barques, a schooner, a brigantine. Because there aren't enough good sailors or hard men to keep 'em at sea, from Spain to the Scillies, all year round and in any weather. It's true. In war time, when they become privateers, like, we even get scared of the big Angliche merchantmen. But you can't make topmen and gunners for a sixty-four gun ship overnight. You'll be telling me about the deep-sea sailors and the fishermen as go to the Grand Banks. But I tell you, at that time, too many of our topmen was dying in the prison ships at Chatham or elsewhere. 'Cause the bloody Saxons had captured 'em, on their merchantmen or their fishing boats, by pure treachery, mind, before declarin' war. Your dad knew that better'n anyone. Two of his brothers was captured like that by Admiral Boscawen. While they was fishing the Grand Banks and doin' no-one no harm. They probably died in them prison ships, like so many others.'

'Well, I didn't know that. My father never told me.'

'That don't surprise me. I never got it from 'im, but from his friend. Your father never spoke 'bout it. That were his way. But once you had to get stuck in, boy, he maybe wasn't a Breton, but you knew you could count on 'im. We was happy to have him at our side.'

'This friend of my father, do you remember him well? Were they good friends?'

'Maybe his best mate. He was a young bloke, not even one of our boys. From the south and spoke with a funny accent, but he was a Marine Guard from the Brest Company all the same. A blondie, a good brave little lad with a big round head and always smiling with it. Even if you didn't know he was a mate of your father's you'd 'ave liked him anyway. That can seem a bit odd that they was friends with such a big difference in age. But they'd served together on *le Célèbre*, a sixty-four, in the Comte de la Motte's squadron, in the Louisbourg campaign, and on the frigate *le Zéphyre*, a thirty-gun ship, in the Comte du Chaffault's squadron, the next year, again at Louisbourg.'

'Do you remember his name?'

'Sure! He was called Lapérouse, but I think that on the ship's register he was du Gallo, or sommat like that. I even thought he was Breton the first time I 'eard his name, like. I never learned to read, you know.'

I recognise the name immediately, of course: Jean-François du Galaup de Lapérouse, Marine Guard. He is the third on the list of witnesses in the Mesquer register of marriages.

'Do you know what happened to him?'

'He was put ashore at the same time as your father and me, five days after the battle, here at Le Croisic. He was looked after at Vannes, and then afterwards come back to the Vilaine, just like your dad.'

'Do you know if he went to India after that with my father?'

'After the Vilaine, I don't know what became of all of them, but Monsieur de Lapérouse stayed in the Navy, him, as he didn't have no problem with his exchange. I was told that the Duc d'Aiguillon had wrote to the Minister to tell him that he should deal with the exchange of the officers of *le Formidable* before anyone else. After the Battle of Saint Cast there was no shortage of Angliche prisoners. As for your father, no one could understand it.'

'And the Chevalier de Ternay, was he on *le Formidable* with you too?'

'No. Ship's Lieutenant he were, aboard another ship in our division, *l'Inflexible*, a sixty-four, that well and truly did for herself trying to get into the Vilaine. But the Chevalier de Ternay weren't commanding. Him, he'd already been in command, of the frigate with your dad and his mate, *le Zéphyre*, like I already said. That's why they wanted to stick with 'im when he wanted to do up our ships in the Vilaine. Your father left because of this business of his failed exchange, otherwise he would have stayed, I think. He got on well with the Chevalier.'

All this raises lots of questions, but I do not want to lose the goodwill of my companion by interrogating him too much. I ask him, therefore, to carry on with his story and promise not to interrupt him until he has finished.'

'...so our crews wasn't well enough trained, and there wasn't enough of us either, and we had lots of convalescents what had hardly got over their scurvy from previous campaigns and not had enough time to rest, like. And that's without mentionin' the big epidemic brought on us by Monsieur de Lamotte's squadron when he come back to Brittany. It's a wonder we managed to find enough lads for the ships we 'ad left. And they still wanted us to go out into the Bay of Quiberon to seek out a fleet of merchant ships loaded with infantrymen and escort 'em all the way to Scotland! You get my drift? But first, we had to sink a little Angliche division commanded by their Commodore Duff, which was blockading the Bay of Quiberon. And all that while their Admiral Hawke was blockading us at Brest. Because you can't get a ship of the line out of Brest when the wind is in the west, d'you see? The channel is too narrow to tack in and what's more there's rocks in the middle of the entrance. Well anyway, the Maréchal de Conflans, who were our commander, he was waiting for the winds to turn to get going. And during that time, Hawke's ships was going round and round outside ready to fall on our backs if we go out. Right then! Nasty blow from the south-west like you can have that time of year. Hawke and his squadron obliged to heave to and take shelter in one of their ports on the other side of the Channel. And when the storm died down, like, and the winds turned north-east, as what often 'appens when the dirty weather is finished, not a single Angliche in sight and we take advantage to go to Quiberon Bay to collect our infantrymen. We got out to open sea at eleven in the mornin' three days after the Feast of Saint-Martin, a Wednesday it were.'

The fish is getting cold on the plates; Old Le Touze had not even touched his glass, he is so engrossed in his story.

'East-north-east the wind, to get out of the harbour, that were good. But then it fell completely. We couldn't get away towards the Bec du Ras and we had to let ourselves drift again on the open sea to avoid being carried onto the Sein causeway. So by the following Monday we was way to the sou'west of Belle-Île. Then the wind backed and freshened from the west, like, and we could at last sail a direct course. We seed eight sails dead ahead of us sailing south-east. It could be that Commodore Duff getting' out of the Bay of Quiberon before being attacked. Well then, *le Soleil Royal* made the signal to give chase, like. We all set off in a right old mess. The wind had risen during the night and the sea too, 'course. And, as Duff 'ad split his division in two, the bastard, we done the same. And there's me having to take off sail in a rising sea and the masts bending. It were blowing and it felt like a storm were brewing. But the weather were still clear and we could soon see Belle-Île from the deck, north by north-west. But what we could see above all, from the masthead this time, this was, to port of Belle-Île, to our west-north-west, were a whole score of sails which at that distance could only be ships of the line. It was Hawke on his way back at the double. They was carrying all sail despite the wind and it was clear they was chasing too, but it was us what they was after. The Maréchal signalled to abandon the chase and rejoin forces. We tried to form a line and us, *le Formidable* division, under Monsieur Saint-André du Verger, a real gentleman that one, we took in sail to get ourselves into the rear-guard which were our place in the order o' battle. That took some time, we was in a right mess as I said and by the time we'd managed it, it were eleven o'clock and we was about eight leagues south of Belle-Île. It were now nearly a full gale with a heavy sea and we'd furled the t'gallants and reefed the topsails. We thought that our Maréchal were going to give us the order to tack so as we'd wait for the Angliches, like we had, on the seaward tack with plenty of sea room. We wouldn't have the advantage of the wind but with that sea we could have used our lower battery while they couldn't. But, instead of that, our Maréchal kept our course, wind three points off the port quarter, heading due north, right between them Cardinal[10] rocks and the du Four shallows. It were an hour after low water and it were spring tides an' all, day after the new moon. We could see the rocks of the Cardinals to our port alright, with breakers everywhere. And on the other side, a fair way to starboard all the same, visible from the mastheads, like, another line of breakers with a great wall of water which were building up on the du Four every time the swell passed

10 Translator's note: *Cardinal rocks: les Cardinaux* in French. The Battle of Quiberon Bay is known in France as *La Bataille des Cardinaux*.

over it. Could be that le Conflans reckoned that the Angliches, without anyone with local knowledge aboard, would lose their nerve on seeing this and stop chasing us. I heard it said too that he wanted to avoid a battle so as to keep the fleet intact so he could carry out his mission to Scotland. But I think he screwed 'imself totally. All the same, he were a good sailor. Maybe he were a bit old and were afraid to fight in that rough sea. Because the Angliches, they weren't in the least bothered by that! They kept on bearing down on us. Us, that is to say, the rear guard. And we could well see that while the head of our line would be close enough to the rocks to make it hard for them to manoeuvre, once they caught us, like, at the rear, we'd be in wide enough water for them to attack us with twenty against ten. In fact, it were worse than that!'

The old bosun dipped his finger in his wine in order to trace on the table the contours of Belle-Île and the submerged rocks around the islands in the southeast of the Bay of Quiberon.

'Towards two o'clock we passed Belle-Île, six miles on the beam to our west-northwest, and ran on with the island of Hoëdic well in sight on our port bow. That were when the two fastest Angliche ships caught up with *le Magnifique,* seventy-four guns, which were holding the back of our line, and then them cannons started to talk! I wanted to find out afterwards all the names of the ships what was in this damned battle. It were their *Derbyshire* and their *Torbay*, both the same size, what kept to windward on port tack while reefing down, then come off the wind to line 'emselves up to windward of *le Magnifique.* But just behind 'em, there was six more arriving at speed, already within cannon shot, like, and who hadn't yet reefed, sails billowing, wind dead astern, great bones in their teeth what I can still see, bringing themselves right across *le Héros* what was between us and *le Magnifique.* So the commander of our division, Monsieur Saint-André du Verger, ordered his Flag Captain, who were his brother, that we 'ad to go help them sailors at the rear. We come back on the wind a bit without moving the yards or the tacks. We was close to going under what with that sea and the wind what there were! And poof! There's *le Héros* and *le Magnifique* gone right past under our wind to starb'd. We put the helm up and found ourselves in line o' battle again, behind everyone else. But we was right in the middle of the Angliches for our trouble. And them, you could say they fair tore into us. We'd done a good move but now they was to starb'd of us and we couldn't use our lower battery on that side 'cause of the wind and the sea what we had, almost a full gale like I said. And them, the bloody Saxons, by the time we'd got up to speed again, they'd opened up proper like! They all passed one after the other within pistol shot under our wind, sailing right up to us, then giving us their whole broadsides, first their *Derbyshire* and their *Torbay*, after that their *Magnanime*, seventy-four guns. Their *Resolution,* what arrived a bit later, had kept to windward to take us on the port side, same time as their fellows was on the other. After that came their *Warspite*, a seventy-four, their *Montague* and their *Defiance*, both of 'em sixty guns. They'd given us such a roasting that they wasn't scared of us no more and had come so close, so as to rip the guts out of us with their biggest cannonballs, that our yards was rubbing with theirs in the roll of the swells, From then on we started to drag our feet. We'd lost our fore topmast; then it were the mizzen mast. There was even a few Angliche ships what was able to pass us under the wind, then done the same thing ahead of us what we'd done at the start, like, slowing down and letting us come back into range to give us another broadside; how many times and which ships it were I've no idea. I'd stopped counting. There were no time to think. It were like a living nightmare. A lot of us was starting to get killed. Monsieur Saint-André du Verger had his head carried away by a cannonball; his brother the Flag Captain were clean cut in two; the whole quarterdeck were killed in two shakes. After a short while there were only the deck Lieutenant left, Monsieur d'Arcourge as he were called. When he took a cannonball square in the chest it were your dad, what was his assistant, as took over. He found himself all alone on the quarterdeck having to command the ship. You could say that it were him what was the Captain for the whole last hour of the battle. Apart from 'im there were only one proper Naval officer left, the Ship's Lieutenant de Kersauzon, what was above him in rank but were too busy commanding what were left of our gunners on the gundeck. By then it were nearly three in the afternoon, with three quarters of an hour left of the flood tide. There weren't much current but the gusts and the big swell was pushing us sideways towards the du Four shallows. We needed a commander to direct our manoeuvres. On the steering deck most of the steersmen had been wounded by flying shards of wood but they was more sheltered than I was on the lower gundeck, and it were just nine- and twelve-pounders, while down there, in the lower gundeck, they was taking the cannonballs from the big Angliche guns at point-blank range from starb'd. They couldn't even fire back, such as with the heel of the ship, like, all the gun ports of our thirty-six-pounders was closed on that side. But the officers commanding the operation on the quarterdeck, they didn't have no protection at all, them. A steersman what were there told me how as Monsieur Dombourg your father were shouting his orders to them from the taffrail, where he had stayed all alone. How he was not sliced by a cannonball, him too, good God! That were a miracle! And then, getting on for four in the afternoon as it was, not that we knowed much about it by then, we'd never even noticed the storm had got worse, and in any case it weren't worth the bother to put in reefs since some of the sails had burned, it started to rain. Anyway, towards four in the afternoon the rudder broke and we couldn't steer no more. We was abeam of the Cardinal rocks, just after the turn of the tide. The ebb tide hadn't yet started to make but the wind and the swell was pushing us towards the shallows. Monsieur Dombourg had the Ship's Lieutenant de Kersauzon called and told him as we had to anchor quick, like, if we didn't want to end up on them rocks. The Lieutenant decided to lower our flag. Our honour were safe were what he said.'

Le Touze banged his wooden leg on the flagstone.

'That were when I lost me leg. We had to anchor and there were hardly anyone left in a fit state. I meself were preparing the end of the port cable at the forward end of the lower gundeck. I dunno how to say it; I found meself stretched out on me back. The pain, that come later. They told me after it were an Angliche nine-pounder what come right through the gun port of the forward cannon of the thirty-six we had to port. Our gun ports was open on that side, and I were hit from behind while I were bent over me work. There was some as clearly saw the cannonball ricochet off the foot o' the foremast. We'd already surrendered but I don't hold it against them Angliches, since even us had gunners still firing, deaf and tired as they was. Their nine-pounders was on the upper gun deck of their sixty-gun ships. The Angliche must have rolled and the cannonball must have headed downwards through our open gun port what with not meeting anythin' until my leg, like! It's fate is what it were. But I were lucky all the same: they didn't have to amputate since that Angliche cannonball had done the whole job. The surgeon just had to put on a rough tourniquet and cut the skin, and I lay there stretched out besides the forward port cannon of the lower gundeck for three days. There was lots of amputees what died. We'd had so many wounded, they couldn't look after 'em...'

The old bosun stopped for a moment and shook his head.

'When the Angliches come to take possession they was surprised, I were told. The starb'd bulwarks was holed like a sieve, they was! The bodies what was still there was piled up as they didn't have time to give them all a proper burial at sea. The blood what should've been washed away by the storm and water flooding everywhere, but it was still slippery to walk around. We had three hundred killed and a hundred and fifty maimed with a lot of 'em goin' to die, and all the rest was wounded one way or another. You can say honour were saved! Them Angliches was respectful towards us, I'll give 'em that. But it took 'em three days to send more surgeons. I remember, I was waked up by one of their surgeons what was looking at me. I still had me tourniquet on, my blood vessels had not been tied off. He got on 'is high horse, did this gentlem'n. He had our surgeon-in-chief called and give him a right bawlin' out. What could he have done, the poor bugger? He hadn't slept for three days, levelling off stumps and putting tourniquets on the most urgent. It was a Lieutenant-Colonel of the infantry we had on board what were the interpreter. He were a miracle escape, that one! All his men either killed or wounded except 'im. They was from the Saintonge regiment. Him, I remember 'im well since he come from Cornouaille, like what I do, from near Faou over Brest way. Monsieur Avelus, the Marquis de Kersalaun were his name. When the Angliches decided to put us ashore at Le Croisic, I mean us, the wounded, a clerk had been sent aboard to write us into the registers and make a report. Colonel Avelus had stayed on board to help the clerk what didn't speak no Angliche. Monsieur Marchais he were called, I remember now. I were starting to be aware of what were going on around me, since after me wound I were unconscious half the time and I don't remember much. I were told afterwards. But there, I can remember the Marquis de Kersalaun said to Monsieur Marchais, while they was passing in front of me the two of 'em, that when he were young he had been at the Battle of Fontenoy with the Royal Ships' regiment, and that had been bloody enough, but besides what had gone on aboard *le Formidable*, Fontenoy were a picnic.'

The narrator suddenly stops with these last words and I realise that the room has fallen silent. Everybody has gone quiet to listen to Old

Le Touze's story. He himself has not noticed. He has gone far from us, no doubt back to the heaving deck of his mortally wounded ship. I try to imagine his suffering: three days left without care, stretched out between two gun carriages, surrounded by the dead and the dying, in the November cold, shaken as one is aboard a ship at an exposed anchorage snatching at her anchors in a big sea. How did he find the strength to survive?

'I was told that my father was wounded too…'

Old le Touze picked up his glass and looked at it. It is still full and the level in the bottle placed between us has not moved either.

'That's true, but it were not noticed at first. When he were on the quarterdeck he were untouched. A miracle I tell you! But before that, he must have taken loads of flying shards from the timber being hit. He had 'em all over. I remember seeing him when he'd had me called to tell me to let go the two forward anchors. His clothes was tored to shreds and he were covered in blood from top to toe. But there were so much blood on the quarterdeck, what with the remains of all the other officers and so many bodies of sojers an' sailors, on deck or hanging from the rigging like pieces of meat, that you couldn't tell if it were his blood or someone else's.'

'How many ships did we have in this battle against the English?'

'Twenty-one ships in three divisions of seven, plus a frigate and a corvette.'

'And the English?'

'I've heard people in the know say as the Angliches had twenty-four ships and five frigates, and there's them what has even counted the number of cannon to say we had less. But that means nothing, it's bloody nonsense! And d'you know why? It's 'cause, apart from three or four of our ships, the rest, or nearly all, never really fought. That's the truth. And then, the Angliches say they sank *le Thésée* and *le Superbe*, but go and find out of it wasn't bad handling. I was told that at least one of the two suddenly started taking water onto the lower gun deck after tacking by accident. In any case, in the blow what had got up, they all went straight to the bottom with their crews. That's already a lot of men, just think! Two complete crews, plus the sojers aboard, drownded in a trice! *Le Héros* copped it less than what we done. All the same, she surrendered an hour after us, like. But with the storm what was already on us, the bloody Saxons couldn't even send a boat to take possession. And night comes quick in November. Everyone anchored at dusk, in the squalls, as best he could, all over the place, in sixteen fathom, battered by the waves. And we was dragging everywhere what with the wind and the current. All what I'm telling you here, I was told, because me, in my state...At daybreak the tide'd already been going out for four hours, there was two Angliches what had given chase was up fair and square on the Four rocks: done for! *Le Héros,* who was also completely aground a bit further on, the Angliches burned her. And we could see *le Soleil Royal* aground at Le Croisic. The Angliches tried to get close to take possession, close enough for the coastal battery at Le Croisic to open fire and she were eventually burned. *Le Magnifique*, what had caused us so much trouble, had disappeared from the start, and she was at Rochefort, intact, with eight other ships. And what in God's name was they doing there, I ask you? And then there was the others what was in the Vilaine after passing the night in Pénerf harbour. Except for *l'Inflexible* what missed the entrance as I told you. There was another what went aground in the Loire estuary, so it seems. Monsieur Saint-André du Verger, him, he didn't waste a second in getting back to rescue the sailors of the rear guard once the engagement began, but he was the only one on that day to react, great man what he was. All them other commanders, what did they do?'

The old sailor shakes his head again. Seventeen years later he still does not understand.

'Anyway, when they tried the Maréchal later, at Brest, and they asked him to account for the loss of *le Soleil Royal,* you can imagine he said what he thought about his commanders who had practically not fired a single shot. Nobody was too proud, you know! And after that, Lieutenant de Kersauzon had his turn in front of that Commission of Inquiry, like, who wanted to know why *le Formidable* had surrendered. Your father couldn't be there as he were still too weak. And when they properly understood what had happened with us, that almost all our fine officers and sailors had been killed at their combat posts, and that your father, just a Frigate's Lieutenant as he were, had commanded his vessel for more than an hour against more than eight enemy vessels, without weakening, at the same time as ten Captains of ships of the line had fled without putting up any real fight, and that even the Angliches spoke well of us, well then, they said it was us what had saved the honour of the Navy, what! And that's how your father were promoted to Ship's Ensign and were given the Cross of Saint-Louis too. And me, Monsieur, when they told me that, I were more than happy for 'im and proud too, because them rewards gave honour to all of us, the living and the dead of *le Formidable*.'

*

I had much to reflect on returning to Kermean that evening, at the half past eight low tide. Old Le Touze's telling of the story of the Battle of Quiberon Bay was truly terrifying. I knew that not everything could be rosy in the life of a sailor, but what I had just been told went well beyond anything I had imagined. My uncle had told me about the sufferings of the French soldiers during the German winters of the Seven Years' War: bare feet under their linen gaiters when it was so cold that the horsemen had to walk on foot, leading their horses by their bridles, so as not to be frozen on the spot, but this did not seem as bad as what I had just heard. And I said to myself too that this description, impressive as it was, without doubt fell short of the reality. On the other hand, I could well imagine my father at his station on the quarterdeck, imperturbable in the midst of hell. He was extraordinarily lucky, that was for sure. But why did the English not want to exchange him?

I knew now that my father's best friend aboard *le Formidable* was this Monsieur de Lapérouse, whose signature I had already seen in the Mesquer parish register of marriages. He had been a Marine Guard at Brest, and as long as he was still alive, I had a good chance of picking up his tracks when I too joined this Company. Old Le Touze had made him sound like a likeable fellow, which was reassuring should I be in his debt.

8

It happened that the Marquis de Becdelièvre was visiting his estates at Mesquer towards the middle of the summer. This visit was expected by the Baron de Kermean, who had already spoken to me about it. It was a rare event as this high and mighty personage usually only stayed at his chateau at Tréambert during the autumn. The rest of the time he lived on his properties near Nantes. I did not know what had prompted this unexpected visit and did not presume to be the cause of it, although I was his godson. However, honesty and modesty oblige me to say that I was by no means the only one in this position, for the great lords are often approached by the heads of families for this sort of favour. Be that as it may, the Marquis de Becdelièvre had offered of his own volition to pay my six hundred pounds a year fee at Brest. It was a goodly amount, but the Becdelièvres are rich. Their estates at Mesquer and Saint-Molf were only a small part of their fortune, and these themselves were considerable. They were made up of the chateaux of Tréambert and Quifistre with their respective parks, lakes, warrens and woods, as well as thirty-eight thousand acres of arable land divided into seven farms, and not forgetting nine hundred salt pans on the saltings and, finally, huge areas of brush and moorland, bursting with game of every sort.

The Baron de Kermean was waiting for this opportunity to go and present me to my illustrious godfather, whom I had not yet met. As well as that, my grandfather wanted to raise the subject of a channel for irrigating his and the Marquis's pans at the end of the Quimiac saltings. For this occasion, he had tied his long white hair back with a velvet ribbon and had dug out of his wardrobe an embroidered jacket, a little out of fashion perhaps, but which well suited him, which I had never seen before. My uncle, the Chevalier, wore a wig along with his black clothes adorned with no more than his Cross of Saint-Louis. As for me, I will say only that I wore my hair *au naturel,* like my grandfather, which I preferred, although I was aware that I would soon lose it once I became a Marine Guard Cadet at Brest. We went on horseback, swords at our side.

The chateau of Tréambert stood in the northern part of a rectangular park, wooded and enclosed by walls, seven hundred yards long and four hundred yards wide. The property was situated between the town of Mesquer and the Quimiac saltings. Coming from Tréambert, we approached it from the south, having come through a salt workers' village. We went along a beautiful straight and well-maintained avenue, six hundred yards long and bordered with horse chestnut trees. The chateau of Tréambert was not as old as that of Kermean, having been constructed by the Marquis's grandfather. It was a large rectangular building of two storeys with mansards on the attics. The entrance, on the left side of the façade, was surmounted by a triangular pediment in the classical style, as was the fashion during the time of Louis XIV.

We were introduced by a liveried footman into a salon whose parquet floor shone in the sunlight pouring through large bay windows open to the ornamental garden. The walls were panelled and hung with gold-framed mirrors. The inlaid furniture on which stood porcelain figurines, the wide, deep hearths in white marble, all bore witness to the wealth and taste of the important figure we had come to visit. It was a far cry from the brick and earthen flooring of Kermean.

After a few minutes the Marquis came to join us. He was close to seventy but bore his years lightly. He was dressed carefully, but with restraint, his wig freshly powdered, and showed truly charming politeness for a man of such importance. His high forehead and dark eyebrows gave him a sombre look, happily softened by his full cheeks and smiling mouth.

The Marquis de Becdelièvre apologised for receiving us on his own, saying that his family had remained at Nantes. He looked at me with kindness when I was presented. After the usual civilities, he invited us to follow him outside, to the end of a terrace where a table was laid for dinner under an arch covered in blossom and from which one had a fine view of the marshes, the small town of Quimiac and, as the Marquis pointed out to us, the channel leading to the Kermean saltings. Servants and a head waiter in white gloves, attentive and silent, served us on plates of Sèvres porcelain.

The Marquis de Becdelièvre recalled the time when my father had been billeted with him, wounded, after the disaster at the Battle of Quiberon Bay. I asked him politely whether he had met Monsieur Marion Dufresne and the Chevalier de Ternay at my parents' wedding. He remembered them well. He told us that de Ternay and Dufresne did not get on well at all. When the latter had suggested to my father that he join the India Company it was he, the Marquis, who had convinced him to accept. On the other hand, he did not remember much about the Marine Guard de Lapérouse. He had joined my father later, directly in the Vilaine, without doubt, and he had never come to Tréambert. The Marquis de Becdelièvre did not know what had become of these officers, and it was I who told him of the tragic end of Captain Dufresne.

I knew that the Marquis de Becdelièvre was a friend of the Duc d'Aiguillon who, in his capacity of military Governor of Brittany during the Seven Years' War, had overseen all the prisoner exchanges with the English after the Battles of Saint-Cast and Quiberon Bay. I asked the Marquis whether he knew why they had refused to exchange my father. He replied that it was inexplicable. The Duc d'Aiguillon had even put on hold the exchange of the Lieutenant-Colonel in command of the infantry aboard *le Formidable*, in order to keep an English officer available to exchange for my father. As a result, this Lieutenant-Colonel had resigned from the Saintonge regiment in which he was serving and taken passage, the following February, as a private passenger aboard a merchant ship loaded at L'Orient for the Île-de-France[11]. Despite this, not only had the exchange not taken place, but the English had

11 Translator's note: Exchanges of paroled officers were often nominal, rather than physical. Once the Lieutenant-Colonel had resigned his military commission, he was no longer paroled, leaving his counterpart paroled English officer free to be 'exchanged' for Laforest-Dombourg's father.

demanded that my father be handed over to them. The Duc d'Aiguillon had interviewed my father, after which he had refused to hand him over. The Marquis had tried his best to find out why the British Admirals were fighting so hard to get their hands on a lowly Frigate's Lieutenant, but the Duc d'Aiguillon would not tell him. My father would only say that there was an old dispute between him and Admiral Boscawen.

I thanked the Marquis for telling me all this and he then turned to my uncle, asking him what was going on at Court. My uncle talked at length about the intrigues and infighting of those around Louis XVI. The end of our conversation was taken up with the problems of my grandfather's channels and I only listened with half an ear.

9

During the weeks which followed our visit to Tréambert, the Chevalier worked hard at training me to fence and to shoot. When I was not working with him at these weapons, I went with my grandfather on his inspections. The estate had entered a period of great activity. It is at the height of summer that the clay diggers put into practice the words spoken by Our Lord to Adam: 'You will earn your bread by the sweat of your brow!'

Haymaking was soon complete, as the hay ripens quickly beside the sea. I have a fleeting memory of several mornings spent in the crisp and salty seaside air, working beside the tenant farmers, piling up the fresh grass dried by the wind. The Baron had his own ideas about how to educate a future officer of the King. According to him, working on the land was a healthy and beneficial exercise. There was nothing dishonourable in it for a young man from a good family destined to an active life. In the fulfilment of these principles, I on more than one occasion ended up with a soaked shirt working beside my grandfather's labourers. And, while on that subject, I would like to know what the great Jean-Jacques Rousseau really knew about working in the fields, and on what authority he maintains that this occupation leads to philosophic reflection because, speaking for myself, I had too many blisters on my hands and was too stiff throughout my entire body to even be able to think about my puzzle regarding Karma. All I could do was hope that our wise rector was doing it for me. I went from time to time to the vicarage to see if he was making any progress, but he had found nothing, certainly not for want of imagination: he had even written out the post-script about Karma several times in Sanskrit in the hope that this might throw some light on the matter. I had admired the beautiful calligraphy and asked for a copy to show to the Chevalier.

Harvest time came. The farm workers toiled from dawn to dusk, the men in hats, the women protected by a towel knotted around their heads. At the Manor, the Baron himself supervised the preparation of the threshing floor, which required a special soft soil that the Kermean carts went to fetch from a spot half a day's drive away from the chateau. During a break between this carting, we went to see the harvesters in action. The fit men were all assembled each day on a single field. They entered the wheat, drawn up in line of battle, scythes in hand. Behind them the ears were gathered by young girls from all the tenant farms. They had tucked up their skirts in order to pass through the stalks, which rubbed their knees and thighs, making them burst out laughing. Some of them smiled boldly at me as they passed by to pile the stalks into stooks. My grandfather said to me with a laugh, 'Laforest-Dombourg, do you still want to spend your life crossing the ocean? I bet you will never see such pretty harvests!' And in the evening, as if to prove him right, all this hot-blooded youth assembled together to dance on the threshing floor, despite the tiring work of the day.

The threshing was the high point of the summer. I ended up barefooted, in a linen shirt, a flail in my hand, elbow to elbow with the other threshers, on a carpet of golden wheat. 'An excellent exercise for the eye and the wrist,' the Chevalier de Kermean had decreed. Between two turns on the threshing floor I took my breath and watched the women taking away the straw we had shelled. The girls had untied their bonnets and bodices to be free to move and I could not resist sneaking a sideways glance at the front of their blouses which they uncovered so generously as they leaned forward to push their wooden forks. I had reached the age when the slightest thing was arousing. Seeing the drops of sweat forming pearls on the curves of these good farm girls had my imagination galloping, far from the mysteries and symbols of reincarnation in the ancient Indian religions.

Fortunately for me our rector was still searching for an answer. On the eve of the Assumption he sent word saying that he had almost certainly found the key to our puzzle and asking me to come to the church, bringing my father's letter with me, so that he could have a final look at it after Mass. I borrowed from the Baron de Kermean an old folder in tattered red Moroccan leather into which I slipped the precious posthumous letter of my father and the rector's attempts at Sanskrit calligraphy, so that I could carry them without creasing them in the side-bags of my saddle.

*

Mesquer, Thursday 15th August 1776, towards half past ten in the morning.

Normally I enjoy High Mass at Mesquer but this time, under the circumstances, the sermon seems to drag on. The rector begins by reminding us that the Cult of Our Lady had been particularly strong in our parish since the twelfth century, long before King Louis XIII made his vow to the Virgin Mary, for that had been the wish of the knights of the nearby Templar Lodge…And our good rector once again launched into a defence of the Templars… '*And they changed their name from the Poor Knights of Christ to the Knights of the Temple, or the Templars, as they had been given quarters in the Temple of Solomon.*' I have heard this many, many times and my mind is elsewhere as I look absently at the pictures on the stained-glass windows.

'*…and Solomon is called Salaun in Breton…*'

I have the impression that while saying that, the preacher looks at me particularly attentively, and I wonder what I have missed.

After the final blessing and the *ite missa est,* instead of going out with everybody else I wait patiently in my place. I know that the rector likes to chat with his faithful under the porch of the church. The smell of incense still floats around me, the sound of conversation drifts in from outside in a confused murmur, the rays of sunshine warm the nave through the blues and golds of the stained-glass windows…and I gently start to fall asleep with the folder on my knees.

'Well, Monsieur Laforest-Dombourg, how did you find my sermon?'

'Oh! Remarkable, rector!' I say, rising quickly from the pew on which I had fallen asleep.

In truth I have scarcely listened to our rector talk about the things which are dear to him, but which I am beginning to get to know very well since spending so much time at the Mesquer vicarage. During these impromptu visits I have endured lessons in Sanskrit and on Karma, of course, but also on the Templars, Saint Bernard, and not forgetting, as the crowning glory, on heraldry and its symbols. The rector has developed a passion for this old-fashioned science, which nobody can hold against him since he himself is a descendant of an old and noble family.

'Have you brought your father's letter?'

I get it out of my folder. He takes it and opens his eyes wide for a moment while bringing it near to his face, then hands it back to me.

'Read the post-script to me again.'

I know this part by heart and read it in a loud voice: 'Karma enjoins reasoned sentiment and lucidity amidst unending night.'

'No, I'm sorry, but you have not read it correctly! Look at the letter properly...'

I do as he says.

'Look how the words are written,' he insists. 'Don't they all have capitals?'

'That's right,' I say. 'But I have never given that much attention.'

'And me neither. And that is why I have wasted so much time searching for some kind of sense to it, when in fact there is none, absolutely none! My first intuition was correct. The sentence is totally meaningless. I told you that your father will have used a very simple method. Listen. If you keep just the first letter of each word it gives us a proper noun: KERSALAUN...Ker Salaun, which means in a way the Temple of Solomon, to which I alluded in my sermon. Does this name mean anything to you?'

I look at the post-script with a new eye: '**K**arma **E**njoins **R**easoned **S**entiment **A**nd **L**ucidity **A**midst **U**nending **N**ight'.

It really is true! And I know immediately to whom it refers: the Marquis Avelus de Kersalaun! Old Le Touze had given me his full title. He had even told me that he was from the Faou region, near Brest. The Marquis de Becdelièvre had also talked about him, without mentioning his patronym, which perhaps he did not know. But there is no room for confusion; it's all to do with the same person. He told us that this officer had taken passage from L'Orient in February 1760, bound for the Île-de-France. But, above all, the request for his exchange had been deferred by the Duc d'Aiguillon because of my father. That is perhaps the reason why my mother had told me that he was under an obligation towards his comrade. But what can I do about it now? The words used in my father's letter and by my mother when she spoke to me seem to indicate that the Marquis de Kersalaun had come back from the Indies in 1772. I ought then, logically, be able to find him in his native area of Cornouaille. I share this last thought with the rector, who advises me to visit Captain Muterse again and learn what I can from him.

*

On the way back to Kermean, riding boot to boot with my grandfather, I asked him about the Battle of Fontenoy. Old Le Touze had told me that the Marquis de Kersalaun had served in the Royal Ships' Regiment when he was young. The Baron de Kermean told me that this regiment had been sorely tested at this battle. When the English forces had broken our lines, knocking aside everything in their way and routing several of our regiments, the men of the Royal Ships had found themselves alone against the main column of the enemy assault. They had almost one hundred and fifty killed and three times that wounded within a few minutes, but they held good. Thanks to their sacrifice, the Army of the King of France avoided a serious defeat that day. The Maréchal de Saxe was able to organise cavalry counter attacks in which the Baron had taken part and which determined the final victory.

I went to Guérande the next day. By chance Captain Muterse was at home. He welcomed me as warmly as the previous time and began by asking me if I liked coffee. He had some coffee from Saint-Domingue that he had had delivered from Nantes and roasted himself. His housemaid filtered it while we talked, so that we could then taste it together on his terrace while enjoying the view over the coast.

The Captain remembered the arrival of the Marquis de Kersalaun at the Île-de-France. He had arrived there aboard a frigate of the India Company, *la Diligente*, five hundred tonnes, commanded by Captain Pierre-Léon Mauguaret, a friend of my host. The arrival in the Indian Ocean of this little ship, safe and sound, in the middle of the Seven Years' War, was thought of as a real miracle. This frigate must have been lucky, for I remembered Captain Muterse telling me, during my last visit, that it had made the same voyage in reverse the previous year, in 1759, and with the same good fortune, under the command of Marion Dufresne. Having arrived at the end of June 1760 at Port-Louis on the Île-de-France, Captain Mauguaret had stayed there for two weeks, then left for Pondicherry where he arrived in mid-August. This was one of the last connections made with this trading port before the English blockaded it completely. When he returned, Captain Mauguaret had told his friend Muterse that General Lally-Tollendal wanted to give a command to the Marquis de Kersalaun, but the latter had scruples about accepting as he had not been exchanged. The Marquis de Kersalaun had left Pondicherry with a group of other adventurers to go into the interior of the Indian continent and nothing had been heard of him since. Later, Pondicherry fell, in January 1761, after a terrible six-month siege. We now know the painful circumstances of this surrender and its vexing consequences, especially for the unfortunate Lally[12]. Moreover, nobody had been in the least worried about the fate of the Marquis Avelus de Kersalaun, one-time Lieutenant-Colonel in the Saintonge regiment and veteran of the Battle of Fontenoy.

*

Guérande, Friday 16th August 1776, towards three o'clock in the afternoon.

We are sitting peacefully on the terrace drinking our coffee when we hear a furious barking and shouts from the courtyard on the other side of the house. Shortly afterwards, a housemaid comes to tell us that someone had managed to get in by the gate which had been inopportunely left open and that he had been discovered beside my horse, which I had left outside. Luckily, he had been chased off before having had the time to unhitch it. Inspecting my tack, I realise that last night I had forgotten to take the red Moroccan leather folder out of my saddle bag, and that it has gone. It is a small loss materially, but I am saddened to lose the only letter from my father that I have ever possessed, especially when I think that the thief will probably throw it in a ditch by the road when he finds out that there is nothing else in the folder he has stolen.

12 Translator's note: *Lally*: General Lally-Tollendal was tried for treason following his defeat by the British in India, and subsequently executed.

*

It had been my intention to wait until at least 15th September before setting off for Brest, but after the rector's discovery I decided to leave earlier to pass by Faou. If I now knew the identity of the comrade mentioned by my father in his last letter, I still did not understand why he had thought it necessary to hide the name of the friend in a code, nor why the latter had not shown up during all this time. All these unanswered questions were trying my patience. I would have liked to have cleared up this mystery so as to have my mind free to concentrate fully on my imminent studies at Brest.

I reserved my passage with a coastal skipper who was to load salt at the port of Mesquer to take to the sardine presses at Concarneau. The harvest in the salt marshes was not yet finished but it had been a good season and the loading of the first consignments had begun. I intended then to follow the main road from Concarneau to Brest, passing through Quimper-Corentin, Châteaulin and Faou. I had calculated that it was about forty miles from Concarneau to Faou. A post-horse can be hired for twenty-five sols for six miles, so I reckoned the journey would cost me about seven pounds. My grandfather advised me to buy a Breton hack rather than hire a second-rate post-horse. He told me that at Concarneau you can buy a good horse for forty pounds. I could then sell it on at Brest. In that way I would be quite independent for my research at Faou.

'Breton hacks,' added my grandfather, 'are not the best-looking, and no cavalry officer would dare be seen on this kind of mount. But they are wrong. And in any case, you are not a cavalry officer. A hack is best for what you have in mind. They are calm, strong, hardy, intelligent, and can go without food for a long time.'

*

Kermean, Monday 2nd September 1776

The evening before my departure, the Chevalier gives me another souvenir of my father about which I knew nothing.

'…it was a gift from him a long time ago. Don't refuse it. I am sure that he would have been happy for me to pass it on to you.'

He offers me a small box made of precious wood. Its carved lid shows a hunting scene in India: at the foot of a grove of palm trees, or coconut trees, an elephant, seen in profile, turns its head to present its tusks to a tiger leaping at its left flank. The elephant is being driven by a mahout astride his neck and carries on his back a mushroom-shaped contraption in which two turbaned men are sitting. One of them is firing at the beast while the other brandishes his spear.

The little key which opens the box is attached by a leather cord and its end is in form of a cartwheel. My heart skips a beat and I pull it out of the lock to look at it more closely. The wheel on the ring of the key has eight spokes and its circumference is lightly filigreed. It is the same as the one my mother showed me.

'Does the key intrigue you?' asks my uncle.

'It is very well made. Is this the wheel of a cart?'

'Not exactly. Your father told me that he had this box made by a famous artisan in Chandernagore who liked to use this decoration on all the keys of boxes ordered from him by Europeans. I have forgotten almost everything your father told me about this wheel. All I can remember is that it is the emblem of a God that the Hindustanis call Vishnu. But open it!'

*

Inside I found, neatly arranged in compartments lined in red leather, two pistols, a little box of flints, an ivory powder case, a tin of bullets, an oilcan, rods, and everything necessary to load and clean them. I took out one of the guns to try it.

It was at least fourteen inches long from the butt to the end of the barrel, which was considerable. It was not light by any means, but that did not bother me as it felt perfectly balanced in my hand. The pistols were decorated with silver, carved with typical Oriental flower motifs. Three gilded lilies surrounded by a shining sun were engraved on the sights. The walnut handle of the butt had at its end a silver cap in the form of a tiger's muzzle. I armed the hammer easily, touched the trigger lightly. The hammer hit the steel with a dry click without jolting my wrist.

'It's a pair of horse pistols that your father ordered specially for me from a gunsmith in Le Havre, whose hallmark you can see on the barrel. He then took them to India to have them decorated over there, have the trimmings changed and this box made. They're very long, even for horse pistols, but they're very accurate. The only complaint I would have about them is that the gunsmith who made them was used to providing the Navy, so they are a heavier calibre than those I used in the cavalry. But that could well suit you…'

10

I was due to embark on my journey to Brest at dawn on the 3rd September, at the port of Mesquer. I was accompanied there by my grandfather, my uncle and Ottmeyer. We got up at five o'clock and rode along the road in the early morning freshness, just after the sun had raised his brow above the horizon. I woke my little Anne to kiss her before leaving. There is not really a port at Mesquer, as the village is more than half a mile from the sea. At high tide the barques came as close as they could to a rudimentary wharf built on wooden posts sunk into the mud above the channel. To go on board, one had to balance along a long and narrow plank slung between the gunwale and the wharf. My baggage was on a packhorse led by Ottmeyer: all the tack for the horse I would buy at Concarneau, a travel bag, my pistols and a mysterious parcel wrapped in canvas: a little rectangular box given to me at the last moment by my grandfather, on behalf of the Marquis of Becdelièvre. At my side I carried the service sword given to me by the Chevalier. Two sailors took care of my baggage. I waited until the last moment before going on board. Our farewells were brief: we were all too overcome to speak.

There was no wind and the ebb tide was still weak. The skipper had the sweeps manned. The little boat turned on the spot and slowly moved away. When we passed the last point before the sea, I saw a group of riders waving to me from the top of the cliffs. They had come along the land. I thought that they must have galloped and forded at least one channel to get there so quickly. That moved me, but at the same time I felt my heart sink. I hurried to unwrap the parcel from the Marquis de Becdelièvre before I started crying. I found a mahogany box about three inches deep. In it was a telescope with two sections made from pewter and brass. The body of the telescope was bound in black marine leather. Extended, it was about two feet long. It was the self-same beautiful achromatic telescope of English construction which Old Le Touze had shown me at Le Croisic.

The coaster on which I had taken passage was rigged as a lugger. She was a little beamier than the one which had brought me from Vannes three months earlier. At first the weather stayed fine, with high white clouds making streaks across the sky. There had been no wind, but now it built up little by little from the south-west and a dark band rose behind the islands. At the end of the day, we arrived at Quiberon on the flood tide under a uniformly grey sky and spent the night on the hard under the rain. The next day the horizon was clear, and the wind had veered to the north-west. The lugger threaded through the usual passage between the islands of Houat and Quiberon, then had to tack interminably to get up towards Groix and the Glénan Islands. The water from the dollops coming aboard worked its way through the deck planks and into the sacks of salt in the hold, making the lugger increasingly heavy and difficult to manoeuvre. We reached our destination on the Thursday afternoon. The sea was a bright blue, crested with sparkling white horses under the low-angled September sun. I disembarked at the port of Concarneau towards five in the evening.

The main activity at Concarneau was sardine fishing. In 1776 the fishermen had to return home each evening as they had been banned from selling their fish to boats going out to collect their catch. Taking a walk on Thursday evening I counted more than two hundred sardine smacks rocking gently in the slight chop at high water, between the jetty of the port and the town ramparts. These fishing boats had no deck. They were about twenty-five feet long with two masts raked backwards, a tall one amidships and a smaller one forward. The masts were unstayed because oars were taken to the fishing grounds for the final manoeuvring with the net. The crew comprised three or four men, plus the skipper.

The place was a hive of activity, as it was the height of the fishing season, which lasts normally from June until Halloween. The end of the summer is the best period for sardines, since, at that time of the year, they have become fat and firm, and are in the best condition for pressing. A thousand or so sardines can be sold for six pounds, whereas they are hardly worth half of that at the start of the season. This short-lived glut attracts a crowd of swindlers from the whole province: street vendors and travelling salesmen, all prepared to profit from the credulity of the fisherman, never hesitating to buy him a drink or two, the better to fleece him. Fortunately, one does come across more honest traders, as well as the country folk from hereabouts who come to sell the produce and foodstuff necessary to feed the seasonal growth in the population. And since the fishermen do not go to sea on Sundays or Feast days, the Concarneau markets are particularly well attended at the weekend. The day after my arrival, I had no trouble finding a horse trader who had come from Rosporden that same morning with his animals. My choice fell to a little piebald stallion with a thick coat, which was not much to look at but whose eye pleased me. I made up my mind after having felt his muscular legs and his hocks, short and dry under their thick hair. The dealer offered it for fifty pounds, but I firmly argued the price down to forty. The negotiation was made in French, which the vendor did not speak well. As strange as it may seem, it is French that is mainly spoken at the Concarneau markets. This surprised me. At Vannes, where I had studied, Breton was the dominant language everywhere. This characteristic perhaps stems from the fact that the sardine fishing and its associated industries have for a long time been controlled at Concarneau by merchants predominantly from Bordeaux, who have imposed their language on their employees and their clients.

I let my horse rest until the next day, intending to get to Châteaulin in one go on the Saturday. I left early in the morning on my new mount. The horse really was small in stature: when I walked beside him my shoulder was higher than his withers. He was not very elegant either, with his wide rump, his overly strong and rounded neckline, but he ambled along at a marvellous gentle trot which was comfortable and steady, and which he could maintain for hours without appearing in the least fatigued.

The main road to Quimper-Corentin was at first easy to follow, with its long straight lines and an eighteen-foot-wide metalled track in the middle. The countryside was enchanting. It was a maze of green, cut with streams running merrily beside the road, wandering off to lose themselves in the luxuriant vegetation, then returning once again to keep me company. The hillsides and valleys, sometimes gently rounded, sometimes cascading down in terraces above the running waters, offered a new and absorbing prospect at each stage of the journey. The church towers of the villages hidden in the woods pointed upwards here and there from a sea of green foliage. When one discovers the country of this part of Cornouaille in the right season, from the top of a rise or the flank of a hill, one has the impression of confronting a virgin land, a huge and joyful forest of oak and beech. But this impression is deceptive as the land is heavily cultivated, and in reality there are fields and meadows everywhere. However, the country folk of this region have had the habit, since time immemorial, of enclosing each parcel of land with raised earthen banks planted with trees. These trees have become majestic over time and it is this which gives the impression of a natural and attractive forest. And this impression is even stronger by dint of the fact that these banks are in no way laid out geometrically; on the contrary they follow the lines of the slopes and the twisting courses of the streams. On the other hand, as soon as one wants to leave the main road, one is confronted with veritable tunnels of greenery winding between the fields and meadows. These paths are too narrow for horse-drawn vehicles. Moreover, they have become rutted over the years by the daily passing of men and their animals, and as soon as it rains, they quickly become quagmires. The branches of the trees planted here and there on the banks interweave so tightly above the paths that they are always in darkness, even in full daylight, and so the stagnant water lying there cannot evaporate. In the end, the network of paths forms a labyrinth which is so hard to get out of that only the locals can find their way.

After Quimper-Corentin, a charming town in which I did not stop, the countryside changed. The land became rougher. The road went over a series of tree-less hills, wastelands covered in gorse, broom and heather, where black cattle wandered aimlessly. I reached Châteaulin at the end of the afternoon by crossing the River Aulne on a dilapidated bridge covered in ivy and undergrowth. This parish was comprised of two ancient churches and a hundred or so pitiful houses, most of them with thatched roofs. The only inn open was the post house, and that was full. A beggar sitting beside the road told me that it was only twelve miles to Faou, a fine town where I would have no trouble finding somewhere. On an impulse, although the day was well advanced, I went and unhitched my horse which I had tied to a ring and set off at once. This was not at all sensible, but I said to myself that it would save me time. I would then be able to start looking tomorrow for the Manor of this Marquis Avelus de Kersalaun, to whom my father was in debt, if the final words of my poor mother were to be believed.

I first went along beside the Aulne before the road left the riverbed and started going up steadily. I put my horse at a walk so as not to tire him too much. After going up for an hour and a half I found myself above a deep valley along whose bottom ran a river. It was still the Aulne – the Aulne which I thought I had left well behind, but which had made a cunning detour while I was labouring uphill. The road suddenly dropped down to meet a little tributary of the Aulne, the Doufine, at a place called the Pont de Buis. Here, for those of a scientific turn of mind, is a very strange establishment – a state-owned company for the production of gunpowder and saltpetre. It is here that gunpowder is made for the Navy at Brest. But, apart from a chapel, a house for the company managers and the powder mill, Pont de Buis is nothing more than a tiny village. What is more, it is a sinister-looking place. This is the land of dark slate. It is everywhere: on the walls of the houses, beside the pathways, on the flanks of the hills. I did not linger, and once I had crossed the bridge, I found myself at the foot of another slope even longer than the one before. At first it was quite steep, then became a kind of bare, miserable-looking plateau which rose steadily towards a line of distant crests which never seemed to get any closer. My horse began to show signs of tiredness. This bold little animal had shown his kind nature for the whole day. His stomach was empty, whereas I had eaten several thick buckwheat galettes which I had bought beside the road when coming out of Quimper-Corentin.

*

The road to Faou, Saturday 7th September 1776, at nightfall.

After walking for an hour and a half I have still not reached the top. The sun has dropped below the horizon and the sky is growing dark. I can see nothing but moors on either side of the road. The dark gorse bushes wave around on the slopes, their rustling merging with the soughing of the wind. I cannot help thinking about all the old tales from this wild land, and shudder from cold as well as from apprehension.

The road crosses a path coming from my right along the line of the main crests. An abandoned house, its walls half ruined, stands beside the crossroads. When I am about twenty paces away, a horseman who seems to have been waiting there expressly for me, and whom I had not seen, comes out from the darkness of the ruins to meet me.

'*Nozvezh vat*[13],' says the apparition in a grave voice.

'*Bennozh Doue*[14],' I reply. But at the same time I draw one of my pistols from my saddle bag and raise it so that he can see it, while carefully keeping the barrel pointing to the sky.

The horseman sees my gesture and stops, raising his hand in a conciliatory way.

'*Meulom oll da jamez Doue hag a vadelez*[15],' he recites solemnly.

He is wearing a big round hat whose wide brim hides his face in the shadow. I can see only that he has long grey hair falling on his shoulders. Apart from his shirt, all his clothes are black: an unfashionable coat with a large Basque waistcoat beneath, such as was worn during the reign of Louis XIV, voluminous breeches that the Bretons call *bragou braz,* leather gaiters and big black shoes. Everything is black, apart from the silver buttons and buckles which shine faintly in the half-light.

'Are you a priest?'

'You are French, then,' replies the horseman. 'However, you well understood what I said.'

'I understand just a few words of Breton. I am going to Brest to enter the service of the King.'

'I speak your language well too, as I travel a lot for my business. I am just a simple thread merchant from Léon, and I too am going to Brest. I saw you from up high on the road when coming from the village of Quimerc'h. I decided to wait for you, as it is better to travel in company across the moors after nightfall.'

---

13 'Good evening.'

14 'May the Lord Bless you.'

15 'Let us praise for ever the Lord and his acts of mercy.'

He is from the Léon region, then, which at least explains his dark clothes and the religious quotation. On the other hand, I have no idea what a thread merchant is, nor how he can be on the road to Brest at this hour. Anyway, I could not care less. I like his calm, reassuring voice. He does not seem lost.

'Is it far to Faou still?' I ask.

'No more than six miles. But it will be night soon and you'll hardly make any progress after that. I know an inn just a quarter of an hour from here at a place called Kervarec. As long as you are not in too much of a hurry and you are not afraid of meeting the *buguel noz*[16], I would advise you to spend the night there, as I am.'

The inn is just a big, low-ceilinged room and a stable where we leave our horses. I take my time to make sure my horse is well settled in, then I go through to the communal room which serves as both a dormitory and a dining room. There are bails of straw thrown in a corner on the earth floor, but no beds. Benches and tables are arranged at the other end of the room, in front of a big fireplace where a log is burning slowly. The scene is lit with the meagre light of a candle. There are only a few guests who can be heard snoring. I can make out several dark shapes rolled up in overcoats or blankets. My companion invites me to take supper with him. I sit down opposite him at a table near the hearth and can now take my time looking at him. He has regular features and a high forehead under his big round hat which he wears at the table like all Bretons. His light but naturally frowning eyebrows, together with the intense blue of his eyes, give him the penetrating gaze of a prophet.

For a few pennies they reheat for us the last of a wheat stew, in which the young serving girl had just thrown a big piece of butter. They also give us bowls of milk to accompany this local dish, and offer us black bread, some squares of bacon and some rather bitter cider. We have only wooden spoons to eat with. My man opposite has already got out his knife. The young girl who is serving us has pretty black eyes and long eyelashes which I rather like. She notices this and rewards me with a gentle smile in return. Emboldened by these manoeuvres, I scrape together the little of the Vannes dialect which I know to ask her where I might find the house of the Marquis Avelus de Kersalaun. She immediately becomes surly and hurries to serve us without even replying.

---

16 A ghost dressed in white who gets bigger as one gets nearer at night.

'What's up with her?'

The thread merchant shakes his head to push his long hair back and looks at me severely.

'You have annoyed her, I believe.'

'But I haven't done anything! I thought that she smiled at me.'

'She did smile at you, it is true...before you started talking so clumsily.'

'My Vannes Breton is very bad. I have trouble making myself understood.'

'On the contrary, she understood you very well. But why would you ask her if she knew where to find the Marquis de Kersalaun unless you wanted to make fun of her, or make her afraid?'

'I don't understand.'

'Everybody around here knows the sad story of the Marquis de Kersalaun.'

'Well, I don't know it, but I would very much like to hear it.'

'How do you know the name of Avelus de Kersalaun anyway? Only the people around here know it. Even in Brest he is almost unknown.'

'It would take too long to explain, and I would rather stay quiet since I don't know what all this is about. Would you like to tell me this story, then?'

'Very well. As soon as we have finished our meal, I will tell you.'

After supper, the merchant rises from the table and goes to sit on a bench by the fireplace. He waves me over to join him. He takes a leather tobacco pouch out of his pocket and a little pipe which he slowly fills. He calmly lights it with a taper from the hearth and starts to smoke while staring into the fire.

'It is a strange story. And yet everything in it is true. From what I have been told it happened not that long ago as well. When exactly I don't know. For myself, I first heard it two years ago and since then I have heard it again, with embellishments, but only in the Faou and Hanvec areas. Even at Daoulas nobody knows much about it.'

The storyteller speaks without looking at me. He grabs the poker and starts to hit the logs at his feet to create some embers. Then he blows on them to get the flames going again.

The serving girl has come to sit on a bench by the nearest table.

'Would you rather hear it in Breton or French?'

'If you don't mind, I prefer French.'

'That's a pity. The story is better in Breton, and easier for me.'

Out of the corner of my eye I can see the dark-haired girl at the end of the table. She seems as interested as I am. Does she understand French?

Realising perhaps that his small audience is complete, the thread merchant begins his story; for I now see that it really is a story and, like many stories, its telling begins with 'Once upon a time...', taking one back to the Flood, or almost...

'...The Kersalaun family is without doubt the oldest in this part of the world. Its origins go back to the start of time, when there were still Kings in Brittany. At the very beginning there was Tristan Avelus, who was the henchman of Lord Solomon. At the request of his overlord, he killed King Erispoë when the latter went to pray at a church in Porhoët. That was how, thanks to Avelus, Solomon became King, the second King of Brittany. But from that moment, King Solomon was haunted by a ghost which was black during the day and white during the night, and he was eaten with remorse. No longer able to bear the sight of the faithful and obedient instrument of his crime, King Solomon exiled Avelus. The latter departed with his family to the other end of Cornouaille. He established himself hereabouts. He raised a tower right beside the sea. But to demonstrate the fact that he remained faithful to his overlord, he called his new fiefdom Kersalaun.

'By tradition the Kersalauns were great swordsmen. It is said that a hermit predicted that all the male successors of this family would die a violent death. For generation after generation the Kersalauns fought for the greatness of the Dukes of Brittany, then for that of the Kings of France. That is how they won their title of Marquis. But they were never rich. And few of them died in their beds. The last of the Kersalauns did not deviate from the rule. He was fifteen years old and an only son when he heard of the death of his father against the Saxons, in Germany. The next year, he kissed his mother goodbye and set out to fight for the King of France. He went further than Germany, over the seas and oceans, as far as India, but always fighting the Saxons. The old Marquise must have died without ever seeing her son again.

'And then, a few years ago, the Marquis de Kersalaun, the last of his line, came home. He did not come alone. Instead of a great fortune, he brought with him a foreign Princess whom he had met in the great and mysterious depths of India. This woman was much younger than he, for sure, and she was very beautiful, more beautiful than you could imagine, more beautiful than anything anyone has ever seen in these parts. All the men of the area who remember her will tell you that. But, listen to me well, there was something supernatural about that beauty. When men saw her in the street, they could do nothing but stare at her open-mouthed, and could not take their eyes off her. Once they had passed her by, they could not get her out of their heads, and once they were home, you could be sure that they would not sleep that night. In this way she acquired a nickname that the women here whispered to each other: the Black Pearl of Kersalaun.

'The Marquis installed himself with his young wife in his tumble-down manor surrounded by ruined ramparts and declared that he was tired of making war and wanted some rest. But his first outlay was for a hunting team. It seems that he had always loved hunting. But not any old hunting and any old game. Oh no! In India he had hunted tigers, but here only one game interested him, the wildest and toughest in these parts, and the most intelligent, the one that one tracks the whole night long in the winter months, when the north wind blows across the frozen moors lit by a cold moon. I call him *Ar Bleiz,* the lordly wolf.

'Every winter's morning, the Marquis set off on horseback with his huntsman, Konan Hurennek. He was a strong fellow, as brave a wild boar, but as quiet as his master, except when he had drunk too much. This only happened when he was not hunting. One sometimes came across the both of them, wild-looking, erect in their saddles, behind the Marquis's pack. And what a pack! We will never see its like again around here. Those dogs never barked. It is said that the Marquis raised young wolves to cross them with bitches from his team. Wolf cullers call them hybrids.

'You know how much Brittany suffered from wolves in the old days, during the Nine Years' War, when our countryside was ravaged by war, famine and plagues. Well, they say that the wolves came right up to the doors of the houses to carry away women and children. These devilish animals were afraid of nothing and even attacked isolated bands of soldiers. So there's no need to tell you how much the Marquis's hunting pleased the country folk. He was well-loved for that from Faou to Landerneau. But as for the Black Pearl of Kersalaun, she really did not like her husband going after wolves. And she had good reason for that, believe me! So she asked him to swear not to hunt, at least on the first Sunday of every year, since on that day she used to make a pilgrimage, on her own, to the tomb of Saint Ronan, to whom she was particularly devoted. Do you understand me? And the Marquis swore an oath.

'The year that I am talking about, not so long ago, on the first Saturday after the new year, the Black Pearl of Kersalaun left the manor to go on her pilgrimage. And the next day, which was the first Sunday of the year, remember, it was snowing at daybreak. The Marquis decided to go to Mass at the Prioré de l'Hôpital and then spend the day by the warmth of his fireplace. But as he was making his rounds of the stable and kennels to discuss the care of his animals with Konan Hurennek, he found in the courtyard a farmer from Kernezur, in the parish of Hanvec. It was a fellow called Tressenec whom he knew well.

'What can I do for you?' asked the Marquis.

'Monsieur le Marquis, I have been sent by the people of Kernezur. A huge wolf has recently arrived in the copse we call the Bois du Gars. We don't know where it has come from. It attacked Le Gouaz who was bringing his animals back along the road because of the bad weather and carried off a big ram right under his nose. But that was nothing. Yesterday afternoon a travelling salesman left his cart at the entrance to the village in order to take a glass or two with us and, well, this wolf attacked his horse and it bled to death in its traces, the poor animal. Everyone came out when they heard the noise and saw the wolf standing in the middle of the road at the entrance to the village, challenging us. But we were too scared to confront it and it went away unharmed. The women and children are scared stiff. Nobody dares go out.'

'Very well,' said the Marquis. 'I will come and kill your wolf. Tomorrow evening, I promise you all, its body will be across the saddle of Konan Hurennek, or I am not the Marquis de Kersalaun.'

'You must come straight away, Monsieur le Marquis. It is in the copse of the Bois de Gars, as I told you. It is too close to us. We've called for volunteers from all around. There are men from our parish, and from Daoulas and even from Irvillac. They will now all be waiting for you at Kernezur to begin the beat in the Bois de Gars.'

'Alas, I cannot, Joz. I am sorry. But I will come tomorrow, that I promise.'

'Monsieur le Marquis, I don't want to offend you, but that is the first time I have ever seen you hesitate when someone has told you about an exceptional animal like this one. Not long ago you would have already leapt in your saddle.'

'That's enough, Joz Tressenec. It gives me no pleasure, believe me, but today I cannot. Until tomorrow then.'

'Our women and children cannot wait until tomorrow, Monsieur le Marquis. And we have the beaters that we have made come from all over the countryside, and on a Sunday too. But don't you trouble yourself, Monsieur le Marquis. I will go and see the son of the Comte de Rosily. He is there at the moment and has already suggested going after wolves several times. He will certainly come. But you'll regret it, for sure, missing out on a wolf of a size that has never before been seen and that will not be seen again for a long time.'

'It is really that big, Joz?'

'Even bigger, Monsieur le Marquis. I saw it myself. It has a shiny black coat with grey tints, and its eyes! As yellow as flames! Even tigers, which they say you hunted in India, could not be as fierce as this beast.'

'The Chevalier de Rosily is just a boy, Joz Tressenec, and a sailor too. What does he know about wolves? I suppose I will have to go. A case of needs must. Go and help Konan Hurennek saddle the horses. He will carry you behind him as far as Kernezur.'

'At ten in the morning the wolf was flushed out. Not in the least intimidated, it began by charging at the beaters, who were terrified of it. But it then found itself face to face with the Marquis and his pack. The wolf was bigger and more fearsome than you could possibly imagine. But listen, as soon as it saw the Marquis de Kersalaun it suddenly turned around and set off at a trot alongside the Camfrout river. It crossed the square in front of the church of the Prioré de l'Hôpital, with the silent pack at its tail, the Marquis on the heels of his dogs, along with Konan Hurennek who was sounding his hunting horn as best he could. It was just after Mass. Can you imagine it? Everybody had gathered there. People were screaming in terror, women were fainting, men were applauding the Marquis, others poured back inside the church. But wait and see what happened after that! The wolf went up the Kersalaun hill and straight into the courtyard of the chateau. And there by the well it stood its ground to confront the dogs. In less time than it takes to say it, it had already killed four or five of them. This sight would have made most think twice. But the Marquis de Kersalaun had never been afraid of anything. He dismounted, drew his knife and marched firmly and calmly towards the beast. Then, listen carefully, the wolf stopped moving. It watched the Marquis raise his arm and looked him straight in the eye as the blade pierced its heart. And suddenly the Marquis had in his arms his dear Black Pearl, with the blade of his sword through her breast. He realised that he had just killed his wife.

'Not long afterwards the King's soldiers came and arrested the last Marquis de Kersalaun. They took him away and he has never been seen since. It is said that he was condemned to the galleys for the murder of his wife.'

The storyteller goes quiet. He waits for my response, keeping his eyes on the dying embers at his feet. The serving girl has fallen asleep, her head in the crook of her elbow on the table. Beside her, the flame of the candle gutters. What I have heard seems so far-fetched that I wonder if it is just a tall story.

'How much is fairy tale and how much is reality in this story?'

The thread merchant turns towards me and I think I see satisfaction in his look. He points a prophetic index finger at me.

'You must understand that every year in our dear Brittany there are miracles whose causes have never been discovered and perhaps never will, even by the wisest men in France.'

'Fine! Let's agree on that. However, I am looking for an Avelus de Kersalaun, originally from Faou, who was a Lieutenant-Colonel in the Saintonge regiment and who left for India in 1760. Are we talking about the same man?'

'There are not too many Marquises by the name of Avelus de Kersalaun who have been a soldier and been to India.'

'But it's not possible! Or else what you have just told me happened very recently! Can you tell me in what year all this took place?'

'Did you not hear what I said a moment ago. I did say that it was recent. I heard it for the first time two years ago. More precisely it was two and a half years ago, at the Rumengol religious fair. But it's getting late. If you want to know more, and you seem to have good reasons to, then I suggest you talk to the prior at the church in l'Hôpital. I don't know him, but he could certainly tell you when it was that the Marquis de Kersalaun's hunt passed his church after High Mass on the first Sunday of the year. L'Hôpital is about twelve miles from here. If you leave early enough tomorrow morning you'll be there in time for Mass, so you'll be able to speak to the Prior. It's easy to get there.

You just follow the main road to Brest for three miles until Faou, keep going straight on through the town and continue along the main road for another six miles until the Bois du Gars. There on your left you'll see a bare earth path which goes through the wood to l'Hôpital. I think that's where the Marquis de Kersalaun first raised his wolf. So you leave the main road and after no more than three miles you'll be in the village of l'Hôpital.'

*

The village had just a single street, lined with a few stone houses, which led to a little port. The biggest buildings were those of an old leper-house built beside the water to the south of the church. The latter was not much bigger than a chapel. Its entrance porch faced west onto a small granite quayside. Two un-decked barques were tied up here, each about thirty-six feet long, of the type which hereabouts are called *traversiers*, with a single mast for a square sail and a bowsprit to take a small jib.

Mass had already begun when I arrived. I tied my horse to a ring on the wall of the leper-house and went into the little church. The faithful were pressed shoulder to shoulder. When I had stopped at Faou to find out the time of the Masses at l'Hôpital, I was told that although the Priory was part of the parish of Hanvec, four miles to the east, people came here for Mass from all the little villages situated between the mouths of the rivers Faou and Camfrout.

The prior was tonsured and seemed to me to be young for his position. He delivered his sermon in French. I had the impression that I was listening to a man for whom reality was a matter of concrete facts. His speech was that of a preacher intelligent enough to keep what he was saying accessible to his rural congregation, while retaining his basic wisdom and cultivation. After Mass, having given a few coins to the inevitable beggars, I went to check on my horse, then waited for the priest to come out. As everywhere, the faithful greeted each other and stood around chatting in small groups before separating and going home. Not seeing the prior come out, I went back into the church, where I found him on his own tidying up the vestry. He had taken off his robes, which enabled me to see that he was wearing a black shoulder cape over his habit. I greeted him and introduced myself, saying that I was an orphan and had stopped in the area to pay my respects to the Marquis de Kersalaun who had been an old comrade-in-arms of my father during the war.

'When I told people that I was looking for the Marquis Avelus de Kersalaun, they told me such an incredible story that I really don't know what to think of it.'

'A story of lycanthropy? Man turning to wolf?'

'So it really happened?'

'Yes and no! I have half an hour before the Sext. I will try and give you an insight into the obscurantism which prevails in this region.'

*

L'Hôpital, Sunday 8th September 1776, towards the end of the morning.

We are sitting on a bench in the shade of a tree, in the middle of the little square which abuts the church to the north. Everywhere is quiet. The churchgoers have gone home and the square is empty. We are facing the port, with the green hills of Daoulas as a backdrop. I can now see the top of the planking of the *traversiers* reaching the level of the quay. The tide has risen during Mass. A turtle dove coos in the foliage above our heads.

'I was not yet at l'Hôpital at the time of the incident you are talking about. I came here in the summer of 1773. The priors here are subordinate to the parish of Hanvec, but we come from elsewhere. I am from the Nantes region. Nonetheless, people have told me about this tragic story. Ask all the questions you want...'

'First of all, Father, I would like to know in what year all these events relating to the wolf hunt of the Marquis de Kersalaun took place.'

'From what my predecessor told me, the Marquis de Kersalaun would have chased a wolf close to the town on a Sunday, just before killing his wife. And that would have been the first Sunday of the year 1773, 3rd January to be precise, and just six months before my nomination here. It was the rector of Hanvec who first told me this unlikely story of lycanthropy. I think that this old wives' tale did not start doing the rounds until after my predecessor had left. Before going any further, I should warn you about two special traits of the people of this region, which are indispensable to an understanding of their behaviour. The first is that there is no country, even in Africa, where men are more superstitious than they are in Lower Brittany. The second is that the storytellers here have the wildest of imaginations. The smallest incident in daily life sets them off. A horse starts to limp after having brought his sleeping master home in his cart after a drunken evening. It's the pixies of the new moon! And a new tale is born. Not only does the owner of the horse not protest and try to give the truth of the matter, but he himself is soon persuaded that everything being said about him really did happen. It is truly distressing. In my opinion, the Church is far too indulgent towards these storytellers. You seem sensible, despite your youth. Perhaps you will be able to give me information which will enable me to put an end to this awful story. What do you yourself know about the Marquis Avelus de Kersalaun?'

'Well, the Marquis was a military man. In his youth he served in the Royal Ships' regiment, and he fought at the Battle of Fontenoy. He then commanded the onboard infantry of the eighty-gun ship *le Formidable.* He was captured in 1759 by the English, who released him on parole. He then left the army and went to India. That's all that I know. I listened carefully to your remarks about superstition and it seems to me that you do not believe the story of the Black Pearl of Kersalaun. I would like to know what you really think happened.'

'Let's say that it is not completely false. As always, it starts from a grain of truth. It is there that one can see the wickedness of the storytellers. There certainly was a wolf in the Bois du Gars at the beginning of the year 1773. And the farmers of Kernezur did send a certain Joz Tressenec as their representative to the Marquis of Kersalaun. After that, the wolf was beaten out of the north-east edge of the Bois du Gars and it was driven by the Marquis's pack towards Kersalaun. They did in fact pass not far from here, on the first Sunday of 1773. Up to this point the story seems based on real fact. But the wolf never came into the village. The hunt just went around the edge. Besides, look for yourself: where can you see room for a hunting pack at full gallop between the quay and the door of the church? Then, it is quite possible that the kill took place not far from the walls of Kersalaun. In fact, having passed l'Hôpital, the animal disappeared onto a peninsula; it found itself trapped between the sea and its pursuers. But there stops the likely part of the story. What follows is nothing but make-believe and silliness, invented by the country folk around here who have always had a weakness for the escapades of the Kersalaun family and refuse to assign any blame to their lord. However, the truth is that Avelus de Kersalaun, Marquis or not, murdered his wife.'

'How can you be so certain?'

'Because it is in writing! A few days after the drama, the rector of Hanvec received a letter from the authorities in Brest confirming that the Marquis had been condemned to hard labour for the murder of his wife. According to this letter, his lands and goods were entrusted to the parish, while waiting, no doubt, for their eventual confiscation for the benefit of the King.'

'Have you seen this letter?'

'Personally, no. But the rector of Hanvec showed it to my predecessor.'

'Do you know what became of it?'

'Oh! I suppose that it has been kept in the parish archives.'

'Well then, who carried out the investigation?'

'I was told that soldiers came by boat from Brest and that they searched the Manor of Kersalaun from basement to attic for a whole day before leaving.'

'Was it the Brest Admiralty which led the inquiry, then? Did the criminal investigator from the Admiralty interview your predecessor?'

'No. He would have said. But why would they have questioned him? He had nothing to do with this business.'

'Well, perhaps they questioned people from the manor. The huntsman Konan Hurennek, for example.'

'No, not as far as I know. Besides, this Konan Hurennek, now you mention him, was, I believe, behind this story of a wolf changing into a woman. You will note moreover, just in passing, that this theme of a stabbed wolf changing into a woman reappears regularly in local legends and is not in the least original. The huntsman had started drinking more than is reasonable, it seems, and his account wouldn't be worth much in any case. But it didn't do him any good, the poor fellow. I never knew him myself since he did not survive the winter of 1773. He was found dead, frozen stiff, in a ditch one morning, hardly a month after the events we are talking about. The last people who saw him alive, the night before, had said at the time that he was blind drunk when they parted.'

'Well then, the Admiralty people perhaps questioned Joz Tressenec or the servants at the Manor of Kersalaun?'

'Not at all! Based on what I heard, for I repeat that I was not there, those who came simply ransacked the chateau. As for servants, apart from Konan Hurennek, they only had one housemaid. The folk around here call her Fantig de Kersalaun because she lives in the little village close to the chateau, but her real name is Fantig Le Goff.'

*

The prior apologised but he had to go; with the hour of the Sext now upon us our conversation had to finish there. All the same, he told me briefly before leaving me that Madame de Kersalaun, 'for she had been married to the Marquis in accordance with the proper religious rites, you know', had been buried at the cemetery of Hanvec. Proof, if it were needed, that the rector and the prior had given no credence to the accusations of lycanthropy and the other defamations directed at this innocent victim.

I thanked the prior and returned to my horse.

My quest had taken on a most unexpected turn. If what I had just learned was true, I would have to visit a jail in order to meet my father's old comrade. I had lots of time left for getting to Brest, and the Marquis's story intrigued me considerably. I still had to find out more about this legend. I decided therefore to spend a few days at Faou, from where I could look around the area, then go to Kersalaun and to Hanvec to try to find out more for myself about this improbable affair. The prior of l'Hôpital had not totally convinced me. He seemed to me to have too many prejudices against the folk of Lower Brittany.

I arrived at Faou in the middle of the afternoon. I found an inn at the port, not far from the church, and put my horse into a comfortable stable. I slept for an hour and ordered a big meal with a bacon omelette, a flat fish and a good bottle of wine. After eating I walked along a footpath which follows the left bank of the Faou river. Lots of boats were at the anchorage: small fishing sloops, *traversiers*, and some bigger craft like bugalets and luggers, all showing how active the port was, despite it being at the very extremity of the Brest harbour. At that hour, all the boats were aground at low water and the river was no more than a wide stream snaking through the middle of a muddy expanse bordered by rocks and grass. I walked for half an hour and stopped beside a stone wall beside the path, to enjoy the evening quiet. The tide was still ebbing and the seabirds floating on the current drifted out into the estuary, revolving round as they went, and watching the banks with their little round eyes. Towards the harbour, on the other side of an arm of the sea, I could see the peninsula where the manor of Kersalaun was situated.

I wandered around the area during the days which followed. I was once again able to hear the story of the Black Pearl. Then I went to the parish of Hanvec where I was received by the vicar. According to his version, the prior of l'Hôpital had come to tell them that the body of the Marquis de Kersalaun's wife had been found, stretched out and dead, in the courtyard of the chateau, with her husband's dagger still planted in her heart. The Marquis had been arrested by soldiers who had taken him to Brest. The vicar had also had the sergeant of the Landerneau Mounted Police alerted. By the time he arrived, the mortal remains of the Marquise had been put in a temporary coffin that had been carried on a cart to Hanvec. The sergeant had started to examine the body of the victim and the knife which had killed her but, as soon as he found out that the Marquis had been arrested by soldiers from Brest, he stopped his investigation, saying that it was outside his jurisdiction. At the vicar's insistence he had however agreed to do what was necessary to obtain permission to bury the Marquise. She was then interred in the Hanvec cemetery. Eventually, a letter confirming the condemnation of the Marquis de Kersalaun had been brought to the vicarage by a high-ranking Naval officer, towards the middle of January 1773. He had introduced himself as the assistant to the Brest Naval Commander. The parish archives were well maintained. When I asked to see this document, the vicar found it without any difficulty. It was a sort of certificate, its upper part decorated with a large vignette representing the King's Seal. This was in the form of an oval placed on gun barrels and surrounded by flags and artillery instruments, all beneath a royal crown. Underneath, an inscription in large, printed letters took up half the page:

CHARLES-HENRY CTE. D'ESTAING,
Knight of the Order of the King
Lieutenant-General of the Navy,
Inspector-General of the Marine,
Commander at Brest.

There followed a hand-written and very terse text…

> *It has been declared that the Marquis Ronan Avelus de Kersalaun has been found guilty of the murder of his wife; in consequence of which he has been condemned to forced labour for life; the management of his assets is entrusted to the parish of Hanvec, made at Brest this day 18th January 1773.*

A small signature was at the end of the text, its letters well-formed and clearly legible: *Estaing.*

The parish had taken good care of the assets of the unfortunate Marquis. Only the hounds and his horses were sold at auction after the receipt of this document. This did not take long as the Kersalaun hunt pack was well known. It was bought by a lord from the Monts d'Arrée, a great lover of wolf hunting. He had come with several carts equipped with wooden cages into which the dogs were loaded with the help of Konan Hurennek. The latter would have preferred to stay with his pack, but the new owner did not want him. The old huntsman was as attached to his dogs as to his master, and this refusal did for him. He drowned his grief in alcohol which, according to the rector, hastened his death.

The Assembly-General of the parish of Hanvec decided unanimously to use the money from the sale of the Marquis's pack and horses for the renovation of a chapel dedicated to Saint Ronan.

*

Kersalaun, Monday 16th September 1776, towards ten in the morning.

My next visit is to Kersalaun. I pass through l'Hôpital without stopping this time and direct my horse along a path beside the Camfrout river. This morning, the wind is from the south-west, and it is raining. The deep grey of the sky brings out the ochre shades of the moors and the moss-covered rock. The abandoned manor house is stood there, all alone, on a rise which overlooks the mouth of the river. The top of its ruined tower rises from the middle of a square of granite walls. I stop in front of an entrance gate surmounted by a narrow arch embossed with a coat of arms, half worn away, which the rector of Mesquer would no doubt decipher thus: *silver sword crossed in black, point down.* Access is barred by a forged iron grille, evidently double-locked for a long time, as it is starting to rust. Through the bars I can see a courtyard overrun by weeds, and at its centre an extraordinary well, its rectangular coping made from huge blocks of stone. At the far end of the courtyard is the façade of a single storey house under a roof of slates half eaten by lichen. The soughing of the wind echoes around the four corners of this deserted enclosure. It is here, then, that the Marquis of Kersalaun would have killed his wolf, if one is to believe the most recent tale of the storytellers of this land.

*

A group of thatched cottages lay huddled together in a hollow a little further to the west, beside a path which wound down between the copses towards the mouth of the river. The hamlet seemed deserted, but the upper shutters of the doors were open. I dismounted and tied my horse to a fence opposite the first house. I was sure that I was being watched and so I took my time. I patted my horse, making sure that I made a loud smacking sound on his neck, then went towards the nearest door without any hesitation and saying a loud *Nozvezh vat*. A soft voice replied from inside, inviting me in. I entered and saw a young woman sitting on a bench. She was spinning wool while at the same time rocking a cradle with her foot. A little child was sleeping in the cradle. Remembering that the prior had lamented the fact that the local people were so attached to their 'criminal' Marquis, I took the risk of introducing myself as a son of one of his friends. Having talked for a while about the weather, a obligatory ritual with country people, I asked if I could see Fantig de Goff. I must have said what was necessary, for my hostess left her work, picked up the baby which was still sleeping despite the noise I had made, and asked me to follow her.

La Fantig, or Fantig Le Goff as I had been told by the prior of l'Hôpital, seemed busy hoeing a little square of vegetable garden behind her house when I saw her. However, I was sure that she had listened to everything and already knew that I was there. I have no idea why I thought she would be an elderly woman. She was certainly no spring chicken, but she was by no means old. She invited us into her house, a single room with an earth floor, furnished with a rough table, two benches, along with several stools by the hearth where a pot hung from a tripod was heating over the embers. The well-polished front panels of three box-beds shone in the gloom. Having been sufficiently prevailed upon to sit down in front of a bowl of cider, thus demonstrating that I knew the local ways, I was able to say why I had come and what I was looking for. The women spoke the Lower Brittany dialect of Cornouaille, to which I replied in the Vannes dialect, not without difficulty. Fantig noticed this and switched to French, which she spoke passably, and for which reason the Marquis had taken her into his service.

I had thought that there was an element of truth in the story I had heard a few days earlier on the road to Faou, and after my conversation with the prior at l'Hôpital, I imagined that there was also a lot of fabrication. I learned that the Lady of Kersalaun had been baptised, that her Christian name was Jeanne and her Indian name Jamna, for she really was an Indian. A princess! – explained Fantig, who had been taken into her confidence. Her father was a Raja in Hindustan, a King, that is, and he had honoured the Marquis with his friendship. There had been plotting and the Raja had been assassinated. Avelus de Kersalaun had saved his daughter and they took refuge in Brittany where they were properly married. It was a beautiful story, but they had no children. The Princess Jamna had confided to her faithful housekeeper that the Marquis had promised that one day they would both return to India. She had told Fantig that the Gods had allowed her to find her father's war treasure and she would be able to raise an army to retake her kingdom. I learned too that there were no domestic servants at the chateau apart from Fantig Le Goff, who went home every evening, and Konan Hurennek, who lived permanently at the manor. On Sunday 3rd January 1773 he had already been away for two days hunting with the Marquis. It was on 1st January that Joz Tressenec had come to tell about the wolf at the Bois du Gars, and the Marquis and his team had set off the next day, 2nd January, before dawn. They followed their prey for a whole day and a whole night. Having made a huge circuit inland, the wolf led them back along the Camfrout river, passed close to l'Hôpital, and found itself trapped not far from Kersalaun. The morning of that famous Sunday, Fantig Le Goff had gone to do her duties after early morning Mass and had found the gate of the manor guarded by men dressed in blue uniforms with red lapels, who all looked like brigands. They took her to their officer in the main room of the manor. She saw the Princess Jamna sitting at the side under the eye of a soldier and a dark, bearded man who was talking to her in an unknown language. He was questioning her, it seemed, but the Marquise stayed silent. She was still in her bed-robe and slippers, her long hair falling untidily over her shoulders. Fantig saw that her night clothes were torn and wanted to give her a coat, but the officer forbade her to go near her. The other soldiers were searching the drawers of the furniture and throwing everything on the floor. They seemed to be looking for something. The officer was very tall, with a brutal air and cruel eyes, Fantig told me, and she was afraid of him. He had asked her where the Marquis was and when he would be back. She had replied that he had gone hunting two days ago and that she did not know when he would return. They locked her in the cellar. She stayed in the dark for the whole morning. Towards midday, the hunting team returned. The dogs never barked but she could hear the horses' hooves in the courtyard. Then she thought she heard cries, but the sounds from outside were muffled, of course. Next thing the dogs began to howl, which they never normally did. That had lasted a long time until finally she heard the voice of Konan Hurennek getting the dogs to their kennels. She had banged on the door of the cellar and cried for help. The huntsman came and set her free. He had blood on his face. He seemed totally confused and was talking incoherently. Fantig understood from what he was saying that the soldiers had ambushed them in the courtyard of the chateau, the Marquis and himself. He had received a blow on the head which had stunned him. He had regained consciousness when he heard the dogs howling.

After liberating Fantig he went off with his arms dangling. Fantig was able to ascertain that the soldiers were no longer there. The grille of the chateau was wide open and the windows were gaping holes. She had seen the body of the Marquise lying on the ground near the well. Madame de Kersalaun lay motionless, half-dressed, her hair still un-combed and spread on the ground. Her husband's hunting knife was still planted in her chest, its handle passing under her left breast. The Marquis had apparently been taken away by the soldiers. There was no sign of a wolf at all. Its body, if there had been one, had disappeared. Fantig had raised the alert at the hamlet, and they had gone to find the prior at l'Hôpital. During this whole time Konan Hurennek stayed seated on a bench, not moving, by the door of the stable. It seems that the blow he had taken had upset his poor brains. Later it was learned that the soldiers had arrived by boat the night before, just before midnight, at high tide, and that they had waited until dawn before disembarking below Kersalaun. They needed horses to carry something or other to the anchorage and had abandoned them near the pontoon. The two animals came back up to the manor of their own accord and had scared Fantig when they galloped into the courtyard. The housekeeper told me that she had told the prior that they had been attacked by soldiers from Brest, but that her husband, who had seen their *traversier* in the harbour, had said to her the night before that he recognised some halberdiers from the jail, a filthy mob, despised with good reason by everybody. Later, some more arrived from Hanvec in relation to the accusation of the Marquis for the murder of his wife. The people here could not believe it. That is why, when the storytellers at the wake created this fable about the wolf, nobody contradicted them. It is less upsetting than thinking that the Marquis had it in him to kill his pretty little Princess, whom he loved so much, in a moment of madness. And it also matched what Konan Hurennek started to recount in his delirium. At the request of the vicar of Hanvec, a clerk and his assistants came to take the key after the sale of the pack hounds and the horses. He made an inventory of the contents of the manor. It was acknowledged that the chateau had been ransacked, but it seemed that nothing had been stolen.

*

Faou, Monday 16th September 1776, in the evening.

There is nothing more I can learn at Kersalaun. All that remains is to try to visit the Marquis when I am at Brest, but there is no urgency now. Given where he is, there is not much I can do for my father's old comrade. Certainly, I still feel myself tied by a kind of obligation, but it is above all curiosity, that powerful motivator, which is stopping me from abandoning my search in this direction. I hope above all that I will be able to see Monsieur du Galaup de Lapérouse, my father's old shipmate. I am looking forward to this meeting, since he was with my father at Louisbourg. He will no doubt be able to tell me about my Laforest-Dombourg grandparents and, as he at one time sailed on *le Formidable*, he will be able to tell me exactly what happened in the past between my father and the Marquis de Kersalaun.

*

Having discovered that coasters ply regularly between Faou and Brest, I decided to make the last part of my journey by sea. Faou being the capital of the Breton horse, I was able to sell my little mount without any difficulty, along with all its tack. I sold the whole lot for sixty pounds. I don't know whether it was a good price or not. I bought a solid sea chest to replace my travel bag and set sail for Brest on 18th September. The *traversier* on which I took passage left Faou towards seven in the morning. The weather was mild, with drizzle and a light wind from west-south-west which would have caused us problems getting out of the Faou river if the tide had not been with us. Having used the oars to get abeam of Landévennec, our barque tacked laboriously to and fro for the whole morning under its square sail. It was almost eleven o'clock by the time we got past Plougastel Point. The sail was then trimmed for a broad reach and the *traversier* at last sped off across the harbour, heading straight for the port of Brest, three nautical miles ahead of us.

*

In Brest Harbour, Wednesday 18th September 1776, towards the end of the morning.

If the Morbihan is truly, as its name indicates, a 'little sea', then in my opinion Brest Harbour merits being called a 'little ocean'. Completely land-locked, with only a single exit via a channel about a mile wide at high water, it is one of the biggest anchorages in the world. Several squadrons could carry out manoeuvres in there at the same time.

As we approach, I look everywhere for the high masts of the King's ships, but I can only see two stationary merchant vessels at the mouth of the Penfeld river. The port and the arsenal are hidden behind the first bend of this river, whose steep-sided bed separates Brest from Recouvrance. The entrance to the Penfeld is defended by a series of batteries constructed on both sides, and it is overlooked, to the east, by the crenellations and machicolations of the old Chateau of Brest and, on the Recouvrance side to the west, on our port hand side, fortifications in the style of Vauban over which floats a huge white flag. At their foot a redoubt in the shape of a half-moon borders the harbour. This is without doubt the Horseshoe, mentioned by Old Le Touze. Looking further west, with my telescope, I discover a rocky coastline whose upper slopes are covered in moors and heather. It is like that right round to the entrance channel, a giant gate cut through the rock and opening to the wide ocean. There are two ships in the channel, heading straight for the port, yards squared to the following wind. They look like merchantmen.

*

Our *traversier* dropped anchor in the middle of a group of coasters anchored below the Chateau. The skipper of the barque explained to me that there were only two small commercial quays in the Penfeld, one at Brest itself and one at Recouvrance. Everything else was reserved for the Navy. One had to wait one's turn to go and load or unload. He himself had to go ashore to announce his arrival and reserve his place in the queue, and so he suggested that he take me and my baggage with him in the ship's boat.

There was a continuous coming and going of boats in and out of the port. I could also see lots of sails of boats plying the harbour: bugalets, luggers, *traversiers, and the two three-masted merchant ships I had seen in the entrance channel. I asked the skipper where the King's ships were and he told me that they were on the Penfeld. He said that normally there was a frigate stationed in front of the Horseshoe, but it must have gone to cruise off the west coast of Brittany.* Moreover, there was a squadron which had left for training manoeuvres six months before but had not yet returned. He pointed out the rows of empty coffin buoys, little reddish dots, kept still in the slop by their mooring chains, five cables from the entrance to the river. Two of these buoys were occupied by the little merchantmen that I had seen with the telescope as we came in. The skipper told me that these were King's transport ships, waiting for a favourable wind to get through the entrance channel. The two ships I had seen coming in under sail were also King's transports.

'...they go for timber from Bayonne and everywhere in Europe for the Naval shipyard. It ain't stopped for a year. The stores was almost empty, I 'ave to say, at the end of the last King's reign. Seems like there were not even enough timber for maintenance and repairs and now they've begun building again at yon end of the shipyard. So they got to bring in more timber. More 'n more! And it ain't finished yet!'

Our boat made its way into the entrance of the port, keeping close to the starboard shore, on the same side as the Chateau. It was low tide. We went along beside blocks of rock covered in green algae and dark tide-wrack. The river was not much more than half a cable wide at this point. The sun had eventually shown itself and its rays were reflecting off the muzzles of the cannons in the embrasures between the stone defences of the Horseshoe, on the other shore. This redoubt was manned by the Army. I could see the greyish white coats of the soldiers leaning on the barrels of their cannons as they watched us. Just after this emplacement, the first part of the Recouvrance quays was defended by a dozen cannons mounted on Naval gun carriages. Their long, dark barrels were aimed to sweep the river abeam of them. This battery was manned by Navy gunners dressed in blue. The skipper of the barque also pointed out the Royal Battery, right at the top of Recouvrance, in the line of fortifications over which flew the big white flag. He explained that it was made up of eighty big 48-pound cast-iron cannons taken off the old *Royal Louis*, and that they had an oven for heating the cannonballs so that they could be fired red-hot.

There were no ships here, just four big ship's boats at the base of the quay with their oarsmen in their places. They were waiting to tow the two transports to the shipyards. Having advanced up the Penfeld, our boat went round a sort of floating jetty formed by a line of small rectangular rafts which served as flotation for the huge links of the port's chain. The skipper told me that, even when open, the chain was always set up to maintain a permanent barrier to a section of the Penfeld. This stopped the ships that were going in and out from hitting a reef situated rather inconveniently right at that spot, and just visible at low water springs. This rock, called the 'Rose', had given its name to the battery that was beside it. After the Rose battery, the river curved in two bends. On the port side, the Recouvrance quays were bordered by the Naval magazines and opposite them, beneath the Chateau, I could at last see some King's ships. The first one we passed was moored fore and aft, just inside the chain. It remained there permanently, the skipper explained, serving as a floating garrison for the port defences. The people of Brest called it *l'Amiral*, or else *l'Avant-garde.* Another ship, a little further on, was tied up beside a huge mast crane, higher than the walls of the Chateau. It was being prepared to receive its main topmast, with a considerable number of riggers and sailors working aboard at this delicate operation.

The commercial quays were just after the mast crane: the Quai de Brest, with the Quai de Recouvrance opposite. The coasters formed a confused mass of hulls pressed tightly together in front of the limited wharf space allowed them by the Navy to unload their cargoes. The Quai de Brest, where we disembarked, was crowded with cases and barrels and crawling with people. They were all waiting their turn for a ferry, as this was the only place where ordinary private citizens had the right to cross between Brest and Recouvrance. This quay was enclosed at the top by the residence of the Commissioner of the Navy, a beautiful building whose elegant balconies in forged iron projected out over the river. To the north it was prolonged by a chapel.

The railings which marked the start of the shipyards began at the walls of this chapel. Putting my nose to the bars I could see a huge pit in the bottom of which sat a ship on its keel, held up by huge props. It had only its lower masts. I could hear a great cacophony of hammers, mallets, saws and adzes.

'It's the old Troulan slipway.'

The skipper of the *traversier* had stopped behind me.

'Slipway?'

'Sort o' dry dock, if you like. The ships come in at high tide then the gates is closed, like them on a lock, like, so that it empties on the ebb.'

'I had heard of them but I didn't think they could take such big ships!'

'Ha! That's only *l'Amphion*, fifty guns, what they're trying to do up. But look you over the river, there at the bottom of the Capucin Hill, in the Pontaniou slipway number one. That be a real ship o' the line!'

He pointed towards the right bank of the river, to the foot of a cliff topped with a wood from which projected a slate roof and two bell towers. I could see an immense hull standing there, it too in a huge dry dock, this one hewn out of the rock.

'That be *la Bretagne*, built to take a hundred an' ten cannon; hundred an' eighty foot long stem to stern, fifty-one foot beam an' drawin' twenty-four foot!'

The skipper of the barque shielded his eyes from the sun with his hand.

'They've got on a fair bit since the last time...She were built here at Brest, fourteen year ago, by that engineer Groignard. Pride of the province, she were. Left abandoned in the Penfeld, she were, fer many a year. They let 'er rot, the shame on it! When the new Navy minister come to 'ave a look round 'ere and they was wantin' to get the Navy back in a decent state, like, they found nine ships 'o the line was completely buggered. An' four o' them had never as bin to sea, like. What a waste that were! The engineers reckoned it'd cost too much to do 'em all up, like, so they decided to knock 'em to bits. And that *la Bretagne*, she were condemned, like, along with 'em. But the Comte d'Orvilliers, who were in command of the Navy at Brest, like, he wanted to save 'er. He convinced the Minister, like, and the King give his agreement too. Bin workin' on 'er a year now, they 'ave. Rotten she were, 'cept the keel and the frames. Soon that big ship'll be like new, like, and the Comte d'Orvilliers, he'll go aboard, he will, and lead the Navy to victory.'

'We're not at war!' I said.

'That be true. But when I sees all this, like, I says to meself that it ain't long comin'. Me, I'm more a peaceful sort o' fellow, and that's as might surprise you, to be sure, but my elder brother, like, he copped it in the Angliche prison ships during the last war....so well then, you as maybe understand...'

I said that I wasn't at all surprised and that, on the contrary, I understood him perfectly. I started to get out my purse to pay him.

'You juss leave that be. You be going in the Navy. You get yerself aboard that there ship when she takes the sea agin. An' think on me when she gets 'er guns a'talkin'.'

I insisted on paying him, all the same, but he wouldn't hear of it. He shook my hand and wished me good luck.

'Be you careful,' he added. 'Brest be a dangerous town, like. Don't you be getting' yerself killed afore as you go to sea. You save yerself for fightin' them Angliches.'

And so that was how I arrived at Brest. I would soon learn that this town was like no other. Brest and Recouvrance at that time were a unique combination, as regards both their fabric and their geographical situation, but also as regards the special atmosphere which overhung the place. It was a restless, feverish town, and dangerous too without a doubt, where life was lived with the greatest intensity. Those who never experienced Brest during those years could never imagine how it really was. And I think that we will never see its like again.

11

Having thanked the good skipper of the barque, I looked for a porter to carry my sea chest. I found two, who wanted to carry my baggage together, and demanded eight sols each, sixteen sols in total. It was more than a labourer earned in a day! I tried to bargain with them, saying that I would rather hire one man with a wheelbarrow, as it would be cheaper. They replied, rather cheekily, that I could have a crack at that if that's what I fancied, but I'd never find one, coz the streets was so steep, like, that I could dream all I liked about pushing a barrow to the Commandement. All this was said in French, as almost everyone speaks French in Brest.

'I just want to go to the Company of Marine Guards,' I said.

'That's just it,' they replied. 'If you're goin' to the Hôtel Saint-Pierre, then you've got to go up the Rampe du Commandement, haven't you? Impossible wiv a barrow, matey.' I had to give in to their demands and I soon found out that they were by no means wrong either.

The Grande Rue of Brest starts at the gates of the shipyards and goes straight up to the town centre. It is lined with stone houses. I could see that there was scarcely room for two carriages to pass each other. In fact, you do not see carriages in Brest, and very few horses. To find a horse to hire, you have to go right to the top of the Grande Rue, near the Landerneau Gate, which is the only entrance to Brest by land, and through which the coaches and all the post services arrive. There is only one other gate, at Recouvrance, on the other side of the Penfeld. In this decidedly odd town, people of quality get around in sedan chairs. I saw lots of little shops and a surprising number of taverns, every single one of them packed with drunken, noisy customers. I had the impression that a great deal of drinking goes on in Brest. I found too that there were a lot of people out, even though it was not a market day. Mainly they were men: a lot from the Navy and the Army regiments, sailors of course, and workmen from the shipyards. As for the women, most of them looked like trollops; there were few honest housekeepers and almost no children.

We went up the Grande Rue until we came to a square which the people of Brest have named *La Place Médisance*[17]. I saw first a fountain, then the much-touted ramp just behind, going up at a right angle. I had to admit that this passage well merited its name. The Rampe du Commandement, so-called because it leads to the Headquarters of the Navy in Brest – the Hôtel Saint-Pierre, when one comes from the port – is a passageway as steep as a staircase but without its steps. It ends at the top of the rue de Siam. The rue de Siam runs more or less parallel to the Grande Rue, but is narrower. It too is lined with fine stone houses, but it does not go right down to the port, bending round to join the Esplanade of the Chateau. The Hôtel Saint-Pierre is on the other side of the street when one reaches the top of the ramp. It is completely hidden from passers-by by an enclosing wall seventeen feet high. Its gate was guarded by two fusiliers from the Royal Corps of Naval Infantry whom I told that I had come to be taken on as a Cadet. One of the two sentries led me to see the Chevalier de Monteil, Ship's Captain and Commander of the Marine Guards of Brest. I asked my two buffoons to look after my chest while waiting for me.

The Hôtel Saint-Pierre is a sombre-looking but elegant building, and huge, despite having only two storeys. Over the entrance is a pediment devoid of sculptures or any ornamentation save a bull's-eye window. Since its purchase by the Navy, two wings have been added which frame the courtyard on the rue de Siam. To be found here are the Commander of the Navy and his staff, the Company of Marine Guards, with rooms for classes and demonstrations, and a drill hall.

---

17 Translator's note: *La Place Médisance:* Scandalmonger Square

I was met by a sly-faced secretary who asked me for my documents. He was worried about how I would pay my fees but was very pleased with my answer. However, he pulled a face when he saw my certificate of nobility, the fruit, to be sure, of the Chevalier de Kermean's ingenuity. He pointed to a chair in the corridor and told me to wait. The Chevalier de Monteil came along soon afterwards and I gave him my letter of convocation as a Cadet.

'That's fine,' he said. 'You have no doubt your proof of nobility?'

I handed him my certificate while trying to hide any apprehension. He examined it carefully from top to bottom, without a word, and declared that it was all in order. He called the secretary and asked him to tell me everything I needed to know about my lodgings and uniform and told me to present myself the following morning at seven o'clock, in uniform, to my Brigade Chief.

My priority was to find lodgings where I could deposit my sea chest. The secretary told me that the Navy housed any Cadets who so wished at the officers' barracks. Otherwise, we could find lodgings in town at our own expense. Many of the Guards preferred the latter option as it gave them more freedom. For myself, given my situation, I chose the barracks.

The Naval officers' barracks, when I arrived at Brest, was once a Jesuit seminary which the Navy had appropriated after the expulsion of the Jesuit Order. To get there from the Hôtel Saint-Pierre, all you needed to do was to go up the last bit of the rue de Siam towards the Landerneau Gate Square, then turn left into the rue de la Mairie. This was one of the most beautiful areas of Brest, where all the town notables and commanding officers lived. You then crossed the Market Square in front of the Saint-Louis Parish church, leaving it to your left. This brought you to the Navy Chapel, which is the former chapel of the seminary, where the Guards attended morning Mass. The barracks were right next door. It took just fifteen minutes to get there with my sea chest.

*

Brest, Wednesday 18th September 1776, towards three o'clock in the afternoon.

The former Jesuit seminary is a monumental building. It is entered on the north-east side by a paved main courtyard a hundred yards wide, whose far side is completely occupied by the façade of the principal building. Its centre is broken by a detached building with a pediment and pilasters surmounted by a slate dome with an open bell tower at its summit. There are two other detached buildings at each end. The huge Cadets' dormitory, where I am lodged, is on the second floor. For the moment I am its only occupant. Its windows look out to the south-west over a garden which slopes gently down to the cliffs beside the Penfeld. This garden ends with a terrace planted with trees, overlooking the shipyard warehouses. The dormitory is divided into little rooms by simple wooden frames equipped with curtains which can be drawn for privacy. Each 'room' is furnished, in addition to a bed, with a box seat and a little desk. Through the window opposite my bed I can see the tops of the masts of the ships moored at the port's military quays, and the houses of the upper part of Recouvrance clustered around their parish bell tower across the river.

I am issued with my Naval officer's uniform, which consists of a royal blue coat edged in scarlet serge and embroidered at the cuffs, a waistcoat and trousers in blue cotton with gold-plated brass buttons to the waist, a hat bordered with gold, a buckskin belt doubled and run through with gold thread, and scarlet stockings. My status as a Cadet is indicated by a gold aiguillette shot through with blue silk and worn on the right shoulder.

Before putting on this fine uniform, I carefully consider once again the question of a wig. Despite the insistence of the Chevalier de Kermean, I was not able to bring myself to adopt this indispensable accessory of military fashion before leaving for Brest. I thought that for travelling I would be more comfortable with my hair worn naturally. I would like just to tie it back with a ribbon conforming to the Regulations, but I am only a Cadet and all the officers I have seen today are wearing carefully powdered wigs. I consider then that it would be wiser, at least at first, to do as everyone else does, and so I make up my mind to have my hair cut and to buy a wig.

*

I found a barber in the barracks. Given the urgency, he agreed to cut my hair there and then and to advise me on the purchase of a wig. I took the opportunity to have the down growing on my chin shaved. From then on, I would have to have myself shaved regularly.

'There are wigmakers at the bottom of the rue de Siam, towards the entrance to the Chateau,' he told me. 'They are all the usual price, about ten pounds for a wig, but I wouldn't recommend them. There's one that does the people of high quality, beside the Hôtel Grand Turk towards the Landerneau Gate, but he's very expensive. You won't get anything for less than twelve pounds there. If you want my opinion, you should go to the jail.'

'To the jail? You are having a joke?'

'I am talking to you very seriously! At the jail you can find craftsmen much more skilled at their art than their bourgeois equivalents in town. And of course, as they are convicts, their prices are inevitably much lower.'

'But how can that be?' I asked.

'You see, Monsieur, it happens that certain convicts, who happened to be skilled craftsmen before they were condemned, are allowed to practise their previous trade as long as they behave well and their crime is not too serious. They are given stalls which they make into shops. They are not, however, excused their forced labour at the shipyards, but they can pay for stand-ins to do extra hours in order to compensate the Navy. As they earn enough money to feed themselves, the Navy saves the cost of their meals. In return, they have the great benefit of not being chained in pairs during the day, like the others. That's why they in the jail they are called 'sock convicts'.'

"Sock convicts'?'

I liked the expression, finding it quite comical.

'Yes indeed! The forced labourers are normally chained in pairs during the day, to make escape more difficult. Those who work at the stalls are alone, of course, although they still have a manacle on their ankle. It is only taken off when they are released. That's why they have this nickname you find so amusing.'

'If I have understood you correctly, they must be very cheap, but unfortunately I need my wig this evening, so as to be able to wear it tomorrow morning at muster. And I imagine that you need permission to go into the jail. That must take time?'

'You have it all wrong, Monsieur! It is Wednesday today and there is plenty of time left. It is open right now. If you wanted to go into the prison itself, I agree with you that you'd have to ask for prior permission from your superiors and you'd have little chance of getting it, in fact. But you don't need it to go to the convict stalls. They are not in the prison itself but in its rear courtyard, accessible by a little door on this side. It's less than a hundred paces away. We are almost neighbours. It's very easy to find. You go left when you come out of the main courtyard and walk straight ahead along the side of the wall of the Navy Infantry barracks. You come to the corner in the prison wall around its rear courtyard and you'll see its door straight away, on your left. You can't miss it because it's guarded by halberdiers.'

*

I found the door guarded by the halberdiers beside the south-east corner of the high wall surrounding the rear courtyard of the jail. This door led to a kind of uncovered corridor nine feet wide and a hundred and twenty feet long. This ingenious arrangement was to allow the halberdiers, of whom there were ten or more, to stop any attempt at escape by the sock convicts, who in any case had no reason to take such a risk, given their juicy position, according to the barber. The halberdiers' guardroom was immediately to the left as you went in. I admit that my heart jumped at seeing for the first time these men about whom I had heard so many bad things at Kersalaun. Their blue tunics doubled in red serge could have resembled the uniform of the Naval Infantrymen, were it not for their yellow leather breeches and twill gaiters. Moreover, they were armed with sabres and the guard at the entrance was leaning on a halberd rather than a Navy-issue rifle. I found out later that they were not there solely to prevent escapes but also, in theory, to enforce the police regulation forbidding access to the jail stalls by ordinary citizens. This regulation had been put in place after repeated complaints from the Brest trade guilds who saw the stalls' business as unfair competition. I have to say that I was still in civilian clothes, and not the only one thus dressed who was there, and that I was not checked. This gives an idea of the level of attention paid by the halberdiers to police regulations.

The rear courtyard of the jail was about sixty feet wide, located between the thirty-foot high outer wall and the jail itself, of the same height and over two hundred and fifty yards long. The windows of this enormous two-storey building were all heavily barred.

The convicts' shops were simple planked stalls built alongside the outer wall, on the right as I came out of the corridor. They were solidly built and well-stocked, not much different from the shops I had seen going up the Grande Rue. I could see the shop fronts of a wigmaker, a watchmaker, a luthier and locksmith. There were also barbers, including a tooth-drawer, and even a tradesman calling himself a 'nature embalmer'. This craftsman, skilled in the art of embalming animals was, I believe, the only one in the whole country.

When I entered the wigmaker's stall, he was sat behind his work bench, intent on plaiting some hair with the tools of his trade. He got up to greet me. He was by no means fat, but he was not in the least pitiful and seemed well turned-out. Were it not for his red cassock and the woollen bonnet, red also, on his shaven head, he could have been taken for an upstanding citizen. On a shelf, a collection of wigs of all sizes were laid out on their display stands. A true craftsman, he soon found exactly what I needed.

*

Brest, Wednesday 18th September 1776, towards the end of the afternoon.

I had not intended to start my search for the Marquis de Kersalaun straight away, but it seems a pity not to take advantage of the current situation.

'I am looking for a convict called Avelus de Kersalaun, or maybe just Avelus,' I say. 'Do you know him?'

Without replying, the wigmaker gets up and goes to look outside, in front of his stall. Partly reassured, he turns towards me and invites me to sit down, while he himself remains standing in front of his door.

'Why are you so interested in a forced labourer?'

He speaks in a low voice, presumably so as not to be heard outside.

I lie.

'The Marquis de Kersalaun is an uncle on my mother's side.'

'A Marquis! What was he accused of?'

'Murder....in principle.'

'In principle? It was not proved?'

'I don't know.'

The convict studies my face closely. He is perhaps wondering if I am setting a trap for him.

'I have just arrived in Brest,' I say. 'I am joining the Marine Guards as a Cadet.'

That seems to reassure him a little.

'Do you know his number on the register?'

'What is the register?'

He points to a tin plaque attached to his bonnet, and I now see that there is a number on it.

'When we are brought here on the chain, them barbers shave our heads, our clothes are burned so they can give us this outfit...'

He taps the sleeve of his homespun red cassock.

'They mark us...'

He says this in a low voice, as if ashamed.

'...And the screws put this nice iron ornament on our ankles. And to finish, they take away our name. We're then nothing but a number. If you don't know your uncle's number, you have to go and see the prison clerk, at the jail. He's the one that keeps the register up to date. He has his office on the first floor. He's the only one as could find who you're looking for and tell you what happened to him...if he feels like it. But you're a gentleman and you just told me you're in the Navy. You just need to get permission from the administration. They don't like that much in principle, but for an uncle, and a Marquis, they'll let you have it. You go in by the main door, on the other side. But don't you mention me. I don't want to lose my place here.'

*

The convict wigmaker clearly did not want to carry on our conversation any longer. However, he asked me my name, to write it in the accounts he kept carefully every day, like all good tradesmen. I paid him and took my leave, carrying under my arm the box in which the sock convict had arranged my wig. I had it for one écu, or six pounds.

*

Brest, Thursday 19th September 1776, six o'clock in the morning.

I am woken by the echo of a cannon shot followed by the chiming of a bell towards the port. I put on my fine new uniform and run, sword at my side and carrying my wig, to the Hôtel Saint-Pierre.

The muster for morning roll call is held in the courtyard of the Hôtel. Leaving aside management staff, the theoretical complement of the Brest Marine Guards is comprised of twenty-five Flag Guards, twenty-five Guards of the First Brigade, twenty-five Guards of the Second Brigade and thirty Cadets. These numbers are quite justifiably 'theoretical', as they are purely indicative and never reached exactly. So, the morning of my arrival, twenty Guards are absent, having gone to sea six months ago with the training squadron. Apart from myself, all the Cadets have been with the Company for one or two years and are working furiously for their Guard examination, which is scheduled for the first of October. I am the only new Cadet to arrive in advance. After muster, we all go together to the morning Mass at the Navy chapel, then my studies begin.

I have scarcely left the Saint-Yves College in Vannes, and now, having for years dreamed of the Navy, I find myself shut up in another college and seemingly no further advanced, despite my uniform. The Cadets meet twice a day, apart from Sundays, in the classrooms of the Hôtel Saint-Pierre, to learn mathematics. We have some fencing sessions, and classes in drawing and English, but above all we are here to learn mathematics. You must become a Guard before taking up more attractive subjects such as naval architecture, rigging, sail and cannon handling, or the use of the rifle.

The main focus of our studies is the textbook by Monsieur Bézout. This famous mathematician, member of the Academy of Sciences, has been designated since the time of the Minister Choiseul as the official examiner of the three Companies of Marine Guards based in Rochefort, Brest and Toulon, and the Company of Flag Guards which is split between Brest and Toulon. In 1772 Monsieur Bézout published, at the royal printing house, his *Course in Mathematics for the Use Of Navy and Flag Guards.* This has become the principal basis of our education and is simply called *Bézout.* The wise author of this highly pedagogic work comes in person once a year to each area to examine the Cadets and the Guards. In this instance, he is expected at Brest at the beginning of October. The textbook is in five volumes. To become a Guard, a Cadet must know the first two volumes perfectly. Only one mistake is allowed. If you fail at the second attempt you are sent home and considered totally incapable of serving in the Navy. One can then very easily imagine that the other Cadets do not want to waste their time, especially those who have already failed once. On the other hand, the regime is very liberal. The fees having been paid in advance, each individual can organise himself as he pleases.

The first volume of *Bézout* deals with elementary arithmetic, from addition, subtraction, multiplication and division through to logarithms; the second starts with geometry and finishes with trigonometry. As the examination is close, the teachers are giving revision classes. The masters allow me to join the classes of my older comrades, saying that I will probably be lost but it won't do me any harm. It is then that I realise how well Father Deniel has trained me. And I say to myself that if I were a Cadet at Toulon, where Monsieur Bézout is due to come at the beginning of next summer, I would be able to pass the Guard examination in June 1777.

On the advice of my superiors, I spend a day visiting the military port, or rather, as the say in Brest, the *Arsenal*. It is on both banks of the Penfeld, below Brest and Recouvrance. Its main entrance is on the Troulan dry dock quay, which I saw when I arrived. Also there is the Naval Academy and the Office for the Administrative Control of the Navy, a single story building, devoid of mansards, whose front has a row of arcades. These buildings are overlooked by a tower with a clock, over which is a bell which is rung to announce the opening and closing of the shipyards, and which I hear every morning as I get up. Both sides of the Penfeld are occupied by warehouses built by the engineer Choquet du Lindu, who also built the jail. On the Recouvrance side are the warehouses for victuals, which I had seen on arriving the first day, the Sainte-Barbe warehouse, so called as it was an artillery depot[18], the special warehouses for the decommissioning of ships of the line, and then the Pontaniou dry dock basins: one huge one where I had seen the ship *la Bretagne*, two other smaller linked ones, and a construction slipway covered by a vast and well-built roof. All these warehouses have been carved into the rocky cliffs which border the Penfeld. At the end of the port are the construction yards, the forges and, on the Brest side, two great ropewalks built side by side across the slope on the left bank of the shipyards. Both ropewalks are a good hundred and fifty

18 Translator's note: *Sainte-Barbe warehouse:* the gun room on French war ships of the time was known as the *sainte-barbe,* Saint Barbara being the patron saint of gunners. The only access to the ship's powder magazine was via a trapdoor in the gun room.

yards long. The jail is above the upper one. The Hospital is to the north of the jail, at the end of the town, on this side of an inlet formed by a prolongation of a bend in the Penfeld, the so-called Powder Mill Inlet, as there was once a powder mill there.

*

The most striking thing for a visitor was the level of activity around the ships. After years of lethargy, which the skipper of the *traversier* which had brought me to Brest had touched upon, the government had decided to put our Naval forces on a war footing. To give an idea of the activity that this represented, I will simply say that since the visit of the Minister Sartine the previous year, in September 1775, two thousand workmen and two thousand five hundred convict labourers had been working without a break in the Penfeld to ready for sea thirty ships of the line and as many frigates, and that the construction of eight new ships of the line and five new frigates had started at the end of the shipyards. The three Pontaniou dry docks were occupied. Every day, ships were brought from the middle of the river to go alongside the quays either to load their cannons, or to have their masts put in at the rigging quay, where the mast crane was in constant use from morning until night. Smoke and the smell of pitch drifted through the air and hammer blows rang out from the forges. Lines of convicts lead by prison guards hauled heavy equipment and cannons ready to be taken on board. Other forced labourers operated the dockside cranes. On the ships anchored midstream, riggers raised the yards and topsails. The sight of all this activity made me think, innocent novice though I was, that war was well and truly being prepared for. I resolved to write a letter to my uncle, the Chevalier de Kermean. I had already realised that his position beside the Secretary of State for War gave him access to information which was not available to the common man. His role at the Ministry allowed him to send mail by the King's messengers who rode constantly between Brest and Versailles. Not only was this system very fast, usually taking just two days to arrive, but it was also totally secure.

I learned from my superiors that the Chevalier de Ternay had been Governor of the Île-de-France for three years, and that the Ship's Ensign du Galaup de Lapérouse had accompanied him there. They were due to return to Brest in 1777, as the Chevalier de Ternay's successor had left to replace him at the beginning of 1776.

As for the Marquis de Kersalaun, his strange story had piqued my curiosity to a devilish extent, and if he had genuinely been a relative, I could have quite legitimately asked to see him. However, this was not the case, and after thinking about it, I concluded that it would be most inopportune to attract the attention of my superior officers by asking for permission, when I had only just arrived, to visit a convict condemned for a bloody crime. I decided therefore to wait before pushing on with my research in that direction. In any case, I had enough to keep me busy as a Marine Guard Cadet, and not only the study of *Bézout*; there would be plenty of other things to occupy me.

12

When you arrived as a Cadet, it was not enough simply to be entered on the Company roll to be accepted straight away as a full-blown member of the Marine Guards. They had their rules and it was first necessary to pass a few tests. The grand master of these rites, almost an initiation, was the Baron de Kilpinnec. He was scarcely two years older than I, but he had become our *senior* after the departure of the older comrades with the training squadron.

For my first test – the word 'ordeal' would be more appropriate, as a Cadet is always by definition guilty in advance – the Baron de Kilpinnec, helped by a small group of Guards, came and ripped off my bedclothes early on the first Sunday after my arrival, while I was sleeping like a log on my first rest day. Having shouted at me that I would never enter the Navy if I adopted these lazy habits, they ordered me to get dressed immediately and follow them at the double.

We first crossed the garden which sloped down behind the seminary. At the bottom we went out through a little door which opened to the left, and for which the Baron had a key. We found ourselves in narrow alleyway in which two men would have difficulty getting past each other. The houses were almost all wooden framed, with projections that hid most of the sky. It was the rough district of Keravel. Originally this quarter, situated on the slope under the parish of Saint-Louis alongside the former ropewalk, had been built close to the shipyards to house the labourers who worked there. They could use a little private entrance, only guarded at night, which gave them direct access to the Penfeld via a vaulted passageway carved out of the rock, and which came out between the general warehouse and the sail loft, and so was right on their doorstep. This privileged state of affairs eventually attracted, like flies to dung, all those who wished to maintain illicit relations with the convicts. Relatives, friends, accomplices, companions or mistresses – although it was strictly against the law – had over the years infiltrated this quarter whose narrow streets hid every sort of traffic and all manner of stolen goods, and from where one could quietly contact convicts engaged in forced labour in the port, having of course first greased the palms of the prison guards and halberdiers. In short, Keravel had a bad reputation, and that is no doubt why the older Cadets had chosen to take me through this place of ill-repute, rather than through the main entrance beside the Troulan dry dock. It was assuredly part of my initiation.

Once we were in the shipyards, these gentlemen stopped at the quay beside the general warehouse, at the top of a slipway which went down into the Penfeld. They started to undress and ordered me to do the same.

I began to understand what they were going to ask of me. Sure enough, once we were all stark naked, they told me that one could not be a good Naval officer without being able to swim. The air was mild and the sky completely grey. There was no wind and it had not yet started to rain. The tide was flooding, but there was little current as it was neaps. Swimming had not been a part of the education offered by the Saint-Yves College. Once we had gone down into the water, up to our chests, by walking down the sloping granite flagstones of the slipway, they pointed to a ship moored in the middle of the river, opposite us, and said we had to swim to it. They immediately dragged me further down the slipway until I had nothing under my feet. They kept me afloat, some pulling me by the arms, others pushing my heels. Now and again they let me sink, and I took in huge mouthfuls of the brackish water of the Penfeld. I then had to grab the end of a rope which hung from the ladder up the side of the ship's hull and haul myself up to the first rung in order to climb aboard. There was a gap of three feet between the surface of the water and the first rung. That does not seem much, but my muscles were not yet trained for that kind of exercise and I had to haul like the devil to pull myself up to that first rung; after that I had to climb another fourteen. On that Sunday morning the decks were deserted except for an infantry guard who just watched us from a distance, trying to maintain an impassive air as we passed in front of him, as naked as the day we were born. He knew well enough what was going on.

Kilpinnec led us to the bow of the ship, up to the rail of the beak head, and ordered me to sit astride the edge of the gunwale and then climb down onto the upper part of the cathead. I stayed there for a moment, balanced and as if suspended between the sky and the surface of the water eighteen feet below. He told me to work my way to the end of the cathead and jump. Or else they would throw me. I ran and jumped with my eyes closed. I heard the water close around my head and felt myself sinking towards the bottom. I swear I thought my last hour had come. Happily, and in line with the well-known principle of Archimedes, I rose to the surface where the older Cadets, who had dived in after me, were waiting. They then dragged me once more to the slipway we had come from, and once our feet were on firm ground, they taught me the movements for swimming. I came back on my own to this spot for the next few evenings to practise and take advantage of the last days of summer before the autumn cold. By the end of a week, I could swim properly.

The next Sunday I was on the alert and was already dressed when Kilpinnec came into my dormitory. He was alone this time and that was reassuring. He was good enough to tell me that he was going to take me to visit a ship of the line. I really thought that the Baron wanted to be friendly to reward me for my good performance the previous Sunday, and that we were going to visit one of the ships of the training squadron which had just arrived in the harbour.

*

Brest, Sunday 29th September 1776, early morning.

I start to worry when I see that the Baron is once again taking us through Keravel. I wonder if I am going to have to throw myself in the water again, which I would rather not as a chilly north wind is blowing on the Penfeld this morning. Coming out from the little passageway at the bottom of Keravel, Kilpinnec stops in front of a big ship moored fore and aft twenty-five yards off the quay, in front of the sail loft. She is *le Magnifique*, seventy-four guns. Last night she was still in the middle of the river. She is now fully rigged but her guns have not yet been loaded aboard. She has no crew, having been towed there to await loading tomorrow. We have to pass over several barges moored between the quay and the ship's hull to reach the latter's ladder. I climb it behind Kilpinnec and find myself at the end of the gangways, with the forward end of the quarterdeck and the main mast to my right and the bow to my left.

My mentor goes and stands at the foot of the mainmast. Its base seems enormous, at least three feet in diameter. Kilpinnec turns to me.

'Laforest-Dombourg, do you know the height of the masts on a seventy-four?'

I join him behind the mainmast and look up. I see firstly the main yard, which seems as big as the mast. It is trimmed square, and its port half must reach right to the quay over the barges we have just crossed. I reckon it is about fifty feet off the deck. The rest is lost in a mass of ropes going up to frightening heights. I multiply fifty by three.

'A hundred and fifty feet?'

'Two hundred and fifteen from the keel to the truck of the topgallant mast!'

Without being able to help it I step back onto a hatch cover, fortunately closed, and almost fall into the ebb tide. This makes Kilpinnec smile; and with a smile that bodes no good.

'Ever climbed that high?'

'Good heavens, no!'

'Well, you're going to. Right now!'

That was said calmly. He could have forewarned me! I could have at least tried to prepare myself mentally. I look closely at him, hoping still that he may be joking. But what I read in his eyes tells me that this is not the case, and that he is even taking a malicious pleasure in observing my confusion.

I ask permission to at least take off my coat and sword and, having got that far, I deposit my wig. That really makes Kilpinnec laugh!

It is therefore in my waistcoat and shirt sleeves, and bareheaded, that I head firstly towards the port shrouds, on the same side as the barges and the quay, where I think, as would any landlubber, that I am more protected.

'Go to starboard! That way, if you let go, you might fall in the water. I also advise you, in your own interest, to keep your hands on the shrouds, not on the ratlines. They are made for the feet only.'

A word to the wise. I straddle the gunwale to climb up the outside of the starboard shrouds and begin my ascent. The first part seems easy enough. There are nine shrouds, with a big space between each one, over a width of thirty feet, with all the space in the world to place my soles. But these shrouds tend to get closer as I go higher. Soon they are just ten feet wide, and I start to grow anxious as a result. I reach the height of the main yard. It is enormous. I can touch it with my right hand as I go past. I would like to stop there to take my breath, but Kilpinnec has said nothing and so I continue.

Just above the main yard is the main top, a platform six feet wide, like a vast ceiling in whose centre I can see, by lifting my head, a hole, just big enough for me, close to the mast. The ratlines lead straight there. It is very tempting to take this route, but there is nothing more shameful for a sailor than to pass that way. And I know it! And Kilpinnec down there knows it too! I sense that he is about to yell at me, and I don't want to give him that pleasure. The Navy, which considers without doubt that easiness is for soldiers and farmers, has put narrow ratlines in the shrouds of the main topmast. This creates little ladders which go up, so to speak, upside down, to the edge of the main top, called the futtock shrouds. I grip the futtock shrouds and try, on my first journey into the rigging of a King's ship, to climb by the outer route, like a real topman. I don't manage it first time, dammit no! My shoes slip and for several seconds I find myself suspended between sky and earth, trying to put my foot everywhere in the void except those cursed reverse ratlines. I finally manage to get a grip on the wrinkles in the dead eyes of the main topmast shrouds and gather my last strength to pull myself up and slide onto the planking of the main top. My arms are hurting, my legs are like jelly, my heart is beating like a drum. I am out of breath as I have forgotten to breathe during my acrobatics. But breathe I have to! A yell, already somewhat weakened by the distance, comes from below.

'Higher!'

I continue my climb. The main topmast seems longer than the mainmast. This time there are only five shrouds across a width of nine feet and they get closer very quickly. I pass the topmast yard, which has been let down to the limit of its lifts, as far as the top of the mainmast. It is slightly smaller than its sister just below, but it must measure at least sixty feet in all. The ratlines start to narrow again very quickly. Now halfway up, I risk a glance below. Bad mistake! Everything starts to turn around me. I clamp my hands on the shrouds, close my eyes, clench my teeth and count to twenty to try to regain control of my mind. I have the impression of having heard a shout from below and I set off again. By dint of climbing on I must inevitably get to the topgallant crosstrees. There are three of them, placed at right angles to the mast cheeks. And, of course, you have to get onto them by means of the futtock shrouds. The trees stick out at least four feet on each side of the mast to spread the shrouds for the topgallant mast and keep it stiff, although right at the moment I could not care less about that! Once I get up onto the trees, I can see that they are scarcely wider than my shoes. I grip the top of the main topmast and stand up very slowly on trembling legs. My head is just slightly below the mast cap. From there I can see, in the foreground, the fore topmast, on the other side of the ship's waist, towards the bows of the vessel; and in the background I can run my eyes over the roofs of the general warehouse, the mast crane and even the Rose battery at the entrance to the port. From where I am, the few individuals walking on the shipyard quay at this morning hour look like insects. But there is a shout from below.

'Laforest-Dombourg! The main topgallant yard!'

Kilpinnec's voice has become very distant. What does he want now? I can see the yard very clearly. It is hauled down to the top of the main topmast, at the end of its lifts, forward of the mast cap which is level with my forehead.

'Climb onto it!'

I can hardly touch the yard and I don't see how I can get a grip on it. The sails and the booms for the studding sails are not yet bent onto *le Magnifique* and so all the yards are smooth, with just a little rope hanging below in loops which the sailors call, no doubt as a joke: the footrope. There is nothing else to grip on to. And this footrope, swinging around in the wind, is about at the level of my chin. I have to step over the void between the crosstrees, bodily grab this cursed main topmast yard, then launch myself into the air. By some miracle I find myself with my stomach across the yard, gripping the hard timber as best I can with my hands, while kicking desperately with my feet to try to catch the wretched footrope. I am looking straight down into the abyss which so far I have carefully avoided looking at, and which now hits me in the face. I finally manage to lodge my feet and I stop there, waiting for my perch to stop moving and my heart to stop thumping, and all the time wondering how on earth I am going to get down. That is the moment I hear, from far, far away, the voice of my torturer.

'To the end! Go to the end of the yard! To starboard! To the yardarm! D'you hear me?'

Alas, I hear him only too well! This topgallant yard does not seem that big even at the mast, but it narrows towards the ends. Moreover, there is nothing to hang on to. I slide, inch by inch, towards the yardarm, rubbing my buttons against the timber. In fact, this yard hardly goes out beyond the side of the ship's deck, way down there, but I am so high up that the deck seems as narrow as a broomstick. I am truly up in the heavens and if, at this very moment and in my present state, I were to see the angels of paradise passing beside me and fluttering in the blue, I would not be in the least surprised. The foot rope goes up towards the yardarm to which it is fixed. Now I must lean on my knees rather than my stomach to balance myself, while pushing out the footrope with my heels, and keeping a grip on the yard with my hands. And so, bent double, the top of my body is tipping further and further forward and I have to clench my fingers to hold on. At the very moment when I think that I am about to let go, I see, at the level of my face, a rope which seems to have fallen from heaven to rescue me. It is the lift. I hang on to it desperately with both hands, while trying to regain control of my panic-stricken mind.

'The yardarm!' shouts Kilpinnec.

Very well, then! To keep on to the end of the yard, I sit astride it and let go of the lift. It is only then that I see that there is another loop in the footrope right at the end of the yard, allowing the feet to be placed lower down, but it is too late.

'Go back to the mast!'

'The worst is over,' I say to myself, but I am badly mistaken. I have hardly put the end of my toe back on the crosstrees when I hear another commanding shout.

'The mast! You have to go to the top!'

God knows but how I hate that Baron de Kilpinnec right at this moment! Above me there is still the main topgallant mast to climb. It is not much thicker than its yard and is held up by only three shrouds, with even narrower ratlines. But I am beginning to get the hang of it. I start climbing again. Twenty-two feet higher the shrouds stop at the hounds. No more ratlines! I stop, thinking I have reached the end of my terror.

'To the truck!'

There are still fifteen feet between the hounds and the mast truck. Fifteen feet to climb with nothing to hang on to. Luckily the mast is not very wide at this height and I am able to grip around it with my hands. I have the impression that it is swaying under my weight, but I am beyond caring. I finish my ascent by shinning up like a monkey and complete the climb by touching the mast cap.

'Come down!'

*

Overjoyed that he had not asked me to sit on the mast truck, I let myself slide down. The descent seemed easier than I had expected.

I reached the deck as relieved as it is possible to be. Do you think that the Baron de Kilpinnec congratulated me?

'You'd better tidy yourself up before High Mass, Laforest-Dombourg. You look like a rag-and-bone man. If ever the Chevalier de Monteil saw you like that, you'd be locked up!'

Since then, I have often climbed in the rigging of the ships in which I was serving. It is something I really enjoy. But I have never forgotten the fear and the cold sweat of my first visit to the aerial kingdom of the topmen.

13

Monsieur Bézout came to Brest, as expected, at the beginning of October. Two weeks after his visit, the mail from Versailles brought the list of the new Marine Guards, signed by Monsieur de Sartine. Those who had failed and had their two chances went home. The new Cadets arrived not long afterwards. They were quickly taken in hand by their seniors, amongst whom the most relentless were of course the newly promoted ones.

The dormitory where I was living quickly filled. In the next bed was Henri Vernon, the Chevalier des Aulnes. He came from Poitou. He had proofs of nobility to spare and almost all his relatives were in the Army. But, being the youngest, the titles and fortune of his family went first to his elders. He had therefore been given a choice between the Artillery and the Navy, both King's Companies, in which it was not necessary to be rich to make a career. He chose the Navy without really knowing why. He was not much younger than I but was smaller and as fair as an angel. It is true that I felt older than my years after all the ordeals I had been through. I decided therefore to share my knowledge of mathematics with Vernon des Aulnes and to take him under my protection to help him, above all, to get through the ordeals waiting for him from our seniors. The latter fellows were soon to learn, at their expense, that he was brave and of a fiery spirit. Despite his small stature, or perhaps because of it, he was good at all physical activities. Besides this, he was an excellent rider and like all those from Poitou, loved the hunt. He regretted having to abandon this pastime by coming to Brest. Finally, he was an excellent musician. He played the violin and the horn fluently, and lots of other instruments. Besides music and hunting, he spent his leisure time writing interminable letters to his *dear Mother.* If the Comtesse des Aulnes, mother of the Chevalier, has kept the letters from her son, she would be able to publish several quarto volumes about the Marine Guards!

I had been lucky to arrive alone before everybody else, as I had been taken in charge directly by the Baron de Kilpinnec. The new Guards hounded the last ones to arrive. All the same, I was not yet out of the woods. I still had to undergo a few more 'tests' in order to be left in relative peace.

To be considered a true member of the Company, a Cadet had to prove his virility. Thanks to an unwritten agreement with our seniors, the ladies of the bordello usually frequented by the Naval officers graciously undertook to initiate the Cadets in the presence of a small jury of seniors there to make certain that there was no cheating. I can already hear the protestations. I was fifteen years old. How could the Navy tolerate such an abomination? I would say first that I looked older than I was, and that the youngest Cadets were spared this test. I would say above all that it was the least of several evils, as it must be remembered that at that time Brest was a monstrosity, not because of its size, but because of the nature of its population. It was a town overrun with unmarried men. I have already mentioned the shipyard workers, the halberdiers, the prison guards and the convicts, but there were also, of course, the mass of rated sailors, to which can be added the Lascars and blacks recruited from the Indies, from the Île-de-France and from the Americas to make up crews decimated by scurvy and yellow fever. There were also the merchant seamen passing through, albeit a small number relative to the six thousand soldiers and sailors of the garrison. And that does not include the parasites, the traffickers and the smugglers attracted to a town where debauchery, drunkenness and villainy had been taken to extremes. This situation had quite naturally led to an influx of harlots and trollops of every kind, whose numbers continued to grow despite the regular clear-outs ordered by the authorities. The

King's sailors and the merchant seamen frequented the steep streets in the Sept-Saints quarter between the Chateau esplanade and the rigging quay. The Keravel brothels attracted a clientele mainly from the shipyards and the jail. The Army had its establishments at the Pont-de-Terre and Recouvrance. Faced with this deplorable state of affairs, our commanders preferred to turn a blind eye and allow us to frequent a house in the rue de Siam with its unequivocal sign: *Aux Dames de la Marine*[19]. They kept an eye on it and the girls were considerate enough to match their tariffs to the rank and salary of their uniformed clients. It was less of risk, then, than going to the houses frequented by the ordinary sailors or, worse, than ending up in the shanty towns on the outside of the Landerneau Gate, where all the girls chased from the town by the authorities had gathered.

Towards the end of October 1776 there remained just one more test to pass but I was no longer thinking about it, as at that time people were talking about nothing else but the King's most recent Decree turning the Navy into a single body. It caused total upheaval.

I make here a slight digression to make what I have just said more comprehensible. Prior to this famous Decree, signed by Louis XVI on 27th September 1776, the Navy had two distinct hierarchies and two commands: the ships' officers, who commanded aboard the vessels and at sea, and who called themselves Sword Officers, and the port officers who commanded on land at the ports and shipyards, and who were nicknamed Pen Officers. These names do not leave much room for doubt as to what the Sword Officers thought of their Pen equivalents! Unfortunately for the ships' officers, not only did their Pen colleagues have control over all the shore side services including, in particular, the building and equipping of the ships, but they also controlled all the expenditure on the King's ships, aboard which they had clerks as permanent representatives. The fine Sword Officers, whom I soon hoped to join, disliked this dependency, towards which they usually adopted a contemptuous attitude. This division of responsibility originated from the wisdom and sense of economy of the great Colbert, but it had become the cause of quarrels and untenable rivalries to which the King wished to put an end. The new Decree gave all the responsibility to the Ships' Officers and simply disbanded the corps

---

19 Translator's note: *Aux Dames de la Marine:* The Navy's Ladies.

of Pen Officers. The latter were either going to be made redundant, if they were older, or integrated into the new body at the same rank. One can well imagine how this last measure, arbitrarily mixing as it did pen-pushers with the noble sword-carriers from the Marine Guards, had aroused consternation amongst the latter. The King had foreseen this, and as he was wise to the world, he had our commanders read the following text to us:

> *'Should any Guard say anything offensive or make any kind of insult to one of the administrative officers, he will be dismissed and not be allowed to return to the service of the Navy...'*

It could not have been clearer!

As for me, you can imagine that I shrunk into myself when I heard my seniors declaring that they would never consider a common born officer to be their superior. Did this reticence make me suspect? I do not know. But they started to create more tests for me. They started picking quarrels with me just for the sake of it, quarrels that I ignored because they were not worth it. And I finally understood what they were after: *You cannot be considered a good Naval officer until you have given or received some sword blows.* I remembered the words of warning given by the Chevalier de Kermean at Prières, and also my revulsion, at that time, at the practice of duelling, which I thought had finished. Thank God I had taken my uncle's advice seriously. I had learned a lot through his lessons and had continued to exercise and keep myself strong in the Company drill hall.

I was well aware that I had no choice but to fight, in order to put an end to the mockery, but the thought was repulsive, and I could never bring myself to provoke a quarrel. However, the basis for a duel soon presented itself of its own accord. Anything other than that would have been surprising, as it would have been attempting the impossible to avoid a confrontation with either sword or pistol in Brest. This town was bursting with swordsmen ready to fight and who were encouraged by the permanent war waged between the Navy and the Army. At nightfall the streets of the port sometimes became places to avoid. For example, the return to land, on 25th September, of the sailors of the training squadron had once again been the pretext for a drinking session which had ended in a pitched battle between the sailors and the soldiers.

At these times, the good folk of Brest shut themselves away and blocked their ears so as not to hear the shouting of the madmen fighting under their windows. At daybreak it was not unusual to find bloody bodies abandoned in the corners of the streets. It was not solely the sailors and soldiers who were responsible for this state of affairs. The shipyards and the jail played their part in attracting to the town a crowd of shady and brutal types. Add to that the fact that duels, although banned by the authorities, had remained very much in fashion. Gentlemen would duel for no more than an ill-judged word or a simple difference of opinion. And do not think that this was the prerogative of the nobility alone. In the port taverns and the soldiers' bars, the landlords kept sharpened foils behind their bars that they were happy to loan to any of their clients who wanted to fight.

My first occasion to duel arose from a provocation which was not directed at me, while I at the theatre with Vernon. The theatre was situated at the side of the Place des Armes, two streets behind the Hôtel Saint-Pierre. Three officers of the Enghien Infantry, recognisable by their white uniforms with scarlet lapels, were in the same box as us. One of them picked a quarrel with my companion, misled perhaps by his juvenile appearance, on a pretext which I have forgotten and which in any event was totally specious, as the events which followed showed. I stood up and said to him that he ought to address himself to me and that it was I who would reply. He seemed annoyed by my intervention and lost much of his self-assurance. I even wonder whether it may have finished without any fuss had he been alone, but I think he dared not back down in front of his comrades. I believe that Vernon could very well have taken care of himself, but he was not under the same pressure as I was. He understood my dilemma and, as a good friend, he had the tact not to interfere.

'Well then,' the officer said. 'Be at the parade tomorrow.'

'That's good enough for me,' I replied.

Almost every day, at midday, regiments of the garrison drilled and paraded on the Place des Armes beside the theatre. The next morning, after Mass, I talked about this with the other Guards and one of my seniors agreed to be my second. At midday we went together to wait for the end of the parade behind the Enghien regiment. As soon as the exercises were over, my opponent met us with his second, and the four of us went down the rue d'Aiguillon, just behind the Carmelite

Monastery, to the foot of the Bastion at the eastern end of the Dajot Promenade. This was a promenade built along the edge of the sea between the Esplanade and the Chateau. Begun almost seven years previously, by forced labour, for the benefit of the commune of Brest, the Dajot Promenade construction had dragged on. It was still not finished in 1776, and the end of the promenade was no more than a wasteland particularly suitable for our unworthy business.

With the instructions and advice of the Chevalier de Kermean at the forefront of my mind, I had been preparing myself all morning. My head was empty and I was almost impatient to cross swords. My opponent, for his part, was by no means as calm as I. That was obvious as soon as my eyes found his behind his blade. I made several quick lunges, but he stepped back each time, well enough that I was not able to touch him. Eventually, my second went and planted his foot behind him. He managed to parry another attack, but his epee slipped from his hand and dropped to the ground. I let him pick it up, but he dropped it again. He took hold of it once more and his comrade tied his hand to the grip of his sword with a handkerchief. I no longer knew what approach to take. I was afraid of killing him. I think that I would have ended up being careless to the point of allowing myself to be wounded by opening up my guard too much, had not our two seconds interrupted us to ask whether we were satisfied. I immediately replied that I fought without any animosity and that I was prepared to stop if my adversary was happy. The latter said that my words were enough for him and the affair ended there.

To win without danger is to triumph without glory. For my part, I had not wanted to be triumphant, and this easy victory suited me well. I congratulated myself on having got through my test without drawing blood. I thought I had now finished with this duelling business, as from then on, I had no intention of being angered by anybody. I preferred to devote myself to my studies. Alas! That would have been too simple.

A week later, the last Saturday of October, while I was crossing the Chateau esplanade with some other Cadets and Guards, we came across a group of Enghien regiment officers who seemed to be waiting for us. One of them came straight towards us and asked to know which one of us was called Laforest-Dombourg. I presented myself. He said in a loud voice which everybody could hear:

'Monsieur Laforest-Dombourg, you are a good-for-nothing!'

He said it with such animosity that at first I was left speechless. Then, getting a grip on myself, I replied:

'I do not have the honour of your acquaintance, Monsieur, but I have always been told that an insult stains he who delivers it rather than he who receives it.'

'You insult me, Monsieur? Well then, so be it! I will await you next Saturday at the parade. And we shall see if your epee is as sharp as your tongue!'

On the advice of my seniors, I went and told the Baron de Kilpinnec what had happened. Having looked into it, he explained the situation. It was extremely serious. The young officer whom I had so easily beaten had been in a similar position as me. He had not wanted to fight. It was under pressure from his comrades that he had sought a quarrel with little Vernon des Aulnes, no doubt intending to do him as little harm as possible. My intervention had upset his plans. The news of the circumstances of his defeat had dismayed the officers of the Enghien regiment, his peers, and they had persuaded their Colonel to send my unfortunate opponent home. After that, all the Lieutenants of the regiment were called together, and they decided to send, in order to provoke me, their best swordsman, their *champion*. He was called de Lestourières. News of our quarrel had been spread around all the officers of the garrison, in case I tried to get out of the duel. Moreover, they had managed to have everyone believe that it was I who had badly insulted de Lestourières by replying to him insolently, and that he was the one who had been offended.

14

The next Saturday was 2nd November: All Souls' Day[20]! Was that purely coincidence or was it an insight into the minds of the Lieutenants of the Enghien regiment? I do not know. In any event, it gave me a week to prepare myself and I intended to make the most of it. Apart from morning muster and the Mass which followed it, we were free to organise our time as we wished. I was by no means behind my fellow Cadets in the study of *Bézout,* and so I decided to devote myself entirely to fencing to prepare for my duel.

*

Brest, Sunday 27th October 1776, towards ten in the morning.

After Mass, I run to the Hôtel Saint-Pierre drill hall. There I find the officers and Guards known to be fanatical fencers. They all know about my duel and welcome me with reserve but also with kindness.

Going to the end of the hall to do some gymnastic exercises before starting to fight, I notice a Naval officer whom I have never seen

20 Translator's note: All Souls' Day, the day after All Saints' Day, is known in France as the *Jour des Morts*: the Day of the Dead.

before. He is fencing against a wall, alone and apart. I soon notice that the other officers there carefully avoid him, and even seem afraid of him. The braided hem of his waistcoat indicates that he is a Ship's Captain. He is very tall, a good five feet ten inches. Well-balanced on his legs, wide of shoulder and chest and graced with an exceptional musculature, he is nevertheless extremely supple. He is aiming at marks drawn on the wall and every time he lunges, the point of his epee lands exactly on target with a truly terrifying precision and force. But what impresses me most is not his dexterity, but the merciless drive and kind of animal power which emanates from his every gesture. He is a man who inspires both fear and admiration. Taken to some tribe of savages in America or Africa, I think that he would soon become their king.

Our fencing master is of course aware of my adventure with the Enghien regiment. He comes to tell me that he will personally take me in charge. I have become, despite myself, the *champion* of the Navy! Before starting my lesson, I ask him who is the new arrival.

'It is Captain Flaharn,' he replies, lowering his voice. 'It's three years since he was last in Brest and I was happy to see the back of him. I don't know when he arrived or why, but if I were you, I would keep away from him.'

It isn't to be. While I am working with the fencing master, the big Ship's Captain whom we have just been talking about comes and stands beside us to watch. At the end of our session, he turns to me. I would say he is about forty-five years old. He is not simply a handsome man. He has a remarkable face with regular and noble features, a high forehead, straight nose, a pronounced chin and a wide mouth which reveals perfect teeth when he opens his narrow lips in what passes for a smile. He is the kind of person in whom one would have unhesitating confidence. He has extraordinary grey eyes: so pale and cold they would freeze your blood.

'You are, I presume, the young Laforest-Dombourg about whom everyone is talking.'

'I am afraid so, Sir.'

'Are you the son of the Ship's Lieutenant Laforest-Dombourg who once commanded *le Triton* for the India Company?'

His voice is serious, rough and slightly husky.

'Yes, that is me. Did you know my father, Sir?'

'I once served in India and I only came across him…at a distance.'

Under different circumstances, I would have like to have found out more and I would have bombarded Captain Flaharn with questions, despite his piercing gaze and his voice.

'I have heard about this business with the Enghien regiment,' the Ship's Captain continues. 'It happens that I am in Brest for a few weeks and can use my time as I wish. I am going to take you in hand. Do not refuse. Your opponent is formidable, and you are risking your life with this affair. But I have seen you working. You are very talented, which I find interesting. I think, if I train you well, that it is you who will kill him.'

*

Kill or be killed. That was the awful choice which I faced, against my will. And I have to say that despite the unsettling gaze of Captain Flaharn, I accepted his proposition without hesitation.

'A duel is not a joking matter,' he added. 'And, in your case, you can be sure that this Lieutenant de Lestourières will give you no chance. The only way to come through this is to give him no quarter right from the start.'

I trained for the rest of the day with my new fencing master, and for the following days too. He taught me little-known moves which would all be fatal if I could not parry them. I asked Captain Flaharn why he took such an interest in me. He replied that it was normal for him to help a *champion* of the Navy. He thought that my youthfulness needed a helping hand against a fighter like de Lestourières. He said again that he thought I was very gifted, and that interested him. These explanations seemed to me to make sense. It is true too that my sessions with the big Ship's Captain stopped me sinking into desperation. At times I felt I was living a nightmare. At the Company and in town, whenever the military met, the talk was about nothing but my duel with Lieutenant de Lestourières. The first assessments had my adversary as the winner. But, once Captain Flaharn had begun to train me, opinions were soon more divided. However, everybody agreed on one point: it would be a fight to the death and one of us would be left stretched out. No Guards were harassing me now! I was treated with respect and consideration, just like a hero on borrowed time. But I myself was too anxious to derive the least satisfaction from it. I applied myself to my fencing with a renewed passion.

The hours spent with the Chevalier de Kermean, the advice of Captain Flaharn, together with, without wishing to boast, a certain amount of natural ability which I had never before wanted to put to the test, quickly bore fruit without me really realising it. On Wednesday 29th October, two days before All Saints' Day, I spent the whole day fencing with desperate energy, even forgetting to dine. During the afternoon I challenged everybody present and beat them all to a man. Then I challenged the fencing master to a bout and beat him too, in glorious fashion, without giving him a chance. When I went to bed on the evening of that memorable day, I slept deeply for the first time in three days.

The next day, Captain Flaharn was waiting for me when I arrived at the drill hall. Previously he had come a little later to give me time to warm up before his arrival.

'You were very stupid yesterday, Laforest-Dombourg. Do you know that all bets now have you as winner against de Lestourières? And that the gentlemen of the Enghien regiment are so concerned that they are having a special meeting about it later tonight?'

'You don't seem pleased about it,' I said, surprised by the severity of his voice.

'That's because they are now afraid of you with the sword.'

'You mean that they are ready to seek a reconciliation?' I asked, full of hope.

'They are looking to change things. Did you really offend him, in fact?

'Absolutely not,' I replied. 'This de Lestourières challenged me in front of witnesses simply because he wanted to avenge the defeat of an officer of his regiment whom I had beaten earlier. I recognise that de Lestourières had immediately made out that I had insulted him, replying as I did, he being a Lieutenant and I just a Cadet. But that seemed so far-fetched that I never really paid attention.'

'Well, that is a pity because, from then on, public opinion has been that it was de Lestourières who was insulted. It is too late to change that and risk losing face.'

'But why is that important?' I asked.

'Important, Sir? It is important because, as the offended parties, they have the choice of arms, and they have now decided that it will be a duel with pistols!'

I felt the ground fall away beneath me. I had not forgotten my uncle's words about duelling with pistols.

'But that is unfair!' I cried. 'All the witnesses will tell you that he came to me deliberately to challenge me and that he called me by my name when I didn't even know who he was! Ask everybody. They will confirm it.'

'Calm down! I think that most people are well disposed towards you, partly because of what you have just told me, and partly because a lot of people have bet on you winning. That ought to allow me to claim the role of arbitrator, in compensation. In that capacity, I have to provide a pair of pistols. You know that, in a duel, it is the custom, first that the pistols should be absolutely identical, and second that the two opponents have the right to try them for a day, the day before, to get used to them. I could therefore propose weapons belonging to you, with which you are familiar, and which you will have handed over to me before, without anyone knowing. That would give you a slight advantage and, considering the way they have behaved, is not really dishonest. Do you have a pair of pistols?'

'Yes.' I replied. 'But…'

'That's enough! We don't have much time. Go and fetch them, with everything needed to load them, and meet me in an hour at the end of the quay upstream on the Penfeld, on the Brest side. I'll wait there with a boat and we can go and train on the right bank at the end of the port.'

I ought without a doubt have explained to Captain Flaharn that I had never used my pistols, but I was so stunned by what he had just told me that I could not think properly. I did as he asked.

*

Brest, Thursday 31st October, middle of the morning.

At the appointed hour I find Captain Flaharn in front of the lower ropewalk amidst anchors of all sizes which are arranged beside the quay at this area of the port. He has borrowed a little yole which he handles very skilfully with a single oar over the stern. There is a bend in the river to our right. The current is weak as it is damned with a holding dyke further upstream, towards the town of Penfeld. We pass to starboard of the massive hulls, completely de-rigged, of the last ships moored there fore and aft in columns of three, in the middle of the Penfeld, waiting to be re-commissioned. We pass in front of the Powder Mill Inlet, barred by a drawbridge. The river goes round to the left and we leave the ramparts behind. It is here that the timber for the shipyards is kept under water. Captain Flaharn comes into the river bank once we are further on. The port is hidden from view by the hills of Recouvrance and its permanent hubbub scarcely reaches us. The place is deserted. I can see only, on the left bank, some building works for terracing where soldiers from the garrison are working. New fortifications are being built to the north of Brest.

The sky is a sombre grey with low clouds pushed by a light breeze from the south-west. It is not cold and is no longer raining. I am carrying my pistol box under my arm. I have wrapped it in tarred canvas to protect it against showers. Captain Flaharn points out a rock sheltered from the wind by a gorse bush.

'Put your case on this rock. We need an area forty paces long. The combat is done on pause and command. The adversaries stand at forty paces from each other. You can go down to fifteen, but I will ask for forty. Loaded pistol in hand, arm beside the body, barrel towards the ground, the butt touching the thigh. It is forbidden to move before the order is given…'

He stops suddenly in the middle of his explanations. While he is talking, I have put my packet on the rock which he had indicated, taken off the cloth which protected it, uncovering the lid of the box and its carved representation of a tiger hunt. Surprised by his silence, I raise my head. His face is impassive, his eyes as cold and inexpressive, but they are fixed my case. I turn the key and open the lid. He starts talking again.

'The judge orders: Fire! You then have to take aim and fire more quickly and more accurately than your opponent. It is simultaneously firing rapidly and firing accurately.'

He holds out a white handkerchief.

'Walk in that direction and count forty paces before putting the handkerchief on the ground. It will do as a target. Weigh it down with a stone. I will load the pistols while you are doing that.'

When I rejoin him, he has already loaded the first weapon and is in the process of loading the second. He has very big hands. I have been able to judge their strength when fencing with him, but he handles the ramrod, bullets and powder horn with a surprising delicacy and precision.

When he has finished, he hands me the first loaded pistol.

'Take up the waiting position as I explained and wait for the order to fire. Don't spend too long taking aim. That is the secret!'

I take one step to the side, put my left foot back and wait while keeping my eyes on the white handkerchief forty paces away.

'Fire!'

I raise my arm while keeping both eyes wide open as my uncle the Chevalier de Kermean has taught me. I pull the trigger as gently as possible as soon as I have the white of my target in the sights. The explosion lifts up the barrel and the handkerchief jumps back, taking its stone with it.

'Excellent! I am pleased to see that you are already well trained with this weapon!'

'Not at all! It is the first time I have fired it...'

The Captain looks at me for a moment without saying anything, then seizes hold of the second pistol. He fires so quickly that I have the impression that he did not even take aim. But our improvised target jumps again.

'They are good pistols, don't you think?' I say.

Captain Flaharn shakes his head.

'They are perfect! With weapons like this you and that fool de Lestourières have a good chance of killing each other. That is not the object of the exercise!'

'I have perhaps enough time to train myself to be quicker?'

I try to put on a brave face, but I cannot stop my voice from trembling.

'Waste of time! Go home and clean your pistols. It would be a pity to ruin such good weapons. I will see what I can do...Trust me.'

*

That same evening, I was summoned to see the Chevalier de Monteil. With him was another Ship's Captain whom I did not know, but who I later found out was on the staff of the Naval Command at Brest.

'Monsieur Laforest-Dombourg! I have just come from the office of the Comte d'Orvilliers who tells me that you intend to fight with

Lieutenant de Lestourières of the Enghien regiment. I am flabbergasted! Do you not know that duelling is strictly against the rules and the law?'

Had I been less conscious of the seriousness of my situation, I think I would have had difficulty not to smile at these words. Since my arrival at Brest, not a week had gone by without several officers or Guards going down to the field to cross swords with an opponent. The last meeting had been between two Guards who had had a difference over a game of cards! And the Chevalier de Monteil well knew it. Just as he must have known that I was to face the *champion* of the Enghien regiment. I had even heard that he had bet five gold Louis on my victory.

'Thank God, I know that you are not responsible for this duel, and that all the fault rests with the Lieutenants of the Enghien regiment. But you ought to have come and told me. In any case, the commanding officer of the Enghien regiment has been held responsible by the Marquis de Langeron. Lieutenant de Lestourières has been posted to the Portzic battery and barred from setting foot in Brest until his regiment departs. As for you, you are of course barred from going to Portzic. I am taking no chances! I formally forbid you, with effect from today, and until any new order, to cross the Penfeld, even just to go to Recouvrance. Do I make myself clear?'

At first, I found the measure a bit steep! But my opinion changed when I learned, not long afterwards, the final word on this affair. At the time that the whole of Brest was talking of nothing but my imminent duel with Lieutenant de Lestourières, the Comte d'Orvilliers, the Navy Commander, and the Marquis de Langeron, the Lieutenant-General commanding the garrison and the forts, had both received a letter from Monsieur de Sartine ordering them, in the name of the King, to put an immediate stop to the quarrelling between the Navy and the Army. His Majesty, it seems, was most aggrieved to learn of the deplorable state of affairs which existed between the two great Corps in his service at Brest. My dispute with the Enghien regiment could not have been known about at such a high level, but both sets of military authorities in Brest had been told of this unfortunate business. One can imagine that they both must have thought that the death in a duel of one of their officers, coming so soon after the severe warning they had just received, would have been extremely detrimental to their futures.

I cannot help noting in passing, that whereas the authorities forced themselves, with a certain amount of good fortune, to impose a minimum of harmony between the Navy and the Army, nobody was in the least worried about the calamitous war that was also being waged in Brest between the Company of Marine Guards and the ordinary folk of the town. Many people think that pageboys are much worse than young sailors and soldiers when it comes to pranks and rowdiness, but they don't know the Marine Guards, next to whom the pageboys are as nothing! At night, when the good citizens were in their beds, the Guards walled up their doors, blocked their locks, covered their doorbells in excrement. Or else they put a ladder against the wall and went up to knock on the blind. If the poor inhabitant was silly enough to open it, they let off a pistol loaded with powder and sprayed him with a little syringe full of blood. He thought he had been wounded, causing great mirth for the onlookers. During the daytime we sometimes danced a big farandole, joining hands with our handkerchiefs, forty or more of us, weaving across the town and pushing into the town's citizenry. Or else we had fun stopping people from walking along the Dajot Promenade. Some of us would carry sticks hidden under our waistcoats, and if they came across some young lad, would give him a good beating. To get their own back, our victims sometimes organised reprisal ambushes. Woe betide any young Guard who was going home on his own at such a time. It could get as far as sword blows and pistol shots. Vernon des Aulnes, my young friend, had been mortified on learning of all these horrors. He told me that it was wrong for us to behave like that, as one day it will cost us dearly.

In any event, I did not have any more duelling to do, and my seniors left me in peace. However, I continued to fence regularly with Captain Flaharn at the drill hall. He had suggested that he keep on with my training with the epee. I did not know what his real motives were, but I accepted since, although he did not seem to be well liked in Brest, he was reputed as a formidable swordsman and, thanks to him, nobody now wanted to seek out a quarrel with me.

I immersed myself once more in the study of *Bézout,* but even this absorbing occupation did not keep me from thinking about the Marquis de Kersalaun and his strange story. Fantig's testimony had not really dispelled the mystery surrounding his arrest. His guilt was by no means obvious. I would have liked to meet him but did not know how to go about it. The simplest way would have been to ask the authorities for permission to visit him, but I could not find a justifiable reason for it. My request would almost certainly have been rejected. Besides, the role played by the Navy command in this affair suggested I should be cautious. It would certainly be unwise to attract attention to myself by pursuing this line openly. I ought first to learn a little more about the Marquis and his situation. Thanks to the convict wigmaker, I knew that the chief clerk at the jail could give me more information. The answers to my questions would surely be in his registers. And in making some discreet enquiries, I discovered that this civil servant would receive visitors like me who wanted to see a convict. He usually asked for one gold louis as his commission. Naturally these meetings took place unknown to the Commissioner of Prisons, Monsieur Testanières. I found out a little about him too. This venerable servant of the King had directed the Brest jail for twenty-seven years. Prior to that he had been clerk for fifteen years at the Toulon forced labour prison. I had heard it said that he was scrupulously honest and exceptionally strict. This was doubtless necessary for a job in which one was surrounded by rogues and men without honour, but it did not help me. I said to myself: if this honest man finds out that I have tried to bribe his clerk and tells the Chevalier de Monteil, who would be the fool? Me, for sure! Moreover, to contact the chief clerk of the jail, one had to go through the halberdiers, and they were certainly not the most appropriate intermediaries for trying to find the Marquis de Kersalaun. I really did not know what to do. Having learned that Monsieur Testanières was to retire at the end of the year, I decided to wait in the hope that the arrival of his replacement might present an opportunity. In fact, I was to have an opportunity much sooner than imagined, but not of the kind I had expected, and it was thanks to, if one could say that, a tragic event that nobody could have foreseen.

15

On Saturday 16th November 1776, the day commenced with light drizzle under a low sky and finished with a gale from the south-west which grew stronger overnight and the following days. On Tuesday 19th, the storm continued with a violent blow from the north-west, rattling the window frames of the Hôtel Saint-Pierre for the whole day. I was happy, for once, to be inside and well sheltered from the bad weather.

That Tuesday, just after three o'clock in the afternoon, when we were once again immersed in our mathematics until the evening, our section leader, Ship's Lieutenant de Clesmeur, burst into the room and interrupted our lesson. A fire had just broken out at the Navy hospital. Buckets had been distributed as quickly as possible to the soldiers from the Royal Corps of Marine Infantry barracks and anybody willing to help in the area, and the port's fire pumps had been brought up.

'…They have also fetched the sailors from their shore barracks. They won't have enough officers with them, so you need to go to reinforce them. All the sick and wounded of the hospital are sailors too, you Cadets! This is a good time for you to show your regard for a class of men who are of the greatest value, despite their modest looks. Remember that without their bravery, the King would long since have been without a Navy.'

We set off straight away. The Navy hospital was built above the upper ropewalk, at the foot of Brest's most northerly fortifications. It was right at the end of the port, beside the cemetery, just past the prison and the Naval infantry barracks. To get there from the Hôtel Saint-Pierre, we had to pass beside the seminary where we were lodged and go along the outside wall of the prison's rear courtyard, where I had bought my wig.

The bells of Saint-Louis were ringing the alarm at full tilt when we passed the church square. Tuesday was market day and abandoned stalls still blocked our passage; their owners had been requisitioned to fight the fire before they had had time to take them down.

The wind was blowing strongly straight down the street. It was right in our faces as we arrived in front of the Navy chapel. Once we had passed the prison, we could see not just smoke, but flames coming from the roof of the hospital where it adjoined the prison. It was about four o'clock. Two of the Brest manual pumps were already sending powerful jets of water against the front of the hospital. Naval infantrymen, helped by volunteers from the town, were passing buckets from hand to hand up the staircase to the hallway of the main entrance. The fire had started in the attic of the first building, the most southerly. Everyone still thought the fire could still be brought under control, but they had not reckoned on the strong wind which was blowing.

Our tars were already there. Lieutenant de Clesmeur had talked about their 'modest appearance' and, for sure, they were not wearing smart uniforms: canvas trousers stained with pitch, blue coats for the most elegant, round hemp wigs or woollen bonnets as headgear. They had all been rapidly equipped with boarding axes.

Lots of sailors had already been assigned to bringing the water to feed the fire engines and the tubs for filling the water buckets going up the stairs. In principle, it is better to use fresh water so as not to damage the mechanisms of the fire engines, but given the urgency of the situation, the sailors were going straight to the Penfeld to fill the tanks and barrels. These were loaded on handcarts and brought up the Grande Rue at the double. They had improvised rope harnesses that enabled them to have ten men pulling a single cart.

Lieutenant de Clesmeur detailed us off to supervise the sailors evacuating the invalids. These sailors met us with a deference I had never encountered since becoming a Cadet, that is to say the lowestof-the-low in the Navy. In truth, they had no need of us to carry out their mission efficiently. The patients in the hospital were Naval ratings like them, their brothers-in-arms so to speak, and so they organised themselves quickly on their own and without an unnecessary word. The skill of sailors has always been proverbial: they had brought lengths of timber and old rope with which they improvised stretchers in two ticks for the sick who were unable to walk. There were about three hundred and eighty patients in the hospital and their evacuation was organised very quickly.

Vernon and I were detailed to head up a small group of sailors to look through the wards to make sure that nobody had been forgotten. A clerk in an office by the entrance drew a quick plan of the building on a piece of paper. The hospital was made up of two long parallel buildings about two hundred yards long and thirty to forty feet wide. They were joined by three transverse wards, creating two rectangular gardens. The sick were all on the ground floor.

We started in the most easterly wing. It was directly opposite the entrance door in the hallway. It was the hospital's biggest ward, the Saint-Louis ward, and went the whole length of the building. Having gone right to the end and gone across the northern connecting building, we came back down the west wing, which had two wards one after the other, the Saint-Jean ward and the Saint-Jean-de-Dieu ward. This took a long time, so that it was getting dark by the time we got to the southern end of the Saint-Jean-de-Dieu ward. We had been intending to come back by the southern connecting building, but its door was locked from the other side. We had to retrace our steps and go through the central connecting building, called the Saint-Claud ward, in order to search the southern half of the Saint-Louis ward. We started to feel a disturbing level of heat and we finished that area in double quick time, relieved not to have found a living soul. We now had only to check the southern connecting building which we had been unable to get into. This was the wing where we had seen flames coming from the roof two hours earlier. We could get to it via another door in the vestibule, to our right in going out, opposite the big staircase where they had been passing buckets since the start of the fire. This time I could push the door open easily, as the locks on the inside were open. I found myself at the entrance to a long dark ward which seemed deserted. The floor was soaking wet where I stood; water had poured down a little spiral staircase which went up to my right. Despite the half-light, I could see that smoke was coming from the top of the staircase and swirling along just below the ceiling to the other end of the ward. It was being blown by a draught, which suggested there was an opening at the other end. I was about to enter the ward to finish the inspection when a nurse stopped me.

'Leave that one, Sir. It's the Saint-Nicolas ward, the convicts' ward. We haven't been able to deal with it and anyway it's too late. Everyone's getting out of here.'

At that moment, we heard the sound of jostling behind us. People were running down the big stone staircase of the hallway. It was clearly impossible to keep fighting the fire on the first floor. My attention was drawn by cries, of female voices it seemed, coming from the end of the Saint-Nicolas ward.

'Are there women in there?'

The nurse seemed embarrassed.

'They'll be the Sisters of Charity. They're the only ones willing to look after those gallows' birds. But I don't understand why they're still there.'

'Is there an exit at the other end?' I asked.

'Yes, there is a little door at the end of a blind alley which opens directly to the shipyards and the door to the Commissioner of Prisons' gardens.'

Without thinking, I took off my coat, my hat and my wig and gave them to Vernon, together with my sword, telling him to take them all back to the dormitory. I knew nothing about fires and thought that all I had to do was to cross this ward quickly to get to the jail side, from where I could not be thrown out. Once there I could talk to these Sisters of Charity. Up until now it had never occurred to me to seek them out, as I had not bothered to find out their exact role in relation to the convicts. One cannot think of everything. I would in any case be more confident in them as intermediaries than the halberdiers.

*

Brest, Tuesday 19th November, towards five o'clock in the evening.

Vernon is adamant that he wants to come with me. I tell him that I have entrusted to him the sword my uncle gave to me and that I would rather that he looks after my things. In truth, I thought at that moment that I would not be in any kind of danger. I learned later that it was thought that I had bravely taken risks in order to rescue the Sisters of Charity, but to be frank, I had no idea of the risks and only wanted to take advantage of this unforeseen situation to try to gain entry to the jail.

The nurse tells me that I will be risking my life. I simply shrug my shoulders. I think that he is exaggerating. I borrow a sailor's axe however, just in case, and launch myself into the Saint-Nicolas ward. I have calculated that it must be about eighty yards long, like the other cross-buildings. The heat has increased considerably. The ceiling is covered by smoke, and it is so dark that I cannot see the wall of the ward on my right. I orientate myself by following the big windows at the front, which I keep to my left. A flickering light comes through them, and I realise that it is not the light of the setting sun but in fact the reflection of the flames from the fire on the wall of the prison just alongside. I can no longer hear voices in front of me, and I quicken my pace. When I get to the middle of the ward, the smoke has already come down to the level of my head. In order not to suffocate, I carry on bent over. I cough and am quickly out of breath walking like this. I start to regret having begun this adventure. I wonder if the nurse was right and whether I should turn back. Without slowing down, I turn my head to look back. This makes me drift off to the right and I bang hard into a bed. I trip. I think that I am going to fall, but, thank Heavens, I keep hold of my axe. My right hand, held out in front, grabs the frame of the next bed and I am able to regain my balance. I stop for a moment to get my breath. I look back but can see nothing in that direction. I realise now that I have stupidly got myself into a real rat trap, but it is too late to have second thoughts. Above all I must see it through to the end. And run for my life!

I suddenly feel something ghastly: something alive is touching my back! I am pulled backwards! For a second, I am paralysed with fright. My hair stands up on my head. I realise that a hand coming out of nowhere has got a firm grip on my belt. And I hear someone speaking to me in the dark.

'For pity's sake, matey, get me out of here!'

Fighting back my fear, I make out a vague form lying on the bed. At that moment other voices come out of the darkness around me.

I shout.

'You mustn't stay here! Whoever you are, walk behind me, if you can. I will guide you.'

'Sorry, Sir, I thought as you was a screw. Where've they gone, them bastards? Run after 'em, Sir! Bring 'em back so as they can unlock us for God's sake!'

The man moves and I hear the metallic sound of chain against the bed frame. I realise the full horror of the situation. These poor men are sick convicts. They have not fled as they are chained to their beds.

An obscene curse rings out a few paces from us and someone begins to shout, his voice filled with a hate and anger that freezes my blood.

'Don't you let go of that toff, matey! He'll leave us juss like them ovvers! Keep a good hold! At least we can take that one wiv us to the fires o' hell!'

The hand holds on more tightly to my belt. Terrified, I hit out blindly with the blade of my axe at the arm which is holding me. I manage to free myself. Cries of pain and anger greet my release. As I move away, I brush against other hands stretched out in the dark to try to catch me.

I try to carry on as quickly as possible, but it is not easy. I have to bend completely double to escape the smoke which is coming closer and closer to the floor. I can no longer guide myself by the glimmer of light through the windows, which are now totally shrouded in smoke. Going along bent double, without being able to look where I am going, I overtake a group of men going in the same direction and whom I bang into in the dark with my head. They are dragging chains behind them. At that moment, smoke fills the room completely. I hold my breath. My heart thumps in my chest. My ears buzz. The terrible smoke burns my eyes. I overcome the need to breathe, knowing that if I do I won't be able to carry on and I will surely die.

My will is not strong enough. I start to weaken. It is finished. I am about to give up. I sense then that the unknown men in front of me are turning sharply left and I keep up with them in a final effort. I let myself be dragged along. The density of the smoke eases, then it disappears. The air is still as hot but I can fill my lungs and open my eyes. Everything becomes bright around me. I realise that my left hand is still gripping the handle of my axe.

We have come out of the building. Is is probably night now but it is as light as day. Huge flames are leaping and roaring straight up from the roofs of the wing I have just crossed. We are in an alleyway or a little courtyard, where a hundred or so people are packed, mainly convicts, going by their red smocks. They are on their haunches or lying on the ground. I see some halberdiers and a group of workmen bustling around near the wall of the prison. They are in fact jailers. I go to the nearest, shouting that there are still chained patients inside. He looks at me without replying, his face startled. He must be wondering where on earth I have come from. I see two wimples amongst the group which has just come out into the fresh air with me.

'Sisters! There are still patients in the ward!'

The nearest turns her face to me. Tears are running down her cheeks, reddened by the heat.

'I know, but it is too late now. We can't go in there. There is too much smoke. We have already made the jailers go and rescue these ones!'

She points to the convicts that I overtook in the smoke. If I had not come across them, I would never have found my way out. As if to show that she is right, we hear a great noise. Flames leap out of the window of the ward I have just crossed. The floors of the upper storeys have just collapsed, blowing out all the ground floor windows at one stroke. I think I hear a single scream, but it seems strangely feeble. I tell myself that the shouting of the unfortunate convicts whom I abandoned there, just a few minutes earlier, must have been drowned in the terrible roaring of the flames. The heat and the light grow stronger in the space where we are. All the convicts who are able to do so are now standing. In fifteen minutes this place too will be deadly. I ask a jailer what we are waiting for. He points to the group I had already noticed by the prison wall. There is an oak door there, which two halberdiers are trying, in vain, to smash down with their sabres.

'It's the door to the garden of the Commissioner of Prisons' house. Our only way out. We can't go via the shipyard now – the heat is too much!'

He stops suddenly. The sinister smell of burnt flesh envelopes us.

'If they don't manage to open it, it will soon be our turn,' he shouts.

My axe! I rush to the halberdiers and hold it out to them. The nearest drops his sabre and grabs it.

*

The door was soon smashed down. The halberdiers who opened it disappeared immediately to the other side, carried by the human tide of the convicts who could walk. The jailers and halberdiers left behind started to beat the crowd with leather clubs and the flat of their swords to form them into ranks and to get them to help those who had trouble moving. It was fortunate that they were mainly sick, weak and lame, otherwise I am sure they would have blocked our only way out by all trying to get through at the same time.

I went through the door with two Sisters of Charity. We were the very last. The jailers were not overly endowed with gallantry! It was about time, for the heat was becoming unbearable in the passageway.

It was not so hot on the other side of the wall, in the Commissioner's garden. The herd of convicts had already crossed it, leaving a wide furrow in the rows of vegetables in the kitchen garden, all the way to the entrance of the house. Its elegant door and mouldings had also been smashed with the axe. Inside the house, on the ground floor, the Commissioner of Prisons' beautiful furniture had been transformed to matchwood scattered everywhere, on the tiling and the now-tattered rugs, amongst the broken crockery, embroidered tablecloths and napkins. In front of the house, on the other side, there was an ornamental garden which was also completely devastated, as the jailers had had to assemble the sick convicts there to make them wait. In fact, the main exit from this garden led onto the street, so could not be opened for the forced labourers. They had to pass through a tiny narrow iron door that led directly to the courtyard of the prison. Normally, only the Commissioner used this secret gate, which allowed him immediate access to the jail at any time. The iron gate onto the street was guarded by halberdiers who would not let me through. I presented myself to a man aged about sixty, dressed in black and still wearing a wig, despite the hour and the circumstances, who was standing on his own on the steps of the house. I thought he was Monsieur Testanières' butler. In fact, it was the Commissioner of Prisons himself, which gave me an idea. I explained my situation and asked whether I could return to the jail tomorrow 'to retrieve the Navy axe which I had loaned to the jailers'. Monsieur Testanières seemed to listen to me sympathetically, but I could see that his mind was elsewhere. Put yourself in his place! In any case, it suited me perfectly. I had been put through so much that I had completely forgotten the Sisters of Charity. I now had only one wish: to get out of this hellish place. The Commissioner himself took me to the gate to tell the halberdiers to let me through.

I got back to the dormitory to find Vernon des Aulnes in a desperate state. They had thought that I had been trapped under the falling ceiling of the Saint-Nicolas ward. For my part, I was still deeply shaken by what I had just experienced. For a long while after I would have nightmares in which convicts smelling of roast pig grabbed hold of me and tried to drag me into the flames of hell. I think that deep down I felt guilty for having abandoned those unfortunates to their horrible fate. There was nothing I could have done, though, but I had been their last hope in this world. It was said that about forty convicts were burned alive in the Saint-Nicolas ward. Afterwards, in giving my account to Lieutenant de Clesmeur, I told him that I was surprised that the poor men had not really shouted. My section leader said that they were probably already dead before the ceiling collapsed, asphyxiated by the smoke, from which I only just escaped myself. I hoped that he was not mistaken.

The end result was that the hospital was completely destroyed. The next day, nothing was left. The upper ropewalk and the prison were spared, against most people's expectation. It had even been thought that the jail would have to be evacuated. It must be said that the news of the death of the convicts still chained to their beds in the Saint-Nicolas ward soon spread round the forced labourers. They were so angered by this and so violently upset that the authorities feared a revolt. To calm them down, they were made to assemble in the courtyard of the jail, where they were told that they would be taken away to shelter in the Brest Chateau until the fire had burned itself out.

This was not a simple business. There were about two thousand nine hundred convicts to move. The Landerneau Gate was closed, and all the guards doubled at the guard posts on the Brest side. There were four of these, not counting the Gate. The convicts were formed into columns which were escorted by Army and Navy personnel with loaded rifles, ready to open fire. They were made to cross the town in several groups, some via the shipyards as far as the commercial port, then across the Sept-Saints, others from the courtyard with the convicts' stalls, past the seminary and via the rue de Siam.

All these men were herded together in the central courtyard of the Chateau, huddled one against the other. For the whole night, soldiers kept turn guarding them, rifle in hand, beside a cannon loaded with grapeshot. The next day at dawn, the fire being extinguished, they were taken back to the jail in the same way.

From what I heard these poor fellows stayed calm the whole time. Maybe the cold that night was too much for them. There was no attempt to escape.

*

Brest, Wednesday 20 November 1776, early morning.

After the muster at the Hôtel Saint-Pierre and the eight o'clock Mass, I ask my friend Vernon to tell Lieutenant de Clesmeur that I am going to the jail to retrieve the axe which I borrowed from the sailors. I am well aware that it is a flimsy, rather illogical, pretext. However, I hope that the strangeness of my behaviour will pass completely unnoticed in the midst of the general commotion caused by the fire at the Navy hospital. Having thus covered my back, I go down towards the shipyards. I have taken the precaution of arming myself with a gold louis as a sweetener for the head clerk of the prison. The wind has fallen away completely after the north-westerly gale which fanned yesterday's fire, but this will not last: the sky is grey and the dawn purple.

A visitor cannot gain access to the inside of the jail through the courtyard where the convicts have their stalls. You have to go around via the shipyards, along the Penfeld quays as far as the ropewalks, then turn right between the last of the warehouses and the lower ropewalk. You then find yourself in a narrow, steep passage with winding steps, which I go up, leaving the ropewalks to my left, until I reach the jail. I have already had the chance to see it from behind, from the stalls' courtyard, but it is much more impressive seen from the front. Its central building is surmounted with an arched pediment whose tympanum is decorated with allegorical sculptures. The flat area at the top of the entrance stairs is at least eighteen feet above the level of the ground where I am standing, between the upper ropewalk and the jail. You get to it by means of two grand staircases which meet below an imposing porch, itself nine feet high. The two storeys of the jail are topped with mansarded attics. The halls containing the convicts take up both floors on both sides of the main building.

It is half past nine when I present myself at the top of the steps at the entrance to the jail. This access point is guarded by a group of halberdiers. I tell them of my involvement with yesterday's events and that I had spoken with Monsieur Testanières. I finish by asking to see the head clerk of the jail. Quite by chance, one of the halberdiers remembers having seen me talking with the Commissioner for Prisons, and so gives credence to my patter. What is more, they have not slept all night an account of moving prisoners between the jail and the Chateau and are too tired to be bothered checking the legitimacy of my request. Monsieur Testanières is not at the jail this morning. From what I can gather, he is busy making an inventory of the damage caused by the forced retreat of the convicts through his residence. According to one of the guards, there was a good thousand pounds worth of damage. I think to myself that the honest Commissioner has good reason to do this task himself, surrounded as he is with unscrupulous subordinates. In any case, this once again works in my favour.

The guard in charge eventually orders one of his men to take me to the head clerk of the jail, whose office is on the first floor. The big iron door of the jail is doubled by a wooden door which is always locked. My guide asks for it to be opened by knocking on a little window.

*

That was how, thanks to a set of exceptional circumstances, I was able to get inside the unusual world of the Brest prison. Everybody talked about it, but few people had ever seen the inside, apart from the condemned and their guards. As yet I had only been able to see the part situated in the central building. On a normal day, I would have come across some convicts and their jailers. But on that day the authorities had decided to wait until the afternoon before sending the convicts to the shipyards. They had not slept during the night as it had been too cold in the Chateau courtyard. Some had fallen ill, I think. It was thought that they were too tired to be able to do their usual forced labour around the port. They were all kept in the prison halls. And I think they must all have been sleeping, as the prison was very quiet that morning.

*

Brest, Wednesday 20th November 1776, during the morning.

On the ground floor, we enter first a deep vestibule, lit only by windows on the front of the building. This area serves mainly as the guard room for the halberdiers. I count about thirty of them, slumped in chairs or stretched out on benches. I suppose that they are there to maintain the security of the jail, but they are all, without exception, following the example of their corporal and snoring loudly. Without bothering to stop, my halberdier takes me to a wide staircase which goes up at the end of the room. It leads to a halfway landing where there is a door which opens on the stalls' courtyard with which I am already familiar. Two other staircases split from there to go up to the first floor. They are extended higher up by two identical ramps going up to the second floor. We stop at the first floor on a long landing lit by windows facing north-east. This creates a kind of corridor at least forty yards long by twelve feet wide. It is enclosed at each end by two big doors, both shut and with little grille windows which are open. That is the access to the big halls where the convicts are locked up. I notice a strange piece of furniture, covered by a sheet and with little wheels. It is standing between two windows against the outside wall in the middle of the corridor. I cannot resist lifting a corner of the cover. It is a mobile altar. The guard explains that it is pushed into the halls when the almoner comes to celebrate Mass for the convicts.

I count seven doors leading off the enclosure on the inner side. The biggest of these is the door of Monsieur Testanière's office. This must be empty as there is no guard. The chief clerk's office is two doors along and the door is open.

The room we go into is divided into two separate parts joined by a glazed door. The walls of the first room are entirely hidden by the rows of carefully arranged registers about which I have heard so much and for which I have come. In the middle is a sort of counter behind which a convict is standing, recognisable by his red smock and bonnet. He is copying from one register to another and seems so absorbed in his work that he scarcely looks at us. He is lean, with dark eyebrows, lively black eyes and an air of cunning despite his sleepless night at the Brest Chateau. He is without doubt a former accountant or notary's clerk who has got involved in fraud of some kind, but whose behaviour has been judged good enough for him to be employed in his old specialty. He is, in fact, a sock convict.

The head clerk is sitting behind a beautiful desk in the other half of the room which is on the front side of the prison and so is lit by a south-west facing window. He is a chubby-cheeked fellow, a little smaller than me, with straight shoulders, a large head and a little round paunch which stretches his waistcoat under his open jacket. When I catch sight of him, through the glass door which separates us, he is totally absorbed in carefully tipping some snuff between his thumb and the index finger of his left hand from a little beaked snuff box. He lifts his loaded hand to his nose and noisily sniffs up his helping. The halberdier who is escorting me stops me with a sign from his hand and wisely waits until his superior has completed this delicate operation before knocking deferentially on the glass pane.

Having presented myself, I wait until the halberdier has gone before telling the head clerk of the jail what brings me here.

'I am looking for a convict.'

'Well then, I am listening, young man.'

'I only have his name. I was told that I could find him if I had his registration number and that you could help me with that.'

'Hmmm. You are asking for a rather tricky service...and unusual...I don't know whether I can help you. What year did he come here?'

'In 1773.'

'Three years ago! Heavens above! That is some searching that you are asking of me! Tricky...yes, very tricky!' he repeats, heavily emphasising the last 'tricky'.

I gently place the gold louis which I have brought on the edge of his desk. He looks at the shining gold coin while rubbing his hands without thinking. He makes no protest. However, he leaves the coin on the edge of the table where I have placed it and gets up, making as if he has seen nothing.

'You seem to me to be a resourceful gentleman. I will try to help you, Monsieur, but you must realise that this is quite out of order, and that you will have to make an additional effort...'

He walks straight into the register room where the sock convict is still writing calmly.

'Wake up, Parisian! Get me the register of the chain for the year 1773.'

The sock convict goes and brings a thick bound volume from his shelves and places it on a corner of his counter. Labels corresponding to the years are stuck on the edges of the pages. He opens it at the appropriate date.

'In 1773, the chain arrived in May,' he began. 'There were four hundred and fifty of them.'

'The chain' is what is called the pitiful convoy of those condemned to hard labour which arrives each year at Brest, having crossed half the kingdom on foot from the Bicêtre prison. The men are attached in pairs by an iron collar to which is attached a metal plate with a ring through it. A long chain passes through this ring and the rings of all the other convicts in the column. There can be up to a hundred unfortunates attached to the same chain, or at least that is what I have heard, although I have never seen it myself. However, as far as I know, the Marquis of Kersalaun did not come to Brest on the chain.

'That won't be it,' I say. 'The one I am looking for came here in January. Probably the first Sunday in January.'

'Ah!' said the chief clerk. 'In that case he was condemned in Brittany and the Mounted Police would have brought him. Good! Bring the register of the inmates. The one we bring up to date every month. We will lose less time,' he adds, turning to me.

The convict carefully puts the register of the chain back and brings another one, marked 1776 on the cover and with the labels on the pages in letters rather than numbers.

'What's his name?' asks the clerk.

'Avelus, Marquis de Kersalaun.'

The sock convict does not move and says nothing. He seems to be looking closely at his chief.

'Well then, you imbecile, what are you waiting for? Look!'

The convict searches under the letter A and shows me the page. There is no Avelus.

On the other hand, there are two Kersalauns. It is a common enough name in Brittany. But the details given for each one leave no room for doubt. The first arrived on the 1772 chain, having been added to the chain as it was passing through Rennes. The other was a former soldier from the colonial regiments condemned for desertion. He had been brought ashore at Brest in 1775, just a year ago, off a corvette from Fort-Royal in Martinique.

At my request, the convict also looks under D for 'de' and M for 'Marquis'. I also suggest he looks under R as the Marquis's forename is Ronan. Nothing!

'Have you a record of those who have died in the jail?' I ask.

I have the impression that the convict is looking at me oddly.

'Well, what are you waiting for!' growls the chief.

The convict goes to the shelves to find another register even bigger than the others. All the dead, accompanied by an explanatory note, have been registered in here, year by year, since the building of the jail. The names are listed in alphabetical order on an index stuck to the end of the book, which it seems is updated annually. The clerk in the red bonnet finds two more Kersalauns.

I hold my breath.

But it is not one of them either. The first died in an epidemic of ships' fever brought by the squadron of the Comte du Bois de la Motte in January 1758. The other Kersalaun died in 1768 on the island of Trébéron, he too victim of an epidemic which hit the chain just before its arrival at Brest. To avert a disaster like that of 1758, Monsieur Testanières, who was already Commissioner of Prisons, had had the chain put in quarantine on Trébéron.

'If he is not inscribed here, then he was not at Brest,' says the clerk. 'It means that perhaps he was sent to another jail. Toulon? Perhaps Marseilles?'

'I am sure, however, that he was arrested in Brittany, in the Brest region,' I say.

'Well, I tell you it is not possible!' The clerk's tone has sharpened. He quickly gets a grip on himself and continues more softly: 'Maybe he was transferred. Listen, I'll write to the office of the Registry General at Versailles. But that will take a long time. I will let you know if I get a response. But I cannot guarantee anything.'

He goes out into the corridor and tells a guard to send an escort for me. Then he goes back into his office and hands me my gold piece without a word. The sock convict is busy putting the last register we have looked at back on the shelves and does not see this. Or at least that is what I think.

I try to insist. I repeat that the Marquis de Kersalaun had been arrested in the Brest region on the first Sunday of 1773, by halberdiers from the jail. I am certain of it! But the clerk says that he has no authority to keep me here any longer. To try to gain some time, I ask for the axe which I had left with the halberdiers the night before. It is Navy property, I say. He tells the halberdier who is to accompany me out to pass on my request to his sergeant-major, and to make sure it is returned to me. Then he takes his leave politely but firmly.

*

The axe was found immediately, which enabled me to take it back to the Hôtel Saint-Pierre. I must say that I was most surprised. I had not expected such efficiency from the halberdiers, especially having seen them at their work. It at least strengthened the pretext I had invented, but it was a poor consolation. I was greatly disappointed, as I was scarcely more advanced than previously. I could not understand what had happened. The clerk had seemed quite willing to meet my request once he had seen me place a gold louis on his desk. He had even let me look at the registers myself. I had found no trace of the Marquis; they had not lied to me about that. I had therefore to find an explanation: could it be that Avelus de Kersalaun had never been at the Brest jail, or had he been registered under another name? But what name? I spent the rest of the day turning this puzzle over in my head.

Then, that night, just before falling asleep, I remembered the document I had in my hands at the parish of Hanvec. It said, quite unequivocally, that the *Squire Ronan Avelus de Kersalaun* had been condemned for murder to 'the galleys', that is to say to the forced-labour jail. This paper, surprising given what I now knew, was dated January 1773, the 18th to be exact. And it had been signed by the Comte d'Estaing, *Inspector-General Commanding the Navy at Brest.*

If it was indeed the Comte d'Estaing who had signed this paper which I had read at Hanvec, this great lord would undoubtedly know what had really happened to the Marquis de Kersalaun. And if the clerk of the jail did not know, then it meant that this business was part of a secret process. A simple Cadet had no chance of gaining access to this kind of information, but my uncle, the Chevalier de Kermean, had the right contacts for that. I had been wanting to write to him for a while. The Commander of the Navy was now the Comte d'Orvilliers. I did not know how many years it was since the Comte d'Estaing had left Brest nor where he had gone to afterwards, but that would not be difficult to find out. I fell asleep more peacefully. I had a new line of enquiry and, this time, I would not be obliged to follow it in secret.

I was firmly resolved, when I got up the next day, to spending my leisure hours asking everyone I knew about the career of the Comte d'Estaing. Towards two in the afternoon, just as I was leaving to go back to class, one of our seniors called me to give me a note from the wigmaker at the jail. He had gone to collect a wig he had ordered and the wigmaker convict had taken advantage of the occasion to ask him to tell me that 'my order was ready.' I certainly had not ordered a new wig. I opened the message and read the following:

Monsieur

You order is ready I will expect you tomorrow at my shop at half after midday.

The hour of our meeting was underlined. My eye was drawn to a sort of post-script written in very small letters at the bottom of the note: *the payot boy will be there, bring six pounds for him.*

I spent the rest of the day wondering what a '*payot boy*' was. I thought that it was no doubt one of the slang names from the jail, but I did not dare ask my officers or friends, for fear of arousing their curiosity. I waited patiently for the next day. In any case, I was beginning to have my own suspicions about the matter.

*

Brest, Friday 22nd November 1776, half past midday.

At the appointed hour, I arm myself with two écus and go to the wigmaker's stall. As he had warned me in his note, he is not alone. At the back of the shop, sitting on a stool, a convict is waiting quietly. He is rather scraggy and of small stature, but this time his black eyes have no hint of tiredness. I recognise the sly-looking little convict whom I saw the day before yesterday at the chief clerk's office. The wigmaker invites me to sit down opposite his visitor and goes to stand by his door, from where he can keep an eye on the rear courtyard of the jail and also listen to what we are saying.

'Well then, so it's you – the *payot boy*!'

'In the clink, that's what they call the jailbirds what do clerking and cushy work. But everyone here calls me the Parisian. I was hitched up to the Pantin chain in sixty-nine. That's seven years I'm in clink and five as a *payot*! That ain't a sob story, it's just to show you that I ain't wet behind the ears. Well, mustn't waste time. I got to get back quick to look as if I've got me nose to the grindstone in them registers before the fat sniffer has finished filling his face.'

'The sniffer?'

'You saw him having a sniff the day before yesterday?' The Parisian imitates taking a snort by sticking his nose between the thumb and index finger of his left hand. 'He ain't told you the truth. Spun you a right yarn, he did.'

'About the Marquis de Kersalaun?'

'Too damn right! The Marquis!'

'What do you know?'

'You've brought a little something, Monsieur?'

'A little something?'

'Yes, or a little sweetener, if you prefer. I ain't asking much. The sniffer, him, he wanted a gold Maltese – eight times as much! That's his usual price, I know him well! And you know what's amazing? That he give it you back! That ain't his usual tune, I can tell you! But he's hoping you'll keep quiet. And in any case, I can tell you that he won't be writing no letter to Versailles.'

'What do you know exactly?' I ask, giving him his écu.

'You're what I call a real moneybags, Monsieur!' says the Parisian as he quickly takes the coin. 'And I'll tell you what I know and without no hogwash. It was the first Sunday of January '73. I was working on me own in me office, late it was. Always like that at the beginning of the year. Have to get all the registers up to date for all the accounting to go to Versailles. And don't you worry, it was just me at it with the sniffer long since gone for his kip. That's when I saw our halberdiers passing on the stairs. They was pushing a geezer who didn't look like he was from our little college, like. A real toff was what you would have said he were! I thought hey up what's all this about and I went out on the landing for a closer gander. He had these swanky Angliche boots, like, a striped jerkin with silver buttons and a big belt over it with an empty sheath for a hunting knife which were banging his sides. Going past, one of the halberdiers says to me with a grin: 'Hey, Parisian! Look at this, would yer! We've caught us a Marquis!' At which the others told him quick like to 'Shut his big gob'. They took him up to the next floor and I heard that they took him to the north hall. I was surprised, the next day, that no one came to register him. Also, when the chief clerk arrived the next morning, him what I call the sniffer, like I said, I made my report. You see, the whole thing was quite out of order. And me, I didn't want no trouble. And I'd had enough trouble getting me place as a *payot*. And my sniffer, who's always on the make, he calls straight off for the head jailer of the north hall on the second floor. Still the same geezer today. Legouez he's called. A real bandit that one! He spots the young nancy boys when they arrive on the chain and proposes himself as their pimp; either that or he'll denounce 'em to the prison authorities. Well! I was in the next room and I hear this Legouez reply cheekily that he was carrying out orders from his superiors and it was no business of the head clerk of the jail. Well, my sniffer, he didn't like that one bit. He were furious! Straight off he dictated to me a report for the Commissioner. He signed it and took it back in his office saying I should take it to Monsieur Testanières as soon as he arrives. It was Monday morning, you see. And then, a halberdier came to say there were a visitor waiting for him at the guard room. I don't know who it were, but when he come back, the fatty were white as a sheet. I saw him through the glass burning his report in the fireplace. And he's never spoke of it since. Well then, when I heard you talking about a Marquis what was brought here first Sunday of January 1773, I thought again about that old story. And the sniffer, too, that's for sure. I could see he were in a fright. That's why he give you back your gold Maltese, and made sure behind your back that you got your axe back straight off.'

'And what happened to the Marquis?' I ask.

'I don't think he stayed long. But when exactly they took him away, I don't know.'

'You didn't see him go?'

'At night I sleep on the first floor and I'm chained like all the others. The first Sunday of January, that were not the usual. And during the day I'm not always in me office. As a *payot* I sometimes even go out into the town. All I can tell you is it ain't normal to keep a prisoner here on the quiet. And the Commissioner sometimes makes inspections on all the floors, like. He wouldn't have tolerated that. That Legouez would never push it too far. He don't want to risk having old Testanières on his back.'

'You've never tried to learn anything from the other convicts in that hall?'

'No-one would talk about it. Legouez give one a right going over, whipped him half to death, as an example, like, so as to put an end to the business. And all the halberdiers of the north wing are behind him… ain't no-one as'll talk. Except…'

The convict stopped talking and stayed quiet for a few seconds. He has a self-satisfied look that suggests he has not yet finished, so I wait patiently. But he is better at this little game than me. I cannot stop myself asking.

'Except...?'

'A convict what were in Legouez's hall were unchained not long after. He'd reached the end of his sentence a month before, but he'd bin forgotten. That happens sometimes. They suddenly remembered him and he were freed on the fifth of January that year. The Commander of the Navy signed in the morning and he were unlocked the same evening. If you could find 'im, he might talk.'

'Can you remember his name?'

'It's me what writes out all the registers here. His number were 2223!' He taps his forehead with his thumb. What d'you say to that? He ain't half got a memory, that Parisian!'

'I'd prefer to have his name this time.'

Instead of replying, the *payot* boy holds out his hand, palm upwards.

'You've still got a little something what you ain't yet handed over, Monsieur. Didn't my friend the rug merchant here put in his note as it were six pounds for the consultation?'

'Yes, but even if you give me his name, how can I find him all by myself?'

'Nothing easier, Monsieur! A lag what's been released has to tell the town authorities where he's living so as the archers can keep an eye on him.'

That did not seem so easy to me, but I cannot leave any stone unturned, and so I hand over my second écu. It is snapped up as quickly as the first.

'This released convict's name is Nicolas Dugoin. He were due to go to L'Orient.'

'Good heavens! I know of him!' I say. 'He was found a few days later floating on the tide in L'Orient harbour. And had he not been killed, he would be far away by now. He said he was setting off for Madagascar with Baron Benyowski. And you must surely have known that. You tried to trick me!'

The Parisian looks shocked and glares at me in a different way.

'You're very harsh, Monsieur, but no doubt you have your reasons for saying that. I underestimated you.'

'You should give me my money back! Aren't I in the right?' I say, turning towards the convict wigmaker. The latter has not moved from his observation post and so far has said nothing, but he quickly agrees with me. It seems that he is already regretting having sent me this compromising note asking for six pounds. And besides, he certainly does not want to fall out with the Marine Guards, who represent a considerable part of his clientele.

The *payot* boy says nothing. His brow is furrowed, his eyebrows drawn together, and he is clearly engaged in some painful reflection. Eventually, greed triumphs. He goes and surveys the courtyard over his companion's shoulder, then comes back to sit opposite me.

'I'm goin' to give you another geezer.'

He is almost whispering now and I have to lean forward to listen to him.

'I'll tell you for nowt, but don't you be tellin' anyone I told you. I'm taking a big risk doin' this. One other person left Legouez's hall after that business. It were his deputy. He's gone for good and I've always thought it was because of that business. He didn't seem to approve of what went on up there. It's true too as he found a good little work number.'

'I'm listening!' I say.

He is starting to annoy me greatly and I want to get out of here.

'He became huntsman for the Marquis de Boulainvilliers, a Ship's Captain…'

'And his name?'

'He's not married. Lives on his own, with a maid of the Marquis, in a house near Guipavas, where the Marquis de Boulainvilliers keeps his dogs and horses. His manor house is at Daoulas. But I think he has left for Toulon…'

The Parisian goes quiet again.

'Who has left for Toulon?' I ask.

'The Cap'n, like, not the huntsman.'

'I'm listening. His name, quickly!'

'He's called Loutre, François Loutre, but here everyone calls him Autumn. Don't tell him I sent you, for God's sake. I don't think as he'll be too pleased to be reminded of this dirty business.'

I now know enough to be able to find this François Loutre without too much difficulty and I get up to leave.

The Parisian gets up too and removes his bonnet to say goodbye. All his initial arrogance has dissipated since I told him that Dugoin had been murdered.

'You be careful, Monsieur. I have to tell you. This Autumn bloke! He would have liked to have joined forces with that Dugoin, him bein' a lad as knew all about horses. And you see what happened to him… But above all, don't you go grassin' on me!'

*

The end of November brought bad news for those Guards and Cadets who, like me, were lodged in the former Jesuit seminary. It was announced that our building was to be taken over to serve as the Navy hospital to replace the one destroyed by fire. The sick who had been evacuated on 19th November had been shared around the hospitals of the town, but these establishments were already too crowded, and this was only ever a provisional measure. Monsieur de Laporte, the Navy Quartermaster at Brest, had made a quick decision: a new Navy hospital would be created, by Christmas at the latest, in the former Jesuit seminary.

We were given one month to find new lodgings, but they could not billet us as there was no room left in the homes of the town's inhabitants. The number of sailors, conscripts and workers at the shipyards had almost doubled since 1775. The citizens of Brest and Recouvrance, who had made their contribution for many years, could no longer respond to the demands of the Navy. It was being said, too, that the Comte de Chaffault had been ordered to form a new squadron, bigger than previous ones, with effect from the start of 1777, which would further increase the number of Naval ratings. The situation was equally bad for the Army, which had started construction work on fortifications for the forts and redoubts around Brest. All that required a lot of men, but the barracks were already full. And that was not all: the garrison was expecting additional reinforcements from the start of 1777.

As for us, the Cadets, our only choice was to lodge at our own expense in an inn. I found a nice clean one near the Chateau esplanade, where they offered rooms for forty-two pounds a month. I could not find anything cheaper. I consoled myself by saying that it was quieter than the port and that the Dajot Promenade was five minutes' walk away. I agreed with Vernon that we would take one room and share the bed, which would allow us to halve the cost. Luckily, I had until then not spent much on my small pleasures, and the little savings I had brought with me, plus the proceeds of the sale of my Breton horse, allowed me to pay the two months' advance rent demanded by the innkeeper. All that remained was for us to write to our respective families for the rent from then on. All this was despite the six hundred pounds they had already paid to the Navy for our upkeep.

I took advantage of this to give my news to the Baron de Kermean. I had not yet done this and felt a little guilty. I wrote too to the Chevalier, at Versailles. I told him that I had picked up the trail of the Marquis de Kersalaun but lost it again almost immediately. I said that he had apparently been imprisoned in the Brest jail in murky circumstances, that he had then disappeared and that I did not know what had become of him. I also asked my uncle for information about the Comte d'Estaing.

The reply from the Chevalier de Kermean came eight days later. It was given to me in the offices of the Navy Command at Brest, at the Hôtel Saint-Pierre, where it had arrived directly with the mail from the Ministry. My uncle had wasted no time in writing to me. As regards the Comte d'Estaing, he told me that he was heir to a great estate in the Auvergne and that he had been raised with the late Dauphin Louis, who was the same age as him. My grandfather, the Baron de Kermean, had met him several times during that period. The Comte d'Estaing had been aide de camp to the Maréchal de Saxe, at Fontenoy, at the age of sixteen! Three years later he was a colonel in command of his own regiment. During the Seven Years' War he was in India with the unfortunate Lally and was taken prisoner by the English at the Siege of Madras. Released on parole, he had mounted, at his own expense, from the Île-de-France, a privateering expedition in the eastern seas. His enemies, of which he apparently had many, reproached him strongly for this, as he had broken his word of honour by taking up arms before having been exchanged. Unfortunately for him, he fell once again into the hands of the English when they captured the ship he was bringing back to France. Considered not to be a man of his word, he was thrown ignominiously into jail in Plymouth. However, thanks to his personal relationship with all the courts of Europe, including that of the King of England, he managed to have himself freed. Once back in France, he was appointed Lieutenant-General of the Army in 1762 and at the same time he was given the same rank in the Navy, in consideration of his marine exploits in the Orient. Then he was Governor of Saint-Domingue before joining the Navy to profit from his equivalence of rank. He was

Commandant of the Navy in Brest from 1772 to 1773. Louis XV put him there expressly to force the officers of the Navy to adopt the new Navy reforms. These reforms centred on aligning the organisation of the Navy with that of the Army. The Comte d'Estaing fulfilled this with a minimum of sensitivity. Since then, he had been doubly disliked by the Navy, firstly because he was seen as an 'intruder', a defector from the Army, and secondly because he had imposed reforms that the Navy did not want. In any event, Louis XV was very pleased with the way that the Comte d'Estaing had brought his sailors to heel. My uncle ended thus detailed biography with these words:

Sailors do not like the Comte d'Estaing; I would go as far as to say they detest him, but they ought not deceive themselves. The King, despite his great devotion to his Navy, still holds the Comte in great esteem and will always take his side in any matter and against anybody. And do you know why? Because in his youth the Comte was the table and study companion of the Dauphin Louis. And Louis XVI has an almost religious veneration for anything remotely connected to the memory of his dead father.

The Chevalier de Kermean was to be believed in this regard. He knew perfectly well what he was talking about. Did he not benefit himself from the benevolence of Louis XVI in memory of the former friendship between the Baron de Kermean and the Dauphin Louis?

A few days later, in the drill hall at the Hôtel Saint-Pierre, where I had been to train as usual, Ship's Captain Flaharn asked me what I had been doing at the jail. I did not know who had told him about that. I told him the story of the axe and that seemed to satisfy him. I continued to fence with him as far as my leisure time permitted. It gave me real pleasure and I think that he too appreciated our bouts. He carefully corrected my faults and thanks to him I continued to make considerable progress. After a while he told me that I had become one of the best blades of the garrison. To demonstrate this, he suggested that we go together around all the drill halls of Brest. In this way, by fencing against all the grenadiers, I would strengthen myself against every move. Wherever I went I trounced everybody. Except Captain Flaharn, of course. Needless to say, nobody sought a quarrel with me.

Captain Flaharn was a strange man. On the one hand he was very attentive towards me. He had even said that he preferred to fence against me to train himself, as the others were too mediocre. This had greatly flattered me. On the other hand, he never opened up; he was as impenetrable as a wall. The first time that I saw his naked torso, when he was changing after a bout during which we had both been sweating, I saw that his wide chest was striped from the right shoulder to the left thigh by the deep gash of a terrible scar.

'May I ask you how you got this awful wound?'

'A sabre blow. When I was in India. Everyone thought I was dead that day...'

There was a small silence, then he added, in a voice that chilled me to the marrow...

'But I had the last word.'

He said nothing else.

I spent Christmas and the New Year at Brest. I would have liked to have gone to see my grandfather and give a hug to my little sister, but with the time taken to travel at that time of year, I would have had to have asked for at least three weeks' leave, which for a Cadet was impossible.

16

We learned at the beginning of January 1777 that Dr Benjamin Franklin, one of the authors of the American Declaration of Independence, had disembarked a month earlier and gone to Paris. Soon afterwards a rumour started to circulate that he had come expressly to recruit French officers, that he did not want any other officers in command of American troops, and that the King had authorised his nobles to fight in the service of General Washington. It was said that captains and even simple lieutenants had been given the rank of colonel in the new United States Army. Downy-cheeked flag bearers, who had never heard a shot on a real battlefield, were dreaming of heading a company or a battalion. The febrile atmosphere soon died down when the Marquis de Langeron published a proclamation to the effect that he had received orders from Versailles saying that any French officer who tried, without the knowledge of his superiors, to approach American emissaries with a view to offering his services, would be arrested and imprisoned prior to being dismissed from service.

On Monday 13th January 1777, I was called early in the morning to the Commandant's offices in the Hôtel Saint-Pierre to retrieve mail sent to me from Versailles, in the Ministerial despatches, by the Chevalier de Kermean. This personal package contained a letter from my uncle and another from my grandfather to which had been added ten beautiful gold louis wrapped tightly in a little parcel. It was the money I had asked for in November and for which I had been waiting for more than a month.

The Baron de Kermean explained that he had sent two hundred and forty pounds to the Chevalier de Kermean, at Versailles, asking him to send it on to me by the usual means. The Baron would have liked to have got it to me sooner by means of a coaster from Le Croisic, but he had not been able to find a boat going directly to Brest. Eventually he had decided that it would be safer to entrust the money to a gentleman from Versailles whom he had met at Nantes, while visiting the Viscount de La Croix de Lormes, the Chevalier's future father-in-law.

In this way I learned that my uncle's marriage arrangements had progressed considerably. The parents of Mademoiselle de La Croix would in their turn be coming to spend a few days at Kermean in May or June. There they would finalise the terms of the marriage contract before taking it to a notary. If all went well, the marriage would take place at the beginning of the summer near Nantes, at the house of the bride's father. As for his fiancée, I learned that she was not much older than me. She was still completing her education in a select convent in the capital and would come from there to be married in Brittany. I remember imagining the Chevalier jumping over the Saint Jean flames watched by his promised one. In fact, he had seen her for the first time in Paris, in October, when she had come out from the convent to visit an aunt. He confirmed in his letter that she was 'quite charming'.

The Chevalier's letter also contained some confidential information that bore on my near future…

> *'…I am fairly confident that I will be able to obtain a regular authorisation for you next June to come to my wedding. It will be possible as by then you ought to be a Marine Guard and, in that case, you will be able to ask for leave prior to joining a ship. In effect, I am about to give you two pieces of news about this which require total discretion for the moment, for as far as I know, not even the Comte d'Orvilliers has yet been told.*
> *There is strong talk here that the brothers of the King will be making a tour of the ports in early June. And Monsieur Bézout will accompany them to examine the Marine Guard Cadets. I know that you are a*

conscientious student and that you will pass your examination first time. That is the first bit of news about your situation. The second concerns your chances of getting a ship.

The Comte du Chaffault has been ordered to keep himself ready to prepare a new squadron for the Antilles. He wrote in his last report that we do not take enough of our Marine Guards to sea. His arguments made an impression on His Majesty who is seriously thinking of sending all the Marine Guards to sea for the next campaigns, leaving only the Cadets on land.'

This meant that the Brest Cadets who wanted to present themselves for examination in 1777 would have to sit it four months earlier, in June instead of October. That would not suit everybody. For my part, I was extremely pleased. I decided to tell my friend Vernon, who at first was somewhat alarmed. But I promised to help him to make sure he had the two volumes off as well as I did.

I acted thus out of pure friendship but, in all honesty, I must admit that Vernon had become very precious to me for other reasons. He possessed two qualities which were of great interest to me as regards my personal situation: he was a hunter and he played the horn. These two characteristics had raised him in my estimation once I had learned that the former deputy-jailer François Loutre, known as 'Autumn', had become huntsman for the Boulainvilliers.

I found out about the Boulainvilliers without any difficulty. They had been well known in Brest for generations, although they were not originally from Brittany. The Marquis de Boulainvilliers was a Ship's Captain in the Toulon squadron. One of his sons, known as the Comte de Boulainvilliers, was a Marine Guard at Brest. He was well known in the Company as both a rebel and a fanatical hunter. The Comte rented the outbuildings of a manor house near Guipavas where he kept horses and a pack of hounds. He went there to hunt several times a week when he was not on sea-going duties.

I had worked out a plan for meeting François Loutre at Guipavas, but I needed some money to put it into action. I had been forced to wait for the funds that I had asked the Baron de Kermean to send me, as I had nothing left once I had paid the advance rent demanded by our innkeeper.

I had thought a lot about the matter. It was out of the question for me to go and talk to the huntsman François Loutre without having got to know his master beforehand. And I did not want to have to explain myself to the Comte de Boulainvilliers. Everything had to happen naturally. The most logical way of meeting the man they called Autumn was to have myself invited by the Comte to a hunting party, but that could only happen if he knew me to be a hunter. I was very happy to start hunting, especially as my friend Vernon was continually asking to teach me. As soon as I had received the package from the Baron de Kermean, I went and explained my plan to Vernon, who was very keen on the idea.

'The trouble is,' he added, looking sombre, 'we don't have the equipment.'

'What do we have to buy?'

'Well, first and foremost, we need rifles. We can find old ones in excellent condition, cheaper than new ones, but we need everything that goes with them. And that is not all; we need ammunition. You can buy readymade shot, but it would be better to have a mould to make it ourselves. We also need the right powder for hunting and above all a gundog. I've been thinking about it for a while and already learned what I can. I've done the calculations. Unfortunately, it costs a lot!'

'How much exactly?'

'Let's see. Twelve pounds for each rifle, six pounds for gun equipment, a mould to make hunting shot, eight pounds; twenty-two pence a pound for powder, replacement flints, and I forgot the powder horns, ten pence, and lead bars…'

'That makes about forty-three pounds,' I calculated. 'And the dog?'

'That depends on whether it's trained or not, and what breed it is. That can double the price. Generally, you can reckon on twenty, twenty-five pounds for a good dog. In any case we can't keep it here at the inn. What would we do with it?'

This question gave me an idea. I got three gold louis out of my savings and gave them to him.

'You look after buying what we need. You'll be better at that than me. Leave the rest to me.'

Towards four in the afternoon, while Vernon went to look for guns and a dog, I started looking for the Comte de Boulainvilliers. I found him easily enough at the Hotel Grand Turc, where he stayed when he was not hunting or not on board his ship in the harbour. This hotel was just beside the Landerneau Gate, which allowed him to get easily in and out of town when he wanted to go to his place in the country at Guipavas. The Comte had already been a Guard for several years and was waiting to be promoted to Ensign after the next examinations at the end of spring. He must have had a considerable income to be able to keep a room for the whole year at the Hotel Grand Turc and maintain a hunting team. That did not stop him being one of the boys. He received me with great warmth.

I told him that my friend the Chevalier Vernon des Aulnes and I were intending to buy a gun dog, but we could not keep it with us. I asked him whether he would accept it as a boarder at his country retreat. I added, of course, that we would pay for the dog's upkeep.

'Well, congratulations,' the Comte replied. 'There's no problem as far as the dog is concerned. I already have eighteen, so an extra one will make no difference. But you said that your friend is the Chevalier des Aulnes? I heard that he plays the hunting horn...'

I was expecting this question.

'That's right,' I replied. 'And he plays it very well.'

'Well I'll be damned! That is interesting! You see, my huntsman is a good man, and not a drinker, which is rare for a Breton, but he murders my ears! You know, I have nothing against shooting, but why don't you come and follow the pack from time to time?'

'That would be a great pleasure for us,' I replied. 'But for that we need horses and once we have bought all our hunting equipment and a dog, we won't have much left for hiring them at the post.'

'Oh, I can lend you horses. Both of you come next Sunday. You can bring your dog. And I'd advise you to bring your guns and equipment and leave them there. It's half an hour's walk from here. That way, you can go anytime you want during the week. There are a lot of woodcock up there at the moment. But tell your friend not to forget his horn!'

He explained that he rented some barns belonging to the Chateau de Coataudon, to the north of the Guipavas road. He had stables for his horses and dogs. He advised us to get up early on Sunday morning to catch the first Mass. 'If you can't do without it,' he added with a knowing look. He was in the habit of being at horse at dawn.

'Wear old clothes because of the brambles and thorns. We'll dine afterwards at my place after the hunt. You'll be my guests. But you can wear your hunting clothes, as we'll be amongst friends.'

When I got back to the inn, Vernon was still out. He arrived half an hour before supper. He showed me the rifles and equipment he had bought. He thought he had found the right gundog for us, but he would go and get it the next evening. While we were eating, I told him about my meeting with the Comte de Boulainvilliers. He asked what sort of game he hunted and what sort of hounds he had in his pack, questions I could not answer. He was pleased to hear that there were plenty of woodcock at Guipavas.

The following afternoon, after class, Vernon went off, saying that he was going to collect our dog somewhere out of town and that he would be back later. For my part I went to the drill hall where I had arranged to fence with Captain Flaharn.

After we had finished our bouts, the Captain told me that he had to go back to Paris, where he was needed. He invited me to dine with him the following Sunday so that we could talk about my future. I thanked him for his kindness, and told him that I unfortunately could not accept his invitation, as I had already arranged to go hunting.

*

Brest, Tuesday 14th January 1777, towards the end of the afternoon.

'I didn't know you hunted,' says Captain Flaharn. 'Who invited you?'

'The Comte de Boulainvilliers.'

He is silent for moment. Then, he says, a little distantly:

'I know a Marquis de Boulainvilliers.'

The Captain's voice is always very deep and slightly raucous. His face remains impassive, his grey eyes as expressionless as always.

'Well, the Comte is his son,' I say.

'Has he kept his father's hounds? They were near Guipavas, I think.'

'He has indeed,' I say.

'The hunt! I have not hunted since I came back to France. It gives me no pleasure. In India, it was another matter.'

'What did you hunt in India?'

'The tiger...the true king of the animals.'

He talks slowly, with an even, neutral voice, devoid of the least emotion.

'Imagine an enormous cat, four feet at the withers and twelve feet long from head to tail. He can cross thirty feet in one bound and jump fifteen feet high. His force is without equal, his hearing infallible. His sense of smell is finer than that of the best gundog. His sight is as effective at night as at day. He moves always in silence. By preference he lies in wait for his prey, close to water. He can spend a whole day motionless in the long grass and bushes where his fawn coat striped with black make him invisible. When his unsuspecting prey comes to drink at the river, he jumps on its back, forces it to the ground and kills it. He is afraid of nothing. He likes human flesh sometimes. And he is possessed of incredible powers of endurance. To give you an idea, I will tell you a story from my own experience. There were twenty of us, all excellent shots. We were advancing towards the edge of a forest where we had been told there was a man-eating tiger. We had with us a hundred blacks of low caste who had formed a circle and were walking while banging pieces of wood and cymbals to drive the tiger towards us. Suddenly the tiger came out of the trees, just fifty paces in front of us. We all fired at the same time. He made a great leap towards the nearest beaters and had torn them to pieces before we had time to change guns. For tiger hunting, we always had a servant behind us with a second loaded rifle. Then, he came bounding towards us and we let him have a second salvo at ten paces. He managed to run another three or four yards before collapsing at our feet. When we cut him up, we found forty bullets in his body. That's why, in general, Indian princes prefer to hunt him from the backs of their elephants...but you already know that!'

He stops talking. It is the first time I have heard him speak for so long. He clearly has a real admiration for tigers, but he has delivered his speech without passion and with a coldness at odds with his words. I find it strange. Why has he suddenly felt the need to tell me this long story about a tiger, he who normally says so little about himself?

'What are you doing now?'

'I'm going back to my inn.'

'It's near the Chateau, isn't it?'

'Yes, that's right. At the bottom of the rue de Siam,' I say.

'I am near the port. If you are not in a hurry, we could go down by the Grande Rue and stop at a bar on the way to chat.'

*

It was already dark outside. The only light came from the windows of the houses by the street. It was not quite freezing, but the cold was damp and penetrating. It was a pleasure to follow Captain Flaharn into a room warmed by a big fireplace. The place was packed, as always in Brest. The amount of wine and brandy consumed in this town was beyond belief.

*

Brest, Tuesday 14th January 1777, towards five o'clock in the evening.

Captain Flaharn orders two glasses of ratafia and a pipe of Holland tobacco, then goes to one of the tables whose occupants quickly clear off when they see him coming towards them. I have already noticed that this is always what happens: wherever he goes, the Captain clears a space, like a solitary wolf wandering through the forest. The crowd in there is nothing remarkable, just what one expects to meet in Brest: a mix of sailors, soldiers, workmen, prison-guards together with the local citizenry. A serving girl brings us two small glasses filled with a brown liquid, and the Captain's pipe. Captain Flaharn goes to light it at the hearth.

'Your father must have told you stories about India as well,' he says, coming back to sit opposite me.

'Not really,' I say. 'He did not talk much. He was often away. And I was still quite young when he died. My mother started to talk to me about him. Unfortunately, she died too, not long afterwards.'

The Captain makes no response to this.

'Your father brought back a chest...from Chandernagore...'

'A chest?' I say, wondering where he is heading with this.

'I meant a case, the one for your pistols, with the tiger hunt. That's what brought back the memories of India I just shared with you.'

'Why do you think this box comes from Chandernagore?'

'From Bengal, anyway. No doubt you have other similar ones at home, not just for pistols, I imagine.'

'The pistol case was not from our house. My father gave it to a friend who passed it on to me as a souvenir of him.'

'A Naval officer?'

'No, Army.'

'This friend, is he still alive?'

'Yes, of course. He is to be married soon.'

The Chevalier de Kermean had so often told me to be discreet about his activities that I dare not mention him by name, even to a Captain.

Flaharn stays silent, then seeing that I have nothing to add, carries on.

'Your father must have amassed quite a fortune with the India Company?'

'Like all the officers of the India Company, neither more nor less. Perhaps less, however, as he never traded on the side...so I have been told. He was certainly better off than when he was on the King's ships, but not much more. So, for example, my Cadet fees are paid by my Godfather, the Marquis de Becdelièvre.'

'That surprises me a lot. Your father did not leave you an inheritance? Or at least some documents, a sort of will?'

'No, not really, except a letter, like a sort of puzzle, in which he talked of India a little.'

'If it is an Indian puzzle, I can perhaps help you to decipher it?'

'That is very kind of you, but I have lost the letter. In any case, I have managed to solve the puzzle with the help of our rector, a very knowledgeable and erudite man of the Church. Can you imagine that he can read Sanskrit?'

'That is remarkable, truly. Would it be indiscreet to ask what the puzzle consists of?'

'Yes! I beg you to excuse me, but it concerns a secret confided to me by my mother just before she died. She was assassinated in our house at Port-Louis when some criminals attacked it.'

'I am truly sorry. You are so young, and life is already so hard for you. I want to help you. As I told you earlier, unfortunately I must return to Paris. But we will have to speak again about you and your future before I go.'

He pauses for a while, seemingly to reflect.

'Since I cannot invite you on Sunday, I will try to see you before. Friday, or Saturday.'

*

Vernon was not yet back when I arrived at the inn. I had gone up to wait for him on our room when I heard shouting down below. Leaning over the landing, I recognised the voices of the innkeeper's wife and the Chevalier des Aulnes and went down to see what was going on. My friend had a big black and white dog on the end of a piece of rope. The mistress of the inn had intercepted him as he was trying to sneak it up the stairs. Our hostess was a big, strapping woman with a loud and powerful voice. She was very proud of her bosom, which she showed off willingly, wearing low-necked bodices that had her male clients leering. This was sometimes useful for winding men round her little finger, but my friend was quite unaffected by that kind of thing, and was getting on his high horse, despite his small stature. The argument was getting heated.

'Out! No fleabags in my inn! And what's more he stinks!'

Eventually I convinced her to give the dog a corner in the stable. The landlady liked me. She was attracted to young men, and I think she would happily have granted me her favours, but I had always ignored her relatively discreet advances. That was why she was not willing to let the dog stay there for the week, and why I had to promise we would find another home for it the next day. However, she refused the fifteen sols which I offered her, and eventually invited us to take some scraps from the kitchen to feed our new companion.

Once we were alone in the stable, I had a closer look at our acquisition while Vernon prepared his food.

'What do you think?' asked my friend.

The dog's shoulder came to my knee. He was strong in the forequarters. He had a heavy muzzle like a pig's snout, a big round head with a prominent forehead, small low-set ears hanging down, a short neck, short hair and a white coat with big black patches on his back and ears. He was sat on his haunches, seemingly completely indifferent to what was happening to him. He looked around with an inexpressive, almost haughty eye, while Vernon explained, with references to the dog's breeding, that he had winkled out an exceptional beast.

'See how well-formed and vigorous he is. He'll be tireless. So much white on his coat makes him a good hunter. He has no fawn patches, which is a sign of good health. Above all, look at this fine nose! The bigger the muzzle, the better. And he is perfectly trained.'

'And what's the name of this marvel?'

'His former owner said he's called Brac.'

In fact, on hearing his name the dog lifted his ears on each side of his big head and for the first time he looked at me.

We had no choice but to take our dog to Coataudon the next day. Vernon suggested that we take the opportunity for a day's hunting, then work a little harder afterwards to catch up. He had been restless since I had told him about the woodcock at Guipavas and said that he would get permission from Lieutenant de Clesmeur.

*

Brest, Wednesday 15th January, at dawn.

Just before sunrise, my friend goes to tell our section leader that we will be absent today. I go to the Hotel Grand Turc to leave a note for the Comte de Boulainvilliers telling him that we have had to go to his hunting lodge sooner than expected.

We set off for Guipavas with our guns at our shoulders, the dog on a leash. The latter has changed completely on seeing the guns. His look has become lively, and he starts to trot energetically, nose in the air, dashing about and alert at the end of his lead as we go up the rue de Siam. The weather is grey, cold and misty. Vernon tells me that we are lucky as these are ideal conditions for woodcock. Once through the Landerneau Gate, we must first go down the slope outside the ramparts, an unwelcoming stretch of bare earth which cuts across the poorly metalled road. Once this is behind us, we pass at daybreak between the high and decrepit façades of the houses of Coatargueven. Everything is quiet. The inhabitants of this infamous place are no doubt sleeping after another night of drunkenness and debauchery. After that, the road rises gently between ploughed and fallow fields surrounded by frost-covered hedges. Once we have left the main road the countryside becomes wilder. The path described to me by the Comte rises towards the north alongside a stream. Moorland takes over from fields and the former entrance to the Chateau de Coataudon takes shape in front of us in the early morning mist. The body of the main building rises above the outbuildings like a keep. The courtyard is bounded by two wings set at a right angle. One of these wings is separated from the main buildings by a passageway wide enough for a carriage. As we approach, the furious barking of a pack of dogs comes from a stable on the ground floor of this last building and a man comes out. He is fairly young, not very tall, solidly built and bow-legged. He still has a currycomb in his hand. His hair flames bright red, despite the morning greyness. I now understand why he is called Autumn.

I go towards him, followed by Vernon with the dog on its leash.

'I am Pierre-Marie Laforest-Dombourg and this is Monsieur Henri Vernon des Aulnes. We are Cadets at the Marine Guard. Monsieur le Comte de Boulainvilliers had given us permission to leave our dog and rifles here. We have also been invited to the Comte de Boulainvilliers' hunt on Sunday.'

François Loutre, for it is indeed him, studies me for a moment with keen attention. The roughness of his features is tempered by a clear, open look. I immediately have confidence in him, and I wonder how such a man could have become a prison guard. The huntsman tells us that he had not been forewarned of our visit, but apart from his first moment of surprise, he shows no animosity and immediately invites us to have a look at the stable with its four horses and pack of dogs. The count has twelve English dogs for tracking and six basset hounds for his occasional fox hunting with guns. When we tell him of our intention to go shooting woodcock, he takes us to the kitchen so that we can leave our equipment there. The serving woman will then put it away for us. This kitchen, with an earth floor, is the main living room of the house. It is there that the Comte entertains his guests after the hunt. Some engravings, a stag's head and a plank on which are nailed several wolf's paws adorn the walls, between the waxed cupboards, a dresser, a rack from which are hung whips, rifles, a horn and some hunting jackets. The big table is covered with various objects: pipes and tobacco pouches, pots of gun grease, spurs, daggers, old cloths, metal and wooden boxes for various things, a coffee mill and a dog-eared hunting manual missing half its binding.

The Comte's housemaid is called Soizic. She looks like a big round chicken with her pointed nose and plump cheeks under her bonnet. She busies herself with the big pot in the hearth and offers some buckwheat porridge for breakfast. She sleeps in a garret over the kitchen. The huntsman has his bed in an attic above the stable. When the Comte spends the night at Coataudon, he sleeps in the house's only bedroom, on the first floor, in a kind of tower that separates the attic of the stable from that of the kitchen.

The weather stays grey for the whole morning. The moors to the north of the chateau are not impenetrable like those of my native Mesquer. There is broom everywhere. The bushes are very big, seven or eight feet high, thin and bare at the base, but rounding into a ball higher up. They thus form a kind of underwood where the woodcock can hide and run about at their ease. I can now appreciate the skill of our dog. As soon as Vernon releases him, he starts to work over the ground, his nose in the air to smell the wind. We wait while watching him from a distance at the foot of the bushes. When he points, Vernon whistles to him softly and he lies down. All we need now do is go forward, rifles raised in the direction indicated by our Brac. The woodcock fly up almost at our feet, zigzagging away with a great whirring of wings. It is a difficult bird to shoot, and at first I miss them all. But Vernon hits them regularly and we soon fill our game bags.

We give part of our game to the Comte's housemaid. Vernon intends to take the rest to Lieutenant de Clesmeur. Soizic serves us a quick meal: salt meat and bread. We are sat at the kitchen table, Vernon and I, busy with our rods and cloths, cleaning our guns before going back to Brest, when François Loutre comes up to me.

'You said this morning that your name is Laforest-Dombourg, Monsieur?'

When I tell him that this is correct, he adds:

'Are you from the family of the lady Laforest-Dombourg who disappeared at Port-Louis at the beginning of the year '73?'

I am so surprised I almost drop my rifle.

'Do you know what really happened to my mother?'

'Alas, no, Monsieur. I know only that the poor Marquis had asked me to have a letter delivered to your mother at Port-Louis, and that it was unfortunately too late. It seems that she had already disappeared by the time my messenger arrived.'

'By 'poor Marquis' you mean the Marquis Avelus de Kersalaun?'

Without replying, Autumn puts a finger to his lips. He takes a stool and makes a sign for me to follow him to the other end of the room. I excuse myself to my friend.

'Forgive me, sir, but this story still frightens me. I had almost managed to forget it. Believe me, when I heard your name this morning, it really shocked me! I've been thinking about it all day while you've been hunting. And then I said to myself: François Loutre, if you keep quiet, you are nothing but a coward! You have to tell everything that you know to Monsieur Laforest-Dombourg. You owe it to the memory of the Marquis de Kersalaun.'

'What happened to the Marquis?'

'He's dead. He killed himself, may God pardon him.'

So, at last, the Marquis really is dead. I was somehow expecting this.

'If you begin at the beginning?' I said.

'I wasn't always a huntsman…'

I know that already, but remembering my promise to the Parisian, I wait for what follows.

'Previously, for five years, and up until the start of that cursed year of '73, I was a guard at the Brest prison. By the end, I was deputy warder of the north hall on the first floor. There are two big halls on each floor of the jail, on each side of the central building. In my hall I had responsibility for the very end, beside the north building. There are solitary confinement cells there. That's how I got involved in all this, you see. If not for them, I would've known nothing. The Marquis was brought in by halberdiers from the north wing on a Sunday evening, very late. I didn't know who he was, but he was dressed like a gentleman.'

'That was the first Sunday of the year, wasn't it?'

'That's right. Everyone was sleeping, except the guards doing their rounds. They woke me to get me to open one of the cells. With the prisoner there was the head warder of our hall, five halberdiers and a man I'd never seen before. He was not part of the prison administration, but everyone obeyed him. They ordered me to chain up the prisoner in one of the cells.'

'Was that normal practice?'

'The cell? There are only two little ones at the end of each hall. Sometimes convicts are locked up in them. To isolate them or punish them, generally. I chained him up in his coat and boots and took off his belt.'

'I meant, is it normal to lock up prisoners who have just been arrested?'

'Oh! Not at all! That's never done. There's a prison in the town for that, in the cellars of the Chateau de Brest. Only those who have been tried and condemned to forced labour can be locked up in the jail. You're right, it was completely irregular! I think that's why they brought him at night and why they put him in a cell straight away. Like that, nobody would know.'

'Do you think the prison authorities had not been told?'

'There must have been someone in authority behind all that,

Monsieur, but it was a secret. In any case, the Commissioner for Prisons knew nothing of it. The whole thing happened behind his back. That I would swear.'

'It's incredible what you're telling me. How can an individual be locked in the prison without anyone noticing it?'

'You're right. In principle it's impossible. But if the head warder is in on it, the layout of the place lends itself to it. The cells are right at the end. To get to them, you have to go the whole length of one of the halls. And nobody can enter the halls without the head warder knowing. Even the prison clerk. Only the Commissioner can have it opened without warning anybody. And you can well imagine that that does not happen every day. In general, he gives advance warning. So, as you see, as long as the halberdiers and prison guards are in on the game, a head warder can do what he likes at the end of the hall.'

'You say that you have to go the whole length of the hall to get to the cells? There is only one way out, then?'

'Absolutely! There is only a single way out: the passageway leading to the central building. This passageway is barred by two successive doors, then a grille on the hall side. They're all permanently locked and the head warder controls their opening. That's straightforward, as his quarters are between the two doors.'

I remember having seen the outside access doors to the two first-floor halls when I went to see the head clerk of the jail. But I have difficulty imagining that the Marquis de Kersalaun could have been hidden there without the authorities knowing. To try to understand what happened, I ask the former deputy warder to describe the place in detail.

'Each hall is about a hundred yards long and sixty feet wide, from the central building to the end building. You follow me? They are split lengthwise into two equal halves each about twenty-five feet wide by a very thick wall. This wall doesn't go right to the ends: it stops about ten feet short of the entrance grille. When you come through that grille, having been checked by the head warder and the guards, you are right opposite the end of this wall, which is about four feet thick. It's so thick because latrines are inserted in little insets along its length, flushed by pipes underneath the building. That is why the *taulas* are built in places against this wall.'

'What's a *taulas*?'

'That's what they call the fifteen-foot square benches to which the convicts are chained during the night and during the day if they're not out at work. Twenty convicts are attached to each *taulas* in two rows of ten. There are about forty *taulas* per hall, twenty on each side of the central wall. With this arrangement, the convicts can get to the latrines at any time by dragging their chains, without having to be detached. To get to the end of the hall, guards and visitors must take one of the two corridors between the edge of the *taulas* and the exterior walls. These walls have barred windows very high up which allow daylight in, but which give no view outside. At night, lanterns are lit. The halberdiers who are on guard duty make their rounds via these corridors. There are archways built into the central wall at regular intervals, between the insets for the latrines, which enable the guards to pass from one half of the hall to the other. Right at the end of the building are the quarters for the deputy warders and deputy guards, along with the two cells. There's also, on the second floor, a staircase giving access to the attics where the halberdiers have their barracks. But there's no staircase going down to the ground floor, so to get in and get out, everybody, even the halberdiers, has to go the whole length of the hall to the door by the central building.'

'How many convicts were there in your hall?'

'Eight hundred, normally.'

'So if I understand you correctly, to take the Marquis to his cell, it would have been necessary to pass in front of about eight hundred convicts.'

'Half of that.'

'That's right, but it's still four hundred. Wasn't there one amongst them who would've talked?'

'Usually, the forced labourers are totally exhausted by the evening. Apart from those who were awake and saw the Marquis and his escort passing, most will have known nothing. And those who were on the *taulas* at the end of the hall, and who were able to see something, said nothing as they were afraid of the head warder. He's called Legouez. A convict was found unconscious under one of the *taulas* at the end, at daybreak the following Wednesday. They said it was another convict who did it, but they never found him, and with good reason! It was the head warder's handiwork. The convict had started making loud complaints about the prisoner in the cell, during the day, in front of some port workmen. The guard had reported him to the head warder. Legouez had given him a good beating with his truncheon until he passed out. After that, I can guarantee that everybody kept quiet.'

'A head warder has a lot of power?' I ask.

'In theory, no more than a non-commissioned prison officer. But, if he's a brute like Legouez, there's nothing to stop him acting like a tyrant. It's a product of the system. Firstly, the head warder has total responsibility for everything that happens in his hall. For that reason, he has the upper hand on his deputies, the guards and the deputy guards and even the halberdiers who help him keep an eye on the convicts. As well as discipline and cleanliness, he supervises the distribution of meals, the provisioning, all that. In the middle of the hall is a kitchen and a bar, both behind grilles. The bar is also the preserve of the head warder. He has the right to sell his wine to the convicts for profit. That's authorised. But Legouez utilises it to profit from the vices of certain convicts. And he makes money from it! I know that he was paid to have the Marquis in his hall. I saw the man who came with the halberdiers pay him off.'

'What did this man look like?'

'Average height, slim but well built, a cropped beard and long black hair held by a ribbon, regular good-looking features, dark eyes, slightly slanting, thin eyebrows and a long straight nose like a knife blade, I'd say. He spoke French with an accent I couldn't recognise.'

'And you say everyone obeyed him?'

'Yes, but I think he was only an accomplice. There was somebody above him who came with him the next night. I was sleeping when they arrived, but I was woken up by the screams of the prisoner. Screams of pain! My God! My room was just beside the cell. I wondered what was happening and got up to have a look. There was light coming under the door. I wanted to know who was there. I was responsible for the cells, you see. The door wasn't locked. I pushed it. That's when I saw them, the one who had come the evening before and another one. The first was leaning over the prisoner. They had tied a thin chord round his neck. Apart from that he was entirely naked. They had pulled his breeches down to the irons I had put on his ankles. His groin was covered in blood. I don't know what they were doing to him. I didn't even dare look. They shouted at me. I backed out and closed the door but stayed there to listen to what was going on.'

'And you heard what they said?'

'I heard the Marquis. He said: 'You killed the father of my wife in order to steal from him. You have no right before God or man. You are nothing but thieves and murderers. I will tell you nothing.' I didn't hear any more, as one of the halberdiers on duty in the hall came to see what I was up to. Well, I was afraid and went back to bed. May God forgive me! But I couldn't get back to sleep. The Marquis was groaning and screaming...It lasted almost the whole night from the Monday to the Tuesday.'

'And the other man? Did you see him?'

'Just a glimpse. He was wearing a wig. He must have been very tall, but he was sitting on a stool, so I couldn't say how tall.'

That reminded me of the description of the halberdier's officer given to me by Fantig at Kersalaun.

'He must have been one of the halberdiers' commanding officers. Did you not see his uniform or his epaulettes?'

'No, he had a big dark coat over his shoulders. But then, the halberdiers don't have officers. They are commanded by a sergeant-major.'

I tell myself that Fantig could easily have mistaken a sergeant-major for an officer.

'Their sergeant-major. Is he tall?'

'Oh no! Besides, I know all the halberdier sergeants and corporals. He wasn't one of them either.'

'Did you get a good look at his face? Would you recognise him?'

'He looked at me when I went in, then turned his face away immediately. Because of his hat, I didn't see his eyes very well. The only light was from a candle on the floor. But I am sure I'd recognise him if I saw him again. I didn't hear them leave as I eventually fell asleep. The next morning, Legouez told me to go and have a look at the prisoner. I found him curled up under the cell's bed-board. They had taken off his bindings before leaving. His only restraint was the chain I had attached to his ankle on the Sunday evening. He had pulled his breeches up himself and put his coat over his shoulders, though he couldn't button it up. I could see the wounds to his body under his waistcoat. They had slashed him and burned him in places. His fingertips were bleeding. They had ripped off several fingernails. There was blood everywhere: on his clothes, on his bench. He was very weak. I went to report all this to Legouez and that seemed to annoy him. He told me to look after him. 'They' had gone off for several days and he didn't want him to 'give up the ghost before they get back.' I told him that this all seemed very suspicious. He told me to shut my mouth if I knew what was good for me. That's just what he said! I helped the prisoner to wash his wounds. I emptied his bucket and cleaned the floor. I went and found something for him to eat and got him to drink a glass of wine. He thanked me. That's when he told me he was the Marquis Avelus de Kersalaun. He asked me to get something to write a letter with. I was taking a big risk. I brought him a scrap of paper that I tore out of the kitchen stock register, and a bit of pencil. I did all that without Legouez knowing. I didn't know this gentleman but in his suffering he had retained a noble demeanour which impressed me. I always had the feeling that he was a good man. The Marquis wrote a message on the paper. He told me to take it to Madame Laforest-Dombourg, widow of a Ship's Lieutenant, at Port-Louis. He wrote the address in big letters on the back of the sheet and gave me his signet ring, telling me to put it with the message. He said I had to get it as quickly as possible to Port-Louis, that it was a matter of life or death. He asked me if I believed in God. He wanted me to swear solemnly to hide the letter and above all not to give the name written on it to his torturers, otherwise the person to whom it was written, your mother of course, although I didn't know it, would be in mortal danger. I swore. He entrusted it to me. I kept it hidden on me all day. I was terrified, I swear. I'm sure that if the others had found out they would've killed me one way or the other. As a deputy warder I couldn't be away from the prison for long. But during the afternoon I was able to get out and went to see the skipper of a barque who I know well and who I trust: he married my sister. He skippers a brig that he uses for coasting, for the Navy. I sealed the letter and asked him to deliver it personally to Madame Laforest-Dombourg as soon as he got to Port-Louis, and above all, told him not to mention it to anyone. I could do no better than that. When I got back to the jail, in the evening, I told the Marquis that I had entrusted his letter to someone reliable. That seemed to relieve him. His spirit was revived. I felt that he had unusual will power but I had no idea to what extent. The next morning, I found him dead. He had made a rope with strips of his shirt. He had attached it to the top of the chain holding up his plank and hung himself by bending his knees. Can you imagine that?

Legouez was very angry, as you can imagine. Not so much as regards the prison authorities, who knew nothing about it, but through fear of the reaction of his accomplices when they came back. The body was taken out at night, wrapped in an old blanket. With the help of the halberdiers, they went in a boat to dump it in the middle of the Penfeld, upstream of the Anchor Quay. I took what chains and weights were needed to sink it. As far as I know it has never resurfaced.'

'And the letter?'

'My brother-in-law brought it back to me three weeks later. He hadn't managed to get to Port-Louis in time. Everything was in chaos there as the house had been attacked and your mother had apparently been kidnapped. I had so impressed on my brother-in-law to speak only to your mother, and that too much talk was dangerous, that he didn't dare speak to anyone and brought the letter back to me.'

'Do you still have it?'

'It's stored away somewhere in my bedroom over the stable. It's been a while and I can't remember exactly where. Don't you worry, I can find it for you. But it'll be dark soon. You'd better hurry if you want to get through the Landerneau Gate before nightfall. I'll look for it tomorrow and bring it to you on Friday, market day in Brest. I always go to buy the provisions for Soizic. She has to prepare the Sunday dinners for Monsieur le Comte and his guests. And if I don't see you on Friday, you can always take it next Sunday, when you come to hunt with the Comte.'

'Do you have any idea what's in the letter?'

'None…I can't read.'

'And the two men who tortured the Marquis – did you ever find out who they were?'

'Legouez knows, probably. I told you what he said to me; and the halberdiers who brought the Marquis de Kersalaun to the jail. But two of them have since died a violent death. And I don't think the ones that are left will say anything, on account of that. Everything was done without the knowledge of the jail authorities. Everything was irregular: the arrest of the Marquis, his imprisonment, and even the way his body was disposed of, without a prayer, without a grave. All that worried me a lot. I was complicit from beginning to end! One of the halberdiers did say to me, to try to reassure me, that the Navy Commandant was behind it all, but it was a secret. Perhaps he was right. Otherwise, how can you explain that nobody ever attempted to find out what happened to our prisoner? All the same. A Marquis!'

'And the two men you surprised in the cell, you never saw them again?'

'I don't think they ever came back, but I'm not sure. I stopped working at the jail immediately afterwards. My father and my grandfather were both huntsmen. It was already a while since the Comte de Boulainvilliers had suggested I work for him. But I was hesitating. Although you may be looked down on, and merely considered a prison guard, even when you are a deputy warder, it has plenty of advantages in compensation: you have a salary of three hundred and sixty pounds a year, and have more or less all your board and lodging. I was able to put money aside to set myself up with later. It was this nasty business that helped me to make up my mind. When I told Legouez I was leaving he told me never to forget that I would be killed if I talked.'

'You said that some halberdiers had been killed. Do you think that is linked to what happened?'

'I don't think anything. I am just saying that two halberdiers have been killed since this business and they were both members of the group that had escorted the Marquis on that Sunday. There were five, at first, all lodged in the attic above Legouez' hall, who took part in that expedition. Of the two who are dead, one was killed by a bayonet blow from a guard from the Royal Corps of Naval Infantry, at the shipyards. At his trial the soldier said, as justification for his action, that the halberdier had insulted him and was about to draw his sabre to attack him. And you know what? He was not even found guilty. The other halberdier was found strangled in Legouez' hall! The convicts were blamed, as the inquest found he had been strangled with a chain, but the murderer was never identified.'

*

On Friday afternoon, after classes, I asked the head guard at the Hôtel Saint-Pierre if the Comte de Boulainvillier's huntsman had left a package for me. He knew nothing about that but gave me instead a note from Captain Flaharn saying that he was leaving Brest the next day and wanted to see me one last time before his departure. He would expect me to have supper with him at the inn *La Dame au Paon*, where he was lodging.

It was dark when I left my inn to go down the steep streets of the Sept Saints quarter, and was snowing. In the light of the lanterns which illuminated the port down below, I could see bigger and bigger snowflakes falling ever more heavily. There was not a breath of wind and everywhere was quiet, with no sound save that of my footsteps. The inn *La Dame au Paon* was on the Brest Quay, close to the mast crane. Clouds hid the moon but the lights of the port, enhanced by the snow, gave out a diffused glow. The snow was beginning to settle on the paving slabs, on the cases of merchandise, on the barrels and casks which always littered the place, and on the decks and planking of the little boats squeezed alongside the quay. I could even make out the yards, picked out in white, of a fully rigged ship of the line moored fore and aft in the middle of the black stream of the Penfeld. It was without doubt a ship for the new squadron and would soon be towed out to the harbour.

*

Brest, Friday 17th January 1777, after seven thirty in the evening.

A square monumental fountain stands in the widest part of the quay, just in front of *La Dame au Paon*. The inn's sign hangs motionless in the light from the windows. It is a painting of an Asiatic woman astride a giant peacock. This strange picture is a souvenir from the visit of an ambassador from the King of Siam, who disembarked here over ninety years ago at the time of Louis XIV. The windows of the big room on the ground floor are fogged up and the inn is crowded. When I open the door, the hubbub from inside spills out into the silence of the snow still falling outside. I quickly close the door behind me and shake my hat and coat. It is warm inside, the bodily heat merging with that of the fire. Thin steam rises from the damp clothes and intermingles with the candle and pipe smoke under the low beams of the ceiling. I hear mainly Breton being spoken. There are mostly coasting seamen here, who will soon go off to sleep in the cold, on their boats moored just opposite. They are not in a hurry to leave. I force my way through to the counter where I am welcomed by the fresh smile of a girl of my age. It is the first time I have seen her, but I am so dazzled that I almost forget why I have come here. I stare at her openly and she holds my gaze without wavering. I have the impression that she likes me too. Alas! When I tell her that I am expected by Captain Flaharn, she knits her eyebrows over her pretty green eyes and pulls a face. She tells me that the Captain is waiting for me upstairs where there is a little anteroom used as a dining room for people of quality who do not wish to be disturbed by the other guests.

I find the Captain sitting in front of a fire. He is alone. A table has been set for two people. Candlesticks have been placed on a sideboard, along with a tobacco pouch and a large package wrapped in tarred canvas. The logs in the hearth crackle and a pleasant warmth suffuses the room. The smell of Holland tobacco floats in the air. Captain Flaharn is smoking a long-stemmed pipe and reading. He puts his book down when he sees me arrive. It is a little duodecimo volume. By leaning my head as I pass by, I manage to read the title marked in gilded letters on its thin sleeve: *Zadig, or The Book of Fate, an Oriental Story.*

He is fully aware of my inquisitiveness.

'Human stupidity is a fascinating subject. The writer describes it extremely well.'

Two serving girls, led by the young girl who welcomed me, put vegetables, fish in white sauce and roast meat in the middle of the table. Captain Flaharn fills two glasses. He has had several bottles of Touraine wine, already uncorked, put in an ice-filled tub on the floor, within hand's reach.

The noise from down below, which had been coming up the stairs, stops. We hear a few notes from a violin before a singer starts a lament:

With all sail set we took our leave
And put to sea on Saint-Jean's Eve...

We sit in silence for a moment to hear the words of the song. It is about one of the many unfortunate sea battles in the last war, recalling the sacrifice of the sailors killed in combat and the wounds of the survivors. There is a silence, then someone with a strong voice sings a more militant song which I do not recognise, but is immediately taken up by everyone there:

Let's go, sailors, Vive le Roi, hunt the Angliches!
Drink a glass, the wind is fair, death to the Saxons!

The Captain has emptied his glass. He invites me to do the same and pours us each another glass for a toast.

'To our revenge against the English.'

That makes me think of the words left by my father:

> *Ten years ago, we had certainly been beaten in combat, but we thought only of redeeming ourselves, while today it's as if everyone sets sail already defeated.*

The dark days have passed. My father would no doubt have appreciated those words of revenge.

Captain Flaharn begins by telling me that he has just learned from Navy Command that Monsieur Bézout will be coming in June to examine the Cadets and asked me if I intend to present myself for examination. I reply that I already feel prepared for the examination and am confident of passing. In the meanwhile, I have emptied my glass again and he has refilled it without asking me. I suspect nothing, and I don't feel like I am drinking a lot since, for every glass I finish, he is downing at least two or three.

'That is perfect,' he continues. 'If you pass, you will be promoted to Marine Guard by the beginning of July at the latest. I hope by that time to have been given the command I am waiting for. I will ask to take you with me. Don't refuse! I have enemies in the Navy, but I also have powerful protectors, and nobody has ever doubted my qualities as a seaman.'

In a lucid moment I wonder why he is confiding all this in me now, whereas before he has always been so guarded, at least up until the story of the tiger hunt.

'You lost your father early,' he carries on. 'I am not married, and I do not have a son. I would very much like to help with your education. And you won't waste your time with me, I promise. These rumours about an imminent war are no doubt well-founded, but I don't think it will happen this year. The squadrons they are going to put together are likely to stay in harbour for a good while yet. There will be time for you to rejoin them before they put to sea properly. But if you accept my offer, you will already have some basic sea-going experience. I can't give you any more details. All that I can say is that I am planning a secret operation in the Channel, which will soon be confirmed, with the command of a frigate. If you agree to join me next June, I can guarantee that you will be in the action long before your friends have left Brest harbour.'

He falls silent. I have the feeling that what he has just told me does not suit me at all, but I no longer know what to make of it. The Touraine wine is starting to have its effect.

'What do you think? Will you accept my offer?'

I mumble a few words of agreement, at the same time as feeling that I should say no.

'Excellent! As a measure of my good faith, I would like to present you with a work used for instructing our King Louis, and which will give you pleasure at the same time as teaching you something.'

He fills our glasses again, then takes the package I had noticed when I came in from the side table and gives it to me. It is a huge quarto volume richly bound in calf's leather. I open the title page and read this:

VOYAGE
AROUND THE WORLD
BY THE KING'S FRIGATE
LA BOUDEUSE
AND
LA FLUTE L'ETOILE
In 1766, 1767, 1768 & 1769

It is a first edition copy of the *Voyage* of Monsieur de Bougainville, the work I had sought in vain at the Saint-Yves College library. I have recently learned that its author is a Ship's Captain who is now in Brest. Quite rightly, he has just been given command of a seventy-four gun ship. Previously he was with the training squadron as second-in-command to the Chevalier de Lamotte-Picquet. He is also a member of the Marine Academy. Captain Flaharn has given me a sumptuous gift. If my mind were clearer, I would be able to refuse it politely. At the moment I am incapable of so doing, and stupidly keep the book on my knees.

*

It had almost stopped snowing when I returned home. The paving stones were covered with a slippery white coating several inches thick.

I don't know how I managed to get up the whole of the lower rue des Sept Saints without falling flat on my face or dropping my book. Next morning my friend Vernon told me that I had snored the whole night. I had a vague recollection of the Captain directing the conversation towards my parents and what they may have confided in me, but I could not remember what I had said. The only thing of which I was sure was that I had accepted to sail with him once I had passed before Monsieur Bézout. Once I had sobered up, I bitterly regretted having made such a promise.

Brest awoke to a covering of snow. I asked Vernon to make my excuses at muster and said I would be at the Mass at the Navy chapel. I ran to the port with my book under my arm. I intended to give the gift back straight away and withdraw the promise I had made. The inn was open when I arrived at the quay. The big communal room was empty at this early hour. However, I could hear voices ringing out from the kitchen.

'Is there anyone there?' I shouted to nobody in particular, to get their attention.

*

Brest, Saturday 18th January 1777, morning.

The young girl who welcomed me last night shows her head at the door behind the counter. My heart begins to thump and I take pleasure in once again seeing her green eyes and golden complexion. I tell her that I would like to speak with Captain Flaharn.

'Again! Well, my little Sir, you like him as much as that, this Captain? I am sorry to have to tell you that he left this morning before daybreak, on a horse brought here by a valet from the post.'

She has a very quiet, soft voice that does not match the self-assurance and confidence of her words.

'And you know where he went?'

'On the Paris road, I imagine. By now, he will already be at Landerneau! And even if you could run quickly, which I very much doubt given the state you were in last night, you would have trouble catching him.'

She is making fun of me. The Captain will not have passed Guipavas yet, but she is correct to say that I cannot catch him up. I feel guilty on account of my inconsiderate behaviour last night. Moreover, this chatterbox, with her feminine intuition, has perfectly divined the feelings she arouses in me, and I sense that she is very happy to exploit pitilessly the windward advantage she has over me. I prefer therefore to turn on my heels and escape her there and then. She acknowledges my flight with a mocking laugh which still resounds dolorously in my head as I rejoin Vernon des Aulnes at the Navy chapel.

*

Our pew was on one side of the transept, opposite a big altarpiece showing the souls of those in purgatory saved by divine mercy. I have to admit that I did not follow much of the service. I was not the only one either. In this Age of Enlightenment it was the done thing, amongst the Guards and Cadets, to be a freethinker as regards religion. It was mandatory to be at the weekday services, but they happily skipped them on Sundays. I myself had never really thought much about the mysteries of the Faith. I respected the Church on account of my uncle, the Father, whom I liked a lot, but I had never asked myself too many questions. But for the moment I was thinking about my evening at *La Dame au Paon.* I contemplated the Holy Spirit gliding above the altarpiece in front of me, like a white kestrel frozen in flight, above clouds filled with puff-cheeked cherubs blowing their trumpets, but I ended up none the wiser as regards Captain Flaharn's behaviour towards me.

Coming out from our classes, which finished earlier on a Saturday, we found the Comte de Boulainvilliers downstairs at the Hôtel Saint-Pierre. It was us he was waiting for, as he came to meet us as soon as he saw us. He said that he had to stand watch on board, and he was already late, but he wanted to tell us as soon as possible that he unfortunately had to cancel the next day's hunt as his huntsman had just been killed. He suggested he walk with us to our inn so that he could explain more as we went. He would then carry on to the port.

As we went down the rue de Siam, which was still snowed up and slippery, he explained that François Loutre had been the victim of a tragic accident while going home from the Brest market the day before. Soizic, the housekeeper, had given the alert when she saw his horse bringing his cart into the courtyard of the Chateau de Coataudon with no driver. The servants went to look for him and found him, stone dead, his skull broken, besides a little stream which runs below the road from Landerneau to the chateau. He stank of alcohol. They concluded that he had got blind drunk at the market and broken his head when he fell from his cart. The good woman Soizic had washed the poor lad's body and dressed him in clean clothes. They had put him on a pew in the chateau's little chapel while waiting for a coffin to be made. The sergeant at the Landerneau Mounted Police had been alerted with a view to him coming to take statements and give permission for burial. All that happened on the Friday. The sergeant had come with a horseman towards the end of the afternoon. Having seen François Loutre's body, he asked to be shown the place where he had been found. He had then declared that the body would have to be examined by two surgeons. He had added that he was going to summon them from Brest before returning to Landerneau, so that they would come on the Saturday morning to Coataudon. The Comte de Boulainvilliers had been forewarned on the Friday evening and had gone to spend the night at his hunting lodge. He had waited all of Saturday morning at the Chateau along with the sergeant and a horseman who had come from Landerneau early that morning. But by ten thirty in the morning the surgeons had still not arrived, and the Comte had had to leave for his shipboard duties. He had passed the two physicians below the Landerneau Gate.

I said to the Comte de Boulainvilliers that I remembered him telling me that his huntsman was of a sober disposition.

'That is absolutely true,' replied the Comte. 'Perhaps the sergeant is not wrong, after all. It's a real pity that I couldn't be there with the surgeons. I would have liked to have known their conclusions. Unfortunately, I'm not in my commander's good books so I can't wait any longer.'

I suggested to the Comte de Boulainvilliers that I go myself to Coataudon to find out what the surgeons said. He replied that he would be very much obliged to me for doing that, but that I ran the risk of arriving too late. The sergeant would probably already have gone back to Landerneau to write his report.

'To make sure that isn't the case,' I replied, 'I will go and hire a horse from the post after dinner. We are free this afternoon, and an outing to Landerneau will do me good.'

'In that case,' replied the Comte, 'if that's what you want to do, the two of you go together and take two of my horses. That will get them out as there is no hunt tomorrow. As long as your friend would not prefer to be revising his Bézout.'

Vernon was delighted to come with me. We ate our meal quickly and by half past twelve we were already saddling our horses ourselves in the Coataudon stable, with Soizic watching us. She had been so upset by events that she seemed to have forgotten all her French and never stopped whining in a Breton of which Vernon understood not a word and I not much more. She told us two or three times that the sergeant had forbidden anyone from going into François Loutre's room. I could see that seals had been put on the trapdoor at the top of the ladder leading to the huntsman's garret above the stable.

It is just a little more than twelve miles from Coataudon to Landerneau. As the sky cleared, we had the sun on our right, a little behind us. The previous night's snow had melted entirely. The track passed through ploughed fields surrounded by bare hedges and broom. We then entered a big forest carpeted with a layer of dead leaves between patches of snow. The road began to descend gently. Soon we saw the Landerneau river shining in front of us through the tree trunks. It was not long after two thirty when we entered the town. The road on which we had arrived went straight down to the port between garden walls and houses faced with white stone and lit by the low sun of a winter's afternoon. The slate roofs were overlooked by a high belltower.

Landerneau is right on the road from Paris to Brest. Its river forms a natural harbour whose end is closed by a bridge lined end to end with big houses. On the banks of the river are two quays, one in Léon and one in Cornouaille, as the river forms the boundary between the two bishoprics. These quays are lined with elegant town houses built by the local shipowners when the town was at the height of its splendour during the previous century. The Landerneau Mounted Police building was on the Léon side.

*

Landerneau, Saturday 18th January 1777, beginning of the afternoon

The sergeant is writing his report when our arrival is announced. He interrupts his work to receive us when he learns that we are there on behalf of the Comte de Boulainvilliers. He begins by explaining that the report of the surgeons confirms his first impressions.

'As soon as I was shown the scene of the accident, I thought immediately that the victim's wound was not natural. There are indeed a few rocks beside the stream, but the slope is not so steep. Even jumping headfirst from his cart, François Loutre could not have injured himself in this way. The doctors' views are conclusive: the wound was made by a blow dealt from behind by a very hard instrument: either a stonemason's hammer or a *penn-baz*. It is therefore a case of murder. Moreover, and again according to the surgeons, the victim had not consumed any alcohol beforehand. According to them, the presumed murderer had deliberately poured a bottle of brandy over his clothes after the blow, to mislead investigators. A crime was therefore committed, and the motive was not robbery. The purse with which the huntsman set off for market was found. The money missing from it corresponded exactly to the provisions he had bought, and which were found on the cart. I am therefore writing a statement for the King's Prosecutor at the Brest Courts. He will of course authorise the burial, but he will then open an inquiry and ask me to look for witnesses. Your visit is opportune as I can take your names. You will certainly be called as witnesses, as will the Comte de Boulainvilliers, the housekeeper Soizic Mateano, and anyone else my enquiries deem to be worth calling. But it is likely that the case will soon be abandoned before reaching its end.'

'Why is that?' asks my friend.

'Well, I think that the inquiry will soon confirm my first impressions from questioning the woman Mateano and a few servants at Coataudon. François Loutre was quiet and orderly. He was friendly by nature and never got angry with anybody. He did not frequent the brothels of Coatargueven. He was not in the habit of getting drunk. From time to time he went to the harvest celebrations, but always acted honourably. He lived alone, certainly, but according to what he had confided in Soizic, he intended to marry a country girl in a year or two. And finally, the housekeeper said that he had put aside some savings with which he intended to set himself up with a house and family. We will probably find these in the loft where he lived, and whose doors I immediately sealed. I believe that the cause of François Loutre's murder is not to be found at Coataudon, but rather where he lived up until the end of January 1773 before entering the Comte de Boulainvillier's service. It is there that the heart of the matter lies!'

Vernon, who knows nothing of Autumn's former life, once again shows his surprise.

'Before becoming a huntsman,' continues the sergeant, 'François Loutre was for five years a deputy warder at the Brest Jail. I believe that it will be by enquiring into that period of his life that we shall find the cause of his death. We will probably find some interesting new elements when we make an inventory of his personal belongings. And that will be the end of the case and the enquiry, as far as I am concerned anyway.'

'I still don't understand why,' says my friend.

'It's very simple. The jail is within the jurisdiction of the Navy Command. The Courts have no competence in this area. The King's Prosecutor will relinquish the file on this matter to the Lieutenant-General of the Admiralty, and I will have to hand over the enquiry to my colleagues at the Chateau de Brest who are answerable to the Navy Provost.'

'Why is that a problem?'

'They are up to their eyes in the disorder and daily fights between sailors, soldiers and shipyard workers, to say nothing of the jail. The dossier on this matter, whose roots probably go back more than three years, will be filed provisionally for an indeterminate period. And, if I believe the rumours of war currently running around the Navy Command, I imagine that the Comte d'Orvilliers will have more important things on his mind than pushing his men to follow up the shady murder of a former deputy warder.'

I think about the message François Loutre spoke about, that the Marquis de Kersalaun wanted to be given to my mother. It had not been left at the Hôtel Saint-Pierre guard room. It must therefore be still amongst the belongings of the huntsman, under seal. When the investigators find it, they will no doubt ask me what I know exactly. I will probably be no longer able to keep silent on this business.

'Have you ever heard talk of the Marquis de Kersalaun?' I say.

The sergeant considers my question.

'You are not from Faou, as far as I know. So, how do you know about this?'

'The Marquis de Kersalaun was a comrade-in-arms of my father, the Ship's Lieutenant Laforest-Dombourg, who died in service in 1771. I tried to find the Marquis when I came to Brest, and I was told that he had been accused of a crime, arrested and put in the jail.'

'I didn't know that he had been put in the jail,' said the sergeant, raising an eyebrow. 'I thought that he was rotting in secret in the Chateau de Brest dungeons...so there could be a link between the death of the huntsman and that affair? It's not impossible, since the dates coincide. I mean François Loutre's departure from the jail and this old business of the Marquis de Kersalaun. If that is the case, then it's even more awkward than I thought...'

I ask him if he knows exactly what happened to the Marquis.

'Well, no. Not really,' he replies. 'It's a rather strange story. Exactly four years ago, at the beginning of January '73, I received a message from the rector of Hanvec. He told me that the wife of the Marquis de Kersalaun had been found dead by her servants in the courtyard of her manor house. She had a dagger in her heart, but not any dagger – it was her husband's hunting knife! The Marquis had disappeared, and the inhabitants of a neighbouring hamlet said that soldiers had come by sea, from Brest, to arrest him, as he had killed his wife at the end of a hunting trip. It seemed to me totally improbable. Not the murder, as I have seen others during my time, alas! But the fact that soldiers from the Navy Provost should come to arrest someone beyond the boundaries of Brest. I immediately left for Hanvec. There, they showed me the body of the victim and the weapon used to kill her. It was indeed the Marquis of Kersalaun's engraved hunting knife. The priority was to bury the deceased, but account had to be taken of what the people of Kersalaun said about soldiers coming from Brest. I have to say that at that stage, neither the rector nor I believed it. But if, by some chance, it was true, that meant that the Brest Admiralty had led the investigation from the start and as a result nothing could be done without the agreement of their Lieutenant-General. Apart from the burial, there was also the problem of what to do with the Marquis's property. I had not even been able to seal the gates because of the dogs and horses there that needed feeding. The rector explained that he had left the key to the gates in the keeping of a certain Fantig Le Goff, a servant at the chateau, for which he took responsibility. She had been told to open up for the huntsman and keep an eye on him every day when he went to look after the pack and the horses.'

I already know all this, but it was what follows that I am waiting for. What exactly was the Navy's role in this? That is the most puzzling aspect.

'What did the Admiralty say to you?'

'Before going to the Admiralty, I went first to see the Lieutenant of the military police, at Brest. He was extremely surprised. He swore that his men had never been to Hanvec and that he knew nothing about this business. And at the Admiralty nobody knew anything either! But as a result of going around and asking questions of everybody, I was eventually called to the Navy Command, at the Hôtel Saint-Pierre. The Navy Commander at Brest at that time was the Comte d'Estaing. I was received by a Ship's Captain, a very impressive man, a kind of giant, who presented himself as the Comte's assistant. I did not take note of his name, but everybody was afraid of him at the Hôtel Saint-Pierre. He told me that the Marquis de Kersalaun had indeed been arrested for having killed his wife, but that he was also being prosecuted for high treason, and for that reason everything about the case had to remain secret. And, to conclude, I was asked with immediate effect to keep out of the whole business. I replied that I had no wish to get mixed up with things that did not concern me, but that it was nevertheless a matter of urgency to get a burial certificate for the parish of Hanvec as regards the wife of the Marquis. I added that the goods, property and buildings of Kersalaun had been abandoned and that it would without doubt be necessary to appoint a bailiff to make an inventory of these assets. And I made it clear that even if this last measure did not of itself seem pressing, it was nevertheless necessary to sort out as quickly as possible the question of the Marquis's dogs and horses. The Ship's Captain had a certificate prepared authorising the rector of Hanvec to do what was necessary, firstly for a Christian burial of the Marquis's wife, and secondly for auctioning off his hunting animals. He himself signed this document which I took as quickly as possible to the rector of Hanvec. After that I had nothing more to do with it. I heard that a month later the rector was visited by the Comte d'Estaing's assistant, who brought a document, signed by the Navy Commander this time, provisionally entrusting the management of the Kersalaun property to the parish of Hanvec.'

'Do you think that the Comte d'Estaing himself covered up the arrest of the Marquis de Kersalaun?' I asked.

'I saw his assistant, at any rate,' the sergeant replies, 'and I can assure you that he was not joking. I took his warning to keep out of this business seriously. That is why I would ask you, Monsieur, not to mention the Marquis de Kersalaun when you go to give a statement to the King's Prosecutor at Brest. At least, not until we have got to the end of due process. Because if you talk too soon, we will straight away be taken off the case. Suppose that the murder of François Loutre had nothing to do with the jail. After all, the surgeons talked about a *penn-baz*, which is the weapon of choice of Lower Brittany country folk. So, even if there is only one chance in a hundred that the murderer is from the parish of Guipavas, I would like to have the time to be certain of that. If we are taken off the case too early, there will always be an element of doubt. That is what I would like to avoid.'

*

We set off again for Brest at about four o'clock. It was less cold, with a sky full of clouds coming in from the sea. Vernon came and rode alongside me. He asked whether it was on account of this story that I had taken such a risk during the fire at the Navy hospital and reproached me for not having confided in him sooner. Vernon was a good friend whom I knew I could trust. There were already too many unexplained deaths in this saga. It was a relief to be able to share my secret. I told him everything: the brutal and inexplicable disappearance of my mother, the research done by my grandfather to try to explain the mystery, the posthumous letter of my father, which had put me on the track of the Marquis de Kersalaun, my investigations at the jail which had led to François Loutre, and finally, this new letter, it too posthumous, of which the huntsman had spoken, and which would certainly be found by the investigators when they made an inventory of his belongings. I explained to Vernon that it was this last fact which had impelled me to talk about the Marquis de Kersalaun with the sergeant of the Landerneau Constabulary. Otherwise, I would have kept silent about the matter.

'Well, if it is on account of this letter that you have eventually decided to ask for my help, then I'm very glad!' said Vernon, to end our conversation.

17

I had been afraid that they would find the letter from the Marquis de Kersalaun to my mother in the huntsman's attic at Coataudon, but as it turned out, I had become anxious too soon. On Monday morning, while I was in class, a Cadet from our unit gave me a flat supple package wrapped in a piece of cloth and tied up with string. He explained that he had had to leave the Hôtel Saint-Pierre for personal reasons towards the end of the morning the previous Friday. When going out, he had witnessed a lively discussion between the guardsmen of the Royal Corps of Navy Fusiliers and a red-haired fellow who was insisting on leaving a package for me. My comrade, being a Cadet, had suggested that he himself deliver it, but he had forgotten to give it to me the next day.

François Loutre had kept his word, after all. At break-time, I got hold of Vernon and we found a corner in which to unwrap the final despatch of the huntsman from Coataudon. Inside, I found the letter of which the poor chap had spoken. It was a scrap of paper, folded in four and sealed with roughly applied wax. The address had been written with a lead pencil in a shaky hand.

To Madame Emilie de Kermean
Widow of the Ship's Lieutenant
Jean-François Laforest-Dombourg

A shiny object fell from the package as I broke the seal. It was a signet ring. Examining it, I recognised the heraldry that I had seen above the gate of the abandoned Kersalaun chateau: *silver sword crossed in black, point down.* I unfolded the letter. On the opposite side from the address was a message a few lines long written in pencil in the same hand as the address.

Madame

The death of your husband deeply moved me and I have not yet begun to find another command to realise my plans. I beg you to forgive my lack of foresight which now puts you in grave danger. The despicable murderer whom I thought I had killed in a duel in Chandernagore has returned like a devil vomited from hell and has me in his power. He wants to know where to find what he calls 'his property'. He found at my house the sketch made by your little boy and understands its implications but does not yet know where to look. His henchman has tortured me to try to make me talk. I have not yet said anything, so as not to compromise you, but I am afraid that I may not have the strength to resist them when they come back. I have decided too to put an end to my life. May God pardon me. I beg you therefore to entrust my package to the King. Be on the alert, as they are furious and will do anything.

Adieu. Pray for me.

Ronan Avelus, Marquis de Kersalaun.

Chandernagore! The Marquis de Kersalaun thought he had killed his enemy there, but in fact he had not. I had the feeling that there was something here I ought to remember, but as is often the case it disappeared as soon as I started searching my memory. I could not get it out of my mind for the rest of the day, during class, then going down the rue de Siam in the evening on our way back to the inn, and finally in our room, where Vernon and I were in the habit of setting each other mathematical problems while waiting for our supper to be served.

'I understand what is nagging you,' said my friend. 'Try not to think about it and you'll find it will come of its own accord. That is often the best way.'

As I did not reply, he grabbed, somewhat in desperation, the beautiful book I had been given three days earlier and which I had

had no wish to open. On its spine a little red rectangle held the title inscribed in gold letters:

VOYAGE
AROUND
THE WORLD
BY
BOUGAINVILLE

My friend put the heavy volume on the table and drew up a chair so that he could leaf through it at his leisure. I was looking on absently over his shoulder. There were more than four hundred pages of text, twenty or so big maps and plans which folded out, and two or three beautiful illustrations. I asked Vernon to open it at the frontispiece, at the bottom of which I could read that the volume had been printed in Paris in 1771 '*with the approval and favour of the King*'.

According to Captain Flaharn, Louis XV had given an identical copy to our present King, his grandson. Why had the Captain been so generous towards me? His overly fine gift troubled me. Moreover, his company had started to make me feel ill at ease, particularly during our most recent meetings. Despite everything I felt I was indebted to him. His questions about my father and his time in India had especially disturbed me. However, he had done a great deal in passing on his knowledge of the use of arms. I thought of all those hours spent in the drill hall, the cramps, the fatigue, the sweat he had shed, he too, at the same time as me, to save my skin, while nothing obliged him to do it.

The sweat! I suddenly had a clear recollection of the time I had come across my mentor with his torso naked; when I had discovered the impressive scar slicing his bronzed body. It was that memory which had been haunting me since the morning and which I had tried in vain to pinpoint. Captain Flaharn had said that he had got this wound in India and that it was from a sabre blow.

He had not wanted to give me any more details, but he had nonetheless added that *everybody thought he was dead.* He had let slip, too, that *he had had the last word.* And then, the following Monday, when we had gone together to a bar on the Grande Rue, he had started to talk to me insistently about Chandernagore. What if his opponent in India had been the Marquis de Kersalaun? *The despicable murderer whom I thought I had killed in a duel in Chandernagore has returned like a devil vomited from hell...* There was no real basis for this hypothesis, but I knew that I would not rest until I had tried to verify it. But how? Flaharn had left. I could do little more than wait to hear from him. He wanted to see me again. That was why he had offered Bougainville's *Voyage.* All I could do for the moment was to try and put a few questions to the young girl at *La Dame au Paon.* Perhaps she could tell me something that would put me at ease.

'What's up?' asked Vernon when he saw me putting on my coat to go out.

'I want to check something at *La Dame au Paon* inn. Don't wait for me. I'll come straight back for supper.'

*

Brest, Monday 20th January 1777, evening.

As I hurtle down the rue Basse des Septs Saints, I try to put my thoughts in order. I do not really know what I am looking for, and it is only by exceptional luck that I have any chance of finding out anything at the *La Dame au Paon* that would shed light on events that happened six years previously at the other ends of the earth. But, just like the sergeant of the Landerneau Mounted Police, I don't want to overlook anything. Also, without openly admitting it to myself, I want to see the girl who made fun of me last Saturday. I had the impression that she did not much like Captain Flaharn and that her hostility towards me resulted from her thinking that I was a close acquaintance of his. I hope that her attitude towards me will change when I show her that she is mistaken and that Flaharn is no friend of mine.

It is half past five in the evening and has already been dark for an hour. It is low tide, with the flood just starting, as I arrive at the quay in front of the inn. There are a dozen or so customers in the room. The serving girls are bustling around them. The one I am looking for is sat at the end, behind the counter, like the last time. My heart once again brims over when I see her. She too has seen me and watches me coming towards her, her face expressionless. I believe I can detect a mocking twinkle in her pretty eyes as I get close. I decide on the spur of the moment to launch straight into the real purpose of my visit. I think that this will help avoid a new round of sarcasm. Anyway, that is the main reason I have come. Having been careful to introduce myself with my full titles this time, which I have never done before, I ask her whether she would mind telling me a bit about Captain Flaharn.

'Really?' she says, somewhat surprised. 'I thought you two were thick as thieves.'

I rush to take advantage of this opening to explain myself.

'Exactly! I have no idea why he has been so friendly towards me. And that troubles me, you see, as I know almost nothing about him.'

'I can tell you straight off that it wasn't your virtue he was after. And buggery,' here she lowered her voice like a little girl caught out saying a rude word, 'is not his vice. I'm well placed to know that, as I've several times had to make a hasty retreat to get away from his wandering hands. Which cannot be said for all the girls who have found themselves in that room. They're not shy, for sure.'

She bursts out laughing. There is still a hint of derision in her manner, but no longer any hostility.

'However, you are quite right to be distrustful, young Monsieur Marine Guard, as this man terrifies me and I hope he won't be back here too soon. And, if you are not a friend of his, so much the better! I would even be happy to tell you about him if I can.'

Hearing her laugh and listening to her soft but assured voice, I almost forget again why I have come. I look for something to say to her and have a bright idea.

'Could you show me the room he occupied? Perhaps he forgot something or left some important clues behind. If it is still empty, that is.'

I would make up any old nonsense just to be alone with her.

'There is still nobody up there,' she replies. 'I am happy to take you up there, but you won't find anything. The room has been cleaned since Saturday. This is a well-run inn. What do you think?'

'At least we will be able to talk in peace,' I say, rushing blindly on with my idea.

'Hmmm. You are not going to jump on me like your Captain, then?'

I wish I were brave enough to do so, but she still intimidates me too much for me to go that far. Apart from the mercenary and indulgent embraces of the ladies of the *Dames de la Marine*, I have no experience of women.

'Not without your permission,' I say feeling my face blush. 'What should I call you, Mademoiselle?'

'Kirwan, Maria Kirwan.'

Mademoiselle Kirwan leads me up the staircase, carrying a candlestick to light the way. Flaharn's room is on the first floor. It is quite big, a veritable apartment, with a bathroom attached and an excellent view of the entrance to the Penfeld during daylight hours. The bed has been remade with clean sheets and the room seems perfectly tidy. At least as far as I can judge by the light of the candlestick held by Mademoiselle Kirwan. Unlike the *Dames de la Marine* she does not use perfume, but the fresh and natural aroma of her young body gives me goose pimples, my heart beats more strongly, and I am lost for words. Clumsily I point out that the hearth has not been emptied.

'As you can see, there was still half a good log left. It was kept, along with the cinders, to make relighting the fire easier for the next occupant,' she replies, while lighting other candles in the room with the flame from her candlestick.

I search in vain for a pretext for getting closer to her and put my face close to the chimney breast to hide my embarrassment. The hearth is very wide for an ordinary room, an observation I share with my young hostess. She replies that this room was once the innkeeper's private quarters. I then notice a piece of wood that looks nothing like a log, in the cinders on the right-hand side. Intrigued, I ask Maria Kirwan to give me more light and lift it carefully out between thumb and forefinger.

'Stop! You'll make everything dirty!' the young girl protests.

I examine my find, holding it at arm's length over the fire irons. It is a blackened object, like part of a walking stick whose handle resembles a big oval apple about three inches in diameter. It is heavy for its size, carved out of very dense wood. It seems to have started to burn, then gone out after rolling away from the flames. This gives me an idea. I put it down on the side of the hearth and take a poker to search through the cinders beside the bricks on the other side of the fireplace. I find a little piece of wood which seems to be the other end of the stick's shaft. I was not mistaken, alas!

'You are making a mess!' protests Maria Kirwan.

'Could you find me a cloth?'

'I'll go down and get one from the kitchen if you promise to wait until I get back before bringing out this rubbish over our nice clean floor.'

While waiting for her to come back, I have a good look at the room. There is a small desk, a wash table with a jug and bowl, a wardrobe, two chairs and a box seat. Now that Maria Kirwan has gone, taking her soft scent with her, I can smell the wax which has been used to polish the furniture and the parquet flooring. The young girl is right. I will find nothing in the room, but what I have just recovered from the fireplace, if I am not mistaken, is unfortunately of great significance. I think again about the Marquis' message to my mother, about Fantig's story, about the words of poor François Loutre, about the assertions of the sergeant of the Landerneau Mounted Police. All this makes me suddenly very sad, and I cannot at the same time stop myself feeling a painful guilt.

With the cloths brought by Mademoiselle Kirwan, I wipe and nervously rub the two objects I have got out of the cinders. They both have the same dense texture and an identical hardness. After a quick clean, I find a brown wood, with a slight patina of age, but still light-coloured. The wood is very fine-grained. The shaft on the ball section matches the stem I retrieved from the other side of the fireplace, except that the latter piece has a little regular groove in it, hollowed out with a gouge, it seems. In this groove is a length of leather cord with about five inches remaining, the rest having been burned to ashes. I have in my hands what is left of a peculiar stick which has no doubt been put on the fire to destroy it and whose two ends have fallen outside the fire irons when the stem connecting them burned. The chimneypiece is about three and a half feet wide. I put down the two pieces of wood, having wiped them carefully, on the marble of the wash table, about three and a half feet apart. I have to bow to the evidence: I know what it is, as I have already seen a similar object in the hands of Old Le Touze, at Le Croisic.

'Who looks after this room?'

'I do,' replies Maria Kirwan. 'Your Flaharn did not want our maids dealing with his personal effects. Monsieur the Ship's Captain was afraid of indiscretions and pilfering. Can you believe that? But it still didn't stop him getting them into his bed, the old pig! And during this time, my uncle assigned me to be the chambermaid for Monsieur the Ship's Captain and his whores.'

'Your uncle?'

'My maternal great-uncle. He owns this inn. What do you take me for? I'm not a servant. My father was an Irish officer in the service of the King! I'm an orphan. My uncle adopted me after the death of my mother.'

'I am an orphan too,' I said. 'My father too was a King's officer. He was lost at sea with the vessel he commanded. He was a Ship's Lieutenant.'

'Mine was a Captain in the Army, in Lally's regiment. He was killed not long after my birth, defending the town of Pondicherry against the English, so I was told. I was born at Port-Louis on the Île-de-France. My mother died not long after we came back to France, when I was five years old. There was an epidemic in the village where we were living. I have no memory of my father. I don't even know what he looked like.'

Her voice has dropped to a tiny whisper. I say to myself that if I let her carry on in this vein, she will end up crying on my shoulder. Despite my current state of mind, that is not at all a disagreeable proposition. But she gets a grip on herself and leans over the two objects I have put on the table.

'What is it?' she asks.

'A common object in Cornouaille,' I say. 'It's usually used as a walking stick. You're not Breton?'

'I know Brest mainly. I didn't live long in the countryside.'

She picks up the length of stick with the oval-shaped end.

'It's really heavy for wood!'

'Yes. I think it's been carved from the trunk of a holly tree. It's not an ordinary walking stick. It is also a formidable weapon for someone who knows how to use it. In Breton, it is called a *penn-baz*. And you say you never saw it before amongst the Captain's things?'

'No. As regards weapons, he had his epee and also an ebony walking stick with an ivory pommel bound in silver. I pulled on it one time and found it concealed a sort of triangular blade filed like a foil.'

'Tell me a little about what else you saw in the room.'

'He had mainly books. He read a lot.'

'You no doubt had a look at what he was reading, even if it was indiscreet of you?'

'Of course. I am inquisitive and I know how to read. Did you doubt that? I can't remember all his books, but I can remember three, one on account of its curious title: *Zadig*. The other two I remember because the titles were almost the same: *Essays on Human Understanding* and *New Essays on Human Understanding*, but one had a sub-title showing that it had been translated from English, from a certain John Locke. They were all of the same kind. The only really interesting one was the book he gave you the other evening. I browsed through it; there are some beautiful pictures.'

'When did he arrive here?'

'The Captain? About four months ago.'

'How did he occupy his time?'

'Heavens, I don't really know. He often went out at the end of the day, but his hours were varied, and he didn't seem to have a regular occupation. He sometimes spent the night away. Sometimes he spent whole days doing nothing; apart, that is, from reading and smoking his pipe. Sometimes he invited officers and gentlemen to play chess. They played in the little anteroom where you had supper with him. They played for money.'

'Did he win often?'

'He always won! Even though he drank an enormous amount, usually rum, during these evenings. But it apparently had no effect on him. I also heard that he had come here on leave to court the young wife of a port officer. If that is true, then the least one can say is that she by no means had the monopoly on his ardour. In any case, I didn't have the impression that he had a job to do at the Navy Command.'

'How did he dress to go out?'

'Usually in his Captain's uniform. But not always. For example, last Friday he went out in the morning dressed like the quartermaster of a merchant ship, with a blue coat and a little round hat. I didn't see him when he came back as I was very busy in the little dining room supervising the preparation of your fine supper. He changed afterwards to wait for you.'

I ask her who looks after the heating arrangements for guests. She explains that a servant makes a tour of the rooms in the evening to make sure there are enough embers in the fireplaces. He comes again in the morning to put another log or two on the hearths. Guests are not allowed to put wood on the fires during the night. In any case, no reserves of wood are left in the rooms, as a precaution. This is all in order to reduce the risk of a fire. And so, of course, the fire in this room had not been relit on the morning of the Captain's departure.

The time has passed quickly. I have to go if I do not want to miss supper at the inn. With the permission of the young girl, I take away my find, wrapped in the old cloth she has given me. I ask her too to see if the servants at *La Dame au Paon* can shed any more light on Captain Flaharn's habits, but this is mainly a pretext so that I can come back. I have fallen completely under the spell of Mademoiselle Kirwan, of her green eyes, her golden skin and her scent of peach, fresher than rose and more intoxicating than musk.

*

I found Vernon at the table with some other Cadet friends who also lodged at the inn. In reply to his questioning look, I put my package between the two of us and showed him its contents, telling him only where and how I had found it. Of course, my friend did not know what it was, but the maid who was passing behind us serving food recognised immediately what I had brought.

'Heavens above! Is that a *penn-baz* that you've broken?'

'No, it was burned,' I said. 'Do you know where I could find a similar one?'

'And why would you want to replace it then? It's not for you to be fighting amongst yourselves. Epees, you've got enough of them for that already, ain't you? You want to hit our boys with it?'

'Rest assured,' I said. 'You know perfectly well that the Chevalier des Aulnes and I don't play those nasty games and that we disapprove of them. I simply want to find out if this walking stick could have been bought here, in Brest. I just want to know, that's all.'

'Well I never! You'll find one at the market, for sure.'

Vernon remembered having heard the Landerneau sergeant say that the weapon used to kill François Loutre could have been a *penn-baz.* I explained to him, showing him the two pieces I had brought back, how this stave of holly could be used as a walking stick and a whip for animals, with its long leather lanyard. But it could also be a formidable weapon when someone trained to use it twirls it round at the end of its lanyard, the latter wrapped round the wrist, giving it the force of a powerful flail.

I told my friend how I first thought that there were remarkable coincidences between the letter of my father, the tragic message of the Marquis de Kersalaun to my mother, the testimony of the unfortunate François Loutre and my discovery of Captain Flaharn's scar; and particularly the few words he had spoken when I had asked him about the wound. I had deduced that the impressive sabre blow that the Captain was on the receiving end of in India could well have been delivered by the Marquis de Kersalaun. Many elements corroborated this hypothesis. In both versions, those of both the Marquis and the Captain, it was a matter of a confrontation in India in which the loser had been left for dead. I had gone to *La Dame au Paon* inn with this idea in mind, and without really knowing what I was looking for, apart from the company of Maria Kirwan, although I kept this to myself, of course. I had no idea whatsoever that I was going to find the remains of a *penn-baz.* This unexpected discovery brought a new and worrying trait to the increasingly troubling character of my former mentor.

There were two market days each week in Brest, on Fridays and Tuesdays. They were held in a little paved square in front of the Saint-Louis church, just five minutes' walk from the Hôtel Saint-Pierre. I went to have a look the next day, together with Vernon, at the midday break. The place was crowded, as always in this town, but the typical Brest weather had dampened the spirit of those there. The snow of the last few days had completely melted. There was not much wind and it was not cold for the end of January. But there was mist, a thick and insidious mist which seemed to hang in the air instead of falling. It soaked us slowly, but more comprehensively than any shower. It muffled the sound of conversation and the haggling of the customers walking round and squeezing under the soaked tarpaulins which sheltered the stalls. The carthorses, tied up around the square, stood motionless between the traces of their carts, heads down, ears flat, from time to time shaking their manes and tails.

It took us a little while to find someone selling *penn-baz.* He was the only one. He was a clog-maker who had a few 'head-breaking' sticks which he had made himself alongside his clogs. He told us he was the only one selling these and that he had no competitors at the Brest market.

'Except when the Fair is on.' he added.

I knew that the Fairs were held at Brest on the first Monday of each month. So, I thought, if Captain Flaharn had bought his *penn-baz* here last Friday, as I supposed, then there was a very strong chance that he had bought it from this good fellow. I got out the two pieces of wood to show them to the clog-maker, making sure that he knew I was not responsible for their present state. The artisan immediately recognised his handiwork and remembered very well having sold this *penn-baz* early the previous Friday morning. Then, as I hoped, he complained about the poor treatment that his work of art had been subjected to. Vernon and I agreed whole-heartedly, as was to be expected. So much so that the clog-maker hardly needed to be asked to tell us about the maverick purchaser to whom he had sold his goods. The first thing he remembered was that his client spoke Breton. However, he was not dressed in the smock and wide breeches worn by a Breton countryman. What's more, he spoke like the people from Vannes. He looked more like a seaman. The rest of his description left no room for doubt. He described a tall individual, well-built and impressively powerful, with very pale grey eyes. This man had weighed up the *penn-baz* like someone who knew all about them and had swung it round a few times in front of the clog-maker, testing it out and showing great skill in the use of this rustic weapon.

That evening I talked at length with my friend. Given what we were starting to discover, it seemed a matter of urgency to find out what we could about the career and real position of Captain Flaharn in the King's Navy. For that we only had to ask our superior officers. We agreed that Vernon would ask Lieutenant de Clesmeur, pretending that he was acting in my interests without my knowledge. He would say that Captain Flaharn wanted me to serve with him once I was a Marine Guard and that I was worried about this as I felt indebted towards him after the help he had given me in relation to my duel.

Vernon soon came back with an initial response. Everybody trusted him, taken in by his innocent demeanour. He was well aware of this and it usually irritated him, but he knew how to take advantage of it when necessary.

To start with, there had been a David Flaharn, a simple First Mate in the merchant navy, working for the India Company. He was a good seaman, a peerless ship handler and afraid of nothing. He would have had all the qualities required to command a ship, except for a total lack of moral sense. His chance came when he happened to be on the Île-de-France when the Comte d'Estaing was launching his privateering expedition. Like my uncle, Lieutenant de Clesmeur considered the Comte's conduct on this occasion to be illegal, as he had just been released on parole by the English after his capture at the siege of

Madras. The Comte had taken over two old ships from the India Company and had also obtained a blank certificate for the captaincy of a fire ship. And so the merchant seaman and ship's mate Flaharn went straight to being a Fire Ship's[21] Captain in the King's Navy, without first having attained the intermediate rank of Frigate's Lieutenant, the rank of my father at the Battle of Quiberon Bay. Lieutenant de Clesmeur did not know all the details of this expedition. The Comte's little privateering squadron had scoured the Indian Ocean as far as Sumatra for six months, behaving like 'pirates', to use Lieutenant de Clesmeur's word. The Captain David Flaharn, who was naturally gifted for this sort of caper, had worked wonders. The Comte had then returned to France on his own. He had been recaptured at sea by the English off the Brittany coast but had been released quite quickly; the Chevalier de Kermean had already recounted this episode in one of his letters. As for Captain Flaharn, he had gone off to India and not been heard of for a while. After the end of the war, in 1762, the Comte d'Estaing had been promoted to Lieutenant-General of the Army, but he was so much in the favour of Louis XV that he also managed to get himself commissioned to the same rank in the Navy, under the pretext that he had proved himself playing at pirates in the Indian Ocean, according to Lieutenant de Clesmeur. In 1764 he had been named Governor of the Windward Islands. He had come back to France in 1766 and decided to stay in the Navy for good. In 1772, Louis XV appointed him both Inspector and Commander of the Navy at Brest. Nobody had previously held these two posts simultaneously. The King had mainly put him there to get his sailors to swallow the Decree of February 1772, which the Comte accomplished with great efficiency, as my uncle had already described. The King was very satisfied with him. The Comte d'Estaing found himself holding the highest rank in the Navy, above a number of experienced and much-decorated seamen. However, the Comte had one problem: he was

21 Translator's note: *Fire Ship's Captain*: This did not mean that Flaharn actually commanded a Fire Ship! The rank of Captain in the French Navy at that time had three gradations, in ascending order: Barge Captain (*Capitaine de Flûte*), Fire Ship's Captain (*Capitaine de Brûlot*), and Ship's Captain (*Capitaine de Vaisseau*). Laforest-Dombourg's father's rank, Ship's Lieutenant (*Lieutenant de Vaisseau*), was a higher rank than both Barge Captain and Fire Ship's Captain, *Vaisseau* in this context meaning a Ship of the Line.

totally incapable of handling a ship. He had absorbed all the theory, as he was very intelligent and had a remarkable memory, but he had had no practical experience and could never acquire it as he was extremely short-sighted. He was incapable of seeing the foremast of a ship clearly from the quarterdeck. How had he managed to direct the manoeuvring of a squadron all on his own? It was also said that he was captured at Madras because he mixed up the red uniforms of the English with those of the Irish in Lally's regiment. He did manage to command his famous maritime expedition in oriental seas but, according to the Brest Navy officers, he could not have managed it without a certain David Flaharn at his side. Flaharn was immoral and unscrupulous but there was nobody who could manoeuvre a ship under difficult conditions as well as he did. Flaharn returned to France in 1772. He had been out of sight in India for ten years. It was said that he had fought as a mercenary in Hindustan for all this time. It could not have worked out better for the Comte d'Estaing. With Flaharn at his side he could manoeuvre any squadron. He had the head for it and Flaharn replaced his eyes. The Comte immediately wanted to have him at his side whenever he mounted the quarterdeck of a ship of war. And, as he knew perfectly well that the officers of the King's Navy, all products of the Grand Corps[22], would not tolerate being under the hand of a Fire Ship's Captain of poor breeding, he obtained directly from Louis XV a commission as Ship's Captain for his protégé. That is how the Fire Ship's Captain David Flaharn became, by the will and favour of the King, a Captain of a Ship of the Line.

It was quickly realised at Brest that Flaharn was not just the 'sailor's eye' for the Comte d'Estaing. He quickly became his righthand man. This unusual position arose because of the foul relationship between the Comte and the Navy officers. And I would add that the fault was not entirely on the side of the Comte, contrary to what Lieutenant de Clesmeur said. We knew something about that at the Hôtel Saint-Pierre. To give an example, on 31st December 1772, when the Comte d'Estaing, as Navy Commander, was to preside over the traditional ceremony of the blessing of the flags, and give a big end of year ball, every single

22 Translator's note; *Grand Corps*: the term used to denote the body of Naval officers who had passed through the Marine Guards and who were therefore of proven nobility.

officer of the Grand Corps refused his invitation. Faced with this inexcusable insult, the Comte had all the Marine Guards and Cadets confined to barracks and ordered them to attend his ball. The Navy officers who came through the Guards hated the Comte d'Estaing and he hated them back. This situation was perfect for a natural intriguer like Flaharn. However, that did not last too long; the Comte left for the Court at the start of January 1773 and did not want to return to Brest. He had heard that Versailles had the intention of fitting out a squadron to help the Turks in their war against Russia and he sought the command of this and was given it. In the end, this Mediterranean adventure did not happen, but all these machinations were only learned later, as the Comte left Brest without saying anything, leaving Flaharn behind. The latter stayed on until the end of January, ruling the roost, as everyone thought the Comte d'Estaing was going to come back. Then the Comte called his righthand man to his side. Everyone in Brest breathed a sigh of relief at his departure.

*

Brest, Thursday 23rd January 1777.

'So, it was Flaharn whom the Landerneau sergeant met when he came to the Brest Navy Command to enquire about the arrest of the Marquis de Kersalaun,' I say, once my friend had told me all this. 'It was he too who must have taken the certificate to Hanvec that the rector showed me. But was it him that the unfortunate François Loutre surprised in the prison cell? Together with the bearded man?'

I don't finish my sentence and still hope that I am wrong.

'I thought about that,' says Vernon. 'Even if I did not hear what the huntsman told you, you spoke to me about it and I remember certain details. And listen to this: Ship's Captain Flaharn had an assistant whom he had brought back from India. He was called 'Master Jack' but nobody here believes it was his real name. The Captain presented him as his secretary but, still according to Lieutenant de Clesmeur, the fellow could not read or write French and,' added Vernon,' I have saved the best for the end. This man was of average height, had a bronzed skin and a beard!'

'Flaharn killed the huntsman François Loutre with a blow from the *penn-baz*,' I say. 'He wanted to destroy the crime weapon immediately.

If I had not had the idea of going to search his room at *La Dame au Paon*, nobody would have known.'

'But why would he have done that?' asks Vernon.

The painful thoughts I had had the other day in the room at the inn come back to me. And once more the cruel evidence hits me between the eyes: it is I who am responsible for the death of Autumn.

'The huntsman had already seen him once, at the jail,' I continue. 'Their eyes crossed, he told me. I believe, alas, that I signed his death warrant by telling Flaharn on the Monday evening that we were going hunting the following Sunday with the Comte de Boulainvilliers. Flaharn knew that the Comte had his horses and hounds at Guipavas. He let that slip. I am sure too that he knew that François Loutre had gone there after leaving his post as deputy warder. He wanted to stop me meeting him as he had guessed that I was looking into the past of the Marquis de Kersalaun. The chief clerk at the jail must have told him. He took advantage of market day to ambush François Loutre on the Guipavas path, where he was sure to pass. Except that he could not have known that it served no purpose as we had already gone to Coataudon…because our landlady did not want a dog in her stable!'

'This story of the Marquis that you told me is terrible,' says Vernon. 'So it is Flaharn who kidnapped him, had him put in jail and tortured him?'

'He didn't really have him put in jail, as everything happened without the authorities knowing. He must surely be the officer that Fantig told me about, who was in charge of the halberdiers at Kersalaun, there is no doubt about that now. But there is more! Flaharn tortured the Marquis because he had discovered, when searching his chateau, a sketch that my father had once asked me to make. The sketch of a hiding place in my parents' house at Port-Louis. That is clearly mentioned in the Marquis's letter. It means therefore that it is Flaharn too who is responsible for the violence of which my mother and old Lénaïc were victims. I have found, without meaning to, the presumed killer of my mother!'

'You yourself were perhaps not meaning to,' says Vernon, 'but as far as he is concerned, believe me, he knew what he was doing in chasing after you.'

'But what I don't understand is why he came to my help in the business with the Enghien regiment.'

'Ah, yes!' adds Vernon. 'I almost forgot. Lieutenant de Clesmeur told me an interesting thing that he got from the Chevalier de Monteil. Do you know how the Comte d'Orvilliers knew that you were in potentially mortal conflict with the *champion* of the Enghien regiment? It was Flaharn! He went to see the Navy Commander and told him that if this duel took place, he would tell the Comte d'Estaing who would mention it to the King.'

'My mother's killer protects me and tries to get me into his service. But why?'

'You don't understand?' replies Vernon. 'He has tortured the Marquis, killed the Marquis's wife, and your mother and governess, because he is looking for something. Something of great value which apparently belonged to the Marquis and which was at your parents' house. But he has not managed to find it despite all his crimes. Your father having been lost at sea, you are now the only living person who could help him find what he is looking for!'

'How can I tell him the whereabouts of what he is looking for, when I myself don't even know what it is?'

'For him to have killed so many people, and for your parents and the Marquis de Kersalaun to have been so secretive, then in my opinion it concerns something of great value. Maybe it is treasure brought back from India! And the last wish of the Marquis had been for it to be entrusted to the King, so he wrote, but as your mother never received his warning, she could not have done that.'

'Treasure! Now you mention it, I remember Flaharn asking if my father had become rich when he came back from India. In any case, treasure or not, I will be able to avenge my mother. All we have to do is denounce Flaharn when we are called to give testimony to the King's Prosecutor for the inquiry into the death of François Loutre.'

Vernon remained silent for a few moments.

'I don't want to upset you,' he said at last, 'but I don't think that is a very good idea.'

'But it is my duty! I have to have justice for my mother!'

'Of course, but you have to be certain of succeeding.'

'What do you mean? Flaharn is a criminal. He deserves to be hung a hundred times for what he did to my parents and the Marquis de Kersalaun!'

'And you think that all you have to do is simply accuse him, just like that, to have him arrested? It requires an inquiry, a procedure. You should know this better than I.'

'But we have witnesses!'

'François Loutre? He is dead. Who else is there? The convicts you interrogated? And suppose they agreed to talk, which I doubt given what you have told me, what value would be placed on their statements?'

'Fantig de Kersalaun. She saw Flaharn. She would recognise him.'

'Yes, if she did not suffer the same fate as François Loutre beforehand.'

'But we have the *penn-baz* that I found at the inn. That is proof!'

'A half-burned piece of wood? And who could prove that it belonged to Flaharn if nobody wants to believe you?'

'The niece of the innkeeper. She was showing me Flaharn's room when I found it.'

'She will really thank you for that! You scarcely know her and you drag her to a courtroom. Not to mention that you will be putting her life in danger too.'

This was the most telling argument. I tried to persist with my idea, but with less conviction.

'What would be the risks? If I denounce Flaharn he will be put in jail while the inquiry is made.'

'And the Comte d'Estaing. What will you do about him?'

'He has nothing to do with this!'

'You told me yourself that the document given to the rector of Hanvec carried the Comte's signature…'

'Exactly! It was dated 18th January. It is evidence of a forged signature, as Lieutenant de Clesmeur told you himself that the Comte was no longer in Brest by then.'

'I grant you that, but Lieutenant de Clesmeur also said quite clearly that the Comte d'Estaing cannot do without Flaharn. You think that the Comte is going to allow you to deprive him of his assistant, when everything seems to indicate that we will soon be at war?'

'But what are we going to do then?'

'You told me that you had an uncle well placed in the Ministry of War. If you trust him, perhaps you could ask him for advice?'

*

I wrote to the Chevalier de Kermean. His job allowed me to use the postal system of the Navy Command. This mail was relatively secure but I would have preferred to speak to my uncle in person. However

I took the risk of explaining to him that reliable information indicated that Flaharn had secretly had the Marquis de Kersalaun locked up in the Brest jail, that he had made forged certificates which compromised the Comte d'Estaing without his knowledge, that there were strong reasons for believing he was behind the violence of which my mother had been a victim at Port-Louis and, finally, that he had killed the Comte de Boulainvilliers' huntsman in order to stop him talking to me. I made a summary of the François Loutre business, telling him that I would be interviewed by the authorities once the inquiry into this case had been opened. I told my uncle that I would very much have liked to denounce Flaharn, but I was afraid of not having solid enough proof to back up my convictions. I asked him whether he thought I ought to take the risk. I told him too that Flaharn did not know that I had in fact managed to meet with François Loutre before his murder, and that the Ship's Captain had suggested that I serve under him once I became a Marine Guard. I gave no hint of the possibility of a treasure but said all the same that Flaharn was very keen to have me at his side. That was perhaps because he thought I held information about the hiding place of an object of great value. I said that I did not know what this object was, but that it may have been entrusted to the safekeeping of my parents by the late Marquis de Kersalaun. I repeated the hints made by Flaharn of plans for a secret operation in the Channel and added that if I did not denounce him immediately, because of insufficient proof, I would perhaps be interested in accepting his proposition. This might enable me to uncover the proofs I was lacking. I also reiterated, without giving his name, the information given by Lieutenant de Clesmeur concerning Flaharn's role alongside the Comte d'Estaing.

The Chevalier's reply came back quickly. My uncle strongly advised me not to try to denounce Captain Flaharn if I had neither sufficient proof nor irrefutable witnesses. If that were the case, then at worst, the Captain would not be in the least troubled and everyone would turn against me; or, at best, he would be put on his guard, would have plenty of time to react, and I would have no chance of finding out what happened to my mother.

As regards Captain Flaharn, the Chevalier gave me some additional information, uncovered by his clerks in the archives kept at the former headquarters of the India Company in Paris. David Flaharn was born in 1729 at Auray, where his parents kept an inn at the port. He had left the family home at the age of ten to sign on as a cabin boy on an India Company ship at L'Orient. After his first voyage, during which his precocious intelligence had been noticed, he was taken on again by the Company as an apprentice officer. He attended a school of navigation and was awarded his ticket as a Captain of the India Company in 1752. Remarkably intelligent, self-taught, of great physical courage, an excellent seaman with an iron constitution, he had no scruples whatsoever. He was criticised for being violent towards his seamen and there were frequent involvements with women, all the more embarrassing as they usually concerned the wives of his comrades or superior officers. That in itself would not have stopped him being given command of a ship, had he not been guilty of the worst crime in the eyes of the Company: making too much money on the side. If the Seven Years' War had not broken out, he probably would have been dismissed from the Company before he was recruited by the Comte d'Estaing for his privateering expedition.

> *...We don't know much about this famous privateering expedition apart from what the Comte d'Estaing himself has said. And we would like to know more.*
>
> *When the Comte's fleet returned to the Île-de-France in 1760, the Governor-General of the India Company, then Governor of the Île-de-France, ordered the Fire Ship's Captain Flaharn to join the officers aboard a supply ship loaded with food for the Pondicherry garrison, to which the English were preparing to lay siege. After that we lost track of him. He did not reappear until December 1772 at the port of L'Orient. He came ashore as a passenger on the last ship of the Company to come from Chandernagore, accompanied by this Indian you call 'Master Jack'. He was immediately called to Brest by the Comte d'Estaing. In relation to this, we greatly appreciated the information on the role of Captain Flaharn alongside the Comte. We do not doubt, of course, that he was of outstanding service to him during this privateering expedition, but the insistence with which the Comte d'Estaing pushed for the promotion of an individual with such a doubtful past was a puzzle to us.*

The Chevalier's reply to my question as to whether it would be opportune for me to join Flaharn's ship was not very clear.

...the allusions made by your Ship's Captain to 'secret' operations in the Channel leave us very doubtful, as this is an area over which we have complete control. We have searched in vain and found no trace of any such activity on the part of the subject. The Comte d'Estaing, whom we discreetly asked about this, confirmed that he had given no orders in this regard. And we well believe it, since the Comte has just managed to have himself named 'Vice-Admiral of the Seas of Asia and America'. In my opinion, this over-blown title is going to upset a few people in the Navy! But in any case, it shows that the preoccupations of our new Vice-Admiral are focussed elsewhere than the Channel.

Additionally, with the agreement of the Comte, who has no need of his seaman for the time being, we have given the subject something to play with in the Channel. This will enable us to keep an eye on him more efficiently.

As for his proposal as regards yourself, do not worry about it. Work quietly for your examination. If, which I don't doubt for a second, you pass, I will know straight away as the list of the fortunate ones comes here for the King's signature. I will then send you, in the same mail that will bring news of your success to Brest, a letter telling you the best course of action...

*

The inquiry into the death of François Loutre lasted until the end of March. As was predicted by the Landerneau sergeant, the case was transferred to the Admiralty and filed for the time being. At my request, Vernon des Aulnes, like me, said nothing about the suspicions we had about Captain Flaharn regarding this matter.

It was confirmed to us that the Comte d'Artois[23] would be making an official visit of the western ports in May. Monsieur Bézout would accompany him and examine in his presence the Cadet Guards at Brest and Rochefort. As for the Toulon Cadets, they would be examined the following month in the presence of the King's other brother[24],

---

23 Translator's note: *Comte d'Artois*: younger brother of Louis XVI and the future King Charles X.

24 Translator's note: *the King's other brother*: the Comte de Provence and the future King Louis XVIII

who was visiting the Mediterranean ports in June and July. We had less than three months to prepare ourselves. Several of our comrades decided to wait until 1778 to present themselves for examination. For myself, I could not bear the thought of spending another year shut up in a classroom without going to sea when a war was perhaps about to start. My friend Vernon shared my view. We spent all the weeks of this period working arduously. There was no question of going hunting at hounds, and in any case the Comte de Boulainvilliers had not yet found another huntsman to replace the unfortunate François Loutre. He was sometimes happy to come shooting with us on Sundays. This enabled us to keep up with what was going on outside the classroom. To tell the truth, there was not much new except that it was said that the Navy had employed additional bakers to prepare huge quantities of hard tack. Were it not for the continuing intense activity at the shipyards, where every week saw work start on a new ship, one would have thought that the rumours of war which were circulating at the end of the previous year were without any real foundation. The Comte du Chaffault, who was now sixty-nine years old and had served in the Navy for fifty years, had solicited and been appointed to the rank of Lieutenant-General of Naval Forces and had been put in command of the Brest Squadron. The rumours which had been running around about a mission to the Antilles had not materialised. For the moment there were only six ships of the line and four frigates in the harbour. All the other vessels of the squadron had remained in the Penfeld. The morale of the officers was feeling the effects of this, according to the Comte de Boulainvilliers, and requests for leave were on the increase.

The end of winter approached. Once again there were pleasant days. The date of our examination grew closer. When my head was reeling from so much time at my *Bézout* and exercise books, I would take a box of paper and pencils and install myself on the rampart walls running beside the Dajot Promenade or, more often, downstream of the mast crane. Amongst our activities at the Hôtel Saint-Pierre we had drawing classes, which I immediately fell in love with. I had first made sketches of the different types of craft passing through the entrance to the Penfeld: barques, bugalets, brigs, sloops, coasters and of course the King's ships. At first I was only interested in copying their shapes and rigs as faithfully as possible. Then I wanted to reproduce their manoeuvres and had started to sketch in the backgrounds against which my boats were moving: the Horseshoe, the entrance to the harbour, the light towards the outer passage, the beautiful façades of the Navy warehouses and houses on the Recouvrance quayside, where I was not allowed to go thanks to Lieutenant de Lestourières. After a while I wanted to add some colour to my drawings and had started to enhance them with gouache.

Maria Kirwan had taken to watching out for me passing in front of *La Dame au Paon* so that she could come and join me. She sat beside me and talked to me, watching me draw and mix my colours…once she had let go of my hands. That is how I found out all about her.

Maria Kirwan's mother was the daughter of a Brest man who became a clerk for the India Company. Born in India, she had got to know Captain Kirwan, of the Lally-Irish regiment, when he had arrived at Pondicherry in 1758 with Lally-Tollendal. They were married in 1759. Captain Kirwan was killed during the siege of Pondicherry, not long before its surrender. Maria was born in June 1761 at Port-Louis on the Île-de-France, whence her mother had been evacuated in January. Maria had never seen her father, not even in a portrait. Nor did she know her maternal grandparents who also perished during the siege. The siege of Pondicherry had been especially hard for the French population. Famine and shortages were added to the diseases and stresses of a climate which was difficult enough for Europeans even in normal times. After Maria's birth her mother had brought her back to France to live with one of her uncles, a Brest innkeeper. For a while she had thought of trying to find some of the former comrades-in-arms of her dead husband, to try to track down her in-laws and also to claim a widow's pension. All that she could discover was that the survivors of the Lally regiment had been incorporated, after the war, into the de Dillon regiment. But she died before being able to take her search any further. That year there had been great shortages followed by epidemics throughout most of Brittany.

As for me, I told her a little about what I knew of my father, and everything I knew about my Laforest-Dombourg grandparents: nothing, or almost nothing! I mentioned the death of my mother without going into the details.

Maria Kirwan had found that our respective stories had points in common: our fathers had both died in the service of the King, our grandparents had likewise been killed by the English during the previous war, at Louisbourg and Pondicherry, India had turned our parents' lives upside down, and we had both been born in a place called Port-Louis.

Maria Kirwan had a pleasant disposition. She talked about weighty subjects without taking herself too seriously and always maintained her smile. She knew how to joke and make light of anything, bursting out in peals of laughter, which I loved. The trials she had had to face at a young age had without doubt taught her to remain strong in adversity and to face up to bad fortune with a good heart. She did not seem to be particularly fierce, but I always felt a little restrained in her presence. I thought that I was in love for the first time in my life and was intimidated by her. I no longer went to the *Dames de la Marine.*

At the end of March, a Monday, towards four in the afternoon, we assembled ourselves on the shipyard quay opposite the Pontaniou dry docks to watch the launch of *la Bretagne*. There were crowds on both sides of the Penfeld to witness this exceptional event. The dock gates had been opened and the big three-decker was floating already but, as soon as they tried to tow her out, she remained stuck in the lock. In something of a panic, they tried to haul her back into the dock. Several tow lines parted during this unforeseen operation. Fortunately, they managed to dislodge the ship and return her to the dry dock. If she had stayed where she was, she would most likely have broken her back on the falling tide. They then had to wait for the spring tides at the beginning of April. She was eventually launched on 7th April, in the early afternoon and moored at the checking quay before having her masts put in.

There were already thirteen ships in the harbour: six of seventy-four guns, one of seventy and the others all sixty-fours. They had not yet finished their fitting out, but the Comte du Chaffault had ordered the commanders to take their powder on board so that they could immediately start training their gun crews in the use of the cannons. The gunners repeated the loading and aiming procedures over and over and, to end the day, they fired at targets towed along outside the lines of ships moored at their coffin buoys. Each evening the ships were quickly surrounded in thick grey smoke and the deafening echoes of the salvos rolled around the harbour and into our classrooms, sharpening our enthusiasm.

At morning muster, we were read a letter from Monsieur de Sartine.

The Minister for War forbade any Navy officers from entering the service of the American colonies. I have to say that this was completely unnecessary as far as we were concerned. Unlike our comrades in the Army, we were sure that we would be offered honourable posts in the front line, and none of us wanted to leave.

At the end of April, I received a letter from Captain Flaharn. He told me that the Navy Ministry had agreed to give him command of a cutter, *le Moucheron*[25], at Saint-Malo. Once I had been examined by Monsieur Bézout, he would have an order sent to Brest for me to join this ship in July, at the same time as I was promoted to Marine Guard. The Captain explained that he would be in charge of the operations of this ship in the Channel. And he added, no doubt to make the proposition more attractive to me, that his second-in-command would be the Fire Ship's Captain Le Meur, who had served with my father during the previous war.

Cutters were small craft with a single mast rigged with a huge gaff mainsail, some square sails for running before the wind and a long bowsprit on which several jibs could be set. They could also deploy galley sweeps from each side in calm weather. At that time the Navy had very few of them. They had for the most part been copied from the English sloops of war currently used by the English coast guard. They themselves had taken inspiration from the Bermudan sloops in the West Indian colonies. The Navy had had three cutters built in 1771, each one by a different yard: one at Bordeaux, one at Saint-Malo and one at Dunkirk. *Le Moucheron* had been launched at Saint-Malo to a design by the architect Groignard, who was also responsible for *la Bretagne*. The three cutters had been trialled together with the 1772 training squadron. None of them was perfect, far from it, but *le Moucheron* could not have been too bad, as she was taken with the 1775 training squadron, under de Guichen, and the 1776 squadron under the Comte du Chaffault. She was therefore well known at Brest, which is how I was able to find out about her. After six years of constant sea service, and having been damaged several times, she had been sent back to Saint-Malo for a total refit. From what people were able to tell me about her, it appeared that *le Moucheron* carried six small 3-pound cannons, she was clinker-built in the English style, about fifty feet long with a low freeboard, a

25 Translator's note: *le Moucheron:* the Gnat.

deep draught for her size, no tumblehome, and reputedly went well to windward. I was told that she sailed with a pronounced heel, often dipping her cannons into the sea. No matter! I considered it a most unusual craft in which to start my Naval career. Moreover, during her two campaigns she had been under the command of young Ensigns. I was surprised that an experienced Ship's Captain like Flaharn should be appointed to such a modest command, and was happy indeed that my uncle was going to guide me with his advice.

The frigate *la Belle Poule* took a coffin buoy in Brest harbour on 7th May. She had made her landfall seven days earlier, at L'Orient, after a four-month voyage from the Indian Ocean. This fine ship was bringing back the Chevalier de Ternay and the Comte de Lapérouse from the Île-de-France. But at that time I was so immersed in my studies that I did not find out about it until the Saturday, the 10th, by which time these two officers had already left for Nantes and Paris. I saw *la Belle Poule* up close when her officers brought her into the Penfeld to deliver her to the King. I admired her lines immensely, finding her very elegant. She had the reputation of sailing as well to windward as off the wind and of overtaking any ship on the same course carrying the same sail. She had already proved this when arriving back in France. When she was four hundred miles west of Belle-Île she had fallen in with an English sixty-gun ship which had changed course and chased her for twenty-nine hours, by which time the English ship was twelve miles astern.

The date of our examination was quickly approaching. The Comte d'Artois arrived in Brest on May 14th. He was dragging behind him a noisy and lively escort of courtiers, most of whose names I have forgotten. These gentlemen were followed by a crowd of lackeys, valets and secretaries who were arguing over who should have the rooms still available in the town. The innkeepers rubbed their hands, as the Comte d'Artois had a reputation for generosity. I don't believe they were the only ones feeling happy, as the Comte d'Orvilliers, the Navy Commander at Brest, received a bonus of twelve thousand pounds, and the Chief Administrator, Monsieur La Porte, was granted six thousand pounds.

Vernon and I were examined by Monsieur Bézout on Friday 16th May. We had the honour of presenting ourselves to the Comte d'Artois, who was presiding over our examination. He was then twenty years old and already a very handsome man. The courtiers said of him that he was the only one of the princes who really resembled his grandfather, with the same looks, charm and politeness. He certainly had the same extravagance.

Monsieur Bézout surprised me greatly by his appearance. I had expected to meet a venerable, white-haired and severe-looking scholar. In fact he was forty-seven years old. I saw a slight man, with fine, distinguished features, unobtrusive, reserved but friendly and who looked with a benevolent air on the young men he was examining. I was lucky enough to answer all his questions correctly. My friend hesitated for a moment on a problem concerning the square of the hypotenuse, but to his credit he eventually got it right. Monsieur Bézout complimented us encouragingly, saying that it was most important that his students go to sea at an early stage and that it was necessary to get the balance right between this and the study of mathematics. The Comte d'Artois congratulated us warmly. All this gave us hope that we would both be part of the next group promoted to Marine Guard. And in fact, on Friday 20th June 1777, our senior officers received from Monsieur de Sartine the list of new Marine Guards, amongst whom were Vernon and I. The only change to our uniform was that henceforth our aiguillettes would be in gold. But things had changed radically. From now on we were members of the Grand Corps of ships' officers, with a salary of three hundred and fifty pounds. The Comte du Chaffault's squadron was now complete in the harbour. It was comprised of thirteen ships of the line, four frigates, two corvettes and two luggers. Almost all the Guards were to join it. It was still not known when the ships would put to sea. Their provisioning was not yet finished and they still had reduced crews, but for the time being the orders were to practise manoeuvres. Fortunately, the harbour was big enough to allow the ships to slip their buoys every day for training. This was better for the new Guards than staying in their classrooms at the Hôtel Saint-Pierre.

My friend wanted to ask the Chevalier de Lamotte-Picquet to accept him into his corps of officers. On the afternoon of 22nd June, towards three in the afternoon, we went together to visit this Ship's Captain. He received us most graciously in the stateroom of his ship, *le Robuste*, a seventy-four. The Chevalier de Lamotte-Picquet was just under fifty-seven years old. At that time he was already admired and well-known throughout the King's Navy for his leadership qualities and his skill in ship handling.

The Chevalier de Lamotte-Picquet was as small as my friend Vernon. He was very thin and his ugliness was legendary throughout the Navy. He had an angular and bony nose, a protruding chin and prominent cheekbones. One cheek had been slashed by grapeshot during the War of the Austrian Succession, which did not help matters. He wore a wig which was too small and which he always seemed to place askew to cover his bald patch; but he was always on the go and his eyes shone the whole time with a remarkable intensity. He was very witty, and alive in every sense, as ready to compliment as to get angry. His rages were famous, but he was forgiven them as they were short-lived and he was the first to admit it when he was in the wrong. However, according to the many testimonies of those who had served under him in the previous war, he was always remarkably calm in battle. Perhaps because he was afraid of nothing, bravery was to him simple and natural. During the Seven Years' War, when he was commanding a corvette, he had been attacked by an English frigate of thirty-six cannons. He had stood up to it aggressively, without getting in the least flustered, for an hour, at which point the enemy frigate, fed up with the whole business, broke combat and went off in search of other prizes. He was one of those leaders who always had authority without ever being authoritarian, and could show limitless energy when required, without taking himself too seriously. If patience was not his best quality, he was always friendly, even when receiving two young Marine Guards like us who knew nothing of the language of the sea. Aboard his ships the Marine Guards ate at the Captain's table, whereas the usual rule was for them to be fed from a mess tin.

I would very much have liked to have embarked, like Vernon, under the command of a leader like the Chevalier de Lamotte-Picquet, but I was already committed elsewhere as a result of acting too precipitately. I had been called to see the Chevalier de Monteil towards the end of Saturday morning. He had received instructions regarding me from the Ministry and also gave me a packet from my uncle. As he had promised, the Chevalier de Kermean had sent his instructions in the same mail which had brought notice of our promotions. He confirmed my embarkation aboard *le Moucheron* for the last week of July, sent me a leave pass signed by the Minister, allowing me to go home in the meantime, and arranged to meet with me at Kermean at the end of the month. He would give me my embarkation order at the same time as my official Marine Guard certificate which he himself would fetch from the Court before leaving for Kermean.

> *...Captain Flaharn was very keen to have you with him. It seems that it was purely with this in mind that he came up with his plan for operations in the Channel. This plan particularly attracted our attention and we have used his interest in you to get it launched. But we have subsequently managed to take advantage of certain favourable circumstances to have Captain Flaharn moved aside from it. It would have been much too dangerous to have left you at his mercy. Henceforth you must avoid him totally. But do not worry, we are following him closely and having him watched secretly. He is on his guard, but I think that eventually we will catch him out. However, we must have patience. In fact, if war finally breaks out, which all of us here think will be the case, Flaharn will have to be with the Comte d'Estaing. So forget him for the moment and trust me. I will tell you more when we see each other at Kermean.*

'You seem to have connections at the Ministry,' said my commanding officer. 'I am happy for you, since it has enabled you to escape from Captain Flaharn.'

The Chevalier de Monteil was not a bad old stick. I knew that his rather strong reaction to the duelling business had more to do with his personal situation within the Naval hierarchy than any kind of animosity towards me. On the contrary, he was very much on my side. He had also welcomed me with great friendliness when I arrived at Brest, despite my contrived certificate of nobility. He knew a little about my father's past and his conduct at the Battle of Quiberon Bay.

The interview over, I ran to *La Dame au Paon* to see if there was a coaster going down to the Guérande area. I was lucky enough to find the skipper of a lugger from Le Pouliguen who was unloading barrels of wine from Le Croisic on the quay in front of the inn. He was expecting to return to Le Croisic with a cargo of Olonne sailcloth, which he would be taking on board at Poul David at the end of Douarnenez Bay. He was happy to take me as a passenger and said he would be leaving the Penfeld the following Sunday at six in the evening and expected to arrive at Le Croisic on the Thursday evening. I did not bother to write to warn of my arrival. The skipper had said we would have good weather for the week. I might well arrive before my letter, but if the skipper was mistaken and we were held up by bad weather, it would serve no purpose to worry my family by making a precise rendezvous that I could not keep. I had my sea chest taken aboard the lugger before going with Vernon aboard *le Robuste.* I paid our innkeeper and doubted I would ever return to the Company of Guards. All that was left was to say goodbye to Maria Kirwan.

The ship's boat which brought us back from the Chevalier de Lamotte-Picquet's ship put us ashore on the quayside in front of *La Dame au Paon*, just beside my lugger. Maria Kirwan was waiting on the quay. When I reached her, she took both my hands in hers and held them tightly, her eyes fixed on mine. Looking into the depths of those green eyes, I suddenly regretted that I was leaving Brest. I promised that I would not forget her. She took off the black satin ribbon that was around her neck and gave it to me.

The lugger slid gently into the current of the Penfeld. Vernon and Maria Kirwan kept up with us, walking along to the end of the Mast Crane quay. My last image was of the slim figure of Maria Kirwan, tiny beneath the ramparts of the Chateau. Our boat passed beyond the Rose battery, leaving me with nothing but memories and a ribbon.

PART TWO

THE DEVIL MAY DIE

1

In the Brest Narrows, Sunday 22nd June 1777, six o'clock in the evening.

Maria Kirwan's ribbon still holds her scent. I take it in both my hands and press it to my nose, holding it for a long moment against my face. I feel I have missed an opportunity, but it is too late to turn back the clock. In any case, I am not one to stay sad for long and am happy to feel a boat moving under my feet again, even if just as a passenger. I put the token in a pocket of my jacket, close to my heart, and give myself up to the strong salt smell of the sea.

*

Having weathered Porzic Point, our boat turned to the west-south-west, with the wind on the starboard beam and a single reef in. We were going directly through the northerly pass of the harbour entrance. For me, it was the door to the ocean, the door to freedom. I felt as if I were leaving a prison. The Cadets did not go to sea, confined as they were to their classrooms in the Hotel Saint-Pierre; this was the price of entry into the Navy. I had been confined too to the east side of the River Penfeld, which stopped me from going near the harbour coastline and the open sea. I would not for anything have taken the overland route.

Coming out of the entrance, the lugger stayed on the same tack, hard on the wind for a while, towards the setting sun and well heeled to port; then she went about to come up to the Bertheaume inlet. Our lugger anchored in clear, sheltered water, in twelve fathoms, our bowsprit pointing to the cliffs along the shore, with the dark mass of the Bertheaume fort to port.

We weighed anchor at eight the next morning. The weather was clear; the bright blue sky reflected in the white-capped waves stretching as far as the eye could see. It was blowing from the north-west, just as the evening before. The skipper had another reef put in and goose-winged the sails. The lugger leapt forward. The skipper pointed his arm to the open sea to show me the sails of a ship sailing a course parallel to ours. I pulled out my telescope to get a closer view: a frigate, t'gallants furled, its lower sails and reefed topsails braced square, leaving a great white wake astern. From the mainmast streamed what seemed to be a blue pennant, and her stern flag was blue too, quartered by a Union Jack. I passed the glass to the skipper.

'An English war frigate! She's moving! On that heading she'll pass to the west of the Porquette in the Race. They just do as they like, these cursed Saxons! They better make the most of it – it ain't going to last much longer.' He spat his tobacco quid into the sea.

The blue water slid in a boiling mass along the lugger's sides, the bow buried itself under the pressure of the wind.

It was the start of the sardine season and we saw lots of fishing boats as we entered Douarnenez Bay. The English frigate was no longer in sight. She must have tacked to take up her station again at the mouth of the harbour entrance. Even in peacetime we were under constant surveillance.

Our lugger left Poul-David at six-thirty on Wednesday morning, just after high water. The weather was still the same as the previous evening: a clear sky with a few round clouds and a strong north-westerly, pushing us on from astern at a hellish rate. As the sun went down, I recognised ahead the coppery-gold face of the cliffs that lie at the starboard side of the entrance to the Vilaine. The skipper decided to anchor in Penerf bay for the night. We were out of the swell, but the north-west wind, still as strong, was howling through the rigging and we were forced to lay a second anchor. We were alongside Le Croisic quay by seven o'clock of the next morning, right at the top of the tide, a day ahead of schedule.

It was good to be ashore in the sunshine, sheltered from the squally wind. I had my chest carried to the house of my grandfather's Le Croisic steward. I asked him to have my baggage taken by mule to Kermean and had a rowboat drop me off on the other side of the entrance to the port, so that I could walk to Kermean alone.

I arrived just in time for lunch. My uncle was just ahead of me, having arrived the evening before. It was moving to be back in the little world of Kermean, with its masters and servants. I felt as if I had been away for an eternity, although I had only been absent for ten months and little had changed since I had left.

Mélanie laid an extra place for me, and so the four of us, my grandfather, my uncle, my little sister and I, found ourselves once more together around the big table in the barons' room. The south-facing doors and windows were open and the bright light from outside lit up the big alcoves between the austere ancestral portraits hung on the walls.

The Baron de Kermean asked me how my stay in Brest had been. I did not quite know how to answer. With my little sister there I did not want to talk about the horrors I had witnessed during the prison fire. Nor did I mention my dealings with the prisoners; my grandfather would not have approved. Clearly, I could not talk about the *Dames de la Marine*. I brought up the subject of the increasing activity at the shipyard, without passing any comment on it. I said that I had learned to draw and to paint, that I had brought in my chest several scenes of the port of Brest. That allowed me to mention my meetings with Maria Kirwan, without arousing more interest than I would have wanted, except in little Anne, who would ask me about her later. The Chevalier and the Baron listened attentively to my story about the duel. I mentioned the name of Captain Flaharn, with my eyes on my uncle, who said that we would talk about it together after lunch. I talked at length about my friend the Chevalier des Aulnes. Little Anne's interest was piqued and she asked lots of questions about him. I finished by describing my examination in the presence of the Comte d'Artois and expressed my admiration for the prince's good looks.

'It is true that he has real presence,' said my uncle, 'but he should try not to keep his mouth open, as it spoils his face a little.'

I replied that I had not noticed.

'My word! You would have made a good courtier!' laughed my grandfather. Then he turned to the Chevalier de Kermean.

'Talking of courtiers, my son, we hardly saw each other last night. Give me the news from Court where, it seems, you pass most of your time.'

'Would you like me to talk about the Court itself or government matters?' asked the Chevalier.

'Well, let's begin with the government. And, first of all, what about these mad rumours I heard at Nantes, where this Dr Franklin, wearing a beaver hat, was so well received at the beginning of December? They say he is the representative of the Bostonians, or the Insurgents, as they are also called. Are we really going to declare war on the English simply to help the northern colonies of America in their revolt against the Crown?'

'Sadly, father, the question is not as simple as it appears. If Louis XVI were able, he would prefer to avoid a new war, obviously. So he would not help the Insurgents. But he has no choice. The King would prefer to avoid a war, of that I am certain. Our sea trade and fishing are only just starting to get going again, and a new conflict would ruin our coastal population once again. Moreover, the King knows that the State lacks sufficient financial resources to take on such a risky venture.'

'Is the treasury as empty as that? What are the figures?'

'I don't know. I've heard it said not just that the State treasury is empty, but that nobody is able to put a number on the exact level of State debt. The deficit has reached incomprehensible proportions.'

'Well then! Why go to war?'

'Because it seems to us to be inevitable since Viscount Weymouth replaced Count Rochford in directing English policy towards us and their American colonies. All our information suggests that the English seriously intend to take on our sea trade and our last overseas possessions. The English want a maritime war against France, and they'll take advantage of the first pretext. Moreover, we are not yet ready to take them on.'

'Which is to say?' asked the Baron de Kermean, somewhat surprised.

'I know my figures in this area, at least. When Louis XV died, we still had forty-three ships of the line and thirty-four frigates and corvettes. But not one of those ships was ready to put to sea! The shipyard warehouses were empty, and the suppliers had not been paid for nearly four years.'

'And the English?'

'At that time, according to our agents in London, they would have been able to line up eighty ships and over a hundred and seventy frigates and corvettes in a very short time. But, since the King has taken control of things, we will soon have fifty-one ships and fifty-three frigates to go against them. And if the Spanish joined us, the advantage would swing to us.'

'Where do the American rebels fit into all of this?'

'Well, according to the intelligence officers that we sent over there, we know that some of them would be ready to make peace with the English, in order to attack us together. The French are the traditional enemy of the English colonies in America. There's still a lot of resistance to anything French. Fortunately for us, the English Cabinet and Lord Weymouth have little desire for a reconciliation at the moment. That's why the King has decided, as of now, to help the Americans. But we have to act in secret in order not to precipitate a war, given that we've not yet finished re-establishing our forces. If London were to discover too early that we are playing a double game...well, they would begin hostilities before we're ready.'

'Be sure not to say anything if it is secret,' said the Baron.

'Ha! What I am able to tell you is unfortunately becoming more of an open secret every day. The King has decided to help the rebels by giving them arms and ammunition. In order to keep this hidden, he himself suggested using private shipowners. The person who has been engaged for this mission is not really a shipowner. He's a man called Caron de Beaumarchais...and quite a character. Having displayed extraordinary talent in clockmaking, he became harp teacher to the daughters of Louis XV, then lieutenant-general overseeing the King's hunting estates. He also showed a talent for secret diplomacy during the reign of Louis XV. Finally, he has also written some successful plays[26]. It was Monsieur de Sartine who had suggested him to the King's Council as an enterprising man whose services he had appreciated during several delicate missions when Monsieur de Sartine was himself head of the Paris police.'

'And this is the man on whom you have placed the management of your secret operation with the Insurgents?' exclaimed the Baron.

---

26 *The Barber of Seville* had already had a successful premier at the National Theatre on 23rd February 1775.

'With good reason. The man is a formidably smooth talker.'

'If I understand you correctly, our ministers are giving this Beaumarchais a free hand?'

'They hang on his every word. Luckily Louis XVI takes no account of all that. In this area, at least, it is he who decides. Just between us, it is a pity he is not so firm with his family...'

The Chevalier sighed and shrugged his shoulders.

'The King's Council allocated two million pounds to Beaumarchais, for him to establish a trading company in his name and load ships to carry merchandise to the Americans. By June of last year, he had already founded a shipping company that he called *Rodrigue Hortalez & Co*. The first sailing was scheduled for last December from Le Havre. Beaumarchais had prepared five ships there which were being loaded with arms and military supplies. They were also going to embark engineers and artillerymen. The English ambassador to Paris, Lord Stormont, got wind of what was going on and sent a threatening letter of protest. The government was obliged to disavow the expedition publicly and on the face of it had the cargoes unloaded. Since then, Beaumarchais has sent several other ships from different ports, this time more discreetly.'

'These rebels are well-established at Versailles?' asked the Baron.

'Not really as yet, but there is now a permanent American delegation in Paris. During the summer of 1776 they sent their first emissary, a man called Silas Deane. And, since last winter, we have the good Doctor Franklin, who has also brought over his London representative, a very active lawyer called Arthur Lee. He's been laying siege to Beaumarchais for months to try to get him to speed up our commitment. Beaumarchais keeps flooding us with memos, castigating us for our lack of action and calling on us in every way to go to war immediately and to pronounce it publicly. But Louis XVI is holding firm. The only concession he has made is to order our vessels to give the protection of the French flag to any American ships which ask for it.'

My chest arrived just at that moment.

It was still fine outside, and the wind had fallen. I had my chest opened on the terrace and pulled out my sketches and gouaches of the Port of Brest. Little Anne was completely taken by my pictures, brushes and paints. I promised to show her how to draw and paint. The Baron examined the different types of ships I had drawn with great interest. He knew absolutely nothing about the sea. As incredible as it may seem for a man who lived so close to a port and who sent off at least part of his salt production by sea, he had never set foot on a boat. As for my uncle, he was more interested in the details of my sketches of the Horseshoe and quays at the entrance to the Penfeld. To be honest he had no interest in their artistic merit. What interested him was their precision. He had already studied drawings of ports and coastlines on Ministerial maps. He questioned me to try and find out how true to life my sketches were. He encouraged me to develop this gift and told me that I would certainly have an opportunity to put it to good use once I was aboard *le Moucheron*. He seemed in a hurry to have a talk with me, and I too was keen to hear him, but little Anne wanted to start learning to draw and make gouaches straight away. The Chevalier felt a little guilty in her regard and we put off our conversation until later. The servants laid out a table outside, with goblets of water and plates for my paints, and my little sister decided that we would make a picture of the blossoms on a rose bush bordering the terrace.

That evening, after supper, my uncle gave me my certificates as a Marine Guard, my order for joining the cutter *le Moucheron* at Saint-Malo in mid-July, and a letter of recommendation from the Chevalier de Fleurieu for the Fireship Captain Le Meur, my future commanding officer. He also gave me a sealed letter addressed to a certain Louis Duval, rue de la Diacrerie, Saint-Malo. He said it was from Captain Flaharn. I showed some surprise, and he told me to pack all these documents into my chest while he waited on the terrace for us to take a walk in the garden.

*

Kermean, Thursday 26th June 1777, evening.

The ornamental garden is situated on the south side of the manor house. Its main path, bordered by shrubs and roses, goes off at right angles to the terrace under the windows of the barons' room. I tell my uncle in detail about all the things I have tried to summarise in my letters: the Marquis de Kersalaun, Flaharn...The Chevalier hears me out, waiting until I have finished before speaking.

'Is it really true, this story about treasure?'

'I don't know. I don't really know if it's a question of treasure, but what I am sure of is that Flaharn is searching for something, and that he hasn't hesitated in killing for it. I think that he is responsible for the death of my mother. On the other hand, he has taken me under his wing and wants me to be near him. I have no legal proof, in that sense, but I'm sure of what I am saying.'

'I believe you. And I have been able to verify that he is trying everything possible to get you close to him. That is why it is out of the question to let you return to his side. The man is too dangerous. As I told you in my letters, allegations about his activities in the Channel have attracted our attention. With the agreement of the Comte d'Estaing, we decided to ask him to a meeting to try to find out more. At our request, the Comte ordered him to meet with the Chevalier de la Rozière, currently in command of garrison at Saint-Malo, and whom we had asked to come to Versailles for this reason. I did not want to see Flaharn myself, because of you. He is not necessarily aware of our family link, but one never knows. The Chevalier de la Rozière earned a considerable reputation for bravery during the last war. He's two years older than me. We served together in Germany, at Cassel, and were awarded the Cross of Saint Louis on the same day. During the peace, in '65, he was sent on a secret mission to England. He was there to make topographical surveys and study the landscape should there be an invasion of England. De la Rozière did a remarkable job, and in recognition of his skills, he now commands the Saint-Malo garrison.'

We arrive at the end of the garden. The pathway stops there, in front of a narrow stone culvert over which one can cross a ditch filled with water covered in lilies. On the other side the moorland stretches to the coast. My uncle rests his elbows on the ivy-covered parapet of the little bridge.

'Flaharn told the Chevalier de la Rozière that he knew someone at Saint-Malo through whom he could recruit some agents well placed to spy on the English Navy in the Channel. At the same time, he wanted to be given a small, fast ship that would allow him to make the most of the intelligence network that he maintained he could set up very quickly. He asked for a small frigate. He didn't want to say straight away what he would do with it, or to give the identity of his contact, but from the start he asked for you. I, along with the Comte de Broglie and the Chevalier de la Rozière, studied his proposition. We liked it a lot. But the problem was you!'

'Me?'

'Yes, indeed! We thought that Flaharn had come up with an interesting project, but you had convinced me from the start that it was no more than a pretext to get hold of you. Our intention was therefore to use you as bait and pull him out of the business as soon as he had told us enough for us to do without him. But this was easier said than done. The man is very cunning. We consulted the Chevalier de Fleurieu, who gave us an idea. He explained that a small cutter was the ideal craft for what we wanted to do. It is the sort of vessel much used by the English and would attract less attention than a lugger, for example. A cutter has yet another advantage: it is too small to be commanded directly by a Ship's Captain. It happened that a cutter that met our criteria had just gone in for a re-fit at Saint-Malo. Moreover, her name was preordained: *le Moucheron!*[27] We shared this with Flaharn and gently prepared to tell him that he could not really command such a small vessel. Unfortunately, rather than discouraging him, this seemed to please him enormously. It was just then that we found out that the Comte d'Estaing had refused to release him to command a frigate, as he was afraid of not being able to get him back quickly enough should there be war. A cutter, on the other hand, presented no problem.'

'Flaharn wrote to me, in fact, to tell me that he was going to have *le Moucheron*.'

'Imagine our predicament! Luckily, towards the end of May, the Comte d'Estaing let us know somewhat brusquely that he had changed his mind. He wanted Flaharn back. And wanted him immediately! Flaharn came in person to tell us that the Comte had ordered him to write a memorandum for an expedition to India. And do you know what? He asked to have you with him, saying that he well knew about India, but that he had some difficulties in actually writing. He said he needed an assistant in whom he had complete confidence in order to help him write his memorandum. In short, he wanted you as his secretary! We told him in reply that your commission for *le Moucheron*

27 Translator's note: *le Moucheron:* a reference to the fact that the French word for a 'mole', in the espionage sense, is '*une mouche*'. '*Moucheron*' is a derivative of '*mouche*', also meaning a fly, gnat or midge.

had already been signed, and that in any case the King had given strict instructions that all the Marine Guards be employed at sea, and that even the Comte d'Estaing could hardly justify sending a Marine Guard, newly qualified, to a Paris office. Flaharn had no choice but to reveal his plan and the name of his contact. But he insisted that it be you who goes to see his contact on his behalf. I think that he hoped by this not to lose contact with you completely. He also asked that you be commissioned to one of the ships of the future expedition to India, once it has been put together, and once you have finished your mission at Saint-Malo. This we accepted as a matter of form. However, I can assure you, that as soon as you have finished with *le Moucheron*, you can ask for a posting wherever you wish and the Ministry will back it, Flaharn or not.'

'So I am still embarking at Saint-Malo?' I said.

'More than ever! And still on *le Moucheron*. I still have a pile of instructions to give you, but first, let me explain this business about India and Flaharn. It should interest you.

'In May, Monsieur de Sartine was told that an envoy sent by a French mercenary in India called Madec, was at the door of his Ministry, complaining that he had been waiting ten days for an audience and that he had crossed the oceans purely for this. Monsieur de Sartine had him brought in immediately and found himself face to face with a Breton gentleman who presented himself as Monsieur Chapelain de Kerscao. This Kerscao said that he had sent him a memorandum and letters written by Madec. Kerscao had travelled with the Chevalier de Ternay aboard *la Belle Poule*, then by coach, still with him, as far as Versailles. Kerscao said that he had made the mistake of leaving with the Chevalier de Ternay all the documents entrusted to him by Madec. Each time he asked for any news about his request for an audience, the Chevalier de Ternay had told him to be patient. And to cap it all, when he had asked the Chevalier de Ternay to give him back Monsieur Madec's documents, he said that he had mislaid them! Kerscao told the Minister that he himself had to rewrite Madec's work, quickly and from memory, and presented him with a badly written and sometimes very confused text. Monsieur de Sartine showed some interest, and offered Monsieur Kerscao a sum of money to compensate him and calm him down. But he had not spent many years as Commissioner of the Police for nothing. He asked Kerscao if he had spoken to anyone else about his misfortune. Kerscao told him that he had been approached by a former lieutenant of Madec, who happened to be in Paris. Monsieur de Sartine had asked what this man's name was. The reply was…Flaharn! Monsieur de Sartine, whom we had already talked to discreetly about Flaharn, had immediately thought that he had there the explanation for the Comte d'Estaing's sudden interest in India. We immediately began to look for Kerscao, as we were afraid of missing him before his departure for the Île-de-France.'

My uncle goes silent. A servant is coming towards us on the path, holding a candlestick and trying to protect the flame with his left hand. Night is beginning to fall.

'It is getting late. I think I will give you your orders for Saint-Malo another time.'

'But uncle, this Kerscao. Did you meet him?'

'We did see him, indeed! I almost forgot: he also spoke to us about the Marquis de Kersalaun. Actually, it's as well that I talk to you about this as soon as possible. Let's go back inside. It's getting cold here.'

A few minutes later we are sitting at one end of the big table. The manor house is quiet. We are alone – everyone else has gone to bed.

'These India stories are terribly complicated. I was continually interrupting Kerscao to make him repeat what he said so that I could take notes. Kerscao had joined Madec's unit in October 1770. He could not have met Flaharn, as the latter had already left for Chandernagore to return to France, but he did hear Madec talk about him. When Kerscao arrived, Madec's men had their quarters at Dig. This is a fortified town, the capital of the Jat country. According to Kerscao, these Jats are a tribe of peasant warriors, installed in the River Jamna valley, between Delhi and Agra in the heart of Hindustan.'

'Did you say Jamna?' I ask. 'It seems I've heard that name before. But I'm sorry for interrupting. Please continue.'

My uncle takes up the story again.

'Madec and his troops had gone into the service of the Raja of Dig in '67, so well before the arrival of Kerscao. These 'Rajous', as Kerscao called them, are a kind of king in India. The Raja of Dig was called Javahir Singh. He already had in his service the troops of a German mercenary called Sombre. Flaharn was one of his commanders. In May '68, Javahir Singh was assassinated in shady circumstances. This Raja had no heirs and had named as his successor his nephew, who was just six months old. Javahir's brother took over the rule of the Jat lands, as his son's guardian. Eleven months later, the guardian was also assassinated. A general called Jakar Singh then proclaimed himself as the guardian of the boy, claiming that he had been designated by the victim. He took Flaharn as his principal adviser. According to Kerscao, it was Jakar and Flaharn who had organised the first two assassinations. For some reason, they became unpopular very quickly. So much so that after about nine months, two illegitimate half-brothers of the Regent were easily able to raise the country against Jakar and Flaharn, who found themselves besieged in the Dig fortress. They threatened to blow up the garrison's store of gunpowder and managed to negotiate their way out. They then took refuge at our Chandernagore trading post. This was in December '69. Kerscao could not tell us anything more. But there is a strong possibility that the infamous Master Jacques, Flaharn's associate, is this general Jakar Singh.'

'And where is the Marquis de Kersalaun in all of this?'

'According to Kerscao, Avelus de Kersalaun had been a personal friend of the previous Raja, called Suraj Mal, the adoptive father of Javahir Singh. Kersalaun became military adviser to Javahir Singh after the death of Suraj Mal, who had been killed in one of the little wars that scatter blood regularly in that part of India. After the assassination of Javahir, Kersalaun had fled with one of Javahir's daughters. Kerscao thinks that they went directly to our trading post at Chandernagore...'

I remember why I know the name *Jamna*. Fantig Le Goff has told me it was the Indian name of the Marquis's wife. So, Kersalaun and his companion have passed through Chandernagore, as well as Flaharn and Jakar Singh. And finally, Chandernagore was a regular destination of my father in India.

'Kersalaun...Flaharn...My father...' I say. 'Something important must have happened between them at Chandernagore. Did your Kerscao have anything to say about this?'

'If anything happened at Chandernagore, the man who would know all about it is Monsieur Chevalier. He has been our Governor there since 1753. Kerscao told us that when Flaharn came to see him recently in Paris, he said that he was on very good terms with Monsieur Chevalier. We were given to understand that our Governor had made a bad impression on Kerscao when he passed through Chandernagore in July '73, on his way to the Île-de-France. He thinks that Monsieur Chevalier is a pen-pusher. In any case, one thing is certain, and that is that Kerscao did not talk much with Monsieur Chevalier when he was at Chandernagore.'

*

I was keen to see the orders for my future sea service, but I had to wait for several more days. The marriage of the Chevalier had been arranged for Saturday 5th July, at the estate of the Vicomte de La Croix de Lormes, near Vertou, three miles south of Nantes. We were expected there on Tuesday 1st July. That meant we had to leave on the Monday. It was quite an expedition and the preparations would last right up until our departure.

The Baron de Kermean had his carriage brought out of the shed where it was stored. It was an ancient coach that had not been used for ages. The country roads were not really suitable for it and my grandfather preferred to travel on horseback. The rear wheels of this antique were taller than I and its running board had four steps. Ottmeyer worked for several weeks to get it back in order. In particular he had to change the springs and part of the wheels. It had also been repainted in black and yellow, with the Kermean coat of arms on the doors. It needed at least four big, strong draught horses to get this contraption up to a trot. However, we only had two at Kermean, and they were needed for work on the land. My grandfather had decided to hitch them up to take us at a walk as far as La Roche-Bernard, where he could hire post-horses for the journey to Nantes. A groom from the stables brought our own horses home. A servant had been sent to La Roche-Bernard during the previous week to warn the postmaster.

We had lots of trunks to carry, as well as my chest. The Chevalier, in particular, had considerable baggage. He was intending to go straight from Vertou to Versailles where he would set up his household. The Baron would have liked him to resign his office at the Ministry and install himself straight away at Kermean, in order to take over the management of the domains, but with a war imminent it was not the right time. My little sister would go with the newlyweds, not returning to Kermean. She was approaching twelve years of age, and my uncle considered that she could not continue to live her secluded life, the only one of her age amongst adults. With the permission of the Baron, the Chevalier had managed to have her entered into the Queen's Convent, at

Versailles. This convent was originally conceived for young persons *of good quality*, particularly the daughters of officers serving at the Court. It was not therefore necessary to be rich, or even of the nobility, to be admitted. This time my uncle had no need to beg the King's Genealogist to perform acrobatics on behalf of a descendant of Laforest-Dombourg. The Queen's Convent had only taken boarders since the beginning of 1773, but it was already well subscribed. As well as the traditional education dispensed as a matter of course to young girls in this kind of institution, the pupils there learned arithmetic and drawing, which pleased my little sister, given that I had passed on to her my taste for this latter discipline. I had even given her all my equipment. Moreover, the Chevalier de Kermean could have her at his house whenever she was allowed out.

My uncle François joined us on the Sunday evening from the Abbey de Prières. The Abbot had given him leave to officiate at the marriage of his elder brother. There were therefore five of us for the outward journey. There would only be two of us, me and my uncle the cleric, to accompany the Baron after the wedding as far as La Roche-Bernard. We would separate there. The priest would go straight to the Abbey, while I would go up to Vannes to take the road towards Rennes and Saint-Malo.

We left at dawn on a rainy Monday. The interior of our carriage was very comfortable, with deep cushions and leather curtains. Each of us had as much space as we needed. The start of the journey seemed interminable. The coach was advancing so slowly that one could climb out and walk, to stretch the legs between the showers. Catching up was easy. We arrived at La Roche-Bernard at about two in the afternoon. From then on, our pace quickened. We went at a trot, pulled by four big Breton post-horses along the King's highway. Ottmeyer now had little to do, as we now had a postillion. The team was changed at Pontchâteau. We stopped at Le Temple, where we spent the night at the Hotel Lion d'Or, the last staging post before Nantes on the Vannes road.

By midday on Tuesday we were at the outskirts of Nantes. The sky cleared and the sun appeared. We arrived at a great esplanade, surrounded by market gardens, which served as a fairground and which the people of Nantes called La Place de Viarme. We then went down a succession of sloping streets to La Place de Bretagne. As we passed, the Baron pointed out the entrance to a Royal garden where they raised exotic plants brought back from distant lands by seafarers. We then went along the left-hand side of the boulevards of the old ramparts, at that time still under demolition. I leaned out of the window. It was my first time at Nantes.

The postillion stopped the team in front of the Hotel de la Poste. We ordered lunch, and while waiting for it to be prepared, the Baron and Ottmeyer having gone to find draught horses to hire for the next two weeks, the four of us – the Chevalier de Kermean, the Priest, my little sister and I – went to look at the commercial port of Nantes on the Quai de la Fosse.

The Port of Nantes is quite different from any I had yet seen, whether L'Orient, Brest or Concarneau. Here, there were no gun emplacements or forts. We were sheltered well inland, over thirty miles from the estuary. The long stretch of the Quai de la Fosse, further lengthened by the Quai d'Estrée, enabled merchant ships to tie up along the whole length of the north bank of the river, one behind the other, prow to stern, for a distance of more than a thousand yards, as far as the busy naval shipyard over which hung the smoke from the caulkers' fires. We walked a third of the way along the port, as far as the mast crane. It was about an hour before high tide, and the hulls of the moored ships rose above the quaysides. Some were unloading their cargoes. They had returned from Saint-Domingue, from the Antilles and from Brazil. Part of the roadway between the sides of the ships and the trees of the promenade was hidden under cases, bails and casks which gave out their perfumed odours: sugar, vanilla, rum, tobacco, coffee, precious woods, cotton, indigo, spices. Sailors and longshoremen were busy in the alleys formed between the piles of merchandise, under the heat of a sun which had reappeared on this first day of July.

Other ships were about to sail. They were loading their victuals: barrels of salted foods, dried vegetables, casks of fresh water and everything else a ship usually needs for a long voyage. Many were also loading their diverse, well-packaged cargoes. They were in the main ships of moderate size: brigs, two-masted snows and three-masters, no more than ninety feet overall. Each carried three to six cannons per side, 6- or 8-pounders, no more. I pointed out to my uncles the very unusual design of the decks of these ships. They were divided in two by an eight-foot high transverse partition that extended beyond each side of the hull. Just one small door in the middle allowed passage from the after part to the forward part of the deck. The top of the partition was composed of niches equipped with forks and stands on which could be rested blunderbusses and swivel guns, which once in place could pepper with grapeshot the forward half of the deck. These ships were slavers.

The priest was interested in my explanations. He had a word with a fellow leaning against a pile of bails. He must have been a bosun or a bosun's mate, as he was supervising the loading of a chest, apparently very heavy, that sailors were hauling aboard the snow at the end of a tackle hitched to the main yard. Once spoken to, the sailor turned towards us with an expressionless face: one would have said it was sculpted in old oak, it was so weathered and tanned by years of exposure to sun and wind. Having looked at us for a moment without showing the least emotion, he turned back to his task and waited until the chest had been deposited on the deck before deigning to pay us any attention. He seemed in no way overawed by my Marine Guard uniform or the Cross of Saint-Louis on the Chevalier's coat, or by our swords, or by the tonsure, the white robe and black shoulder cloak of Father François de Kermean. Nor was he in the least mollified by the large eyes of my little Anne. The Father asked him what was being loaded.

'That interests you, Father? Well, for example, what's just gone aboard, that's little iron bars. There's three hundred of 'em in all. That's what's used for money in Africa. In the other chests there's rifles, pistols and sabres for trading, along with lead balls and gunflints. The gunpowders, they get loaded at the last minute, on the river. There's also clothes, hats and there, in them sacks, there's bouges[28]...

'Bouges? What are they?'

'A shell money used in India. Them's also called 'virgins'[29] in the Indian Ocean. The blacks love them 'cause of their shape like. Ha! What I mean is for them it's a symbol of fertility...we got twenty sacks of 'em. We also got ornaments, necklaces made from bits of red coral, six chests' worth; and there's glass stuff too, necklaces with glass beads of every colour like, and then, above all, loads of cloths of every kind – crimson satin, velvet, Guinea, India and Siam-style cloths...all them made here in Nantes. And then, of course, masses of bottles and demijohns filled with kill-devil and rosolio. Them's are ratafias made

28 Translator's note: *bouges*: derived from the Dutch word for a cowry – *boesjes.*

29 Translator's note: *virgins:* probably because one of the main sources of cowries for the slave traders were the beaches of the Virgin Islands.

with sugar and grains and mixed with rose petals and orange flowers, as a tip, what! It's the little extra we give to get ahead of the competition.'

'And to whom are you going to sell all these beautiful things?' asked my uncle.

The bosun smiled for an instant. The wrinkles around his tight lips stretched to his cheekbones and he chortled.

'Them's for the black kings. We give 'em that, and in exchange, like, they give us their good and bad subjects and even their own wives when they wants to get rid of 'em, beggin' your pardon, Father. It's a load of junk, ain't it, our load for bartering!'

In my turn I asked the bosun about the length of the voyage and the best times to leave. He replied that a *circular* voyage varied, from fifteen months to two years on average. It was a matter of luck. It depended on the amount of time lost in the calms of Horse Latitudes, south of the Equator. And also on the number of blacks immediately available and on the spot when the ship arrived at the trading posts. Sometimes it needed three or four long stops to fill the between decks to the required level, but it varied. With luck, you could even do the whole thing in a year, or even seven months. It had been done. As for the departure times, there were none in particular.

'That depends on the owner and the cap'n, like. Some as prefer to leave in autumn. You can have storms in the Bay of Biscay, but you arrive at the best season on the coast of Africa. Then you can leave before the rainy season, which is May to December. Rains the whole time during the season, with tornadoes at the beginning an' end. But the main trouble is it's the time the sailors gets them nasty diseases what we don't have 'ere. It's good to get away from there, but then we gets to the American Islands in the hurricane season and that's a different story from the tornadoes on the African coast! That's as why a lot of 'em, like us, prefer to leave now, in July. We'll go to San Tomé, at the bottom of the Gulf of Guinea. If we can fill up quick with blacks, like, we'll go and spend the end of the rainy season at Saint Antonio on the Île d'Annobon, south of the Île de Prince. The climate's good there, like, for lookin' after our cargo and give 'em a little rest so as they's in good shape for sellin' at Saint-Domingue. After that we'll head up north to catch the Trades. That way we'll be out the Sea of Antilles well before them big tropical storms and with good weather get back to Nantes in less than a year, God willin', right back to the Quai de la Fosse.'

Lunchtime was approaching. We thanked our slaver and returned to the Hotel de la Poste.

'I don't understand these Nantes shipowners!' said the Chevalier de Kermean as we walked along. 'They gave Dr Franklin the warmest of receptions last winter. I also know that Mr Thomas Morris, the Insurgents' agent here, never stops talking about the enthusiasm of the Nantes people for the American fight; the struggle for liberty, as they call it. They must surely know that there is a strong risk that it will end in a war with the English. And they continue preparing ships for the slave trade! What are they thinking of? Have they forgotten the Boscawen caper[30]? They seem to be doing all they can to have our sailors made prisoners of war, while we will soon need them for the King's Navy. It's beyond me!'

'But, brother,' replied my uncle François, 'you really don't understand? It's called the profit motive! The rumours of war about which you talk are surely bound to raise the price of slaves at Saint-Domingue. That pirate we were just talking to said they hoped to finish their round voyage in less than a year. They think they have a chance of doubling their money and are tempted. What I don't understand is that these people who are so attached to the notion of liberty continue to enrich themselves by depriving men, women and children of that very same liberty!'

'Well, François, are you on the side of our philosophers who only love our enemies?'

'I am no more than a priest, my dear brother, happy just to read the Gospels and to try to apply the words: '*Diliges proximum tuum sicut teipsum*[31]'.

'But do you think that should also be applied to the blacks?'

'I can guess what you are going to say to me: one cannot accept that God, the wisest of beings, would have put a soul, especially a good one, in a black body.'

'I think I have already heard that somewhere...In any case, it's not without foundation, you must agree. I'm sure I have another argument

30 Translator's note: *the Boscawen caper:* before the Seven Years' War had officially started, the English Admiral Boscawen captured all the French fishing and merchant ships he could, in order to deprive the French of sailors in the imminent war.

31 'Do unto others as you would do unto yourself', from St Matthew.

that you won't refute so easily, but I can't quite remember it. I know it well and it's on the tip of my tongue. Oh, how annoying!'

We arrived at the inn. My grandfather was already waiting for us. He had hired four draught horses from a wheelwright. Ottmeyer had stayed to supervise their hitching to the coach. We were served pike in clarified butter, and the Chevalier de Kermean recommended a bottle of Muscadet to accompany it. He told us that his future father-in-law owned a number of vineyards that produced this wine. My uncle François told the Baron about our walk along the quay. The Chevalier was very quiet and seemed to be thinking about something. Suddenly he interrupted us.

'That's it! I've got it!'

We turned to look at him. His blue eyes were shining, and his face was lit up by a triumphant smile.

'What have you got?' asked the Baron de Kermean, who also could not resist smiling at seeing the joyful face of his elder son.

'It's Saint Paul! He said that slavery is not forbidden! What do you say to that, Father? Surely you are not going to doubt the word of Saint Paul?'

Far from seeming discomfited, the Father of Kermean smiled in his turn.

'I ought not to be amused by such a serious matter. Nevertheless, neither you nor I can help it for the moment. So you have become a Doctor of Theology, brother? Citing to me as you have Paul's Letter to Philemon? The shortest letter that Saint Paul ever wrote but, it seems, not the least known! It is true that having baptised an escaped slave, Saint Paul, then in prison in Rome, sent him back to his master, Philemon, one of his disciples, with a letter asking him to act well towards his slave. That does not mean, however, that he advocated the practice of slavery, and even less that he would have approved of the Trade as we practise it today. I think we have to put Saint Paul into the context of his time. Slavery had been practised for many years and was one of the foundations of the ancient world. Saint Paul had no intention, therefore, of attacking the society of the day head on. But that does not mean that he approved of its faults. What did he also say? '...We have been baptised only to form one single body – Jews, Greeks, slaves and free men, all of us imbued with a single spirit.' And he also said 'Each of us should rest in the state we have been called to the Faith.

Are you a slave? Do not let that afflict you, but if you can become a free man, make the most of it.' I would add that the Church has made a big contribution to the emancipation of slaves, but rather than calling on them to rebel, the Church baptised them and defended them. I see nothing there that justifies this horror called the Trade.'

'Well, let's leave it there, brother,' said the Chevalier. 'I admit defeat, but for pity's sake, don't mention it in your marriage sermon. The Vicomte de la Croix has no direct involvement in the Trade, but his wife's family has plenty, and there will be shipowners amongst the guests.'

'I will do as Saint Paul, dear brother, keeping everything in proportion. I certainly won't attack the basis of Nantes society in my sermon. All the same, I would like to talk about it in private with any of the wedding guests who would like to debate it with me.'

'So be it. If it encourages them to cancel their sailings this year you will be doing me a service. But don't go at it too strongly, I beg you.'

The Chevalier de Kermean had very firm, and sometimes rash, ideas, but to his credit he did not like arguments.

We arrived at the de la Croix de Lormes estates towards four in the afternoon. The weather was fine and hot. The entrance gates to the estate were on the right side of the road from Nantes to Vertou. A straight and carefully raked avenue, between double rows of poplars, led southwards from the gates for almost six hundred yards. It then went through a wonderfully maintained garden. The garden's flowerbeds, surrounded by bushes trained on wires, were set in geometric shapes right up to the steps of the main body of the house's north-facing façade.

A lackey in a powdered wig led us across the marble tiles of the entrance hall, and then through a panelled sitting room decorated with inlaid furniture and rare plants from overseas. The Vicomte lived on the income from his estates, mainly his vineyards, but, without the prosperity of nearby Nantes, his situation would have no doubt been less rosy. The master of the house, along with his wife and his daughter, the bride-to-be, were waiting for us on a balustraded terrace overlooking a garden in the English style followed by a gentle grass slope that descended to the edge of the river.

Monsieur de la Croix was a man of average size, plump but not overly so, affable and without affectation. He had perfect mastery of the art of putting whomever he was talking with at ease. His wife was a petite blonde woman, pretty and as pleasant as her husband. As for Mademoiselle de la Croix, soon to become Madame de Kermean, she was a very young girl, the last-born after four or five boys. At first sight she seemed to me much more reserved than Maria Kirwan. But are we not told to be wary of still waters? She had just come out of the convent of the Abbey aux Bois at Paris. According to my uncle the Chevalier, the fees at this educational institution were six hundred pounds a year, the same as for the Marine Guard cadets, but there they were much more demanding as regards proof of nobility. The Chevalier was afraid of being too occupied during the coming days to be able to give me my detailed orders regarding my future mission at Saint-Malo, so he asked the major-domo to wake us before everybody else the next day and asked me to meet him at six in the morning on the terrace.

*

Vertou, Wednesday 2nd July, early morning.

At the bottom of the garden there is a little rotunda made of white limestone, erected in the water in the middle of the rushes, and linked to the bank by a short stone passageway. We sit down there on a circular bench, our backs against the balustrade that goes right round the structure. A light mist floats above the river. Our shoes and stockings are soaked from the dew covering the lawn that we have crossed. It is pleasantly cool but the day promises to be hot. After the rain during our journey, summer seems to have settled in for good.

Firstly, the Chevalier hands me a heavy purse.

'There are fifty louis in here.'

My eyes widen. Fifty louis! That's twice the cost of my cadetship as a Marine Guard. Personally, I only have enough to cover six months of my expenses, which are only three hundred and fifty pounds a year.

'It is to cover your outlay for the mission. Make good use of it, it is the King's money!'

He hands me a little notebook with a cardboard binding.

'Note down carefully all your spending, and the date, in this notebook. If you give money to someone you must note down the reason why you thought it the right thing to do, but never mention any names. Remember that well. You can record the names in your memory, but, above all, no written traces! You must hand the notebook back to me once you have finished, along with what's left of the twelve hundred pounds.'

While he is saying that, the Chevalier has pulled out of his pocket a sheet of paper which he carefully unfolds before handing it to me with a serious air. I find a short note, written in a clear hand, but I cannot tear my eyes away from the big letters at the top of the document: *Louis, by the grace of God, King of France and Navarre.* I skip the two or three lines of the text, without reading them, and go straight to the signature at the bottom, a simple signature: *Louis.* I have never had occasion to see the King's signature. My hands start to tremble. I lift my head and look at my uncle.

'Uncle? This signature?'

The Chevalier cannot help smiling at my disbelief.

'It is the King's!'

'He has written expressly to me?'

This time my uncle laughs aloud.

'Not exactly, but that's really none of your business. Read!'

I examine the contents of the document:

Monsieur Laforest-Dombourg is hereby charged with my secret orders. The discretion and speed with which he executes them will be the most pleasing proof of the zeal he affords me in my service.

It is dated 20th June, scarcely twelve days ago!

'It is a safe-conduct which gives you the right to act in the King's name. Keep it carefully hidden on you at all times. Never be separated from it, as from now on it is your responsibility. You will have to hand it back at the end of your mission. I'm going to tell you when and how to use it. Apart from that, show it to nobody. Don't even speak of it.'

He then hands me a detailed map of Saint-Malo. On it can be seen the ramparts, the chateau and the street names, but not the port or its access points. I can't help remarking on this.

'You'll have the naval charts once you are on board your ship. You will need this map so that you can quickly find your way inside the city.'

The surprises are not yet finished, for my uncle then hands me a dubious document which immediately disquiets me. It is a printed form, a kind of certificate with a fine coat of arms at the top and, as is usual, the blank spaces filled in by pen by an officer of the Naval administration. It says that Monsieur Laforest-Dombourg has been detailed to embark at Saint-Malo as a Volunteer, aboard *le Duc de Choiseul*, a merchantman bound for the Guinea Cays. A slaver brig!

'We at first considered giving you a false identity for your activities in the town. That's why we first asked the Chevalier de La Rozière to provide this certificate with the name left out. But after some reflection we decided that a false name can be a source of unnecessary complications if one is not accustomed to it. Eventually, we wrote in your proper name. I can assure you, you are still a Marine Guard and not a Volunteer, but you must tell people you are the latter if asked what you are doing in Saint-Malo. This is to put any English spies off your track. The document is authentic; the signatures and seals on it are real. All the same, it is obviously a false certificate. The real one will be produced later, with the name of the boy who will in fact embark on *le Duc de Choiseul* once she has returned to Saint-Malo. Ships which take Volunteers have to be registered at the Navy Office. *Le Duc de Choiseul* is a real vessel. She is under the command of a Captain Royer, belongs to the shipowner Dubuys, and it really is intended that she take a Volunteer for her next voyage, if it is not cancelled because of war. But be assured that the brig left in July of last year and we have been told that she will not be back before next autumn. There is no cause for concern on that count. By the time the real Volunteer has been named, your mission will certainly be over…'

My uncle suddenly takes back the document and examines it more carefully.

'It's only now that I see that our secretary did not see fit to imitate the handwriting of our good officer at the Navy Office at Saint-Malo. Damn! Well, it doesn't matter. In any case, you will only be showing this paper if the military police or gendarmes are making checks. But above all, don't show your safe-conduct signed by the King! It is reserved for another purpose that I'll tell you about later. And of course, you mustn't go about in uniform down there. That's why you are going back to Nantes this morning. The Vicomte will lend you a mount. Go to the tailor David in the rue des Capucins, near to the Quai de la Fosse. He is expecting you and will take your measurements with a view to making, over the next two weeks, one complete outfit in nankeen, and another winter one in ratine. The cloth is ready. I ordered blue, the preferred colour of sailors.

While you are there, you should also order an un-braided hat, shirts, stockings, waistcoats, shoes, boots, a rain cape. In short, everything you would need for a long sea voyage. Make the most of it. It will all be of use to you later on and it's in a good cause. Monsieur David will prepare all that for you and you can pick it all up while passing through Nantes with the Baron de Kermean and the Father on the way back to La Roche-Bernard. While I think about it, your sister told me that you had given her all your drawing and painting equipment, which was very kind of you, but while you are in Nantes, also buy some paints, crayons, charcoal and parchment paper, for your mission. Buy the best. You will certainly be able to make use of them during your stay at Saint-Malo. Pay for all this with the King's money and record it in your notebook, starting tonight. I will help you for the first entries.'

To finish off, he hands me a bundle of papers on which I recognise his handwriting. Unlike my father's, of which I have unfortunately lost the only example I have known, the Chevalier's handwriting is difficult to read.

'What I'm now going to tell you is written in these papers. Reread them up until your departure, to fix everything firmly in your memory. I would ask you to burn them before leaving Vertou.'

I have always respected and admired my uncle Jean-Baptiste, but I think that here he is going a bit too far. All the same, I take the package with deference, without saying a word, but he has guessed my thoughts.

'Don't think that I'm being unnecessarily cautious. I told you the other day, at table, the speed with which Lord Stormont, the English ambassador, found out about our fitting out of *le Havre de Grâce.* In fact we realised we had no idea how *Lord All Eyes All Ears*, as we have christened Lord Stormont, came to possess the complete list of names and competencies of the officers participating in this first expedition. This means that the English have some very well-placed agents, and as long we don't know where they have recruited them, we have to take every precaution and constantly mistrust everybody, everywhere. This is true at Versailles and will be even more so at Saint-Malo.'

The Chevalier stops for a moment to see if I have anything to say, then continues.

'When the Comte d'Estaing recalled him, Flaharn gave us the name of his contact. It is this Louis Duval, for whom I have given you a letter written by Flaharn. We have opened this letter, along with another one that Flaharn sent to Duval, and which we intercepted and then sent on to its addressee. The sealed letter which I have given you only contains what Flaharn has already told us. As for the letter he sent to Duval, it simply informs him that the Ship's Captain is not able to come and see him as arranged, and that you will be his representative. He also explains the password that you have to give him. We found nothing else. Flaharn seems to be playing straight with us. In any case, we look at all his correspondence. Just be aware, for your own good, that it is very easy to open a sealed letter and reseal it without any trace visible to the addressee.'

'Even those you send by Ministerial post?'

'Of course, but we don't need to open them since it's us sending them. On the other hand, yes, any letters sent by the post can be opened.'

'By the Black Office?'

'You could call it that. It's a special service for the King, that I work with...very closely. But if we can do it, others can do it too. That's why one must always be very careful when sending mail by the ordinary post.'

'Is that how you manage to keep an eye on Flaharn?'

'We are watching him. Now, listen carefully. Everything is in the papers, but if you need clarification on anything, now is the time for that. Firstly, when you arrive at Saint-Malo, you will present yourself to your commander, the Fireship Captain Le Meur. You will give him the letter from the Chevalier de Fleurieu that I have given you and answer any questions he wants to ask of you. Although he is only a Fireship Captain, he needs to know everything you will be doing, in the spirit as well as the letter, since the future operations of his ship depend on it. You will leave your all Naval dress aboard, including your sword, and put yourself quietly ashore with everything you need to get by for a week. Use the King's money for all your expenses but remember to keep a record of everything. Don't forget your certificate or your safe-conduct.'

'Is Captain Le Meur an agent of your service?'

'He is...an initiate...his whole crew is hand-picked. Now, secondly! You will look for discreet, modest lodgings in the town that accord with your supposed position as a Volunteer. Use the whole of this first week to learn to find your way around Saint-Malo with the least hesitation. You can use the town plan I gave you to help with that. The object of the exercise is to enable you to lose anybody following you when you go to meet the man called Duval, later on. If enemy spies start to take an interest in you, despite all our precautions, they will want to follow you to find out what you are up to and whom you are dealing with. If they are experienced in this kind of work, you will never notice them. I'm going to tell you how to thwart anyone following you. Firstly, you change direction two or three times, one after the other, each time having a quick look behind you. If the same person is always behind you, he is following you. I call that 'going round the houses.' But there could be several of them taking turns. In that case you won't see a thing. So, next, after 'going round the houses', you arrange things so that you cross a deserted space in which you can see a long way. That will force your followers to keep further back from you. You can then change direction very quickly so as to lose them, then go to your rendezvous. Of course, all this has to be done as naturally as possible, without attracting attention, which we quite rightly want to avoid. Do you now understand why you need to know perfectly the layout where all this will take place? I think a week should be enough to prepare several routes. Have you understood?'

'I follow everything, uncle.'

'Good! Thirdly, you have to make contact with Monsieur Duval. Flaharn has given us his address, in the rue de la Diacrerie. But he told us that the best way to find him is to go at midday to the inn called *La Malice*, where he usually has his lunch. This inn is on the north corner of the Petit Placître, in the rue de Crevaille.

It's marked on your map and you won't have any problem finding it. According to Flaharn it's an old wooden building from the last century, with a sign depicting a woman, a monkey and a cat…'

The Chevalier suddenly stops, his eyes crease with pleasure, a big smile appears on his lips and he slaps his thighs with two hands in a rush of hilarity he cannot suppress.

'Oh my God! A woman, a monkey and a cat: *La Malice*[32]! I had never noticed before! These Saint-Malo people are priceless!'

'I think, uncle, you had better start avoiding thoughts like that.'

32 Translator's note : *La Malice*: A *malice* is a mischievous joke played on the unsuspecting, the kind of things perpetrated by monkeys, cats and women. The inn and the sign existed in Saint-Malo at that time.

'Yes, but it won't be easy. I have been a bachelor for too long. Right! According to Flaharn's description, this Louis Duval has a pock-marked face. He was blond-haired when young, but since he has been bald for a number of years, he usually wears a wig. Once you think you have recognised him, introduce yourself by saying that you have a letter for him from Captain Flaharn. But, before giving it to him, say that Flaharn has asked you to pose a question, as a kind of confirmation. In fact it is we who asked Flaharn to find a suitable password. You have to ask Duval who it was who took the ship *Merry* out of the port of Muscat on October 4th, 1759. He will reply that it was he himself, using a manoeuvre involving the raising of the jib, or something like that. I don't know for sure, not being a sailor, but if it really is Duval, he will give you a convincing answer. Make sure you get him to tell you exactly what happened that day at Muscat. It was the start of the Comte d'Estaing's famous campaign in India.'

'This Duval took part in that?'

'Yes! There are few survivors left today from that expedition. That's why Duval is of even more interest to us. I'll come back to that in a minute. Once he has given the Muscat password, show him your safe-conduct. That will force him to take you more seriously, given that you are so young. Once you know what it is he is proposing to us, your job is to pass on all that information, and anything else he may tell you, to the Chevalier de La Rozière. Obviously, there is no question of you going to see him at the Commander's office, or not until you have finished your mission. There is a way of corresponding secretly by depositing written accounts in agreed places, but it's a difficult technique to master and you'd have to learn to use code, which would take too long. So you are going to have to make your reports orally. With that in mind, we are sending someone to Saint-Malo to whom you will make your reports, and who will direct your interviews with Duval. He will be in charge of our operations once we know enough to start. He is called Dumouriez. He is thirty-eight years old, a colonel since 1772, attached to the Lorraine regiment. He should really be called a 'detached attaché', since he has never set foot in the Lorraine regiment. It's just a pretext for paying his salary. We have to live somehow!'

The Chevalier cannot resist laughing again at his little witticism.

'Recipient of the Cross of Saint-Louis in 1763, he fought in the last war, where he was lightly wounded. He then carried out several secret missions for the King's diplomatic service, notably in Corsica and Poland. None of this stopped our dear friend, the Duc d'Aiguillon, from issuing a *lettre de cachet* against him and sending him to the Bastille, without any opposition from Louis XV. The honest Louis XVI had him brought out of prison and even agreed to have him write a memorandum on our coastal defences. He is still working on it with the Chevalier de La Rozière. Colonel Dumouriez is very intelligent and well-educated – a hard worker. He speaks English well, and has always kept impeccable accounts for any spending of the King's money, and so has all the required skills for running an intelligence network across the Channel. But he can't go unnoticed. He will stay with the Chevalier de La Rozière. You will meet him aboard *le Moucheron* with Captain Le Meur. Now, just between us and because you are my nephew, be very careful with this Dumouriez. He is whiter than white as regards his accounting of the spending of the King's money, but for the rest, he is ambitious, unprincipled, cunning, ingratiating, secretive and only looks after his own interests.

'There it is,' concludes my uncle. 'I've finished. Do you have any questions?'

'I think you were going to tell me something about the Comte d'Estaing at Muscat?'

'That's right, I had forgotten. Try to gain the confidence of this Duval so that he is willing to tell you a bit about the Comte d'Estaing's India campaign. But be sure not to send me anything about it in writing! You can tell me what you find out when we next meet.'

*

I went to Nantes for the day, as instructed by the Chevalier. The tailor took my measurements and then directed me to a shop for seafarers, where I could buy all my linen and utensils for my forthcoming missions. I bought a larger chest than the one I already had. I also acquired a leather bag of the type sailors use to carry their clothes. On seeing some sailmaking equipment, I had a bright idea and selected an assortment of needles and threads, the best I could find, and a sailmaker's palm. I then went into the town to find someone who sold paints and brushes.

This allowed me to have a better look around Nantes. Not all the Nantes shipowners are slave traders. Trade in more worthy goods, especially sugar, was also widely favoured. But the Trade dominated most of the other activity of this flourishing town: factories for Indian cloth, arms, bottles, pewter pots; all the diverse junk taken on board by the slavers, for bartering on the African coast, was made by Nantes workers.

While buying my paints, I came across a traveller's writing desk. It was a light but solidly built box, in varnished redwood, decorated with a brass anchor inlaid into the lid. It contained goose quills, a penknife, a sand holder and a large bronze inkwell which could be sealed tight. A little board, inserted inside, wedged all the contents to stop them moving about while the box was being carried, and could be taken out and unfolded for writing on. A draw for storing paper opened to the outside. On a sudden whim I bought this little treasure on the spot. I went and sat down on a crate beside the Loire, on the Quai de la Fosse. There, I wrote a letter to Maria Kirwan.

> *Mademoiselle*
>
> *Your farewell of the other day touched me and went straight to my heart. I guard the gift you offered me as if it were the most precious treasure. I would be most happy if, on reading this, the first letter I have the honour of writing to you, you could forget the coolness and lack of attention of which I am guilty in your regard. I leave soon for Saint-Malo to join the ship on which I will be sailing. God only knows when we will see each other again but believe me when I say that my only care is to be worthy of your understanding and friendship.*
>
> *There remains just one favour to ask of you, which is to accept my assurances of the deepest respect with which I am, mademoiselle, your most humble and obedient servant.*

Pleased with myself, I took this *billet doux* to the nearby post office.

The marriage was held the following Saturday. It was a wedding ceremony without excessive pomp. There was Mass in the morning, in the Chateau's chapel, followed by a grand banquet in the main rooms of the house. All the windows had been opened to allow the air to circulate. The countryfolk and workers of the Vicomte were fed on trestles which had been set up under the trees of the avenue, where they were probably more comfortable than we were, as it was very hot. The guests of honour were the old Marquis de Becdelièvre, my godfather, and his son, at that time First President of the Brittany Chamber of Accounts. But there was also a good number of Nantes shipowners, in their gently toned silk outfits, immaculate white stockings and silver-buckled shoes, all carrying swords like true gentlemen. Many of them were, in fact, of stock ennobled two or three generations ago. Seeing my Marine Guard's uniform, they surrounded me to try to find out what was being said in the King's Navy about the war in the Americas. With my uncle's words still ringing in my ears, I took on a knowing air and said that a direct war between us and the English was not out of the question. They all agreed, but the question was 'when?'. My uncle, the priest, had been correct: most wanted to make a profitable voyage just before hostilities commenced, when rumours of war would have made the price of prime slaves jump in the colonies. They were tempted by 'double or quits'. Many of them would later regret it.

2

We stayed for a week at Vertou, after which we had to think of leaving. The Chevalier had to get back to Versailles without delay. The Father, his brother, had only a little more freedom. As for me, I was expected in Saint-Malo.

The Baron took us all in his coach, driven by Ottmeyer, as far as Nantes. We lunched together for the last time at the inn in the rue de Gorge where we had stopped on the way to Vertou. The newlyweds then set off for Versailles with my little sister. The Chevalier had hired a coach along with post-horses from Nantes, just as we were doing in the opposite direction. After their departure, Ottmeyer went to collect my chest from the tailor David and we in our turn took to the road, hitched once again to four horses with a postillion. We spent the night at La Roche-Bernard, at the post inn.

The Baron de Kermean had been forcing himself to put on a jolly front, but once we were alone with him, just the Father and I, we felt that his heart was not in it. The irascible old Baron, who had once thought of petitioning for a *lettre de cachet* against my parents to stop them marrying, had become very attached to my little Anne. She had brought a breath of fresh air to the old manor house. Although he denied it, we could feel that the Baron feared being alone without her. Not that he was always of an especially tender disposition. Sometimes he had been somewhat of a despot. In particular, he had tried to give her lessons in arithmetic and geometry during which the poor thing had more often than not been scolded. When the Chevalier had suggested putting Anne in the Queen's Convent, the Baron de Kermean had apparently been very enthusiastic about the idea; and when my little sister started saying that she loved her grandfather too much to think of abandoning him, he had condemned her 'stupidity' in his gruffest tone. At the moment of separation, the Baron had managed to put on a brave face and cover his feelings, but neither the Father nor I were fooled.

On the Tuesday morning, at daybreak, I kissed my uncle and grandfather goodbye and took the first coach to Vannes. The weather was still pleasant at that time of the morning, but the day promised to be as hot as those which had preceded it. Everybody wanted to be inside the coach, to be sheltered from the sun once it had warmed up. Seeing this, I decided to sit outside on a raised bench, beside the head coachman. During the first two hours of the journey the dew all around helped to keep the air cool. The trotting of the six horses, hitched in three pairs, made a dull sound on the still-damp earth of the road. This part of Brittany has a particularly wild look. There is not a single tree anywhere in the countryside, and no fields. A traveller new to these parts would soon feel lost, without even the means of asking directions, since most of the locals do not speak French.

We arrived at Vannes early enough in the evening for me to pay a courtesy call to Father Deniel, who had introduced me to mathematics when I was a boarder at the Saint-Yves College. He was very touched that I had not forgotten him. We talked mainly about the education I had received at Brest. My old teacher listened with interest as I gave a detailed account of my examination by Monsieur Bézout. He did not raise the question of the death of my mother. Although he had been involved in my initial research into what had happened to her, he did not know that things had taken a new turn once I had learned of my father's posthumous letter.

The next morning, I left for Rennes on the stagecoach. The countryside was now more varied. Woods and forests alternated with moorland and marches. We stopped for lunch at Malestroit and spent the night at the Guer inn. I took a private room as I needed to be alone in order to secrete the King's safe-conduct in the lining of my nankeen jacket. For this I used the sailmaker's kit which I had bought expressly for this purpose at Nantes. It took a while as I was not used to sewing, knowing only the techniques used by the Navy sailmakers I had watched at work in the Brest sail loft. I was quite pleased with myself once I had finished the task.

That summer of 1777, just like the previous year, was remembered for its extreme heat. I had decided always to travel on the seat beside the coachman and did not regret it. I did not envy the other passengers enclosed in the stuffy cabin of a coach thrown around by the uneven paving of the road. This became truly hellish once we had left Guer on the Thursday morning. About a mile and a half after the town, after crossing a bridge, there was nothing but an earthen roadway. The dryness had made the ruts as hard as stone, and they jolted the big rear wheels of the coach mercilessly. Our passing threw up a pall of yellow dust which hung in the scorching air behind us. On my raised bench I was a little above the dust where the air was still breathable, while beyond my feet I could watch the sweating backs of the postillions. These fellows were being shaken like puppets by the trotting of their mounts. The horses' backs were flecked with white sweat from the rubbing of the harnesses. There were two postillions on the three pairs of horses, one on the left of the rear pair, the other on the right of the leading pair. I think this must be one of the worst jobs imaginable.

We stopped for the night at Rennes. From the little that I was able to see of it, it seemed a well-built town, a harmonious combination of grand buildings and wide avenues. The Louis XV Square, where we stopped, makes an imposing ensemble. The food there is good. We were offered a two-course meal, a dessert and wine, the whole lot costing two pounds with the lodging included.

There are six staging posts between Rennes and Saint-Malo, and the journey can be made in a single day. Coaches leave three times a week, on Monday, Wednesday and Friday. The public coach leaves at four in the morning, with the lunch stop two thirds of the way along, at Plesguen. I wore my uniform for this last stage, as I wanted to make the best impression possible on my commanding officer when presenting myself at the end of the day. The countryside between Rennes and Saint-Malo is rich in greenery. On the upper slopes there are copses of oak, beech and sweet chestnut, while in the valleys are fields of rye and buckwheat, rather than corn, and pastureland.

At our midday stop, at the Plesguen coaching inn, I was approached by two travellers whom I had seen at supper the previous evening, at Rennes, but who had not paid me any attention. I think that my Marine Guard uniform had attracted their interest, but as I was travelling beside the coachman, they had not been able to talk to me during the journey. They were both dressed in the latest Paris fashion, at least that is what I supposed: wigs, beaver hats, silk jackets, one with brown stripes, the other flowered, bronze-coloured velvet breeches and English boots. But they did not carry swords.

'Good day, Sir, or rather, young man,' said the brown-striped one. 'Forgive me if I am wrong, but is that a Naval uniform you are wearing there?'

'Marine Guard, to be precise,' I replied.

'Perfect,' he said, turning towards his companion. Then, addressing me once more, asked, 'Would you dine with us?'

'That is very kind of you,' I said, forcing myself to be polite, as I would rather have remained alone in my corner, not drawing attention to myself.

'Thank you, young man. Maxime de Bauflert at your service. This is my travel companion, Gustave Ducamp.'

'Your servant, Monsieur,' said the aforenamed Ducamp, sitting down at the table at the same time as his friend.

Maxime de Bauflert had a large round head that he kept raised as he looked down on me with bulging blue eyes half covered by heavy eyelids. This gave him a somewhat dominating air. His companion had hollow cheeks, a more direct look, and a little beard.

'You see, young man,' continued Bauflert, 'we are on this journey in order to study maritime trade in France. We spent the whole winter in London, which enabled us to study in depth the admirable way in which English shipowners and merchants organise themselves. At first we were going to write a memorandum on this subject, but we then thought that it would be even better first to look at the French system too. That way we could make comparisons to enable us to improve the faults in our maritime trade. We decided to start our tour in Brittany, or more precisely Saint-Malo, which is, it seems, a big commercial port. We arrived from Paris the day before yesterday, hired a carriage and…'

'Can you imagine that the public coach takes more than a week from Paris to Rennes?' said Ducamp, interrupting his companion.

'...We decided to start with Saint-Malo,' continued Bauflert, tapping his finger impatiently on the table to indicate that he had not finished talking. 'Then, we will go to L'Orient and to Nantes. My friend also suggested going to Brest, but from what I understand, it is exclusively a military port, and so has no interest for us. What do you think? Do you know Brest?'

'I know Brest well, in fact, and I can confirm that it is a military port, perhaps the biggest on the country. Private commerce is limited to coastal trade.'

'You see?' said Bauflert, turning towards his friend. 'Wasn't I right?'

'All the same, 'I added, 'it seems to me that your study would be incomplete without also looking at the Navy. What do you imagine, Sirs, is the principal requirement for a prosperous sea trade?'

'Well,' replied Bauflert. 'Competence! Seriousness! And fearlessness in business! Pragmatism, as they say in England! In short, all the qualities found in shipowners in London and Liverpool!'

'Certainly,' I replied. 'You are absolutely correct, Sir, but I ask you, how would these English shipowners have got on, despite their boldness, if their Royal Navy had not been able to support their interests by force across all the oceans? Have you heard about Boscawen's campaign at the start of the last war? Without squadrons capable of protecting our merchant ships wherever they want to go, our shipowners can accomplish nothing. What we lacked during the last war was a powerful Navy. The result was that we lost our colonies in Canada, while in India we are left with the crumbs. And if our enemies want to take over our possessions in the Antilles, our only major commercial outlet, how can we protect them without warships?'

'Thank you, my boy!' exclaimed Ducamp. 'I have always said that it is the essential point on which everything else depends.'

'Regarding the matter of war,' said Bauflert, suddenly keen to change the subject, 'are you familiar with the *European Courier*?'

'No, but I have heard about it. It is a newspaper, is it not?'

I had not read this paper, but the Chevalier de Kermean had told me about its creation, so I was interested to hear what the Parisian had to say about it.

'It's a paper written in French by the English. It is printed on broadsheet, like the other London papers, but there is no need to understand English to read it. It allows us to have the same news as the London gentlemen. That is yet another demonstration of how up to date our neighbours are. Our *Journal de Paris* was inspired by the *London Evening Post*, but our leaders still have a lot to learn from the English in this area. To come back to the *European Courier*, it reveals all the mistakes made by the Court of St. James in their policies towards the brave English colonies in America. And I think, despite my admiration for the British, that we will not find a better reason for going to war against England than that. And we seem to be in agreement on that, which is why I wondered whether we had been reading the same material.'

I said nothing. The Chevalier de Kermean had told me that the *European Courier* had been launched on the orders of Louis XVI, after discussion with his privy council. Following the experience of the previous war, during which we had seen some of our philosophers deliberately siding with our enemies as regards Canada and the Indies, and knowing how keen Parisians are on anything emanating from London, the King's advisers feared that His Majesty would not be supported by the makers of public opinion should he be forced to declare war on the English Crown. So they decided to launch a newspaper in London. Secret funds had been provided to Beaumarchais – how indispensable he is! – with instructions to launch a French language paper, but edited in London, so that people would think it was genuinely English. They had even been so ingenious as to create the impression that the *European Courier* was being smuggled illicitly into France. In this way our great minds would be convinced that the paper was edited by the English, those serious and intelligent people, and not by the vulgar French. It seemed as if the operation had achieved its ends.

'Where do you intend to stay in Saint-Malo, Sirs?' I asked.

'We have a letter of recommendation to a shipowner and will be staying with him in the rue d'Orléans.'

I promised myself to look at my town map as soon as possible, in order to keep clear of that quarter. I was regretting having put on my uniform. Luckily, I had kept my wig on, which might stop me being immediately recognised by these fellows if, by chance, I came across them in town, without a wig, dressed as a Volunteer for a merchant ship.

'What is the name of the shipowner?' I asked.

'Monsieur Blaize de Maisonneuve. Do you know him?'

'No. As yet I don't know anyone in Saint-Malo,' I replied.
At least it wasn't Monsieur Dubuys. Another stroke of luck!

*

On the road from Plesguen to Saint-Malo, Friday 18th July 1777
After Plesguen I fall into a half-sleep before drifting off completely, sat on my bench, hat over my nose, my back resting against the trunk of the coach, exhausted from the constant jolting and lulled by the heat. I am dragged from my stupor by the voice of the coachman sat beside me.

'Sorry to disturb you, Sir...but we'll soon be at your destination.'

The turn of phrase used by the coachman, talking of *my* destination, strikes a curious note in my ears, as it suggests that I am now the only passenger left on the coach! But my mind is still groggy. I can see that the coach is still making its way north, as it has done since we left Rennes. It must be about five in the evening; the shadows are starting to lengthen. We pass several elegant properties built on the banks of the River Rance, which can be seen below the road amongst the greenery. There are fields and meadows, an abbey built on a pretty rise overlooking the estuary and, looking inland, towards the east, several chapels are visible. It seems to me that the horizon towards the north is becoming clearer.

Ahead, in the distance, the tree-lined road that we have followed since Rennes stops at a crossroads before an inlet of the sea. This is heralded first by the brightness reflecting behind the land, and comes into view, along with a fortified town on the other shore, as we cross the final ridge. The city seems quite close, like a mirage; its granite walls seem to thrust out from the mirrored water. I can make out the upper parts of house fronts and their big windows; they are higher than the walls of the ramparts. Of the pointed bell towers rising above the slate roofs, the highest is topped with a dome shaped like a candle snuffer. I can see ships anchored to the right of the town, at the foot of a massive keep. The town is joined to the mainland by a long, thin strand of sand, on which neatly aligned windmills turn their sails to the sea breeze.

The coachman tells our two postillions to stop. They shout at the horses and in unison lean back and pull hard on the reins. The six big post-horses slow their trot, scraping their horseshoes on the paving stones to counteract the inertia of the heavy coach. They ease down to a walk, and then stop completely, breathing heavily through their nostrils.

We have stopped about two hundred yards from a tidal inlet linked to the Rance. It is completely filled with water and is the port of Saint-Malo. The walls of the town and the band of sand with its windmills form the northern limit of this natural harbour. Its eastern side is enclosed by a spit of land to the right of the basin, separated from the mainland by marshland. On this spit I can make out a rope walk and several ships under construction. The King's highway gets around this basin and the marshes by means of a dike which leads to a road on the sand besides the windmills, and which seems to be the only land access to the city.

'That's the commercial port you're lookin' at there, Sir,' says the coachman. 'Over there, opposite, where them windmills are, it's the Sillon[33]. That's where you've got to pass to get into the town. In front of us, you've got the shipyard and the Talard ropeworks. But the military port is at Solidor, behind Saint-Servan. You, you've got to go to our left, over there!'

Saying that, he points out a path which crosses the road and heads off west towards the outskirts of a big town, about two-thirds of a mile away, built along the top of a ridge.

'It's there! At Saint-Servan!' insists the coachman.

The houses of Saint-Servan extend right down to the water besides a little, low point oriented to the north-north-west, at the end of which stand two windmills on a kind of stone base. This point forms a natural mole which encloses the port anchorage on the west side, leaving only a narrow passage of navigable water, two or three cables wide, between it and the southern bastion of the Saint-Malo ramparts. A merchant ship is making its way through the passage towards the Rance, helped by the tide. In the weakening sea breeze she is carrying her topsails and mizzen t'gallant sail, all braced hard on starboard tack. Lots of little sail and rowing boats criss-cross the anchorage. Several other merchant ships have slipped their moorings and are drifting gently on the top of the ebb, canvas still brailed up, waiting their turn to make for the passage. It is just an hour after high water; the right time to exit the Rance.

---

33 Translators note: *Sillon* – furrow or ship's wake.

'You see the tower furthest to the left, Sir?'

The coachman turns on his seat and points with his arm.

'The one just above the top of the ridge behind that windmill? That's the bell tower of the Sainte-Croix church. Well, the military port is just below, on the other side of the Saint-Servan houses, beside the Rance.'

'But I was told that my ship would be in the port of Saint-Malo,' I say.

'It's a ship of the King's Navy, Sir?'

'Of course,' I reply.

'Well then, she can only be at Port Solidor. That's where you'll have to go, Sir. I'd be happy to take you the whole way on the other side, but what's the use if you then have to return to Saint-Servan with all your baggage?'

'But,' I reply, 'just how am I supposed to get over there with all my stuff?'

'Oh! Don't you worry about that, Sir. Just leave your chest beside the road, long enough to go and find a cart to get you over to Saint-Servan. Nothing will happen to it. That's what everyone does.'

*

That wouldn't do at all! On the contrary! My chest contained my nankeen jacket, with the King's safe-conduct sewn into its lining. My uncle had told me never to let it out of my sight. Moreover, I didn't have much time to think, as the other passengers inside the coach were growing impatient and leaning out of the doors to protest to the coachman and the postillions. I was still hesitating, not knowing what to do, when five men, whom I had not noticed previously, stood up beside the road and came towards the coach. The one in front was of medium height, about thirty, with regular features and auburn hair under a little round felt hat. He was wearing brown breeches buttoned at the knee and an overcoat of the same colour over a blue and white striped waistcoat. Fixed to his buttonhole was a shiny metal badge, with a little chain going from it into his pocket. I knew that the badge was the King's arms, and that it was not holding a watch but a whistle. The four men behind him were wearing woollen bonnets. They had rolled up their sleeves on account of the heat and were wearing wide, blue and white striped sailor's trousers which came down to mid-calf level.

Their feet were bare in their pumps. They were all as bronzed as North American Indians and walked like sailors, swinging from one foot to the other. The man with the whistle, seeing my uniform, addressed me while raising the back of his hand to his hat.

'Monsieur Laforest-Dombourg?' he asked politely.

'That's me,' I replied, happily surprised to see that my problem seemed on the way to being solved.

'Couet, Jacques Couet, at your orders, Sir. Bosun's mate on the King's cutter *le Moucheron.*'

Couet had given the name of his ship with as proud a tone as if he were talking of a ship of the line. Hearing that, one of the passengers, who was watching what was going on from the door of the coach, repeated, imitating the bosun's mate's voice with a certain irony, 'the King's cutter *le Moucheron!*' That set the other passengers laughing. Hearing them, the sailors came up to the coach and I saw the biggest of them, a strapping fellow with his sleeves rolled up over huge forearms, place a pair of hands as big and hairy as bear paws, on the bottom of the door. Seeing this, the joker ducked back inside the carriage. I just had time to see that it was Monsieur Bauflert.

'In God's name! Who's making fun of us in there?'

The question was followed by a wise silence.

'Well then, get Monsieur Laforest-Dombourg's chest, you others, instead of trying to scare these silk-covered shopkeepers!' shouted the bosun's mate.

'How did you know I would arrive this evening?' I asked Couet.

'Simple, Sir. The Captain was expecting you this week on the Rennes coach, so we came to wait for you on Monday and Wednesday evening.'

I went to the back to show the sailors my chest. They grabbed it and took it away from the coach, joking amongst themselves. They had already completely forgotten the incident.

Going back to the front of the coach, to pay my fare to the coachman, I overheard Monsieur Bauflert, who was sitting on my side, say:

'Our trade will be well protected with imbeciles like this!'

I had no wish to find out whether these words were spoken for my benefit. I passed by without turning my head, hoping only that Bauflert could not read my face. He was not wearing a sword, and that was lucky. Had Bauflert been armed, as I was, I would have found myself in a real dilemma: react to the insult and call out its instigator, thereby compromising the mission entrusted to me by my uncle in the name of the King, or be seen by the world as a coward for letting an insult go unpunished. Yes indeed! That's how I now thought after a short year with the Marine Guards!

The sailors took turns in twos to carry my chest. It took us nearly half an hour to get to Saint-Servan. As we walked, the bosun's mate explained that the Navy had reserved for itself the only sheltered harbour at Saint-Malo where ships could stay permanently afloat.

The military port of Saint-Malo, also called the Solidor Anchorage, is formed by a channel between Saint-Servan and a sandbank which dries to a height of ten feet at low tide. There is always a minimum anchoring depth of three fathoms. The military port, as Couet then explained to me, also includes three well-protected inlets where one can dry out at low tide. As for the commercial port at Saint-Malo, it is affected by a bad chop when there is a strong wind at high tide, but the main thing about it, he added, is that it dries out completely at low tide. The transport ships that I could then see on the other side of the basin, in front of the quay under the ramparts between the Chateau and the Main Gate of the city, would all have dried out at the next low tide. I was used to tides, of course, and since my childhood had seen brigs and coasters aground in the Port-Louis inlet and along the quays of Le Croisic. At Brest, they took advantage of the biggest tides to pull ships of eighty guns or more into the dry docks, but how they could be handled without mishap in an anchorage that dried out completely seemed to me to be beyond belief. I could not resist mentioning this to the bosun's mate.

'It's that here, Sir, the rise and fall of the tide is twice that of Brest. At the moment, the tides are average, but there's already a twenty-four foot range. In a week's time it'll be springs and we'll 'ave thirty feet. And when the tides is exceptional it can go to forty or even forty-two. I agree you wouldn't risk it with a seventy-four gun ship of fifteen 'undred tons. But a fifty-gun ship can manage it. In any case, the biggest merchant ships is never more than three or four 'undred tons, with a draught of fifteen feet, so they manoeuvre quite happily here at high tide, over a bottom that'll be completely dry six hours later.'

In order to pass in front of the Sainte-Croix church, as we crossed Saint-Servan, we descended a street whose upper part was already in shadow, while its other end, open to the west, still shone in the fiery light of the setting sun. Port Solidor, when we arrived, was bathed in a quiet evening splendour. The first thing which caught my eye, when we arrived at this magical spot, was the Solidor Tower, stood at the end of the northern branch of an inlet of the same name. It was an old keep whose crenelated top floor stood sixty feet above sea level. The tower is built on a rock base which is surrounded by water at high tide. It is linked to the shore by means of a passageway built on a huge earthen ramp enclosed in eighteen-foot high stonework and joined to the quay by a stone bridge.

The shore of the upper part of the inlet was entirely taken up with a shipyard that Couet had us cross. I counted six construction slipways. They were built side by side on the slope above the shoreline. The left-hand slipway was empty. The next two had no more than keels on blocks, with just the stem and stern posts assembled. Next, there were two partially planked hulls. The final slipway, under the Tower, held an almost-completed ship. It was clearly a fourteen-gunport frigate. By that time the shipwrights had gone home.

An elegant little clinker-built ship's boat was sat on the sand between the slipways. It was *le Moucheron's* ship's boat. The sternpost of the frigate on the nearest slip was already standing in two or three feet of water. Surprised, I looked at the other slipways. It was the same story. The bosun's mate had seen what I was looking at.

'Well, if you'd been 'ere three hours ago, there'd 'ave been another three or four foot of water. That's the big trouble with this 'ere shipyard. The after end of the ships built here are five or six feet in water twice a day. That's why they can only build frigates and corvettes 'ere.'

The sailors took off their pumps and slid *le Moucheron's* boat along the sand, inviting me to board before launching it into the water. I took my place in the sternsheets, facing for'ard. I could see two unrigged ships moored on big buoys opposite the Solidor inlet, in line with a little rock that could be seen sticking out of the river a little further on.

'The Bizeu rock,' said the bosun's mate, sat at the tiller, and added that the two vessels had been named *la Résolue* and *la Prudente*. They were two 12-pounder frigates, launched the previous week.

'You saw the slipways with just the keels laid down, Sir? *La Résolue* and *la Prudente* was still on 'em a week ago! An' they've already started two more! They ain't losing time! Never seen owt like it.'

For my part I wasn't surprised. It was exactly the same at Brest.

Since the Chevalier de Kermean had explained to me how far we were behind the English Navy, I understood the reason for this frenzy of construction. I asked why the left-hand slipway was empty.

'It's a haul-out slip, for dry-dockin' an' refittin'. That's where they pulled out *le Moucheron.*'

La Résolue and *la Prudente* had been launched and christened at the same time. Had the man who had decided on such dissimilar names thought that it might influence their respective fates[34]? In any case, they didn't really interest me at that moment, as I had eyes only for *le Moucheron.* She was moored to a coffin buoy a little further north about three hundred yards out from the Solidor Tower, in front of a little creek nestled between the Tower and the rocky slopes of the Cité d'Aleth peninsula. The exit from this creek was marked by a post fixed to a rock sticking out of the water about a hundred and eighty yards from the shore. Couet explained that it was the Mercière Reef, which dried to a height of eighteen feet at spring tides. We were arriving at the middle of the ebb, and our boat was drifting crabwise towards the bow of the cutter.

*

The Solidor Anchorage at Saint-Servan, Friday 18th July 1777, evening.

After hearing about her for so long, she is finally before my eyes: my first ship. In the tidal flow she is pulling at her mooring lines like a tethered colt. I find her quite small: fifty feet long and fourteen feet in the beam. But her quivering bowsprit adds another twenty-five feet, and her boom overhangs her stern by seventeen feet. Her mast, including her topmast, must rise seventy feet above the surface of the Rance. The lower mast is hewn from a single tree trunk and comprises two thirds of the mast height, given that the gaff spanker is the principal sail for this kind of rig. For the moment this sail is furled between its yard and boom, laid horizontally one above the other, above the taffrail. To my eyes, with her black hull and strong sheer, underlined by the white antifouling of her clinker hull, and her aft-raking mast, making a right

34 Translator's note: *their respective fates:* They would both be captured by the English, *la Prudente* in 1779, when she was a King's frigate during the American War of Independence, and *la Résolue* much later, in 1798, under the Republic.

angle with her slightly raised bowsprit, *le Moucheron* seems perfectly constructed for the mission to which she has been assigned.

*

The ship's boat came alongside to port, beside the chainplates. These were more or less amidships because of the rake of the mast. Ten or so sailors, gathered forward around the bitts, watched our arrival in silence. We used the channels like a stepladder to climb aboard, pulling ourselves up by gripping the lanyards between the deadeyes. The guard who welcomed me aboard was not from an Army regiment, as was usual on most Navy ships at that time, but was a genuine member of the Royal Corps of Navy Infantry. It seemed insignificant, but this little detail immediately put *le Moucheron* in a class apart.

According to the Regulations, when boarding a King's ship, one is required without fail to turn towards the poop and salute the flag. The cutter was of such modest proportions that I found myself right beside the three officers who were waiting for me between the binnacle and the big open tiller. I immediately recognised my new commanding officer, by the two gold stripes sewn onto the scarlet cuff of his sleeves. He took a step towards me and stopped at the hatchway just forward of the binnacle. The two other officers remained where they were, their backs resting against the portside rail, heads turned towards me. The nearer of the two wore, like the commander, a scarlet-lapelled Navy jacket, but with a single strip on his sleeve. As for the third, he was wearing the blue uniform of a merchant seaman; he was an auxiliary officer commissioned just for this campaign. I had about six paces to take to get to them, through a narrow passageway between the two chocks for the ship's boat and the quarterdeck. The boat was not yet in place but its supports were taken up with its rigging and oars. I also had to get around two little 3-pounder cannons facing aft, held by gun breeching. There were six in all, three on each side. The whole ship smelled new, with its fresh paint and tar[35].

---

35 This tar is not to be confused with coal-tar. What was called tar in the Navy of old was derived from the resins of pines, firs and larches. It was mainly used for coating rope and for making pitch that was mixed with cotton tow for caulking. The tarred rope took on an attractive colour somewhere between chestnut and orange-brown.

Besides the Fireship Captain Le Meur, the command of the ship comprised a Frigate's Lieutenant and an auxiliary officer. I was the only Marine Guard. There were no Volunteers. The Captain must have been in his forties. With his bulging chest, wide shoulders, sleeves puffed out by his biceps, and narrow waist, he gave an impression of power combined with lightness, just like Flaharn. There was just this difference: Flaharn stood a head above everyone else, while Le Meur was a little below average height. The Fireship Captain had a face bronzed by years at sea, two clear brown eyes, prominent cheekbones, a strong nose and a determined chin. His black hair, thick and curly, was attached behind by a ribbon that failed to control it. I saluted him by raising the back of my hand to my hat and gave him the letter from Monsieur de Fleurieu. He presented his two officers to me. The Frigate's Lieutenant de Kerlaziou was from Brest, at least thirty, quite big, with rough, almost brutal features softened somewhat by a clear gaze. Monsieur Chollet, the auxiliary officer, was over forty, rugged and solid, of average size. In particular I noticed the scar which intersected his forehead. It came from underneath his hat straight down above his nose and stopped by his left eyebrow. It had probably been made by a boarding sabre. This gave him a fearsome look that contradicted his stated role as a peaceful merchant seaman.

Having quickly read my letter of recommendation, Captain Le Meur opened the flap of the hatchway by which he was stood and without further ceremony invited me to go down with him into the 'great cabin'. The bottom of the ladder rested on the sole of a four-foot wide passageway where an infantryman stood guard under the light of two heavy little lanterns hanging from the deck beams. This was, as I would later find out, the only place below decks in the cutter where a man of average height could hold himself upright without having to lower his head. The 'great cabin' was entered by pushing open a door in the forward bulkhead, which led to a seven-foot square space almost entirely taken up by a table and two benches fixed to the sole planking and to the transverse bulkheads. A skylight, the only one of its type on board, allowed a little evening light to filter in. A lantern with clear glass, for the moment unlit, hung above the table. To the left of the door a metal instrument in a varnished wooden box was fixed to the bulkhead. It was a bronze u-shaped pipe – a nautical barometer. Once again, this detail suggested that *le Moucheron* was no ordinary cutter, as the Navy had only just begun to equip its ships with this advanced instrument. The forward part of this square was taken up with the Captain's bunk. The rest of the crew, including the officers, had to make do with hammocks. The officers' hammocks were hung at night in two little 'cabins' – two tunnel-like spaces three and a half feet wide adjoining the corridor and formed by the gap between the bulkhead of the 'great cabin' and the ship's bulwark. These two 'cabins' were separated from the passageway by a simple canvas curtain. As we passed, the Captain showed me the port hand one and told me I would be sharing it with Monsieur Chollet. Captain Le Meur had also opened a second door, this time in the after bulkhead of the passageway, opposite that of the 'great cabin', in order to show me a dark little space that occupied the full width of the ship as far aft as the sternpost. This area was much more important than an officer's quarters, as it served as both armoury and powder room.

*

The Solidor Anchorage, Friday 18th July 1777, evening.

The Captain settles himself on the port hand bench and indicates I should sit opposite him. His face is illuminated by the evening light, while on my side I am in shadow.

'Off you go. I'm listening.'

As my uncle has advised me, I start by explaining as clearly and as completely as possible what I have been sent to Saint-Malo to do. The Captain cuts me off.

'You have a safe-conduct?'

'Yes, Sir'

'In the King's hand?'

'Yes, Sir.'

'You have it on you?'

'No. I have hidden it in the jacket I will be wearing in town.'

'Go and get it.'

Saying that, he gestures with his thumb to the bulkhead behind him. While talking, I have heard several people come down the companionway and drag a heavy object into the nook corresponding to the quarters that I had just been assigned. I go out and do in fact find my chest in the portside tunnel. It takes up almost the full width. I will have to sling my hammock above it. I go back with my nankeen jacket under my arm. The Captain signals me to put it on the table in front of him, and feels it with his hands for a few seconds...

'Look in the locker behind you. There's a knife...Give it to me.'

I find a wide-bladed knife in a leather sheath. It has a long wooden handle, like the knives that sailors stick under their belts. I hand it to the Captain, and with two or three quick and precise little cuts he snips through all the threads sealing the lining, that I had so much trouble sewing. He pulls out the precious paper carrying the signature of Louis XVI and smooths it reverentially on the table. Then he lifts it to the light to read it and refolds it carefully. He unhooks the lamp and calls the sentinel.

'Have Master Deyo called. And light that,' he adds, handing him the lantern.

We can hear the sentinel climb to the top of the companionway and shout along the deck: 'Master sailmaker for the Captain!'

'The lining, that's always the first thing they look at...'

The Captain looks me straight in the eye.

'What shoes will you be wearing in Saint-Malo?'

'The ones I am wearing now, Sir,' I say.

'Take them off.'

His tone is polite but there is no room for argument. There is the sound of a footstep coming down...a silence...then a knock on the door. The guard brings back the lamp that he has lit and the master sailmaker enters, his hat under his arm.

'Give him your shoes!' Captain Le Meur orders me. 'Master! Have a good look at this bit of paper. I want it hidden in the shoes of our Marine Guard.'

He shows the paper, folded in four, with his right hand. The master sailmaker examines it, without any attempt to take hold of it and without asking any questions. I will soon learn that the crew of the cutter are never surprised at anything they are ordered to do.

'Right...I could make insoles out of thin leather.'

'Do it now and at the same time resew the lining of this jacket. We'll wait for you. Carry on, Monsieur Laforest-Dombourg,' he adds, once the door is closed.

I take up my story again. This time the Captain hears me out to the end without interrupting. He looks me straight in the eye the whole time. He keeps silent for a few moments after the end of my account.

'Good! Interesting! Have you ever done this sort of…work?'

'No. I'm ready to follow any advice you may have for me, Sir.'

He gives a funny little suppressed laugh, almost silent. There is nothing offensive about it; on the contrary. He looks away from me, his eyes narrow, and two clefts form between the corners of his mouth and his cheekbones.

'I should hope so!'

He looks at me again.

'You are going to have to stay ashore until we have finalised our plans with this Duval. Monsieur Chollet has found discreet lodgings for you, above the port where we are now. It's on the Point of the Cité side, with an aunt of his, the widow of a corsair who will keep quiet, and who you'll pay with the King's money.'

I tell him that I had rather thought of lodging in Saint-Malo, at *La Malice* inn. The weather-beaten face of the Captain creases again, two openly mocking folds forming from his cheekbones to his half-closed eyes.

'That way, you'll be just beside the rue des Moeurs[36]? Won't you?'

I tell him that I have been given a map of Saint-Malo, and the only thing I have so far learned from it is that it will be difficult to find one's way around the town. It is only for that reason that I had thought of installing myself inside the walled city right from the start. That would allow me to familiarise myself with the layout of the place. As for the rue des Moeurs, I've not even seen it on my map. I wanted to go first to *La Malice*, as this would give me a chance to observe Duval while staying incognito, in order to choose the best moment to approach him.

'Not a bad idea. And I agree it's not easy to find your way around Saint-Malo if you don't know it. The street names change all the time. When you ask the way, you don't know if you'll be given the current name or the previous one. Go to *La Malice*, then, if that's what you want. It doesn't bother me, since we are putting to sea. I've had a lot of things changed during the refit and it all needs testing. The crew needs training too. The Navy is not used to cutters. It's Friday the 18th. Tomorrow, Saturday, it will be high water just after five in the morning. Monsieur Chollet will put you ashore at four o'clock. He will

36 Translator's note: *rue des Moeurs:* the ironically named rue des Moeurs – Morality Street -was in those days the Saint-Malo red light district.

show you your lodgings in the Cité and give you a key. We'll get under way as soon as he is back on board. If all goes well, I expect to be in the Saint-Malo entrance channels at the start of the flood on Saturday 26th, after the evening low tide. That gives you a week to sort yourself out and make contact with this Duval. From Saturday 26th onwards I want you lodging with Chollet's aunt. The room that she will rent to you can be seen from here. Every evening, once it's dark, I'll send the ship's boat into the Port Saint-Père creek and you will without fail come and meet it, without making yourself too obvious, of course. However, if I want you on board straight away, I'll have a blue flag hauled up to the masthead. At night it will be a lamp at each end of the spare yard. If, from your end, you want the boat sent urgently, hang a sheet from your window. At night, put two candles side by side behind the windowpane. Understood?'

'A sheet and two candles! Yes, Sir.'

'Another thing. You said you have a notebook for your accounts. Leave it with me and we'll do your expenses together.'

Did he want to keep a check on me?

'I don't know if they chose you deliberately for this mission, despite your young age. But it's an excellent idea, as you will attract less suspicion. So let's not take any unnecessary risks. There is nothing more compromising than an notebook full of accounts. And those who sent you here are at least right on one point: the English are certainly watching Saint-Malo very closely. The bad peace that we made with them after the last war gave them too many opportunities to establish agents and you can be sure they will have done everything possible to that end. To attack Saint-Malo has always been an obsession of theirs, even though it's a poor port that dries out. But it's inhabited by Malouins[37], which no doubt makes all the difference. You said you had also been given a false embarkation certificate?'

I have this on me and hand it to the Captain, who examines it carefully.

'It's not absolutely perfect...but it would have been hard to do any better.'

Once again he smiles oddly.

'You have to use it carefully. Did they tell you that?'

---

37 Translator's note: *Malouins:* An inhabitant of Saint-Malo is known in France as a Malouin.

I reply that I was told only to take out the certificate if I had no other choice, but that I had not been told why.

'You'll soon find out why. You see, at the moment, in Saint-Malo, there are not many openings for getting on board a ship. Moreover, even if a Malouin goes to sea regularly, it's generally not from Saint-Malo. The ships leaving here are usually after cod. They leave for the Grand Banks in April and return in the autumn. So, that sort of sailor, the kind you are most likely to find at Saint-Malo, is away at the moment and as far as you are concerned, they have done well not to include you amongst them. That's the first thing. After that, the second biggest activity of the port, by size, is the trade in cloth, but for the moment there are no sailings in prospect. As for the famous expeditions to the South Seas, there haven't been any for a long while, even though that's the first thing everybody thinks of at the mention of Saint-Malo. That just leaves trading with the Americas and the Slave Trade. Usually there are a few sailings in early autumn. But, in this day and age, with all these rumours of war, the Saint-Malo shipowners are probably going to delay their plans and see how things turn out, seeing as how, in time of war, the big game here is privateering. It's the speciality of the place. In any event, most of the sailors waiting for a ship, that you are likely to come across here, fall into the last category I mentioned, that of slavers. So in one sense, your certificate is fine. However, as I have just explained, the shipowners engaged in the Trade are few, relative to the other activities. That means that most of the crews of the slave ships know each other well and their officers even better. And *La Malice* is frequented by the long-haul merchant officers. It would be better therefore not to have to rely on your false certificate with them. We will have to create a more elaborate cover story for you. This letter says that you can draw and paint. What's all that about exactly?'

I tell him that I have in my chest some of the pictures I made during my stay at Brest and he asks to see them straight away. He looks at my work without making any comment. He pauses, however, over the drawings I have made of different types of ship. Then he carefully examines my drawing box.

'Well then,' he finally says, handing me back my box, 'here's a good alibi. You are a young man of a good family who wants to become an artist, much to the despair of your grandfather. One of your uncles considers that there would be nothing better than a sea voyage to stiffen your spine and so he has undertaken, with the agreement of your family, to have you shipped aboard at Saint-Malo. You are not at all happy with this. Naturally, once left to your own devices, all you want to do is to paint and draw. Walk around with this box under your arm. That will be your best certificate. You can show the other one to the innkeeper and to the military police if they want to check on you.'

There is a knock on the door. It is the master sailmaker bringing back my jacket and shoes. He shows us the right insole in which he has made a little pocket into which the safe-conduct can be slipped. After he has left, and while I am putting my shoes back on, Captain Le Meur tells me that he will explain my position to the other officers, but that they will not ask me anything in that regard, as he has cautioned them against it. Then, looking at me thoughtfully, he asks about my links with the Ship's Captain Flaharn.

'The only thing I know for sure,' I say, 'is that Captain Flaharn seems to have an interest in me. When I asked him the reason for this, he said that he didn't have a son, that he wanted to help me because I was an orphan...that kind of thing. But, between us, I don't think that is true. Although he maintains that he has never met my father, I think that he is lying about this too and that something happened between them at some point. Something serious. Captain Flaharn wrote to me that you knew my father well at Louisbourg.'

'I don't know who told him that,' replies Captain Le Meur. 'In truth I never knew your father 'well'. But it's true that our paths crossed over there in the summer of 1758. Under his command I even exchanged fire with the English for a whole day.'

'I was told that when he was paroled by the English, after the Battle of Quiberon Bay, the English government refused to exchange him and even demanded that he be returned to them, as if he had been released in error. I had still not been born, but according to my grandfather, my father told him that he had a personal dispute with Admiral Boscawen.'

'He didn't give any more details to your grandfather?' asks Captain Le Meur.

'I don't think so...I mean...I'm sure he didn't!'

Captain Le Meur suddenly becomes much more serious. The mocking look has disappeared from his eyes. I even think I can detect a hint of sadness in them.

'Yes, I understand. I think I know what happened with your father at Louisbourg, or at least in part. But it would take a long time to explain. I don't have the time to talk to you about it right now. Because of your arrival, I have put back the officers' meal and we can't wait any longer. As you are the only Marine Guard, you will eat with us when you are aboard. But, before that, you will have just enough time to prepare your bag for going ashore tomorrow. Then you must get some sleep as it will be a short night. I promise I'll tell you everything I know about your father and Louisbourg later. But I don't think it has anything to do with Flaharn.'

*

The night was short but calm. In harbour, the crew of *le Moucheron* kept a simple watch system. I was tired after my journey and slept right through until a sailor woke me. The night before I had packed away my sword and my beautiful Marine Guard uniform in my chest and prepared my bag for Saint-Malo. The Captain had told me that he and his officers had put on their uniforms to receive me aboard ship, but from now on we would all dress like normal merchant seamen aboard *le Moucheron,* including the men of the Royal Corps of Navy Infantry. I was soon up and dressed in the light of the muted lamps lit permanently in the corridor. I tied up my drawing box with a piece of twine, threw my sailor's bag over my shoulder and climbed the ladder onto the deck. It was half past three and the night was bright; it was the eve of the full moon. The cutter was moving gently on the end of its taut mooring line. The crew was up and silently preparing the ship for departure. Lieutenant de Kerlaziou, accompanied by the bosun, was inspecting the ship. The bosun's mate Couet pulled on the painter of the tender, which had been left afloat, to bring it up level with the port stays. As I was about to climb down into the boat, Captain Le Meur appeared on deck. I put down my bag to salute him.

'Good luck,' he said. 'I don't know what you are going to bring back, but if it is what I think it is, *le Moucheron* will have to be quicker and handier than everybody else. And I guarantee that we will spend the whole of this week doing all we can to achieve that. The rest is up to you.'

*

Saint-Servan, Saturday 19th July, 1777, towards half past four in the morning.

The boat lands at a little slipway at the foot of the Solidor keep. I walk behind Monsieur Chollet, stumbling along the rocky footpath that climbs up from the end of the slipway, through bushes and overgrown weeds, to the first houses built between the Cité headland and Saint-Servan. The rest of the crew has stayed with the boat. My guide turns to the left in a little paved street that goes up a gentle slope. It is still quite dark in the shadow of the houses. At first everything is quiet and bare, but little by little one can start to distinguish things: the detailing on the façades, the branches of trees above the garden walls; a motionless cat in a basement window. Birds start to sing. We pass the last of the houses. The road is no longer paved: we are on a pebbly path which goes up the middle of the ridge towards the dark mass of the fort at the top of the peninsula. With my bag on my shoulder I am starting to sweat. Daylight starts to appear along the horizon to our right, gently illuminating the commercial port, now filled by the tide. Chollet stops and turns east to wait for the appearance of the sun. I let my bag slide to the ground. A pleasant little breeze is blowing from the north-east. Little by little the countryside comes out of the shadow. I can make out the houses of the northern outskirts of Saint-Servan, built on rock right down to the sea. They make a continuous wall along the shore, describing the shape of a rounded inlet as far as the rocky headland with its two windmills that I saw last night. The entrance to the port is now visible to the left of the windmills. A hazy light reflects off the water flowing past the foot of the black Saint-Malo ramparts, still in shadow. The cone of the cathedral tower stands out against the background of clear sky, at the opposite end from the Château, to the right. Gulls circle and mew over the surface of the anchorage. Chollet points out the inlet and the headland.

'The Bas Sablons inlet will be completely dry in six hours' time. Everything is uncovered at low tide here, except for a little gully in the entrance passage that one can cross on foot to get to Saint-Malo, by means of a little culvert of flat stone. There are seven culverts in all and several pebble pathways crossing the port. But they are all under water at the moment. To get into town this morning, you'll have to hire a ferryman. The crossing costs one sol[38]. Their boats are on the other side of the Nose. That's what we call the headland in front of us, the one with the windmills at the end. But there's no point going before seven o'clock, as there won't be anybody there. When the tide has dropped a bit, you can cut across the sand in front of the Saint-Servan houses. That'll shorten the route and save you going back around the suburb.'

It is still too dark for me to be able to look at my map. I ask him if *La Malice* is easy to find.

'It is in the rue de Crevaille, just before the rue de la Diacrerie, north of the Petit Placître, in the town centre, south of the Bishop's Palace. The ferryman will put you ashore between the Old Quay and the Main Gate. Once you have passed the ravelin[39] and gone through the Gate, go straight on up the Grande Rue to the cathedral, then turn left into the rue de la Petite Boulangerie as far as the Place du Martroy, then right, going up on the south side of the Bishop's Palace in the rue des Bès, after which you take the third street to the left, then first right where you'll see the sign straight away.'

Well, that is a lot of help! It seems a bit complicated, and I hope I can find it by means of my map, once it gets light. I also ask him if the rue d'Orléans is far from *La Malice*, and he tells me that it is at the opposite end of the town, towards the Saint-Louis Bastion.

Monsieur Chollet turns towards the west and we set off again. On this side everything is still dark, but it won't last. He takes a footpath bordered with strong-smelling wild plants. The path first descends towards the Rance, then turns to the right. We stop in front of a little two-storey stone house, all on its own to the left of the path. To our right, the steep slope, covered in yellow weeds and bushes, drops down thirty feet to the rocks washed by the dark waters of the anchorage.

The light is strengthening quickly. In the distance the surface of the sea is growing bright. The door of the house faces south-west, overlooking the little creek where I came ashore beneath the Solidor keep. The cutter is sitting on the sheltered stretch of water of the Solidor

38 Translator's note: The *sol*, which later became the *sou*, was one twentieth of a *livre* (pound), so perhaps equates to about five pence.

39 Translator's note: *ravelin:* a triangular fortification placed in front of the entrance to a fort, to divide an assault force and give a position from which defenders can fire down on the attackers.

Bank anchorage, easily visible and about a cable and a half from the shore. Monsieur Chollet opens a ground floor door.

'On Monday we sent two sailors to clean up a bit, but it's not yet perfect. It's a long time since the place has been used.'

We go into a low-ceilinged room which smells of wax polish. My guide takes a candlestick and tinderbox off the mantlepiece. He takes out the means to make a flame and strikes the flint. With just three tries he has the charcloth alight and the candle burning. Apart from Mélanie, at Kermean, I have never seen anybody get a flame so quickly. He tells me softly that his aunt is sleeping above us, but that I don't need to worry as the staircase to the first floor runs up the outside of the house. He gives me the keys and leaves, suggesting I should sleep a little while waiting for seven o'clock.

Once he has left, I have a look around: two box beds, a table, benches, some chairs, chests, a big fireplace. The usual interior of every Breton house, apart from a floor which is tiled rather than bare earth. The room has been swept and the furniture polished. The copper nails on the closed doors of the box beds shine in the candlelight; the fireplace has been cleaned and some dried flowers hung in the chimney.

I go outside again and sit down on a stone bench in front of the door. It is now day, but the sky is still pink. The ship's boat is already back, lying off *le Moucheron's* stern. The boat's crew is being passed a cable that will be used as a stern line by threading it through the ring of the mooring buoy and passing it back to the ship. As they bring the boat on deck, the dull echo of one or two bangs, wood on wood, reach me through the calm early-morning air lying above the surface of the water. The cutter swings to face north-east as it plays on its mooring lines. The yard goes up the mast at the horizontal, deploying the unbrailed spanker. The sail snaps quietly in the breeze as the peak is swayed right up. The jib is quickly hauled up. I hear one blast on a whistle. The cutter turns its bowsprit seawards and starts immediately to pass slowly in front of me along the length of the Solidor Bank, on starboard tack, heading north-north-west, at the same time slipping her bow and stern lines. The King's flag is hauled up to the end of the peak. Apart from the blast on the whistle I have heard no order or shout. Carried by the current and the light wind from the north-east, *le Moucheron* slips between the de la Mercière beacon and the Cité peninsula before being lost to view.

I would have liked to have left with them, but I have a task to accomplish on which the cutter's mission depends. I have not the faintest idea what is going to happen. I don't really know whether I have the ability to fulfil what is expected of me. In principle that ought to worry me, but the calm and determined confidence of Captain Le Meur has erased my misgivings. With a leader like that, it seems to me, nothing can stand in our way. What mainly plays on my mind is the meeting with this famous Duval. What exactly are his links with Flaharn?

3

At high water, the Boatmen's Guild had the monopoly on the crossing between Saint-Malo and its Saint-Servan suburb; at low water everybody could cross on foot. The ferrymen were usually old retired salts who had sailed to Newfoundland or Cadiz or the Americas, and also sometimes into the southern seas, India or even China. As Captain Le Meur had said, the Saint-Malo seaman was a local speciality that was ripe for export. The boatman who took me in charge that morning was no exception to the rule. He was an old shellback, the kind that can turn his hand to anything, his skin tanned and salted by years of voyaging on every ocean. It was seven in the morning and I was his first customer of the day, being the only person wanting a boat at that early hour on a Saturday. Once he had hauled in the sheet to sail close-hauled to the Old Quay, he studied with a knowing air my new blue nankeen coat, my cowhide sailor's bag, just as new, and took me for exactly what I was pretending to be – a young man from a good family about to go to sea. He looked disapprovingly at my painting box.

'So, my little fellow, you've come to look for a ship?'

It was difficult to avoid the conversation that was coming. I replied that I already had a ship in mind.

'What ship's that, then?'

'*Le Duc de Choiseul*,' I replied.

At least, I thought, I'll have a chance of seeing whether the clever plans of my uncle will work of not.

'A big brig, and a good sailor, she is! She got in two weeks ago. They've already put her on the drying posts at Rocabey. But I'm afraid you as might be disappointed. I'd be surprised if she sails this autumn, seeing as what folks are sayin' in town, that there'll like as not be a new war with them Angliches. If that happens, her owner'll want to fit her out as a corsair. Won't take much to alter her. She's already got eight gun ports so she can easy carry sixteen 8-pounders if they want.'

I said to myself that my uncle's forecast was not quite right, but that his plan wasn't too bad despite that. I decided to play the game suggested by Captain Le Meur.

'Ah well, so much the better,' I said. 'You see, I'm not too keen on the sea. It's my family that wants me to be a sailor. What I really like is painting. I want to be an artist, not a seaman!'

Saying that, I showed him my painting box.

The boatman looked disgusted and thereafter left me in peace. Captain Le Meur had got things right.

*

Saint-Malo, Saturday 19th July, eight o'clock in the morning.

The houses in the town seem to me to be packed together so tightly that I wonder how there could be any room for the streets. Their grey façades, they themselves topped by high roofs, rise much higher than the ramparts. Huge chimney pots, lined up like rows of soldiers on parade, crown everything. My boatman gently slides the bow of his boat in amongst the other craft moored to the right of the Main Gate, on a drying-out ramp at the foot of the ramparts between the ravelin and the Old Quay.

When I go ashore, there do not seem to be as many ships as I thought I had seen, from afar, the previous evening. There are only about ten vessels. Moreover, just as the bosun's mate Couet has said, they are of modest size, mostly brigs, snows, ketches and one or two merchant frigates of no more than three or four hundred tons.

Having paid my ferryman, I throw my bag over my shoulder and head towards the Main Gate. The Gate is framed by two very old round towers. Monsieur Chollet has advised me to take the Grande Rue, once through the Gate, in order to get to the Cathedral. This Grande Rue, one of the biggest streets in Saint-Malo, is no more than fourteen feet wide. Its paving is plunged into the shadow thrown by the two rows of buildings and overhanging rooms that dominate it. I can see, at the end of the street, the Cathedral tower, topped by its cone and standing out against the blue July sky. The rue des Bès, a little further on, is scarcely any wider, although its houses are of four or five storeys.

*

There were plenty of people in the streets. I think that, according to the censuses, there were about seventeen thousand inhabitants within the walls of Saint-Malo. Brest, which was four times bigger, had a population of twenty-two thousand. But here, everything was the opposite of Brest. The latter port was inhabited mainly by unmarried men, while in Saint-Malo, with a thousand or so sailors away fishing on the Grand Banks, you came across women and children rather than grown men. The seamen and shipowners who made up the larger part of Saint-Malo's population had always been in the habit of producing large families which filled up their houses from top to bottom. Little boys and girls ran about everywhere, shouting and laughing under the somewhat severe but half-amused eyes of passers-by.

The street into which I turned to seek out my inn was even narrower than those I had walked along. Its houses were so high and so close to each other that the top floors were almost joined. It was one of the oldest areas of Saint-Malo, where mainly there were still old wooden houses, with big windows, glazed with tiny panes, and set between long panels that went the whole width of the successive overhangs. These houses had been built during the time of Louis XIII and Henry IV, or even earlier.

In the heart of this quarter was the rue des Moeurs, so called because it was the only place in the town where the police allowed harlots to ply their trade. As a consequence, the street level of the neighbouring alleys was full of bars and the lower saloons of inns. These were the haunts of sailors looking for diversion, as well as those wanting to escape the eye of the military police. Everyone knew that a new war would inevitably mean additional pressing to man the King's ships. It goes without saying that the matriarchs of the town forbid their many offspring from entering this infamous part of the town. Luckily, *La Malice* had its easily recognisable sign, otherwise I would have spent a lot of time trying to find it amongst all the drinking holes lining the rue de la Crevaille and the rue de la Diacrerie.

The public room of the inn was entered by going down a step. As with most very old houses, the beams were scarcely higher than a ship's between-deck. The front windows were in the ancient style: little squares of bullseye glass assembled on a frame and crimped into lead surrounds. These window panels were all wide open when I arrived, letting in the fresh air and noise of the street. The floor was paved with dark brown tiles. A bucket of water had just been tipped over it and a barefoot employee was drying it with a mop. Everything seemed clean, in any case, and the walls were even decorated with a few prints of sailing scenes.

I wrote my proper name in the inn register, as had been agreed with my uncle. The innkeeper asked to see my certificate, but only glanced at the seal and the signature of the official who had issued it, before giving it back to me. At least that was the impression I had at the time. He told me that he was once a bosun in the merchant navy. It must have been a long time since he had swallowed the anchor; he certainly had the air of a bullyboy, but he seemed to me to be all fat. Be that as it may, he seemed to appreciate the tinkling of my purse when I put it on the counter in order to take out two new white crowns as a down payment. To reassure him on my account, I told him that I had heard that the ship on which my family wanted me to sail was without doubt going to put back its departure, and that, as a result, I hoped to go back home quite soon. But, I added straight away, I was going all the same to stay for a week at the inn in order to make the most of my visit to Saint-Malo by doing some drawing and painting. As he was looking at my box, I pulled out a little sketch that I had done at Brest. It was a lugger under full sail. I gave it to the landlord as a present, to get him on my side, or at least keep him neutral. To thank me, he asked if I had breakfasted, and treated me royally to a glass of wine and a fillet of pickled herring, along with a piece of bread and a raw onion.

The room I was renting was on the fourth floor. It had no fireplace, but at that time of year that didn't bother me. The single window took up the whole street-side wall of the room. I could quite easily have knocked on the panes of the house opposite. The sea was not visible, but the cries of the gulls perched on the rooftops were a constant reminder that this was a port. I got the map of Saint-Malo out of my box and decided to start exploring the town straight away.

I realised very quickly that the geography of Saint-Malo was ideal for the methods outlined by the Chevalier for losing potential followers. A good part of the northern half of the town was taken up with the estate of the bishopric, comprised of the canons' houses, a dovecot, a tower and gardens. This area could be by-passed and in principle was never crossed. As well as the bishopric, other religious communities were spread throughout the town: those of Saint Aron, Saint Thomas, the Benedictine monks and nuns to the north, the Ursulines to the west, with the Hôtel-Dieu, Saint-Saviour and the Recollets to the south. The bells of all these chapels and churches rang out throughout the whole day, merging their sweet sounds with the raucous cries of seabirds and, at high tide, the murmur of the sea around the ramparts. Three parts of the city were delineated by streets which were more regular, straighter and a little less narrow than the others. These quarters had been built at the time of Louis XIV, or even later, for various reasons. The first was the area surrounding the Rue Saint Vincent, near the Chateau and the old emplacement of the Port de Mer Bonne. Then there was the quarter around the Grande Rue, which I had walked up on my arrival, and which had all been replaced after a fire a century earlier. Thirdly there was the area occupied by the shipowners' houses, built scarcely forty years previously, at the southern end of the town. These houses lay behind the Bastion de la Hollande and went the whole length between the Saint Phillippe and Saint Louis Bastions. It was here that the shipowner Blaize de Maisonneuve had his house. The old quarters with wooden and glazed houses, the original kernel of the town, were to be found around my inn, to the south of the town, between the Recollets, the rue d'Entre les Deux Marchés, and the meat market. They were made up of a maze of tiny, dark alleyways between the overhanging fronts of houses from another age. There were also several dead ends; very useful for applying the Chevalier de Kermean's techniques. This assortment would have allowed me to construct all sorts of permutations if that had been my sole aim when staying in Saint-Malo. Moreover, the possibility of going up onto the top of the ramparts to make a complete circuit of the town hugely facilitated the 'going round the houses' so dear to my uncle. I was feeling quite jaunty when I returned to the inn for my supper. I would have been less so, had I known what awaited me.

The innkeeper had told me that he only dealt with people of quality. That was not entirely untrue. I didn't see the most important shipowners of the town in there, but the average standing of his customers was far above that of the sailors and workmen who frequented the bars and brothels of the rue des Moeurs. There were two sorts of guest at *La Malice*: people passing through, like me, who had their dinner and supper at the little tables in the corner of the room, in silence, and the regulars, mostly unmarried men, for whom the inn was a kind of club where they had their set habits. There was a table for the smaller merchants and shipowners' clerks. There was one for the merchant navy officers, the 'navigators', as they were called. And finally, there was a table for the 'Africans', that is to say the close-knit circle of masters and mates of the slave ships. They were in a minority in Saint-Malo, and it was at *La Malice* that they gathered when not on a voyage.

The slaver captains were distinguishable by their healthy financial position. They were even better off than some shipowners. My explanation for this odd phenomenon was that the Trade required considerable investment on the part of the ship owners, and although it could yield good profits, it could also cause crippling losses. The captains, for their part, were spared this circumstance, for their principal investment was their ability; the only capital they risked was their skin. The shipowners engaged them and paid them a considerable price for this. The captains knew that they were indispensable, and that bankruptcy was impossible for them as long as they stayed alive. Those who were still here had survived hurricanes, tornadoes, murderous slave revolts and, above all, the deadly fevers of the African coast which could cut down whole crews and against which European remedies were powerless. This was not to be sniffed at!

To survive in this profession you had to be unscrupulous. To feel pity was a weakness; to have worthy feelings was a defect. The world of the Trade was so oppressive that most of those who tried it gave up after one or two voyages, despite the high pay and the famously lucrative perks. Those who ended up at *La Malice* were the cream of the business. From the very first evening I was struck by the way they carried themselves. They were show-offs, behaving like great lords. They affected to believe neither in God nor the Devil. One could admire them, or secretly hate them, but nobody dared to confront them. They inspired a kind of respect, mixed with revulsion, or the inverse. They put me in mind of Flaharn. From that first evening, while remembering my uncle the priest's pronouncements on the Trade, I wondered how there could be such a divide between these roughneck adventurers and the powdered, polite shipowners I had met at the marriage of my uncle Jean-Baptiste. I have since found the answer, and it is simple. A shipowner can certainly have nightmares when lying between his silken sheets and thinking of the dizzying sums he has invested in fitting out his ships, but the Trade is still for him an abstract notion; he raises his children as good Christians and he has his personal pew at the Parish church. For the captain of a slaver, the Trade was by no means the same thing. For him the Trade had its own smell, its own faces – those of the terrified captives chained up in the stink of the between-decks; for him, the investment was not a number at the bottom of a column; it had a tangible reality called 'junk'. He well knew that if he could easily find slaves for sale at the trading posts on the African coast, it was due to the constant wars between the inhabitants, and that, if a large part of his 'junk' was comprised of swords, rifles, gunpowder and brandy, it was to ensure that the fighting never stopped. It was difficult to play the good family father when returning from a long voyage in the inhuman world of the Trade, especially if you had to set off again so soon. That ground a man down, not just physically, but morally as well. The cod fishing also had its share of suffering and risk, but it was not the same: you did not lose your soul. But it was less profitable!

Amongst the slaver captains who dined at *La Malice*, the wildest, the most brilliant, the proudest and the most incisive of the gang, who had only returned to Saint-Malo two weeks before, after an exceptionally fast and profitable voyage, was Captain Royer, commander of *le Duc de Choiseul.* You can imagine that I made myself invisible behind my little table, on learning that. I would have liked to have hidden myself behind my plate. And there was more to come. At the 'navigators' table, the talk was only of the rumours of war. These gentlemen were fired up at the thought of soon being able to start privateering. One of them commented to Captain Royer that he was lucky to be in command of the fastest brig in Saint-Malo.

'...Once you've replaced those six useless 6-pounders with sixteen good 8-pounders, if you need officers to train your gunners, I'll volunteer!'

'You're right, young man! *Le Duc de Choiseul* is fast,' replied Captain Royer with a rasping voice, 'and I'm sure that with her I can outrun the English frigates as long as I have water to sail in. But why would I run the risk of being trapped on the coast by enemy cruisers in order to try and catch a ship whose value I'm not sure of? If war happens, the price of a cowry shell will at least double in Haiti! Given the profits we made on the last voyage, I had no trouble persuading Monsieur Dubuys to have *le Duc de Choiseul* copper-bottomed. That's why we have careened her. Have you heard about putting a layer of copper on a ship? It's little known here, but the English are doing it a lot. Last year at Rochefort Monsieur Dubuys bought the former King's corvette, called *l'Expérience,* that the Navy had built to try this new method. The copper was stripped off here so that we could try it out on *le Duc de Choiseul.* Our shareholders are all confident and the next cargo of junk is pretty much all financed. I'll sail on 1st September for another voyage to the Guinea Cays. I'll leave you to play hide and seek in the river mouths of Finisterre, hoping to capture a cargo of rotten cocoa or sodden coffee! Your health, Mister Corsair!'

And Captain Royer, pleased with himself, burst out laughing and grabbed the waste of a pretty young girl who had just entered the inn and come up to him to make a show of applauding his speech. This was another fundamental difference between the captain of a slaver and an honest Grand Banks man. The latter rejoined his wife and children each autumn and spent a peaceful winter fussed over by his family, while the former usually had nobody waiting for him on the quay when he returned. He found consolation, then, with pretty fancy women. These were quite dissimilar to the sailors' whores of the rue des Moeurs. They were young, beautiful and spirited, and they dressed like ladies. They had no fixed price. In fact, they had no price. They freely picked out the wealthiest men and spent their time plucking them bare in the most agreeable way. There were several fine specimens of these courtesans in *La Malice's* dining room that evening. The best of the bunch were of course at the 'Africans' table, and Captain Royer was favoured by the most beautiful amongst them. She was a smooth-complexioned blonde, with limpid blue eyes speckled with silver, which gave her a falsely angelic look. She had a waist as flexible as a reed, a smooth, rather musical voice which could turn a man's head, and a bust which had men looking at her as if they were in love. This dream creature called herself Elizabeth de Malaga, an allusion, no doubt, to the Malouin trading posts in Spain.

Sat in my place at the end of the dining room, my nose in my plate, I thought back to my uncle's assurances that *le Duc de Choiseul* would not be back before the autumn. And I myself had trumpeted into the ears of the innkeeper, that very morning, that the ship on whose manifest I was to be entered would not be leaving on account of the risk of the war about which everybody was talking. Every time that my host appeared in the room, I thought that it was to tell Captain Royer that one of his future Volunteers was here. Monsieur de la Rozière had thought of everything, for sure, but who could have foreseen that *le Duc de Choiseul* was going to beat all the records hitherto recorded for a 'circular' voyage?

I was so appalled by this awful turn of events that I almost forgot my main reason for being in Saint-Malo: to talk to Louis Duval. He was at the 'navigators' table. Once I had collected my thoughts, I recognised him from the description I had been given. He did have some smallpox marks on his brick-red face, although they were not too evident. He must have had a mild form of this terrible disease when he was young, and therefore found himself immunised for life, with no other consequences than these scars, which were only a minor annoyance for a man thirty-eight or forty years old. So, from that point of view, fate had favoured him. His baldness was plain to see, as he had hung his wig and jacket on the clothes stand by the door. He had just a half crown of hair pushed back behind his ears, leaving the rest of his head smooth. He had regular blue eyes, prominent ears and a long nose that gave him a juvenile, malicious look that was somewhat at odds with his general appearance. He was of average size, slim to the point of being skinny. All the same, from where I sat I could see him eating like a horse and knocking back glass after glass without it seeming to have the slightest effect on him. Between each course he would light a cheroot from the candle flame and blow the smoke into artistic spirals. But he did not seem to be a talker. He was happy just to listen and only interject when asked. It had been my plan to watch him covertly for the week and approach him quietly on the last evening, but the presence of Captain Royer had thrown this into confusion. Moreover, it seemed to me that with each evening spent in the dining room I increased the risk of having the innkeeper announce my presence to the commander of *le Duc de Choiseul.*

That evening, before going to sleep, I carefully folded my embarkation certificate and slid it into the pocket in my right insole, alongside my safe-conduct. I had decided that if by some bad luck my host mentioned me to Captain Royer, I would play innocent, saying that I had thrown my certificate from the top of the ramparts after hearing about the risk of war and that I no longer wanted to go to sea. It was lucky that the innkeeper had not paid too much attention when I had shown him my certificate and that I had not had to tell him the specific names written on it; I was prepared to swear black and blue that I had never heard of Captain Royer or *le Duc de Choiseul.*

The next morning, I got up at dawn and went out with my drawing book, paint box, brushed, pencils and a bottle of water. I had decided that this was not the time for 'going round the houses' in the way my uncle had foreseen. Given the way things were turning out, I had decided to adopt Captain Le Meur's plan and to play to the full the role of the budding artist. Despite my great respect for the Chevalier de Kermean and his friends the Comte de Broglie and Monsieur de la Rozière, I had finally concluded that, as far as common sense was concerned, nothing could beat that of a mariner who had spent several decades at sea. In fact, I was both right and wrong at the same time. I was soon going to find out that while Captain Le Meur's advice was priceless, so too was that of my uncle.

*

Saint-Malo, Sunday 20th July 1777, seven o'clock in the morning.

I set myself up on the Bastion de la Hollande. Last night, while walking around the ramparts, I had noticed the view to be had from here over the entrance channels to the Rance. They are defended by forts built on the rocky islets surrounded by sea: the Grand Bé and the Petit Bé. There are others further out, too far for my drawing, and there is the Royal Fort, to the north of the town, but I cannot see it from where I am. The wind has turned to the west. The weather is good: neither too hot nor too cool. Little round clouds parade across the sky. It is high water. A strong smell of the sea and tangled seaweed rises up to where I am sitting. I think of *le Moucheron.* She will perform well in this weather. I am sat on the parapet, my legs stretched out on the granite, facing north. I draw the high façades of the houses, the path around the ramparts and the slits in the walls, the little round Notre-Dame tower on the middle of the wall to the north of the Bastion de la Hollande. At the end of that section of wall, after the Notre-Dame tower, the north-west battlements of the town describe a triangle facing seawards, with another tower at its apex. That is where the garrison's powder is kept. It is backed up on the inside of the triangle by an old raised ravelin, on which is a turret facing the powder store, whose merlons[40] had been knocked down to create a gun emplacement. From my observation point I can see the tips of the cannons projecting from their embrasures, aimed at the Rance entrance channels across the wall of the ramparts.

*

During my time at Brest I had developed my own method for making gouache drawings. Firstly I made a general sketch. At the same time, I made other drawings of interesting details on another sketch pad and mixed my colours on yet another sheet. Once I had found a shade I liked, I gave it a number and noted it in pencil on my main drawing. That way I could reproduce it later, working quietly in my room. This kept me busy for a good part of the morning.

As it was Sunday, I went to Mass at the nearby Benedictine Convent de la Victoire. This convent is in the north part of the town and I got there by going straight round the top of the ramparts. I am not particularly given to finding comfort in religion; what I really needed was a quiet place to help me calm my emotions after the discovery of Captain Royer. I would otherwise never have gone to the Cathedral. I was not disappointed. There were not many people and the Benedictine choir had its own marvellous and individual style. The nuns who were singing were hidden behind a grill in the choir and so were invisible to the ordinary mortals. I found their soft voices so much more moving by dint of seeming to come from nowhere. After this break I went back to *La Malice* to have my lunch.

While eating, I watched Louis Duval from the corner of my eye. Spirits and wine were flowing and empty bottles were lined up on both the 'African' table and the 'Navigators' table. The women were drinking

40 Translator's note: *merlons*: the solid parts of a crenelated battlement.

much less than the men, of course, but all the same I could see that Elisabeth de Malaga was holding up her end, glass in hand. By the time I got up to leave the room, some of the guests were already completely intoxicated. This was not the case with Duval, although I had seen him drink like a fish. Despite his thinness, he had a prodigious ability to hold his drink. Nonetheless, he never became talkative. Basically, this was a good thing for what we had in mind for him, but I still wondered how I could approach him without being noticed.

*

Saint-Malo, Sunday 20th July 1777, towards one o'clock in the afternoon.

When I return to the Bastion de la Hollande with my painting gear, the morning scene has changed. The sea has receded beyond the Petit Bé. This makes the fort on it look like an eagle's nest on a rocky outcrop. There has been a thunderstorm and heavy rain during lunchtime and a mass of black cloud is now crossing Saint-Malo. To the north the sky has stayed blue. Its extraordinary brightness, contrasting with the temporary shadow cast across the town, brings out all the tints of the landscape: the greyish-yellow of the ramparts, the orange-grey of the granite at their base, the black patches of seaweed, the blue with emerald reflections of the sea beside the wide beach of white sand uncovered by the ebbing tide; even the thin vegetation on the top of the Grand Bé has taken on a green, almost blazing, colour. I take out my brush and gouaches and rush to capture the shades of this fleeting palette. The clouds pass and the colours return to normal, giving the landscape its usual look. I spend the rest of the afternoon reproducing the identical drawing I made this morning at high tide but adding all the changes which have appeared at low tide. There are many new details to take note of and it keeps me occupied until dinner time.

*

The next morning, I decided to stay in my room to work on the colours for my two drawings, aided by the notes and sketches I had thrown together on my paper. I started with the scene at low tide. I wanted, without delay, to capture again the special light which had so taken me at the end of the thunderstorm the day before. Towards ten o'clock the housemaid arrived, along with the odd-job man who was to take down the buckets. They were surprised to find me there. They admired my work and were quite complimentary. I gave twenty sous to each of them as a tip. I made this gesture without thinking, using the King's money, and I was not to regret it.

Painting is such an absorbing occupation that one does not notice the passage of time. I finished just in time to go down for lunch. There was a surprise waiting for me at my table. When I picked up my table napkin, I found a note folded in two hidden in it. I had the presence of mind to slip it into my pocket straight away, without reading it, but I had to control myself not to rush down my meal too quickly, so impatient was I to return to my room. Once I was alone, I looked first for a signature. There wasn't one. This is what I read:

Be at the Bastion St. Philippe at six o'clock, before dinner. I will be wearing a tailored pink cotton jacket and a blue-grey hat.

My first thought was that it must be Louis Duval, but the mention of a pink jacket[41] did not match him at all, as I had never seen him in anything other than a threadbare brown rateen coat. I had five hours to wait. I went back to my paints and attacked the view at high tide, but this time I had trouble concentrating. In the end I abandoned the scene at high tide before it was finished and went back to the one I had worked on earlier, the thundery sky at low tide. There was nothing more to be changed but I continued to contemplate it blissfully until it was time to go.

*

Saint-Malo, Monday 21st July, six o'clock in the evening.

The Bastion Saint Philippe is located at the south-west angle of the ramparts to the south end of a wall just below the Bastion de la Hollande, which is reached by a big flight of steps.

The sky has cleared, but an unusually cold breeze from the north-west has got up. The coolness of the wind and the late hour must

41 *Pink tailored jacket*: men's jackets, particularly those worn at Court, were often likely to be pink. This was not the exclusive preserve of women.

have discouraged any strollers, and there is nobody on the ramparts at my meeting place. I feel a little tense. I wonder if I am about to do something very foolish and wish I had my pistols. I have left them on board *le Moucheron* so as not to weigh down my bag. I hear footsteps coming up the stairs from the rue Saint Philippe. A grey hat comes into view, and the back of a spare and slim-waisted person in a pink coat and breeches. This apparition has a sprightly gait and carries a sword at its side. It reaches the path around the bastion and turns towards me.

'Good evening, Monsieur Dombourg. Follow me, I am inviting you to dinner.'

If I have any doubt, it is dispelled by the singularly honeyed tones of that voice. I have before me the woman who calls herself Elisabeth de Malaga. She is even more unnerving in her disguise as a gentleman of the Court, a disguise which sits so well with her strawberry blond curls. I want to object, but she silences me with an intense look of her strange blue eyes. To have found out my name, she must have looked in the innkeeper's register. I say to myself that in future I must be careful with that dubious character. She leads me to the nearby entrance of a shipowner's house at the western end of the rue Saint Philippe. She then takes me through a courtyard to a little door of which she has the key. This door opens onto the foot of a hidden staircase. At the top, she ushers me into a room which has a door to the top floor landing. A cold collation awaits us, set out on a round table in front of a fireplace from which a little porcelain figurine seems to be studying me with an ironic look. The walls are decorated with printed cotton. A big window, facing the sea, to the west, allows the direct entry into the room of the still bright early evening sun. Against the wall at the end of the room, opposite the door, is a four-poster bed, its drapes painted with Chinese motifs, and just beside it is a doorway covered by a curtain which La Malaga pulls back to reveal a little bathroom decorated with painted tiles. The centrepiece of this room is a copper bath already filled with hot water. The servants who had set the table had also prepared the bath for the mistress of the house. Having tested the temperature of the water, my hostess takes hold of a porcelain pitcher filled with a perfumed liquid and pours its contents into the bath. Then, without any ado, she undresses completely and sinks into the bath with a sigh of relief. She gets out before long and invites me to follow suit, which I do without much persuasion, for a bath is a luxury which is completely lacking at *La Malice*.

*

Even the most intimate crannies of La Malaga's body gave off the aroma of rosewater. She was possessed of treasures worthy of a King and used them with the greatest skill. Once she had turned me upside down and inside out, in her own particular way, without even giving me the time to wonder why I was deserving of such generous treatment, she pulled on a diaphanous silk robe, handed me a dressing gown and invited me to eat with her. She pointed out a carafe half filled with a beautiful dark liquid.

'It's a Bordeaux wine given to me by a captain I know. It has been to the Americas and back at the bottom of the hold, which has enabled it to age incomparably. I am sure you will never have tasted anything like it.'

I took hold of the carafe and, like a gentleman, made to fill her glass before mine, but she stopped me straight away and poured water into her glass, while saying, somewhat flirtatiously:

'Thank you, my young friend, I am not in the habit of drinking wine, and moreover, you have taken care of me so vigorously that I am still reeling.'

Everything considered, the initiation that my former friends had imposed on me at Brest, at the house of the *Dames de la Marine*, although dubious from a moral point of view, had been of itself an excellent thing. Without it, I am sure that I would have lost all common sense and taken as the unbridled truth everything that she was saying to me. Not only did I remember seeing her emptying her glass like one of the men the day before, at *La Malice*, but I was also capable of realising that she was telling barefaced lies as regards our lovemaking, given that she had taken the initiative right from the beginning and directed all operations, imposing her own rhythm from start to finish. So I wisely put down the carafe of wine and poured myself some water too. In any event, she did not hold back from serving herself first and attacking her plate. That was a little more reassuring. I copied her with a will, for our little diversion had given me an appetite. But I wasn't going to get off so easily! As soon as I had put down my empty glass she quickly filled it with her famous wine.

'If you don't drink some of it, dear heart, you will upset me. I have uncorked it especially for you.'

Ever more distrustful, I looked around, trying to find a way out of this impasse. My eye fell on the magnificent sunset over the Rance. I took my glass and stood up, offering my arm to my hostess.

'Come, Madame, I would like to drink to your health while admiring this sublime spectacle.'

Without giving her the time to react, I opened the casement window and leaned on the sill, at the same time drawing La Malaga's supple waist close to me. The sun was dropping out of sight and the north-west wind, quite cool at this late hour, took us in a cold embrace. We could hear the sound of the waves against the foot of the ramparts eighty feet below us. I felt my friend shiver in her light gown. To reassure her, I brought my glass to my lips and pretended to drink.

'Come in quickly. It's cold and people will see us,' she said, pushing me away to escape my hold.

I relaxed my grip and she turned quickly away to find shelter inside the room. I used the moment to pour the contents of my glass into the street below and followed her back into the room. She closed the window straight away and looked at my empty glass with what, it seemed to me, was a certain satisfaction.

'How do you like my sea-going wine?'

'Exceptional,' I said. 'I have never drunk anything like it. But I am feeling tired all of a sudden.'

'Lie down, then, my dear heart.'

'All alone?' I said, playing the innocent.

La Malaga was conscientious, I have to give her that. She did all she could to get me off to sleep. Nonetheless, although she made a noble effort to appear willing, I could feel that she had not foreseen that things would drag on for so long, and her heart was no longer in it. As for me, I was not in the least unhappy to give her a taste of her own medicine. Following which I stretched, yawned, closed my eyes and started to breathe regularly as if falling asleep.

Having watched me for a while, no doubt to be sure that I was properly asleep, my seductress got up. I had stayed on my back, my head turned out from the bed, so that I could watch her through half-closed eyelids. She went straight to my jacket and searched the pockets carefully. She then had a look at my breeches and waistcoat. Not finding anything, she went back to my jacket and ran her fingers carefully over all the seams. She found nothing, of course, and that seemed to vex her, as she repeated the operation several times. Eventually she blew out the candles and got back into bed beside me, not having thought to inspect my shoes. She pushed me freely towards the wall with her elbows and feet so as to have more room, all the while grumbling to herself: 'What a greenhorn! I hope that fool of an innkeeper hasn't picked the wrong ship and that the others find something.' Then she fell asleep without the slightest misgiving. This confirmed to me that I had done devilishly well not to taste her wine. At the same time I thought about Captain Le Meur and his master sailmaker with the greatest of gratitude. Nonetheless, I tried to keep watch for the whole night.

*

Saint-Malo. Tuesday 22nd July 1777, morning.

I wake with a start. Sleep has overcome my mistrust. La Malaga is already dressed; as a woman, this time. She has put on a dress of Indian cloth with flounced pagoda sleeves. It is probably a gift from her slaver. The 'junk' cloths are not sold exclusively to the petty kings on the coast of Africa; they are appreciated just as much by the beautiful Creoles of Haiti and by the ladies of Europe.

'Up and out!'

I sit up, stretching and rubbing my eyes…and all my clothes land on my head.

'Did you hear? The party's over, you big halfwit!'

Elizabeth de Malaga's eyes are flashing and have lost all their charm. This does not surprise me, given what I heard her say before I fell asleep last night.

'I've wasted enough time with you! This morning I have to meet a man, a real one, not a spring chicken! You want to know who it is?'

I take my time to dress. I know very well who she is talking about. It is certainly the man who gave her this dress. I also have the feeling that La Malaga is waiting for my answer while watching me closely to see how I react. I have no desire to give her what she wants. In this kind of exchange the loser is always the one who speaks first. As I put on my right shoe I experience once again the secret satisfaction of feeling under my foot the insole made by Master Deyo.

'Captain Royer! That rings a bell, doesn't it?'

'Not at all,' I reply, forcing myself to look as vacuous as possible, which seems to annoy her enormously.

'Don't you have to embark on his ship?'

'Who on earth told you that?'

'I have a friend at the Maritime Office. He let me look at the lists for Saint-Malo. When I want to know something, I'll always find it, you know! Don't try to lie to me!'

She is of course lying. My name could certainly not have been entered into the Maritime Office lists for Saint-Malo, since the real Volunteer for *le Duc de Choiseul* has not yet been assigned and my certificate is false. What is more, my uncle has told me that the certificate had left Saint-Malo with its holder's name left blank. That meant that only the innkeeper could have told her. And she mentioned him when talking aloud last night. Why is it such a serious matter to be assigned to *le Duc de Choiseul?*

'Once again, I don't have the faintest idea what you are talking about,' I babble.

'I'm talking about your embarkation certificate, you little pipsqueak!'

Now she is really shouting and getting angry. She seems to me to be increasingly losing her composure the more she uncovers the extent of my pretended stupidity. I think to myself that it is best for me to keep on bolstering her mistake.

'Do you mean that printed piece of paper that my uncle gave me and that I was supposed to present to my commander in order to embark? I didn't read it properly, but I don't think the name of your Captain Royer was on it. Anyway, it's not important. As soon as I found out there was a risk of war, I tore up the paper and threw it over the ramparts. I didn't want to go to sea anyway; but to fight as well? That's not for me! I want to be an artist.'

Hearing that, Elizabeth de Malaga cannot hold back a scream of rage. It seems that this fiery girl hates cowards. She catches sight of the sword that she had been carrying last night to come to our meeting. It is lying on an armchair where she has thrown it before undressing. She grabs it by the handle and swings the scabbard with a whipping motion that shows a strong hand and some practice in swordsmanship and, in an instant, even before the scabbard has hit the floor, I find myself with the point of the sharp blade under my chin.

'Listen well, my lad. There has maybe been a misunderstanding but know that what happened last night ought never to have taken place and that you have had a lucky chance that many more deserving men than you would envy. So here's some advice. Forget everything and never say a word. And above all, don't go boasting about it. If Captain Royer hears of it, you'll be dead within the hour. Do you understand me?'

I don't need to force myself much to look terrified. For a fraction of a second, I really think I have gone too far and that she intends to slit my throat.

*

When I got back to my room on the fourth floor of the inn, I at first noticed nothing out of the ordinary. Everything seemed to be in its place. It is true that I had not quite recovered from my adventure at La Malaga's house. After a while, though, once I had calmed down, I began to think that my things were a bit too tidy...except for my two paintings, which were still on the table where I had left them, between my paint box, a pitcher of water, my brushes and the piece of cloth I used to clean them. It was then that I saw that on my painting the tide had risen of its own accord. I remembered very well having put the picture at high water aside, before I had finished it, in order to contemplate the low tide version, with which I was so satisfied. This meant that somebody had searched my room while I was with Elizabeth de Malaga. Somebody very conscientious who had looked at everything, then arranged everything carefully to hide any trace of a search. Unfortunately for him, he had made a mistake when putting the paintings back. He must have thought, quite logically, that the unfinished one would be the one on my worktable in front of my chair. Overcome by disquiet, I took my purse out of my bag to check the King's money. Nothing had been taken. I was relieved but thinking about it more, found that even more disquieting.

In order to be sure, I waited for the housemaid and her assistant the bucket emptier and thanked them warmly for having given the room an extra clean the previous afternoon. They were visibly pleased at this, but said, with great honesty, that they did not deserve my compliments as they had not been in my room since the previous morning. Besides, they added, even if they had wanted to they would not have had the time.

I asked them how long the current innkeeper had been the proprietor at *La Malice*. They replied that he had inherited the inn about ten years earlier, following the death of the previous owner, whose sole relative he had been. Once again, I gave them a little tip.

All this needed thinking about. La Malaga had, according to the evidence, concerted with one or several accomplices so that they could search my room while she took care of me. As for the innkeeper, 'this fool of an innkeeper', he had been there long enough to make it all seem natural to me. The courtesan must be leading him by the nose. I saw him more as an unwitting accomplice rather than an active participant in a dark plot organised by the English...or organised by Flaharn? I had to admit, despite the injury to my self-esteem, that my good fortune of the previous night owed nothing to my own attractiveness.

Who were La Malaga and her accomplices working for? If it was for the English, on the supposition that they had got wind of a mission organised by the King's secret service in Versailles, how the devil had they managed to find me so quickly? It was black magic!

And what if Flaharn had laid a trap for me, with La Malaga and Duval as its agents? But this idea did not sit well with the courtesan's attitude towards me. If I analysed the few words I had heard from her the previous night, she thought she must have mistaken me for someone else, and that I was far too young and too stupid to be the one she had been asked to seduce. And after all, she seemed to have total belief in the authenticity of my certificate of embarkation for *le Duc de Choiseul*. Her sole interest seemed to be in this famous false document. And, even if Flaharn did not know that I had a false certificate, he knew well enough who I was and why I had come to Saint-Malo.

The only way to get to the heart of the matter was to talk with Duval. It was no longer a matter of quietly waiting at *La Malice* until the end of the week. It was absolutely imperative that I approach Louis Duval that same day. If the advice that the Chevalier de Kermean had given me at Vertou had seemed somewhat exaggerated at the time, that was no longer the case. I could still feel the tip of La Malaga's sword under my chin. This mission was not just a game. There was one point, however, on which I had cause to feel relieved: if what the beautiful Elizabeth had said about Captain Royer were true, he still knew nothing of my existence.

*

Saint-Malo, Tuesday 22nd July 1777, ten o'clock in the morning.

I stretch out on the bed and stare at the ceiling, trying to find a way in which I can approach Duval without attracting the attention of my unknown adversaries. I would only be able to see him in the inn's dining room, during lunch and therefore, so to say, under the eye of La Malaga. I think about waiting for him outside so as to follow him and then approach him. But that is too risky. Elizabeth de Malaga was not born yesterday. If she notices my manoeuvre, all will be lost, unless, once again, they are all in it together and Duval is part of the gang. Thinking about the courtesan gives me a good idea. She had slipped a note into my table napkin. It is of course impossible to do the same thing and approach the 'navigators' table without being noticed and, moreover, I won't know beforehand which place Duval will be sitting at. On the other hand, I am familiar with his jacket, which he always hangs on the same clothes stand along with his wig and hat. I could slip a note into his pocket while going out, without anybody noticing; that is possible.

All the same, I must not forget that Duval himself could be a danger to me. For that reason, I have to choose a meeting place which will allow me to react quickly in the event of danger, whatever it might be.

I sit down in front of my drawings and suddenly that gives me an idea. I had made my picture of the Bon Secours beach at low tide on Sunday, towards one in the afternoon. That Sunday there was a full moon. It is now Tuesday. The tides will still be big and low tide will be a little after two in the afternoon. I have it!

I cut a little piece from my best drawing paper and write the following words:

> *I will be waiting for you near to the rocks at the entrance to the Royal Fort at low tide today. Come alone!!! I will give you a letter from F... if you can reply to the following question: who took the Merry out of the port of Muscat on 4th October 1759?*

Drawing paper has the advantage of being strong and thick. Even if Duval does not normally put his hands in his pockets, he will feel my note as he puts his jacket on. I prepare my bag and put it under the bed. With a pencil I make a discreet mark to show its position on the floorboards. I do the same thing with my drawing pad that I leave leaning against the bed frame. This time, I take all my money with me. Lastly, I take my safe-conduct from its hiding place and slip it into my jacket pocket.

*

While going down the stairs for lunch, I came across the odd-job man, who was waiting for me. He told me in a low voice that as he was crossing the courtyard to empty the buckets into the sand-filled pit reserved for this purpose, two men had called him to the door leading to the street and asked him 'if the young man on the fourth floor was still in his room or whether he had gone out'.

'They gave me one sol!' said the servant with disdain.

I gave him an ecu and asked him what they looked like. He said they were dressed like clerks, with flat shoes and black hats. The good man had told them that I was there and they had left. Distrustful, however, he had gone through into the inn's dining room to observe the men through the slit in the door and had seen the two individuals about ten paces apart leaning against the wall opposite, one watching the door to the courtyard and the other the main entrance into the dining room.

I ate quickly, keeping my head down. La Malaga arrived on the arm of Captain Royer and did not look my way. Louis Duval was at his place. I went out while the regulars were still at their first course. I managed to slip my message into the pocket of Monsieur Duval's jacket and went out into the street. Although I was well ahead of time for getting to my meeting point, it was not too much as I would have to make some detours. In fact, if accomplices of Elizabeth de Malaga were watching me in the street, it was now or never as far as applying the advice my uncle had given me at Vertou was concerned.

I saw nobody as I came out of the inn. I started by walking slowly towards the rue de la Diacrerie as if I were out for a stroll. I then turned north into the first street on my right. This little alley was called the rue du Point du Jour[42], as it was so narrow and the upper floors of its houses so close to each other that it was always very dark. Moreover, there were

42 Translator's note: *rue du Point du Jour :* Daybreak Street

never many people here, and as it was still lunchtime, it was deserted. I kept walking just as slowly. Once at the end I turned right again into the rue des Bès. I glanced back and saw two men coming out of the rue du Point du Jour. They were walking one behind the other about ten paces apart. They took the rue des Bès in the same direction as me. The first was wearing a dark blue jacket with a waistcoat and chamois breeches. The other was dressed in black with white stockings. They had the look of clerks or secretaries. It may just have been coincidence, but after what the lad at the inn had told me, I decided to stop to make sure. This was one of the techniques recommended by the Chevalier de Kermean.

I was just coming to the top of one of those tiny little gardens that the Malouins tend with such care and which are found in the least space between the high walls of their houses. The centrepiece of this one was a cherry tree. It was not very big, but as it had to stretch high to seek out the light, on account of the houses hemming it in, its greenery was spreading at least six feet above the ground over a remarkably thin and straight trunk. It was the end of July, so its fruit had long since been picked. However, it had attracted the attention of a gang of little scallywags gathered there, all looking upwards at one of their number who was climbing up the trunk like a monkey. From their shouting, I gathered that it was one of those challenges that kids like to make to each other. I used this as an excuse to stop, as if I wanted to watch the attempt. But the rascals did not have a clear conscience: seeing my sudden interest in what they were up to, they skedaddled in a flash, while the little climber slid down to the bottom of the tree in one go and ran off after them. As they were going up to towards the western ramparts, I was able to watch them quite naturally, and was able to confirm that my two fellows had stopped in unison, each of them contemplating the façades of the houses at their respective levels. There was no doubt about it: I was being followed.

It was out of the question to lead these two all the way to Duval. I absolutely had to get rid of them. On the other hand, if I suddenly started racing along, they would know immediately that I suspected something and was not as innocent as I looked. My moves had to appear natural. The reconnaissance that I had made the previous Saturday, although brief, was now going to be very useful. The rue des Bés, along which I was walking, led to the Place du Martroy. This square, situated to the south of the Cathedral, is the central point to which all the streets lead from the different gates of the town. Someone, like me, arriving here from the west, could turn left, due north, towards the Cathedral porch; or else continue straight on towards the Croix du Fief or the Main Gate; or else turn right to go down due south as far as the Dinan Gate. However, there was another possibility. Forty yards before the Place du Martroy, the rue des Bés was crossed by an eight-foot wide alley called the rue de la Lancette. Bordered with old four-storey wooden houses similar to *La Malice*, and housing several bars, it went south for forty yards before turning east at a right angle where, after another forty yards, it opened up onto the main thoroughfare going down from the Place du Martroy to the Dinan Gate. This section of the street was called the rue d'Entre les Deux Marchés. I approached the crossroad, walking slowly and trying to look as relaxed as possible, and then turned as quietly as possible into the rue de la Lancette. As I had hoped, my two followers had hung back a bit more after the incident with the cherry tree. They had almost caught up with me by being too close; now they made the other mistake and let me get too far ahead.

As soon as I was out of their sight in the alleyway I started to walk more quickly. I resisted the desire to run, as that would have drawn the attention of the many townsfolk walking about. When I reached the right angle in the street, the blue jacket had not yet reached the intersection between the rue des Bés and the rue da la Lancette. I went faster until I got to the rue d'Entre les Deux Marchés, turned right towards the Dinan gate, without slowing my pace, then ducked into the first street on my right, bringing me back towards the west. At best, my followers would be searching for me in the inns of the rue de la Lancette; at worst, they would lose time in the rue d'Entre les Deux Marchés, wondering whether I had left for the Dinan Gate, or whether I had continued east towards the Main Gate or the Bastion Saint Louis. I walked at a good pace, at each turn making for the western ramparts, which I reached via the rue de la Crosse at the top of the north end of the Bastion de la Hollande. I then did not have any time to lose, since to get to the Royal Fort I had to go out via the Saint Thomas Gate, which was at the opposite end of town from where I now was. Following the ramparts on the inside, I had to cross the end of rue de la Diacrerie, not far from *La Malice*, and the end of the rue des Bés. I looked carefully to my right before crossing these delicate spots, fearing that the blue jacket and the black jacket might have doubled back after losing my tracks. Finally, I passed to the north of the Bishopric buildings, in front of the Benedictine church. Breathing hard and sweating, I reached the Saint Thomas Gate, to the north-west of the Chateau.

*

Saint-Malo, Tuesday 22nd July 1777, afternoon.

The Royal Fort is built on a rocky island, called the Islet, eight hundred yards to the north of the Saint-Malo Chateau. Like the Grand Bé and the Petit Bé, it is surrounded by water at high tide. At low tide one can get to it by walking across the shore. Access is by means of a strip of white sand, bordered on each side by clear water in which shoals of little fish can be seen swimming. I am the first there. I sit down on a rock, back to the Fort, facing Saint-Malo. I have a good view of the walkers coming out of the Saint Thomas Gate to get to the Sillon by means of a strip of earth along the foot of the huge fortifications of the Chateau. To come to the Royal Fort it is necessary to leave the groundwork and come down onto the shore. I have chosen this spot because Duval will have to cross an empty space about two hundred yards wide to get to me. If he is not alone, I will see that straight away and have time to make off along the shore to the north of the Sillon. I do not have long to wait. I recognise him easily from a distance. He is coming down onto the sand. I would like to have my telescope with me, to see whether he has left one or two accomplices to wait for him at the Gate, but it is in my chest aboard *le Moucheron.*

I stand up when Duval is thirty paces away. He has already seen me, as there is nobody else about apart from me.

'Good day, Monsieur Duval,' I say.

His face shows the greatest bewilderment.

'Well, then, it's you! The devil take it! Not what I was expecting…'

'What were you expecting then?'

'I would never have imagined that Flaharn would send me a stripling!'

Stripling! Greenhorn! Pipsqueak! I start to have my fill of being taken for a little boy.

'You know that if I had my sword, you might adopt a different tone?'

'Don't take offense. I simply meant that knowing Flaharn I would have been less surprised to find a nasty horned devil than a young man with your sweet face. And you certainly weren't born in 1759...do you have the letter from him?'

'Yes, but first you must tell me about the *Merry.*'

'That's right. He warned me. But let's not stay here. The tide will be rising soon. Shall we go to the Grande Grève? We can talk and walk as far as La Hoguette.'

We walk to the north-north-east along the immense expanse of white sand exposed at low tide to the north of the Sillon levée. We pass the big piles dug into the sand by the Malouins to protect the roadway from the destructive assault of the sea.

'At the end of the year 1759, the Comte d'Estaing had chartered a ship and a frigate from the India Company...'

'I know that,' I say, 'It was at the Île-de-France and Flaharn was in command of the ship. But please continue. Tell me all the details. It will be interesting and we have plenty of time.'

'Good! Well, the ship was called *le Condé* and the frigate was called *l'Expédition*. In fact, Flaharn was normally only the first lieutenant aboard *le Condé* for the Company, but the Comte had arranged for him to be given a commission as a Fireship Captain. We sailed on 1st September. Four weeks later we boarded and searched a Portuguese merchant ship, the *Mamoudy,* which was coming from Muscat. Flaharn had declared it a valid prize, since it was flying the English flag. That was not true at all, but as the Comte was too short-sighted to verify it, he said nothing. Flaharn spoke a little Portuguese and he began to interrogate the Captain of the *Mamoudy*. You know Flaharn? I wouldn't like to be interrogated by him! When the Portuguese skipper had seen the kind of man he was dealing with, he quickly let out that there was a valuable English merchantman, the *Merry*, anchored in the port of Muscat. So Flaharn made for the Arabian coast. After five days we arrived at Muscat. It's a very sheltered harbour, bordered to the east and west by steep rocky mountains, dark brown as far as I remember, with the town at their base. At the entrance to the anchorage, on the left, on a rocky, sheer island, were several small forts, and about six hundred yards opposite, to the right, on a spur of the mountain, was a bigger fort with five naval artillery guns. Under these cannons, half a gunshot away, lay the famous *Merry*. *Le Condé* raised the English flag. We anchored a cable's length from the *Merry* and waited until nightfall. As soon as it was dark enough, we launched the ship's boat and her sloop. The Comte went aboard the boats with fifty men and rowed towards the mooring buoy, at the same time letting out a cable astern that *le Condé* would then use to tow us out of the port with our prize. At first everything went well. The surprise was total and we quickly overcame the crew, who were chained up in the hold. But then, disaster! The tow rope had been badly hitched and it ended up in the water. We began to drift towards the rocks under the fort. On top of that, some boats had pulled out from the port to stop us, which we fired at with rifles and pistols. Suddenly, the port cannons opened fire. By the sound, I'd say they were 24-pounders. It was soon panic aboard! Everyone was rushing everywhere. As for the Comte, he remained quite calm, but like a good infantryman, all he could think of doing was aiming the *Merry's* 8-pounders at the fort in order to return fire. Luckily, a little breeze started to get up off the land. Seeing that, I grabbed a quartermaster and five or six sailors who seemed a bit calmer than the others. We hauled up the foretop staysail, I told the quartermaster to take care of the sheets and I took the helm. I steered seawards and Flaharn came with *le Condé* to pass another towrope for'ard. For that I was promoted from Volunteer to Ensign, on *le Condé's* crew list. There you are! Will you give me that letter?'

I hand him Flaharn's letter, the one whose contents the Chevalier de Kermean had summarised for me at Vertou. Duval stops walking in order to read it. When ha has finished, he looks at me with a shake of the head.

'Well, yes, it seems like him, but it's you he's recommending to me? He must have changed a lot in seventeen years. Really, I have trouble believing it.'

'Is it that long since you have seen him?'

'Not since May 1760, at Port-Louis on the Île-de-France, when we got back from that expedition. A voyage into hell, I should say. I was twenty years old and saw so many horrors that I still have nightmares. And I think it will be like that until I die.'

He studies me again with a disbelieving look. I look around. There are carriages and pedestrians on the Sillon, but the Grande Grève is empty apart from us. It would seem that Duval has come alone to our meeting. I get out my safe-conduct signed by the King and give it to him. He whistles through his teeth as he realises what it is.

'This signature…'

'You have seen it well enough,' I say. 'It is the King's.'

'The King of France! My God! Ah, I understand better now. You are a protégé of the Comte d'Estaing, isn't that it? A noble! That's why you were talking about your sword just now? I beg you to forgive me. I couldn't have known, with you dressed the way you are.'

'There is one thing I don't understand,' I say to him, taking back my precious document. 'If you have not seen Captain Flaharn since 1760, how is it that he is asking us to make contact with you now?'

'Everything is done by letter. It's me who wrote to Flaharn proposing the business for which you've been sent here. At first, he was going to come himself, but then he wrote to say something had come up and you would come in his place.'

'When did you first write to him?'

'The first time? It was in September last year. I'd heard that he had a prominent position alongside the Comte d'Estaing. That's why I thought of him when we had the idea for our project. I wanted to ask him whether his position would make it possible for him to act as an intermediary between us and the Navy Office or the War Office. He replied straight away saying that he was very interested and that he would come to see me at Saint-Malo as soon as he could. Then, in the end, his last letter said you would come as his representative, that you would have a letter from him to give to me, and that you would ask me about the old story of the *Merry*. That was all a sort of password to avoid anything going wrong.'

'But why did you not go straight to Monsieur de la Rozière, the commander of the Saint-Malo base?'

'We feared a refusal, because our plan is rather unusual. Excuse me, but on whose authority are you acting?'

'What! Have you not read the signature on my safe-conduct? Is that not enough for you?'

'I'm sorry,' replied Duval. 'You're quite right. It is true that I have never had occasion to see the King's signature, but it seems authentic. In any case, I don't think there would be much to gain by making a forgery of this calibre. The risks are too high.'

'Well, I'm listening,' I say, forcing myself to take on a conciliatory tone.

'Right. Firstly, I am acting for Monsieur Régnier, Jean Régnier, of Granville. He owns the biggest of the Chausey[43] Islands, the only inhabited one. In this capacity he operates a granite quarry, whose stone is much valued for the King's fortifications. He also does some trade with the Jersey Islanders…all above board, I can assure you!'

'And that's why you didn't want to talk about it with Monsieur de la Rozière?'

'We have nothing against Monsieur de la Rozière himself, but amongst those around him there could be some who are…narrow-minded, let's say. Anyway, these commercial dealings have allowed us to establish contacts with Jersey men who are able to keep us informed of ship movements within the English ports. This could obviously be of great interest to the Navy Ministry, especially if we are to have a new war with England. That's why we wanted to get in touch with the Minister.'

'And what are you asking for in exchange?'

'Oh, nothing! Absolutely nothing! Monsieur Régnier is acting out of pure patriotism. The only thing is, we have had some problems with the Ferme Générale[44] and in particular with their intendant at Caen. They have already tried to issue an injunction forbidding Monsieur Régnier from continuing his activities on Chausey! And that in time of peace! Imagine what it would be like if we were really at war.'

'In short, you want immediate cover for Monsieur Régnier's activities on Chausey, and continuing protection during the war, should it break out?'

'Solely for the good of the Kingdom! So as not to deprive the King of the precious intelligence that our Jersey agents could provide. But that is not all. Monsieur Régnier has a pretty little lugger at the port of Granville. If war breaks out, as you say, we would like a letter of marque so that we can fit her out for privateering.'

'And that is all?'

'Absolutely! I would just like, for myself, a commission as Frigate Lieutenant, for as long as the war lasts, anyway. With that, Monsieur Régnier can give me the command of his lugger.'

---

43 Translator's note: *Chausey Islands*: an archipelago of mainly tiny islands located to the south of the Channel Islands, about ten miles out from Granville on the Normandy coast.

44 Translator's note: *Ferme Générale* – under the *ancien régime*, a private company that collected customs and excise and other duties on behalf of the King.

'Well,' I say, 'I will pass all that on to my superiors. But I won't be able to contact them straight away. I propose that we meet again next Sunday, at ten in the morning, in front of the entrance to the Sainte-Croix church at Saint-Servan. Does that suit you?'

'Why not at Saint-Malo?' he asks.

'Because I think I am being watched. Are you sure you weren't followed yourself when coming here?'

'I don't think so...For sure, I believe you, but who could it be? Some sniffers from the Customs and the Ferme Générale?'

I say to myself that his activities on Chausey are not as innocent as he makes out, and that's why he thinks immediately of this possibility.

'I don't think so,' I reply. 'Why would the Customs be following me? Anyway, I am sure that two individuals tried to follow me when I came out of the inn just now. I managed to lose them. They wouldn't work for you, by any chance?'

Duval assures me, in a grave voice, that this is not the case. I believe him. Since I showed him my safe-conduct signed by the King, he has behaved quite deferentially towards me, and seems sincere. I am convinced that if Flaharn is behind La Malaga and my followers, Duval is unaware.'

'What do you know about the courtesan who calls herself Elizbeth de Malaga?' I ask him.

'I don't know if she really is a courtesan. She appeared after the return of Captain Royer from the Americas. Before that, nobody had ever seen her at Saint-Malo. But she quickly made a big impression at *La Malice*. It's true that she has some irresistible selling points.'

'Do you know where she comes from? Does this name 'Malaga' ring any bells?'

'Oh! As far as that's concerned, I think it's just an assumed name. It's unlikely she has ever set foot in Spain. On the other hand, I've heard her use typical expressions from Normandy. But I don't know anything more. I don't even know where she lives.'

'She has her rooms in a private house just beside the Saint Phillipe Bastion.'

'Beside the Saint-Phillipe Bastion, you say? Then she is at the house of Monsieur Dubuys, the shipowner.'

We arrive at the end of the Sillon. In front of us, facing the sea, is a shoulder of sand on which stand the remains of an old gallows.

'We'll part here,' I say to him. 'Do you think it is still possible to cross the port?'

'It's possible but you risk getting wet feet. The tide is rising quickly! I'd advise you to go via the Sillon.'

'Thanks for the advice. Don't forget: next Sunday at ten o'clock in front of the Sainte-Croix church at Saint-Servan. I won't approach you. Follow me at a distance once we have seen each other. If ever you think you are being followed take out your handkerchief and wipe your nose. I will do the same and if I have any doubts, our meeting will be put back to the next day at the same time. Try and find out about Elizabeth de Malaga, and above all don't trust her. I don't know who she is working for, but it could be the English, and if ever they get wind of what we are planning, your Jersey connections will be exposed. And for your part, you can kiss goodbye to everything: trading, letter of marque, a commission and whatever comes from them.'

*

I returned to the Main Gate, then strolled around the quays. Eventually I found a ferryman and asked him at what time could he take me across to Saint-Servan. He replied that half past six would be a good time, so I arranged to meet him then at the Old Quay. I walked on the ramparts to kill time. At six I was at the inn. I went to find the innkeeper to pay my bill. I told him that I had booked a passage on a barque that was going to Dinan the next day, and that I was going aboard at high tide at twenty minutes after seven as the master wanted to anchor in the Rance before nightfall. To help allay any mistrust on his part, I also paid for my dinner in advance.

I went up to my room. Thanks to the marks I had made, I was able to be sure, this time, that nobody had been through my things. I packed my bag and my drawing box. There was nobody in the dining room. The servants had not yet begun to set the tables and the innkeeper was in the kitchens supervising the preparations for dinner. I went by the most direct route to the Main Gate. I did not get the impression that there was anybody behind me, this time. This was lucky, for, loaded as I was, I couldn't see how I could have got rid of any followers.

I had only spent a couple of hours in the little house above the Port Saint Père, but so much had happened to me at Saint-Malo that

I seemed to be returning to a haven of peace, or rather, a kind of lair. The aunt Chollet was sitting on the bench in front of the house when I arrived. She was a woman of about fifty, her skin tanned by the sea air. After introducing myself, I told her that I would be going out as little as possible up until the end of the week and asked her to take care of my food as well as my lodgings. She did not ask any questions. I even had to insist that I paid her.

I decided to stay inside until the following Sunday. I was convinced that I had got rid of my followers in the rue des Bés in fine fashion. I had tried to behave as naturally as possible, but it was quite possible that they thought they had been tricked. If they had had to report this to La Malaga, I could easily imagine the violent anger it would have provoked. If that were the case, it could very well be that she had ordered her accomplices to move heaven and earth to pick up my trail again. What use would it have been to have taken all those precautions to cover my meeting with Louis Duval, only to have the henchmen sent to look for me surprise me at Saint-Servan?

I did not put so much as my nose outside and it was hard. I tried to allay my boredom by drawing the landscape that I could see through my open window. And I reflected on what had happened to me over the previous days...

Everything seemed to revolve around *le Duc de Choiseul.* La Malaga had appeared in Saint-Malo just after this brig had returned from the Americas. The innkeeper had spoken to the pretty courtesan about my embarkation certificate aboard the same ship. Having learned of this, she had decided to set a trap for me with the sole intention of searching my clothes and allowing her accomplices to inspect my room at their leisure. What would have happened to me if I had drunk the drugged wine and if Captain Le Meur had not advised me to change the hiding place for my safe-conduct? La Malaga would have found the precious document and perhaps, had that been the case, I would never have woken up. Then, I had been followed. By accomplices of La Malaga, for sure. Probably the same men who had searched my room.

From what I already knew about Flaharn, it was not at all impossible that he was organising a twisted plot against me. He knew that at some time or other I would go to *La Malice* to find Duval, and he could easily organise my kidnap. The search of my clothes by La Malaga, and of my room by her henchmen, could also be explained by something I remembered well: the interest the Captain had shown when I had told him, in a bar in Brest, that my father had left a letter for me in the form of a puzzle.

But there was something not quite right in this reasoning. La Malaga's interest in me seemed to stem from the fact that I was in possession of an embarkation certificate as a Volunteer aboard *le Duc de Choiseul*. Moreover, knowing the distrust held by my uncle and his friends the Comte de Broglie and Messieurs Fleurieu and de la Rozière for Flaharn, it was very unlikely that they had told him about my false papers.

That left the other hypothesis: that La Malaga and her gang were agents in the pay of England. But Duval had told me that the beautiful Spaniard – or Norman – had appeared at *La Malice* just after the return of *le Duc de Choiseul,* that being two weeks before my arrival in Saint-Malo. At that time, I didn't even know myself that I was going to stay at that inn. Did the agents of King George know what I was going to do even before I knew myself? Could they have been so efficient? It seemed inconceivable to me. In any case, it was all a mystery. I was going to have to relate everything to Captain Le Meur and to my uncle, including my adventure with La Malaga, of which, I admit, I was not in the least proud.

4

As planned, *le Moucheron* returned on the Saturday evening, with a westerly wind and a clear sky. I was watching out for her from my window. There was nothing else for me to do. When I caught sight of her, she was sailing along the left bank of the Rance, reaching along under spanker, topsail, fore staysail and her two jibs. I watched her drop her topsail before gybing to cross the anchorage towards the Cité headland. She got in her fore staysail and big jib and tacked again around the end of the Solidor Bank, before easing her mainsheet and coming gently up to her mooring buoy. Before departing, Captain Le Meur had left a length of hawser hitched to the mooring buoy and supported by a pickup buoy that I could now see floating in the current twenty yards further on. The cutter tacked in the lee of the mooring buoy, bisecting the length of line with her bow, allowing it to be picked up, and came to a sudden stop, her sails head to wind before they were dropped. There was nothing for me to do except wait patiently for nightfall.

The sun stayed yellow throughout its descent. As soon as it was dark enough, I went down to the port. It was half tide. The ship's boat was waiting for me at the foot of the Solidor Tower, with the bosun's mate Couet in command, as usual.

*

Saint-Servan, Saturday 26th July 1777, at dusk.

This time we climb aboard up the starboard channels. I am welcomed by the same infantryman as before, but he is not carrying arms and is dressed like an ordinary merchant sailor. I am met by the same smell of paint and tarred rope. The crew is just as quiet and discreet. The running rigging is all carefully coiled in place. The square sails are furled in the bunt and the spanker is tight to its boom.

The Captain receives me in the 'great cabin'. He has the same controlled voice, slightly sardonic, and, behind his deadpan face, eyes creased in a constant inner smile. I ask him whether the trial cruise was satisfactory. After a silence, he tells me that he wants to alter the rig, with taller and more solid masts, reinforce the topmast with backstays and stronger running backstays, and to cut some bigger sails. He says that the cutter is not yet at maximum speed and that she can still carry more canvas.

'So the trials did not meet your expectations?'

The Captain does not reply immediately. He seems to be dreaming, his eyes unfocussed.

'Oh no…it was good…very good even…But how about you? How did you get on?'

*

I recounted my adventures in detail, omitting nothing, not even my sordid encounter with Elizabeth de Malaga. I finished by telling him that I was due to meet Louis Duval the following morning.

'As regards Duval and this Régnier. I have an idea. We will probably talk about it tomorrow afternoon with Colonel Dumouriez. He has arrived at Saint-Malo and will come to see us. You can tell him everything you have told me. Go to your meeting with Duval and see what else you can find out. You can tell him that as yet you haven't had a reply from Versailles and that you need to fix another meeting during the week on a day which suits him. Tell him to tell his boss that we will need to see him face to face as well. And that the best place for this would be at Chausey. Do you know Colonel Dumouriez?'

I replied that my uncle had told me that Dumouriez was thirty-eight years old, a Colonel in the Army, a Chevalier de Saint Louis; that he had fought in the previous war in Germany and carried out secret missions in Corsica and Poland. I added that the Duc d'Aiguillon had had him sent to the Bastille during the time of the late King Louis XV, but that Louis XVI had rehabilitated him. I did not repeat what my uncle had said about his character: 'ambitious, unprincipled, cunning, ingratiating, two-faced and totally self-interested...'

'Good!' said Captain Le Meur. 'We'll soon see. As far as the business with the girl is concerned, the search of your room, the men who followed you and your first meeting with Duval, you can write a detailed report right now. We'll have it taken to Monsieur de la Rozière tomorrow morning so that he can have his secretary encode it and have it sent without delay to your uncle in Versailles. Perhaps he will be able to add other details we don't know about and shed some light on the affair. Despite your doubts regarding Flaharn, I don't think he is involved. It is the English who are behind all this. I'm thinking in particular of Lord Stormont, and also the English Commissioner in Dunkirk. But, like you, I wonder how they got onto you so quickly. Duval told you that this Elizabeth de Malaga is from Normandy. That interests me. Ask him to find out a bit more about this.'

The next day, Duval was waiting for me as agreed, in front of the huge tower of the Sainte-Croix church, at the top of the street leading down to the Navy shipyards. The bells were ringing full blast, for the good parishioners were going in for Grand Mass. I signalled to him from a distance and walked towards a path that goes around the headland to the south of the Solidor port. Tall weeds, hawthorn bushes, elderberries and honeysuckle stood as high as a man on each side of the walkway.

*

Saint-Servan, Sunday 27th July 1777, ten o'clock in the morning.

The sweet perfume of wild flowers hangs over the whole length of the footpath, giving me the feeling, or the illusion, that life can be good. I stop twenty minutes later beside a gap in the bushes that gives a view over the mouth of the Rance. Having glanced behind me to make sure that Duval is following, and that there doesn't appear to be anyone behind him, I go and sit down a little way down the slope below the path. There is still about half an hour to go before high water. From my viewpoint I cannot see the slipways with their hulls under construction. I can see the Solidor anchorage: *la Prudente* and *la Résolue* in the foreground, and further away, *le Moucheron,* all lined up on their coffin-buoys. The lower masts of the frigates are now in place; the riggers have frapped the stays. The wind is from the south. Diaphanous white clouds stretch out over our heads towards the sea, gradually veiling the blue of the sky.

'The weather's going to change,' said Duval, joining me. 'I wouldn't be surprised if it rains soon.'

Before I can ask him, he assures me that he has not been followed from Saint-Malo. I tell him that I have nothing new for him at the moment and that I won't have any answers until Monday or Tuesday. I repeat what Captain Le Meur said about the possibility of a meeting with Monsieur Régnier at the Chausey Islands. He replies that he will have to go to Granville to let him know and suggests we meet the following Wednesday at nine o'clock, at the morning low tide. That would give him time to get from Saint-Malo to Saint-Servan and back on foot. I tell him that this time I will wait for him at the foot of the fort on the Cité headland, beside the Bas Sablons inlet. In that way, I think, I could watch from a distance with my telescope and see if he is being followed. I ask him if there was any news about La Malaga and he replies that she is always seen with Captain Royer. I pass on Captain Le Meur's suggestion that he try and find out more about the Norman origins of our pretty adventuress.

'Well, there's nothing for it but for me to return to Saint-Malo,' says Duval in a resigned voice when I have finished. 'All that distance just for a few minutes of conversation! But I don't know what else we could have done. It's a pity you no longer want to come back into the town.'

'Well then, stay a bit longer,' I say to him, 'since you seem to have time on your hands. I'd like to talk about Captain Flaharn, if you don't mind. I imagine you're intending to go to *La Malice* for lunch. What time do you have to be there?'

The officers' meal is at one, as usual.'

'Fine! It's ten o'clock and slack water. You'll have plenty of time to tell me what you know about Flaharn before getting a ferry back at the Nose.'

'Flaharn! I don't know if I could still say that I know him. I knew him well for nine months, that's for sure, but that was eighteen years ago during the Comte d'Estaing's operation.'

'That doesn't matter,' I say. 'We don't have much information about him.'

In fact, from what I gathered from my uncle, this is exactly the period that interests us, but I keep that to myself. I tell him that Flaharn came to see us of his own accord, on the recommendation of the Comte d'Estaing, with a proposal for an intelligence operation against the English, based in Saint-Malo. That is not quite correct, but neither is it wholly a lie. Apart from that we know very little.

'...so tell me in detail about this famous expedition of the Comte d'Estaing. I'm keen to hear the story. It has been talked about a lot. It was even as a result of this glorious undertaking that the Comte was admitted directly into the Navy with the command of a squadron, which had never happened before. But in the final analysis, nobody can say exactly what happened.'

'And for good reason!' replies Duval. 'Of us thirty-three officers who left Port-Louis, only five came back. Three died from their wounds or from illness after our return to the Île-de-France. So that now Flaharn and I are the only surviving officers. Along with the Comte d'Estaing of course...'

Duval settles more comfortably, takes a little metal flask out of his pocket and throws back his head to take a swig. The willingness with which he told me about the Muscat business makes me think that he is one of these silent types who becomes unstoppable once he is given the chance to tell his life story to someone willing to listen.

'In March 1758,' he began, 'I had embarked at L'Orient as a Volunteer aboard *le Neptune,* five hundred and forty tons and sixteen guns, belonging to the India Company. But my ship had been decommissioned at the Île-de-France at the end of May 1759, so I found myself at a loose end. At best, I risked being pressed aboard one of the King's ships, which was not a very attractive proposition. We had been at war for three years and our merchant ships were no longer plying the routes. Well, as soon as I heard that the Comte d'Estaing was recruiting officers for a privateering operation financed by himself, I signed on straight away without giving it much thought. With the result that, once I found out that Flaharn was to be the commander, it was too late to change my mind without being reckoned a deserter. I had never met Flaharn, but I had heard all about him. He was well known amongst the India Company crews. The managers of the Company had even tried to get rid of him, despite his qualities as a seaman, on account mainly of his brutality towards the men. In one sense, the Comte d'Estaing took the right decision by taking Flaharn with him. He had gathered up those who were left at the Île-de-France, that's to say the dross that neither the Comte d'Aché nor the Comte de Lally-Tollendal[45] wanted to take. In all, there were a hundred and sixty soldiers and 'volunteer' fighters. There were a few honest sailors in the pile, but as for the rest – scum! I've never seen such a bunch of pirates! The numbers were made up with two hundred kaffir slaves, for whom some cases of rifles had been piled in *le Condé's* hold. He needed a Flaharn to keep the thumb on such a raggle-taggle mob.'

He stops to clear his throat and take another swig.

'After the *Merry* affair, which I've already told you about, we went to attack an English fort in the Straits of Hormuz. Bandar Abbas, it was called. We put ashore soldiers and cannons at night. At dawn, we issued a warning and then attacked. In fact, the Comte had mounted this operation solely to capture some English officers alive, so that he could eventually be exchanged for them should he be captured. Eventually, after the English had captured him at Madras, he was released on parole while waiting for the French to have an English prisoner available of the same rank as him. The Comte was a Brigadier, that's to say a General, for God's sake! And you were lucky to find two or three English Generals in the whole of India at that time, let alone capture one! During the last war it was our Generals who got themselves captured. So the Comte had decided, off his own bat, that freeing several English officers at the same time would have the same value. At Bandar Abbas, we took seven prisoners who the Comte d'Estaing had freed after giving them a good lecture. That set off a fair few arguments, later on. Even for me, who knew nothing about these things, it seemed to be stretching matters, but it was none of my business really. Between the fort and the *Merry* we had picked up a fair bit of booty. They were in fact the best prizes

45 Translator's note: *Comte d'Aché* and *Comte de Tally-Tollendal:* Vice Admiral and General commanding France's failed offensive against the English in India during the Seven Years' War.

we took during the whole damned campaign. I have to admit, though, that the Comte d'Estaing, who had fitted out the expedition at his own expense, most nobly gave his share of the prize money to his officers. And since, by the end, there were only two of us, I would have had no cause to complain...but I wasn't rich for long, alas! I'll tell you why in a moment.'

Duval sighs and pulls a horrible face. Even more than ten years later he has trouble talking about it.

'We sent our booty to the Île-de-France aboard the *Mamoudy* and the *Merry* and crossed the Indian Ocean with *le Condé* and *l'Expédition.* The Comte d'Estaing's idea was to pillage the English settlements on the west coast of Sumatra. For that he was relying on the influence and neutrality of the Dutch. We spent three months making our slow way to Sumatra in calms, storms and adverse winds. And Flaharn showed what he was capable of. I told you that we had shipped aboard a crew of pirates. You can imagine what that could lead to aboard a ship becalmed for day after day on the Equator; sooner or later there'll be a mutiny. Flaharn didn't wait for that to happen. He had foreseen it, you could say. He used a very effective but brutal strategy. This is what he did...Among the crew, he had picked out right from the start the biggest troublemaker on board, a potential leader. He was a Provençal who everyone called Cavalet.A big lad, a bit like Flaharn, but nowhere near as strong, and, above all, less unscrupulous. Flaharn began by putting him under the yoke more often than the others, then began to reprimand him unjustly, increasing the level of humiliation and at every opportunity showering him with the kind of insults used by westerners against people from the East, and worse. It is said that an insult only defiles the one who makes it and that it is not easy to insult someone effectively, even a Provençal, but Flaharn had a special gift for that too. He is a man who knows no limits! He doesn't follow a single rule! He is inhuman! And eventually we saw that. One evening, when Cavalet had been summoned once again to the quarterdeck by the Captain to be abused on some pretext or other, clearly untrue, he lost his composure. He pulled out his knife and attacked his tormentor. Flaharn was expecting it. He easily disarmed him and began to hit him, first with his fists, until the poor fellow fell to the deck, and then with his feet. This was done quite methodically; purposefully I would say. He seemed calm and focussed. All those who were on deck at the time, officers, sailors, soldiers, were aghast. When he had finished, Flaharn left his victim stretched out unconscious against the lee rail and went back beside the helmsman. Without a word, he took the ship's log from the binnacle and began to inspect it as if nothing had happened. When the surgeon, after some time, came and nervously asked permission to attend to Cavalet, he just shrugged his shoulders. The poor bugger was lifeless, with blood pouring from his nose, mouth and ears. He died during the night without ever regaining consciousness. But after that, I swear to you, the crew was on best behaviour!'

Duval undoes the top of his flask and takes another mouthful.

'With the slaves, Flaharn used a different method. Which proves that with him, everything is worked out, especially wickedness. Our kaffirs were extremely deferential towards one of their number, a giant with bronzed shoulders and arms like iron, called Bama. Flaharn made an effort to get him on his side. He favoured him by making him his personal servant. And he behaved in the same way towards all the kaffirs, treating them not as slaves, but as warriors. He never had any problem with them. I think they took him for either a god or a devil. They attributed supernatural powers to him. Above all, they were impressed by his animal strength and his rare cruelty.'

'And the Comte d'Estaing, what did he say about it?'

'He didn't say anything, but I think he too was fascinated. At the time, they were both about thirty, in their prime. But, if I could dare to make a comparison, I would say that Flaharn was the wolf, while the Comte was only a fox. You see, the Comte d'Estaing had unwavering courage and an iron will. At five feet eight or nine inches he was almost as big as Flaharn, but he seemed rather thin and narrow in the shoulders compared to the other. Despite that, he did not move with such lightness. Above all, he lacked the kind of wild and unbridled power that characterised Flaharn. I've seen the Comte d'Estaing, like all of us, have his moments of weariness, weakness, headaches, without mentioning tropical fevers, which it's best not to catch whether you are a Comte or a matelot, but Flaharn! Him! He seemed untouchable by anything like that. The least of his gestures showed unimaginable energy and life. Incredible! It was...how can I explain it to you? Look, I'll tell you something to try and get you to understand. As well as a surgeon, we had on board *le Condé* another doctor who prided himself on his knowledge of anatomy and what he called 'animal physiology'.

He had managed to acquire, through the local fishermen, the recently extracted heart of one of those big sea crocodiles that are sometimes found in the river estuaries from southern India to Borneo; fearsome and very dangerous animals that can hide underwater for hours without breathing. This surprising ability had drawn the attention of our doctor, who had kept the crocodile heart in a bucket of water with a view to dissecting it once he had finished studying it. After several days, the heart would still jump in the bucket if you touched it with a scalpel! It was impressive. Well, every time I watched Flaharn walking and moving on the *le Condé's* quarterdeck, I thought of that crocodile heart. D'you see what I mean?'

Duval is about to take the stopper from his flask, but he stops, looking at the flask in his hand.

'I've never seen anyone drink like Flaharn. In the usual run of things, he ate and drank like everyone else. But, sometimes, he wanted to drink as if to get himself drunk. This was unpredictable but was always in the evening. He would sit in front of us, at the end of the table in the great cabin and have a fresh bottle of rum and a glass brought. Jesus! He would drink the whole bottle, glass after glass, calmly, all the while staring at us without a word. When the bottle was empty, he would get up, go on deck, walk up the scuppers to the foremast and climb up to the foretopmast. I never saw him take an unsteady step. I think he did that to impress us. Or to challenge us. But who would be so crazy as to confront a Flaharn? At those times, after his rum, people kept clear of him. He seemed more dangerous than usual…'

Duval shakes his head and eventually takes a swig.

'It wasn't really the best time for going through the Malay archipelagos. It was still the north-east monsoon, so we had a lot of contrary winds. It would no doubt have been better if we'd waited another month or two. All the same we got to exactly where we wanted to go. Flaharn was an officer of the India Company and he knew his business. We made our landfall between Mintao Island and Bonne Fortune Island, just below the Equator, where we went to resupply at the Dutch trading post at Ayer Bongis, at the top end of this strait on the west coast of Sumatra. It was about time, as we had quite a few cases of scurvy. We were able to get fresh food. The Dutch even gave us a guide and interpreter. He was a Malay who looked like a real pirate, so he wouldn't have felt out of place with us. Then we went along the coast to get to a little English trading post thirty miles to the north, called Natal. It was held by forty Europeans and about sixty local auxiliaries. This was a kind of hors d'oeuvre. In fact, they didn't even try to resist. We boarded and pillaged all the ships anchored there, then took over the place. We left *le Condé* there as she needed some repairs, and piled the healthy soldiers and kaffirs aboard *l'Expédition*, with a view to attacking another English trading post about eighty miles further north. This trading post was called…oh! Damn and blast!'

Duval tries to recall the name of the trading post, without success. He takes up his story again.

'I can't remember the name, but what I can't forget is that it was in Batak territory. You'll soon learn why. There are several tribes in Sumatra. The Malays are the majority in the southern half, but in the north and centre there are different peoples who probably arrived before the Malays. The Bataks are one of them. They live in the middle part of the north west of this big island. It is said that the Bataks have a well-developed society, with laws and their own writing system. They are reputed to be hospitable, gentle and peaceful, and it seems that they have real poets writing real poetry, just like us, though in their own language, of course. But they are strange people! I'll tell you in a moment something about them that I saw myself and which will make you shudder…Well! It took us seven days and six nights to get there. We had flat calms during the day, and storms with squalls and heavy showers at night, but we were sheltered from the swell of the Indian Ocean by a big island to the west called Nias. We arrived at daybreak on a Thursday in mid-February, just off the trading post. Before seeing it, we came across three little two-masted Malay boats rigged with lugsails of a kind. We hauled up the English flag and took possession of the first boat. Seeing that, the other two turned tail and sailed off towards the trading post. We had no way of catching them with our sluggish old frigate. The chance to take the post unawares had gone! We arrived at the anchorage towards the end of the day, the anchorage of…oh damn and blast! My memory is going!'

I feel like telling him he has drunk too much but hold back.

'Well, in a nutshell! I remember a nice little well-sheltered anchorage at the end of a bigger bay, protected by two headlands and a string of little islands covered in coconut palms. There were well-arranged groves of coconut palms around a pretty Batak village. These villages are comprised of beautiful wooden houses built on piles, with high sloping roofs and carved beams, all very strange. We saw this from the end of the bay, beside a big expanse of grass and rice paddies, all of a magnificent green! When the mist began to part and the sun broke through the clouds, we could see hills and mountains further back, completely covered in forest and encircling the village about twelve miles away. It was a beautiful scene. The English had set up there to trade in gold powder, camphor and gum benjamin. All in all, it was a little paradise. And we had arrived to create hell. The anchorage had just one entrance, defended by two batteries, one on each side. According to the information given to us by the Dutch, there were ten 18-pounders for each battery. The garrison had forty European gunners and two battalions modelled on the Sepoys, one composed of Malays, the other of Bataks, who one of their Rajas had put at the disposal of the English.'

Duval breathes in noisily and takes another swig.

'The first thing we noticed were several plumes of smoke rising over the bay. With our telescopes, we could see that the English had already set fire to some of the merchant ships anchored there. The Comte d'Estaing and Flaharn wrote an ultimatum to the Governor, saying that if he continued to burn 'our prizes', we would put the whole garrison to the sword. We released the Malay boat and told its skipper to take our little message to the Governor, while we moored outside the entrance, out of range of the guns, to block the exit, each laying out two anchors. The sea was calm, but as you'll see, we would have been better to have lain to single anchors with a warp rigged to haul us broadside on. We thought that the Governor had taken our threat seriously, as we saw no more fires. But after nightfall, as the tide turned at about half past eight, we saw two new conflagrations. They made two balls of fire in the night. We quickly realised that it was two blazing ships drifting towards the passage, straight towards us anchored in the way. The Governor had released these two improvised fireships on the ebb tide in the hope of snaring us. The rise and fall of the tide is not very much in those waters, no more than seven of eight feet, so the ebb tide is not very strong, but on this coast there is always a little breeze off the land as night falls. In something of a panic, the small ship's boat was launched to lay out an anchor to port. A hawser had been bent on that was used as a stern spring. By quickly hauling on the capstan we just managed to get the ship out of the way. Luckily they weren't real fireships. They didn't explode, but they passed close by! We could feel the heat!'

Another mouthful from the flask. I wonder what it contains. It smells like white rum. I understand now why Duval holds his drink so well at the inn: he has plenty of practice.

'The Comte d'Estaing was not pleased! Before night had fallen, we had the time to see that there were shining white sandy beaches the whole length of the coast, with no outlying coral reefs. We launched the sloop and the second ship's boat and filled them to the gunwales with soldiers and kaffirs, even the little boat. The Comte d'Estaing and Flaharn came with us. It was forbidden to load the rifles in case one went off accidentally and gave the alarm. Everything by bayonet! We headed for the shore behind the battery to our left. The rear of the little fort was defended by a simple earth trench and a little palisade the height of a man. We approached in silence and lay there until daybreak. The doctor had told me that there were lots of tigers hereabouts, and I admit I was a bit on edge, but there were too many of us to be at risk.'

Duval shook his flask and pulled a face. It was almost empty.

'As soon as we could see a little more clearly, we ran to the palisade and we all crossed it. The Comte was the first to jump into the trench. I was just behind him. This fort was held by the Malay battalion. Remember that, as it's important in what happened. The Malays were still half asleep. They were under the command of a young European lieutenant. Jesus! He was the first to react. I can still see him going for his pistol in his belt. But the Comte was too quick for him. He charged him and put his sword through his body with such force that the blade broke off inside him! When the Malays saw that they broke ranks and fled for the battery. We followed them and arrived inside the fort at the same time as they did, and began to play with sword and bayonet. There were fewer of us, but they panicked. It was a real slaughter. All by the blade! The only ones who saved their skins were those who managed to jump into the entrance channel and swim off. As our rifles were not loaded we could not fire at them. We turned the 18-pounders, which were all ready for action, towards the battery on the other side of the channel and opened fire. That fort was held by the Bataks. They all ran off through the coconut trees behind and we never saw them again. The Europeans who were with them, officers and gunners, had little choice but to follow them. We thought that it would be left at that, but that was not to bring Flaharn and the Comte d'Estaing into the reckoning. Out of the question to let them run off unchallenged! We quickly got back into the boats, crossed the channel to the other fort and set off in pursuit of those running away. Behind the coconut palms there were rice paddies still flooded with water, then marshland as far as the edge of the tropical forest. We began wading through. We hadn't caught a single Batak; this was their territory and they weren't going to let themselves be captured so easily. But we had already taken all the English before midday. It's now that I'm going to talk about those Batak bastards. Better brace yourself!'

Duval grabbed my arm and turned towards me, putting his face close to mine. The least one can say is that his breath was not sweet-smelling.

'The Comte d'Estaing had had the prisoners taken to the frigate, which in the meantime had entered the anchorage. As for the hundred or so bodies lying around the fort, we had to collect them all together and set fire to them, as it was too much trouble to bury them. So we started to collect the bodies of the Malays and drag them inside the fort. We began to notice that many of them had been mutilated in a strange way: ears had been cut off, in some cases the entire head, to take them away, apparently. The soles of their feet and the palms of their hands had been sliced off to the bone. Others had their chests split open! The English Lieutenant that the Comte had killed was untouched. Our Malay interpreter explained that those responsible were the villagers, who had come during the morning while we were splashing around in the swamps. They had taken advantage of the fact that the bodies were nice and fresh to come and take their favourite bits: the ears, the soles of the feet, the palms of the hands, the heart and the brains! Those Batak buggers love human flesh. They grill it or marinate it in lemon juice and pepper. They don't execute criminals; they eat them raw. And when they don't have enough of a supply of criminals, they deliberately go to war amongst themselves so as to take prisoners they can roast on the spit. Our Malay even told us the story of a Raja who would not eat anything else, and when he had no more left, he would send soldiers out into the countryside to collect some more two-legged meat. Perrault's[46] fairy tales are not so far off the mark, with their ogres...But I haven't finished! Wait till you hear the rest!'

---

46 Translator's note: *Charles Perrault* (1628 – 1703): French writer who invented the genre of the fairy tale. His creations include Cinderella, Puss in Boots, The Sleeping Beauty and Little Red Riding Hood.

He emptied his flask and put it back in his coat.

'Flaharn was with us. The Malay's explanation put one of those damned perverse ideas that only he can have into his head. Oh! What a godawful bastard! He had us cut and sharpen fifty or so bamboo stakes that were set in the ground around the fort. And he ordered us to impale the mutilated Malays and the English Lieutenant on them. He told us to strip the Malays completely but to leave the uniform on the Lieutenant, 'so that it looks good' as he said. I knew that they were already dead and so could not feel anything, but it was sickening, I swear. I'll spare you all the details, but we had to split their arses with a cutlass in order to skewer them more easily. The sky was clear and they had been in the sun the whole morning. They were emptying out...you can imagine the stink...and what it looked like! I puked out everything and couldn't eat for two days after that. When we had finished, the result was horrible... but...how can I say? Sublime? Imagine those fifty mutilated bodies, some headless, lined up six feet above the ground, all completely naked, with the English officer in uniform in the middle and the burning fort behind, and all that in the middle of an idyllic landscape!'

'Did the Comte d'Estaing see it?' I asked.

'God yes! I think so. But wait for the rest! After this first mission, we returned to Natal. The Comte d'Estaing organised a little ceremony to hand over the trading post officially to the Dutch. Then we went to lay waste to all the other English establishments on the south-west coast of Sumatra, an area inhabited mainly by Malays. That's when the idea of impaling, which had so disgusted me, turned out to be a stroke of genius. It took a while to get down the coast in our tired old ships; our reputation had the time to go ahead of us. As soon as we appeared off a port, the Malay auxiliaries, who provided most of the manpower for the English garrisons, ran off scared into the interior of the country, abandoning their European officers. Even the biggest place, Fort Marlborough, which defended the settlement at Bengkulu, was taken without a fight! When the fifteen hundred Malays at the garrison saw *le Condé* arrive at the entrance to the port, they all deserted! It was like that all the time. In the end, if we had just burned down the trading posts we attacked, we would perhaps have had fewer casualties. But, each time, the Comte d'Estaing had us chasing the deserters. Sometimes that took several days. He also had us make incursions into the interior to burn down secondary posts. The west coast of Sumatra is made up of a flat coastal strip backed by a chain of mountains extending from the north-west to the south-west. This strip is nothing but marshes and mangrove swamps infested with mosquitoes and often drowned in thick foul-smelling mists. There you catch exactly the same nasty fevers[47] as on the Guinea coast in the rainy season. Their effect is so devastating that men in good health in the morning can bury their comrades before midday and die the same way as them by the evening. It's not for nothing that the sailors engaged in the pepper trade called this Sumatran coast 'the plague coast'. And that's why the Comte d'Estaing's expedition was so murderous and why so few of us returned to the Île-de-France. It's because of Flaharn and the Comte!'

Duval shakes his head. He takes out the old butt of a cheroot from his pocket and begins to chew on it.

'Real mad dogs! Indeed! That's what we became! The fierceness with which we threw ourselves into the marshes for whole days at a time, in pursuit of deserters, was completely incomprehensible to the Malays. Although I do recognise that it helped to maintain the terror which we inspired in them. They had convinced themselves that it was us who had eaten bits of their fellow countrymen before impaling them, up there in the north, and when they saw us chasing after them like that, for no apparent reason, well! They thought we wanted to eat them too. There you have it! We had become the ogres of Sumatra! Nothing to boast about!'

'What became of Flaharn after your return?' I ask.

'When we arrived at Port-Louis, the Governor had just had some very alarming news about our post at Pondicherry. The English were preparing to lay siege to it, and so a supply ship was being loaded to take reinforcements, and above all, food. As Naval officers were in short supply, Flaharn was ordered to join the ship to make up its complement of officers. He was furious. Before leaving, he told me he intended to desert at Pondicherry. He had heard about European mercenaries who offered their services to the Maharajahs of Hindustan. He said to me: "You know what, Duval? The Maharajahs take their war booty in diamonds and precious stones. They don't take up much space. In a little casket you can carry ten times more than chests and chests full of

47 Nasty fevers: It was thought at the time that malaria was caused by the mists and miasmas produced by evaporation in marshy areas.

coins. I'd like to get hold of one of those caskets. Afterwards I can take it home under my arm. And I'll be able to afford the good life to the end of my days, while watching those around me slaving away." That's the last time I saw him.'

'And you, did you not go to Pondicherry?'

'I was no more than an Ensign in the merchant service, and very weakened too. I didn't have Flaharn's constitution. Nobody wanted me. And anyway, I'd had enough of the Indian Ocean. I had a good little nest egg with my share of the prize money. I had enough to set up at home. I wanted to buy a barque or a brig to do some coastal trading. I came back to France on the same ship as the Comte d'Estaing. Unfortunately, we were captured by the English just as we arrived off the Brittany coast. They soon knew who we were, the Comte and me; the reports of our exploits in Sumatra had already reached England. The Comte, being a great lord, was soon released, but I had no powerful friends in high places. They took everything out on me. It made no difference that I was a merchant Ensign. They stuck me in one of their damn prison ships as if I were a common pirate, right to the end of the war. I fell so ill there I thought I was a goner. So much for having escaped the plague coast! And, of course, they took my prize money. When the war finished and I at last got back to France, I was as poor as when I left! The only thing I had acquired was my Ensign ticket on the long-haul merchantmen. That allowed me to ship out from Saint-Malo as a mate. I was asked several times to make voyages to China or India, but I always refused. I agreed once to go to the Guinea Cays, but I didn't want to go again. I've seen too many poor lads dying of the deadly diseases you catch in these far-off places. So I just limited myself to the Cadiz route.'

*

I let Duval go off on his own along the path to Saint-Servan. I needed to remember everything he had said, which was not easy. But it was absolutely necessary that I repeat the story I had just heard to my uncle without any errors. I thought that it must be very close to the truth. Duval had not tried to inflate his own role. What is more, he had not made any judgement of Flaharn or the Comte d'Estaing, simply recounting the facts of the story. In a way, Duval had left me free to make my own judgements. What I drew from it, above all, was that Flaharn was truly dangerous. Everything I had heard was worthy of my attention, but there was a tiny niggling detail, buried somewhere in the story and which I could not quite recall, that suddenly seemed likely to be important, so important that I had to try to remember what it was.

I was trying to get my thoughts in order when my glance fell on *le Moucheron.* A flag was going up to the masthead, beneath the white ensign of the King's ships. From my position, with the wind from the south, I could not see it very well, but I knew that it was blue.

5

I found the bosun's mate Couet at the end of the Solidor slipway. He told me that we were expecting a visit from Colonel Dumouriez. The ship's boat put me aboard before going off again to wait alongside the quay. The cutter's five infantrymen and their sergeant were lined up along the port rail, in uniform for once.

Half of the crew were squeezed up for'ard. The other half were waiting below. *Le Moucheron* had a crew of about thirty – petty officers, topmen and able seamen. This was fewer than the norm aboard a fighting cutter, but it was, all the same, a lot of men for a ship fifty feet long and fourteen feet wide.

The two lieutenants were waiting aft. I saw Lieutenant de Kerlaziou in dress uniform, sword at his side. I went below to change and came back on deck to join them. The Captain had remained alone in the great cabin.

The hours passed. A huge band of grey cloud came up from the south. Soon the sky was completely covered. The wind went round to the south-west, blowing more and more strongly. Our Colonel arrived at half past five in driving rain. He had come in a carriage, having taken the long way round. To stop him getting soaked, the sailors had put a heavy tarpaulin cape over his shoulders, which he got tangled up in while climbing aboard. He would probably have fallen in the water had not the bosun let go of his whistle in order to grab him. When he took off his cape, he revealed a frock coat, double-breasted in the latest Paris fashion, with stripy sailors' sleeves, leather breeches and Hungarian boots. He was no taller than me, with a trim waist. He had a sallow complexion and regular features with a hooked nose and prominent cheekbones. He was forever frowning and tensing his jaws, creating jowls at the corner of his lips that gave him the look of a mastiff about to bite. I thought that he was in a bad mood because of the rain, but I was soon to learn that this was his normal face. The Captain invited him to take shelter in the cabin, offering him the chair backing onto the corridor while we, the Captain, the two lieutenants and myself, squeezed into the two benches on each side of the table.

Captain Le Meur made the presentations. Dumouriez started by advising the greatest discretion over what we were about to hear.

'Everything we are going to talk about concerns the future mission of my crew, does it not?' asked Captain Le Meur immediately.

'Obviously!' replied the Colonel, somewhat curtly. 'Otherwise I wouldn't talk to you about it. But nothing we are going to talk about here must leave this room!'

I caught an amused light in the Captain's look, as fleeting creases appeared between his cheekbones and eyes. This was his discreet way of smiling. But Dumouriez, who did not know him, noticed nothing and went straight to the heart of the matter.

'I have read the report of young Laforest-Dombourg. What do we know about this Régnier? Can we trust him?'

'My second lieutenant knows him well enough,' replied Captain Le Meur, inviting Lieutenant Chollet to speak.

Lieutenant Chollet had taken off his hat, completely revealing the sabre scar that ran down the middle of his forehead. This sight drew our visitor's attention, who asked where he had won this fine decoration.

'It's a souvenir from our English friends during the last war, Sir.'

Dumouriez smiled, causing his bulldog jowls to disappear for a moment, and raised his right hand, palm open. Half his middle finger was missing.

'As for me, it was the Prussians, at Klostercamp...Carry on, I beg you.'

'Jean Régnier is registered as a ship's captain in Granville, but he is best known around here for holding the concession for the Chausey

Islands. His father had established an inn in the ruins of the old castle on the Grande Île, which the English had pillaged during the war. To try to get reparations, Régnier senior had the idea of asking for permission to cultivate the Chausey Islands. He made a request for this through the Abbot Nolin, Canon of Mâcon and a member of the Agricultural Society, who was said to have a good relationship with Versailles. Eventually the Canon managed to obtain the concession for the Chausey Islands – but for himself! He had even tried to have the Régniers evicted. Everything was normalised, if I could call it that, after the death of the Canon. Four years ago his beneficiaries sold the Chausey concession to the younger Régnier. Since then, he has built a farm, a chapel and stables on the Grande Île. He raises cows and sheep, and during the summer he brings in workers who burn seaweed to extract soda, and stonemasons to restart the granite quarries. And finally, it's true, he trades with the Jersey people. He sells them brandy which the Jersey islanders smuggle into England. To finish I would dare to say, Sir, that in my opinion Régnier is a patriot who is worthy of our trust, since all of his assets are to be found on a French island.'

'A French island, certainly, but one that the English can pillage whenever they like, which gives them a hold over our man. You have to acknowledge that no-one is in a better position than him for playing the double agent. And how would we know if that is the case?'

'If you would allow me, Sir,' said Captain Le Meur, 'I have a suggestion to make. I know how the Jersey people get Monsieur Régnier's brandy into England. Régnier's men throw barrels overboard, with buoys, at agreed places. The Jersey smugglers are in the know, pick them up, and in their turn deposit them on the English coast where their accomplices come and pick them up at night. Naturally, orders follow the same path in the other direction, and that is exactly how, I think, we can get information on the preparations of the Royal Navy. This is what I propose: we ask Monsieur Régnier to help us get in touch with the English smugglers, so that they can give us a place on the English coast where I can go myself and pick up the barrels with *le Moucheron.* They can put their reports in well-sealed bottles.'

'And how will we check them?'

'Firstly, remember that our offices in Versailles regularly receive detailed reports from our London spies on the state of the British Navy. It would be very interesting, I think, to compare the intelligence from those sources with what we expect to obtain here. Moreover, once we have had our first deliveries, and while we are still at peace, nothing would stop me, in fair weather and under the English flag, from heading from time to time to the Isle of Wight and the St. Helen's Roads. That way I could have a quick look at Spithead, to verify the truth of the initial information we will have had. This would not give an absolute guarantee for the future, but it would show them, at least at the start, that they can't tell us any old thing. Each time I pick up their reports I can leave a payment that will change according to the quality of the intelligence they have provided. I have a good idea of the type of person we will be dealing with. They are more or less honest in business, if that's what you can call something close to treachery, but they are very greedy. The question is whether we will have the means to pay them.'

'The intention,' replied Dumouriez, 'is to pay them in piasters[48]. I haven't yet decided the amount we will let them have, but I have plenty in reserve.'

'If you don't mind, Sir,' said Captain Le Meur, 'that is a subject we can discuss later, at your offices in Saint-Malo.'

'As you wish.'

Dumouriez looked surprised, but he did not object. He then turned towards me.

'What are Régnier and Duval asking for in return for their patriotism?'

'Well,' I replied. 'I was given to understand that above all they want protection against the Caen Commissioner.'

'Pardon me for interrupting, Sir,' said Lieutenant Chollet. 'The Caen Commissioner is a Monsieur Esmangard, who was a personal friend of the late Canon Nolin, and I think he will use every means possible to damage the Régnier family interests.'

'I see,' said Dumouriez.

He turned to me.

'What else did they ask for?'

'They wanted Letters of Marque for their privateer when the war starts and a Frigate Lieutenant's commission for Duval.'

48 Piasters: the reference is to Spanish piasters. Spain held huge reserves of currency thanks to her silver mines in Mexico and Peru. This was her main export. The legitimate trade was doubled by a high level of smuggling. The piaster was current throughout Europe, the whole continent of America, and in India. It was the international currency of the time.

'And when do you see Duval again?'

'We have a meeting arranged for next Wednesday. He asked for a delay once I had told him we wanted to meet with Monsieur Régnier at Chausey.'

'Good! You can go and tell him we will give them everything they are asking for. We will tell Esmangard to desist, and if he continues to make trouble for Régnier, the latter only has to let the Duc d'Harcourt[49] know on my behalf. They will have their Letter of Marque when they want it, and also the Frigate Lieutenant's commission. But pay attention! There is one condition: Régnier must organise a meeting between us and the English contacts of his Jersey accomplices. And I want to see those who will be seeking intelligence at Portsmouth. If this doesn't happen, you will make it clear to Duval that not only will we not help Régnier, but we will set the tax authorities and Customs onto him. He will have no choice but to close down his little smuggling business and the rest with it: the Chausey quarries, the soda, the whole shooting party!'

'Do not forget, Sir,' said Captain Le Meur, 'that you must be clear from the outset that we want the English smugglers to give me the exact coordinates where they will anchor their goods, so that I can retrieve them myself.'

'Of course, do whatever is necessary. Now...' Dumouriez turned to me. 'I would like to come back to this girl who is running amok at *La Malice*. Although you showed great discretion in your report, I was given to understand, reading it, that she got rather close to you?'

I felt my face reddening.

'Good, I'll take that as my answer,' continued Dumouriez, with a sardonic little smile. 'It seems too that you have a talent for drawing and painting. Try and do two or three portraits of this beauty, with a good likeness. These are not for my private collection. I would like to send one to your uncle's office in Versailles, and you can give another to Duval to pass on to Monsieur Régnier. That might help him find out more about her.'

Colonel Dumouriez seemed about to leave, but Captain Le Meur had something else to say.

---

49 Translator's note: *Duc d'Harcourt:* French general and peer. Also, incidentally, the subject of a Fragonard portrait that sold for over £17 million at a Bonham's auction in 2013, the highest price for a work by the artist.

'One last thing, Sir. You have not said anything about the special pay for my sailors.'

'I was told that they are permanently enlisted.'

'Only the petty officers, Sir. I am speaking on behalf of the whole crew: the petty officers, the able seamen, the ordinary seamen. The Chevalier de Kermean promised me that they would be considered. You see, we are in a time of peace and my men already run considerable risks. If we are captured and the English learn what we are up to, it will be the rope for them. And then, later on, when we are at war, they will have no chance to participate in any prize money, as we won't be taking any ships.'

'I understand. How much do you want?'

'Five sols per man per day for every member of the crew, irrespective of any other pay.'

'Do you not think that is a little excessive?'

'It comes to exactly ninety pounds a year. The pay of one lackey. It's not much for risking the rope.'

'I'd like to! Except that a lackey gets ninety pounds only, while your sailors already have their pay. What you are demanding here is a bonus.'

'Well then, let's say it will be the cost for their silence.'

Colonel Dumouriez considered this for a moment.

'You will have it.'

On saying that, he really did look like a bulldog about to bite.

As soon as Colonel Dumouriez had been put ashore, the Captain had the crew assembled on deck. The men all looked very happy.

'I am not going to repeat what we were just talking about, since I see that, as usual, you already know. Let me add a few comments. Since you were listening to us, you will also know that there are English spies swarming all over Saint-Malo. If even one of you talks too much, instead of a bonus it will be the rope that you will earn once the English have laid a trap as a result of your foolishness. I know that you are all capable of understanding this and that you can hold you tongues when sober. But a drunk man always talks too much. So, watch yourselves. Don't get drunk in the taverns, and if you see a comrade doing so, stop him before it is too late. If, on my side, I hear that one of you has drunk too much in any bar, he will find himself immediately in the hands of the Commissioner of the Lists, even if he has stayed silent. Don't forget that I have recruited each of you personally, and that I have the full power to replace you whenever I wish.'

The weather stayed bad for the whole of the following week. In any case, Captain Le Meur had not intended to sail immediately. He had the topmast sent down, then sheerlegs set up to lift out the main mast. While this was going on, the Captain had been to the Tallard shipyard to select bigger, more solid spars in the best Baltic timber. Nothing was too good or too expensive for such a special mission. Naturally, this new rig was a little heavier than the previous one. To those who objected that this risked unbalancing his ship, the Captain replied that he would rather sink than break his mast by forcing on sail to escape the English. He also ordered best quality sailcloth from which the master sailmaker Deyo had to cut a new sail wardrobe corresponding to the cutter's new dimensions. Since the sail loft at the Solidor yard was already overflowing with the sails for the two frigates being fitted out, our Deyo and his men installed themselves in a covered battery at the Cité fort. Since the last refit of *le Moucheron,* in June, Captain Le Meur had already added a false keel and deepened the rudder to increase her draft and reduce leeway. All that allowed, in theory anyway, for a corresponding increase in sail area, as long as extra weight, rather than volume, of ballast was added. The cutter's ballast was amidships, directly below the mast, between the forward and after holds. Initially it was made up of four old 6-pounder cannons, placed on the linings at the bottom of the hold and completely covered under a layer of stones. The Captain had decided to replace them with three 12-pounders and to secure them with chests full of scrap metal. It was necessary to lift out the stone ballast and take it ashore in a lighter borrowed from the shipyard, wait until the new mainmast was in place before setting up hoists to change the cannons, before putting a layer of pebbles over the whole lot. The six little 3-pounders that served as armament for the cutter were taken from their positions and installed as movable ballast, along with their carriages. Captain Le Meur asserted that they were more useful thus, since the role of his cutter was not to attack little boats, but to escape big ones, English frigates and ships of the line, for which a 3-pound cannon ball was no more effective than an insect bite. The Captain had another good reason for this, linked to *le Moucheron's* particular mission; what was the use of not flying a white flag at the masthead, in order to pass for an innocent coaster, if the cannons were kept on deck? This doing away with our artillery greatly upset Lieutenant de Kerlaziou, but he felt better once the Captain told him that he could use as much powder as he wished training his men in rifle fire. As for the ten swivel-guns which completed our armament, I never saw them taken out of the lazaret during my whole time aboard *le Moucheron.*

All of this took us to 15th August. For my part, after Colonel Dumouriez' visit I had installed myself at Aunt Chollet's house with my pencils and paints. I had to make at least fifty sketches of La Malaga before I had her face right. I finished with two small portraits, of a good likeness, that I highlighted lightly with gouache to bring them more to life. Lieutenant Chollet found some little round frames for me, so they could be kept under glass. I also wrote to my grandfather and to my friends from my Brest days, Vernon des Aulnes and Maria Kirwan, although I did not really know what to say to them. That was the problem with being on a covert mission for the King. I was not even allowed to mention the name of my ship; although they knew it already. As for Maria Kirwan, I also felt guilty on account of my adventure with La Malaga. I got over the problem by sending her gouaches of the sea and Saint-Malo.

On the morning of 13th July, the wind was blowing from the north-west with such violence that I could hardly walk straight on the path along the crest of the Cité peninsula. I wanted to go and shelter to the east of the walls of the fort and found the place already taken up by a flock of sheep that had the same idea.

At low tide the port had an ethereal look: a huge expanse of muddy sand towards the interior, beautiful white sand to the west of the ramparts, with seaweed covered rocks and big pools. There was nobody out on this grey and rainy morning, until I saw a lone figure come out of the Dinan Gate and descend the steps leading to the shore. With my telescope I could see that the man coming was wearing a cape and wide trousers in waxed tarpaulin, such as sailors wear in showery weather, but in place of clogs he had kept on his city shoes and stockings, which were already soaked. Once he had reached the shore at the Bas Sablons, the man changed direction to take the path to the Cité. He stopped for a moment in the shelter of the houses to take out a flask and drink a mouthful. It could only be Duval, and he seemed not to be followed. I left my shelter to go and meet him.

Duval's face lit up when he recognised me, but he was soon scowling when he had heard what I had to say.

'But it's impossible, what you are demanding! Our English links will never agree to that. I will relay everything to Monsieur Régnier, but I think, with these conditions, he will want to put a stop to everything.'

'I am afraid it might be too late and that he won't have any choice. Did you hear what I said about the tax people and Customs?'

'You are worse than Flaharn, by God!'

'Don't be unfair. You well know that I am just an intermediary.'

'But it will take months!'

'Let's say a month at the most. But we have the time,' I replied. 'And anyway, to show that we are not total devils, we will hold back Esmangard until you have arranged what we are asking for. That apart, do you have anything new regarding La Malaga?'

'I mentioned her to Régnier. He told me he would see what he could find out about her. But once he knows what you are asking of him, I doubt he will be as well disposed.'

'Let's see,' I said. 'I'm sure everything will work out. As soon as you are ready, leave word with the Port Commander. Address it personally to Monsieur de La Rozière. Just put 'Your wine order has arrived'. No name, no signature. You will understand that if La Malaga and the men who followed me in the street the other day really are English agents, one can be sure there are others in Saint-Malo, including in the port offices. As soon as Monsieur de La Rozière has passed your message on to us, I will wait for you the following Sunday, like last time, at the ten o'clock Mass at the Sainte-Croix church.'

I handed him a little bag of waxed cloth containing the portrait of La Malaga. He whistled when he opened it.

'How did you manage to get hold of a portrait of this girl?'

'That's of no importance,' I replied, trying to hide my satisfaction. 'Do you find it a good likeness?'

'It's spot on, with her angel face and witch's eyes!'

'In any case, this will show Monsieur Régnier that we take the matter seriously. Give him the picture, as it will help him in his search.'

*

Le Moucheron put to sea again on 16th August, and this time I was aboard. Captain Le Meur had decided to test his new rig in all weathers. With her huge spanker, gaff topsail, staysail, jib and flying jib, she could go to windward just four points off the wind, while the best frigates could only manage six. The ship's rail was protected with strong canvas up to waist height. This was just as well, for when going to windward in a strong breeze, the water poured over the rail to the height of the gunwales, and to leeward one could almost walk along the inside of it. The first time, I found this quite frightening. I wasn't the only one, for our sailors too were unused to this kind of experience, but we soon took it for granted. The cutter also had a topsail and a t'gallant sail, and for downwind work, a huge square sail, which we called the *square foresail* and which was set below the topsail. In light weather the Captain could also play with a whole range of studding sails for the topsail, the t'gallant sail and the square foresail. He also had one that could be set on the leech of the spanker.

At last, I was really sailing. Up until then I had made no more than modest coastal passages. Those who go to sea for the first time usually have a price to pay but I discovered, with some pleasure, that there are exceptions to every rule: I never got to the point of being sick.

In fair weather, one could find luggers as fast as *le Moucheron,* but they were too lightly built to take the kind of reinforcement that Captain Le Meur had imposed on his cutter. The point of this refit was to allow us to hold on to our canvas longer in a rising wind and sea. This improved our chances of escaping any frigates or ships who wanted to seize us. The longer the boat, the greater its speed. There is no escaping this rule, but in a heavy blow a light and fine-lined craft can outpace a big ship. This advantage disappears completely in a full gale. In fact, the main advantage of the cutter was the minimal leeway she made. That was her best guarantee of escaping any eventual pursuers.

The two lieutenants ran the ship watch on watch. I was assigned to Lieutenant Chollet's watch. He made the most of it to teach me ship handling and the practical aspects of navigation. It was extremely interesting for me, as our second lieutenant knew the Channel particularly well. The master pilot taught me how to use the log and the octant. The first lieutenant instructed me in gunnery, a purely theoretical education aboard *le Moucheron.* The Captain, meanwhile, had me working on various navigational calculations. I learned more quickly than I would have aboard a frigate or a ship of the line, as I was the only pupil. The main disadvantage of this education was that the handling of a cutter had little to do with that of most ships used in the Navy. For ships, frigates, corvettes and all square-rigged ships in general, tacking through the wind is a complicated manoeuvre, and not advised in a big sea, as there is a risk of breaking the topmasts if the ship is taken aback while pitching heavily. It is usual practice to wear the ship round, downwind, if possible. Cutters, on the other hand, tack very nimbly. All that is required is to put the helm up, soon bringing the ship head to the wind which, as soon as it hits the other side of the sail, of itself shifts the boom to the other tack. The staysail is held back for a moment, to help bring the head round. On the other hand, cutters don't like the wind from astern so much. *Le Moucheron* was somewhat more stable than similar ships on this point of sailing, thanks to the modifications made by her Captain. All the same, gybing on this point of sail was still a delicate operation, if the precaution had not been taken beforehand of brailing up the spanker and setting the big square sail. Moreover, by increasing the power of the cutter's rig, as well as her draft, her tiller was harder to hold in a strong wind, and so it was necessary to attach it with lines run through blocks fixed to the gunwales on each side.

The cutter returned to Saint-Malo on Saturday 6th September, at the end of the afternoon, on the flood tide. We must have been watched out for, as we had hardly moored to our coffin buoy when a boat came out from the Solidor inlet and headed in our direction. Colonel Dumouriez requested that we, the Captain and I, attend a meeting without delay at the office of the Port Commander. Having discussed it with me, the Captain decided to go alone. It was night when he returned on board and explained what was going on. The previous day Louis Duval had delivered the message agreed at the end of July to the Commander's office. Since then, Colonel Dumouriez had been champing at the bit. Monsieur de la Rozière had had the greatest difficulty stopping him from going himself to *La Malice* inn to find out what was new. I met Duval on the Sunday morning and we talked on the footpath bordered by honeysuckle and hawthorn on the Chergères headland. Monsieur Régnier had managed, as we had hoped, to persuade the Jersey people to bring their English accomplices to Chausey. If we agreed, the meeting was to take place on the Grande Île on Wednesday 10th September. If not, we would have to wait until October as we were a fortnight away from the equinox and the weather was changing. I gave him our agreement.

Duval had kept the best until the end. Régnier's research on La

Malaga had yielded success, thanks to the portrait I had made for him. She was indeed called Elizabeth, but her real surname was Lesueur. She was from Saint Hélier and had left Jersey some years before to set up in London. This seemed to indicate that it was not Flaharn who was controlling her, but the English, just as Captain Le Meur had suggested. That did not explain, though, how the English agents had managed to home in on me so quickly. As soon as I was back on board the cutter, my commander had me write a report to be taken to Monsieur de La Rozière, for encoding and sending to Versailles. Perhaps my uncle might find the key to this mystery.

Captain Le Meur asked Colonel Dumouriez to sleep on board on the Tuesday night as he wanted to sail on the morning tide. Having been reluctant at first, the Colonel finally agreed and came to install himself in the great cabin. The Captain had to sling a hammock in the starboard cubby hole alongside Lieutenant Kerlaziou.

We had to cover about twenty nautical miles to get from Saint-Malo to Chausey. On 10th September the cutter sailed at first light, two hours after the start of the flood. The currents were more or less on the nose, and the north-east wind created lines of cloud over the Channel. We had to put in a fearfully long starboard board to the north-north west, close-hauled, the ship heeled in a grey and confused sea. Colonel Dumouriez, by now quite pale, clung to the windward rail, taking the spray right in his face. *Le Moucheron* tacked when south-east of the Minquiers Islands and set her course south-east for a second board. This was much easier, thanks to what were now favourable currents which took us to the south of the Chausey Islands before our final turn to the north-north-west. Luckily it was blowing hard, filling out *le Moucheron's* sails, and thanks to her windward ability we were soon sheltered from the open sea, in the lee of the south coast of the Grande Île. This is really only an islet. We anchored for the day in clear water, sheltered by two rocky headlands.

We went ashore in the ship's boat, landing on a little beach of fine sand at the end of a creek. The sun had finally appeared. A footpath bordered with ferns led us to a group of houses built in front of the inner Chausey harbour. This was no more than a place for drying out at low tide, but the first time I saw it was at high water. The boats anchored there were moving around in a chop whipped up by the wind. They were in the middle of a multitude of rocks surrounding several tiny granite islands, crowned by grass and fringed with foam in a luminous blue sea. There were several small barques, a big lugger, which must have been Monsieur Régnier's, and two tough-looking little sloops, which Captain Le Meur told me were *smacks*, from Jersey.

There were two men representing the English smugglers. They were big, black-haired fellows with bushy beards and features that looked as if they had been hewn with an axe out of the brick-red wood of their faces. Their eyes shone clearly. At first sight, they looked to me like real wreckers, but I then remembered how deceptive was Flaharn's noble face, and told myself not to judge people on their appearance. They were from Cornwall, speaking to each other in a dialect that resembled Breton, although I still understood nothing. The conversation was in English, of which Dumouriez and Captain Le Meur both had a command. The two Cornishmen told us that they would be able to supply us once a week with details of the English warships in Portsmouth and Plymouth, as well as their movements. Apparently they were already paying accomplices in these two ports to keep an eye on the Navy coast guard and Customs. They repeated the words '*Revenue Service cutters!*' several times, shaking their heads angrily. They proposed putting their written reports in well-sealed bottles that they would hide in weighted boxes attached to a warp under a buoy.

There was a long and bitter argument over how much they should be paid. This was their main concern. They seemed not in the least restrained by any sense of patriotism. Or perhaps they did not feel truly English. It was finally agreed that they would be paid forty piasters for each weekly delivery. Captain Le Meur would place that sum each week in the box attached to their buoy, on condition, of course, that there was a package in it. Captain Le Meur, supported by Colonel Dumouriez, added that the information provided would be evaluated, and that there was the possibility of an extra payment for any intelligence of particular interest. Once the terms of the deal had been agreed, they gave Captain Le Meur the coordinates of the spot where they intended to leave the documents. This was off the south coast of Devon, six miles east of the Salcombe river, along an uninhabited stretch of coastline west of Start Point, between Pear Tree Point to the east and Prawle Point to the west. We had to get into an exact alignment between Great Sleaden Rock and the southerly tip of Prawle Point. These two bearing points were about three nautical miles apart, and the buoy would be placed exactly halfway between the two, in four fathoms of water at low tide. The buoy would be the usual cork type used by ships to mark their anchors. It would be lengthened by a warp held up by a netted glass float. They explained that Great Sleaden Rock was an isolated rock three hundred yards off Pear Tree Point. Once you got to Start Point you could see it easily to the west-south-west of a big rock, called Black Stone, which protruded from that point. You had to be sure not to get too close to this rock, especially in a strong easterly during the flood tide, which runs to the west in this area. Our two 'wreckers' assured us that the coast here was uninhabited, but that it would be better to operate at night on account of the Revenue cutters which sometimes came past during the day. These arrangements could not have been better for Captain Le Meur. For all sailors in the Channel, Start Point was a prominent landfall, situated about a hundred and twenty nautical miles north-west by north of Saint-Malo.

It was about four in the afternoon when we got back to *le Moucheron.* The wind had died away completely, it was hot, and the sun was veiled. After we had weighed anchor, the cutter drifted for a while at the whim of the ebb currents carrying us towards the Minquiers Islands. We could hear thunder in the distance. A little later fine drizzle began to fall and the wind settled into the south-west, straight from where we were heading. We had no choice but to tack from one board to the other in an awkward chop. Lieutenant Chollet predicted a gale from the west that night, which was confirmed by the barometer. Even in good conditions, we would not have arrived at the Saint-Malo entrance before dusk. It was already a delicate operation, even for those practised in it, like Lieutenant Chollet, to enter the Rance at night in good weather, but with a storm threatening, it was too risky. The Captain decided to head south-south-east, taking advantage of a wind now stronger than the current, to anchor in the lee of the Grouin headland. He had the topsails and t'gallant sails set, as well as the spanker, the gaff topsail, two jibs and staysail, and *le Moucheron* soon picked up speed, close-hauled on starboard tack in a freshening south-westerly. That night, Lieutenant Chollet brought us into a sheltered inlet between two steep headlands. We anchored in two fathoms close to a wide sandy shore uncovered by the falling tide. According to our second lieutenant, there was a unit from the coastal militia on each of the headlands protecting our anchorage.

Colonel Dumouriez ordered me to go and ask the coastguards where one could find horses for hire. The ship's boat put me ashore and I chose to go to the post to the south of the shore. There I found six militiamen with their equipment and arms. They were on their way down to check, having seen me disembark. They told me that there was a man who hired out carts and carriages at Cancale, and that it was possible to find a mount for hire there for going to Saint-Malo. But of course, they added, you would have to wait until tomorrow, as at this late hour the establishment would most certainly be closed.

When I returned on board to report the results of my reconnaissance, Colonel Dumouriez wanted to go to Cancale right away, under the pretext of getting his reports to Saint-Malo as quickly as possible. I had to escort him with two of our infantrymen. He made us put on our uniforms. Night had fallen, a squally wind was blowing and it was raining. We walked for nearly an hour over the moorland in the light of a lantern, on a slippery, muddy path, and were soaked and filthy by the time we arrived at Cancale. The town was silent and in total darkness. Colonel Dumouriez made the first inn we arrived at open its doors and we left him installed in front of a fire while an omelette was prepared for him. I think that rather than an urgent report, he was impatient to get ashore because he had been sick as a dog for the whole crossing. Nothing would have forced him to spend another night on board. All there was for us to do was to return to the cutter, which we did by midnight.

We spent the whole of the next day at anchor. On the Friday morning, at low tide towards half past seven, we set sail. Captain Le Meur wanted to make a daylight reconnaissance of the Cornishmen's buoy and, above all, to check all the bearings in order to be able to find it at night. It was blowing hard from the west, and we had to beat until one in the afternoon, under spanker and the three jibs, to clear the Minquiers Islands. The current was in our favour, but it was raising a steep sea against the wind. Things went better once we could head north, with the wind and current abeam. We raised Start Point on Saturday, late in the afternoon. *Le Moucheron* stayed close-hauled to bring us to the west of Pear Tree Point. We picked out Great Sleaden Rock and Prawle Point, and hove to in the swell at the place our intermediaries had designated. There was our buoy dancing on the green and white-streaked waves. Without doubt it had served for a long time as a pick-up point for tons of contraband. We immediately carried on, so as not to attract attention from any potential observers, although there did not appear to be a living soul on land. It was a wild and steep coastline, crowned with short grass, devoid of trees or bushes, with grey and white cliffs falling straight down to a scattering of rocks. The sea was breaking along the length of the shore, except for the inside of the two headlands to the east and west, where there were two narrow, enclosed creeks. In the western one I saw a barque moored to a coffin buoy and a low stone cottage with a thatched roof. With my telescope I saw a man come to the threshold to watch us. Could he have mistaken us for the coastguard? Living there, he was probably an accomplice of the smugglers.

The cutter returned to Saint-Malo on Sunday at the top of the flood tide. Captain Le Meur wanted to leave again on Tuesday, as the full moon was due on Wednesday and he wanted to make a night reconnaissance of what we were already calling the 'smugglers' anchorage'. But the weather deteriorated again, becoming quite awful. As low tide was in the middle of the day for the next three days, the crew took advantage of this to dry out the cutter in the Solidor inlet, in order to careen and re-caulk her.

I received two letters from Brest. Vernon told me that his ship, *le Robuste,* under the command of the Chevalier de Lamotte-Picquet, and five other vessels, had received orders to remain in the anchorage, with five months' supplies aboard, ready to depart at any moment. The ships were not leaving the bay but were training regularly in gunnery and manoeuvres in little divisions of three or four vessels. They had even done a disembarkation exercise recently at the Roscanvel headland. My friend had given up for good the room at the inn in order to install himself permanently on board. This did not stop him going hunting regularly with the Comte de Boulainvilliers whenever he had permission to go ashore. He hunted mainly by tracking, and played the hunting horn for the pleasure of the Comte. The latter had engaged a new huntsman, but he missed poor François Loutre. Our guns and dog were still at Coataudon. Brac was fine.

Vernon still saw Maria Kirwan, and he enclosed a letter for me.

Nothing is more honourable, Sir, than the manner in which you make me aware of my feelings. Your discretion is all to your credit. I bear your distance from me by contemplating the pretty gouache drawing that you so kindly sent me since your letter of last June. You wrote beneath it that you painted the sea while thinking of my eyes. That is most kind of you. Thus am I assured that you will think of me every time that you look around you aboard your ship.

I have the honour of being, Sir, as completely as is possible, your most humble and obedient servant.

It was her response to the letter I had written at Nantes, beside the Loire, at the start of summer. God knows how much I had wished for it and waited for it, this charming letter, written by a young girl who thought nothing but good of me. Unfortunately, since then, there had been the Saint-Malo episode with La Malaga. I was beginning to realise that I was feeling considerably less shame about this memory. I took up my pen again to try to correct my aim.

Mademoiselle

Your kindness towards me touches me boundlessly, but sadly I fear that I am not worthy of it. Moreover, I am a sailor, called by my vocation to depart before long to the other ends of the world where I will be incapable of providing the affection you deserve. In your own interest forget me, Mademoiselle, or at least think of me as a friend, a caring one indeed, but one who will never be able to do justice to your most beautiful and pure feelings, and preserve them for someone more deserving.

I ask you simply to accept my assurances of the deepest respect with which I will forever remain, Mademoiselle, your most humble and most obedient servant.

Towards mid-September I received a letter from my uncle de Kermean by the post which passed through Monsieur de La Rozière's office. The Comte de Saint-Germain had resigned on the first of the month. The back-biters, so numerous at Court, had also made out that the Comte had been disowned by the King. The Chevalier assured me that there was nothing in this, that the King and his Minister of War had in no way fallen out, and that they had worked together on these famous reforms attributed to the Comte. In reality, the Comte had been ill for some time. He had tried to carry on working but he was suffering too much to be able to fulfil his duty properly. My uncle had always remained loyal to him since being under his command in Germany, and he did not get on well with his successor, the Prince of Montbarey.

We went to sea again at the end of September. *Le Moucheron* was in constant service, since she had to cross the Channel every week. After the improvements made by her Captain, the cutter really showed her qualities. She sliced easily through the waves and her additional ballast gave her an inertia which kept her moving in light airs. Captain Le Meur had her careened whenever possible. Our intermediaries seemed to be honouring their contract, to the satisfaction of the Versailles offices. From time to time we cruised off Spithead. There we met many English ships of war. Their corvettes and frigates had little interest in us, at worst taking us for common smugglers, small fry to be left for the ships of the Revenue Service. We sailed without a white flag, without any ensign, or else an English one, without uniforms for the officers and infantrymen, without cannons on deck.

The crew now had the cutter well in hand, and *le Moucheron* responded to the requests of her commander with the same suppleness and the same precision as a well-trained war horse. Monsieur de Fleurieu had been right: she really was the ideal craft for this type of mission. The men of the crew were all qualified seamen from Saint-Malo, selected individually by Lieutenant Chollet and Captain Le Meur, who even knew their families. The devotion and discretion of the sailors were absolute, and they were overjoyed to be able to serve their time aboard a ship of the King while staying close to home. They had no wish to do something silly which would cause them to lose this plum job and the bonus of ninety pounds promised by Dumouriez.

Then we were into autumn, with its gales, cold hands, rain, first frosts and its fine days too. When the sun warmed the deck during the midday watch we could have ourselves believe for an hour or two that it was spring rather than November in mid-Channel. I began to appreciate this life, aboard a good ship, with a good Captain, surrounded by a happy crew.

6

At Saint-Malo, Colonel Dumouriez kept us up to date with what was going on in the outside world. The war was continuing in New England. It took a month to have any news from the other side of the Atlantic. Our government continued to give secret aid to the Insurgents, mainly by means of the seaborne activities of *Rodrigue Hortalez & Co.*, under the direction of Monsieur Beaumarchais. Not everything was going well. Lord Stormont continued to know all about our embarkations, supposedly clandestine, to New England: *Lord All-hearing-all-seeing*, more than ever!

'To think,' fumed Dumouriez, 'that Monsieur le Marquis de Lafayette, when he left Paris in order to embark at Bordeaux, did not even dare tell his young wife, of whom he is very fond, through fear of alerting our enemies! Yet our Lord Ambassador of His Majesty George III learned of his departure before Madame de Lafayette and before Renoir, the Paris Police Commissioner! And if it were only that! More than fifty of our merchantmen carrying secret supplies for the rebels have been intercepted. Their crews are in the prison ships at Portsmouth and their cargoes lost to us and our allies. All that money spent for nothing! Stormont has placed agents everywhere, especially around Benjamin Franklin, the doctor of the lightning rod, the darling of Paris and the philosophers, the wearer of a beaver hat!'

Dumouriez was almost choking.

'He has been told so many times to be careful with his mail! We may as well whistle in the wind!'

I often heard this kind of talk at the meetings organised by Colonel Dumouriez at a house in the rue des Juifs, where he had established his headquarters. The Colonel had in effect decided that he would not go aboard *le Moucheron* again, and that it was up to us to make the journey to him. In his defence, I knew that our short cruise to the Chausey Islands had left a bad impression on him.

The Colonel requested a special meeting on the first Thursday of December. Captain Le Meur would have liked to postpone the meeting, since we had returned to Saint-Malo that same morning, at dawn, after a freezing night in the Channel. The room where we met in the rue des Juifs was still unheated. Colonel Dumouriez had other things to think about than laying in a supply of wood for lodgings in which he did not live. He had categorically refused to put back the meeting and seemed quite exhilarated as he invited us to sit at the table used for our deliberations.

'I can quite understand that you are tired, Sirs, but I have important news to tell you. Firstly, the English have lost a battle against the Insurgents, at a place called Saratoga. General Burgoyne – Gentleman Johnny as he is known – surrendered unconditionally! You are amongst the first in France to hear this news as it is quite fresh, having been brought to Nantes the day before yesterday by an American war corvette commanded by their Paul Jones. I give you his name as I will be coming back to him in relation to the second thing I have to talk to you about. We have also received a confidential letter from your uncle.'

Dumouriez turned towards me.

'He explains at last how and why the girl Lesueur picked up on you so quickly when you arrived in Saint-Malo last July.'

I forgot my tiredness and the cold. God knows how many times I had asked myself about this puzzle.

'I have often spoken to you about the disastrous lack of prudence of Benjamin Franklin as regards protecting the secrecy of our diplomatic exchanges about English spies. Well, there are leaks in our own offices in Versailles! Except that we for our part have managed to uncover the source, thanks to the Chevalier de Kermean.'

Dumouriez turned to me once again.

‘As he was unable to ferret out the moles installed around the good Franklin, because of the total lack of cooperation of the man, your uncle set off a false rumour in our own offices to try at least to entrap any Stormont agents who may have infiltrated us. It worked. In truth, the person who was caught in the net is not really a traitor, but more of an idiot. One of our secretaries, a young man of good family, whose name I will withhold out of regard for his relatives, had become so infatuated with the struggle of the Americans that he thought our government too slow to take the rebels’ side. He got tied up with Beaumarchais’ secretary, another scatterbrain of the same type, and they egged each other on. Our two champions of liberty were approached at the Palais Royal by an accomplice of Lord Stormont who represented himself as being an Irishman close to Silas Deane. This false Irishman, in reality English, asked them to keep him informed of our secret operations, for the good of the American cause. This was, you understand, to make sure it went well! Stormont’s agent made out that the ‘honourable decisions of the King’, made as a result of Silas Deane’s requests, were being wilfully frustrated in our offices by the malice of some of our officials acting on behalf of His Majesty. He therefore asked our young fool to give him all the documents about secret operations which passed through his hands. Of course, Silas Deane had asked for nothing of the sort and had nothing to do with it. In fact, the information provided by our young idiot went straight to the office of *Lord All-hearing-all-seeing*.’

On hearing all this I no longer felt cold. I even thought I was sweating. My eye caught that of Captain Le Meur, who seemed equally dumbfounded.

‘You mean the English know all about our mission?’ asked the Captain in a hoarse voice.

‘Rest assured, that is not yet the case. Here’s what happened. As our naïve idealist could obviously not pass on the originals of the documents he handled, he made copies, without always understanding them, on small sheets which he gave to his good friend the ‘Irishman’. He admitted to us that he had copied, in particular, the embarkation certificate for *le Duc de Choiseul*, that Monsieur de La Rozière had sent to Saint-Malo to be given to Monsieur Laforest-Dombourg. I can remind you that the name of the certificate’s beneficiary was left blank. And our imbecile stupidly transcribed on the same sheet a letter from

Benjamin Franklin. In this letter, Franklin asked for administrative and financial support for acquiring at Saint-Malo a fast warship for the American Navy. Franklin explained that he wished to give the command of this ship to Lieutenant Paul Jones, of whom I have just spoken. I have to say that this Paul Jones has become something of a bête noire for our English neighbours. He captured sixteen cod-fishing schooners from them in six weeks during the last fishing season on the Grand Banks! In short, the English thought firstly that Benjamin Franklin wanted secretly to buy *le Duc de Choiseul* to turn it into an American privateer operating out of Saint-Malo, and secondly that the King's secret office had prepared a false certificate for Franklin's representative charged with supervising this mission. Note that *le Duc de Choiseul's* reputation as a fast ship made the idea quite credible, especially as she had gunports from outset, having been fitted out as a privateer, and that Dubuys, her owner, had had her copper-bottomed to increase her speed. The English were already choking on their tea every time they heard mention of Saint-Malo. Imagine their reaction when the name of Paul Jones was added to the mix! So you can see why the English Cabinet at St James was stirred up to the extent of ordering their secret services to deal with the matter urgently. And that is how the beautiful Lesueur arrived at the house of the good shipowner Dubuys, whom she probably took into her bed, at the risk of exploding his old heart, and then got her claws into the dashing Captain Royer...and others I won't mention! Note that she could not know the name of the bearer of the certificate as it was blank when Lord Stormont's stupid agent copied it.'

'Good! I prefer it like that,' said Captain Le Meur. 'I was also thinking that our little intelligence operation with Monsieur Régnier was hardly big enough to attract the attention of the English so quickly.'

'Yes indeed!', replied Dumouriez. 'Monsieur Laforest-Dombourg was taken, through no fault of his own, to be an agent of Benjamin Franklin, on account of his embarkation certificate for *le Duc de Choiseul*. Who have you shown the certificate to, Monsieur Dombourg?'

'To the innkeeper,' I replied. 'But it is true I wondered how the English could have got interested in me so quickly. I could not understand it at all. In any case, I am pleased that this business is over.'

'Not at all! It isn't at all! Do you still have this famous embarkation certificate?'

'Yes, I still have it. My uncle told me to keep all my documents and hand them back at the end of the mission.'

'And he did the right thing! Well now, you will go back to *La Malice*, where Captain Royer is still up to his usual tricks, and you will present yourself to him while clearly showing your certificate.'

'I thought Captain Royer was setting sail again in September,' I said.

'He was supposed to be. But if you came to Saint-Malo more often, you would have seen that *le Duc de Choiseul* is still moored in front of the Saint Vincent Gate, under the Chateau. And do you know why? Because a merchant ship cannot put to sea without having all its papers signed and in order. And following that business with you last July, as we were not sure what was going on, we withheld the signing of the documents, to the extreme annoyance of her owner. In any case, there's no cause for complaint, as the Ministry has forbidden any sailings to the Grand Banks. They want to avoid a repeat of the Boscawen affair.'

'But why don't you simply arrest this girl?' asked Captain Le Meur.

'She is not acting alone. Thanks to Monsieur Dombourg, we know that she has at least two accomplices and that she has infiltrated the Office of the Lists. I want to get to a position where they cannot do any damage before they set up shop in Monsieur de La Rozière's anteroom. In short, I want to catch the whole gang! And to achieve that, I have kicked the ants' nest. I have sent a letter on official notepaper to the shipowner Dubuys, telling him that the government intends to requisition his ship and that he will be compensated. Of course, this is not true, but it will get old Dubuys shouting, and I hope La Malaga will hear him. And when Monsieur Dombourg reappears on the scene brandishing his famous certificate of embarkation, I reckon she will quickly round up all her sidekicks.'

'But what use will that be?' asked Captain Le Meur again.

'I have a plan. Laforest-Dombourg shows up at *La Malice*, takes his meals there and afterwards comes here, to this house. The girl Lesueur will soon have him followed. We will have put one of our men behind her henchmen to identify them and once they are watching from down below, in the rue des Juifs, we just have to pick them up. Then we will go and arrest La Malaga, in old Dubuys' bed if necessary!'

'I don't agree,' said Captain Le Meur. 'This will create unnecessary risks for my young Marine Guard. This girl wishes no good for him and may even want to take revenge against him.'

'Another good reason for it! If that is the case, we can be even more sure she will react. Monsieur Dombourg risks nothing, since, as I have already said, his back will be covered. However, to limit the risks, he will only go to eat at *La Malice*. The rest of the time he can stay here where he will be well looked after and where he will be under the protection of the military police. And in any case, don't forget that as far as this business is concerned, including your ship's mission, it is I who gives the orders and who decides! To give La Malaga time to return, we won't start until tomorrow. I don't think she will react straight away. We may have to wait a week. Monsieur Dombourg, you will disembark and install yourself here. You can go and get your bag from the ship. I will send a carriage for you to the Solidor port during the afternoon and will expect you here this evening, to give you your instructions.'

I was ready to go ashore with my bag towards four in the afternoon. I was wearing my blue ratine jacket and a big woollen scarf. Captain Le Meur told me once again how much he disapproved of Colonel Dumouriez' plan. I could not take my sword, but he advised me always to have two loaded pistols on me and he gave me a dagger that I could slide under my belt behind my back between my waistcoat and my jacket. I could not take my beautiful cavalry pistols, as the barrels were too long for my pockets. I was issued with two standard Navy pistols from *le Moucheron's* armoury.

'We will be staying at Solidor tomorrow and the day after. With low tides at midday I want to make use of them to careen. Don't hesitate to come and see me or to send me a message if you have any worries. We will leave on Sunday morning with the tide. I aim to be at Start Point at nightfall, then we will head up towards the Isle of Wight for a final quick cruise off Spithead before the end of winter. I think we will be heading back to Saint-Malo on Tuesday 9th.'

I regretted having to go ashore, knowing that I would be there for at least a whole week while *le Moucheron* was cruising in the Channel.

On Monday, at half past twelve, I went to *La Malice*. At my request, Monsieur de La Rozière had had Duval warned and told to behave as if he did not know me. I told the innkeeper that I had spent the last few months at Dinan and that I had come back to embark on *le Duc de Choiseul.* I told him that I was lodging in town, but I intended to have lunch at his place every day during the week. He was surprised, of course, but once he had heard the tinkle of the King's money, he refrained from commenting. Things were going somewhat differently for Captain Royer. He was less cocky than when I had first seen him. With his ship confined to port, that was understandable. I presented myself to him as a Volunteer designated to his ship and showed him my certificate. He asked me what I had been told when I had presented myself the port offices. I replied that I thought that *le Duc de Choiseul* would probably be released within the next few weeks. As vague as it was, this answer seemed to please him. It would not have taken much for him to have kissed me! La Malaga was not there. I was given to understand that she had left off him somewhat on learning that *le Duc de Choiseul* had been confined to port by the authorities.

I checked my pistols on going out after lunch. I could feel the dagger given to me by Captain Le Meur in the small of my back. When I went past the bar next to my inn, I saw an individual come out and fall in step behind me at a distance. He was wrapped up to the ears in a big blue Prussian three-collared overcoat. It was Colonel Dumouriez' private secretary. His job was to watch my back and keep on the heels of any potential followers. He was called Martin and was a serious young fellow. He had told me that he spoke several languages and that he had travelled widely across Europe. He was friendly and seemed intelligent, but I would have preferred a real and illiterate soldier. The rue du Point du Jour was as dark and deserted as ever. In any event, nobody would have wanted to be out walking in this cold.

The next day, La Malaga came to the inn. Monsieur Dubuys must have told her about the letter sent by Dumouriez about the potential requisitioning of *le Duc de Choiseul.* The colonel had kicked the ants' nest and the queen of the ants had come out from her hole! Captain Royer seemed quite cheered up. He invited me to lunch with him and I found myself sat at his table opposite La Malaga.

'My dear friend, allow me to present to you this young man who has just told me of his happiness at having been assigned to embark very soon under my orders as a Volunteer. And he has just come from the port offices! Isn't that marvellous? I really think our troubles are nearly at an end!'

Elizabeth Lesueur gave me an icy look.

'What did you tell the Captain?'

'I only said that *le Duc de Choiseul* would soon be putting to sea,' I replied, staring straight into her eyes.

Outwardly she remained impassive but I knew that I was playing with fire annoying her in this way. Having already felt her blade at my throat I ought to have been more careful but, after all, had not Colonel Dumouriez said that he wanted to provoke a lively reaction? After the meal I took my leave, telling Captain Royer, loudly enough so that La Malaga would hear, that I was lodging in town but that I intended to eat every day at the inn. My head was heavy. In his good mood, the slaver Captain had not stopped refilling my glass and encouraging me to empty it. Martin was watching out for me from the window of his bar. I was on the alert, but I thought it was still too soon and that things would not start to get serious until the next day.

On Sunday morning I went along the western ramparts to get to the rue de la Diacrerie. The tide would be ebbing from ten o'clock and I wanted to watch *le Moucheron* depart. It was fine and very cold, without a cloud in the sky. An icy wind was blowing from the north-east. *Le Moucheron,* freshly tarred, was passing through the Main Gate entrance, reaching under her spanker, all her jibs, gaff topsail, topsail and t'gallant sail, along with their studding sails. This spread of canvas glistened in the white sunlight of this winter morning. She was magnificent! I went to the inn before lunchtime, in order to get a table on my own. In this way I could avoid another invitation from Captain Royer. He would have had me drinking like the day before and I wanted to keep my head clear for anything that followed. I was nervous, I admit, entering the rue du Point du Jour. But nothing happened that day, or the next, or on Tuesday. Nothing either on Wednesday 10th December. The weather stayed just as cold. I noticed that Martin had relaxed and was following me from a closer distance, but that had no consequences; with that weather we were most of the time walking along alone one after the other. As a result, I forgot to check my pistols and renew the charge of powder in their flash pans.

On Thursday the wind fell completely and went round to the south. The temperature became milder and a thick, damp mist enveloped Saint-Malo. I was concerned, as nothing had been heard from *le Moucheron.* Monsieur Dumouriez had sent his private carriage several times to Solidor, but each time the coachman had returned to say the ship's buoy was empty. She would normally have returned the previous morning. This time I could not avoid lunching with Captain Royer. La Malaga was not there. Captain Royer told me he had not seen her since the previous day.

*

Saint-Malo, Thursday 11th September 1777, towards three in the afternoon.

I go out of the inn. The fog is just as thick and seems even wetter than this morning. One cannot see further than ten paces. Martin has already come out and is waiting for me, standing in a doorway, wrapped in his big blue coat. I pass in front of him without stopping and lose sight of him straight away. I walk slowly to make his job easier. I am almost halfway along the rue du Point du Jour when I seem to hear a muffled groan behind me. I stop and turn round. I wait a few moments. I have lost any sense of time in the cotton-wool universe which engulfs me.

I see, with some relief, Martin's big blue coat emerge from the mist. He seems to be hurrying. Then he stumbles. His knees give way. He crumbles like a doll on his bent legs and lies stretched out on the cobblestones. I run to him, thinking he is ill. He is lying on his side. I take off his hat and lift his head. He tries to speak to me and I lean towards him, feeling his breath, but blood suddenly streams from his mouth. I try to pick him up to turn him over, and feel something hard in his back. The handle of a dagger is buried between his shoulders. His gaze becomes fixed and he stops breathing. I realise with horror that he has died in my arms and that it was his last breath which I had felt on my face.

The shock is completely unexpected. I can see and feel this horn handle at my fingertips but I cannot believe it. The mist makes everything unreal. Nothing around me seems solid. For a few seconds I am frozen to stone. Then I feel as if I am about to give way to fear. Above all I must think and keep a cool head. I look towards the end of the street drowned in a veil of suspended moisture. I listen carefully to the silence. I hear breathing close to me and I jump up. I was looking in the distance and 'they' are right beside me. Three motionless shapes in the mist, stopped just a few paces away. How long have they been looking at me? I point one of my pistols in their general direction.

'Who goes there?'

Without waiting for a reply I pull the trigger. As in a nightmare, the flint strikes the plate but nothing happens. I turn on my heels and run off. I tell myself that I will get a dagger in the back too, so I weave as I am running. The muscles in my back are so tense they hurt. Strangely, 'they' do not seem to hurry. I hear a calm but strong voice behind me. I hear something like: '*don't let…'m…go*'. In any case, it is English. I soon see who these words are for. Other shapes appear in front of me, coming from the rue des Bés. I am cornered! I back into a doorway, drop my first pistol and grab the second. I draw my dagger with my left hand and shout as loudly as I can.

'The first who comes near, I will kill!'

Ottmeyer had often told me that you should shout in a fight. It allows you to concentrate your energy and unsettles your opponent. My attackers stop several paces from me, barring the road to left and right. There are six in all. Two are dressed like townsfolk, with three-cornered hats and knee breeches. They look like the two henchmen whom I lost in the rue de la Lancette six months ago. The other four are dressed in bonnets, woollen overcoats and wide trousers, like ordinary seamen, but they have broader shoulders than the norm, huge arms and a terrible look about them. Although they are only carrying knives they are as frightening as war machines.

One of the two townsfolk is holding a knife by the blade. It must have been he who had killed poor Martin. I point the barrel of my pistol at him. He speaks to me calmly in good French.

'Do not try to resist, Sir. Throw down your weapons and you will not come to any harm. We want simply to talk and do a deal with you.'

I am not totally taken in by this, but I think to myself that if they really wanted to kill me I would already be dead. The English sailors wait without moving. I try to think while keeping my weapon pointed at the knife-thrower.

'Don't come any nearer, I…'

A loud bang cuts off my words. The man who spoke to me seems to jump in the air and is thrown violently onto the cobblestones two paces to the left of me. It isn't me who has fired.

'Throw down your arms!'

*

I seemed to be dreaming as I recognised the voice of Lieutenant de Kerlaziou. During the stand-off with my attackers a group of about ten men had come up on us from the south end of the street. I recognised the sailors from *le Moucheron.* The crew of the cutter, and her infantrymen, were equipped with the latest 1777 model rifles. One of them had been fired at the knife-thrower. The second 'townsman' tried to escape by running towards the rue des Bés. Lieutenant de Kerlaziou grabbed a rifle from one of the sailors beside him and shot on the fly, as if he were hunting. The man fleeing made a complete somersault and rolled like a rabbit. The English sailors dropped their knives, with a look that said they knew the game was up. Lieutenant de Kerlaziou asked me if I was wounded. I was fine. Windows opened above us, with the curious leaning out to see what was going on. Lieutenant de Kerlaziou shouted for a handcart to be brought. Soldiers from the Chateau garrison soon arrived, their bayonets fixed, and the Lieutenant turned the prisoners over to them. He told me that Captain Le Meur had alerted the garrison as soon as they had started following the English. He told our sailors to take care of the dead. There were at least two – poor Martin and the knife-thrower. The latter's accomplice was in a bad way, but was still alive. It seemed he had taken our first lieutenant's bullet in the right shoulder blade. Walking towards the rue des Juifs, Lieutenant de Kerlaziou told me how he came to be there.

'It was a matter of chance. As you no doubt know, Captain Le Meur had decided to have a last look at Spithead. Arriving at the Isle of Wight, we saw a big cutter coming out from Portsmouth. At the masthead she was flying her 'commissioning pennant' as they call it, and a red ensign at the peak. For a moment we feared she might change course to give chase to us, but she ignored us completely and carried on to the south-west. That was on Monday, towards four in the afternoon. The next day, at dawn, as we arrived at the Saint-Malo entrance, who did we see ahead of us? The cutter from the previous day, which we had caught up with overnight. Except that she was no longer flying her pennant and had raised a Dutch flag. We saw her anchor in the Rance bay, opposite the Saint Philippe Bastion, seemingly to wait for the tide before entering the Saint-Malo commercial port. So we decided to do the same. While we were both waiting for the tide to rise in the entrance passage by the Nose, we saw our cutter sending up signal flags. We could not read them, but the signal was clearly for someone in the town. That's when Captain Le Meur thought of the girl you had to make a portrait of, the one who works for the English and lives just on this side of the ramparts. That, of course, got us even more interested. We came into the port after him and guess what? Our man anchored alongside *le Duc de Choiseul.* We anchored close too, so that we could watch what was going on. During the evening, three people came on board once it was dark, and stayed there. In the morning, before dawn, they laid hold of *le Duc de Choiseul.* Then, towards one in the afternoon, we saw a group put off in their boat to go ashore. We did the same. Luckily there was the fog, otherwise the ten of us, standing squeezed together in the boat, would not have gone unnoticed. We soon caught up with them and followed them quietly from a distance. That was easy for our Malouin sailors…'

Captain Le Meur had alerted the port authorities and the town Commander. Soldiers from the garrison boarded the English cutter and *le Duc de Choiseul.* The English had intended to seize her and sail her out on the tide. They might well have succeeded, with the assistance of the fog. They also wanted to take me with them to London to interrogate me. They still thought I was mixed up with Paul Jones. Their scheme was bold and it almost worked. But they made a big mistake that would go against them. The shipowner Dubuys had left two Malouin sailors to guard his ship. Their bodies were found against the old quay, near the ravelin, at low tide. Both had their throats slit cleanly. The English had left nothing to chance, but now that their mission had failed, they were in an awkward position. With the killing of poor Martin, there were rather too many French deaths for an operation directed, in principal, against the Americans.

Elizabeth Lesueur was found on the cutter and was arrested along with the crew. La Malaga's two accomplices, the man killed and the man wounded by Lieutenant de Kerlaziou, were from Jersey, like her. She had presented them to Monsieur Dubuys as distant relatives from Cherbourg. As they had some knowledge of accounting and clerking, Monsieur Dubuys had employed them in his offices, where they were much appreciated. They had declared the English cutter as the *Walrus,* from Amsterdam, and presented the port authorities with a false bill of lading, according to which the vessel was bringing Dutch beer for the private consumption of Monsieur Dubuys. They were renting a little house at Paramé, where the sergeants of the military police found cages containing pigeons by which they sent any urgent reports to Portsmouth. Otherwise they gave them to an agent of the English Commissioner at Dunkirk, who came regularly to see them at Paramé. That was how they had sent the message to Portsmouth that had decided the English equivalent of our secret service to mount the operation with the *Walrus.* This was probably not the real name of the cutter, if it had ever been registered with the Royal Navy. Like *le Moucheron*, this vessel obeyed two masters. She was declared a prize and refitted by the port Commander under her new name: *la Guèpe*[50].

Colonel Dumouriez was without doubt badly affected by the brutal death of his faithful secretary, but his strong sense of duty forbade him to show it. He spoke to us about 'the total success of his plan' and intervened personally to have *le Duc de Choiseul* authorised to depart.

Le Moucheron resumed her missions across the Channel. We still had our meetings in the rue des Juifs. Colonel Dumouriez kept us up to date with the government's policies and the negotiations between the French and Spanish cabinets over the adoption of a common position as regards the Insurgents. Spain had not yet made up her mind, but incidents between French and English ships began to multiply. The impression that we were heading towards a naval conflict with England was borne out more and more and, in this context, *le Moucheron's* activities were followed with great interest by the highest authorities. The King himself had told Monsieur de Fleurieu how pleased he was with the success of this operation and asked for this to be made known to Fireship Captain Le Meur.

I received a letter from the Chevalier de Kermean. It had travelled with the Ministerial packages for Monsieur de La Rozière. This mail contained a letter from Flaharn, sent by him via the ordinary Post, and already opened. This kind of thing no longer surprised me, following my conversations with my uncle. Captain Flaharn wanted me to know that he had several plans for expeditions to India in preparation and that he was working on this under the orders of his 'superior', as he wrote, with an eye to discretion. Ships would certainly be designated in the spring of 1778 for leaving for India. He strongly advised me to keep an eye on the fitting out that was going on at this time and to try and get myself appointed to one of these vessels, whether a ship or a frigate. My uncle added that he was sending me this letter purely so that I knew that Flaharn had written to me, but there was of course no question of me leaving for India, if Flaharn was going too.

---

50 Translator's note: *La Guèpe – The Wasp*

7

La Résolue and *la Prudente* left Saint-Malo at the end of 1777 after completing their fitting out and their sea trials. The first was given to the Chevalier de Pontevès and the second to the Vicomte des Cars. The next frigate, the one whose slipway was closest to the Solidor Tower, was launched on the first Monday of January at ten in the morning, at high tide. She was christened *la Gloire.* We watched her launch from the deck of the cutter. That day we were due to sail after lunch on the last of the ebb, with a view to making our usual landfall on the Devon coast the next day.

*

The Solidor anchorage, Monday 5th January 1778, towards eleven in the morning.

It is very cold. I help the boatmen get the ship's boat aboard, to give myself some exercise. I have put a cape over my coat. Our Malouin sailors, for their part, are wearing sheepskin cloaks and woollen bonnets. The wet timber and rope are freezing for my bare hands, which I have to shake constantly to warm up. The night in prospect will be hard, in the cold waters of the Channel. The Captain and his two lieutenants are talking quietly to each other, leaning on the taffrail and watching the port boats towing *la Gloire* to her mooring buoy. As the cutter is small, I can catch the end of their conversation.

'We mustn't complain,' said Captain Le Meur. 'Two years ago at the same time, the sea had frozen up to three miles out from the coast. The swell was carrying ice floes as far as you could see. You would have thought it was the Baltic Sea. But that is nothing compared with New France[51]. One time, in the middle of May, at Louisbourg, I saw so much ice develop in our ship's rigging during the night that when it fell onto the deck the next day, we reckoned its weight to be twelve thousand pounds.'

On hearing the word Louisbourg I stop moving and look aft. The Captain sees me and stares back. At first he says nothing, then frowns and signals me to join him.

'Monsieur Laforest-Dombourg, I recall that last July I made a promise to you that I have not kept. True, we have scarcely had a free moment since then. We have a little time before lunch. Follow me, I beg you. I will try to make amends.'

He gives a few last orders to the two lieutenants regarding our imminent departure and invites me to follow him into *le Moucheron's* tiny great cabin. It is pleasant below. The master caulker has hung a brazier under the deck beams, to heat our little dining room before the officers' lunch.

'You heard me talk last time about a legal dispute between Admiral Boscawen and your father, and you asked me what I knew about it. I think I can give you the reasons for it…'

He signals me to sit on one of the benches fixed round the table under the skylight and settles himself opposite me. Since my arrival in Saint-Malo, all the questions I had about my father have been overshadowed by the somewhat dramatic events in which I have been closely involved. It only needs me to hear Captain Le Meur mention Louisbourg to revive the pained curiosity I have so often felt deep inside myself since the last words my mother spoke to me before her disappearance: '*You know nothing of his story, but it ought to be told.*' I remember too the advice given to me by the Chevalier de Kermean in the garden of the

51 Translator's note: *New France* (*La Nouvelle France*). The name given to France's extensive colonies in what is now Canada. They were mostly ceded to the British in 1763.

Abbey des Prières: '*I believe the answers we are seeking are to be found in the story of your father, at Louisbourg*'.

'Did you know my father's family, Sir? I lost my parents very early on and I have never yet met anyone who could tell me about my grandparents from Louisbourg. I know absolutely nothing about them.'

'I did not know your family particularly well, but I am happy to tell you everything I know. Especially as regards this business with Admiral Boscawen. Before beginning, though, I should warn you. What I am going to tell you might at first displease you, but you mustn't hold that against me. If you have the patience to listen to me to the end, you will change your mind.'

He went quiet. He had lost his usual sardonic look.

'This takes us back twenty years, to Louisbourg, in June 1758. We were besieged by the English forces from 8th June of that year. At the start of the siege, the Governor ordered your father to take charge of a little party of Indians that was to make sorties at night. He wanted them to search in the woods for a group of soldiers who had not managed to re-join us before we were encircled. He also ordered him to harry the rear of the enemy encampment. Our allies, the savages, made war in their own way. You have no doubt heard of their terrible habit of taking scalps. Well, during one of these night expeditions, a young English infantry officer had the misfortune to be scalped. To make things worse, he was a close relative of Admiral Boscawen.'

He stops and looks me right in the eyes. Despite his warning, I am caught off-guard. I am too dumbfounded to react.

He carries on.

'The English quickly found out, nobody knows how, that it was your father who was commanding the unit responsible for this 'act of barbarity', as the English Admiral called it in the letter he had sent to the Governor. The Admiral simply asked for your father to be handed over to him. In some ways, I can understand his resentment. I have seen the bodies of men who have been scalped the way the Canadian Indians do it, and have been told how they go about it if you have the misfortune to fall into their hands. They lay you on the ground on your stomach and put a foot between your shoulder blades. They take a fistful of hair to pull your head back and quickly cut the skin from the skull by going right round with a knife a sharp as a razor...'

He moves his finger round his head to show me the movement.

'....and then, they strip the whole lot off in one go, complete with the skin, by pulling hard on the hair. It seems that it is possible to survive this horror, but generally the death throes that follow last a long time, so I have been told. It is not a pretty death.'

He goes quiet again. His words make me feel awful. They seem to sully the memory of my father. It is much worse than when I thought he had been making money on the side. If I had not learned to respect Captain Le Meur, I think I would call him a liar, there and then.

'With the greatest of respect, Sir, are you absolutely sure of what you are telling me? I thought my father was a Frigate's Lieutenant in 1758. How could he have been ordered to make these land-based expeditions that you have told me about?'

The Captain passes both hands over his face and sighs.

'Your father was a Naval officer, certainly, but he was born in Louisbourg. Not only did he know the countryside perfectly, he was one of the few French officers at the garrison, if not the only one, who could speak the language of the Indians there fluently. That's why, without doubt, he was assigned this particular mission.'

'My parents never said anything about it. My father spoke the Indian language? How is that possible?'

'I don't know. I am only telling you what I heard. He was born there, after all. As for the rest of it, you are right, as a sailor he was in theory only subject to the orders of the Marquis des Gouttes, our squadron commander. However, unfortunately for the Navy, the King had given overall command to the Governor of Louisbourg, the Chevalier de Drucourt. I myself often witnessed the lack of agreement between the Marquis des Goùttes and the Governor, but the Marquis was too honourable a man to disobey.'

I cannot help thinking that it is a familiar tune. I remember my grandfather's comments in this regard: 'Argument! It is the great French disease!'

'As for your father, I saw him with my own eyes on the morning of his last expedition. He was coming in, at dawn, through the postern between the King's Bastion and the Queen's Bastion. He was dressed like a trapper amongst his Indians, with his black hair falling over his shoulders. On my word of honour, you could have sworn he was one of them!'

I admire my commander and I have appreciated his rectitude, but I still cannot swallow what he is telling me. After all, this bears no relationship to what I was told by old Le Touze, at Le Croisic!

'You talk about this Marquis des Gouttes, Sir, but I have been told that at the time my father was an officer aboard *le Zéphyre,* commanded by the Chevalier de Ternay, in the Comte du Chaffault's squadron. If that is true, how could he have found himself under the orders of another squadron commander?'

'What you say is quite right. But your father had been ordered to take a letter from the Comte du Chaffault to the Governor. At the same time he was to act as a guide, through the woods, for the Second Battalion of the Cambis regiment, that the Comte had disembarked at the end of May to reinforce our garrison. Your father arrived on foot at Louisbourg on the morning of 1st June. I was there. He was with Captain de Guéron of the Second Battalion. They had walked day and night.'

'They had come on foot through the forest? I thought Louisbourg was a port.'

'The Comte had not wanted to disembark at Louisbourg itself, as the English had already arrived downwind of the town, with the intention of attacking us. From the Princess Bastion, to the south of the ramparts, we could see their ships tacking to try to weather Cape Black, to the south-east of the town. They had come from Halifax. Luckily for the Comte, the wind was north-north-east. We counted seventy sails at first, then more than a hundred. Amongst them were at least twenty-two ships of the line. The Comte's squadron had just four or five, no more, plus a few frigates, for escorting transport ships and merchantmen up to Quebec. That's why, rather than stay locked up in the Louisbourg trap, the Comte du Chaffault preferred to anchor out of reach of the English, further north. He went to the other side of the Île Royale[52], to Port Dauphin in Sainte-Anne's Bay, two days' march from the fort. He got together all of the squadron's sloops, for landing the troops of the Cambis infantry. As there was not enough depth for the ships of the line at the end of the bay, the Comte had designated the frigate *le Zéphyre,* under the command of the Chevalier de Ternay, as you rightly said, to escort the sloops and cover them while the troops were landed.

52 Translator's note: *Île Royale* – what is now Cape Breton Island

The squadron sailed off immediately. The Chevalier was to re-join it as soon as he had completed his mission, bringing the empty sloops in tow, if he had time, before the arrival of the English forces. If this wasn't the case, or if the winds went to the west or south-west, he was authorised to abandon them. This meant that the disembarked troops were left to their own devices in a country they did not know. When a Naval officer had to be chosen to land with the battalion, guide it to Louisbourg across the interior of the Île Royale, and carry a message from the Comte du Chaffault, the choice naturally fell on your father. He knew the area very well and was already aboard *le Zéphyre.* That's how he found himself under the orders of the Marquis des Gouttes...'

And he spoke the savages' language! I am saddened and feel like crying. The Captain sees this and for a second places his hands on mine.

'I can see that my story about the scalping has upset you. No need to be! Imagine how combat is in the woods, at night, blind, with the knife and tomahawk. One can well imagine that under these conditions an officer cannot control everything going on around him. Particularly if he has to direct an Indian war party. I am not in any way questioning you father's honour. On the contrary! In this affair, I think he simply carried out his orders, as every officer should, and reluctantly too, for I've heard he warned the Governor about the Indians' way of fighting.'

'You can tell me the truth, Sir. I'm no longer a child.'

'But that is the truth! Besides, I myself saw Monsieur Laforest-Dombourg, your grandfather, vigorously upbraid the Governor, the Chevalier de Drucourt, at a full council meeting, asking him not to use his son or our Indian allies in this way. He said that it risked setting off a chain of useless violence that would inevitably lead to reprisals. In his view, the game was not worth the candle, as it would not even delay the fall of Louisbourg, which was inevitable as we were outnumbered ten to one and the town was too poorly fortified for us to hold out for long.'

I no longer feel upset with the Captain. Twenty years after the events he is telling me about, I can see that it is still painful for him.

'Did you meet my grandparents then?'

'Only your grandfather. He was a leading light in Louisbourg. He was a Captain in the militia, too, and in this capacity took part in the war councils at the garrison headquarters. I saw him several times, when the Marquis des Gouttes took me to these meetings.'

'If you please, Sir,' I ask him, 'this is the first time that anyone has ever really talked to me about my grandfather Laforest-Dombourg. What was he like?'

'He was on the big side, with very blue eyes…still well-built for his age, for I think at that time he was nearing sixty. In any case, his hair was white.'

'My grandfather had blue eyes?' I was surprised. I had imagined them dark brown, like my father's and mine.

'He came from the old Acadie[53], where his family had lived for more than a century. He had come to the settle on Île Royale before the birth of your father, and distinguished himself in the previous war, the War of the Austrian Succession, which the English and the Indians in Canada called 'King George's War'. He had a fine reputation in Louisbourg and was the leading shipowner in the town. He had fast fishing schooners that in peacetime went as far as the Antilles and even La Rochelle, to sell their cod. I found him very active and decisive when I saw him for the first time. He had been through some great misfortunes, but never talked about them. He was very patriotic, like most colonists in New France.'

'Yes, I knew my uncles were captured by the English.'

'At the start of the war, in fact, his two youngest sons were taken by the English, with one of his schooners, on the Grand Banks. He never found out what became of them.'

'Somebody at Le Croisic told me that it was thought they died in captivity.'

'That's quite likely, and that's why, I think, your father decided to enter the service of the King. He had a deep-sea merchant Captain's certificate, and the ship he was commanding had called in to La Rochelle when he left to become an auxiliary officer in the Navy. Later he became a Frigate's Lieutenant. But, as you may know, your grandfather Laforest-Dombourg suffered an even worse misfortune, in 1757.'

'Worse than the loss of two of his sons?'

'As bad at least, as he lost in one stroke his wife, your grandmother, and his young daughter, your aunt. Both caught a putrid fever while at the Royal Hospital, nursing the sick of the Comte du Bois de la Motte's squadron. The only family Monsieur Laforest-Dombourg had left was

53 Translator's note: *Acadie*: the French name for what is now Nova Scotia.

your father, his eldest son…whom the Chevalier de Drucourt wanted to send on the most dangerous of missions. As you no doubt know, your grandfather was killed not long afterwards, in his own house, during a bombardment of the town, once the English had managed to get close enough to reach the centre with their mortars.'

'Can you tell me anything else about my grandmother?'

'No. But I remember well how sad Monsieur Laforest-Dombourg was.'

Captain Le Meur has told me everything he knows about my grandparents. Nonetheless, I don't want the conversation to end. The Captain has opened up such a new landscape that I want him to carry on telling me about Canada, this distant country where my roots are to be found.

'And you yourself, Sir, what was your rank at Louisbourg?'

'At the start of 1758 I was still a young second pilot. I had served in Canada since joining the Navy, and despite my age I had a lot of experience of the Saint Lawrence River up to Quebec and even as far as Montreal. I had returned to France with a convoy and was waiting at Rochefort for a ship when the Marquis des Gouttes was ordered to Louisbourg. I had never been to the Île Royale before, but I knew the approaches to the Gulf of Saint Lawrence well. The Marquis asked me to go with him as master pilot on *le Prudent*, seventy-four guns, that he was in command of then. For me it was an unexpected promotion.'

I listen to the Captain saying these words so loaded with history: Louisbourg, the Saint Lawrence, Quebec, Acadia; a world lost to France and of which I know nothing except that it is very far away, over the sea. Up until now, in my mind, the Seven Years' War had mainly been associated with my uncle's army campaigns in the Lower Rhine. Now, however, I realise that, from Pondicherry to Louisbourg, this disastrous conflict had a much wider theatre than Europe alone.

'…we left Rochefort in early March bound for the Île Royale, accompanying a convoy of the King's supply ships and merchantmen with cargo for Louisbourg,' the Captain continued. 'Soon after we arrived we were joined, at the end of May, by Monsieur Beaussier de L'Isle, who had also escorted a convoy with his four ships-of-the-line and an armed frigate. Even then, we could see ten or twelve enemy sails every day cruising off the Île Royale. In all, in Louisbourg, we had just five ships of the line and a frigate, plus one armed supply ship.

The commander of this modest squadron was the Marquis des Gouttes. Our original mission had been to escort reinforcements for the town. But, instead of letting us leave, the Governor ordered us to stop enemy ships entering the port. The Louisbourg anchorage is almost completely enclosed except for an entrance passage scarcely six hundred yards wide. It was therefore quite possible to anchor our ships in the bay in a line broadside on, within cannon range of the entrance, and supported by our batteries placed on land on each side, one on the mainland, the other on a small island. To do this, the garrison had of course to keep hold of both shores of the entrance.'

'And this wasn't the case?' I ask.

'Alas, no! Unfortunately it wasn't, at least as far as the north shore was concerned.'

The Captain falls quiet, long enough to sigh, then takes up the story again.

'This was twenty years ago! It all seems so far away now. Despite our preparations, the English managed to disembark their troops in a creek three miles to west of the fortress, overrunning our defences. They were able to occupy the north of the entrance passage, where there was a hill called the Crête de la Lanterne, as a lighthouse had been built there. The Governor had not considered defending this crucial spot, which he should have held at any price. As soon as the enemy artillery had set up on this emplacement, the position of our ships quickly became untenable.'

'You told me last summer that you had spent a day under the command of my father.'

'Yes...it was just after the English soldiers had taken control of the Lanterne ridge. Several of their ships were then able to come in close to the shore to the north of the entrance passage, outside the anchorage. This put them within reach of a handy beach for disembarking their men. Their intention was to land their heavy artillery, notably mortars, to reinforce their position on the Lanterne. If our ships had tried to leave the anchorage, they would not have been able to get back in and would certainly have been either destroyed or captured. Unless, of course, they had immediately sailed out to sea. But the Governor had formally forbidden this. Your father had therefore proposed, for want of anything better, that he go and disrupt the enemy disembarkation with a bomb vessel.'

'A bomb vessel?'

'Yes, it's a barge which has been reinforced and fitted out to carry a small calibre cannon that fires incendiary devices. It's a kind of floating mortar, if you like. Your father said that he knew the reefs and currents well enough to get to a firing position that the enemy frigates and corvettes would be unable to approach. The rest of us had been ordered to abandon our ships to fight on the ramparts alongside the soldiers. As I wasn't too happy about that, I volunteered to go with your father. He got our barge anchored inside a scattering of reefs that gave us some protection and we began to fire our mortar shells at the inlet where the English were landing. That really messed them up, you can be sure! One of their frigates came close to the line of rocks and gave us a complete broadside, but she was far too far away, and her cannon balls simply whipped up the sea well away from us, without causing the least alarm. They then sent in two small cutters. These were able to anchor close to the breakers but their little cannon balls bounced off the rocks surrounding us. Finally they used grapeshot. Luckily it was getting dark and they couldn't see too well. We were almost out of range too, but they did manage to hit us from time to time. We had several wounded and one killed before nightfall. Your father didn't seem in the least affected by this. He told us to look after the wounded and calmly carried on firing. I didn't know him. I had only seen him from a distance on the morning he returned with his band of savages, as I told you. That day, on the bomb vessel, I was impressed by his calmness. After that, I never saw Lieutenant Laforest-Dombourg again. His sally with the bomb vessel gave some ideas to the commander of a little ship from Le Havre. He was called Vauquelin, and like your father he was a Frigate's Lieutenant in the King's Navy. His frigate was called *l'Aréthuse.* She was fast, but above all she had a shallow draft and tacked really well in light airs. Lieutenant Vauquelin proposed that your father join forces with him with his boat to create a sort of floating mobile artillery, to bombard the approach works of the English infantry. Lieutenant Laforest-Dombourg knew the depths and contours inside the harbour perfectly. Thanks to that, the two of them, with *l'Aréthuse,* were able to get close to the shore at night or in fog. They directed their fire towards the English positions, then moved immediately, so that the enemy return fire could not reach them. The two of them did a good job, but it wasn't enough. Towards mid-July, when it was clear that the end was near, Lieutenant Vauquelin asked the Governor to authorise him to leave. Your grandfather had just been killed and your father also asked if he could leave on *l'Aréthuse.* The English were already asking for him, following the scalping business I told you about. If he had been handed over, he could well have been tried and hung. That's the only reason why the Governor agreed. Vauquelin decided to leave one Saturday evening. Just before nightfall, I saw Vauquelin's frigate weigh anchor and un-brail all her canvas simultaneously, bracing everything to starboard. She shot out right under the nose of the English on the Lanterne, who fired everything they had in her wake. Seeing *l'Aréthuse* disappear seawards, I had a heavy heart, believe me. I would have given anything to have been with them. After they had gone, we held out for another eleven days. Then we surrendered. I was a prisoner for the rest of the war. I was just twenty! I never saw your father again.'

'And this Lieutenant Vauquelin? Do you know what became of him?'

'*L'Aréthuse* made a quick crossing. I know that Vauquelin came back to Canada to help in the defence of Quebec. He finished the war as a Ship's Lieutenant, like your father. He died of an illness six years ago, at Rochefort. Admiral Boscawen, too, is dead. He died in 1761, at home in England.'

I understand now why my father had been so quiet when his exchange had been refused, just a year after the dramatic events of the siege of Louisbourg. Even in France nobody would have understood his position and would no doubt have seen him as being in the wrong. What I have just heard corroborates, in part, what I have already been told by Old Touze and Captain Muterse. Except, of course, this unexpected story about the Indians and the scalping. It is the first time I have heard about the Canadian Indians and their 'savage customs'. And I have learned at the same time that my father was quite familiar with their language! I did not know either that my grandparents were born in Acadia and that this had been the family's home for more than a century. I don't even know where Louisbourg and Acadia are.

The Captain's sad demeanour has vanished. His eyes are shining again.

'But, for the rest of it, what a country! My greatest regret is only having been able to look at it from the deck of my ships. But I have been as far as Lake Ontario in a ship's boat: huge prairies, hills and mountains covered with forest as far as the eye can see. There you can find caribou, moose, lynx, bears and wolves, lots of them. The lakes and rivers are teeming with salmon, perch and sturgeon. And, of course, beavers and otters whose furs are sold here. Our lakes and rivers are tiny compared to those of Canada. The waterfalls there are huge. And then…there are the Indians.'

'Apart from those who were with my father, have you seen many up close?'

'Very few, in all honesty. I have always been a sailor, while the Indians are trappers. They watched us from the banks when we went up the river but normally we didn't see them. I really didn't have the chance to get up close to them, except on one occasion. It was summertime, and they had tied up beside our sloop, at Montreal. They got around in narrow boats about twenty to thirty feet long. These boats are made with a skin of birch bark stretched over a light frame of cedar.'

'Were they Hurons?'

The Captain smiles, wrinkling his eyes for the first time since the start of our conversation.

'For the French, Canada is inhabited by Hurons. It is true that they have been faithful friends of France for more than a century; but there is only a handful of them compared to the great Iroquois nation. These I was telling you about were Iroquois. There were about forty of them, all warriors. They were annoyed with their English allies and had come to propose an alliance to the Governor-General. They were almost naked apart from a sort of loincloth in cloth or leather passed through a belt and whose ends hung down in front and behind. Their heads were completely shaved with just a tuft of hair decorated with feathers and deer hairs. They were lithe, with magnificent slender limbs. At the time I was strongly impressed by how healthy they looked. Then I saw that they were all carrying bundles of scalps in their belts. They kept the hair of their victims, still with its original skin, this horror serving as an ornament to show off. They had bows and arrows, daggers, big clubs and tomahawks. Apart from that, I can't tell you anything.'

Captain Le Meur stops talking. He looks at the little room around him, as if he had just come back to it. He had gone away in fact…a long way.

'To find out more you'd have to ask the officers who served in the

Army there during the last war. Did you ever come across Monsieur de Bougainville in Brest?'

'I have read his 'Voyage Around the World',' I reply. 'But isn't he in the Navy?'

'A very educational read! Yes, he is in the Navy now, but before, during the last war, he was in the Army. If you ever get the chance, ask him about the Indians. You'll see that he knows a lot about them.'

8

Our mission on the Devon coast continued, with about three or four round trips each month. In good conditions it took little more than twenty hours to make the crossing. The ideal situation was to arrive off the coast at dusk, which allowed us to move in discreetly and lift our private mail at about midnight. We then sailed straight for Saint-Malo, arriving in the morning the day after. That gave a cycle of two or three days. Captain Le Meur organised the use of his time according to the tides. For a destination like Start Point it was rare to have an unfavourable wind. But in winter, storms are frequent and we were constantly having to confront them. Even if familiarity with the Channel allowed Lieutenant Chollet to recognise the advance signs of a change in the weather, it was nonetheless very difficult for him to predict its strength. On a small vessel like *le Moucheron* conditions were often rough at this time of year, and our cockleshell danced around on waves which would scarcely have had any effect on a ship-of-the-line. On each return to Saint-Malo we had to inspect the cutter, check her rig, change any damaged spars. The men too paid their dues, with boils, dislocations, bruises of all sorts. However, these things were of little consequence as we always came back to shore between two short cruises. Above all, our sailors were not subject to the much more serious illnesses usual on long voyages, especially scurvy and fevers. Nevertheless, Captain Le Meur had decided to suspend our reconnaissance of Spithead, as it needed one or two extra days. He preferred to use the time for the maintenance of the cutter and the health of the crew. These were indispensable, he said, if we were to keep on with the regular weekly collection of our intelligence, against wind and tide, in all weathers. We knew that the information provided by our Cornish agents was well appreciated at Versailles. This was confirmed once again in a letter to me from the Chevalier de Kermean that I received at the end of January 1778.

Sailors know that routine does not exist where the sea is concerned, but Colonel Dumouriez was an infantryman through and through. Having seen *le Moucheron* going back and forth across the Channel without any problems, he concluded that our existence was a little too regular. Like a good soldier, he decided one day to put an end to it. He wasn't quite so abrupt about it. He talked to us about Patriotism and a sense of Duty.

This took us by surprise during one of our meetings in the rue des Juifs house. He organised them for the end of the week, after the intelligence we had brought back from Devon, essentially lists of ships and their movements, had already been studied and coded by Monsieur de La Rozière's secretaries and send to Versailles via a relay of horsemen. We sat ourselves around the big table and the Colonel settled in opposite us to debrief us. We could well have done without these meetings, but the Colonel liked to hear the verbal reports of the Captain and his officers, as this allowed him to write additional memoranda to which he could add his personal touch. Since his stay in the Bastille, Colonel Dumouriez loved to write memoranda[54].

'Gentlemen,' began the Colonel. 'Having heard the detailed account of your last crossing, I must say that *le Moucheron* is a remarkable ship. She has the best equipment to be found in the Saint-Malo shipyards, her crew is hand-picked and well paid…'

Colonel Dumouriez scowled as he said that last word – *paid.* We knew he was alluding to the bonus squeezed out of him by Captain Le

54 Translator's note: *Colonel Dumouriez loved to write memoranda:* After a long and chequered career, in which he rose to the rank of General, Dumouriez ended his days in England, advising the War Office in its war against Napoleon. He died near Henley-on-Thames in 1823.

Meur, and which he still had trouble accepting. We were all wondering where this was heading.

'All of this, Sirs, thanks to the kindness of the King. And what are we doing to merit it? We play postman across the Channel! And that's not all! This mission keeps us busy for three days, while, if I am not mistaken, a week is made up of seven! Is this a good use of the resources entrusted to us by the King? Certainly, there is no question of stopping the collection of the documents sold to us by Régnier's Cornishmen, but this is not enough! From here on, you will not make do with simply collecting your letters and heading straight back to the stable. You will spend an extra day reconnoitring the Isle of Wight area, before the imminent war makes it impossible. It is of the highest importance!'

The Colonel stood up and began to pace up and down the room, obliging us to twist our necks to keep looking at him. It was always like that once he got talking; he could not stay in his seat.

'There are three harbours on this island: Yarmouth, Newport and St Helens. The last two are difficult to get close to, being, so to speak, in the antechamber to Portsmouth, where the English naval forces are concentrated. But this does not seem to be the case with Yarmouth. I therefore want a precise report on the approaches and defences of this port. You will use this occasion to take full advantage of the drawing talents of Monsieur Dombourg. Moreover, I would also like a description, as precise of possible, of the whole south coast of the island, from the Needles rocks to Whitecliff Bay, to the south of St Helens. Nobody has ever envisaged a landing on this part of the Isle of Wight, as it is thought by us to be fringed with inaccessible cliffs. And it is accordingly less well defended. If there is even one little creek suitable for a surprise landing, I want a map of it. I would also like you to take a very close look at Compton Bay and Brixton Bay. Your report must include drawings made by Monsieur Dombourg.'

'Are you aware, Sir,' replied Captain Le Meur, 'that the King's geographers already have excellent maps of the Isle of Wight, notably those of the Chevalier de Beaurain, as well as those of Monsieur Bellin?'

'Of course, but the best of them are twenty years old, and lots of things will have changed since then. In any case, our Naval officers really don't know the Channel, which is to be regretted.'

It was not the first time he had said this to us, each time getting a strong reaction from our two lieutenants. At first, our commander had strongly protested against this allegation. Over time, we realised that the Colonel was simply repeating the fine words quoted freely in the salons of Versailles and Paris.

'At least the soundings will still be correct,' offered Captain Le Meur.

'Well, I'm not asking you to check them all, only those at the places I have indicated, along with everything else you can find out by means of a careful examination of the coast. I have trust in your experience as a sailor. Finally, I'd like drawings of the coastal defences. These must have changed at least.'

'The job you are asking us to do cannot be done in one go, Sir. To do it properly we will have to make a number of visits. To check soundings we will have to launch a ship's boat, which we can only do at night so as not to attract attention. That is tricky work, especially at this time of year.'

Colonel Dumouriez adopted his angry bulldog look.

'I well understand that it is not easy. Why do you think you have been given the job?'

'Have you at least talked to Monsieur de La Rozière about it?'

'Monsieur de La Rozière has plenty of other things to do besides worrying about your mission. Leave him in peace. His job is already complicated enough. Get on with your own work!'

'Very well,' said Captain Le Meur. 'I had already decided to leave next Monday, in the middle of the afternoon. Tuesday evening we will be at our usual rendezvous. The next day, Wednesday, towards midday, I can be off the south of the Isle of Wight. If the weather allows and we are not chased by the English coastguard, I can cruise until nightfall within view of the coast. If all goes well we will be back in Saint-Malo on Friday night, but at the moment the wind is in the west and I'm afraid we may have to wait until Saturday morning.'

'Wait until Saturday. Out of the question!'

'Listen, Sir. If you really want me to make a detailed reconnaissance of the south coast of the Isle of Wight, I cannot do it faster than that. But seeing as you are so keen on the Isle of Wight, I could head back to Cherbourg, which is half the distance and far better placed for the Isle of Wight. If you could send a despatch rider there I could give him our packages. Of course, we would then have to come back here, since for the coast of Devon and Cornwall it is better to leave from Saint-Malo.

Maybe the Isle of Wight is more important than what we are doing now but, whatever the case, it is a new and different mission. Of course, I expect you intend to give us written orders.'

Dumouriez looked more than ever ready to bite.

'Captain Le Meur! Previously, you were perfectly well able to make the round trip with a detour to Spithead. And that did not seem to create any problems for you. It was even you who proposed it at our first meeting, I well remember. Why this change of heart?'

'It is because, Sir,' replied Captain Le Meur, 'we were then in midsummer. It was only a matter of passing quickly well offshore of the bay, just once from time to time, when the visibility was adequate. We were just taking a quick look to make sure that our Cornish agents were not pulling the wool over our eyes. While now, you are asking us pretty much to make a map of their coastal defences, which is not the same thing at all. It will take much more time and will necessarily be much less discreet. It could even compromise our mission on the Devon coast.'

Colonel Dumouriez thought for a moment.

'Very well, here's what we will do. You leave on Monday and come straight back to give me the Cornishmen's despatches. Then, instead of spending several days in port, as you have done previously, you will leave straight away for the Isle of Wight. In future, if it takes too much time, we will alternate the missions, one to Devon, one to the Isle of Wight.'

Before returning on board the cutter, Captain Le Meur got together the three of us, his two lieutenants and myself, at Aunt Chollet's house.

'Gentlemen, God knows I am not a man to refuse to do my duty, whatever its price may be. But what Colonel Dumouriez is asking of us is in my opinion impossible to do without seriously compromising the mission for which *le Moucheron* was originally designated. If the focus is now to be on the Isle of Wight, we should be based in Cherbourg. But we can't at the same time make regular crossings to Start Point and to the Portsmouth approaches. Moreover, what we are being asked to do seems of little use, given that it has already been done since the end of the last war. I know that the Comte de Broglie sent several officers on a secret mission to make a survey of the south coast of England and its coastal defences. One of them, and by no means the least, was Monsieur de La Rozière. You heard what Colonel Dumouriez said when I asked him about Monsieur de La Rozière?'

'But what's his aim in all of this?' asked Lieutenant Kerlaziou.

'I think I can guess. But that's not the point. If I refuse to obey, we will all be in trouble. Even if he doesn't want to give us written orders.'

'What can we do, then?' asked Lieutenant Chollet.

'Above all, we have to be sure that the mission given to us today by Colonel Dumouriez is in line with new orders from Versailles.'

'But how can we find that out?' asked Lieutenant Kerlaziou.

'By contacting the person there who looks after the file on our mission and who writes the orders for Colonel Dumouriez.'

'You want to go over the head of Colonel Dumouriez? Isn't that risky?'

'We might have a way of getting around him without him knowing.'

The Captain turned to me.

'Monsieur Dombourg, the person I am talking about is your uncle, the Chevalier de Kermean. It's he who has directed our operation from the beginning. I think it would be a good idea if he were to come here personally to check on what is going on. Could you suggest that to him discreetly? How do you usually correspond with him?'

'Well,' I replied, 'I send my letters with the mail carrying coded letters from the port Commander.'

'So they will pass through Colonel Dumouriez' hands! In that case you had better write via the normal post. But you must not be too precise, otherwise you might be accused of negligence or treason if the secret service were to open your letter before it reaches your uncle.'

It was not easy to warn somebody without being able to use words freely. Having thought about it, I finally had an idea that Captain Le Meur approved of. I wrote two letters that I sent at the same time, one via the King's private mail, the other via the normal post.

In the first letter, which would be seen by Colonel Dumouriez, I reminded my uncle that my mission with Duval had finished, and asked him to come to see me in Saint-Malo, *as soon as possible,* so that I could give him my safe-conduct, the King's money which I had not spent, and the vouchers for my expenditure. I hoped that my scrupulousness would puzzle my uncle without raising any suspicions on the part of Colonel Dumouriez. The Chevalier de Kermean had always said that there was no hurry in returning the money and the documents. I added that at the same time I was sending him a letter by normal post containing a poem that I had copied just for him. With a bit of luck, that would encourage him to go and collect his post at Versailles without too much delay.

It was trickier to write the letter travelling via the post horses, as I had to avoid any reference or indiscretion that might alert a reader other than the intended recipient. I took particular care since, as far as I knew, those most likely to intercept any mail from Saint-Malo to Versailles probably worked in shady offices close to the Chevalier de Kermean's place of work. It would have been annoying for him, as well as me, if my little ruse were discovered by a colleague who was badly disposed towards him, as sometimes happens in Ministerial offices.

The 'poetry' that I had chosen to copy for him was a fable from La Fontaine: *The Coach and the Fly. Think about the last word of the title,* I wrote. I hoped my uncle would see the allusion to *le Moucheron*[55].

Upon a sandy, uphill road
Which naked in the sunshine glowed
Six lusty horses drew a coach…

In fact, I only copied these initial lines and jumped straight to the end of the fable, taking a few liberties with the original text of Monsieur de La Fontaine…

Thus certain soldiers[56]*, bustling noddies,*
Jump into every great affair,
And, being fools and busy-bodies,
Really should be chased from there.

I added a post-script in the form of a puzzle, inspired by the last letter of my father.

Post-script: Don't Underestimate Man Or Urge Reason In Endless Zealotry

55 Translator's note: *Allusion to Le Moucheron*: the last word of the title, Fly, is *Mouche* in French.

56 Translator's note: *Certain soldiers*. The original says 'certain people' (*certains gens*).

It was not very subtle, I admit, but it had the advantage of being at first sight very opaque for anybody except my uncle and myself.

We left for our 'postman's' crossing the following Monday, as Colonel Dumouriez had ordered. Lieutenant Chollet pointed out to us that the weather was uncertain and that the Colonel's brilliant plans risked getting a good ducking, for this week anyway. The wind had already begun to strengthen considerably from the south-west as the Devon coast came into view. However, we managed to fish out our sunken packet without much difficulty.

At midnight, when I took my watch with Lieutenant Chollet, the wind had risen even more, passing from half a gale to a full gale and raising a big sea against the opposing current. The Captain had put us hard to windward, straight for Saint-Malo, as far as this was possible given the wind and sea. The cutter worked her way laboriously along, under deep-reefed spanker and staysail, heading south by south-east in total darkness. From time to time the white flash of a breaking wave, closer than the others, surged out of the gloom, allowing me to gauge the unusual height of the waves that we were climbing relentlessly, one after the other. When we reached a crest the gusts snapped our tiny staysail, although it was sheeted in hard, with such force that each time I thought I was hearing a salvo of rifle fire. Then, having dived into the deep trough which followed, the bow took one or two head butts that resounded through the rig.

We had two teams permanently working the two ship's pumps. The men were relieved every hour, four replacing four. They had to be tied on so as not to fall down the sloping deck swept continually by big seas. As for me, I was huddled in a corner aft under my soaked cape, teeth chattering, chilled to the bone, eyes full of salt spray, deafened by the wind. I was hanging on to the nearest lifeline, muscles permanently tensed to cushion *le Moucheron's* pitching.

The helmsman had rigged the tiller's blocks and tackles. Lieutenant Chollet helped him from time to time, to stop the cutter coming up into the wind when the pressure on the rudder was too strong. He shouted to me to go and get a man from the orlop to help them. I hauled my way carefully along to the hatch to the crew's quarters, just forward of the mast. I waited until the cutter had passed over a crest and opened the scuttle to slide down as quickly as possible, letting the hatch fall back down above my head before the next wave. The lower deck was weakly lit by a little lantern. As a precaution, most of the crew had been sent down here. There wasn't space to hang hammocks for those on watch. The sailors were sitting on the sloping cabin sole, legs bent to their chests, chins buried in their knees, braced against each other as well as they could be with nothing to hold on to, trying to follow the violent motion of the ship. Behind their shoulders, the compact mass of the hammocks of their resting comrades was so tightly packed that it swung in one movement to the brutal pitching. The topman nearest to me got up to go out on deck, having heard my shout. After the tumult and cold outside, I at first appreciated the apparent warmth and calm of this refuge, despite its oppressive atmosphere. But that did not last long. There was a lack of air in this confined and juddering space where the men had been piled up, waiting for hours with nothing they could do about it. I admired their patience and calmness. As for me, I was still not fully hardened to the sea. After a few minutes my throat tightened, painfully, from the anxiety of hearing the infernal rushing of the water along the planking and the dull and regular blows of invisible waves hitting the hull. It was almost a relief to have to go up on deck again.

The next morning the sea was streaked with white under a low, black sky. The waves were less high than at midnight, as the current was now with the wind, but it was blowing just as hard, and as a result, our leeway was now greater. In the pale light of day the officer of the watch could see that several tears had appeared near the tack of the spanker, just above the upper reef points, despite the sail being cut from number one canvas. The Captain, alerted to this, called the master sailmaker Deyo, who said that the sail could hold, or it could blow out in one go, but it was impossible to say when.

'Once we're back in port,' said the master sailmaker, to finish, 'if they give us what we need, we should try and make new sails out of cotton. It's only used for little boats as it's expensive, but it don't rot like ordinary sailcloth.'

Captain Le Meur was worried. Our packages were awaited at Saint-Malo, but the wind and sea didn't look like abating. In this bad weather, close-hauled, it was difficult to be sure of our course sailed. The cutter was being set strongly to port, as the Pilot had foreseen, but it was impossible to be sure to what extent. The Captain was split between his wish to fulfil his mission, at all costs and on time, and the risk of having his spanker blow out within an hour or two, thereby finding himself unable to manoeuvre, with the Channel Islands under his lee and the breakers of the Minquiers Islands dead ahead. He did not hesitate for long. The bosun called for extra hands and the cutter came up into the wind to allow our topmen to furl the spanker. We then bore off, rigging the little heavy weather square sail. *Le Moucheron* ran before the storm, now in clear water, well to the north of the Channel Islands and the Raz Blanchard[57].

Things improved immediately. We were still buffeted, but it was quite comfortable compared to the blows we had suffered for the whole night. We no longer had to put up with the dread of masses of green water hitting us up for'ard and the showers of freezing spray that ensued. With the weather now coming from astern, the waves were catching us up and pushing us from behind, their crests curling and breaking around us. The spanker was unbent and rolled up so as to pass it down the scuttle into the petty officers' quarters, where the sailmaker and his assistant repaired it, sheltered in the dry. Our point of sail was much more comfortable, but we were hurtling along. So much so that by the time the spanker was repaired we were miles from anywhere in the middle of the Channel, somewhere north of Dieppe and off Beachy Head, whose chalky cliffs Lieutenant Chollet had identified with his telescope. The wind veered to the north-west.

By midday Friday we were back in the Main Gate entrance channel, at the start of the ebb and with just a light breeze from the west to push us. Luckily it was still slack water. Colonel Dumouriez was champing at the bit for his documents. However, he didn't send us off immediately to survey the south coast of the Isle of Wight, as he had promised. He was not as cruel as we had been given to believe. He was happy to call us to a meeting the following Monday, to make our report, leaving us the whole of Sunday to put the cutter back in order and to lick our wounds.

On Monday I followed Captain Le Meur and his lieutenants to the house in the rue des Juifs, where we were to have our meeting at nine in the morning. Arriving in the room where our meetings were usually held, I was pleasantly surprised to find the Chevalier de Kermean there. I would have shown my joy without any restraint had not my uncle,

57 Translator's note: *Raz Blanchard:* the Alderney Race.

looking at me in a particular way, given me to understand that I must keep silent.

Colonel Dumouriez made the presentations, since the Chevalier did not know the officers of *le Moucheron.* My uncle said that he was enchanted to meet his nephew's commander and expressed a desire to visit the cutter.

'In all the time since Monsieur Laforest-Dombourg and the Chevalier de Fleurieu have talked to me about the Navy,' he said, 'I have never been aboard a ship of the King!'

When it was my turn to be presented, last, by virtue of hierarchy, Colonel Dumouriez did it very carefully. He knew my links with the Chevalier, and had probably seen my letter to him. My request was, of itself, a good pretext, but it could certainly not explain the promptness with which my uncle had raced to Saint-Malo. Colonel Dumouriez was too intelligent and too subtle not to sense this. The Chevalier had also announced, tapping a file that he was holding under his arm, that he had come to read us a message from the Chevalier de Fleurieu, giving us '*good news that concerned us all.*' I did not think that the Colonel looked at all at ease as he invited us to sit down 'to listen what the Chevalier de Kermean has to say to us'.

The Chevalier unfolded a headed letter and, having repeated that the letter had been written and signed by the Chevalier de Fleurieu, he began to read:

> *His Majesty has tasked me to tell you how satisfied he is with the speed and zeal with which Colonel Charles-François Dumouriez has completed the most delicate mission which was entrusted to him at Saint-Malo. This has encouraged His Majesty to expect further demonstrations of his zeal and therefore His Majesty has the firm intention of very soon giving him a commission as Commander of the Port of Cherbourg, with the rank of Field-Marshall. In order to allow him to prepare himself fully for this new task, His Majesty, with effect from this moment, releases Colonel Charles-François Dumouriez from his obligations at Saint-Malo and authorises him to leave this place as he sees fit.*

Learning of the King's satisfaction, which he clearly did not expect, the subject of the letter tried to remain impassive, but his eyes were shining, even more so once the Chevalier de Kermean had told him that his promotion to Cherbourg was likely to bring with it a salary of six thousand pounds. But the happiest of all with this news was very careful not to show it. I speak, of course, of the Fireship Captain Le Meur.

Colonel Dumouriez wanted to go to the Chateau immediately to tell Monsieur de La Rozière of his change of situation. He asked Captain Le Meur to come with him, as henceforth the latter would be taking his orders directly from Monsieur de la Rozière. Before leaving, the Captain of *le Moucheron* invited my uncle to come aboard the cutter towards midday, along with Colonel Dumouriez, to lunch with us.

'That would be perfect,' said the Chevalier. 'We will be alone, away from indiscreet ears, and I can use the time to bring you up to date with my office's political and tactical plans.'

'Do my sailors need to be told?' asked the Captain.

'It is not strictly necessary,' replied my uncle, a little surprised by the question.

'Then in that case, Sir, I can start by showing you *le Moucheron,* but afterwards we can go and eat somewhere more discreet. Since, you see, in the Navy it is often said, with good reason, that two people cannot talk together aboard a ship without the whole crew knowing what was said within minutes, irrespective of any precautions taken. That is even more true for our ship, it being so small.'

Dumouriez gave a start.

'What? You said nothing about that the first time we met aboard your ship, last July!'

Captain Le Meur's eyes creased up to his ears and he laughed silently.

'If you remember, Sir, I asked you whether what you were going to say to us concerned nothing but our mission, and you confirmed that was the case. It was not without benefit for my sailors to know the truth about the particular dangers of the undertaking. From then on they knew perfectly well what they were getting into, more so than if we had told them ourselves.'

Colonel Dumouriez took this in good part. In any event, the news of his promotion had put him in an excellent mood. He excused himself, saying he was unable to eat with us, and even offered to arrange a carriage.

The meeting between Colonel Dumouriez, Captain Le Meur and

the Port Commander was likely to take some time, and I wanted to talk to my uncle alone. It being low tide, it was possible to walk to Saint-Servan. I invited the Chevalier to walk with me and suggested to Colonel Dumouriez that the carriage be kept for Captain Le Meur. As for the two lieutenants, they had already gone off, intent on their business, having received orders from their commander.

*

Saint-Malo, Monday 23rd February 1778, ten o'clock in the morning.

The north-westerly breeze is very cold. I decide not to go round the top of the ramparts and instead take my uncle through the town. We cross the entrance passage to the port on foot, following the stone path and the culvert as far as the Nose. The Chevalier is amazed at the wide expanse of the port uncovered at low water, with the merchant frigates canted over on the shore to our left and the sea lapping gently on the sand to our right.

'I understood immediately from your letter that you had problems with Colonel Dumouriez. But what's it about, exactly?'

I tell him what Colonel Dumouriez had proposed regarding the Isle of Wight. I explain that Captain Le Meur was quite alarmed by it.

'He asked me to alert you discreetly. I had the idea of sending you the two letters, seemingly harmless, in the hope of getting your attention.'

'The Isle of Wight! Well! I should have thought of that. Of course you did the right thing, you and your commander.'

He tells me that he had received my letter sent via the King's mail on 17th February, and had found my other letter at the normal Post only three days later, the Friday. He admits that my first letter had puzzled him, but once he had read the second letter he had understood, thanks to my ruse of the post-script, that Colonel Dumouriez was causing us great concern. Without knowing exactly what it was about, he had a feeling that the situation was serious and so alerted his friend the Comte de Broglie straight away.

*

The Comte had left Metz, where official business had held him up for a while, and soon arrived at Versailles. He had come to rehearse the presentation that he was shortly to make in front of the King about his famous plan for a landing in England. I say *famous* because the Chevalier de Kermean had already spoken to me about it several times although, of course, the plan was a great secret.

The Comte de Broglie knew Colonel Dumouriez well, having previously sent him on a secret mission to Poland. The Comte had learned, the hard way, not to trust this exceptional officer, brilliant, for sure, with an inventive mind, but impossible to control. The Comte and the Chevalier had guessed the nature of his latest idea, and were convinced that it would threaten the success of *le Moucheron's* mission if left unchecked. It came at a bad time as the Comte and Monsieur de Vergennes had just learned, with great dismay, that the English had just arrested one of our best agents in London and were about to hang him. This unfortunate spy was regularly copying highly secret documents on the state and movements of the Royal Navy. This was bad enough on its own. But, after this fateful blow, *le Moucheron's* mission was now the sole source of intelligence on the movements of the English squadrons. So that Colonel Dumouriez' initiative was not well timed.

The Comte and my uncle had gone to see the Chevalier de Fleurieu. By chance, the King had just asked him to write a confidential memorandum giving his opinion as to whether Colonel Dumouriez ought to be named as Port Commander at Cherbourg. It was unanimously agreed that the best way to keep Dumouriez quiet was to give him this post, which he been soliciting for a long while and for which he was perfectly qualified. The Chevalier de Fleurieu had backed the Colonel to the King, who had written, on the spot, the letter which the Chevalier de Kermean had just read to us. And my uncle had left for Saint-Malo in the middle of the Friday night, in a carriage drawn hell for leather for two days and three nights by the horses of the King's mail.

*

Saint-Servan, Monday 23rd February, morning.

'I will have to explain this Isle of Wight business and everything else to your commander and fellow-officers. How do you find them?' said the Chevalier.

I told him all the good things I thought about them, and the admiration in which I held them, despite the fact that they had not come through the Marine Guards.

'Yes,' replied my uncle. 'To an extent that is why Monsieur de Fleurieu chose them. Not that he has anything against Marine Guards, as he was one himself at Toulon, but he is of the opinion that their education does not fit them for an intelligence operation like *le Moucheron's.* There is no honour to be won in an activity like this. Those who do it must already have it, hidden deep in their hearts, and be ready to accept that nobody will ever know about it. It is not for everybody! That, at least, is what Monsieur de Fleurieu said. I think you have it too, seeing you, your commander and your fellow-officers of *le Moucheron* dressed like ordinary folk the whole time. When was the last time you put on your beautiful Navy uniform?'

I had to think back before replying.

'It was at the end of July, when we received Colonel Dumouriez aboard ship.'

'I think you have done your job well and that you have to start thinking about signing up to a real warship soon. Think about it. And let me know what you decide. I promise you will have my support, along with that of the Director-General of Ports and Arsenals[58]. Now let's talk about other things. I have a letter here for you from Flaharn.'

He pulls the letter from his jacket pocket and gives it to me. We have reached the Sablons shore to the west of the Nose. We walk in front of the big blocks of rock which support the walls of the first of the Saint-Servan houses. I head towards the foot of the buildings to our right to find some shelter, where I examine the letter's seal. It seems intact.

'I haven't touched it. It's the original seal,' says my uncle, amused by my reaction. 'Our men have just collected it from the Paris post office where Flaharn usually puts his letters. We collect all the letters he sends, which are normally brought to my office where I check them and reseal them before putting them back in circulation. When possible, we have them taken by the King's mail. So sometimes they arrive more quickly than if they had gone by the normal post. This one has not yet been opened, and as it was for you I brought it with me without knowing its contents.'

Ship's Captain Flaharn writes that the *Comte*, whom he still

58 The official title of the Chevalier de Fleurieu.

does not name, has asked him to keep a very close eye on the work of *Monsieur de T…*regarding the plans for an operation in India. He confirms that the *Comte* intends to ask to be named as commander, and that he is certain he will be appointed. In fact, the forces which are being earmarked for this great enterprise are too big for someone of *Monsieur de T…'s* rank. Flaharn says that he has heard, from a reliable source, that two frigates, currently under construction in Saint-Malo, will be included in this force, and as I am on the spot, he asks me to be on the alert in order to use any influence I can to get myself enrolled on one of them when the time comes.

I can very well see where all this is leading, and give the letter to the Chevalier to get his opinion.

'The plans for the operation are those of the Chevalier du Ternay. The Chevalier had asked for twelve ships of the line and six frigates, as well as ten thousand troops. The command of the troops would be given to Monsieur de Bussy, and not to the Governor of Chandernagore. Ternay was hoping, as a result, that he himself would be promoted to Lieutenant-General. Flaharn's argument is well-founded. But he is a bit behind the times, as less than a month ago, because of our lack of resources and this problem of rank, the Chevalier de Ternay lowered his sights. He is now only asking for six ships of the line and three frigates. And I can assure you that Monsieur de Sartine and the Chevalier de Fleurieu are now seriously thinking of backing the project. At one point there was even talk of the expedition leaving next August. But where Flaharn really surprises me is in relation to these two frigates being built in Saint-Malo. The Chevalier de Fleurieu is certainly intending that they join de Ternay's expedition to India, but I thought that only two or three of us knew that. We haven't even told de Ternay, as we were still not sure whether they could be given to him. In any case, our man is right on one point: if the Comte d'Estaing asks to be given command of the India squadron, he will get it! I didn't know that the Comte d'Estaing was still interested in this India business. It seems that he is. Flaharn is in a better position than us to know this, and I think we can believe him. But if you want my opinion, the Comte d'Estaing could still change his mind in the coming months…'

Saying that, my uncle takes on, without realising it, that conspiratorial air that he sometimes affects, the air of someone who knows things that others could not know and never should know.

‘Do you think I should try to get myself aboard one of these frigates?’ I ask.

I ask the question purely as a matter of form, as I already know the answer in advance.

‘For the moment I would say no! And again, no! Why? Because it seems clear that Flaharn is doing his utmost to snare you in his net. Of course, I am curious to know why he is chasing after you like this, but it is too dangerous to go along with him at the moment. Besides, I cannot act against Flaharn without first discussing it with the Comte d’Estaing, and that would not be appropriate. As I have told you, we have to be patient because of the imminent war.’

*

It was already after half past eleven when we arrived at the port at Saint-Servan. There we found the bosun’s mate Couet, who told us that he had been ordered to wait until midday for the Captain. It being low tide, the ship’s boat was aground on the empty shore, in the full blast of the wind. The boat’s four oarsmen were trying without success to warm themselves up by stamping their soles on the wet sand. While waiting, I took my uncle to shelter behind the tower. We managed to find a less cold spot, pressing our backs to the rock and facing the sun. From there we could see the naval shipyard and the two frigates Flaharn had mentioned. Their construction was well advanced, with the outer and inner planking finished. All the deck beams were in place. The frigates were for 12-pounders, with fourteen gunports per side. As we were alone, I took advantage of the wait to relate to my uncle the incredible story of the Comte d’Estaing’s campaign in Sumatra, as told to me by Duval.

Captain Le Meur arrived at midday and the ship’s boat took the three of us out to *le Moucheron.* It was the start of the flood and so the cutter presented her starboard side, allowing us, for once, to follow the rules of naval etiquette.

Visiting a modest cutter can never be a grand affair. There is no comparison with a ship of the line or even a frigate. The majestic height of the rig, the muzzles of the cannons showing through the gunports, create a natural respect. *Le Moucheron* had nothing of that. She was tiny and not even armed. Nonetheless, her general look inspired confidence from the very first sight of her, even for the most unknowing of visitors. She seemed solid and trustworthy. This first impression was without fail confirmed when talking to her officers and petty officers, by the look of her sailors and soldiers, by the orderly arrangement of her deck gear, her lines and her sails; even the most insignificant objects seemed to be perfectly located, each one in its place and in total harmony with the rest of the ship. This did not give the impression of being a show simply to impress a superior; it was quite natural. Before going into foreign affairs, the Chevalier de Kermean had been a soldier long enough to appreciate this kind of order for what it really was. He went everywhere; he talked with the sailors; he examined the ship's logbooks, charts and navigational instruments. Lieutenant de Kerlaziou patiently answered all his questions. The visit lasted a long time. It was already two o'clock when the Captain, who had been waiting for a while on deck, announced that the ship's boat was ready to take us ashore.

A meal was waiting for us at Aunt Chollet's. Our second lieutenant had engaged Saint-Servan's best wine merchant and caterer. With the help of his aunt he had put together a solid buffet in the downstairs room, the one I had stayed in when I first arrived. Everybody felt better once they were inside. Big logs were burning in the fireplace. Bottles and plates of food covered a big table laid across trestles. Through the tiny panes of the windows, the cutter could be seen at her mooring. Her flag and her pennant streamed out in the icy wind sweeping the Rance.

Once we were all warmed up again, a glass in hand, well installed on the chairs and benches, our Captain thanked the Chevalier for having got us out of a tricky situation, and asked him why Colonel Dumouriez was so interested in the Isle of Wight. Was a military operation against the island being planned in the Chevalier de Fleurieu's offices, or was it a personal initiative of Dumouriez?

My uncle stood up and turned his back towards the fire to face us.

'No plan of campaign has been decided. We are in the process of studying the options before presenting them to the King. All ideas are welcome. Colonel Dumouriez had come up with the idea of the Isle of Wight. I think he intended to write a memorandum about this to the Ministry and the King. We will give it all the attention it deserves. I imagine that once he is at Cherbourg he will be in a good position to keep working on his plan. We hope so, but that is none of your concern. Your current mission is of the greatest importance. I'll come back to that but first I'd like to give you an overall picture of the political situation. What I will tell you is still secret. I hope you won't get caught by the English, and that if you do you will hold your tongues. Firstly, we are convinced that a war with the English is inevitable. Simply because that is what they want…'

I had already heard him say this.

'And we even think that had their colonies not revolted against them, forcing them to send part of their military resources to America, they would perhaps have already attacked us. I can say without any doubt that their rebellious subjects in New England have been de facto allies of ours right from the start, whether that pleases or not those who are against rebellion in principle.'

The Chevalier went silent for a few moments to allow any objections, then continued.

'If we cannot escape this conflict, we have to do our best to keep it as short as possible. Why is that? It's very simple: we cannot launch an overseas war because the state finances don't allow it. Our war aim cannot therefore be to annihilate the enemy at any cost, but to force him, as quickly as possible, by means of unarguable military victories, to negotiate a treaty that will give lasting peace and have done with the disastrous 1763 Treaty of Paris[59]. That is the gamble we have to take.'

We all looked at each other, shaking our heads and looking concerned. A poor man's war! Always this question of money! The deficit! It was the only thing being talked about in the news sheets. It was true then?

'As the war is being made against England, the pinnacle of naval power,' continued the Chevalier, 'we obviously have to concentrate all our efforts on the naval side. We must not repeat the mistakes of the last war. At that time we wanted to make land offensives in Europe and carry out overseas operations at one and the same time. Since we could not manage them both simultaneously, it resulted in the loss of India and Canada. That was by no means compensated for by our campaigns in Germany. This being the case, I have assembled some different plans to be presented to the King. For the moment, two proposals are competing

59 Translator's note: *Treaty of Paris*: the treaty which ended the Seven Years' War and under which France formally ceded its North American territories to the British.

against each other. The first is to send all our squadrons to sea at the same time to try and make gains in several theatres simultaneously: the first to America, to support the war of the Insurgents and at the same time defend our possessions in the Antilles; the second to the Atlantic and the Channel, with the help of Spain, to underline the strength of our flag; and the last to India, to force the English onto the defensive. The central point of this proposal is that an unfortunate defeat somewhere could be offset by a happy victory somewhere else. The second proposal is the Comte de Broglie's. The idea is for our Spanish allies to create a diversion in the Atlantic, while we concentrate all of our naval forces in the Channel. This should give us temporary superiority here, long enough for us to land sixty thousand men in Sussex. If that succeeded, the war would soon be over. That's the main advantage of this option. But it is all or nothing. If our army is beaten on land, the war is well and truly lost. This latter proposal has variations, one of which is to attack the naval ports of Portsmouth, Chatham and Plymouth, to destroy the Royal Navy installations and shipyards for the long term. In every case, we would propose withdrawing in return for an honourable peace. Colonel Dumouriez' plan is another variation on the latter proposal: to seize the Isle of Wight, allowing us to threaten Portsmouth. So that's an outline of our policies. You can well see that whichever option is adopted, the intelligence you are regularly collecting on the movements of the English fleet is of primary importance for the preparation and conduct of our operations.'

The Chevalier paused to drink a glass of wine.

'Now,' he said, 'I get to the main news. About three weeks ago Monsieur Gérard de Rayneval, our First Secretary for Foreign Affairs, met with the American representatives, led by Benjamin Franklin. In the name of the King, Monsieur Gérard countersigned two treaties with them, between, on the one hand, the King of France, and on the other, "the representatives of a sovereign and independent America".'

The speaker stopped a moment to give time for his audience to absorb what he had just said. You could have heard a pin drop.

'They are exactly the terms used! The first treaty was for commercial objectives, and also to give protection with our warships to any American ships who ask for it, and vice versa. The second is no more and no less than a formal military alliance between the Insurgents and France, against England. For the moment these accords are still secret, but once they are revealed you can be sure it won't be long before hostilities begin.'

*

The next day *le Moucheron* did not leave port. Nor did she go out on the following days, as low tide was around midday and Captain Le Meur wanted to take advantage of this by careening the cutter in order to renew her white lead antifouling and to check the rudder pintles which may have suffered after the storm of our previous outing. My uncle invited me to have lunch with him at Saint-Malo. He wanted to see *La Malice*, whose name had so amused him. We were seated, alone, at a little table at the end of the room, with a bottle of Bordeaux before us. My uncle quietly explained to me, between the poached sole and the mutton stew, that France's situation was a little more complicated than he had let on to Captain Le Meur and his officers. The year 1777 had not ended with the best of outlooks for the politics of the Kingdom.

Firstly, the Spaniards were abandoning us. Having wanted to drag us prematurely into a war against the Portuguese and their English allies, when we had made it clear that at that time we were not yet ready, the King of Spain, Charles III, had done an about-turn. He no longer wanted to join forces with his nephew, King Louis XVI, to help the Americans. He had written to Louis XVI to say that it was immoral to help the rebels.

As if that were not enough, at the same time, towards mid-December, the British Prime Minister, Lord North, in one of those unforeseeable reversals so typical of English pragmatism, had announced that he was ready, not simply to make a reconciliation with the Americans, but to grant them independence. At the same time as the despatch from our London Ambassador announcing this annoying news was arriving in France, our agents in Paris had already spotted and followed a British emissary who had come from Dunkirk. The chap was an English loyalist from New England, and righthand man of the head of British intelligence services. He had come to suggest that the Americans make peace with King George and join forces with him against us. The thing we had most dreaded was about to happen. As soon as he was told of this, the King asked his ministers to give absolute priority to drawing up a treaty with the Insurgents. It was this text, dictated urgently by the King himself, that

Monsieur Gérard de Rayneval signed with the American representatives.

Last but not least, war was about to break out between Prussia and Austria. And Vienna was demanding that France stick to their alliance. Luckily, Louis XVI had no intention of repeating his grandfather's mistakes.

There was one bright spot, if one could call it that, in this gloomy picture: Monsieur Necker had announced that in his estimation we could fund a war without raising taxes. All it needed was for the Swiss banks to issue a guaranteed loan. That was still worrying for the King, but did we have any choice?

I asked my uncle what he thought about this plan for an invasion of England. He replied that he did not think the King would keep on with it.

'For sure,' added the Chevalier, 'I put myself on the line in doing what I could to ensure that the Comte de Broglie could present his plan to the King. Although he gave a brilliant presentation, the Comte did not manage to convince Louis XVI. All the same, the plan is very well thought through. If followed, sixty thousand men could be landed in England. Even the King agrees with that. That was not the problem.'

My uncle already knew the question that the King would ask the Count: 'And now that you have managed to land your army, tell me, my dear Comte, what will you do with it?' My uncle had himself discussed this at length with the Chevalier de Fleurieu. Together they had studied the landings made by the English at Saint-Malo, Cherbourg and Saint-Cast in 1758, during the previous war. The English had landed quite modest forces – ten thousand men at the most. At first everything had gone well, for them at least. They had burned and pillaged our defences and ports, but then, each time, they had got into difficulty as their fleet could not keep on supporting them when the weather changed. This was despite it being a good time of year, between June and September. Moreover they had nothing to fear from our Navy, as the few ships of the line we had were either confined to port through lack of crews, or deployed too far away to be able to intervene. The Battle of Saint-Cast, in particular, ended disastrously for the British, with several thousand killed and hundreds of them taken prisoner. Yet at the start of the conflict they were only facing local coastal militias.

'Tell me,' continued my uncle. 'You are getting to know the Channel. Could one reasonably guarantee, and I mean guarantee with certainty, that the weather and the Royal Navy would allow our own Navy to give adequate support to our infantrymen, dragoons and artillery, once they have landed on the south coast of England?'

'One can generally predict a change in the weather a day in advance,' I said carefully.

'Yes, but can you predict how many storms there will be? During the course of a month, for example?'

'You would have to ask Lieutenant Chollet,' I replied. 'There are always at least one or two storms a month, except in midsummer. They are fairly rare then. But from October, the bad weather returns without fail.'

'In other words, if the weather stays good for the three months of summer, and if the Spanish manage to immobilise the Royal Navy for three months – and I remind you that for the moment they have abandoned us – our invading troops have to force England to capitulate within that time. Otherwise we will have lost the war. That's the crux of it. But I think the King will be happy just to concentrate our land forces in France, along the Channel coast. He will allow the diversionary tactics to proceed but, contrary to what the Comte is recommending, it will be just to give the English the impression that they are threatened on their own soil. It won't go any further than that. I think the main theatre of war will be in America. This will allow us to make sure our enemies don't help themselves to our last colonies in the Antilles. Above all, this will be a naval conflict. That's why, if I were a young man today, I would choose to be a naval officer, like you and your father.'

9

The winter passed. Storms became less frequent. The cold was no more than a memory. *Le Moucheron* continued her mission. Vernon had written a long letter to me after returning from a training exercise held in February. When they were anchored in Quiberon Bay, the Comte de Lamotte-Picquet, who had become commander of the squadron, had replied with the required nine-gun salute to the thirteen-gun salute from the privateer *Ranger*. She was flying the American flag and was commanded by the famous John Paul Jones, who Colonel Dumouriez had told us about. It was the first time since the Declaration of Independence that the flag of this young nation had been saluted at sea by a foreign warship. Since the squadron's return to Brest, the training was still continuing, within the confines of the harbour. Manoeuvring in divisions still left something to be desired, but the intense gunnery training was starting to bear fruit. My friend was still hunting whenever he could with the Comte de Boulainvilliers, but he had permission to go ashore a lot less frequently than before and he had always to be ready to re-join his ship at a moment's notice. Now they could only hunt with guns on the outskirts of Brest, so as not to be too far away. The hound Brac was doing well.

Between each double crossing of the Channel I went regularly to visit the slipways at the Saint-Servan shipyard in order to observe progress on the building of the two frigates. I happened to meet Monsieur Chevillard, the naval architect in charge of construction. He gave me permission to go into the two hulls to have a look at them. I talked with the shipwrights. They were still using adzes and augers, but only for the finishing touches. They had finished with their axes and saws. The decks were finished, the beak heads complete; they were mounting the capstans, the main bitts and the channels. Workers were finishing off the cabins with hand saws and planes. The caulkers had started work. At the top of the shore they had set up huge pots in which they mixed their pitch. Its heady odour overrode the sweet perfume of the oak, pine and cedar which up until then had dominated the two slipways.

These two beautiful ships were identical. Their hulls still had the paleness of fresh wood. They seemed to me to be similar to *la Belle-Poule,* which I had admired at Brest the previous year: same length and same beam, to the inch, same armament and, judging by the gun port openings, the same elegant sheer line and cross-section. This was not a matter of chance, as Monsieur Chevillard was working from plans drawn up by Monsieur Guignace, the builder of *la Belle-Poule.* It was therefore reasonable to expect that these two Saint-Malo frigates would sail as well as their elder sister from Brest.

In March, a master carver and his assistants arrived at the yard to decorate the bow, the taffrail and the breast work, using mouldings, bas relief, fleurons and various types of scrollwork. I found the names of the two ships under the rows of windows of their respective great cabins. The Ministry had finally decided to call then *l'Amazone* and *la Gentille.* I liked these two names a lot. I said them to myself in a low voice, imagining warm and turquoise blue seas such as those my father must have known during his times in the Mascarene Islands. I already loved these two elegant ships and was impatient to see them fully rigged. There was just one thing that displeased me: with such names they could well have been adorned with beautiful figureheads of ancient Goddesses, of the type loved by all sailors, their proud and naked bosoms exposed to the caresses of the salt sea. But at this time it was no longer the fashion. To the great disappointment of the carvers and the sailors, the Ministry had for a year imposed the same design on all ships: a lion rampant, its rear paws gripping the stem head and its fore paws joined at the top of the cutwater on a badge carrying the French arms, and to top it all off, a big round head like a mastiff's.

On Friday 27th March, Monsieur de La Rozière called all the Naval officers then in Saint-Malo to the Chateau. We were able to attend the meeting, as low tide was at midday that day and Captain Le Meur, adhering to his principles, had decided to make use of it to careen *le Moucheron*. The Port Commander told us that diplomatic relations with England had been broken off on the 13th of the month, and on the 19th, following the decision of the King's Council, the Prince de Montbarey was tasked with telling the English Commissioner in Dunkirk to stop all activity immediately. These words were followed by a deep silence, after which everybody began to applaud. When things had calmed down, Monsieur de La Rozière also announced that Benjamin Franklin and his companions had been received by the King.

As we were about to leave the Chateau to return to Saint-Servan, Monsieur de La Rozière called me over, to give me a letter from my uncle which had arrived in the last Ministerial post.

'The Chevalier de Kermean is proposing a ship for you. He has asked me to let him know your answer as soon as possible...'

Excusing myself, I broke the seal of the letter. My uncle told me that *l'Amazone* and *la Gentille* had been designated for the Chevalier de Ternay's expedition to the Indies. The former would be commanded by the Comte de Lapérouse and the latter by Monsieur Mengaud de la Hage. The lists of officers for these two ships had not yet been finalised, as it had not yet been possible to inform their commanders of their nominations. Monsieur Mengaud de la Hage was at sea, commanding the old frigate *le Zephyre*, while the Comte de Lapérouse was expected at Brest after a Channel patrol, and was to relinquish his corvette back to the King. However, my uncle had spoken about me to the Chevalier de Ternay and the latter, remembering my father, was happy to recommend me to the Comte de Lapérouse. My uncle ended his letter by strongly advising me to let Monsieur de La Rozière know my answer as quickly as possible. There would be many volunteers for these two ships as soon as their departure for the Indies became known.

I did not waste time wondering why the Chevalier, who had been so unfavourable to the idea of seeing me go off on this expedition to India, had suddenly changed his mind. I had already decided, some time ago, to do everything possible to get myself aboard one of the two Saint-Servan frigates of which I was so enamoured. And now I was learning that one of them would be commanded by the Comte de Lapérouse, the old friend of my father aboard *le Formidable.*

'I am happy to sign aboard *l'Amazone,* Monsieur.'

'Good. My congratulations,' said Monsieur de La Rozière with a smile. 'I will warn Captain Le Meur.'

He held out another sealed envelope.

'This too is from your uncle. He asked me to give you this letter should you agree to go to India. I know its contents, but I will leave you in peace to acquaint yourself with it by yourself. I wish you good luck, Monsieur Laforest-Dombourg.'

The package contained a letter and a notebook. In the letter, my uncle explained that I had a good chance of leaving for India. The booklet was a code book.

I can confirm what I said the other day about a landing in England. All the troop movements which have been decided for the Channel coast are nothing but a diversion. But that must remain secret. I know you well enough now to know that you will keep total silence on this matter.

The King's main objective, which has priority over everything else, is the war in America. However, that does not exclude secondary operations designed to interfere with English interests in India. We don't have anyone over there. Certain characters on the Île-de-France do not always exhibit as much loyalty as we would expect from them, notable as regards Monsieur de Ternay. Past history has shown us the damage that scheming politicians can do to military men who are guilty, in their eyes, of doing everything possible to accomplish their mission. The sad injustice of which Lally-Tollendal was a victim during the last war must not be repeated. The Chevalier de Ternay has our full support but he has no protection from slander. When he was over there as Governor of the Île-de-France he made enemies as well as friends. That is why we thought there would be a benefit from having in our files, later on, a daily account of the situation, written by somebody above suspicion, like yourself. This would allow us, if required at some later date, to be able to back up the Chevalier's reports in the face of any scheming civilians who might wish to damage him.

My superiors have already had a recent opportunity to confirm your honesty and your writing talents during your Saint-Malo mission. All we will ask of you is to provide a regular and faithful account of the events you witness. You will keep strictly to the facts, avoiding any opinion, analysis or commentary of any kind. Of course this has to remain totally secret, especially as far as Monsieur de Ternay is concerned, even if our sole aim is to help him defend himself later against any possible plots against him.

I enclose for you a simple code that you will use for this. You will send me regular letters, devoid of anything of interest, addressed to your uncle, that is to say, me. You will put your coded reports as addendums, presenting them as your thoughts on certain mathematical problems. This ought not to attract attention, coming from a student Naval officer keen to learn his trade. Keep the codebook and give this letter back to Monsieur de la Rozière, who will take care to destroy it...

The code given to me had no doubt been worked out by associates of Monsieur de Fleurieu. It was principally based on combinations of numbers and mathematical formulae. A real sailor would not have mixed them up with a calculation of longitude by lunar distances, but to the unversed, they resembled it closely. However, one thing surprised me about these orders: there was no mention of Flaharn, not even a veiled reference.

At the beginning of May I received a letter from Vernon. He told me that a huge naval force was being assembled at Brest. It was under the command of the Comte d'Orvilliers. The Comte de Lamotte-Picquet had been promoted to the rank of Squadron Commander. He had left *le Robuste* to go aboard *le Saint-Esprit,* eighty-four guns, where he had the pleasure of raising the blue flag of the Commander of the Third Squadron of the fleet. However, he did not have much time to enjoy it, as the command of this squadron was finally given to the Duc de Chartres, who had just been made a Lieutenant-General. The meteoric rise of the young Duc in the Navy was mainly due to his being a prince of the blood, not to his nautical knowledge, which is why Monsieur de Lamotte-Picquet was kept at his side to advise him.

Vernon had asked to follow his commander to *le Saint-Esprit.* Not only had his request been granted, he had shortly afterwards been promoted to Flag Guard. This distinction, he explained honestly in his letter, had been accorded by His Highness the Duc de Chartres to all the Marine Guards serving on *le Saint-Esprit*, on the day he joined the ship. But my friend had not written to me simply to tell me all that. Above all he wanted to let me know that Monsieur de Bougainville had been ordered, in March, to give up *le Bien Aimé* and go urgently to Toulon. Vernon had just heard that this was to enable him to take command of a new seventy-four gun ship in a squadron which was to sail as soon as possible, under the command of the Comte d'Estaing, to wage war on the American coast. This news had been kept secret as long as possible, which is why we had heard nothing about it. I realised, reading the letter, that the Comte d'Estaing must already be at sea. Maybe he had already passed Gibraltar. I now understood why the Chevalier de Kermean had changed his mind so easily and why he had been so quick to support my signing aboard *l'Amazone.* He knew without doubt that Flaharn was at that very moment sailing for America and that, as a result, there was no obstacle to me going off to the other side of the world where I would be out of his reach. I was not annoyed at my uncle for his secrecy. I was too happy at the idea of departing for India, in the wake of my father, and under the orders of a Captain who my father had said had once been his best friend.

L'Amazone and *la Gentille* were launched on Monday 11th May, towards six in the evening, at high tide. I watched the event from the deck of *le Moucheron*, while we were preparing to sail on the ebb. When we returned, on the following Thursday, both of them were on their mooring buoys. Derricks had already been rigged for getting their masts in. *La Gloire* had left Saint-Malo under the command of Ship's Lieutenant Bavre, for sea trials before re-joining the fleet at Brest.

During the strange spring of the year of grace 1778, despite the simultaneous and reciprocal breaking off of relations between us and England, war had not been declared either at Versailles or in London. On each side of the Channel, each Court was waiting for its opposite number to do something wrong which would then allow the offended side to affirm, haughtily, the rightness of its cause and invoke the protection of the Gods of War.

In the previous conflict, Admirals Boscawen and Hawke had started attacking our fishing boats and merchant ships in 1755, and had made a surprise attack on two of our armed supply ships, which were forced to surrender. Despite this, Louis XV had waited until May of 1756 before making a formal declaration of war.

In May 1778, however, the situation seemed quite different for us.

Certainly, the Royal Navy had started to attack our merchant ships, on the pretext of stopping trade with the Insurgents, but Louis XVI, on his side, did not seem to want to delay things as long as his grandfather. Everything seemed to indicate that we would not have to wait long, even if appearances seemed to be saying to the patriots in the Paris salons that the slowness and indecision of the government was causing the loss of our ships and the ruin of our shipowners. Firstly, there was the departure of the Comte d'Estaing. Vernon had been the first to tell me of this. Later we learned that the Comte had clear orders authorising him to act with hostility towards any English vessels he came across in the Atlantic. This news had been widely broadcast by the Secretary of State for the Navy as soon as the frigate *la Flore,* sent off by the Comte, had confirmed in France that our Levant fleet had passed the Straits. The English learned of this at the same time, but it was already too late for them, otherwise they would certainly have tried to stop our ships from passing Gibraltar. For my part, I thought that this latest piece of news had been released deliberately in order to stir up feelings in London since, according to the newspapers, its announcement led to a stormy session in the English parliament. In any case, it could not have been kept secret forever.

In France, Louis XVI had not yet given the Navy an order of the type received by the Comte d'Estaing. In any case, while waiting for that day, which was sure to come soon, he modified in advance the rules regarding the sharing of prize money. That did not go unnoticed, above all in Saint-Malo! The King would from here on buy any warships captured by his crews at a new tariff ranging from fifty-four thousand pounds for a frigate to five hundred and ninety thousand pounds for a three-deck ship. As for merchantmen, they would be sold at their market value, as before. But that was not the main change. The new aspect was that the King was giving up his share. The old rules had always allowed for a third share of the prize money to go to the King, a third to the Disabled Seamen's Fund, and just a third to the crews. From here on it would be a third for the Fund and two-thirds for the crew. For the moment, this only applied to the Navy, but that's all I ever heard talked about in Saint-Malo. Everybody was hoping that privateering would also benefit from it, once war was officially declared. And the sooner the better since, following previous orders, sailings for fishing on the Grand Banks had been cancelled, the ships had had to remain in port, and so the Saint-Malo sailors and shipowners were left with nothing to live on. They were therefore waiting impatiently for the declaration of war, so that they could once again feed their large families by means of the only way now possible: privateering.

The weather was good and the storms were less strong and less frequent. All the same, war was in the air. From here on we had a man on permanent lookout in the maintop during daylight. As soon as he spotted a sail on the horizon, the men on deck went quiet and serious. Luckily the sea is big and our cutter was tiny. Usually we had only to tack to keep out of sight. We no longer regretted *le Moucheron's* modest proportions.

We were chased once by a corvette which was working its way along the coast from Plymouth. She had suddenly popped out from behind Bolt Head while we were hove to off Start Point waiting for nightfall. We had lost her easily by sailing to windward much closer than she was able. She had not kept on with the chase, turning away to head once more for Portsmouth. It has to be said that we were not properly at war at that time. No cannon had as yet been fired, but this could not last forever. In fact, everything was going to change radically on 17th June 1778. That day would produce what at first sight seemed a small incident, but one which produced a dramatic turn of events and which caused a strong reaction from the King and the whole of France. It had an effect even on the hairdressers of the most fashionable women in Paris. *Le Moucheron* was to be an involuntary witness to the arrival on stage of the actors in this drama.

We had left Saint-Malo on the morning of 14th June, on the half past nine tide. Contrary to his usual habit, our Captain had decided to sail on a Sunday, as Lieutenant Chollet had predicted a change in the weather, with a very light northerly wind. That could lead to a very slow crossing of the Channel, and it was imperative that we pick up a package from the other side every week. For the whole of Sunday, and the following night, we had a good breeze, and Lieutenant de Kerlaziou gently teased his fellow-officer. At dawn on Monday the wind fell, fulfilling the predictions of the second lieutenant. We were about halfway across the Channel. The cutter was heading north-west, sailing as close as she could to the wind, towards Plymouth. This was a little too much to the west for our taste; even taking into account the usual ebb and flow of currents, we would have to tack if the wind did not shift. However Lieutenant Chollet was hoping for a south-south-westerly the next day. The sea had scarcely a ripple and the cutter was dragging herself along in miserable fashion, despite all the sail we had been able to put on her: big jib, staysail, flying jib, gaff topsail, topsail and topgallant sail braced hard, spanker and its studding sail. The master sailmaker Deyo had even pulled out of his store a new triangular water sail that I had never seen before and which was set under the boom aft of the poop deck. Despite all this washing we were making less than two knots since morning. It was hot; too hot. A heat haze drowned the horizon all around in a milky, dazzling light in which sea and sky seemed to merge together.

*

At sea aboard le Moucheron, Wednesday 17th June 1778, towards ten in the morning.

Towards ten in the morning, the mist suddenly starts to lift and the lookout shouts that there is a three-masted ship ahead on our starboard bow. She is so close that we can clearly make out her hull from the deck of the cutter. She must have seen us too. Captain Le Meur sends me to the maintop with my telescope. On a little cutter like *le Moucheron* there is no platform, just two narrow struts, parallel to each other and at right angles to the mast, which is itself raked aft. You have to hang on well when you are up there. However, on this day it is easy to remain standing, as the sea is so calm. I can even lean my shoulder calmly against the mast, holding my telescope in both hands and focusing it on the unknown ship clearly visible to starboard of our topsail.

I can see straight off that she is a frigate. She is heading south-west, broad reaching on starboard tack. Her course is at right angles to ours. She has furled her topgallant sails and raised her topsails to the mastheads. She seems stuck on the sparkling surface of the sea, but watching her more closely I can see her moving imperceptibly to my left. I count fourteen gun ports on the port battery facing us. She probably has twenty-eight cannons on her gun decks. It is not possible to make out the flag on her stern as it is hanging flat against its pole on account of the lack of wind. Her masts seem lower than those on a French frigate, her yards wider. She is English, for sure. I shout all that down to the Captain listening below.

'She looks somewhat like one of our 12-pounder frigates, Sir. But I'm sure she's English.'

The Captain also has his telescope trained on the unknown ship. Now knowing that she is a frigate, rather than a ship of the line, he voices his estimation that she is hardly more than three miles ahead of us.

'Perhaps a hundred yards more,' he clarifies.

The fog has played a nasty trick on us. With a fresh wind, this English ship could be on us in an hour. We would be in a most difficult position. What's more, she has the advantage of being to windward of us. Luckily, in the present conditions it would take her three hours to get to where we are – if we were to wait for her. Observing the frigate, I see a row of coloured square flags appear, making a dotted line between her poop deck and the starboard end of her main topsail yard. Normally flags are raised vertically to the masthead, but as there is no wind, they have sent them up diagonally.

'She is signalling, Sir!' I shout down to the Captain.

The mist continues to clear. Now I can see other sails further on, three miles to windward of the frigate: seven big ships. They are sailing in each other's wake, maintaining an exact distance of one cable, each astern of the other. Only ships of the line could sail in such strict formation. Behind them, at the very limit of the misty horizon, there are more, but I am unable to count them in the poor visibility. I bring my telescope back to the frigate. I have seen her signal our presence to the squadron in whose lee she is sailing, but she does not seem willing to alter her speed or course. She calmly holds her heading, her canvas deliberately reduced. We are too small to be of any interest to the commander of this fleet. No doubt he takes us for common smugglers, like the rest of them. And he certainly has much more important plans in mind to be concerned about small fry like us. That, at least, is what I think while going back down on deck to make my report.

'According to the information given to us last week by our Cornishmen,' says Captain Le Meur, 'Keppel[60] would have weighed anchor last Saturday at Spithead, but he would have remained stuck in the Saint Helen's Roads because of lack of wind. They said he had twenty-one ships of the line. You say you counted seven? And there are others in parallel behind? It could only be him. They are sailing in the

60 Translator's note: *Keppel*: Admiral Augustus Keppel (1725 – 1786). Long-serving British Naval officer and Parliamentarian who became First Lord of the Admiralty in 1782.

classic order – three columns. They don't want to waste time and, thank God, we are of no interest to them. I would like to know where they are heading. The Brittany coast? Or America?'

*

The breeze which had cleared the fog brought our speed above two knots. The Captain had an English flag sent up, just in case. There really wasn't enough wind to fly it properly, even though I could now see, as I leaned on the taffrail, little whirlpools revolving gently but regularly behind the after end of the rudder. *Le Moucheron* went about, heading north-east to pass astern of the English fleet. The lookout's voice came down once more from above.

'Cutter in sight!'

We grabbed our telescopes again. The said ship was appearing slowly from behind the frigate. Up until now she had been hidden from us. It was a big cutter, armed for war. She had a yellow hull with a wide black band along her topsides. I counted six cannons projecting from the open gun ports on her starboard side. There must be twelve in all, but of what calibre? The cutter must have been almost twice the size of *le Moucheron.* She was finishing wearing ship, coming across the wind onto a square reach, piling on canvas and heading due east. Clearly, our ruse with the English flag had had no effect. She intended to cut us off. For sure, in this light wind, everything would unfold very slowly, like those nightmares in which you have the impression of moving so sluggishly. Captain Le Meur had the ship brought two more points off the wind, to sail on the same heading as our pursuer. If she wanted to intercept us, she would have to overtake us first.

The wind was still from the north, a gentle breeze, scarcely enough to ripple the mirrored sea. But we were no longer immobile. For half an hour, the two cutters sailed exactly parallel courses, three miles apart, heading due east at the same speed. We were advancing gently together, without either of the two ships making any positive gain on the other. The two lieutenants had joined the Captain aft. Suddenly, as I was observing the English cutter with my telescope, she seemed to be gaining on us. When I looked with the naked eye, this didn't seem to be the case. I pointed this out to the Captain.

'He has come off the wind one or two points more to reduce the gap between us,' said Captain Le Meur. 'If he does it again, we will luff up till we are hard on the wind. We'll see how that works out.'

The day continued thus. The mist had completely cleared. Visibility was now twelve miles or more. The English fleet moved off slowly to the west while we progressed, just as slowly, in the opposite direction. Towards half past two the masts of Keppler's ships began to disappear below the horizon. Apart from the seabirds, there was now only the big cutter and us. From time to time, our pursuer bore off to a broad reach while we came up hard on the wind. As soon as she resumed her square reach, we did the same thing. At that rate, she was not catching us up, but each time reducing the gap that separated our courses. I could not work out what our Captain had in mind. He had had a long talk with Lieutenant Chollet and they had both agreed that we were about equal with the English ship with the wind on the beam, but perhaps quicker than her on the wind.

'In principle, she should beat us on all points of sail, as she is bigger, but there is not much wind, we are lighter, our hull has been recently scrubbed down, and *le Moucheron* has been set up for windward work. That is her strong point. The English cutter would certainly beat us with the wind dead aft, as she is heavier, with greater momentum, even in this light weather. That is why I avoided taking flight at the start. I'm sure that's what they wanted us to do. Whereas now, they are forced to play our game. If he comes right off the wind, we will continue as we are. He will end up astern of us but having lost the windward advantage. We will come hard on the wind and I hope we might lose him that way. If not, we have the option of using our sweeps...but if she has them too...we'll just have to fight!'

By four o'clock, the English cutter's bow was following our stern directly. Only a thousand yards separated us. We could see her crew with the naked eye. Our men had stopped talking. They had eaten in silence at one o'clock. Those who were not needed for running the ship had been sent below.

'Following us like this she's going to lose her squadron,' said Lieutenant de Kerlaziou. 'Why is she sticking to an inoffensive little cutter like *le Moucheron*? Her Admiral will lose her!'

'Keppel probably has good reason to think they can re-join each other easily,' replied Captain Le Meur. 'And I'd like to know that reason!'

'As for why she doesn't want to let us go,' added Lieutenant Chollet, 'that's not difficult to guess. She must be thinking that *le Moucheron* sails too well for such a modest ship. They think we are top class smugglers. That our cargo is worth its weight in gold! That's what she thinks!'

Captain smiled at him, with a flash of his usual ironic air.

'And you think we are worth nothing? What would you do with all those piasters I carry in my strong box?'

'But do you think her Admiral agrees?' asked Lieutenant de Kerlaziou.

'Without doubt!' said Lieutenant Chollet, and continued on. 'With them, the squadron commanders get a share of all the prizes taken by their officers.'

'Oh!' said the Captain. 'Maybe she just wants to make sure we are not a scout from one of our squadrons in Brest. And our behaviour must intrigue her. A normal scout would immediately have headed south to report to her superiors. As I just said, what really bothers me is why Keppel thinks the cutter could re-join him easily. Maybe we'll find out the answer to that in our Salcombe letter box...if we ever get there.'

He had said those last words very quietly, so as not to be heard by the man on the helm.

By five in the evening, the English cutter was less than four hundred yards off in our wake. She was not giving an inch, and seemed to be gaining on us a little. Lieutenant Chollet was surprised she had not opened fire with her bow chasers.

'She's still a little too far off,' said Lieutenant de Kerlaziou behind us. 'We're not yet quite within her range. And that's just as well, I can tell you!'

He had just come down from the maintop, where he had climbed with my telescope to try to get a good view down onto the deck of our pursuer. Just at that moment, as if to contradict him, a brief orange flash lit up the English cutter's bow, which was immediately lost in a cloud of white smoke. A loud bang put up all the seabirds sitting on the water thereabouts and a projectile slashed the calm surface of the sea less than a hundred yards from our stern.

'My oath! She's firing 12-pound balls!' shouted Lieutenant Chollet.

'Let's not exaggerate. They are what the English call 'double fortified 6-pounders'. That is to say 6-pounders, but they have twelve of them. That's a lot for a little ship like that. Since we are unarmed, it would be enough to destroy us, if she gets any nearer.'

'You're right,' said Captain Le Meur. 'As for what to do, it would be better to avoid that. Now she's lost the windward advantage, let's see how she gets on close-hauled.'

He gave new orders and *le Moucheron* came up hard on the wind, heading north-east. Our pursuer did the same thing, but stopped gaining on us. By seven o'clock she was much further astern. As night fell, we saw her bear off and wear round, heading off due west.

It was just two days after the full moon and the night was very clear. The English cutter lit a stern light. Our Captain waited another hour before we tacked and headed north-west, close-hauled, to bring us to Start Point. After midnight the wind backed to south-south-west, as Lieutenant Chollet had predicted, but it was still a light breeze. At dawn, the sea was completely deserted. On Tuesday 16th, at three in the afternoon, our destination was in sight. There were still no other ships visible. We waited until nightfall before picking up our package under a waning moon. Captain Le Meur told us to stay on the mooring buoy, keeping the pick-up buoy on board, while he went below to read the documents we had retrieved. When he came back on deck, he looked pleased and said he had doubled the usual payment for our informers. The sailors threw the buoy back overboard. *Le Moucheron* slowly moved away from the coast, on starboard tack, pushed by a light land breeze.

The Captain called us around him to share what our agents had written.

'Their report says that Admiral Byron left Plymouth at dawn on Tuesday 9th June, just after high water at five in the morning. He has thirteen ships of the line, one of ninety guns, the others of seventy-four, plus a frigate. The report gives the names of the ships and their commanders. Most importantly, it says that Byron has been ordered to the Americas to thwart the Comte d'Estaing's squadron. The English ships already over there will come under his command. As for Admiral Keppel, he finally sailed from the Saint Helen's Roads last Friday towards one in the afternoon. He has with him twenty-one ships of the line, of which one has a hundred guns, four have ninety and one has eighty. He also has four frigates and a 'sloop of war', that is to say a corvette, the *Alert,* whose captain is a Commander Fairfax. Here too they have provided a list of the ships and their commanders, as well as a description of this fleet's mission. Keppel has to cover the rear of Admiral Byron's fleet against attack from the Comte d'Orvilliers' forces. To do that, he has to get to the entrance to the Channel as quickly as possible and cruise off Ushant in order to stop the Comte sending a squadron in pursuit of Byron. They say that the *Alert* is rigged as a cutter. She is certainly the ship that chased us, and why her commander was sure of being able to re-join Keppel off Ushant. That's why she kept after us for so long. The main point of the report is that Byron and Keppel have not joined forces. That means we are even with the English in the Channel, but that the Comte d'Estaing will be facing a superior force once Byron has added the ships already in America. We've got to get this news back to Saint-Malo as quickly as possible.'

Alas! The wind dropped completely again. At the rate the cutter was dragging herself along we wouldn't get there until the middle of the next Friday. Midnight had passed and it was already Wednesday 17th. Byron had left five days ago and we had seen Keppel go past a day and a half ago, almost two days in fact.

Captain Le Meur had the sweeps manned – the 'galley oars[61]'. They are well-named! Everyone had his turn, even the officers: one hour of rowing, one hour of rest. We were in the Saint-Malo entrance passage at six o'clock on the Thursday morning. We could hardly stand. My hands were covered in blisters. I slept for the whole of Friday, and Saturday as well.

On the Sunday morning, I was woken up unceremoniously by the two lieutenants, who had just come back on board. They were very excited and impatient to tell us the big news about which everyone was talking on land. Before that, though, Lieutenant de Kerlaziou quickly told me that he had seen a letter for me from Brest at the Post office.

It had just been learned that there had been a fight the previous Wednesday, off Ushant, between *la Belle Poule* and an English frigate which had been detached from Keppel's squadron. *La Belle Poule*, commanded by Ship's Lieutenant de la Clocheterie, had gone out of Brest harbour at the head of a light reconnaissance division comprising the 8-pounder frigate *la Licorne*, the corvette *l'Hirondelle* and a lugger, *le Coureur*. They had fallen upon Keppel's squadron, that we had seen ahead of us two days previously. Our ships, under chase, dispersed.

61 Translator's note: '*Galley oars*': '*Avirons de galère*'. This is a kind of pun in French, as '*la galère*' also has the metaphorical meaning of 'misery, hard times'.

Only *la Belle Poule* and *le Coureur* stayed together. They had been caught up at six in the evening by a frigate and a cutter from Keppel's fleet. The action had unfolded in calm weather on a flat sea. The two frigates were moving very slowly, beam on to each other, firing their cannons at pistol range. The combat lasted until ten in the evening and was murderous. The English ship had finally tacked, taking advantage of her superior speed, due mainly to her being copper bottomed, and thus admitted defeat. To escape from the enemy ships bearing down on him, Lieutenant de la Clocheterie had anchored his ship, riddled with cannon shot and leaking everywhere, amongst the rocks close to the coast off Plouescat. In his report, written the next morning and sent ashore, he said that the English ship had opened fire first, and that he had no choice but to return fire, that his crew had fifty-seven wounded and forty killed, that he had seen *le Coureur* lower her flag and surrender to the English cutter that she was fighting and that he thought that *la Licorne* had been captured but that *l'Hirondelle* had managed to escape.

It was perhaps only a duel between two frigates, but it was the first real engagement of the war and, not only had the English frigate fired first, a crucial factor in the eyes of the King and his Cabinet but, above all, it could be considered that she had been beaten, having broken off the battle of her own free will and sailed back out to sea. Since the last war the English had acquired such a reputation for invincibility at sea that this little victory, a single frigate of ours against a single English frigate, was already being unanimously fêted, by general public opinion, as a divine intervention. Lieutenant de la Clocheterie's report, written by him at the Plouescat anchorage on the Thursday morning, had reached Brest the same evening. It had been copied and sent immediately by special post to Versailles. Other copies had gone out to the other western ports, including Saint-Malo. Lieutenants Chollet and de Kerlaziou were certain that *la Belle Poule* and *le Coureur* had fought with the frigate and the cutter we had seen the previous Monday.

'They had 3-pounders on *le Coureur*, eight in all, and they must have had a nasty surprise when they found themselves within pistol range of the *Alert's* twelve 'double-fortified 6-pounders'. I wouldn't have wanted to be in their shoes. But there will be promotions and rewards for those on board *la Belle Poule,'* said Lieutenant Kerlaziou in conclusion.

On Monday morning I went to the post office to collect the letter I had been told about. It was from Maria Kirwan and was dated 1st June.

Sir

Your last letter made me cry. Do you believe me to be so self-centred to the point of not appreciating the greatness, as well as the difficulty, of your calling? You will see that I will always busy myself with everything that pleases you before thinking of myself. Wherever you may go, Brest is a place through which every sailor passes. Do not refuse the support that a young and unselfish girl, who wishes only your happiness above her own, can provide.

I have got to know a young lady of quality who has come to stay at the inn while she finds living quarters in Brest. Her fiancé is a Naval officer who at present is at the Ministry in Versailles, and who will soon take command of an armed ship in Brest. They met each other on the Île-de-France and she made the voyage here all alone in order to be with the object of her affection. For reasons beyond her and her fiancé's control, they will probably have to wait until the end of the next campaign before marrying. Well then! She does not complain. She stays gentle and good-natured, with never a cross word. That's how a Frenchwoman loves a sailor. I have benefited greatly from her company and she has honoured me with her friendship.

You can see very well that you have no cause for concern as regards myself and my affection for you. I aspire to nothing more, Sir, than the honour of being your most humble and most obedient servant.

Le Moucheron sailed again on Monday 22nd June, at five in the evening. The crossing passed without incident, despite our fears. For the whole time there was a light breeze from the east, enough to move the cutter along. According to Captain Le Meur, if the wind stayed like this, Keppel would be unable to come back up the Channel and we would be left in peace. The report we fished out on the English coast confirmed this view. There had been no movements in Plymouth or Portsmouth during the previous week. It was a crossing of the type we had not had for a long time: magnificent weather, a slight but regular breeze, with nothing to do on deck but sleep in the shadow of the sails. On the other hand, we were not progressing very quickly. It was only on Friday 26th June that we were able to enter the Saint-Malo entrance passage, having had to wait for the second hour of the flood, as it was not a big tide that day. When Captain Le Meur returned on board that evening, he brought back orders concerning me. I had to present myself at the office of the Port Commander on Monday 29th June, before midday, to receive my embarkation order for the King's frigate *l'Amazone.*

On Sunday afternoon I packed my chest and began to say my farewells to the crew of the cutter. Before signing my disembarkation order, Captain Le Meur asked me to swear solemnly that I would never talk about *le Moucheron's* mission, not even to my future commanding officer, Ship's Lieutenant de Lapérouse.

'Our safety lies in secrecy,' he explained to me. 'Those who are not part of it could never understand. If you tell them that we often cross the Channel in order to pick up letters attached to a buoy on the other side, they will think there is nothing to it and will pass on this amusing little story to a friend, not thinking they are doing any harm. This friend will mention it again by chance at some social gathering. And in the end, sooner or later, it will reach the ear of one of your Malaga's cronies. Think, too, about that cutter that chased us two weeks ago. We got away from her, didn't we? But if she had really known who we were, do you think she would have let us go so easily? She would have done everything possible to capture us! That is certain! And there would have been no mercy towards us, just as we show no mercy towards them. And by the way, since we are talking of La Malaga, do you know what happened to her? She was hanged, And her accomplice too. As for the sailors from the English cutter, they would have been hanged as well, had not Colonel Dumouriez intervened personally. He wanted them to have a soldier's death: they were given the firing squad.'

That was the moment when I really began to understand the sound reasoning behind the advice to be careful given to me by my uncle at Vertou, all the precautions that had made me smile at the time; the false papers, the 'going around the houses'. This was not a game.

10

At seven in the morning on 29th June 1778, the ship's boat took me ashore. It had been agreed with Captain Le Meur that the bosun's mate Couet would wait for me at the foot of the Solidor Tower to take me back on board and pick up my baggage. He would then take me directly to my frigate, whose mooring buoy was just a cable and a half away from the cutter, opposite Saint-Servan. I had put on my blue and red Naval uniform, while at my side was the old regulation Musketeer sword given to me by the Chevalier de Kermean. My hair had grown long again, just long enough to be able to be tied by a ribbon, as the regulations required. I had decided to keep my hair long, not wishing to have to put up with the torture of a wig.

The offices of the Navy and the Commissioner of Lists were beside the quay of the military port at Saint-Servan. I was the first visitor at this early hour and the Port Commander was kind enough to see me straight away. He was called Obet, a Ship's Ensign of about forty years of age. He was a one-time auxiliary officer who, just like my late father, had fought his way to becoming a ship's officer on merit alone. I gave him my debarkation certificate, along with another certificate from Captain Le Meur saying that I could not present my sailing record as it was to be sent directly to the Chevalier de Fleurieu, the Director of Ports and

Arsenals. The Commander doubtless knew the situation as regards *le Moucheron* and made no comment on this. He just asked how long I had been a Marine Guard, how long I had served on the cutter, and made a note of this. He then gave me my embarkation order, requiring me to join without delay the King's frigate *l'Amazone,* commanded by Ship's Lieutenant de Lapérouse[62]. I was about to take my leave when a secretary announced the arrival of the Comte de Lapérouse himself. I thought I would be asked to leave, but the Commander asked me to stay, saying that he would be pleased to introduce me to my new commander. In came a Ship's Lieutenant, wearing a working uniform, of average height, stocky and rather plump.

'I can guess what brings you here, Sir,' said the Commander. 'Tell me if I am right. Before even having heard you, I can already present to you one of your Marine Guards. This is Monsieur Laforest-Dombourg, who is burning to serve the King under your orders.'

'So that's what you are up to! Don't think that you will get away with it so easily, Sir!' replied the captain of *l'Amazone.* 'I have not come to look for Marine Guards. I was given my sailors last night. Where are the thirty trained gunners that I spoke about when we last looked at the Lists?'

He spoke with a firm and direct tone, but remained friendly nonetheless. Without waiting for the reply to his question, the Comte de Lapérouse turned towards me. He had a big head, with a wig which was too small crammed down on it. His eyes were a shining blue, with an open, direct look that went straight to the heart. His mouth held a natural smile and the dimples at the corner of his lips gave him a slightly juvenile and deceptively candid air. I knew that he had been about my age when he was a Marine Guard aboard *le Formidable*, in 1759. He must therefore have been between thirty-six and thirty-seven years old.

'I am most honoured to have you under my orders, Monsieur Laforest-Dombourg.'

'I understand your reaction perfectly, Sir,' began Ensign Obet, somewhat embarrassed at being of a lower rank than the man he was

62 Translator's note : *Ship's Lieutenant de Lapérouse* : Jean-François de Galaup, comte de Lapérouse (1741 – 1788?). After an illustrious career in the French Navy, Lapérouse led a two-ship scientific and exploratory expedition on a voyage around the world. Having spent some time at the British colony at Botany Bay, the expedition sailed for the South Pacific and was never seen again.

talking to. 'Believe me, I am on your side. Alas, since we last looked at the Lists there has been a change of circumstances against which I am powerless: an announcement from the Secretary of State for the Navy regarding privateering, which the King must have signed only five days ago.'

The Comte de Lapérouse turned to him quickly.

'A Royal announcement? About privateering? A few days ago?'

'I know, it will only be made public in a week or two at the best, which is why I have not yet received a copy. But the Saint-Malo shipowners who, as you know, have plenty of connections, know about it already.'

'Explain, Sir. I fear the worst.'

'It will say that sailors serving on board privateers will have the same benefits as those serving on our war ships, and that volunteers who have served on privateers will no longer have to serve for one or two campaigns aboard the King's ships.'

'What do you mean by 'volunteer'?'

'Precisely! That is the heart of the question! Unfortunately, as I have told you, I have not yet received the text of the declaration, but it is certain that the sailors from here would rather serve on a Saint-Malo privateer than run to the other end of the earth in the service of the King. And the local shipowners, well knowing this, have very quickly started rumours that those serving on privateers will soon be untouchable and out of reach of the Commissioner of the Lists. And since then, what do you expect? The sailors are staying at home so as not to miss their chance. It is not within the law, but I cannot find anyone else and your gunners are ignoring their call-up. They have certainly been bottled up by the less scrupulous shipowners. And that is not all. His Majesty intends to authorise private citizens who fit out privateers of more than ninety-five feet in keel length, to take free of charge from our arsenals as many 12-pounder and 8-pounder cannons as they need.'

'And how will you have enough to equip everybody?'

'I don't know for sure! But it seems it will be a matter of lending some money to those who arrive too late, when there is nothing left in our armouries. However, you can be sure that I will not release anything before I have received official written orders. In any case, I will put what you need to one side. If you could send one of your officers to choose himself, while there is still a choice, that would be better for you.'

'And my gun carriages?'

'They are finished, exactly as your first lieutenant ordered: thirty-six brand new carriages, twenty-six for 12-pounders and ten for 6-pounders. They just need painting.'

I thought I had been forgotten about when the Comte de Lapérouse turned to me.

'Monsieur Dombourg, when will you be coming on board?'

'Immediately, Sir. I need only go and get my chest from the cutter, after which the ship's boat will put me straight aboard *l'Amazone*.'

'Excellent! Wait a moment...Monsieur Obet, could you give me something for writing a note.'

The Ensign got up and offering his chair to the Ship's Lieutenant, put in front of him a sheet of paper and an inkwell. He wanted to cut a new quill for him, but the Comte de Lapérouse had already picked up the one which was there and had started writing.

Having sanded his text, my new commanding officer shook the sheet and folded it in four, then wrote a name on it and handed it to me.

'Before going to get your chest, give this to my boat master. He is waiting for me on the quay right opposite the door. You will tell him to return directly to the frigate, give this note to my first lieutenant and come back here with him. I will be waiting for him.'

I looked at the note. The Ship's Lieutenant had written: *For the attention of Monsieur de Tromenec.*

Once I had carried out my task, I re-joined Couet and his oarsmen, who ferried me back to the cutter. I saluted *le Moucheron* and her crew for the last time and the ship's boat took me, along with my chest, to *l'Amazone*.

*

The Solidor Anchorage, Monday 29th June, morning.

It is a beautiful summer morning. The piercing cries of the swifts mingle with those of the seagulls. The tide is high and has just begun to fall. The start of the ebb is gently turning the stern of the frigate in our direction. From where I am sitting I can make out topmen working at the fore topgallant crosstrees. An officer whom we cannot see is shouting instructions from the after deck. His voice, amplified by a speaking trumpet, reaches us across the surface of the water. The bosun's mate Couet explains that they are installing extra stays, so-called 'false rigging'. He says it is a necessary precaution before putting to sea in a new ship.

'It ain't possible to get things taut. A new rig is always stretchin'! The false rigging is deliberately made with old rope as can stretch. It's temporary, like. Don't look pretty an' it's hard work, but better do that than have the masts fallin' on yer 'ead in the first blow when you puts to sea for the first time.'

There are several craft moored alongside *l'Amazone,* on her landward side. Seeing that, the bosun's mate pushes the tiller to bring us to the other side. The boat passes under the elegant horseshoe-shaped stern. I can see that the rudder has been shipped. It wasn't there yesterday. The chop splashes noisily under the transom. The reflections from the sea throw stars of light which glitter on the windows of the great cabin and the gilding of the taffrail above. We pass into the shadows of the quarter galleries and the starboard topsides. Her flanks are painted in a smoky black, with a wide ochre and yellow stripe highlighting her open gun ports, as yet empty of cannons.

A sentinel in a white infantry uniform with a dark trim and collar, hails us from the quarter deck. I give my name and rank before taking hold of the boarding ladder. Standing up in the ship's boat, the first rung is at the height of the buckle of my belt. There are eight rungs to climb. I feel a new sensation. This isn't even a ship of the line, just a 12-pounder frigate, but after *le Moucheron,* the difference is enormous.

The frigate's main deck is not deserted. I can see a crowd of sailors, unmoving and silent, some sat on their kitbags, other standing. They are in a long line which disappears into the forward bulkhead of the after deck and are watched over by five or six armed soldiers ranged along the sides of the ship.

I take off my hat and turn towards the quarterdeck to salute the King's flag, then I look ahead to my right. That's where I see the officer that I have heard. He is standing a few paces from me, with his back to me, speaking trumpet still in his hand, his head looking up to the foretopmast. He is wearing a working uniform with the epaulettes of a Frigate's Lieutenant.

'The officer of the watch is over there, Sir, if you please,' says the soldier, pointing aft.

I ask the soldier to help *le Moucheron's* boatmen lift up my chest, and head towards the officer of the watch. There is an ordinary civilian dressed like a clerk, no doubt a supernumerary, beside him. The two men are absorbed in a plan that is spread out in front of them on top on the hatch to the main companionway.

*

The Lieutenant lifted his head once I was standing in front of him. He must have been in his forties. Of average height, he had the tanned face of the professional sailor, chestnut hair tied simply behind his neck with a length of twine, a square chin and blue eyes.

'What may I do for you?'

I presented myself and he apologised, with a calm and deliberate voice, for not having welcomed me aboard. He presented himself too. He was called Guillemin. The man with him was the ship's master victualler. The two of them were studying the complex problem of how to arrange everything in the holds, as lighters were soon to arrive bringing the ship's food, water, wine and all the endless gear that a ship putting to sea for the first time must take on board. The Lieutenant invited me to follow him to the great cabin to meet the Chevalier de la Jonquière, Ship's Ensign, the second captain[63].

Once below I saw the rest of the line of sailors that I had seen from the side deck. They were waiting their turn to go into the great cabin. There were two doors leading into it, one on each side of the main companionway, and set into a bulkhead just aft of the mizzen mast. A young lad, his head bare, was calling men from a list he had in his hand. These were going in by the port door, while those ahead of them came out by the starboard door. A sergeant and two fusiliers were keeping an eye on proceedings.

I followed Lieutenant Guillemin in through the starboard door. The great cabin was entered by two symmetrical passageways corresponding to each door. It was a real stateroom, taking up the whole width of the frigate right up to the stern. It was panelled, and the deck planking was overlaid with parquet. The space was well-lit by the five windows set into the transom at one end, and on each side a gun port enclosed with a

63 Translator's note: *second captain*; at that time French warships had two commanders, possibly as a response to the high mortality rates in sea battles.

glazed shutter. The hooks and buckles projecting from the hull around these gun ports were a clear indication that two cannons would soon be installed there.

A Ship's Ensign and a Ship's Lieutenant were sitting, backs to the stern windows, behind a wide table in the middle of the cabin. They were quickly asking each sailor what his skills were and assigning him a role on board. The sailors then had to put their signature, or else their mark, beneath their name, and were then given three months' pay in advance. This had to be done to be able to get a full ship's complement.

The Chevalier de la Jonquière could only have been four or five years older than me. Carefully turned out, he had powdered his wig and put on his dress uniform in order to give an appropriate welcome to the sailors who would form his crew. Despite his youth, he had the assurance of a noble, which had its effect on the sailors, petty officers and middle-ranking officers who had been at sea much longer than he had, but who were below him in the social hierarchy, such as the officer to his left, or such as Lieutenant Guillemin.

'Sir, here is Monsieur Laforest-Dombourg, our Marine Guard,' announced Lieutenant Guillemin.

The Chevalier de la Jonquière signalled to the infantry corporal beside the door to hold back the next sailor, and held out his right hand with a friendly smile.

'Monsieur Laforest-Dombourg, welcome aboard *l'Amazone.* It is an even greater pleasure to welcome you, as my father at one time had your own father under his command, and he always spoke supremely well of him.'

I had not expected such a reception.

'You are surprised?' he continued. 'My father commanded *le Célèbre,* in the Comte de La Motte's squadron, in '57.'

That's when I remembered that Old Touze, at Le Croisic, had talked about this ship, and that my grandfather had said that the Comte de Ternay had told him about a Ship's Captain called Taffanel de la Jonquière, under whom my father had served. I had not made the connection with the Chevalier's name.

'I was still young when I lost my parents,' I said simply.

'I understand...please forgive me. I have had more luck than you in that regard, for although my mother passed away four years ago, my father is still going strong. He is a Squadron Commander and hopes soon to be made a Vice-Admiral.'

He pointed towards the man beside him.

'This is Ensign de Caudam, out third lieutenant. You may already have seen our second lieutenant, Monsieur Restif, up aloft.'

I nodded respectfully to Ensign de Caudam. He had a brick-red face and rough, craggy features, in complete contrast to his second captain.

'Ensign de Caudam, like Lieutenant Guillemin,' continued the Chevalier, 'has already been in the Indian Ocean. Speaking of which, you know that is where we are going? Have you everything necessary? In particular you'll need a light uniform to be able to bear the tropical heat.'

'As far as uniforms go,' I replied, 'I only have this one that I was issued at Brest. I have scarcely worn it since leaving the Hotel Saint-Pierre. I have come from the cutter that is moored just behind you.'

'I know. I saw that in your papers. She's called *le Moucheron*, isn't she? A pretty little ship, very well maintained. Don't worry, I won't ask you what she was up to. I know simply that she was of great importance to Monsieur de La Rozière.'

The Chevalier turned to the rear of the cabin. Two young boys in Volunteer uniforms were sitting quietly on the box seat under the stern windows.

'Monsieur de Thomas, come here, I beg you.'

The youngest of the two Volunteers got up and came towards us. He was possibly thirteen years old. The ribbon knotted behind his neck failed to contain the blond curls floating around his angel face.

'Monsieur de Thomas, this is Monsieur Dombourg. He will be your mess chief, as he is older than you and because he is a Marine Guard. What is more, his father served with honour under the command of your great-uncle alongside the Comte de Lapérouse. You will help him make a list of everything he needs for the voyage. You will show him his quarters and you will then give him a complete tour of *l'Amazone.*'

The Chevalier de la Jonquière had me inscribed on the ship's roll, in Lieutenant de Tromenec's watch. The only Frigate's Lieutenant amongst the officers, he served as the ship's first lieutenant.

'He is not on board at the moment, as he has gone to select our cannons at the Saint-Servan arsenal.'

Little Thomas did me the honour of showing me the ship, after having advised me very conscientiously on everything I would need to make up my sea chest. He knew what he was talking about. With his piping little voice, his look of an innocent angel straight out of a religious painting, he had already seen plenty of things that many adults would never encounter. He had been born at Port-Louis on the Île-de-France. His father was a relative of Monsieur de Taffanel de la Jonquière, my father's old commander. Youngest son of a big family, he had no hope of any inheritance, and so his father was happy to have him enrolled as a Volunteer on the King's ships. He had known storms to the south of Mozambique, seen seals at Simon's Bay at the Cape, tasted turtle soup on Ascension Island, crossed the calms of the Equator, been swept by gales in the Bay of Biscay, and disembarked on a rainy May morning at L'Orient, in a country where he knew not a soul.

L'Amazone was three times longer than *le Moucheron,* but she carried a crew of two hundred and seventy-eight, eight times more than the cutter. Not only did everybody have to be quartered, they had to be able to fight effectively. The set-up of a 12-pounder frigate was the result of a century of reflection on this thorny problem.

The most important and most characteristic part of a frigate was her gun deck, which was partially enclosed and which the sailors called simply 'the deck'. This deck was situated below the poop and fore-castle, and above the lower deck. The holds were below everything, between the lower deck and the keelson. The living space was the lower deck, while on 'the deck' were twenty-six 12-pounder cannons, thirteen to each side, constituting our principal armament.

It was down below, on the lower deck, that the hammocks of the crew and soldiers were hung at night. In fact, there was only ever half the crew sleeping at any one time – those who were off watch. The others had to stay on deck, even if they had nothing to do, as there was no room elsewhere. At the end of the watch they slept in the hammocks still warmed by the sailors they had relieved. Every morning at seven, the hammocks were unhooked and stored in nets alongside the passageways.

The 'false gun room' was the name given to the part of the lower deck situated at the bottom of the main companionway. The officers' cabins were arranged against the hull to port and starboard on each side of this space. These were also the quarters for the Volunteers and myself. It was there that I would hang my hammock at night and take my meals. In fact, while the lieutenants, the surgeon, the master victualler and the chaplain were fed in the great cabin, at the Captain's table, for which the King paid a supplement to cover the cost, the Marine Guards and the Volunteers ate from their mess tins. But we had the right to two ship's boys to serve us, which saved us having to pay for a cook and a steward.

Our complement of officers comprised four lieutenants, of whom one was a full Frigate's Lieutenant, the other three having been commissioned just for the duration of this campaign. Add to that a Marine Guard and three Volunteers and you have a relatively low number of officers. This was an inconvenience from a watch-keeping point of view, but an advantage as far as our quarters were concerned. The Infantry Lieutenant on board was attached to the officer corps, as were the surgeon, the master victualler and the chaplain. The Infantry Lieutenant was called Frémont. He was a young man who was conscientious and very strict in the execution of his service. He was from the Auvergne Infantry. Lieutenant Frémont was serving for the first time aboard a ship of the King and could not hide his disquiet. He had no fear of the eventual dangers of war at sea but was concerned about the pernicious influence that the sailors could have over his elite soldiers.

I had received a hundred and seventy-five pounds, a six-month advance on my pay. This sum would allow me to complete the acquisition of what was lacking from the equipment I had on *le Moucheron.* My uncle, when he had come to see me in February, had given me part of what remained of the King's money, as a bonus. Without that, my advance would probably have been eaten up by the purchases I still had to make: a regulation summer uniform for the tropical heat, a costly spare working uniform, some scarlet silk stockings, linen, utensils and even some tablecloths. As I had plenty of money, I also bought some foodstuffs to improve the usual fare when eating with my future table companions, the Volunteers: spice bread, marmalade, dried fruit and a little barrel of Concarneau sardines. It was my welcome present as their future mess chief. I ordered my uniforms from the military master tailor at the Saint-Malo chateau. I had a little time to spare. The two frigates were to put to sea at the end of the month but as yet they had not received their orders.

The following weeks were devoted entirely to fitting out the ship. The shrouds and stays were tightened up and systematically doubled with 'false' stays. The sails were brought on board and the summer canvas bent onto the yards.

Lieutenants Guillemin and Caudam supervised the loading of ballast and stores. Casks were stowed in the water hold and the wine hold. The food for the voyage was stored and the gear for the various petty officers was packed away in holds and chests. The anchors were shipped and the cannons installed under the careful eye of Lieutenant de Tromenec. They were loaded one by one onto their carriages from the outside of the hull, through a gun port close to the boarding ladder, by means of heavy blocks and tackles suspended from the main yard. The crew then rolled them to their final emplacements which were marked with a number. The shot racks were loaded with their cannon balls. All of this required a great deal of delicate and complicated use of blocks and tackles, sometimes requiring fifty men at a time, during which each of the lieutenants showed his knowledge and seamanship. It also gave an opportunity to check the abilities of the sailors and to make any final corrections to the crew's roles.

Powder was brought aboard on Monday 6th July. While not all our sailors were gunners, most of them were well used to working high in the rigging of a three-masted ship. The able seamen of Saint-Malo, the majority of those on board, had all sailed on deep sea fishing boats and merchantmen. They learned voice and whistle commands very rapidly and were quick to their manoeuvring stations. As far as ship handling was concerned, the main difference between a frigate of war and an equivalent-sized fishing boat or merchant ship was that a frigate had ten times the men, and therefore, in principal, could manoeuvre ten times as quickly. It was a different matter as far as fighting stations were concerned.

When the decks were cleared for combat, I had to be on the covered part of the deck forward of the mainmast. This did not please me much; I would have preferred to be handling the ship, out in the fresh air. But, for the Comte de Lapérouse, a 12-pounder frigate, in time of war, which we were now almost in, was there to carry 12-pounders, and the rest could look after itself! It is true that in normal times I would have all the time in the world, during my watches, to learn the finer points of sailing a square-rigged ship.

My combat station was overseeing the third, fourth and fifth cannons of the gun deck. This meant six cannons in all, counting those to port and starboard, but only one side was ever used at a time. I was under the orders of Ensign de Caudam, who looked after the first two cannons, right forward, and who in addition to me supervised the Volunteer Laborde, who oversaw the sixth, seventh and eighth cannons. Lieutenant de Tromenec was in charge of firing overall, assisted by the master gunner and a master gunner's mate.

While we were moored in the harbour, Lieutenant de Tromenec, from dawn 'til dusk, mercilessly trained in gunnery those who had no particular task connected to the fitting-out of the ship: pull the gun back to the end of its breech rope, swab out, go through the motions of loading, run the gun out, aim…and do it all over again. A 12-pounder on its carriage could weigh more than three thousand pounds. It needed eight men to get this weight moving, by hauling on the tackles under the direction of the gun captain. To those who complained of the boredom of an exercise which consisted of moving around a dead weight for hour after hour, and who maintained that the only worthwhile training was real target practice, Lieutenant de Tromenec replied that *la Belle Poule* had lain alongside her adversary, the *Arethusa,* while the two fired broadsides at each other, from six in the evening until half past eleven. The wind was so light they scarcely had steerage way.

'Under those conditions every shot counts and the advantage goes to the ship that can send her adversary the most weight of metal in the shortest possible time. When evenly matched, it's the rate of fire that makes the difference. That's what gave victory to *la Belle Poule.* And the only way to get that is to move the guns more and more quickly for longer and longer. In any case, if we want to practise live fire, we have to leave the harbour.'

This would soon happen. Gautier, our master pilot, promised us a week of fine weather with a smooth sea and favourable winds – the ideal conditions for getting our apprentice gunners firing. The Comte de Lapérouse asked the Port Commander, and Monsieur Mengaud de la Hage, who as the senior officer had the say over the command of the two frigates, for permission to sail the next day after the morning high tide. *La Gentille* would put to sea the day after for her own trials.

*

Solidor Anchorage, Monday 13th July 1778, morning.

Hammocks have been struck at four. Dawn rises on a cloudless sky. The preparations for putting to sea take the whole of the morning watch. At eight o'clock, the little bell mounted on the rail at the forward end of the quarterdeck rings eight times. We are at slack water at the top of the tide. The current at the Solidor anchorage has already turned to the north-west. The frigate swings gently on her buoy, her bow facing the current and the light land breeze from the south.

The Comte de Lapérouse positions himself just forward of the starboard mizzen chains. He himself will direct the operation for this first time. The Chevalier de la Jonquière stands behind him, a little way away, ensuring that he is not between the Captain and the helmsman. The lieutenants are spread around on the fore and after decks and the main deck. The bosun, standing at the aft end of the starboard side deck, is ready to repeat the orders for the manoeuvre. The Volunteers and I are on the port side, with nothing to do, ready to execute any orders given to us, and also ready to shift our positions smartly should the Captain move, as since time immemorial in the Navy the custom has been that we should always be on the opposite side to the commander or the officer of the watch. Lieutenant Frémont comes and stands beside us. The men silently take up their positions around the ship. In the King's Navy it is forbidden to talk or sing during a manoeuvre. The commanding officer's orders are repeated by the bosun with a speaking trumpet and a whistle.

I keep my eyes and ears as open as possible. It is the first time I have been able to witness close up the functioning of this marvellously complicated machine: a three masted square-rigger. Leaving harbour is made simpler this time by virtue of being on a mooring buoy and therefore not having to raise the anchor. For this reason, the ship's sloop and gig have been brought aboard last night. To leave, the frigate must make a complete turn in a corridor a hundred yards wide. The slightest error would mean her going aground on the military port side, or on the Solidor Bank. In principal, there is little chance of this happening, but *l'Amazone* is a brand-new ship and nobody knows for certain how she will behave. All the same, it is reassuring to know that all our Saint-Malo sailors are experienced in handling this type of rig.

Firstly, a hawser is passed to the ship's boat through the starboard aft gun port but one. This is then passed through the mooring buoy and back to the ship, where the end is taken to the main capstan. As soon as the ship's boat has brought back the line, it is lifted aboard and stacked on top of the other boats.

'Turn the capstan!' orders the Comte de Lapérouse.

The order is repeated by the bosun from the top of the side decks, and by Lieutenant de Tromenec down on the main deck. The sound of the sailors' feet on the deck as they circle round, leaning on the bars of the capstan, reaches us through the hatchway of the main companionway. The frigate starts to turn slowly. The silence is such that one can hear the clicking of the pawls, the creaking of the cable and even the increasing chop on the starboard side of the hull as it is brought beam on to the current. The little bell is struck once, its clear ring making me jump.

'Hold there!'

A blast on the bosun's whistle stops the frigate. Her bowsprit is pointing towards the Solidor quayside.

'Let go topsails and mizzen t'gallant!'

The sailors climb the ratlines and untie the gaskets on the designated sails, letting them drop into their brails, then return to deck in silence.

'Raise and sheet the foretopsail! Brace hard forward to starboard! Raise the outer jib! Sheet the outer jib to starboard! Wheel hard a-port! Raise and sheet the main topsail and mizzen t'gallant sail! Brace back to port!

The orders follow each other rapidly, punctuated with long blasts of the whistle which echo in the calm early morning air. The sailors, bare-footed, silent, haul and pull in unison, ranged in lines along the falls of the halyards, braces and sheets. Blocks are groaning everywhere. The jib flaps briefly and is taken aback. The fore topsail fills. The hull judders.

'Let go the bow line!'

The frigate turns on the spot. The Solidor Tower passes quickly from left to right in front of the bowsprit.

'Let go jib sheets! Let go the stern line! Brace around forward! Square off everywhere! Wheel a-starboard! Sheet the jib to port!'

L'Amazone, suddenly released from her bonds, slips along the Solidor channel, passing closely alongside *le Moucheron.* Lieutenant Chollet is watching us. I wave as we pass. The cutter will sail later to be at the English coast that night. The frigate turns slightly to port, to miss the end of the Solidor bank, leaving the Mercière withy to starboard. She heads first for the Petit Bé to avoid the still-submerged Rance Rock. The foresail and the mainsail are un-brailed and sheeted home as we pass in front of the Cité fort. The master pilot Gautier has remained standing beside the helmsman. He once again sends one of the Auvergne Infantry fusiliers to the bell: two bells already! The t'gallant sails and the mizzen topsail are unfurled, hauled up and sheeted. The entrance to the port of Saint-Malo passes slowly to starboard. All the decks are spread with ropes, the falls of the halyards, braces and sheets that have been hauled on. The sailors and petty officers are coiling them neatly and hanging them on the pin rails along the bulwarks and around the masts.

The master pilot takes the wheel and steers us well clear of the rocky shore of the Petit Bé, avoiding the Frogs rocks, which are also still entirely covered at this state of the tide. He then steers due north to leave the Grande Conchée fortress to port. The land breeze eases and then drops completely. The frigate bobs about for a while in front of the huge walls of the fortress. The little bell strikes eight bells. It is midday. The sun shines straight down onto the deck planking between the shadows of the sails. The smell of tossed seaweed rises from the depths. The wind then comes in from the west, rising to a fresh breeze. The Captain has the tacks of the lower sails brought to port, the lee braces hardened, all the jibs and staysails set, the spanker raised, and everything sheeted to starboard. *L'Amazone* gradually picks up speed, her deck leans to starboard and the water starts to sing along her sides. The blocks squeak, the ropes stretch and vibrate, the halyards whistle, the sails billow out, noisy and full of wind, straining their sheets and bringing the whole rig to life.

'Brace a little more!' orders the Captain.

The Grande Conchée falls away astern. A long wake stretches out over the sea behind us, showing the course we have traced. The white flag snaps at the peak, right aft of the spanker. The frigate keeps accelerating as she goes. I never had such an impression of power when on *le Moucheron.*

'Could you give me your opinion, Captain?' asks the master pilot Gautier. 'She seems to me to be a slightly more frisky than *la Belle Poule,* but she responds more quickly too.'

The master pilot, as well as being from Saint-Malo, is also one of the permanently enlisted petty officers. He has been to the Île-de-France and the Indies with the Chevalier de Ternay at the same time as our Captain and knows *la Belle Poule* very well.

'We manoeuvred with the use of a stern fast, so it's too early to draw conclusions. But we will soon see what she's made of,' replies the Comte de Lapérouse, grasping the spokes of the wheel in both hands.

His face is glowing. His eyes sparkle with an intense blue when he raises his head to look at the sails. I cross the quarterdeck to the leeward side, as Naval etiquette demands, and find myself beside the Chevalier de la Jonquière. He leans towards me and murmurs:

'Have you seen how happy he is! I am pleased for him. Thank God! He was so sad when I first met him.'

I dare not ask why the Comte de Lapérouse had been 'so sad'. It is neither the time nor the place. The bell rings seven times. The men of the port watch go off to get their meal before taking the afternoon watch. I have to do the evening watch from six until midnight. The routine of life at sea imposes itself on the brand-new frigate.

*

The main purpose of this cruise, which lasted a week, was to give everybody some gunnery practice. Initially, we fired one cannon at a time, to teach the gun captains how to aim, and to show the men what happened when you fired a cannon in earnest. It was no longer the great inert mass that they had spent hours moving around in port. Its recoil could be fatal. It was necessary to check that nobody was caught behind it. When the linstock was brought to the touch-hole, the three thousand pounds of the gun jumped back in its breech ropes with an explosion that split your eardrums, a thick grey-white smoke clouded the gun deck and the acid smell of the powder caught your throat. It was worse when we moved on to firing broadsides on command: the whole side in one go. We exercised by mooring a weighted barrel with a flag on it, which gave a target to aim at as the ship manoeuvred around it. The Comte de Lapérouse could now see that his frigate, although in many ways the equal of *la Belle Poule,* both to windward and downwind, went about more nimbly and more surely than the latter.

We returned to Saint-Malo on 17th July. The Comte de Lapérouse had his gig launched and went to get his orders. When he came back, he assembled the whole crew and told us that on the tenth of the month the King had written to the Admiral of France, ordering him to *attack the vessels of the King of England and to give commissions as privateers to those of his subjects who asked for them.* The Captain also told us that the Comte d'Orvilliers and his fleet had left Brest on 7th July on the order of the King. And, on the 8th, two of our frigates, *la Curieuse* and *l'Iphigénie,* had chased and captured an English corvette in the entrance to the Channel. We were now properly at war.

The following days were spent in short exercises in the mouth of the Rance and in perfecting our gunners. At the end of the fourth week of July, Monsieur Mengaud de la Hage received the order to prepare himself for a cruise of several months, with *la Gentille* and *l'Amazone* under his command. We replenished our stores. Everybody was required to stay on board. On the 26th we were joined in the harbour by the cutter *la Guêpe*, who was to be part of our little division. This vessel was the old *Walrus*, on which the unfortunate Elizabeth Lesueur had been captured. The cutter had been completely re-rigged and now belonged to the King. She was commanded by an auxiliary officer, a Saint-Malo man, whose name I have forgotten.

Monsieur Mengaud de la Hage sent us his new signal book, which the Comte de Lapérouse asked me to copy for the officers. I made ten little notebooks held together with sailmaker's twine. I used pastels to colour the flags, so that they would not be destroyed by sea water, and illustrated the covers with a drawing of *l'Amazone* under full sail. The Captain complimented me on this work and was so pleased with it that he asked me to make another copy for his friend Mengaud. On this one, I of course drew *la Gentille* with her white flag on a staff at the stern.

11

Monsieur Mengaud de la Hage got his orders on Friday 31st July. We were to cruise the Channel and the North Sea until October, in order to reconnoitre English waters and to capture or destroy any English vessels that we met, whether warships or merchantmen. It was specified in our instructions that we should leave fishing boats alone. That was a particular wish of the King. At the end of this cruise, the division was to return to Brest. Our two frigates would then be copper-bottomed in preparation for our voyage to India. As for the cutter, she would rejoin the Comte d'Orvilliers' fleet.

We also learned that the Comte d'Orvilliers had returned to harbour at Brest with his fleet, after having faced Keppel's thirty ships off Ushant the previous Monday. Both sides had fired vigorously for three hours. We had a hundred and sixty-three killed and five hundred and seventeen wounded, including the old Comte de Chaffault. This Battle of Ushant, as people were starting to call it, was by no means the decisive victory some would have liked. In truth we had not beaten the English, but they had buckled in a battle of squadrons, which was something. That had not happened since the great Tourville[64]! Coming

64 Translator's note: *Tourville*: Anne-Hilarion de Costentin, Comte de Tourville (1642 – 1701), French naval commander under Louis XIV. He inflicted several defeats on the English and Dutch Navies, notably at the Battle of Cape St. Vincent.

so soon after *la Belle Poule's* battle, this half-victory was a surprisingly heartening boost for the French sailors.

The Chevalier de la Jonquière and Lieutenant de Tromenec were nonetheless somewhat put out that their comrades had been in action while they had been confined to the Rance anchorage, waiting for orders. As for me, I was of course thinking of Vernon. According to the accounts published in the broadsheets, the French fleet had tacked at the last moment in order to bisect Keppel's ships in reverse order. It was therefore the rear-guard squadron, the blue squadron led by *le Saint-Esprit,* which had joined battle first. My friend, in his capacity as Flag Guard, must have had his baptism of fire on the quarterdeck of a ship at the head of the line, that is to say in the most dangerous spot, as that is where warships direct their first broadsides simultaneously.

The Comte de Lapérouse, for his part, consoled himself by thinking about our eventual departure for India. The Chevalier de Ternay had sent a letter to our two commanders along with their orders. The King had it in mind to give him a seventy-four gun ship, as well as a sixty-four. The Chevalier de Ternay hoped to take them himself, before the end of the year, to the Île-de-France where they would be copper-bottomed. At the same time, the details of our mission over there were starting to become clearer. It was no longer a matter of sending us to the Malabar coast in order to support land-based operations there. The talk was of us destroying the English trade with India and China.

On Saturday 1st August *la Gentille* fired the departure cannon and at midday signalled to us to weigh anchor. The wind was blowing hard from the south-east. Once we had passed the Porte rocks, we set all sail, pushing ourselves to nine knots. In the evening we took our departure from the Île de Bréhat and set a course to the west-north-west to start our cruise.

Monsieur Mengaud de la Hage's plan was firstly to spend two or three weeks patrolling the entrance to the English Channel and the Saint George's Channel[65]. After that we would go up through the Irish Sea and around the north of Scotland into the North Sea. We sailed in a column for the whole night. On Sunday 2nd August our three ships

65 Translator's note; *Saint George's Channel*: the stretch of water linking the Celtic Sea to the Irish Sea.

took up a line formation, fifteen to eighteen miles wide. *la Gentille* was at the port end, *l'Amazone* to starboard, both regulating their speed to that of *la Guêpe*, sailing between the two to relay signals.

Towards nine o'clock we were sixty miles south-west of the Scillies. The cutter relayed a signal to us from *la Gentille* to chase two ships she had seen under our lee. The wind was from the east and the ships we were pursuing were heading north-north-east, close-hauled. We piled on sail and by eleven could see them clearly from the deck of *l'Amazone*. They were a three-masted corvette and a brig. *La Gentille* was already manoeuvring under the stern of the corvette to give her a broadside, but the two ships quickly lowered their flags and hove to. The corvette was a letter of marque of five hundred tons carrying fourteen 12-pounder cannons. She had come from Jamaica with a cargo of rum, sugar, madeira, cocoa and logwood. The brig was four hundred and fifty tons and was loaded with cases of sugar from Havana and wine from Porto. Within three weeks we had taken a dozen English merchantmen in all, of various sizes, from cutter to frigate. The cargos were of varying value. One of the cutters was loaded with cork, while the frigate was carrying three thousand bails of Pernambuco cotton, a thousand cowhides, and above all, two hundred elephant tusks, one of which was five feet long. We had not seen a single enemy warship.

We now had twelve prizes in our wake, which was hampering our ability to manoeuvre. We had put a third of our crews aboard them. If it was purely a matter for them, the Comte de Lapérouse and Monsieur Mengaud de la Hage would have put all the prisoners aboard the frigate and sunk the other ships, to leave our hands free should we meet a warship. But that would have been disastrous for our Malouin sailors, who from petty officers to ship's boys had begun to calculate their share according to the new rules issued by the King: a third of the sale value to the Disabled Seamen's Fund, two thirds to the crews. That was all that was talked about on the gun deck during mealtimes. By the end of three weeks our commanders thought we had done enough. We took our convoy, which was now a burden, to Morlaix harbour, under the shelter of its defensive forts. We kept just one fast schooner which would sail astern of *la Guêpe* in our cruising formation. She was put in charge of one of *la Gentille's* lieutenants.

Lieutenant Restif, because of his previous experience as a Saint-Malo privateer, was left at Morlaix with a handful of sailors to do what was necessary, together with the port Naval authorities, for the ransoming or exchanging of prisoners and the sale of the prizes.

Our two frigates, along with the cutter and the schooner, sailed north once again. Once again we saw no warships; it seemed that all the King of England's ships had gone off to the other side of the Atlantic.

As for me and the Volunteers, our Captain supervised our instruction personally. He was not happy simply for the master pilot to give us lessons in navigation. He also had us climbing about the rigging like the ship's boys and sent us up one at a time onto the t'gallant sail yards, to see what happened. He was happy to see us handing and reefing the sails along with the sailors.

The Comte de Lapérouse was an affable man. He seldom got angry and was very patient. But that did not stop him being demanding, as every good sailor should be. He applied to the letter, and even beyond, the instructions given by the King and his Minister: *the Captain will make sure that everything possible is done to ensure cleanliness and maintain the good health of the crew. He will make sure that he often has the decks cleared and will see to it that the call to action stations is carried out with the same care and precision as if it were for actual combat.* Usually, these exercises finished with gunnery practice. When we chased merchantmen, one of the second captains would take any interesting documents off them: signals, charts, logbooks, nautical instructions. The English crews were then transferred to the schooner and the abandoned ship used for target practice, as we could no longer weigh ourselves down with prizes.

This new way of doing things was accepted wholeheartedly by our Malouins. They even developed a taste for it and were keen to train seriously, given our future campaign. They had by now learned that our mission in the Indian Ocean was to 'destroy English trade with the Indies and China'. This word association – *destroy, Indies, China* – had our sailors' eyes shining as if they had been shown the Golconda[66] diamonds. When the petty officers were eating in the gun room, they often asked the master pilot Gautier to tell them about the *Indiamen,* as the English called the ships of their East India Company.

---

66 Translator's note: *Golconda*: Fortified city of the Moghul Empire known for its mines that yielded some of the world's biggest diamonds, including the koh-i-noor.

'They have two-deck ships carrying 24-pounders on the lower gun deck and 12-pounders on the upper gun deck. Somewhat like a ship of the line with fifty cannons. What's more, they often paint them like Royal Navy ships and even add false cannons made of wood to discourage pirates. But they are not really that dangerous! Their crews are too small to be able to handle all their guns at once. And often the space between the cannons is taken up with bails of merchandise as there is not enough space in the holds for all the cargo. An Indiaman is well within the reach of our two frigates combined, especially if our gunners keep on training as they are.'

'And the cargo? Tell us about the cargo!' There the master pilot took on a falsely disinterested tone.

'Oh…coffee…pepper…indigo…porcelain…silk. And diamonds, of course, and barrels filled with piasters; everything you usually find in these countries.'

There was only a small bulkhead between the gun room and our quarters, and the master pilot had a voice that could be heard from one end of the deck to the other. It wasn't long before his words were circulating around the ship. That was why our Malouins had no objection to sinking brigs full of dried fruit in order to improve their gunnery.

With us, the master pilot talked above all of the voyage we would make from Brittany to India. He explained that the return route, the one that young de Thomas had told us about, was quite different from the one we would take on the way out.

'When you leave, you have to think about the monsoon season over there. That's really important for ships that want to go straight to the Coromandel Coast, to Pondicherry, or to Chandernagore in the Bay of Bengal. There are also those that want to go to Canton, passing by the Sunda Strait. People leave from the end of October until the beginning of April. For us, that will be less important, as we will go quietly to the Mascarene Islands. When I say 'quietly' it's just a manner of speaking. First, we have to avoid getting trapped in the Bay of Biscay by a storm from the south-west. Once out of there we go on to pick up Madeira and the Canaries, then on into the trade winds: a strong and regular wind in which you can sail all day long without having to touch a rope. You have to make the most of those, as afterwards, around the Equator, there are variable winds with lots of calms. Men have spent weeks revolving on the spot with the sails stuck to the masts. Then suddenly they are hit by a squall coming out of nowhere with no warning, which can knock the masts by the board. To escape that, the best way is to go towards the coast of Brazil to cross the Line well to the west of Ascension Island. Then you go south to the thirtieth parallel. There you catch the big winds from the west and you head off due east to pass the southern cape of Africa. You don't see it, though, as you keep well to the south. The seas there are enormous. Sometimes the swell is as high as the masts. It's the home of the albatross, a giant seabird that follows us, mocking us poor men on our mad boats. You tear along with the wind dead astern, a devilish wind, and you have to keep a fair bit of canvas on to stop the ship being submerged by the huge waves coming up behind. You mustn't be going at less than eleven knots or you're done for. So then, with our exposed helm, we can't have a weakling at the wheel, I'll tell you that! If he can't keep the ship on course…in that part of the world you'll soon get caught beam on, and with the canvas you're carrying and the speed you're going, you risk going under, and then! Holy Mary! You're sure to be clinking glasses with old Father Neptune! Luckily, this voyage is not too long. Once you reckon you're at fifty-five degrees longitude east of Paris, you turn north-east to get to the Mascarenes.'

One time I asked him whether he had met anybody at Chandernagore who had known my father.

'I don't know Chandernagore. You should ask the Captain. He's been there.'

I made up my mind to ask the Comte de Lapérouse about this once this cruise is over.

On 13th October, towards the end of the afternoon, our little division anchored in Brest harbour, alongside the main fleet, having left our prizes at Morlaix. I was off watch. I spent a while doing nothing, leaning on the starboard rail of the quarterdeck, contemplating Brest. The wind had fallen. A coaster, under sail, was going slowly into the river in front of the Horseshoe. The calm waters of the Penfeld were already in the shadow of the high walls of the Chateau, whose top was still bathed in bright light. The days had started to shorten. I remembered that I had left this port in a little coasting lugger in July 1777, scarcely more than a year ago.

The duty watch, spread through the rigging and the decks, was finishing off putting everything in order after anchoring. Lieutenant Frémont was checking on his men and giving them their instructions for our time in harbour. The big ship's bell on the foredeck rang the Angelus for supper. The Comte de Lapérouse's valet came to tell me that the Captain was expecting me in the great cabin. That morning I had made a request to see him. I was hoping that he might be able to give me some interesting details about my father's last voyage to Chandernagore. I still thought that something bad had happened over there, involving my father, Flaharn and the Marquis de Kersalaun.

*

Brest Harbour, Tuesday 13th October 1778, evening.

The reflections of the evening light on the calm water of the harbour illuminate the great cabin. The stewards have not yet laid the table but they have lit wax candles in silver chandeliers, giving a celebratory atmosphere to this end of campaign meal in harbour. The chaplain is deep in thought, leaning on the port cannon, breviary in hand. The officers, sat on benches around the table, wait for supper, chatting in low voices so as not to disturb the Captain, who is reading, sitting alone on the aft window box, his back against the stern windows. Through their panes I can see the ships of the fleet anchored in three columns. There are about thirty of them, plus twelve frigates. It is an imposing force, although this is hard to realise, lost as it is in the huge Brest harbour.

Seeing me arrive, the Comte de Lapérouse closes his book and lays it on the bench.

'Sit down, I beg you,' he says.

He turns his head towards me and studies me for a long time. His smile has gone. I start to feel embarrassed.

'You resemble him a lot...physically at least. It is surprising! It is the first time I have really noticed it. I never saw your father again after our time holed up on the Vilaine. He went off with the India Company, as First Mate to Marion Dufresne. That was in December 1760. Eighteen years already! Each of us was taken up with his ships and we had no opportunity to meet again. That is the sailor's lot. But we continued to write to each other. I was interested in his experiences navigating beyond the Capes. In August 1771 he wrote to me at Brest.

He had decommissioned his ship at L'Orient and was going to have a long leave, as the India Company had stopped trading. He invited me to come and see him at Port-Louis. He wanted to talk about his last voyage and some plans he wanted to share with me.'

I hold my breath.

'Do you know what these plans were, Sir?'

'No. He didn't say anything else and I let it lie. Also I didn't get the letter in time since I wasn't in Brest. I had left on 1st May as a lieutenant on *la Belle Poule.* The same *la Belle Poule* that was so much talked about in June. I found your father's letter when I got back to Brest, in mid-October. I would have liked to have gone to Port-Louis, but Monsieur d'Orves had relinquished his ship to the King and the Comte de Ternay took her immediately, to fit her out for the Île-de-France. I went with him. I was a Ship's Ensign, acting as a first lieutenant. Moreover, I had two tasks: decommissioning one ship and fitting out the other. In any case, I didn't have the time to go to L'Orient. Particularly as the ship was being copper-bottomed and the Comte de Ternay had asked me to oversee what was a new technique in France. I had no idea your father had been recalled to Brest by the Navy. He had been ordered to take command of a King's corvette, *la Fouine.* This ugly little ship was to go to the Saint-Domingue station with a light division commanded by Monsieur de Monteil, the brother of your commander at the Marine Guards. We were both in Brest at the same time for three weeks, without knowing it, he aboard his ship and I at Pontaniou, supervising the work on *la Belle Poule.* Monteil's division sailed during the second week of November 1771. *La Belle Poule* left Brest for the Île-de-France in February 1772. Just before we left, we heard about a despatch from Monsieur de Monteil, saying he was very concerned about *la Fouine.* His division had been hit with a bad storm and atrocious seas just after leaving Brest, and had lost sight of *la Fouine* during the second night of the storm. I only came back from the Indies last year.'

'The master pilot said you had been at Chandernagore. Did you hear any talk about my father over there? From the Governor perhaps?'

'I was in Chandernagore from September to December 1773. About five years ago. Your father had spent the winter there, with his India Company ship *le Triton,* from September 1770 until the beginning of January 1771. And you're right: Monsieur Chevalier, the Governor of

Chandernagore, asked me if I had any news about the outcome of some affair that indirectly involved your father. He even said some rather disagreeable things about it, I remember. He could not have known that we were friends.'

'He talked about a duel, I assume?'

'Not exactly, but something like that. He accused your father of having helped a mercenary escape. A man who was probably guilty of killing an Indian Prince and of trying to kill a man called Flaharn. In fact, it was this Flaharn himself who made the accusations. I have never met Flaharn, but I know he has made a reputation in the Navy as something of a schemer, especially when he was the Comte d'Estaing's righthand man when he was the commander at Brest. But the Chandernagore Governor, Monsieur Chevalier, himself seemed to think highly of him. He never doubted a word he said.'

'What exactly did he say about Flaharn?'

'You know him?'

'Yes, in fact I know him very well. I think he is a dangerous man.'

'Dangerous? Really? It's very possible. I have never met him personally. He had arrived in Chandernagore in 1770. According to the Governor Chevalier, he had said he had been in the service of an Indian Prince. His contract had terminated and he wanted to return to France. But it was too late in the season. He had to wait for the next ship from the India Company, which wasn't expected until September. By chance, this was *le Triton,* commanded by your father. Flaharn stayed at the Governor's residence for six months, along with a Hindu who was with him and whom he was taking with him to France. At that time, Governor Chevalier was very interested in what was going on in Hindustan. He was trying to contact some Frenchmen who were there, in particular a Monsieur Madec, and a mercenary called Sombre. It seems that Flaharn knew everything about Hindustan, and the Governor spent many hours talking about it with him.'

'And what about these accusations?'

'Well, if I am to believe what the Governor said, Flaharn and his Indian companion went aboard *le Triton* at the last moment, the day before she sailed. The next morning, after the Company's ship had left its mooring in the river at dawn, the Indian who was with Flaharn arrived at the Governor's residence with porters carrying Flaharn on a stretcher. He was unconscious and covered in blood. When he came round, he said that he had come across a Frenchman who had embarked at Chandernagore without telling the Governor. This Frenchman had attacked Flaharn without warning, to stop the latter from denouncing him to the authorities on the Île-de-France. According to Flaharn, this Frenchman, who he said was called Vayu Sahib by the Indians, had seduced the daughter of a Raja and run off with her after having killed her father. The Governor was therefore squarely accusing your father of helping a criminal by not delaying his departure from Chandernagore. It is true that some people at Chandernagore told me that Flaharn had challenged this Vayu Sahib to a duel and that he had been beaten fairly. Vayu Sahib therefore had a legitimate defence, in that he had left thinking that he had killed Flaharn. But the Governor did not want to believe this version because, as he told me, if you had seen the kind of man Flaharn was, you could never believe that he could have been beaten other than by unfair means. This point of view always seemed a bit far-fetched to me. Especially as the Governor had proposed writing a damning report on Vayu Sahib and your father, but Flaharn had declined, saying that it was not necessary and that he had faith in the justice system of his country. Eventually, Flaharn and his Indian left a year later, aboard the last India Company ship to leave Chandernagore.'

'The man you call Vayu Sahib was the Marquis of Kersalaun,' I said.

'Kersalaun! Ronan Avelus de Kersalaun, who was an officer in the Saintonge regiment?'

'Yes, the same person who served with you at the Battle of Quiberon Bay.'

'And how do you know all this?'

'I had heard about the Marquis of Kersalaun from a former bosun on *le Formidable,* and a man called Kerscao had told my uncle, the Chevalier de Kermean, that Vayu Sahib was his Indian name. You doubtless know this Kerscao, as last year he came back from the Île-de-France with you aboard *la Belle Poule.*'

'I do remember, yes, but I never spoke with him. The Comte de Ternay advised me to steer clear of him, as he was a fantasist. But if this Vayu Sahib really was Kersalaun, he could well have beaten Flaharn in a regular duel. I remember that the Marquis was excellent with both epée and sabre. I never saw anyone last more than two minutes with him.'

'Kerscao had indeed talked to my uncle about the murder of a Raja, from Dig, I seem to remember,' I added. 'But according to Kerscao, the killers were Flaharn himself and his Indian accomplice.'

'If this really is Kersalaun, then I can see why your father took his side. He was indebted to him as the Duc d'Aiguillon had deferred the Marquis's exchange on account of him. That's why Kersalaun had resigned from the army.'

'Yes, I know all about that,' I said. 'It's all because of an incident to do with a scalping.'

The Comte de Lapérouse cannot hide his surprise.

'Really? You know this story?'

'It was Captain Le Meur, the commander of *le Moucheron*, who told it to me. He was in Louisbourg when it happened. What I still don't understand is how they couldn't find an officer who spoke the Canadian Indian dialect better than my father. After all, he had been in the King's Navy for a number of years, while some of the army officers, like Monsieur de Bougainville, for example, must have known the savages' customs better than a naval officer.'

My commander does not reply immediately. He shakes his head gently.

'In that case you don't actually know everything. What you don't know was your parents' big secret. There were only two of us whom they shared it with; myself and Monsieur Taffanel de la Jonquière, my second captain's father.'

The Comte de Lapérouse let out a long sigh.

'If I had known, I could have kept it secret, as your parents did. Monsieur de la Jonquière would have said nothing, and would have helped me not to say anything to anybody. But now it's too late.'

*

At that interesting point in our conversation, we were interrupted by the Chevalier de la Jonquière. He came politely to remind the Captain that dinner had been on the table for a good while and that it was starting to go cold. I took my leave, excusing myself from the officers, and went down to the false gun room, where my Volunteer shipmates, showing more sense than their officers, had got the master cook to keep our food hot.

12

We spent the day of 14th October at anchor. A little lighter came out to take off our remaining gunpowder.

Towards eleven, a boat left one of the fleet's ships and passed under our stern. It was the pinnace from *le Saint-Esprit* and was going ashore. A Marine Guard, sat in the stern with the passengers, asked our officer of the watch, Lieutenant de Caudam, if Monsieur Laforest-Dombourg was on board. It was the Chevalier Vernon des Aulnes, who had come to visit me. Once I had embraced him, I looked at him closely. I had the impression that he had grown a little, but above all he had taken on an air of solidity and confidence. And his voice had changed. I suggested he stay to eat with the Volunteers. The Comte de Lapérouse gave his permission. I took my friend down into our quarters, where I presented him to our shipmates.

Vernon told us that *le Saint-Esprit* was preparing to leave harbour the next day, along with *le Conquérant,* a seventy-four gun ship, and *le Solitaire,* a sixty-four. They would be cruising for a month.

'The Comte de Lamotte-Picquet is in a good mood again,' said Vernon, 'but we had some difficult moments.'

He lowered his voice.

'I think that he is very pleased to have got rid of His Highness the Duc de Chartres.'

'Were relations between the Comte de Lamotte-Picquet and the Duc de Chartres as bad as that?' I asked.

'At first, no. The Duc de Chartres got on well with everybody. He was friendly to the officers. He knew how to talk to the sailors. It was the incident of the manoeuvre that went wrong that ruined everything, along with the punishments that the King wants to hand out to his commanders who make mistakes in battle.'

'You are talking about the Battle of Ushant?'

'Of course! It was the only thing people were talking about in August and September. Especially in Paris and Versailles, it seems, if one is to believe the papers. Well, not about the battle itself, of course. All the arguments were about the Duc de Chartres and Captain de Trémignon[67], who was court-martialled and acquitted. Nonetheless, three Captains were demoted on the King's orders!'

'We don't know anything about all that! We arrived last night and so far nobody has gone ashore. When we left Saint-Malo we heard that there had been a battle between Keppel's fleet and yourselves, and that it was a victory for us. Is that not the case?'

'Oh yes! We won. There is no doubt about that. But not as well as we would have wished.'

'Could you tell us about it in detail, Sir?' asked Volunteer Laborde.

Vernon looked around. We were no longer alone. Our neighbours the petty officers, who were preparing to eat in the gun room, had heard through the bulkhead that we were going to hear about the Battle of Ushant, and had left their table to come and listen.

'Speak freely,' I said. 'We all really want to know what happened in the battle.'

My friend bit his lip. The presence of the petty officers was making him nervous. He could not say any old thing in front of them. Ship's Captains had been punished, and a Prince of the blood had become the target of rumours and debate. It was all very delicate.

'Just try and give us the facts,' I said. 'The facts and nothing else. You can tell us later about the Duc de Chartres,' I added quietly.

Vernon gave me a knowing look and began to talk.

---

67 Translator's note: *Captain de Trémignon*: Commander of the 64-gun ship *l'Aléxandre,* part of the Comte d'Orvilliers' White Squadron during the Battle of Ushant.

'We left Brest on Wednesday 8th July and were patrolling between Ushant and the Scillies. Good weather, at first, with scarcely enough wind to get us moving. On the Friday it was blowing a gale from the west, with a big sea and poor visibility because of the rain squalls. At dawn on Monday 27th, same weather with a big sea, rain squalls from the south-west, under nothing but reefed topsails, we caught sight of the enemy fleet. It was in three columns, sailing the same course as us, nine miles to leeward on our beam.'

'Your Admiral judged it well, then,' said the master pilot Gautier. 'You fell in with them again, still with the windward advantage, after three days of sailing by dead reckoning. That's not bad!'

'We wore round to head towards them and immediately took up a line of battle. Then we completely lost them from view in a huge rain shower. When they came back into sight, they were just astern of us. They had all tacked in the squall and were chasing us. The ships of their rear guard were sailing more closely to the wind than us, and more quickly too. Clearly, they wanted to overtake us, passing us simultaneously to port and to starboard. When I say 'we' I mean our blue squadron, which was the rear guard, and which would have been caught between two lines of fire. The only way to stop this was to turn round and face them. The Admiral signalled for us to all tack together.'

'Tack through the wind in a big sea?'

'The waves were steep and it was blowing hard.'

'My God!' said the master gunner Morvant. 'Did you manage it first time?'

'All except *l'Artésien,* a sixty-four, the last of the white squadron, so the first in reverse order. She made it eventually and the Admiral signalled us all to ease up a little and form a proper line.'

Vernon used his hands, one behind the other, to show the ships slipping into line to starboard.

'Just like that! So we all formed a line again, with *l'Artésien* not far behind *le Saint Esprit.* At that moment, the head of the English line was already level with us and she crossed eighty or a hundred yards to leeward, on the opposite tack. The gunfire started. *L'Intrépide* opened fire first, but I have to say that we got a lot more, as the enemy held back their first broadsides for *le Saint-Esprit*, as she was flying the squadron commander's pennant.'

'Was it hard?' asked little de Thomas.

'For me, it was the first time, and I think in that case it's always hard. It shook me, I can tell you! I had never before seen men killed before my eyes. The English were to leeward and had kept their lower gunports open, while we had had to close ours because we were heeling heavily to starboard. Luckily, our manoeuvre had forced them to change their plans in a hurry, and they were a bit disordered. And that's when we had the incident that the Duc de Chartres is being blamed for.'

Vernon suddenly went quiet, having seen Lieutenants Guillemin and de Tromenec coming down the stairs to their cabins to wait for the officers' mealtime. They had stopped to listen at the foot of the main companionway. My friend began to bite his lip again, realising that he had forgotten to keep silent on this delicate subject, the most contentious part of his story.

'Carry on, I beg you, Monsieur Marine Guard,' said our first lieutenant. 'We went ashore last night and that was the only thing people were talking about. But every version was different. We are happy to have the luck of meeting an eyewitness. And,' he added, seeing Vernon glance at the petty officers, 'this matter concerns us all and I'm sure the petty officers are as interested as we are. So, speak freely.'

'Well, Sir,' said Vernon, taking up his story again, 'it happened like this... We had already sailed past the first two English squadrons and we saw that as we arrived at the tail of their second squadron, *l'Intrépide,* ahead of us, had stopped firing completely. There was a hole in their line! Their third squadron had not managed to catch up. The Comte de Lamotte-Picquet came up to me and told me to keep an eye out for any signal from the Admiral. Then he began to explain to the Duc de Chartres that he had to bear off and charge into the gap, to cut the English line. He was getting ready to make the manoeuvre, without even waiting for the signals. The gentlemen in the Duc's entourage then intervened. They said that a Prince of the blood could not be exposed to such danger and that the Comte de Lamotte-Picquet did not have the right to make the manoeuvre without being sure of having received a signal for it. And they all crowded around me to watch me decode the Admiral's signals. Contrary to what some people are saying, we could see them perfectly well. As we had the windward advantage, the smoke from our cannons was being carried away immediately, towards the English, so we could see clearly along the whole length of our line. When the signal to cross to leeward of the English rear guard had been sent, I passed it on straight away, but we had already lost time and the manoeuvre had to be explained once again to the Duc de Chartres. The moment was lost because of this. We were already in danger of passing their rear guard to windward. The firing began again with a vengeance. I don't know whether any of you know the Comte de Lamotte-Picquet. He gets angry very easily! He threw his hat and wig on the deck and trampled on them. After that, he never mentioned it again. It is something he would like to forget, I think. He feels guilty, without a doubt.

'And the Duc de Chartres?'

'He didn't say anything. He was calm under fire, on the quarterdeck, but I think things happened too quickly for him. I am only a Marine Guard and a novice, but to decide to cut the enemy line like that, right in the middle of a battle, needs a quick and sure vision that can only come with experience, I imagine. There's no need to wait for the Admiral's orders. It has to be done immediately. The Comte de Lamotte-Picquet is capable of that, but not the Duc de Chartres. He was not experienced enough. He should have let the Comte de Lamotte-Picquet get on with it without posing questions. But the man notionally in command of the division was still the Duc de Chartres. And when we had passed the end of the English line, the Duc's courtiers insisted that the Comte de Lamotte-Picquet go alongside *la Bretagne* to ask the Admiral to repeat his orders. As if we hadn't been able to understand them, d'you see? The Comte de Lamotte-Picquet kept quiet but he was fuming for days. The Admiral then ordered us to wear ship and put ourselves to leeward of the English, but the problem with that position is that you can't go on the attack, you have lost the initiative, especially against the faster English ships. You have to wait until the enemy wants to come down on you before re-joining battle. And they didn't want to do it.'

'And you say that there have been punishments?' asked Lieutenant Tromenec.

'Not immediately. When we returned here the first time everyone was very happy. The Duc de Chartres went to Paris to announce the victory and was treated like a hero, so people said. When he came back to Brest, in August, we put to sea with twenty-eight ships. We came back after a month and it was then that we heard that the King was asking for punishments. He had the commanders of three vessels demoted.

'And what about the Duc de Chartres?'

'I don't think that one can punish a Prince of the blood. I think I heard that he had left the Navy to take up a command in the Army.'

*

At dawn on Thursday 15th October, we began to get our number one anchor aboard. We then towed the frigates into the Penfeld with the ships' boats, before the midday high tide. It was cool, with a wind still from the north.

We tied up the two frigates at the quay in front of the main arsenal in order to get them ready to be careened. The cannons were taken off, along with everything movable. All the false gunports were sealed. Everything else was secured, especially the stove and galley. A bulwark of tarred planks was erected on the side decks to seal the main deck. The t'gallant masts and topmasts were sent down. Then we moved the ships to the other shore, to the Recouvrance side, just below the Pontaniou dry docks.

Careening is a matter of forcing a hull over until its keel is exposed. This is done alongside a pontoon specially constructed for the operation, with strong capstans, derricks and tackles. Scaffolding was erected beside the frigates, as it was not just a matter of careening *l'Amazone* and *la Gentille;* they were also to be copper-bottomed.

Originally, doubling the planking of a hull was done mainly for protection against shipworms and all the other parasites which eat the hulls, especially in warmer waters. The India Company used to preserve the underside of its ships by putting a second layer of planking on them, into which were hammered stud nails. This procedure was efficient and not too difficult to apply, but it slowed the ships' speed considerably. Putting on a layer of copper, on the other hand, aided the flow of water along the hull. The procedure had been little known in France, while the English had been using it since the previous war. It was after having seen the superior speed of their copper-bottomed ships over ours that we wanted to imitate them. The Navy had done two trials. The first copper bottom was put on at Le Havre, on a corvette. Having made a single voyage to Rochefort, the ship had been decommissioned and had lain forgotten for many years. The Saint-Malo shipowner Dubuys had bought it, at a knock-down price, to use it as the basis for coppering his ship *le Duc de Choiseul.* The second attempt had been made with *la Belle Poule,* at Brest in 1771. When she had had her copper removed in order to inspect the hull it was noticed that all the ironwork, especially all the planking nails and the rudder pintles, had rotted away three times faster than normal. According to the Comte de Lapérouse, the English had partly resolved this problem by replacing iron fittings with bronze and replacing the iron nails in the planking with copper nails. That was where we were when in July 1778 the frigate *l'Iphigénie* had captured and brought to Brest an English cutter with a copper bottom. It was found that her planking had been attached with copper nails, that the hull had been daubed with white lead, and the copper sheeting laid directly on top. *L'Iphigénie* was then coppered using a new technique to try to stop the deterioration of the iron nails in her planking. This consisted of applying white lead below the waterline, then laying tarred canvas on the hull before placing the copper sheeting on top. This was the method that the Naval engineers had decided to use on *l'Amazone* and *la Gentille.*

Our sailors and petty officers were lodged in a shore barracks built on the rise just above the pontoons where the two frigates had been careened. The officers were staying in Brest at their own expense. I was with the Volunteers in the Recouvrance barracks of the Auvergne regiment to which Lieutenant Frémont was attached. This Lieutenant was a very friendly young man. After his initial reticence at Saint-Malo, he had come to appreciate the Comte de Lapérouse's style of command, a happy mix of benevolence and firmness. I took up the habit of practising swordsmanship with him during our free time. He enjoyed fencing and thought of himself as a skilled exponent. He was surprised to find that I surpassed him in this discipline but, far from taking umbrage at this, he was happy for us to be friends, despite the difference in our age and rank.

13

I had not dared to go and see Maria Kirwan again. I really wanted to meet her, but I was not sure whether I could show her the level of affection that she deserved. I was afraid of taking advantage of her kind nature. I was still very attached to the ribbon that she had given me. To try to forget her, I went once or twice to the *Dames de la Marine*, where I was welcomed with open arms, without having to make any payment. The girls were always very generous towards me. They said that they could allow themselves to do a favour for a young Marine Guard like me, as they had been overwhelmed with gifts from the Duc de Chartres. He had been one of their most regular customers during his stay at Brest. He had honoured each one of them in turn, one after the other, without exception and without any favouritism. As they were not the ungrateful kind, they remained 'faithful' to him, as one might say, in his adversity. 'It is shameful, this argument about the Battle of Ushant!' they complained. 'Such a handsome man!' I felt at ease in their arms. Nonetheless, despite their friendliness and kindness, they failed to cure me of Maria Kirwan.

The Auvergne regiment was the best-looking and smartest in the garrison. It was also said to be the most competent, and the best-drilled on parade. Lieutenant Frémont sometimes invited me to dine with his fellow-officers. I was surprised to discover how much more rigid was the hierarchy in the Army, as compared to the Navy. The sub-lieutenant waited respectfully until the lieutenant spoke to him, while the lieutenant was on the alert to reply to his captain, and so on. When Lieutenant Frémont invited me into this company, with its extreme rigidity and rules, I did my best to uphold the honour of the Navy, while at the same time remaining as discreet as possible, so as not to draw attention to myself. These meals with the Auvergne infantry officers were not much fun. Because of the traditions which I have just mentioned, the lieutenants' and captains' tables only talked very quietly, so as not to disturb the colonels, lieutenant-colonels and majors, who enjoyed the privilege of talking amongst themselves without restraint. This meant that one could hear everything they said. This particular circumstance lead to me committing a grave error. What can I say? It could not have been worse had I insulted the King!

During one of these ceremonial and rather punctilious meals in the Auvergne regiment's officers' mess when, as usual, all one could hear at the lieutenants' tables was the sound of cutlery on plates, and whispered demands to pass the salt or the bread or something similar, my ears picked up the particularly loud voice of a guest at the commanding officer's table. His slightly song-song voice was rather like that of the Comte de Lapérouse, though a little less exaggerated. From what he was saying, I understood that he was a former officer of the regiment. He was called Colonel de Guypair[68]. From what I could make out, he was now at the headquarters of the Duc de Broglie, at Bayeux, and had come to inspect the Army units and fortifications at Brest, along with Monsieur de la Rozière. If I may make a small digression: more than six thousand troops had been mobilised on the Normandy and Brittany coast, and quartered across more or less all the camps and garrisons on the Channel coastline. It was said that this force was destined to land in England once our Navy had chased the English ships out of the Channel. The command of this invasion force had been given to the Duc de Broglie, who had asked Monsieur de la Rozière to assist him. This latter, I imagine, had not been particularly impressed by this

---

68 Translator's note: *Colonel de Guypair*: *Guibert* in modern French spelling. Jacques-Antoine-Hippolyte, Comte de Guibert, was a brilliant and renowned soldier, tactician, writer and member of the Académie Française.

show of esteem, as he himself must have known what my uncle the Chevalier de Kermean had already told me in confidence at Saint-Malo: that Louis XVI had no intention of invading England and that this was all no more than a diversion. Moreover, this must have been a great disappointment to him, as he was a fervent supporter of the idea of an attack on England.

This Colonel de Guypair had started by saying that apart from the Auvergne regiment, and to a lesser extent, the Chartres regiment, which was garrisoned at Landerneau, the other regiments hereabouts were in a poor state.

'I recognise, however, that there are a lot of problems for the regiments at Brest. On the one hand, as a result of the predominance of the Navy over the Army, but above all, because our soldiers are exposed daily to the terrible example of the indiscipline and relaxed dress of the sailors and the marines; who scarcely obey orders on board and who once ashore are totally undisciplined. In the streets we have met groups of poorly turned-out and drunken sailors who couldn't care less that we were officers. And our best soldiers, whom we have to send on detachment from our garrisons onto their vessels, soon take on the same attitudes and come back to us totally corrupted.'

The speaker continued, explaining that the main culprits for this state of affairs were the Naval officers.

'No rank obeys another! There is no obedience aboard: the ensigns, the lieutenants, the captains, the rear admirals, the admirals, they are all chums! They should start by forbidding captains from choosing their own officers. Naval officers are snobbish, rude and dissolute. The Marine Guards, in particular, are quite derelict. They are not taught the least decency. Nobody supervises them. They lodge wherever they see fit once they have come ashore. They come home at whatever hour they like. Despite having been strangely privileged by birth, they are all devoted to vice! And if these officers were at least good at their jobs, or even simply brave fighters! Far from it! Look at this stupid action they pompously call the 'Battle of Ushant'.'

I then heard a long exposition on all the qualities of the English Navy and all the faults of our own.

'Our frigates are all poor under sail, all inferior to those of the English; this is because of the poop deck cabins that they are hampered by. Monsieur de Sartine has ordered them to be taken down, but it won't be done and do you know why? They are the officers' quarters. None of them will obey because, for them, it's always comfort and ease that wins the day. In any case, we don't know how to use our frigates and corvettes. Look at the last engagement! The English knew where we were, while Monsieur d'Orvilliers himself was incapable of calculating his own position! This famous Battle of Ushant that we never stop hearing about! A victory? What a joke! It was just an exchange of fire. No manoeuvres, nobody obeying signals, pitiful, mediocre leadership from the Comte d'Orvilliers, an accumulation of mistakes. They'd hardly fired a few cannon shots before they were back in port, with nobody able to get them back out again. Frigates, at least, should stay at sea. The English ones are always out there. But no! Not ours! They stay in port under the pretext of making repairs that could be made at sea. They want fresh food, they want to see their women, their mistresses, they want to go to the theatre. This is the real reason: they don't want to fight, because they are idle and soft. I even think they are afraid!'

While listening to this speech, I was aware of the side glances of the lieutenants sitting around me. Some were sniggering, those well disposed towards me felt pity. After a moment, I said to myself that I could never again show myself amongst them, my head held high, if I did not react. I stood up, by myself, without permission, an inconceivable act in the Auvergne officers' mess and went, hat in hand, to stand before the table where this Colonel de Guypair was continuing his oration. He was seated to the right of the commanding officer, wearing the epaulettes of a colonel and an infantry uniform similar to that of the Auvergne regiment, except for the pale orange collar. Becoming aware of the shocked silence descending on the room, he raised his eyes and saw me standing in front of him, in my blue and scarlet Marine Guard uniform, my hand already placed nervously on the handle of my sword.

'Monsieur,' I said simply, 'I could without doubt disprove point by point all your allegations about the Navy. But I am no more than a Marine Guard, that is to say someone, in your view, beyond saving. However, I can at least prove to you that we do not lack courage, and the best way to show that will be sword in hand at a place and hour of your convenience.'

At first Colonel de Guypair was dumbstruck. I saw disbelief in his eyes. This disbelief was then replaced by anger, quickly controlled, and he looked me up and down with an ironic and hurtful expression. He was a man in the prime of life. He had a big round head, his neck set into his shoulders, a dimpled chin and a straight nose continuing the line of his receding forehead, which gave him the look of a Roman Emperor on an old medallion.

'My dear Vicomte,' he said, in a seemingly calm voice, turning towards the regiment's colonel. 'This seems to me to be a legitimate challenge. But if I am not mistaken, duels are forbidden. And, moreover, this is a challenge to a superior! I am surprised that one could put up with such insubordination here. Ought I retract all the good things I have just said about the glorious Auvergne regiment?'

An indignant murmur spread through the room.

'Call the guard!' said the colonel.

After disarming me, the guard took me first to the regimental prison. The next day I was transferred to the Marine Guard prison on the other side of the Penfeld, where I waited three days without knowing what would be done with me. On the third day, they came to take me to the Hôtel Saint-Pierre, to the office of the Marquis de la Prevalaye, the interim Navy commander at Brest.

*

Brest, Wednesday 28th October 1778, morning.

'Monsieur Laforest-Dombourg, could you tell me what wasp has stung you?'

I have for a long time thought and rethought about this affair in my cell. Although I am against duelling, on principle, I could not see any other way out of the difficult situation in which Colonel de Guypair had placed me with his public defamations. I try to explain all this to the Marquis.

'What Colonel de Guypair said is unacceptable. But all the same, you ought to have remembered that one does not challenge a superior officer to a duel...and that this offence is normally punishable by twenty years in prison.'

The Marquis de Prevalaye has adopted a cold, dry tone. I look at him hopelessly. He does not seem to be joking. Up until now, I had thought that I would be released with a reprimand after a few days.

'Twenty years?'

'You should have thought of that before! What are we going to do with you?'

I have the impression that his voice has softened, and I start feeling more hopeful. That's it! He doubtless wanted to give me a fright.

'In any event, it's not me who will decide. The Marquis de Langeron has asked to see you. You will be escorted immediately to him and I have told him that I will go along with whatever he decides about you.'

Hearing that, I believe that I am well and truly lost. The Marquis de Langeron commands the town and the forts. As the representative of the Army in Brest, he is known for fighting continuously against the dominance of the Navy in the garrison. On this point, at least, Colonel de Guypair had not been exaggerating. The Navy is not entirely innocent.

The Marquis de Prevalaye calls for the infantry sergeant who has brought me here.

'Sergeant! Take Monsieur Laforest-Dombourg to the Brest Château. The garrison commander will see him.'

I think to myself that I am done for. The Navy is deliberately abandoning me!

I go down the rue de Siam between two Navy riflemen. It is drizzling, and water flows gently down the paving stones. My serge uniform will soon be wringing wet. It is my best uniform, which I usually put on to honour the Navy when I go to dine at the Auvergne regiment. My sword, the beautiful standard issue sword given to me by my uncle, is still at Recouvrance, confiscated. During my three days in the cell I have done my best to keep my uniform in a good state. At night I took off my stockings, breeches, jacket and coat, despite the cold. Now I no longer care. Twenty years! Drummed out of the Navy, without doubt. The war will be finished long before I am released. And the India that I dreamed of discovering? My adventure is ended before it had even begun. I cannot believe it.

The Chateau de Brest looks forbidding under the rain and the dark sky. My sergeant shows his orders to his Army counterpart, who detaches a private to guide us. The soldiers look at me with curiosity. Having crossed the first bastions, the moat and the ravelin, we pass under the old entrance, between two massive crenelated towers squeezed against each other. An icy wind blows down the dark tunnel and I shudder, saying to myself that I will no doubt have to spend the night here in some dark and dripping wet cell. After the gate, we have to cross a wide courtyard to reach the offices of the commander of the garrison and the forts.

The Marquis de Langeron is a lieutenant-general. His office is on the first floor. The duty lieutenant has been forewarned, and takes us in immediately.

The Marquis is sitting behind a big desk at the end of a vast room. He is studying papers and annotating them. It is cold and the fireplace is empty. We are only at the end of October, but the candles of the two big chandeliers have been lit, at one end of the room and the other, in order to permit the Marquis to work.

The sergeant salutes, bringing his hand to his hat and uncovering his head. I do the same. The Marquis raises his head. He seems closer to sixty than fifty. He is wearing a wig and town clothes: a pink coat trimmed with gold.

'Thank you, Sergeant. You can go back and tell the Marquis de la Prevalaye that you have been discharged of your prisoner. Now, leave me alone with Monsieur Laforest-Dombourg.'

Without thinking I look around me. Maps and plans have been hung on the walls, along with sketches of fortifications. Books, registers and more maps are spread on several work tables along the walls. Behind the Marquis de Langeron's desk, in the weak light of this rainy autumn day penetrating the window panes, I make out a big motionless shape placed on the marble of a console against a wall. I know immediately what it is and where it comes from. But it is not important and my eyes pass over all these things without my brain lingering on them.

'Monsieur Laforest-Dombourg! Two years ago you nearly caused us a lot of trouble by reason of a duel with Army officers. Here you are hardly back in Brest, with nothing better to do than once again provoke one of our officers. And not any old officer! Colonel de Guypair! A colonel known and appreciated throughout the Court for the pertinence of his books on military tactics. And, I may add, you are reputed to be a dangerous duellist. What have you to say in your defence?'

I am unable to speak. I start to tremble from cold, or maybe from fear. I no longer know.

'Sit down.'

I do not move, having thought I had misheard.

'Sit down, I tell you!' the Marquis repeats.

I see a chair beside me. I let myself fall into it and once again start shaking. The Marquis de Langeron looks at me closely.

'What did they tell you at the Navy headquarters?'

'Twenty years in prison.'

'And that has shaken you, by the looks! At least it will teach you a lesson. You had a problem, two years ago, with the junior officers of the Enghien regiment. Well, today you can thank those of the Auvergne. The lieutenants of this regiment went to see their colonel in your defence. And then, you are equally lucky that Monsieur de la Rozière happens to be in Brest at the moment, and he was recently Colonel de Guypair's commanding officer. Monsieur de la Rozière likes you a lot. He has managed to persuade the Colonel not to make a complaint. Without which, you would probably have had them, your twenty years! Colonel de Guypair was very upset with you. He has just been given command of a regiment and he does not take discipline lightly.'

Have I understood properly? I am afraid of getting it wrong.

'You are going to release me?'

'You are free. You have paid with the three days you have done.'

It is too much for me. I start to sob. The duty lieutenant has come back into the room. He leans towards the Marquis to tell him something in a low voice.

'Bring him in,' replies the Marquis de Langeron.

*

I was crying silently, unable to stop myself. I heard someone sit down in the chair beside mine.

'I give you back your Marine Guard, Captain. The fighter has become a good little boy.'

'Thank you, Marquis. I am infinitely grateful to you,' replied the Comte de Lapérouse.

'Oh! Don't thank me. My friend Monsieur de la Rozière is acting as guarantor for this boy. But the colonel of the Auvergne regiment was quite right to arrest him on the spot. Otherwise, God knows how it might have ended.'

The Marquis stood up and went to take something off the table behind him. When he brought it back I recognised my sword. It was all there, complete with its sheath and loop. It had even been polished and its golden hand guard was shining.

'You have a regulation sword of an officer of the old First Company of Musketeers, which is not normal for a sailor.'

'It was a present from my uncle, the Chevalier de Kermean.'

'Monsieur de la Rozière also spoke to me about your uncle. If you want your sword back, swear solemnly that you will never duel again.'

I swore with all my heart.

'The sailors will be very grateful to you for this gesture, Monsieur le Marquis,' said the Comte de Lapérouse.

'You, without doubt, and some of your comrades, I don't doubt. However, I would like the Navy to put a stop to all this carping and pettiness against me. I can tell you, though, that I have little hope. But don't worry; I will do my duty despite it.'

'They are lucky to have you as garrison commander, but they don't realise it.'

The Marquis de Langeron had been appointed to Brest because he was an expert in fortification. His previous post had been at the fort of Briançon. The fact that his elder brother, now retired, had served as the King's Lieutenant in Brittany had no doubt also helped his appointment. Nonetheless, the Navy was hardly helping him in his work. It constantly reminded him of its predominance, down to the minutest details. Moreover, his private quarters were provided by the Navy command, and he was regularly reminded that he could not keep them, as the Navy needed them.

The conversation turned to the Auvergne regiment. The Comte de Lapérouse expressed his satisfaction in the excellent behaviour of Lieutenant Frémont's detachment.

'I will send a few words to the Vicomte, their colonel. That will please him. You are right; it is a good troop, well commanded. Sadly, they have finished their service at Brest. They will be relieved at the end of the month. I am working on that right now.' The Marquis gestured to all the correspondence spread out over his desk.

As their conversation continued, I could not stop myself from getting up to go and examine more closely the extraordinary object behind the garrison commander's desk, which I had caught sight of when coming in, and which now concentrated all my attention to the extent of making me forget all the elementary rules of politeness.

I had already heard that it was possible to stuff animals in such a way as to give them the same attitude as if they were alive. But it was a little-known process, and apart from some very poor specimens of deer or boars' heads, I had never seen an entire stuffed animal. This one was a wolf of extraordinary size. I could never have imagined that such a beast existed. Yet it seemed quite authentic. It would have been impossible to fabricate such a perfect imitation, above all the magnificent black fur, shining and flecked with grey. It had been made as if standing still, with its jaws open, its tongue hanging between its sharp teeth, as long as ivory daggers, its head turned sideways. It seemed to be staring at me with its wide yellow eyes, slit like almonds.

'Excuse me, Marquis,' I said, 'did you kill this wolf yourself?'

'Good heavens! You have made a quick recovery, my boy! As for this monster, it was not I who killed it. Good Lord, no! I am not a hunter. It was a personal gift from the Comte d'Hector to mark my arrival here in 1776, as a token of the good relations between the Navy and the Army. The Comte himself is a great hunter, despite being a sailor. He commands a ship in the Comte d'Orvilliers' squadron.'

'And was it the Comte d'Hector who killed it?' I asked.

'It wasn't him either. He told me that he had bought it because of the exceptional size of the animal. It had been offered to him by a shrewd tradesman whom he uses to conserve his hunting trophies. In truth, I think he also gave it to me because his wife wanted rid of it. This stuffed wild beast had place of honour in his entrance hall for three years and it gave his nephews nightmares when they came to visit.'

'Does this taxidermist work in Brest?' I asked.

'Oh, you must certainly know his shop, if you have ever been to the forced labour stalls.

'Ah! He's a forced labourer? I remember now,' I said. 'It's almost two years since I last went to the prison stalls. He is still there?'

'As far as I know he has not finished his sentence, luckily for hunters like the Comte d'Hector and above all for all the amateur naturalists aboard our ships. I think he is a unique craftsman. He is said to be well known in the little world of enlightened amateurs, as far as Paris and throughout the realm. His works are sought after by the owners of curiosity shops. In the Navy, his main clients are doctors and surgeons. They bring half rotten little creatures from the ends of the earth, preserved in alcohol, more or less, that our prison taxidermist excels, it seems, at restoring to their original state. Without doubt, Comte de Lapérouse, you have aboard your frigate one of these doctors obsessed by zoology?'

'I don't think that's the case with mine. He is happy to write and to study the habits of foreign peoples. He is a humanist; a philosopher, one might say. He has written a treatise on bandaging, which is too hard for me to understand, and also published a travel journal in which he relates his two voyages to India and China with the India Company. In fact, it was after having read it that I invited him to join me.'

Coming out into the courtyard of the Chateau, I looked at the sky, still just as grey, and considered with relief that I had thought I would no longer see it for a long time. It had stopped raining, but I felt cold. I suddenly realised how wet my clothes were. They had certainly not dried out in the Comte de Langeron's cold office. I shuddered, shaking my shoulders. The Comte de Lapérouse noticed.

'Do you not have an overcoat?'

'I was arrested as I am now.'

'We shall go back to the Marquis. He will have one given to you.'

'Please, do not go to the trouble,' I said. 'I would like to get out of here as quickly as possible.'

The Comte de Lapérouse asked me where I would like to go. He said that he had had my chest and personal things collected, and that they were at the inn where he was lodging.

'I imagine that you have no wish to go back to the Auvergne quarters. The young lady who runs the inn where I am knows you very well and was very concerned when she heard of your arrest.'

Saying that, he smiled.

'She told me,' he continued, 'that she would be happy to lodge you free of charge once you were set free. But I'm not sure whether that would suit you.'

'And what is the name of this inn?'

'*La Dame au Paon.*'

'It's just that…I would not like to abuse her hospitality.'

'She warned me that you would say something like that and she asked me to reply that, given your current situation, you ought not to feel that you owe her anything.'

'But how did she find out what had happened to me?'

'Because the whole of Brest is talking about it, dear boy! Lieutenant Frémont and his comrades have told your story in every detail, including

Colonel de Guypair's speech and the challenge you threw down to him. You have become famous! Several captains, and by no means the least important, have told me that they would have you aboard, if you ever wanted to leave my ship. But listen carefully. You must not let this go to your head. The role of Navy Champion is perhaps tempting, but you must not forget the promise you made to the Marquis de Langeron.'

I replied that he need not worry, and that my reputation as a 'duellist', to use the Marquis of Langeron's expression, was based entirely on a misunderstanding. But it was true that Colonel de Guypair's speech had caught me completely off guard. If one believed the Marquis de Langeron, this officer had a brilliant mind. Moreover, I did not understand how he could have spoken such words in my presence were it not with the intention of provoking me.

'I don't believe he wished to provoke you,' replied the Comte de Lapérouse. 'I think he believed what he said to be true. There is, on the part of Army officers, some bitterness and a great deal of misunderstanding as regards the Navy. France has always been a great country of landlubbers. Military men like de Guypair are naturally jealous to see that now all the credit goes to the Navy, and that the Army is relegated to second place. That has never happened before. As for this mutual ignorance between Army officers and us, it reminds me exactly of your farmworkers from deepest Brittany who consider the fishermen of Douarnenez to be lazy good-for-nothings, simply because they don't work to the same rules as them. Colonel de Guypair said that the Comte d'Orvilliers did not know how to manoeuvre at Ushant. But for a sailor, to tack through the wind, all together, as he had ordered the fleet to do, is as difficult a manoeuvre to get right as all the clever tactics, with marching and counter-marching, that de Guypair admires so much. I know that he has written a lot on the use of artillery in military campaigns and on the complicated formations that the infantry must adopt to take account of it. I haven't read his books, but he is certainly justified in being very proud of them. However, he talked of Ushant as a simple exchange of fire. He seems ignorant of the fact that a single seventy-four gun ship, in one broadside, can launch a weight of metal greater than all the artillery of the Duc de Broglie's army put together, if they could ever line up all their guns simultaneously on the field of battle. You look frozen! Would you like to borrow my coat?'

We were going down the ramp which descends directly from the Chateau esplanade, besides its bastions, down to the Brest quayside.

'That is very kind,' I said, 'but it's not far. If we hurry, I will soon be warm in your inn.'

'It's the same thing with the superior speed of the English frigates over ours,' continued the Comte de Lapérouse, increasing his pace. 'It's all down to their copper-bottoming, and not the deck cabins, which in any case most captains have refused. You'll see! Once *l'Amazone* has been coppered, I'm ready to wager with anyone that no English ship can beat her.'

The Comte de Lapérouse stopped talking. We had arrived at the quay, beside the mast crane. We went into the main room of *La Dame au Paon*. I saw Maria Kirwan coming towards us. She took my hands in hers, squeezing them. Once more I fell under the charm of her eyes. All my scruples evaporated. I said to myself that it was fate which had reunited us. But I started to tremble, my teeth chattering, helpless to stop myself.

'Pierre-Marie Laforest-Dombourg! Your hands are frozen and you are shivering! And you are soaked! You have taken a chill in prison!'

I could no longer stand. Marie Kirwan put me in the best room of the inn. It was the one in which Flaharn had stayed. The young girl's uncle, a childless widower, let her do as she pleased. She had a roaring fire lit in the hearth that the hotel boy was ordered to keep permanently fed. The Comte de Lapérouse sent Monsieur Le Choquet, the ship's surgeon, who prescribed extract of juniper and maidenhair syrup. Nature would do the rest. Luckily for me, Monsieur Le Choquet was not one for bloodletting, so at least I escaped that.

The crews of the two frigates had been permitted to go home for four weeks. They were handed their part of the prize money just before leaving. They could have been given it sooner, but Monsieur Mengaud de la Hage had deliberately held back the hand-out. That way, the families of our sailors had a better chance of seeing some of the money. Without such a wise precaution, this unforeseen mana would without doubt have disappeared entirely into the pockets of the brothelkeepers of the rue Haute des Sept Saints.

I stayed in bed until the end of November. Maria Kirwan spent a lot of time at my bedside. She forced me to swallow the concoctions and syrups prescribed by our surgeon. These potions tasted horrible, like all good medicines, but with Maria Kirwan close beside me, everything went down. I never tired of looking at her. Not being able to kiss her, I breathed her breath, drank in the music of her words, though I was too intoxicated by her presence to remember the details of her conversation and to grasp the implications of certain allusions which she made, and which only came back to mind later on.

She talked in particular about the letter she had sent me in June. Not to remind me that I had not replied, but to tell me that the *young lady of quality* whom she had spoken of in the letter was my commander's fiancée. This girl was called Eléonore Broudou. She was twenty-three and had got to know the Comte de Lapérouse on the Île-de-France. They had sworn to marry each other and she had come all alone to France to enable this to happen. In the meantime, however, Monsieur du Galaup, the Comte de Lapérouse's aging father, had formally opposed their plans. He considered it a mismatch for his son, whom he preferred to marry a young noblewoman from Albi. Mademoiselle Broudou had nonetheless stayed in France and continued to see her beloved in Paris, thanks to the kind complicity of the Marquis de la Jonquière. My commander and his lady friend both intended to wait until old Monsieur du Galaup, who was nearly blind, changed his mind or was no longer in a state to oppose their union. She had come to Brest to spend some months close to her great love before his departure for India. On arrival, she had the good luck of coming straight to *La Dame au Paon.* Maria Kirwan had helped her to find a little upstairs apartment, behind the Dajot Promenade, and they saw each other often. Eléonore Broudou knew hardly anyone in Brest. For my part, I thought the Comte de Lapérouse to be overly dutiful for a man of thirty-seven, but Maria Kirwan thought his attitude was quite acceptable. She considered it unthinkable that children, whether adults or not, should marry without the consent of their parents.

We had not exchanged any promises, Maria Kirwan and I, and this possibility was not a priority for the moment. In any case, a Marine Guard was forbidden to marry and, even without that, the Comte de Lapérouse's situation gave me pause for thought. My only living predecessor was my grandfather. I well knew that he had opposed my parents' marriage, raising exactly the same objections as Monsieur du Galaup. There were a lot of parallels between their story and that of my captain, except for the role played by the Chevalier de Ternay. My father had had more luck with him than the Comte de Lapérouse.

I went back to the shipyard to see the work on the two frigates, as soon as I was back on my feet. They had finished coppering one side of each hull, and had turned them over in order to copper the other sides. For the first time I met our Rear-Admiral, the Chevalier de Ternay. He was fifty-five years old, austere-looking, with a strong nose planted firmly above a permanently pursed mouth framed by two deep folds. His square forehead was also wrinkled. He was the very picture of duty. Youngest son of the Marquis d'Arsac, he had even served as a page to the Grand Master of the Order of Malta[69], before then becoming a Chevalier of the Order himself. At the age of fifteen, as was the rule, he had taken vows of celibacy which for his whole life, I believe, he had observed. He was a straight, uncompromising man. I better understood why the Baron de Kermean had complete confidence in him.

The Comte de Lapérouse and his friend, Monsieur Mengaud de la Hage, were very attached to their Rear-Admiral. This at least proved that the Chevalier de Ternay, despite his look of a tight-lipped, gloomy monk, was a good commander and a humane leader. My father must also have held him in high regard, as he had asked him to be a witness at his wedding. All the same, I thought, as the Chevalier de Ternay, after having returned my salute, evoked precisely this memory... all the same...neither my father nor the Comte de Lapérouse had confided in him as regards my parents' *great secret.* Would the Chevalier have refused to accede to my father's request, if he had known what it was, this secret? This was another interesting question to put to the Comte de Lapérouse at the first opportunity.

Vernon came to visit me on the last Friday of November. His division had returned to harbour two days previously. They had brought in ten prizes with them. At my friend's request I took him to the shipyard to see our two frigates, still hove down against the Recouvrance quayside. He looked at progress on the work with interest. This question of copper-bottoming hulls was at that time a matter of great fascination to all the officers of the Navy.

'All the English ships are coppered,' Vernon was saying. 'We saw

69 Translator's note: *Order of Malta*. A Roman Catholic religious order, founded in the XIth century and still in existence today.

that at Ushant. They could do whatever they wanted. It's because they caught us up that we were forced to tack at the last moment.'

'You're right,' I replied. 'It was the same with the action involving *la Belle Poule.* If she had still had her copper bottom, the *Arethusa* would never have been able to catch her and give her a broadside.'

'That's what Monsieur de la Clocheterie wrote in his report, at any rate,' replied Vernon, 'but in fact, between the two of us, I know, through a friend who was in the battle, that the first broadside of the war was definitely fired by *la Belle Poule,* and not the English. There's no doubt about that, even if nobody has dared to tell the King.'

After visiting the shipyard, I suggested to Vernon that we go to the forced prisoners' stalls. I wanted to see the extraordinary convict who had stuffed the Marquis de Langeron's wolf. We walked along the right bank of the Penfeld to the Recouvrance Quay and hired a ferryman to take us over to the Brest side.

The taxidermist's stall was the last one, right at the end of the courtyard, next to the little gate that led to the prison governor's garden. Unlike the others, this shop had glazed windows and a real door that could be kept closed. Going in I was surprised by the balmy warmth that pervaded the place.

'Shut the door, gentlemen, please!'

The little room was heated by two copper braziers hung from the beams. Lanterns fixed to the walls lit this little shop, or rather, laboratory.

'I beg you to wait a moment, gentlemen.'

The convict taxidermist turned his back to us. He was seated at a sort of workbench placed against the planked wall at the end of the shop and was skinning some kind of web-footed bird that he had laid in front of him. It was clearly a delicate operation, consisting of removing the skin from the body of the bird without tearing it, and without losing any feathers.

Vernon and I took advantage of the wait to look around this remarkable booth. Huge bottles full of different coloured liquids, alcohols, spirits, various oils and powders, were placed on the floor. Each one was labelled. An indefinable odour, a mixture of camphor, acid and newly tanned leather, hung in the air. Tools were carefully arranged on a little table. They were simultaneously those of an apothecary, a surgeon and a cabinetmaker: scalpels, different sized pliers, scissors, pincers, hand saws, brushes, wood rasps, files, rolls of wire of different sizes, tow, oakum, cotton…

Vernon pointed to a huge snake placed on the floor in a corner. Its body was thicker than my arm. It rose up in a spiral, balancing on its tail curled on the ground. It must have been eight feet long and its big triangular head, stretched out horizontally at the level of my face, was six inches wide. It was brown-coloured, with dark grey patches on its back. A straight black line went from each eye to the base of its jaw. Even stuffed, it made me shudder. Other animals awaited their future owners on rows of shelves fixed to the walls. The birds were kept separately in a sort of big glazed cupboard, its doors sealed with oakum. Vernon pointed out woodcock, but there were also seabirds. There was a bit of everything, in fact, according to the wants of his clients: fish, shellfish, plus a few sets of antlers, of course. Fox or dog skins were soaking in a vat. Labelled sacks held carefully cleaned skeletons. The Marquis de Langeron was right to have said that the taxidermist had orders from all over France.

The convict got up and turned to us, taking off a pair of spectacles.

'It's a diver. I've cut its skin down the back, as I want to have it standing up, showing its puffed up chest. For more common birds, like gulls, I make the incision on the belly so there's no risk of seeing the stitches later on. It's very important to present animals in their natural pose. Like the snake you were just looking at. It was the surgeon-in-chief of the frigate *la Blanche* who brought it back from Martinique. Following his description, I've made it as if it's attacking. Over there it's called a 'spearhead'. Its bite is generally thought to be fatal, but not always.'

The convict naturalist was taller than average, but incredibly thin. Everything about him was stretched: his legs, arms, hands and his neck from which protruded a prominent Adam's apple. His head, viewed in profile, formed a roundish shape ending with a bony nose that curved above a sunken chin. He had big round eyes, half veiled by heavy lids. He put fear into the other convicts, who called him the Tortoise. It was whispered that he had been condemned for embalming human bodies, including women and little children, without the permission of their families.

'What can I do for you, gentlemen?'

'To be honest, we just wanted to get some information from you.'

It was a clumsy introduction and I immediately felt his distrust.

'A short while ago in the Marquis de Langeron's office I was admiring the unusually big wolf that you prepared for the Comte d'Hector,' I said hurriedly, 'and I simply wanted to know who had killed it.'

His face grew calmer and he grimaced, even though it was meant to be a kindly smile.

'I understand! I've tried to find out too. But the man who brought it to me would never tell me.'

'Are you able to tell me who that is? I assure you that I know how to be discreet.'

'I can tell you who it is because he is long since dead and buried. He has taken his secret to the grave. It was a halberdier. He quarrelled with a Navy infantryman who killed him with a bayonet.'

'When did this happen?'

'Oh! At least four years ago.'

'And the wolf?'

'He brought it to me in January 1773. He thought that an animal of this size should interest a rich collector. He proposed that I stuff it and we share the proceeds. He wasn't wrong, but to tell the truth, I only accepted the deal because of the uniqueness of the animal. First, as you've seen, it's an incredible size. You'd only see a wolf like that every hundred years. Or more! And then, it wasn't damaged in any way. That's mainly what interested me. I've handled lots of wolf remains. Often they're a mess! Battered with spear or even trident blows, when they've not been shot cleanly. But that one! It was unmarked! One dagger blow to the left flank. The blade had passed between the ribs without touching them and pierced the heart. To do such a thing, you have to approach the beast head on and strike upwards with your dagger in your right hand, at the very moment he leaps at you. Even with a normal wolf, that needs calmness, amazing vision and a strong wrist. But with such a monster! The hunter who did that was quite exceptional! That's why I would have liked to know who it was. Men nowadays are a disappointment. When you get the chance to meet somebody out of the ordinary…I've always been a keen student of man, you see. I should have lived at another time. You know that I once wrote a treatise on mummies and Egyptian embalming? Humanity has gone backwards since…'

My intuition had not been wrong. From the moment I saw it, I had a strong feeling that the Marquis de Langeron's wolf was the same one killed by the Marquis Avelus de Kersalaun on the banks of the River Camfrout on the first Sunday of 1773. The halberdiers who had attacked Kersalaun had not pillaged the manor house, but they had carried off the remains of the wolf. Whoever was in charge of them had without doubt allowed them to do so, at the same time as stopping them from ransacking the manor. But why? Had he foreseen that the disappearance of the wolf's body might cause the storytellers of Cornouaille to create the legend of the Black Pearl of Kersalaun? The more I thought about it, the more I was convinced that this detail carried Flaharn's signature. It reminded me of the story of the Sumatra impalings told to me by Louis Duval.

14

L'Amazone and *la Gentille* were both completely coppered by the beginning of December. The crews had returned at the end of their leave. Able seamen rarely deserted but, since these were Saint-Malo men, there was the fear that they would be waylaid by the privateers and enterprising shipowners who would then have squared them with the law. The prospect of a campaign designed to ruin English trade in the Indian Ocean was, I think, a sufficiently powerful bait to stop sailors being tempted elsewhere.

We were lucky with the copper-bottoming of our frigates, but the five ships destined for the Brest division of the India fleet were less fortunate when they were hauled down for theirs. Not only was it done late, but at the last moment it was realised that the stock of copper available at Brest was insufficient for the job. In the end it was decided that only the lower part of the hulls would be covered in copper, while the four higher strakes would be provisionally studded instead. The rest would be completed on the Île-de-France. The Chevalier de Ternay could hardly believe it, but he put on a brave front in the face of misfortune. The main thing was to get under way. At the end of December there was another setback. The two ships that were to join him at Brest had already put to sea. In the Bay of Biscay, they had

had an engagement with an English privateer which had attacked them, thinking they were merchantmen. The privateer had escaped, but the rig of one of the ships had been damaged, forcing her back to L'Orient for repairs. The other ship had continued alone, to wait for orders off the coast of Brazil. I had never quite understood what happened, but it seemed that they were now lost to the Chevalier de Ternay's squadron.

The refitting of *l'Amazone* and *la Gentille* was started. The two ships came over to the Brest side, alongside the quay in front of the general warehouse by the entrance to the arsenal. The foremasts and mizzenmasts were reinstalled, the guns were taken aboard, along with everything that had been taken off for the careening. The two crews worked aboard during the day, and were lodged and fed ashore. This meant a lot of movement of the ships' boats morning and night, crossing the port, but our commanders wanted to embark our fresh provisions and water at the last moment.

Each evening at dusk I got back to *La Dame au Paon,* together with the Comte de Lapérouse. My captain saw Mademoiselle Broudou regularly. He seemed to have completely forgotten the sadness evoked by his second-in-command at the time of our first sortie from Saint-Malo. One evening, just before Christmas, I took advantage of this to try to revive the interrupted conversation we had been having when we arrived at Brest.

*

Brest, Wednesday 23rd December, dusk.

'I know,' I say, 'since I was told by my family, that if the Chevalier de Ternay had not recommended my father to the Baron de Kermean, my maternal grandfather, he would never have allowed my mother to marry him.'

The Comte de Lapérouse stops. We are at the end of the Brest quay, where porters are finishing filling handcarts with the last cases of provisions unloaded from the Breton coasters and which will ensure the daily feeding of the town.

'When we returned from our last mission,' I continue, 'you told me that my parents had a secret. I have thought a lot about that since. I remember very well what you told me when talking about yourself and Taffanel de la Jonquière. My conclusion is that the Chevalier de Ternay had no knowledge of this secret. If he had known it, he would never have agreed to help my parents get married. Am I not mistaken?'

'If I remember correctly,' replies my captain, 'that remark about Monsieur de la Jonquière slipped out because I was surprised to learn that you knew about the scalping business in which your father was involved.'

The dusk light is fading completely above Recouvrance. I no longer feel the freezing damp rising along the quay. My heart beats more strongly. I am about to find out the answer to the question which I have been asking myself for so many years.

'You were surprised, I believe,' continues the Comte de Lapérouse, 'that your father, a sailor, had been asked to command Indian warriors in a land-based operation. And you found it odd that he was the only officer there who spoke their language properly.'

My captain pauses.

'These savages, as you call them, had asked for your father. Amongst all the officers at the Louisbourg garrison he was the only one they trusted. And he could not refuse, just as he could not have forgotten their language. Because it was his maternal language and he was a half-brother to them. His mother, your grandmother, was a pure-blood Micmac.'

'Micmac? What's that?'

'It's the name of a Canadian Indian tribe that once dominated a huge territory covering what we have called New France, Acadia, the island of St. John and Newfoundland.'

'My grandmother…?'

'Yes indeed, Pierre-Marie Laforest-Dombourg! Yes! The blood in your veins is a quarter Indian. The blood of a savage, to use your term from the other day.'

The Chevalier de Lapérouse bursts out laughing, seeing my face.

'And I think that explains a lot of things. Colonel de Guypair got off lightly!'

He laughs again, then becomes serious once more.

'Your grandfather, in case you don't know it, came from a long-established Acadian family. When the English got control of this territory, Monsieur Laforest-Dombourg, your grandfather, perhaps more foresighted than the others, did not believe their promises and decided to move to Louisbourg with his young Indian wife. The

Acadians were free men. They did not consider the Micmac to be outright savages, but as allies worthy of the same respect as themselves, no more, no less. They intermixed. Unlike their Acadian friends, who were mainly farmers, the Micmac lived traditionally by hunting and sea fishing. That's perhaps why your father was always a sailor at heart. The Micmac hated the English even more than we did. They never believed in the peace treaties we signed with the English. And the latter made them pay for it. During the last war, the English governor of Nova Scotia offered a bounty of ten pounds for every Micmac scalp collected by his allies, the Mohawk, and by Major Gorham's Rangers. These rangers were a body of white irregulars created specifically to fight against the Micmac and the Acadians. I learned all this from your father.'

'If the Chevalier de Ternay had known all this, he would never have supported my father, would he?'

'Oh no! No more than he will support me.'

And, I think, deep down, that the Baron de Kermean would also not have given his daughter in marriage to a 'half-savage'. I now understand why my parents had always been so secretive about my father's past in Louisbourg. I was too young to be able to keep this secret and, if the Baron de Kermean had discovered the truth, then my father, even though a married man and a Chevalier de Saint-Louis, would have merited a *lettre de cachet* which would have sent him straight to the dungeons of the Saint-Malo Chateau or the Grande Conchée fortress.

'You said that you and Monsieur de la Jonquière knew all this, but the Chevalier de Ternay did not. How could that be?'

'Monsieur de la Jonquière and I met your grandparents when we went together to Louisbourg with La Motte's fleet, in June 1757. Monsieur de la Jonquière was in command of *le Célèbre,* sixty-four guns, and had asked your father, at that time a simple auxiliary sailor, to join his officers. Your father had a Captain's ticket and knew the waters between Newfoundland and the Gulf of Saint Lawrence very well. I was a Marine Guard, like you, and Monsieur de la Jonquière, a distant cousin of mine, was my guardian in the Navy. Your grandfather was one of the leading lights of Louisbourg. We were invited to his house.'

'That's how you found out that my...grandmother...was not French. I mean...was it obvious?'

'She was already quite old, I believe, but you could not put an age on her. She had been mostly spared wrinkles and had a very fine complexion when I saw her. It was obvious that she had been a great beauty. It was understandable that your grandfather had fallen in love with her. Of course, one could see that she was of Indian birth, with her hair, eyes and the natural ease of movement that your father and his sister inherited. She was also very dignified, despite having already lost two sons, taken by the English at the start of the war. It would be an understatement to say that she hated the English! She had strongly encouraged your father to give up the command of his ship and enter the service of the King.'

'And Monsieur de la Jonquière was not embarrassed by all of this?'

'Not in the least. He had already married a Creole from the Île-de-France. He is a great man. He himself would happily have married a Micmac Indian!'

We have started walking once more towards the inn. The Chevalier de Lapérouse puts his hand on my shoulder.

'Yes, I was very impressed by your grandmother, but her daughter, who looked like her, but with the blue eyes of her father, was quite marvellous. I think we were all a little bit in love with her. But they were enjoying their very last days. We only found out about it much later, a long time after the Comte de La Motte's squadron had returned to Brest. An outbreak of the putrid fever[70] had decimated the sailors of the squadron, contaminating Louisbourg, and also contaminating Brest and the whole of Brittany when our ships returned to France.'

'You're talking about the great epidemic of December 1757?'

'Yes. It had started in Louisbourg. Your grandmother and aunt were amongst the first victims. We escaped by chance, without knowing it, having left Louisbourg just before the outbreak. We were nine ships in all, blockaded in Louisbourg harbour, under the command of the old Comte de La Motte. The English Admiral Holburne was waiting for us outside with twenty ships. Our Rear-Admiral had decided not to go out, in order to avoid an engagement. We stayed like that for some months without doing anything. This was not to Monsieur de la Jonquière's liking. Through his insistence, he was finally authorised to try to break out, to take his ship back to France. It was the end of September, I remember. One morning there was a completely red sky at dawn and

70 Translator's note: *Putrid fever*: what we would now call typhus. There were 10,000 deaths in the Brest region alone.

not a breath of wind. The English were all becalmed. Your father assured Monsieur de la Jonquière that we would have strong south-easterly blow that night and that he would be able to pilot the ship out. Thanks to him, we were able to prepare ourselves in advance. The commander of *le Bizarre* had decided to join us. By evening the sky was as black as ink. Towards midnight the wind suddenly got up, the darkness was total and we passed like lightning through the English fleet. Your father was promoted to Frigate's Lieutenant on account of that. That's how we escaped the putrid fever which shortly afterwards struck down the Comte de La Motte's squadron and the town of Louisbourg.'

*

The Christmas celebrations were even more joyous than usual, as the Queen had just given birth to a little girl. The ships were dressed and lit up at night. In mid-January we learned that the Pondicherry stronghold had surrendered to the English after a four-month siege. Chandernagore, which had no defences or garrison, had been occupied by the English since the start of the war. This all caused some concern for the Comte de Lapérouse as regards our mission, as he had always thought that an India campaign should be supported by Pondicherry. And that was not all. At the end of the first week of February we saw the frigate *l'Alliance* enter port. She was carrying the Marquis de Lafayette[71], who left immediately for Versailles. He had just asked for reinforcements for America.

These developments were not enough to create doubt over our departure. It was still possible to disrupt the English trade from the Île-de-France and to operate on the Malabar coast that our captain knew well. He had met Hyder Ali Khan, the Sultan of Mysore, and an ally of France, during a call at Calicut. Hyder-Ali was as important a card for France as the Moghul emperor in northern India, if not more so. We still had some advantages in India. The Comte de Grasse had just left to reinforce Martinique with four ships. That reassured our commanders: they still had no need of us over there, and so our departure for India was still valid.

71 Translator's note: *Marquis de Lafayette*: Marie-Joseph Paul Yves Roch Gilbert du Motier, Marquis de La Fayette. French military officer who fought in the American Revolutionary War, commanding American troops in several battles.

Our squadron was now formed and was smaller than expected, being no more than a division. But at least it existed: *l'Annibal*, seventy-four, commanded by the Chevalier de Ternay; *le Diadème*, also seventy-four, commanded by Monsieur Dampierre; *le Réfléchi*, sixty-four, commanded by Monsieur Cillart de Suville; *l'Amphion*, fifty guns, commanded by Monsieur Ferron de Quengo; and not forgetting our two 12-pounder frigates.

Our crews left their shore billet. The Comte de Lapérouse and I gave up our rooms at *La Dame au Paon* and reinstalled ourselves in our quarters aboard *l'Amazone.* The two frigates completed their provisioning and went out to anchor in the harbour. A detachment from the Royal-la-Marine came aboard to replace that of the Auvergne regiment. We loaded our powders. The ships of our squadron started to come out of the Penfeld shortly after us.

Monsieur Mengaud de le Hage and the Comte de Lapérouse received orders to have themselves ready for immediate departure for a reconnaissance of the Mascarenes. The Chevalier de Ternay would join us over there with his five vessels and a convoy of transport ships. I began to make my last farewells to Maria Kirwan, without knowing when they would be for real. On Friday 12th February the Port Commander, along with the Chevalier de Ternay, came to review our two ships. I doubt they had ever seen crews so keen to get their sailing orders. It seemed as if there was nothing left to delay our departure. We had carried out some trials with the two ships in the harbour. The coppering worked marvellously well. One thing was sure: once we had passed out of the entrance to the harbour, no French ship would be able to catch us to order us back.

Nonetheless, the sailing order that we were awaiting did not come, neither the next day, nor the following days. Instead, we learned that the news from the Americas was bad. The Comte d'Estaing had allowed the English to seize St Lucia and had failed to retake it, despite a provisional but clear advantage in numbers. The Comte de Lapérouse was worried. He even went so far as to ask me whether I had heard anything from my uncle that might put our minds at rest.

The Chevalier de Kermean had in fact written to me via his official post. Above all he wanted to tell me that Colonel de Guypair would not be lodging a complaint against me... *Otherwise I guarantee that it's to me that he would have had to explain himself and he would not have been able to hide behind the idea of discipline. I know him well as we worked together for the Comte de Saint-Germain. We did not always see eye to eye, but he was always an honest supporter of the Comte. He is clever, but ever since acquiring a mistress who enjoys the company of philosophers, he has developed a taste for writing, and become somewhat pretentious. Thinking, no doubt, that his talents were not sufficiently appreciated in France, he has sought the flattery of foreign royalty. It would have been enough if he had been satisfied with the Emperor Joseph of Austria, who is, after all, the brother of our Queen. But no, he could not stop himself from going off to lick the boots of Frederick II, just like his philosopher friends. At the moment he is in command of the Neustrie regiment in Normandy.*

My uncle had appended to his letter a summary of the political situation in France, using the code that he had had passed to me at Saint-Malo by Monsieur de la Rozière. The King definitely did not want to invade England. Even less did he want a 'pirate' operation designed to attack one point on the English coast and lay waste to it, in order, as had been suggested by Colonel Dumouriez, to demoralise the English by bringing terror to their soil. His Majesty had not ordered his Navy commanders to leave the English coastal fishermen in peace in order to send soldiers to burn and pillage their homes. Nonetheless, Louis XVI hoped to obtain the same result by having the English believe that this threat existed, and that is why he had concentrated his armies along the Channel coast. Obviously, for this diversionary tactic to work, it had to remain credible, and so nobody knew the King's real strategy in this regard, apart from those in the Comte de Fleurieu's office.

The war was centring more and more on the Americas. In fact the cost of the conflict, of which he was constantly reminded by his Minister of Finance, Monsieur Necker, was seriously worrying the King. According to our Sovereign, France's only hope for avoiding the financial disaster it was facing was to ensure that, once there was peace, we would have privileged trading links with the young American nation[72]. Louis XVI was very much attached to this idea, which is why he had insisted from the beginning on the commercial nature of the

72 Preferential trade with the United States: The idea that grateful Americans would cede to France the position traditionally occupied by the United Kingdom was Louis XVI's big mistake. The laws of trade and economics evolve by their own mechanisms which have nothing to do with feelings. After their defeat the English continued their preferential trading links with America, just as before.

treaties signed with the rebels' representatives. But first, he had to help them gain their independence. According to my uncle, this was not a threat to our secondary expedition to India, as its aim was to weaken our enemy's economic resources. It goes without saying that I could not divulge this information. And despite my friendship and respect for my commander, I said nothing to him, apart from the fact that we could still hope to leave for India.

Winter had its final sting at the end of February. Cold engulfed the harbour and it snowed. We had to clear the decks and rigging for several days. The Comte de Lapérouse's fears were confirmed: our orders were changed. In his last reports, the Comte d'Estaing had maintained that he had insufficient forces to protect the merchant convoys between France and the Antilles. Receiving these dispatches on the heels of the Marquis de Lafayette's urgent appeals, Versailles had finally decided to send the Comte a supplementary force of ships and soldiers. The Chevalier de Ternay's division was the only one available in the short time frame. The India expedition was not officially abandoned but was put back to a later date, and the Chevalier de Ternay received orders to sail to Martinique.

Aboard *l'Amazone*, this setback was received in different ways. There were those who would rather have gone to India, especially our Saint-Malo sailors who saw their dreams of prizes loaded with piasters and pearls fade away; and there were those, like the Chevalier de la Jonquière and Lieutenant de Tromenec, who were overjoyed to go and fight in America where, rather than riches, they could earn glory. For myself, I was a little sad not to go to India, but I largely shared the officers' feelings. Anything was better than staying in Brest.

Unfortunately, this view was not shared by the Chevalier de Ternay, who loathed the Comte d'Estaing more than anybody. He immediately asked to be re-attached to the Brest fleet, keeping just two ships and two frigates to make up a small division. He said that he would was ready to go and fight anywhere on earth, rather than put himself under the command of an 'upstart' Vice-Admiral who, he announced to anyone who cared to listen, *had cruelly ripped his flag halyard from his hands.* And, to crown the whole lot, the height of misfortune, or a fit caused by this turn of fate and the disappearance of the promotion he had so much hoped for: the Chevalier de Ternay slipped awkwardly on the frozen snow on his ship's boarding ladder and damaged his ankle falling into the boat that was waiting to take him ashore. He could no longer even walk.

The Ministry and the Naval Command did not hesitate for long. The Comte de Lamotte-Picquet was detailed to replace the Chevalier de Ternay, at a moment's notice, with the two Rear-Admirals ordered simply to exchange ships. The Chevalier de Ternay switched to *le Saint-Esprit* with extremely bad grace, while the Comte de Lamotte-Picquet, with scarcely concealed joy, hurried aboard *l'Annibal,* a brand new and partially coppered sixty-four. He kept his officers, including my friend Vernon des Aulnes.

To my great dismay, the Chevalier de Ternay managed to keep his two valued frigate commanders, the Comte de Lapérouse and Monsieur Mengaud de la Hage, along with their ships. We were staying in Brest!

The Comte de Lapérouse tried to raise his officers' morale by explaining that leaving for India would have made us miss the high point of the war – the invasion of England. And by remaining in Brest, we were now certain of taking part of it, with all the attendant honour. These words of comfort had little effect on me, as I knew the truth about this great invasion. When ashore I went to see Maria Kirwan, who did her best to console me. I found this very touching, as she could easily have been pleased that I could stay with her longer than foreseen.

Our luck suddenly changed. On Monday 12th April, while taking the sunshine on the Brest quay, together with Maria Kirwan, I saw *l'Amazone's* pinnace coming into shore, with the Chevalier de la Jonquière at the helm. Seeing me, he ran towards me and asked me to help him find all the officers who were then ashore. Seeing how excited he was, I asked him what was going on. He knew nothing apart from the fact that the Comte de Lapérouse had new orders and wanted to see us all aboard at the double. When we were all finally assembled in the frigate's great cabin, the Captain told us that *la Terpsichore,* one of the Comte de Lamotte-Picquet's frigates, had put to sea the previous day, for a brief sortie, but that her mission was being extended through unforeseen circumstances. With the departure of the Comte de Lamotte-Picquet's fleet imminent, the Comte d'Orvilliers had designated *l'Amazone* to replace her immediately. We had just one day to prepare and not a minute to lose.

Thus, fate sent me back to the Comte d'Estaing's squadron and the troubled waters frequented by his righthand man, Ship's Captain

Flaharn. The Chevalier de Kermean had not foreseen this. By the time he found out it would be too late for him to send me his advice. All the same, I could easily guess what it was: to keep myself as far away as possible from my former mentor and to stay permanently on my guard.

15

We remained stuck in the harbour for more than two weeks. This was the great drawback with the Brest harbour: only luggers, cutters and other small craft able to beat through the entrance passage were capable of putting to sea if the wind was not completely favourable.

Every morning, having looked closely at the sky, the commanders allowed those who were not on duty to go ashore. We had to be on the alert, though, for the slightest change in the weather, and not go too far from the quay, so as to be able to get back on board as soon as our division fired its cannon. I had a guaranteed place at *La Dame au Paon*, where I could meet Maria Kirwan. Vernon des Aulnes often joined us. We had a mild and rainy spring that year, of which I have fond memories. We took innocent advantage of this last respite before setting off on what we thought would be a great and beautiful adventure.

I was at ease with Maria Kirwan. She was a straightforward girl, and virtuous. The first time that I tried to kiss her she stopped me, putting her hand to my lips.

'Do you love me?'

Taken unawares, I did not manage to say 'I love you' straight away, those words so light and simple, yet so serious at the same time.

'I think that you love me,' she continued, 'but you love risking your life in a war even more.'

And, as I remained stuck there, like an idiot in front of her, my arms dangling and my mouth closed, she laughed her fresh little laugh that I loved so much.

'Well then, Pierre-Marie Laforest-Dombourg! Are you going to give it to me, this kiss?'

We would walk, hand in hand, along the Brest quay, or on the Dajot Promenade ... if it was not raining too much. We would often meet Mademoiselle Broudou there. I would point out the ships due to leave the harbour, lending her my little eyeglass, so that she could look at *l'Amazone* and try to spot her beloved. As commander, the Comte de Lapérouse had much less free time than we did. His 'promised one', as Vernon, Maria Kirwan and I called her between ourselves, despite the poor girl not being quite that to the extent she that would have liked, was a charming person. She was approaching twenty-three years of age but seemed much younger. She got on extremely well with Maria Kirwan, who was not unlike her in temperament. Mademoiselle Broudou had been born in Nantes but had spent her youth at Port-Louis on the Île-de-France, while Maria Kirwan was also born on the Île-de-France, even though she remembered little of it. It helped, I think, to bring them together.

At daybreak on Saturday 1st May we finally had a north-easterly. But it was a heavy blow, with squalls and showers sweeping the harbour. It seemed unlikely that our Rear-Admiral would risk going through the harbour entrance in these conditions. I saw a pinnace pulling away from *le Diadème*, carrying those given shore leave. This example was soon followed by the several transport vessels moored in line behind the four ships of our division. We wondered whether the Comte de Lapérouse would follow suit. He did nothing of the sort.

'They don't know the Comte de Lamotte-Picquet very well, if they think that he will be put off by a paltry breeze like this.'

He was right, for shortly afterwards *l'Annibal* signalled to us to weigh anchor, and raised the pennant for the commanders to come aboard for orders. The Comte de Lapérouse occupied himself with that while we raised the anchors. On returning he said that we were ordered to anchor at Bertheaume[73].We went out just before the turn of the tide. By one

73 Translator's note: *Bertheaume*: fortified island to the west of the Brest harbour entrance.

o'clock we were all anchored below the fort in the Bertheaume inlet, except for *le Diadème* and the five transport ships who had had to wait for the boats injudiciously sent ashore. Luckily for them, and for us, the wind stayed in the north-east for the whole day and they were able to get through the harbour entrance that evening on the start of the ebb.

The next morning, before daybreak, we started to get our anchors. The wind had settled into the west. Two hours later the whole division, complete with its transport ships, was sailing towards the Bec du Raz, wind on the starboard beam, under all plain sail with the studding sails being prepared. As for us, we had our topsails set as low as possible but even so, we had regularly to ease the sheets and bowlines so as not to get too far ahead of the convoy. This was not doubt due to our new copper bottom. This put the Comte de Lapérouse and the whole crew in the best of humours, given that there is nothing more important for a mariner than to have the advantage of speed.

We were joined by *l'Artésien,* sixty-four guns, who had been waiting for us at L'Orient with a convoy of merchantmen for Martinique. The Comte de Lamotte-Picquet's division now comprised five ships and three frigates. We went straight to the Aix harbour, off La Rochelle, to pick up more merchantmen.

On 7th May we left La Rochelle with more than fifty-two transport ships and merchantmen. We had a new passenger on board: the Vicomte de Noailles. Originally he had embarked at Brest aboard *l'Annibal,* but along the way the Comte de Lamotte-Picquet had decided to use the superior speed of *l'Amazone* to detach it ahead of the fleet once we got close to Martinique. The Comte de Lapérouse could then pick up local pilots and bring them back to the convoy. The Vicomte de Noailles, for his part, was charged with delivering to the Comte d'Estaing the precious packages, sealed and hidden away, containing the latest orders from the Ministry for himself and the Governor of Martinique.

Shortly after our departure from La Rochelle I was invited to dine at the captain's table, in *l'Amazone's* great cabin, at the request of the Vicomte de Noailles. He had heard my friend Vernon tell the story of the Colonel de Guypair affair and as a result he wished to make my acquaintance.

The Vicomte de Noailles was seated to the right of the Comte de Lapérouse, at the end of the table. I had been asked to sit opposite him, at a slight angle, beside the Chevalier de la Jonquière. The Vicomte was twenty-two years old. He was a handsome man, quite tall, with jovial features and a clear, bright gaze, somewhat dreamy. A young man of the highest nobility, his life had always been divided between the Court and the various cavalry regiments in which he had served. He had started as a second lieutenant, but always in a privileged regime, on account of his prestigious name and his wealth. He was currently commander of a cavalry regiment. In principal, there was no reason for him to go on a campaign which only involved infantry. His chance had come because the Ministry had decided not to mobilise his regiment for the time being, and only to retain a handful of senior officers who could act as the backbone if the decision was changed. This left the Vicomte completely free, as for the moment there was nothing for him to do. And, as he had connections at the highest level of the realm, and as he was friend and brother-in-law to the Marquis de Lafayette, nobody was able, or even wished, to stop him accompanying his friends in the de Dillon regiment.

'I would have loved to have seen de Guypair's face when you called him out. He has always thought he was made from Jupiter's thighbone! That said, you were lucky it was him. If it had been me you would not have ended up in prison, but you may not have got out of it unscathed.'

I was on the point of replying but caught a look from the Comte de Lapérouse and remembered just in time the promise I had made to the Marquis de Langeron. In order to reward me for holding back, no doubt, my commander remarked that nonetheless I had a reputation as a good swordsman.

'Really!' exclaimed the Vicomte. 'What luck! That means I'll have someone I can fence with to pass the time during the voyage.'

The crossing of the Bay of Biscay was heavy-going, with contrary winds, but fortunately no gales. We thought ourselves lucky to weather Cape Finisterre on 20th May, my eighteenth birthday. Our convoy then dragged along at the pace of the slowest ships, heading south-west by west. It took us twenty days to get level with the Canaries. The sails of the fleet and its escort formed a trail of white six nautical miles long. Usually the frigate *la Fortunée* went ahead, *la Blanche* carried up the rear, our five ships were divided up on each side, while *l'Amazone* ranged from the head to the tail.

The Vicomte de Noailles had found, in the person of the Baron de Boismorau, commander of our infantrymen, a fencer as fierce as himself. When the weather was calm they fenced every day across the main deck, between the capstan and the officers' ladder. I joined them from time to time and always beat them fairly and squarely, which never failed to surprise them. The Vicomte de Noailles joked that it was a pity that the commander of the Auvergne regiment had stopped me from fighting Colonel de Guypair, as it might have saved a number of sub-lieutenants from having to study his boring book of tactics. I kept quiet on all of that. I could not forget that my skill with the sword came partly from my private lessons with Flaharn, about which there was nothing to be proud.

We had passed between the Canary Islands and the African coast when, early one morning, we heard a cannon astern. At that moment we were level with the middle of the convoy. The Comte de Lapérouse ordered us to go about and we piled on more sail to get to the rear of the fleet. An unknown ship had used the darkness to catch us up and was trying to capture one of our straggling merchantmen. Monsieur de la Galissonnière, the Ship's Lieutenant commanding *la Blanche,* was up to the situation, being the nephew of the Rear-Admiral who had fought Admiral Byng at the Battle of Minorca in 1756, one of the rare successes of the last war[74].Without hesitation he launched his frigate against the attacker, a ship of war. When we got to the merchantman, which had just managed to escape capture, *la Blanche* had broken off from the fight and was heading north, chased by the enemy vessel. We lost them from view within an hour. The merchantman told us that the English ship was the *Jupiter*, fifty guns.

By then the convoy was covering a hundred and twenty to a hundred and fifty sea miles per day. A week after the attack by the *Jupiter* I saw flying fish for the first time. These fish only fly two hundred feet or so, but they had wings and really did fly. Some fell on the deck. The sailors would collect them to take to the chief cook.

'You can eat this, Sir, and it's good!' they told me.

The next day, after noon, the master pilot Gautier, while looking at our calculations for latitude, said that we would cross the Tropic of Cancer during the night.

'The weather's clear, and we'll take advantage of it by measuring the angle between the sun and the moon on the Tropic of Cancer, in order to calculate our longitude.'

---

74 Translator's note: *Battle of Minorca*: Admiral Byng was later court-martialled and executed by firing squad for his perceived failings at this engagement.

This announcement from the master pilot aroused no enthusiasm from our Volunteers, who would rather have spent their time watching flying fish than fighting with cosines, or the sines of spherical angles, but soon everybody on board was aware of it. Nothing said aboard a ship escapes the notice of the sailors. The next morning at dawn the officer of the watch and the helmsmen were subjected to 'tropical hail', dried peas provided from the ship's stores and thrown from the masthead. A 'coachman' came down from the main top with a message for the captain from the *bonhomme Tropique*[75]. This messenger was wearing imitation seven league boots made from sailcloth, and a hat of boiled leather. He carried a big whip that he cracked on the deck. The Comte de Lapérouse was too good a seaman to refuse to pay his tribute to the *bonhomme Tropique*. Shortly afterwards he himself came down from the main top, with a long beard, oakum hair trailing behind him, and wearing the kind of sheepskin jacket favoured by the Saint-Malo sailors in winter. He was escorted by his 'children', the ship's cabin boys, their hair plastered with sea water and their bodies wound round with rope, so that they looked like Tritons. Those of us who were making their first crossing were baptised in tubs ranged along the side decks.

The Surgeon le Choquet was a great supporter of these entertainments. He told us all the time that it was healthy to oblige the crew to take baths, whether on deck or in the sea. Besides the bathing keeping them clean, it was generally healthy for Europeans who have left their cold or temperate climates to cross the tropics. We were now in a perpetual summer, with the cold of the north Atlantic a distant memory.

On 22nd June we saw our first tropicbirds. According to our master pilot these graceful birds, recognisable by the two long feathers adorning their tails, showed that we were close to the American islands. On 23rd June, at the start of the afternoon watch, just after the sun had passed the meridian, *l'Annibal* ordered *l'Amazone* to pass under her stern. The frigate placed herself to leeward of the ship, level with her port quarter, and matched her speed to that of *l'Annibal.* I saw Vernon leaning on the woodwork of the poop deck cabin and we exchanged a friendly wave. We had been in the same waters for the whole time but had not

75 Translator's note; *bonhomme Tropique*: The Man of the Tropics – the French equivalent of Father Neptune for the baptism rituals of crossing either a Tropic or the Equator for the first time. French fishermen new to the Grand Banks were also 'baptised' by the *bonhomme Tropique.*

seen each other since leaving Brest. A petty officer skilfully threw a weighted package containing our orders and all the despatches for the Comte d'Estaing and the Governor of Martinique. The Comte de Lamotte-Picquet himself took hold of the speaking trumpet to address our commander.

'Monsieur de Lapérouse! Have you calculated our latitude?'

'Fourteen degrees and forty minutes north, Sir!'

The water boiled noisily between the two hulls travelling at close to ten knots through the great blue swell of the Trades. The Comte de Lapérouse had to repeat himself.

'Good! I have the same result as you. According to my estimated longitude we ought to be nine hundred nautical miles from Martinique. Do you agree?'

We could determine our latitude precisely, but longitude was more difficult. It took hours of detailed calculations, with the results often a matter of luck. Unless one had the benefit of several nautical chronometers, as had *l'Annibal.*

'We saw tropicbirds yesterday!' replied the Comte de Lapérouse.

'Ah, the birds? I remember now! Good! Off you go! Head due west! Don't lose any time and send us some good pilots. And above all make sure you go around via the north! Don't forget that the English are now at St Lucia. Thanks to the Comte d'Estaing! You can thank him on my behalf for this voyage!'

The Comte de Lapérouse gave orders to set all the sail we could carry. I went up with the Volunteers to throw off the main t'gallant sail gaskets. We considered our mission an honour. The starboard studding sails were run out too.

*

At sea, Wednesday 23rd June 1779.

After all these weeks continually reducing sail in order not to get ahead of the convoy, the frigate seems to hurtle off like a racehorse held back for too long. The crew is jubilant. The ship's log is regularly showing twelve, thirteen and even fourteen knots. The sails of the fleet drop quickly below the horizon astern.

There is little to do to maintain our speed. Sway in a little there, ease a bowline there, check a sheet now and again, that is all. All the same, I go up several times to the main topsail yard purely for the pleasure of it. It is hauled up hard, and the footrope is no more than a thin and unstable line swinging permanently under my shoes. It is a long time since I have paid that any attention. But what an incredible sight! The hull of the frigate seems to me like a thin rocket framed on the deep and intense blue of the sea by two streaks of foam. I cannot see the bowsprit, but I have the impression that that is what is pulling the masts, regularly swinging them forward. The great rise and fall of the ocean swell lifts the ship by its starboard quarter, making the hull slide forward in a great boiling of water, as if wanting to propel it even more quickly to its destination. Below me, the white sails, filled with the powerful wind of the Trades, stretch out like sounding boards. The yard to which I am holding myself rolls to the rhythm of the swell, its collar, sliding around the mast, producing a repeated moaning. And the regular pendulum movement traced across the sky by the masthead just above my head, more than a hundred feet above the deck, gives me a sensation of flying.

We went thus at an unbridled speed for three days. On the third, the Comte de Lapérouse had lookouts posted on each mast. By evening we had still not sighted land, but the master pilot said that the colour of the water had begun to change, a sign that we were close to Martinique. I could not see much difference myself. The Comte de Lapérouse had the studding sails run in and the main and topgallant sails clewed up, which reduced us to a more sensible speed.

The next morning, during the brief tropical dawn, we saw a huge dark mountain blocking our course across the horizon. It looked like a flattened trapezoid with a band of thick cloud hiding its summit: the island of Martinique.

The captain once more had all the sail the frigate could carry set and she soon started racing again. After an hour the trapezoid resolved into a chain of mountains. Their summits were still hidden in the shadow of the clouds, but bright sunshine poured over the coastline. The coast was now clearly visible through a telescope. The master pilot Gautier estimated that we were about forty-five nautical miles from land. He reckoned that we would have been able to see it at one o'clock the previous night, and that had we not reduced sail we would have piled into it before dawn.

Towards ten in the morning, having raised our big white ensign at the spanker peak and our recognition signal at the masthead, the Comte de Lapérouse and the master pilot headed us towards a headland they had identified as the Caravelle. The Captain had decided, in agreement with the Vicomte de Noailles, to put him ashore with his packages in the sheltered bay behind the Caravelle peninsula, in front of a town called La Trinité. A road connected La Trinité directly to the town of Fort-Royal, crossing the middle of the island. With a good horse, the Vicomte de Noailles could be with the Comte d'Estaing at Fort-Royal harbour within three hours. We would need twelve hours to get round the north of the island.

The Vicomte de Noailles got himself ready. As he liked me, he asked my commander to let me go with him, saying it would be useful for my future education to get to know the interior of Martinique. I was of course very keen on the idea after all those weeks at sea without seeing land. But the Comte de Lapérouse replied with a hearty laugh that it would be better, for my *future education* as a sailor, to get to know the north coast of Martinique and the entrance into Cul-de-Sac Bay at Fort-Royal.

*

East coast of Martinique, Saturday 26th June 1779.

L'Amazone shortens sail again, keeping just her topsails, jibs and spanker. We pass beside the Caravelle islet, which lies about ten cables to starboard. From what I can see of it, it reminds me of the Leviathan of the Bible, its head turned towards the entrance to the bay, tossing up foam with its powerful flippers. Looking at it through the eyeglass, I see that its back is covered with white droppings and that it is surrounded by seabirds, amongst which I recognise the frigatebird. The sea is changing colour. A transparent royal blue has replaced the Prussian blue of the ocean. The water grows lighter and lighter as we progress. And I can smell the land. It is still faint: whiffs of vegetation mingle with the trade wind. The peninsula to port is covered with green shrubs and close-cropped bushes, with shoulders of grey rock showing through. The echo of a gunshot, muffled by the wind and the surf, resounds across the surface of the bay. A flag goes up the pole above the palisade of a small fort. Two other flags rise a little further away, along the coast to our left. The Comte de Lapérouse has a cannon fired to answer this salute.

*

We saw a sloop under sail coming to meet us, flying a big white ensign. With undisguised relief, the Comte de Lapérouse gave the order to heave to, to wait for her.

The sloop told us that *la Blanche* had arrived at Fort-Royal the evening before, having shaken off the *Jupiter* near the Canaries. The Comte d'Estaing had already sent off three frigates and a cutter, with orders to sail east in as wide a line as possible in order to meet the Comte de Lamotte-Picquet. The first part of our mission was accomplished. The Vicomte de Noailles went down the boarding ladder with his precious packages in his hand and jumped nimbly into the sloop which was dancing on the transparent waves. *L'Amazone* got under way again, hardening in her staysails to sail northwards up the coast.

*

Harbour of the Fort-Royal, Martinique, the night of Saturday to Sunday 27th June 1779.

We arrive well after nightfall in the entrance passage to the Royal Cul-de-Sac Bay. More than three nautical miles wide at its mouth, the passage faces west and is well-sheltered from the trade wind swell. Having had unstable winds coming down the coast, we have, as we arrive at the entrance, a light but well-established breeze from the east, which allows us to sail gently into the heart of the anchorage. The crew is all in place for anchoring. The anchor is uncatted. Our pilot puts us on starboard tack to head towards the little lights coming from the windows of the town. Some ships, marked by their stern cabin lights, are already anchored here. Our jibs are hauled down, our mainsails and topsails brailed up. The frigate comes up into the wind, helm down, yards squared. Our mizzen topsail swings over. The anchor drops to the bottom and the men go aloft to gasket the sails. The damp, humid air makes the night sticky. Our clothes are soaked. The wind carries the smell of rotting vegetation mixed with the perfume of vanilla and frangipani blossoms. It is more than fifty days since we left the harbour at the Île d'Aix.

*

At dawn, the weather was cloudy. The light of day showed a harbour full of ships of war lying to their anchors. The ensigns and commanders' pennants floated in the easterly breeze, bringing some brightness to the background of grey sky. *La Blanche* was moored three cables off our bow. Behind her I recognised the four ships of the Comte de Grasse's division, that I had seen leave Brest. A little further away was the Marquis de Vaudreuil's division. He too had left Brest during the winter. Beyond his ships there was an empty space where a spur of Fort-Royal projected out, and after that, almost in the middle of the harbour to the south-west of the fort, lay a dozen ships of the line: the whole squadron that had left Toulon the year before with the Comte d'Estaing.

The Comte de Lapérouse had his gig launched. Nobody could go ashore until he had returned. He was going to pay his respects to the Comte d'Estaing aboard *le Languedoc.* This huge eighty-gun ship was anchored in the middle of the bay, not far from the walls of the Fort-Royal. She was recognisable by her Vice-Admiral's insignia – a big square white ensign raised at the main masthead. A little while later the gig came back without the Captain. The Comte de Lapérouse had sent a message to Lieutenant Guillemin to join him with a full list of everything left aboard in the way of water, provisions, powder and ammunition.

We waited once again. It began to rain, just some big drops at first, then in successive showers which drummed on the fore and after decks and washed the salt from our sails in an instant. Towards noon the sky cleared. A heavy sun lit the harbour. The whole frigate began to steam, until the heat became so strong that the Chevalier de la Jonquière ordered tarpaulins to be rigged over the deck so that Father Aymé, our chaplain, could celebrate mass out in the air.

Lieutenant Guillemin returned for his lunch, alone. Our Captain had been invited to eat with the Comte d'Estaing. He had asked that his boat be sent back as soon as his boatmen had finished their meal. The third lieutenant told us that the Comte de Lamotte-Picquet's convoy had been sighted and was expected that evening. He added that we had to rig the water pipes, as the floating tanks would be coming during the afternoon to replenish our water reserves. We were still forbidden to go ashore until further orders.

When he returned, the Comte de Lapérouse gave no indication what his orders were. This surprised his officers, as it was not his normal habit, whereas many captains, on the contrary, liked to surround everything they did with an air of mystery. While Lieutenant Guillemin supervised the taking aboard of water, the master pilot Gautier assembled myself and the Volunteers on the after deck, in order to show us the harbour.

The Fort-Royal harbour was surrounded by hills covered in greenery. The highest mountain was far off to the north-west. It had three peaks which at this time of year were usually hidden in cloud. The town had been built at the edge of unhealthy marshes which stretched from the foot of the mountains to the harbour. There was very little tide here, which was surprising for a Breton. The frigate hung on its cable, facing the easterly breeze. To port we could see the houses of the town, single- storeyed and built on piles. They nevertheless formed a regular unit, with straight streets. The town was limited to the west by the mouth of a river bordered with pink frangipani trees, whose scent had reached us the night before. On the other side stood the fort's citadel, built on a steep spur that dominated the bay. Between the town and the fort was a wooden jetty where one could come alongside with small craft like corvettes or cutters, and where the ships' boats came ashore. Gautier called this jetty the Savannah Quay. Behind this quay stretched a huge lawn bordered by tamarind and coconut trees. It was the favoured place amongst the townsfolk for taking a stroll. There were no vessels moored in front of the fort on account of the shallows there. Behind the fort was a deep inlet, called the Cul-de-Sac, that we could not see from our anchorage. It acted as a shelter during hurricanes and it was there that the King's ships were careened. Above the Cul-de-Sac, on a hill overlooking the town and the anchorage, was a fort, the Bourbon Redoubt. Its construction had been started after the last war and it had still not been completed.

The fleet and escorts under the Comte de Lamotte-Picquet's command began to enter the harbour towards the end of the afternoon of that day, the 27th June. The frigate *la Diligente*, which had been sent by the Comte d'Estaing to meet the convoy, was ordered to anchor close to us. She was part of the Martinique station and normally moored to a coffin buoy at the mouth of the Cul-de-Sac. On Monday 28th we were ordered to prepare for taking aboard the light infantry company of the Champagne regiment. That was why we had taken on water so quickly. *La Diligente*, for her part, was to take aboard the grenadier company from the de Dillon regiment, which had left Brest at the same time as us. We learned that we would be putting to sea the day after that for a mission whose length and objective we did not know. The Chevalier de la Jonquière confided in me that for the moment the Comte de Lapérouse knew no more than we did. On hearing this, the Surgeon le Choquet asked to see the commander and told him that we were now two months out of Brest, and if our fresh food was not renewed within a month, all our sailors would be incapacitated by scurvy.

'You said it yourself,' replied the Comte de Lapérouse. 'We still have a month's worth left. So you don't need to worry.'

On Tuesday 29th, when the Champagne regiment infantrymen came aboard, we were pleasantly surprised to see the Vicomte de Noailles at their head. He told me that we were going to attack the island of Grenada and take it back from the English in compensation for the loss of St Lucia.

'We had a narrow escape,' the Vicomte told me. 'Imagine! In the letter that I took to the Comte d'Estaing, the Minister told him to return to France, escorting the return convoy from Martinique, to leave the Comte de Grasse on station here, and to send the Comte de Lamotte-Picquet to hold station at Saint-Domingue[76]! We would have made the whole crossing for nothing! But luckily the Comte d'Estaing is a real fighting man. You know what he said to me after reading this letter? He said it made no sense! Moreover, we have had too many losses trying to retake St Lucia. I've talked about it with the officers of the Martinique regiment. They made a bayonet charge against the English defences who massacred them firing grapeshot from their cannons. We were unable to land our artillery. We have to get our revenge! They don't understand that at Versailles!'

The Vicomte also told me that he had been approached by the Ship's Captain Flaharn, who had asked him if I was aboard *l'Amazone.*

'He asked me whether you had said anything about him. He said he likes you a lot and thinks of you as a sort of son. All the same, he seemed very pleased, even relieved, when I told him that you had never spoken about him.'

I explained briefly why Flaharn might present himself in this light, and asked him what he thought of my 'protector'. He replied that he

---

76 Translator's note: *Saint-Domingue*: French colony on what is now the island of Haiti.

could not make a judgement in so short a time. In fact, I think that he was split between his friendship for the Comte d'Estaing, who was very much on Flaharn's side, and the unpopularity of Flaharn amongst the officers of *le Languedoc.* I also asked him whether he had met Flaharn's secretary, the so-called Master Jacques.

'I have not had the honour, but the second in command of *le Languedoc* told me that he is a native of India, touchy and introverted. He refuses to share quarters with the other supernumeraries and was given permission to sleep in one of the ship's boats when they are aboard. He also refuses to eat the usual ship's food, cooking his rice and dried vegetables himself, with no meat! He is left alone as he always has his hand on the handle of the dagger in his belt. He scares people. He looks angry the whole time and he has even been seen quarrelling with Flaharn. At least that's what the officers of *le Languedoc* thought; he and Flaharn speak a language nobody understands.'

The Comte d'Estaing was in command of a strong squadron, composed of twenty-five ships of the line, ten frigates and three transports. For his expeditionary force he took the best units from the regiments stationed at Martinique, leaving virtually nothing to the Governor for the defence of the island.

16

On Thursday 1st July, as soon as the troops had been embarked, we set sail with a following wind. The weather was magnificent. A huge crowd was gathered on the heights overlooking the harbour exit. The whole population of Fort-Royal seemed to have gathered to watch us leave. The ships formed themselves into three columns, with the transports following. The frigates and lighter craft were distributed along the flanks. The wind was from the north-east. Having passed Cape Solomon we altered to port tack, running due south. An English corvette sent from St Lucia to observe us was chased by *l'Iphigénie.* This vessel was, along with *l'Amazone* and *la Gentille,* the only copper-bottomed French frigate. She rapidly caught up with the corvette, who struck her colours after a short exchange of cannon fire. We certainly would have been as successful, but both we and *la Diligente* were under orders always to stay within a cable's length of *le Languedoc.* This was so that at any moment we could get our specific orders, which our commander-in-chief was still working on.

The master pilot Gautier explained to us that navigation in the American islands differed from elsewhere, because of invisible squalls, called over there *white squalls.* You always had to be on your guard, ready at any moment to let go the t'gallant and topsail halyards and to ease all the sheets. He also taught us that from July onwards we would be entering the winter season, a dangerous period because of the hurricanes that mount up during this time. Normally, at this time of year, our ships were either taken into the Cul-de-Sac at Fort-Royal or sent to Tobago, where the hurricanes are less frequent. Grenada is not far from Tobago. I do not know if that is why the Comte d'Estaing had chosen it.

At five in the evening we passed to the south of Saint Lucia. Just after dusk the sky grew as dark as ink and at eight in the evening a violent thunderstorm hit the squadron. We could scarcely make out the stern lights of the ship immediately ahead. After a period of squalls, the wind died towards ten o'clock. The sea was then flattened by torrential rain. Tremendous flashes of lightning lit up the hulls of our neighbours. This was followed by terrible claps of thunder, and a moment later, completely blinded, we found ourselves in unmitigated darkness. In one of these doomsday lightning flashes we saw a seventy-four gun ship pass across our bowsprit. It was *le Marseillais.* We thought she was going to collide with *le Languedoc,* when we saw lightning strike her mainmast. In the ensuing chaos, her main yard was broken.

In the end, incredible as it may seem, there were very few collisions. At midnight the storm cleared and the good weather returned. At dawn a bright sun allowed us to pick out, on our starboard quarter, the green mountain on the south coast of Saint Vincent, which we had passed without seeing. The wind had eased and we were now advancing in our usual way. *Le Languedoc* raised her order flag for *l'Amazone* and *la Diligente* and with her loud hailer asked us to send on board the Vicomte de Noailles and the Comte Edouard de Dillon. When our ship's boat brought back the Vicomte, he was accompanied by a Martinique mulatto, originally from Grenada, who was to act as our guide. There was a council of war in the great cabin. Beforehand, the Vicomte de Noailles had taken me aside to tell me that the Comte d'Estaing had asked each of his two frigate commanders to detach a liaison officer to be with the infantry companies on their disembarkation. The Vicomte wanted to ask the Comte de Lapérouse for me, but he first wanted my opinion, since, before he had left *le Languedoc*, Flaharn had strongly advised him not to recommend me. My 'mentor' was still concerned about my safety, against my own wishes. I told the Vicomte that I'd be only too pleased to accompany him and that it was not for me to take orders from Captain Flaharn. This time, the Comte de Lapérouse did not deny the Vicomte de Noailles' request.

The Comte d'Estaing intended to disembark before nightfall in the Beauséjour inlet on the west coast of Grenada, about three miles north of the Saint George Fort. The Champagne regiment light infantry, along with the grenadiers of the de Dillon regiment, were to go ashore beforehand a mile further south in the Molinier inlet, below a headland called the Bois Maurice Point. They were to secure the heights to the south of there, so as to cover the disembarkation of the army across from the Saint George garrison.

The two frigates anchored outside the Molinier inlet, ready to pound the Bois Maurice Point with their cannons. An English flag was flying at the summit, and it was possible they had a battery there.

L'Amazone's sloop made the first landing with a detachment charged with gaining a foothold to the north of the Molinier inlet shore. The Vicomte de Noailles and I were aboard. We rowed towards a little beach of greyish-white sand surrounded by coral reefs.

*

West coast of Grenada, Friday 2nd July 1779, end of the afternoon.

The weather is fine and the clarity of the water is incredible. There is nobody on the shore; the place seems deserted. At the end of the inlet a wide footpath goes up through the dense vegetation. At the other end of the beach, the de Dillon grenadiers have already found a little goat track that weaves up the cliff.

Everything is quiet. The two ship's boats loaded with soldiers join us. The sloop and the two boats make two more journeys, after which our whole detachment goes up the footpath in single file. After ascending for several minutes we arrive at a wide cart track which follows the coast, and which we use to head off southwards. Down below to our right we can see the sea, while to our left fields of sugar cane rise up the slopes. When we reach the top of the ridge leading down to the Bois Maurice Point, the Vicomte de Noailles has us leave the road to head due north across young waist-high sugar canes. Our guide explains that these are cuttings.

It is very hot. My shoes and stockings, soaked in sea water, soon dry, but I am perspiring freely and my canvas uniform is drenched in sweat, sticking to my back and armpits like a second skin. After walking for half an hour, the Vicomte de Noailles tells his captain to stop. We are overlooking a little bay which curves eastwards – the Grand Mâle inlet, according to the guide. Directly below us, a stream coming from the interior of the island runs down the bottom of a valley between two slopes planted with sugar canes. The track that we had left crosses this watercourse by means of a bridge. On the other side is a kind of hamlet. It is the settlement of a French planter, Monsieur Olivier. Our guide also points out the Strongton farm, named after its English owner, a little higher up the stream. From our position the buildings look like dolls' houses, but they are real little villages. The master's house and outbuildings, the stables and the buildings for processing the sugar are all in stone. They are surrounded by the lightly-built huts of the blacks. All the fields are empty. The inhabitants and their slaves must have fled, or else are hiding in their houses. The ridge across from us, on the other side of the valley, is called the Saint Eloy Hill. That is our objective. Saint George is just behind it. All the heights overlooking the cultivated slopes are covered by impenetrable tropical forest whose edge starts half a mile to our left. We can see, in the distance, the de Dillon grenadiers. They are taking up a position much lower than ours, between the road and the summit of the Bois Maurice Point. The English flag has already been replaced by a white ensign which stands out against the light blue background of the sea. Behind us, the disembarkation of the Comte d'Estaing's seventeen hundred men has begun in the Beauséjour inlet. Not a single shot has been fired.

*

Two roads led to Saint George. The main one was the one we had taken before turning left. It went down further, and along the edge of the sea below the fields of sugar canes. A second track, starting at the bottom of the valley, zig-zagged up the Saint Eloy Hill, passing through the forests on its northern flank, to get to the top.

The Vicomte de Noailles had been instructed to seize the ridge of the Saint Eloy Hill at daybreak. As soon as the sun was down we descended to cross the valley and its stream, before going up the other side through the woods. Towards nine in the evening, gunshots ahead of us echoed round the night. They seemed to come from the other side of the slope we were climbing. The Vicomte de Noailles made us press on more quickly, but once we had reached the ridge we could hear nothing more. The Vicomte told the captain to position his men along the edge of the forest, facing south, and have them sleep and eat in turns, while rotating the guard.

The soldiers had supply bread. I had only brought a few sea biscuits, but I was not hungry and I did not want to make myself thirsty by eating. I had already drunk two thirds of the water in my canteen. The air was still hot, despite it being night. We had not come across any snakes, but I thought suddenly of the mounted 'spearhead' that I had seen in the booth at the Brest prison. The convict taxidermist had said that it came from Martinique, which by no means meant that there were not any on Grenada. I could not sleep all night, mindful as I was of every crackling in the undergrowth around me.

Dawn found us on open ground at the edge of the thick woods which crowned the summit of the Saint Eloy Hill. We retreated into the edge of the tropical forest to hide under its cover. The vegetation was extraordinarily dense. Tree ferns and flowering trees with huge leaves, interwoven with vines, created impenetrable thickets in which the soldiers used their swords to cut paths between the observation posts. Tiny humming birds buzzed from flower to flower. The calls of unknown birds echoed under the green vault behind us. I had forgotten my night-time fears. Besides, even though I had seen scores of lizards, I had not seen the tail of a single snake.

Having inspected the company's dispositions, the Vicomte de Noailles had a sort of room thirteen feet square cut in the forest, completely covered by foliage, from which he could observe the Saint George fort. With his eyeglass he observed the English positions in front of us. Our emplacement overlooked a valley parallel to the Grand Mâle inlet, into which flowed a little river. Besides the river was a strange collection of buildings comprising several barns and vats set up on terraces. Our guide explained that it was an indigo dye works and the river was called the Saint-Jean river. The right bank of this watercourse, from our side, was also planted in sugar cane cuttings. The left bank rose straight up in a steep slope, under a hill whose summit was about half a mile from us as the crow flies. It was called Hospital Hill, as the Saint George hospital was situated on the ridge of its western spur.

Some have since said that Hospital Hill was a sugar loaf mountain. This is an exaggeration. It is a horizontal ridge, from east to west, about two thirds of a mile long. At its highest point, no more than six hundred feet above sea level, it bends to the south. It is true that the English had carefully cut down all the vegetation on its steep slopes to make a talus, and that they had enclosed the whole summit of the ridge with lines of palisades from which they could cheerfully shoot down anyone foolhardy enough to try to climb up that way. They had also constructed a permanent battery on the western spur, above the hospital. They had installed four 24-pound guns, facing the sea, to stop any entry into the port, but they were of no use against a land attack coming from the interior of the island.

We had a good view of the Saint George fort. It was built on a rocky headland which overlooked the entrance to the port, for the moment hidden from sight. We could not see a single sail. The English ships had all taken shelter in the port, under the protection of the fort, while ours were still at the Beauséjour anchorage to the north. We could easily see the movements of the English at the gate of the fort and in the part of the town built beside the sea, as well as along the summit of Hospital Hill. We could hear their voices echoing, without understanding what they were saying. It looked like they were emptying the fort in order to reinforce the hill. Eventually I fell asleep.

*

On the ridge of Saint-Eloy Hill, Grenada, Saturday 3rd July 1779, early afternoon.

I am woken by the sounds of men clomping towards our position in the forest edge. I open my eyes. It must be midday. The sun has pierced the grey clouds. A group of men, talking amongst themselves, are coming along the path cut into the forest. There are five of them. The Vicomte de Noailles quietly tells me who they are before going to greet them: the Comte Arthur de Dillon, commander of the regiment that carries his name, his brother Edouard, who disembarked at the Molinier inlet with the de Dillon grenadiers; the Comte de Pondevaux, wearing the uniform of a lieutenant-colonel of the Auxerrois regiment; the Comte de Durat of the Cambrésis regiment; and our general-in-chief himself, the Comte d'Estaing, Vice-Admiral of the Seas of Asia and America. He is in shirtsleeves with a simple white waistcoat and the blue sash of the Order of Saint-Esprit around his neck. It is the first time I have seen him. He seems as tall as Flaharn, but without the latter's shoulders. He still has youthful features, not yet being fifty: a square, dimpled jaw, a straight nose, big but finely drawn, light brown eyes that he alternately furrows and opens wide as he looks around him. He is weathered from the months spent at sea since his departure from Toulon. He has the determined look of a general who has knowingly disobeyed his government's orders, and who is gambling everything in full knowledge of the risks he is taking and the means at his disposal. Flaharn is not there. No doubt he has remained aboard *le Languedoc.* He fears neither God nor the Devil, but he is not the kind of man to take unnecessary risks. He must have thought that I had stayed aboard *l'Amazone.*

*

The Comte d'Estaing had come with his principal officers to look at the enemy dispositions, that could be seen very clearly from the Saint-Eloy Hill, and to hold a council of war. He listened with interest as the Vicomte de Noailles said that the English seemed to be emptying the Saint George fort in order to reinforce the defences of Hospital Hill. The Comte d'Estaing announced that our principal objective would be Hospital Hill. It had to be taken first, after which the Saint George fort would fall easily. Having decided this, he presented his plan of attack: approach at night, attack at dawn from the east, where the slope was less steep, having first launched a diversionary attack from the west, between the indigo works and the hospital.

The Comte de Pondevaux was assigned to the diversion with two hundred men who were waiting behind us near the Olivier farm. He left us, together with the Comte de Dillon, in order to relieve the de Dillon regiment grenadiers, who were at that time positioned to our right, opposite Saint George at the top of the coast road. The grenadiers had already reconnoitred the approach route for the diversionary attack the night before. It was during this reconnaissance that they had fired the shots we had heard. The Comte d'Estaing considered this to be a good thing, as the English would be even more convinced of an attack from that quarter.

I followed the Comte d'Estaing, together with the Comte de Durat and the Vicomte de Noailles. Seeing me there, the Comte d'Estaing said he was pleased that the Vicomte de Noailles had brought me with him as directed. I introduced myself as the son of the Ship's Lieutenant Laforest-Dombourg, killed in action, and added, deliberately, that my father was a friend and companion in arms to the Marquis de Kersalaun. As this did not arouse any particular reaction from the Comte, I carried on, saying that the marquis had been an officer in the army and had fought at Fontenoy in the Royal des Vaisseaux regiment.

'I never had the honour of meeting this Marquis de Kersalaun,' replied the Comte, 'and the name means absolutely nothing to me. But I strongly encourage you to follow the example of your late father, who has shown you the right path. I heartily approve of good relations between naval officers and their army counterparts since to be fully competent, a naval officer must have an understanding of land-based warfare and not remain solely obsessed with navy methods. After all, of what use is a naval force if not to land troops to carry out land-based operations?' This idea of the role of the Navy was particular to the Comte d'Estaing, and if one considers his campaigns, it had often guided his actions.

We found our troops bivouacked at the Pradine farm, the muster point for the attack. Monsieur Pradine was French, like many of the wealthy landowners of the island, which had only been occupied by the English since the Seven Years' War. The force assembled by the Comte d'Estaing was a disparate collection. Apart from the de Dillon regiment, which was almost complete, with its colonel and its flags, the rest was composed of detachments raised from different regiments, mainly from Martinique, which he had left practically defenceless, much to the anger of the Governor. We had about seventeen hundred men ashore. The English garrison had just over six hundred, making things three to one in our favour. Given that we were attacking a well-defended enemy, that was not too disproportionate, but the big difference was that the English garrison on Grenada was mainly composed of militiamen, while the Comte d'Estaing had elite and battle-hardened troops at his disposal.

The orders for the attack were given before dusk. We were told that the English were well-entrenched and had cannons. Since we had none, we were ordered to carry on our backs navy slingshots and their supports, for an eventual attack on the palisades. We were to go up the eastern spur of Hospital Hill in three columns. The left would be made up of the de Dillon regiment, preceded by an advance guard. The other units would be split between the two other columns, one in the centre, commanded by Monsieur Edouard de Dillon, the other on the right, commanded by the Vicomte de Noailles. The Comte d'Estaing had announced that the English had carried all their valuables into the Hospital Hill bastion, and that the soldiers could have it by right of pillage. It was just the kind of thing one would expect from such a person...

We only had supply bread to eat, with water. There was no wine, but the owner of the farm had some rum barrels opened and each man had his tot. The signal to move was given at eleven o'clock. The companies formed up in the darkness, silently, and set off at a march one behind the other. The plantation owner had provided guides for us. The change of position did not give many difficulties, as the sugar cane plantations are crossed by cart tracks for taking the harvest to the mills for processing. This was not like the sunken roads of Brittany, where everyone would soon be lost.

By midnight we were at the foot of the hill. The columns of attack separated to get to their departure points at the foot of the steep slope that rose towards our objective, lost in the darkness above us. With the Vicomte de Noailles, we were on the edge of Hospital Hill's north-east flank. Everyone rested where he was. I slept deeply. In this kind of situation, where the body is tired from marching and from lack of sleep, you find oneself overcome by a sort of beneficent numbness which makes you insensible to fear, but which does not diminish the sharpness of your mind.

*

The north-east flank of Hospital Hill, island of Grenada, Sunday 4th July 1779.

We are woken towards two in the morning with a low word from the officers and sergeants passing from group to group. Each man checks his arms, in the dark and in silence. We wait for a long time for the signal to begin the attack. It is given by the sound of lively gunshots which suddenly ring out, creating echoes which reverberate right to the seaward end of Hospital Hill. It is the diversionary attack launched by the Comte de Pondevaux's soldiers. Drums begin to beat. We launch ourselves forward. The slope is steep and we have to haul ourselves up by pulling on the stalks of the half-burnt bushes which stretch right up to the top of the redoubt. It is a benefit at the start, as one is less confused by the darkness when using one's hands to make progress, but the effort is extreme, and I am soon dripping with sweat. Daybreak comes quickly. The sky lightens to my left. The English start to spot us from the top. I hear the sound of their guns. The drum rolls get faster. They are our drums. How on earth can you play the drum on such a gradient? A single cannon goes off, somewhere on the other side of the ridge. I no longer feel any tiredness. I no longer think of anything. I hang on to the roots with both hands to pull myself more quickly towards the palisade that I can see, lit by the rising sun, at the top of the ridge. The shooting intensifies. Bullets ring out noisily all around me. I sense, rather than see, men rolling down the slope beside me, their grey-white coats suddenly starred with purple. Our soldiers shout *Vive le Roi*[77]*!* I start to hear cries of pain, but I have no fear. I feel as if I am dreaming and at the same time I am well aware that everything is real. It is a strange sensation. Grenadiers armed with axes, picks and ropes rush towards the relative shelter at the foot of the palisade. Our light infantry, lined up along the slope, aim at any Englishman who puts his head above the parapet. The roar of a huge heavy artillery salvo rips through the air, drowning the sound of gunshots and shouts. The grenadiers pull down the posts of the palisade. Another salvo, as powerful as the one before, roars out again. This time I recognise the sound, and realise what is happening: a ship of the line, off Saint George, is firing broadsides one after the other. As we are the only ones with such ships here, they must be ours. The grenadiers have opened a breach. The Vicomte de Noailles rushes unto it. The infantrymen start climbing again, brandishing their rifles, bayonets fixed, and shouting. I follow them, shouting, as they do, at the top of my voice: *Vive le Roi!*

*

Somehow or other I got to the flat area at the brow of the hill. I could see a confused melee going on at the top of the west spur. The Union

77 Translator's note: *Vive le Roi!: Long Live the King!*

Jack had disappeared from its pole at the end of the hill. The soldiers of the English militia still alive were throwing down their arms and raising their arms in surrender. Everything seemed to calm down. The sergeants were assembling the prisoners. The white flag rose in place of the English colours. There was silence, the calm after the storm. I went along the ridge. An excited group had collected at the foot of the flagpole. The Vicomte de Noailles was there, as was the Comte d'Estaing, recognisable by his height. He was bare-headed and still in shirt-sleeves and waistcoat, with his blue sash across. He was being presented to a grenadier sergeant to whom he gave a round hearty praise.

'I promote you to officer!'

There were shouts of *Vive le Roi!*

A lieutenant explained to the Vicomte de Noailles that the Chevalier de Vence, who had arrived first at the top of the redoubt, had run without stopping to the other end, where he had cut the flag halyard with his sword. The fight was still raging on the east end of Hospital Hill and, with the element of surprise now lost, the English soldiers had surrounded him with their bayonets. He would certainly have succumbed had not the grenadier sergeant arrived and fought with him like a lion until our soldiers arrived, thereby saving his life.

The business was by no means finished, however. Some of the English defenders had gone down the west spur of the hill and taken position in the Saint George fort, over which the English colours were still flying. The fort was built on a rocky headland which formed the north mole of the port entrance. The Governor, Earl Macartney, sent an officer carrying a white flag to parley. He suggested a twenty-four hour ceasefire and negotiations. The Comte d'Estaing took out his watch and said to him in a loud voice, clearly articulating every word, that if the fort had not surrendered within two hours, he would attack it and the garrison would be massacred. At the same time he had the four 24-pound cannons at the end of the ridge, that the English had not had the time to spike when they retreated, aimed at the Saint George fort. It was possibly no more than an empty threat, but it came from the man who had laid waste to Sumatra, and it was taken seriously. The English Earl did not insist, and surrendered. This was just a week after *l'Amazone's* arrival in Martinique.

The Comte d'Estaing had promised the soldiers that whatever was found on Hospital Hill would be their booty. It was clear that the

Governor and the richest English townsfolk had brought their most precious possessions to the Hospital Hill redoubt, thinking they would be safe there. The collected goods were then sold at auction, being mostly bought back by their owners, including Earl Macartney. The proceeds of this sale were to be transferred to the Army strongboxes and distributed later to the soldiers, or to the families of those killed, as a bonus. It was a similar system to that applied to the prizes taken by privateers.

I was not present at this sale as I was keen to rejoin my ship. The Vicomte de Noailles was to stay with the Comte d'Estaing and return with him to *le Languedoc.* I had no wish to go with him and meet Flaharn. The tension which had sustained my mind and body for many hours was draining rapidly away, and I felt an immense and sudden tiredness. I asked permission from the Vicomte to go down to the port to find a boat which could take me back to my frigate, which I assumed was still anchored behind the Bois Maurice Point.

I had already seen several ship's boats go past below the Saint George fort, so I went down to the quay to find a boat to take me to my ship. I had the good fortune of coming across the Chevalier de Lantivy, a senior of mine at the Marine Guard school. He had already been promoted to Ensign. We had not seen each other since I had left Brest in 1777. He was one of those who had thrown me into the Penfeld to teach me how to swim. It was strange to meet again on this distant island, at the other end of the earth, after so much sound and fury. We scarcely knew each other but we hugged like two brothers. He told me that *l'Amazone* had not remained at anchor, but had been ordered to cruise on the leeward side of Grenada to stop any smaller English craft trying to get to sea. I had a good chance of seeing her pass by without being able to stop her. He proposed that I go with him to *l'Annibal.* This was better than dragging my feet at Saint George, with the risk of the Vicomte de Noailles changing his mind and ordering me to accompany him aboard *le Languedoc.*

Going aboard a sixty-four gun ship, I was met by the familiar smells, sounds and atmosphere. But I was also completely lost. There is a world of difference between a little frigate and a ship of the line with its crew of seven or eight hundred men. Luckily, Vernon looked after me. It was lunchtime. The Comte de Lamotte-Picquet, who was in the habit of having his Marine Guards at his table, invited me to join them. Once it was learned that I had been part of the land operation, I was immediately bombarded with questions. For three days I had eaten nothing but ship's biscuits and drunk nothing but warm water and my ration of rum at the Pradine farm. I thought I was hungry, but my stomach knotted at the first mouthful and after a single glass of wine I felt unwell. I asked the Comte de Lamotte-Picquet to excuse me, and Vernon took me to the gun room, where the Marine Guards and Volunteers sleep on a ship. This has an advantage for them, as the deckhead is taken up with the steering lines from the ship's wheels, and so hammocks cannot be hung there. So these little gentlemen sleep like lords in proper bunks. The gun room on a ship is on the after part of the lower gun deck, the first deck, where the big 36-pound cannons are housed. This means that when the decks are cleared, its bulkheads, furniture and partitions are all dismantled and taken down to the orlop. I would soon witness this.

I slept late that morning and was left in peace. Vernon gave me the necessities for washing myself, loaned me a clean shirt, and had me shaved by a barber's assistant. I then went up to the quarter deck and presented myself to the officer of the watch, who told me that the ship's second captain, Monsieur de Rivière, had wanted to see me once I was up. He added that I was lucky not to be disturbed in my sleep, as we were expecting the order to go to battle stations at any moment. I had noticed, when coming up from the gun room, that they were winching nets full of cannonballs to the bulwarks and that in the centre of the gun decks they had deposited stocks of reserve cannonballs for combat. I waited on the quarterdeck while the second captain was told of my presence.

The second captain received me in the great cabin and told me that I could not return to my frigate for the moment. The Comte de Lamotte-Picquet and the Comte de la Croix, his Flag Captain, were attending a council of war aboard *le Languedoc*, to which the Comte d'Estaing had returned. They feared that Byron[78] was on his way. Monsieur de Rivière asked me what was my combat station aboard *l'Amazone*, and when I told him that I was on the gun deck, he assigned me to the

78 Translator's note: *Byron*: At that time Rear-Admiral and later Vice-Admiral John Byron, grandfather of Lord Byron, and a distinguished naval commander. His attack on the Comte d'Estaing's fleet at the Battle of Grenada was his last major action, after which he resigned.

lower gun deck to replace a Marine Guard who had had to disembark at Martinique.

The drums beat us to action stations at half past two during the night of the 5th to 6th July, just as we received the signal to weigh anchor. While the partitions were knocked down I went forward to the middle of the lower gun deck to present myself to Ship's Lieutenant de la Bourdonnaye, who was in charge of the lower deck guns. He assigned me to guns nine to eleven, situated level with the lower windlass of the main capstan. I introduced myself to my three gun captains. My role was to act as a messenger between them and Lieutenant de la Bourdonnaye. It was the first time I had seen a 36-pound cannon up close. It bore no resemblance to the 12-pound guns I was used to on my frigate. This monster was as high as my shoulders on its carriage and weighed nine thousand pounds. It needed fourteen or fifteen men, including the gun captain, to manoeuvre it. The gun captains showed me the line that was not to be crossed when the guns were firing if you did not want to be made into mincemeat by the recoil. 'As long as the breech ropes don't break, of course', they added. The battery was made up of twenty-eight cannons, fourteen on each side.

*

At sea off the west coast of Grenada, Tuesday 6th July, three in the morning.

The Marine Guard looking after guns five to eight shakes my hand in a friendly way. He has freckles, round cheeks and a turned-up nose – the face of a child. He gives the order to ready the starboard guns. The gunports have been left open overnight because of the heat. As the sea is calm they are left like that. Boys bring charges of powder handed out through bulkheads on the orlop deck by the armourers. These bulkheads are guarded by armed sentinels, bayonets fixed.

The starboard guns are loaded and run out. The smoke from the linstocks collects under the deckhead in the dim light of the combat lamps fixed to the planking between the open ports. After all the noise of clearing for combat, a great silence descends. The men and the officers try to interpret the orders and whistles coming from the quarterdeck, two decks higher. All the same, we have no sense that we are moving. The heavy ship seems totally immobile. There is not a breath of air. I can see nothing and have no idea what is happening outside.

The light of dawn pierces the gun ports, eclipsing that of the lanterns. I feel the ship move under my feet. Looking over the shoulder of the gun captain, along the barrel of gun number ten, I recognise the Bois Maurice Point passing gently by. I cannot see our other ships.

The two leading hands of gun number ten gun crew exchange a couple of words and lean towards the corner of the gun port to look forward.

'Quiet!' says the gun captain.

I move a few paces to the side to have a look too. I can see several of our ships, recognisable by their white flags; they are hard on the wind, three or four cables ahead of our starboard bow. I recognise the last one. It is *l'Amphion*, fifty guns, a ship which came across with us from Brest. We should have been in line with *L'Amphion*, but six places behind her. This means that the rear guard, of which we are the back marker, has fallen to leeward of the line of battle, leaving a big hole in our formation.

The sea is beautiful and the ships are advancing majestically, all sail set, in a light breeze. The sky, which has so often been covered since our arrival, is completely clear. The blue water surrounding us is luminous and transparent. We can hear it running gently along the side of the hull; its music drifts in through the gun ports and flows along the gun deck. It is truly the start of a magnificent day. It must be about half past seven.

We hear the sound of cannon fire, still quite far ahead. It quickly gets closer. Looking again through the gun port, I see *l'Amphion* amidst a cloud of thick smoke through which gunfire flashes intermittently. The first English ship comes out of the smoke. The rest of the English line follows, in good order, bowsprit to stern, except for one or two ships whose rigs seem to have been damaged, and which are drifting away dangerously towards the coast. We are too far away for them to target us; they file away towards Saint George, astern of us. Is it already over?

The gap between us and *l'Amphion* is growing smaller. She is too straight ahead of us to see without leaning out of the gun port. We have caught up with the line of battle. Or rather, it has eased off to allow us so to do. We hear random cannon fire far astern. As we are last in line, I assume that Byron and the Saint George fort are exchanging fire. Then we hear nothing.

I am starting to wonder why we have not tacked in order to go after the English when I see a Marine Guard rush down the main companionway and run towards Lieutenant de la Bourdonnaye. It is my friend Vernon. He gives a note to the Ship's Lieutenant who shouts to us to prepare the port guns as quickly as possible. The gun crews cross the deck and furiously haul back the guns on that side in order to load them. Soldiers from the onboard garrison come to help them, quickly dividing themselves up amongst the teams of sailors behind each gun, and enabling them to manoeuvre the guns more quickly, with more manpower on the tackles.

'Ready! Port, aim to dismast! Fire on command! Gun captains, hold back with your linstocks!'

The lieutenant inspects all the guns. He has his watch in his hand. He sees that I am trying to look at it and turns its face towards me as he goes past. Half past ten already! Everybody is tense now. The atmosphere on the gun deck has changed completely. Everyone looks at his neighbour in silence. I know that the crew of *l'Annibal* has already been under fire. For my part, this is my first naval battle. I wonder what it will be like. In a few moments, the world will be set ablaze. There won't be time to think. My nerves are on edge. I remember the terrible story told to me by old Le Touze, at Le Croisic. Shivers run down my spine, making me tremble. I start to perspire freely. I am not the only one! I can hear someone's teeth chattering in the silence. The fear is palpable. I can truly feel it in the air all around me. It is quite different from what I felt before the attack on Hospital Hill. I go and stand behind gun number ten, port side, making sure to be beyond the recoil of the breech ropes. The reflections on the sea contrast sharply with the shadow on the lee side of the ship. The starboard gun ports behind me throw great pools of almost blinding light onto the gun deck beneath my feet. I feel a sort of stirring to my left. A ship's bowsprit starts to pass by to leeward. Its figurehead is a leaping lion. One of Byron's ships must be called *Lion.* Then I can see nothing but her hull through the gun ports. She is sailing faster than us, overtaking us steadily, even though she is less than three hundred feet to leeward. I can clearly see her guns and aimers through the open gun ports of her lower gun deck. Her cannons look a little smaller than ours. They too are holding fire. She must be a sixty-four.

That's only a few guns less than us, but the weight of metal that she can discharge is considerably less than ours.

She lets go her broadside: a belt of orange balls of fire in a great horizontal cloud of smoke, a brutal deafening explosion. I feel the shock of the cannonballs pounding into *l'Annibal's* hull. Shards of timber fly everywhere, spinning around the gun deck. She has fired at our hull but the cannonballs have not passed right through. The patrols who remove the wounded and dead from the decks carry away several bodies. One of them has had his neck pierced by a splinter. One of his carriers tries to close the wound and I see blood spurting between his fingers like wine from a burst goatskin. I tell myself that he is finished. All the same, I have time to reflect that the shock of the salvo was not as terrible as I had feared. It is definitely a sixty-four! At that moment the big loud-hailer gives the order to fire, and the thirty-six port-side guns, the 18-pounders on the upper gun deck, along with our own, let go all together. My two feet jump on the decking and I feel as if I have been deafened. The wind carries the smoke towards the English. As it clears, I see that her mizzen topmast has been carried away. They are already cutting away its stays. Our gunners, helped by the soldiers, have quickly reloaded; they run the guns out for the next discharge. *Lion* is sailing less rapidly now, but she persists in going broadside to broadside. It is a mistake. The loud-hailer orders a new broadside before she has had time to release her own. This time, her main topmast goes by the board and she veers off, leaving her place to the next in line. Well done! I say to myself; she would have been better to have disengaged immediately. I feel an irrational hatred for these English who want to kill me.

Another bowsprit appears. I don't see the figurehead passing, but from the first glimpse I feel that this is more serious. A seventy-four, like us! She fires her broadside just as our guns are run out. I cannot help closing my eyes. I feel a kind of breath to my left, as if air had been sucked suddenly into a pipe. I am hit hard in the face by a sharp object which cuts deep into my cheek and falls to the deck, leaving a bloody trail. I touch my cheek with my hand and find a gaping hole. My teeth seem out of place. Strangely, I feel no pain. My fingers slide easily over my skin as if it had been buttered. The object which hits me has fallen at my feet. It is a big piece of bone, with hair still attached to it, and bits of sticky jelly. That is what has buttered my cheek: half the head of the leading hand of the crew of my number eleven gun. He has had his head taken off above the ears by a 36-pound ball that has crossed the ship and buried itself into the starboard planking. I wipe my eyes and feel as if I have brains in my mouth. I spit out as hard as I can. I feel as if I am going to be sick.

'Wait! Aim to dismast!'

The seventy-four is also faster than us and is overhauling us easily. Opposite, I see her gun crews working like devils to reload their guns at the end of their breech ropes. I have not been sick. Our loud-hailer orders us to fire. Our two port batteries go off again, in perfect unison. The English ship slows down, her sails holed by our cannonballs. She can no longer overtake us to leeward. Now it's the turn of our crews to swab out and furiously ram in the wads and ball. Opposite, we can see them starting to run out their guns. Thanks to the help from the soldiers, we are quicker at handling our cannons. The English have hardly begun to fire, at will this time, with well-spaced shots, when our next broadside, just as powerful and well-aimed as the previous ones, hits them again. This time, she suddenly veers off downwind as her mizzen topmast falls completely. I have time to read her name under the stern rail: *Cornwall.* Already, a third English ship is coming up on our port side, a sixty-four. We give her two broadsides to her one, and she falls away rapidly. A fourth ship takes her place. Like the others, she easily out-sails us. She takes our salvo before being able to release her own and her gunners reply with disordered fire. For a moment she is side to side with us, under our lee. I have the feeling that she wants to use her superior speed to overtake us and continue on along to leeward of our line. But *l'Annibal* has found her rhythm. She fires complete broadsides, one after the other, as regularly as a metronome and twice as quickly as the English ship, which finally breaks off. She wears ship and disappears astern.

Nothing else comes up under our lee. I think we can all have a breather, but I hear the sound of feet running on the main companionway and a shout.

'All hands to the starboard guns! At the double!'

I oversee the change of side and the reorganisation of our gun crews. We have had some losses. Bodies are dragged away and piled on top of each other at the foot of the main companionway. Blood! Blood! It is everywhere on the deck and easy to slip on. The ship's boys have been waiting for this moment, and throw buckets of sand around to soak it up. They look understandably terrified; luckily their mothers cannot see them right now. Thanks to the infantry reinforcements we still have enough men to manhandle the guns.

This time, it seems as if the whole English squadron is coming up to windward of us, ship after ship. We can no longer stop them as they are taking our wind. We switch to firing at will. Our guns aim at the horizon through thicker and thicker smoke, both ours and the English, all of which is now blowing back at us through the gun ports. Splinters of wood fly everywhere despite the nets laid over the planking. Bodies are continuously dragged away behind me by the patrols charged with keeping the decks clear. The gun captain of my number nine gun falls. While he is being taken away I get close to the barrel. I put my chin on it to check the aim but pull it away immediately. The metal is scorching hot. The number ten gun captain pulls me by the sleeve and points to his deputy, who takes over from me. He seems to know what he is doing. I take up my position behind. Only one thing counts – to fire more rapidly than them! The infernal din of guns being fired is never-ending. The huge masses of metal leap back one after the other. Swab! Charge! Rammer! Ball! Wad! Rammer! Run out! The gun hits the sill of the gun port: nine thousand pounds moved by the gun crews' arms! There is no longer any need to aim, as the English, with the windward advantage, are crowding ever closer and we are scarcely a pistol shot away. Fire! Every shot hits home. We are now firing at the hulls, just like the English. At six hundred yards a 36-pound cannonball can pierce three feet of oak and we are now at a hundred yards. It seems that the sailors of the Royal Navy call it the *slaughterhouse*, the main battery of a man of war in combat. I can believe it!

Suddenly the breech ropes of gun number eight part. The huge mass of metal leaps backwards unhindered. The little red-haired Marine Guard posted to my left leaps aside, but not quickly enough. The great weight catches his left leg and sends him sprawling onto his back. He now has just one foot, and the other is a shapeless mass of flesh and bone, flattened along with his shoe. I see his open mouth. He must be screaming, but nobody can hear him, or else I am completely deaf. I go to pull him away but the surgeon's crew has already arrived. An Ensign who is going round all the guns gives me a shake to get me behind my guns again and shouts in my ear that I must cool down the cannons with a mix of water and vinegar kept in barrels on the gun deck, if I don't want the same thing to happen to me. The English ships, faster sailors, are still passing us inexorably. Our forward guns are still firing at those who have just passed while our rear guns are aiming at the bow of the next one. My throat is choked with smoke. It stings my eyes. Everything is dark as night. The heat is hellish and I can scarcely breathe. It reminds me of the fire at the Brest hospital – but worse.

A little ship's boy carrying a powder charge slips on a pool of blood and falls over to my right. I bend down to help him up and feel a terrible blow to my shoulder which knocks me backwards. I find myself on the decking, unable to move, buried beneath a disordered pile of bodies. There is no air to breath. Violent pain suddenly arrives and I half lose consciousness.

*

I came round as the men charged with picking up the wounded pulled me from the horrible pile in which I was buried: torsos, haunches, half-bodies emptying themselves onto me. One of my legs was caught in a pile of guts which one of the buckles on my shoes ripped as I was pulled free. A cannonball which had come straight through the gun port of gun number ten had cut in half all the crew to the right of the gun and would have done the same to me had I not bent down to help the powder boy. My concern for him had saved my life. I had been sprayed from head to toe with unmentionable liquids...and with blood. It was everywhere. I could feel its bitter taste in my mouth; it was rolling down my neck under my clothes. It was in my eyes too; I could no longer see.

Two men dragged me to the scuttle down to the orlop where the surgeons had their post. Lieutenant Bourdonnaye, seeing me pass by, had me smell some salts, which seemed to revive me somewhat. A sergeant helped me down. The orlop deck of a sixty-four is level with the waterline. I could still hear the infernal rumbling of the cannons, but it was muted. The ship's sides resounded from the shock of the cannonballs hitting the hull above us, but there were no longer spinning shards of timber flying about. I was holding my left forearm with my right hand. The pain in my left shoulder was becoming unbearable. I did not dare touch my arm above the elbow. The surgeons' post is situated below the main passageway in the heart of the ship, above the holds and below the lower gun deck. It is not very deep but it is as long as the ship is wide. It is also called a *theatre* on account of the big platform in the middle. The unfortunate 'actors' who put on performances there do it against their will: this platform is made up of the boards on which the ship's surgeons carry out their mass amputations.

The place was crowded with wounded, with more being brought in every minute. I leaned against the ship's side to await my turn. Those who were being amputated were screaming like madmen. I could see piles of arms and legs under the bloodied planks of the theatre. I said to myself that my left arm would soon be joining them.

The Surgeon-in-Chief had dined with me the evening before at the commander's table. He recognised me and came over. I was so covered in the blood of the poor number ten gun crew, that he did not know where I was wounded. I said it was my left shoulder and it felt as if my arm was detached from my body. He tested out my shoulder and assured me that it was still in place, not cut off at all, or even cut open. But he was going to bandage it as it was swelling rapidly. I tried to explain what had happened to me, and he said that the cannon ball that had killed my gun crew must have ripped off a big lump of wood from the gun port cover, or from the corner of the gun port, as it passed, and that is probably what had wounded me.

I was so happy to learn that I was not going to lose my arm that the pain seemed to ease. I wanted to get out of that terrible place full of amputees and those about to be amputated, and where the screams of suffering almost drowned out the sound of battle. The surgeon held me back and made me sit on a stool in order to clean the wound on my cheek and sew it up. He said I would keep the scar for the rest of my life. That did not bother me, considering that I had thought I would no longer have my left arm.

I went up to the lower gun deck to take up my battle station again. Everything had already been cleared up. The bodies of the killed gun crews had been taken away and their replacements were busy around gun number ten. The battle was moving ahead of us. *L'Annibal* stopped firing. I could still hear occasional gunfire towards the head of our line. This was followed by an unworldly silence. Rear-Admiral Byron had turned hard on the wind to head north, leaving us where we were. It was one in the afternoon. There were still a few shots fired against the English ships too damaged to follow their squadron and trying to escape individually. I heard it said that we could easily have captured them, but the Comte d'Estaing did not want to. The next day we returned to anchor off Grenada.

This battle has passed into history as the Battle of Grenada. Vernon, who witnessed it from the quarterdeck, and was surprised to have survived, said to me, in all seriousness that, by comparison, the Battle of Ushant was no more than a skirmish.

He told me that Byron had arrived at Grenada with a convoy of fifty ships carrying troops to reinforce the Saint George fort. He had left his fleet to the north of the island and had come down with his squadron to see what he could find. He had given the general chase signal on coming across us and had engaged with our advance guard and main body of ships, running past them on the opposite tack. He had then continued to the fort, which had opened fire on him. The English had then all worn ship together. As a result of this manoeuvre, their rear guard found itself at the head of the line. They had caught up with our line, with the apparent intention of passing us to leeward so as to catch us between two lines of fire once the main body of their fleet had caught up and overtaken us on the other side, to starboard. This attempt to overrun us was stopped in its tracks by the murderous broadsides from *l'Annibal.* Byron had then settled for running along us to windward and firing. He had then turned to windward, leaving us behind, and gone to re-join his convoy. *L'Annibal's* resistance had been decisive, but she had paid dearly: fifty-nine killed and ninety wounded. The Comte de Lamotte-Picquet had a thigh wound, and Ship's Lieutenant de Marguery, who was in command of the battery of 18-pounders on the upper gun deck, had been killed. This battle aroused a lot of argument. In my opinion there was only one lesson to draw from it: the incontestably superior speed of coppered ships as opposed to those that weren't. That ought to have alerted us for the future.

'That's true,' said Vernon, 'when I think about it. At Ushant it was the same story, except that it was less obvious because we had strong winds and a big sea. While here, in that light breeze, it was blindingly clear that they were faster than us.'

'For sure,' I replied. 'And if there had been a big sea *l'Annibal* would not have been able to operate her lower gun deck to leeward and send the 36-pounder broadsides that disrupted their battle plan.'

'That's a really good point,' said my friend. 'At Ushant they could sail closer to the wind than us and they had tried to do exactly the same thing: catch us up from astern and take us from both sides. It's because the Comte d'Orvilliers saw the danger of this that he gave the order to tack. That's why nobody understands why the Comte d'Estaing didn't do the same thing when we met the English at dawn. He had plenty of time; nothing stopped him from doing it. We could have trapped Byron between Saint-George fort and ourselves. He wouldn't have been able to make use of his better speed and we could have pounded them a bit with our heavy broadsides. Instead, they almost succeeded. Without the rapid firing from *l'Annibal* the others would have had time to get to windward of us and we would have been attacked from both sides simultaneously. Can you imagine that? I don't know how we would ever have got out of it[79].'

I was able to rejoin my frigate the next day. Her role in the battle had been to relay signals from under the lee of *le Languedoc.* Little de Thomas confided to me that the Comte d'Estaing's orders were incomprehensible. Even the phlegmatic Monsieur de la Jonquière had become agitated. The Comte de Lapérouse had finally had to raise his voice to silence the criticisms of his exasperated officers. All the same, when I suggested to my commander that the Comte d'Estaing might have been better to have tacked after the initial engagement, he replied that that would have put us even further to leeward of the enemy.

The squadron remained at Saint George for four days, during which time *l'Amazone* cruised nonstop between Grenada, the Union Islands and Carriacou. We were then sent ahead to the island of Guadeloupe to get the latest information on the convoy from the Windward Islands that the Comte d'Estaing would normally have been escorting to France, had he deigned to obey his written orders from Versailles. We, of course, knew nothing of that.

I was completely preoccupied by my shoulder, which had me in constant pain. It had become purple and the slightest movement was agonising. I could not use a hammock and had bouts of feverishness. The Surgeon le Choquet tended me with various unguents and gave me concoctions of quinine to drink. He even bled me, which was against

79 Gun crew numbers were designed for them to operate just one side at a time; there were not enough to work two sides simultaneously. Hence the naval tactic of trying to attack the enemy rear-guard from both sides.

his principles. He asked permission from our commander to put me in a foldaway bed on the deck.

Our next destination was to be Cap-François at Saint-Domingue. While we were at Guadeloupe I was invited to present myself aboard *le Languedoc* to see Ship's Captain Flaharn. I declined the first invitation, saying that I was having trouble recovering from a wound sustained at the Battle of Grenada. The Vicomte de Noailles, who was now aboard the Admiral's ship but who often came to see us, passed on Flaharn's proposition that I be transferred to *le Languedoc.* This time, I asked the Vicomte de Noailles to reply that I wanted to stay on *l'Amazone* and did not want to see Flaharn in the immediate future. I added, deliberately, that if he insisted I would ask for the Comte d'Estaing's view on the matter. I heard nothing more.

17

On the morning of 31st July the green hills overlooking the town of Cap-François[80] came into view ahead. The land breeze had dropped away and the weather was mild. A cloud of brightly coloured butterflies was fluttering around the upper sails. I would have liked to have made a painting of it all, to show my little sister, but this fairylike scene would have been impossible to render with brushes and gouache.

The Cap-François harbour is protected by a reef with only two passages through. The safest is the northerly one. The Comte de Lapérouse had already been to Saint-Domingue and our frigate was the first to go through. The anchorage was in the middle of the bay and about half a mile to the west of the town. The houses were aligned along the strip between the base of the hills and a line of straight quays overlooked by tree-lined promenades. We could not go in further on account of the shallower water by the quays, which could only be reached by sloops and ships' boats. It was ten in the morning.

L'Amazone was the first to drop anchor, at the edge of the shallows near the shore, in seven fathoms of clear water, four cables to the south-

80 Translator's note: *Cap-François*: Later Cap-Français and now known as Cap-Haïtien in what is now Haiti.

east of the Royal Battery. We were off a quay bordered by palm trees, on which a big and colourful crowd was waiting for us. As the Comte d'Estaing went ashore, he was saluted by all the forts and batteries. *Le Languedoc* signalled to us to return the compliment. The Comte was carried in triumph by the crowd. We were welcomed as victors.

My wound was troubling me less. I was starting to move my shoulder without worrying about the pain and my fever had fallen. However, the Surgeon Le Choquet still thought I was weak and on his advice the Comte de Lapérouse sent me ashore to convalesce for a few days. I was to go to a hospital run by the Fathers of Charity, which had links with the Navy.

I did not really see the need, but the idea of a few days rest paid for by the King was not unattractive, especially considering Flaharn. Although I had no real proof, I still considered him to be extremely dangerous. He was not pursuing me for my own good, but because he thought I could give him the information for which he had already tortured or killed several people, including, no doubt, my mother. As he knew that I was aboard *l'Amazone*, that is probably were he would start to look for me, just as he had done during our stop at Guadeloupe. He had enough influence and cunning to send me a request to meet that this time I would have difficulty in refusing. My view of Flaharn had changed since Brest. Everything I had learned about him combined to put me on my guard. I was in agreement with the Chevalier de Kermean on this point. Flaharn was like a formidable chess player, capable of advancing the most complex and twisted combinations far in advance. The impalings at Sumatra and the wolf of Kersalaun were good examples. I thought therefore that a stay with the Fathers of Charity would give me a welcome respite. In fact, the Comte de Lapérouse had told us that the Comte d'Estaing intended to wait at Saint-Domingue for a frigate bringing despatches from France. She could arrive any day, and once she was there, the Comte d'Estaing would probably revive the furious rhythm imposed on us since Martinique. This might mean that Flaharn would no longer have time to concern himself with me.

On Sunday 1st August, having heard the obligatory morning Mass aboard the frigate, I got a few personal things out of my sea chest and put them in the leather bag I had bought at Nantes. I added my writing box and paints and colours, along with my telescope and the chest containing my pistols. It was still too soon for me to think of fencing, and the Surgeon Le Choquet had strongly advised against it. However, I hoped to find a quiet corner where I could practise my shooting. That would do instead of exercise. Moreover, I felt I had to be armed during this stay at Saint-Domingue, so happy in appearance, but where the threat of Captain Flaharn stalked.

L'Amazone's boat put me ashore at a quay between the Royal Battery and the Round Battery, by the entrance to the artillery depot. There was a fountain there from which the King's ships took their water. The Royal Battery had its guns lined up in front of a beautiful esplanade shaded by three rows of palm oil trees. The wealthy residents of Cap-François had put their cabriolets at the disposal of any of the squadron's officers who wished to go for a ride. There were always two or three awaiting our pleasure on this esplanade, at the start of an avenue which left from here and followed the harbour to the southern exit of the town.

The town of Cap-François was built to the west of the harbour, on a gentle slope below hills which, at this season of frequent rain, were covered in vivid green woods and forests, right to their summits. The streets and squares were all paved. The houses were built of bricks or dressed stone and seemed to me to be as elegant, although more modestly proportioned, as those I had seen at the Quai de la Fosse, at Nantes.

My cabriolet trotted along the promenade beside the harbour. We came out of the town after taking a straight road bordered on both sides by pavements shaded by palm trees. The end of the bay, to the south of Cap-François, opened onto a huge fertile plain where the most beautiful houses on the island were to be found. The Fathers' hospital was set at the start to this plain, in a slight declivity at the base of the hills. The officers' house, where I was admitted after presenting my papers, was separated from the rest of the hospital by a magnificent garden planted with frangipani, logwood and lemon trees, and by a field bordered by acacias. It was an elegant colonial style building that put me in mind of a manor house. It was also the quarters for the Father Superior himself, who kept a sumptuous table there to which the best society of the town was regularly invited. I too became a guest. It was a far cry from Lent at the Prières Abbey! I was given a very pretty room with a bathroom and a black domestic to look after me. He was one of the many slaves at the hospital. There were only convalescent officers in the house. Those who were sick, with fever or contagious illnesses, were kept apart in the infirmary.

The Father Superior certainly did not live in penury. The King paid the Fathers twelve pounds a day for a sick officer. And the hospital also had sugar and coffee refineries staffed by an army of slaves, and which brought in more than two hundred thousand pounds of income a year. My uncle the priest, in his holy innocence, could never have imagined the Fathers of Charity leading such a lifestyle by making so many slaves work for their benefit.

Through dining with the Father Superior, I got to know two rich inhabitants of the island who were cavalry officers in the local militia. They pressed me with questions about the expedition to Grenada. I gave a more or less factual account, but stressing the heroic side so as not to disappoint the expectations of my military audience. My account of the promotion given on the battlefield to the grenadier sergeant, for having saved the Chevalier de Vence, went down very well and I had to repeat it several times.

After lunch, these gentlemen invited me to visit the Cap's plain in their carriage, drawn by three horses side by side. My hosts did not refer to 'sugar fields', but 'sugar gardens'. Each cultivated piece of land was surrounded by orange and lemon trees. The sides of the surrounding hills were not in fact covered in woods, as I had thought, but by coffee plants edged with banana, mahogany and palm oil trees. The biggest farms, which had up to two thousand slaves each, were like big villages.

I was curious to learn how they made the sugar. They showed me their refinery, with its ovens, horse-powered mill and watermill. While I was admiring the grindstone and mechanisms of the latter mill, my attention was drawn to an axe, placed obviously beside it.

'It's a dangerous job, feeding this machine,' explained one of my guides. 'We have seen blacks dragged in and crushed, through no more than being caught by their little finger. The only way to save then is to cut off their arm. That's why an axe is always kept at hand. It's for their own good.'

I thought it an odd way to show goodness to one's fellow man. There was a lot to think about here! I now understood why my uncle was so strongly against the slave trade. I decided to note down my observations, for his benefit.

That night there was a violent thunderstorm over the hills. Flashes of lightning lit up the countryside for several seconds, followed by terrific thunderclaps. There was wind and torrential rain. I was soon to find out that this happened almost every night, it being normal for the season.

On Monday morning, everything was calm again. The overnight rain had left things agreeably cool. Under the window of my room was a kind of sheltered area, with a balustrade. It is a feature of colonial houses, and is called a 'veranda'. It was a very pleasant spot, with a table and benches. I felt good as my shoulder was no longer hurting me. I took my box of pistols out of my bag and put it on the table, remembering that they had not been out of their case since Brest and so might need cleaning. I decided first to make some notes on what I had seen and heard the day before, that I could give later to my uncle. I wanted to help him in his fight against the Trade. I took my writing box out of my bag and set myself up at the table under the veranda, determined to put down on paper my views on the state of the sugar islands.

*

Cap-François, Saint-Domingue, Monday 2nd August 1779

I try to find the right words, dipping my quill into the inkwell. I have trouble concentrating on the difficult subject that I want to deal with and cannot stop my eyes wandering to the surrounding countryside, enjoying the light and the morning peace after the storm. That's when my attention is drawn to a man who has just appeared on the path leading to my house. He speaks to a servant who points to where I am sitting. The visitor comes along the path. Another glory-seeker, I think to myself, taking on a preoccupied air and lowering my nose into my paper. I have no wish to describe yet again the taking of Grenada. I hear the steps of the interloper coming closer along the boards of the veranda.

'Monsieur Laforest-Dombourg?'

His accent is strange, though not unpleasant. He rolls his r's a little. I raise my head.

'At your service, Sir.'

He takes off his hat in response to my greeting. He does not look like a rich settler from Saint-Domingue. He is about my size, a little bigger perhaps, well-built, his skin bronzed like all the sailors who sail in the Tropics. He has a handsome face, with black eyes slightly slanted towards his temples. His carefully trimmed beard is as black as his hair which is collected into a little cloth-covered bun behind his head. He is wearing a blue cotton waistcoat striped with silver, from under which bulge his well-muscled shoulders. His shirt is an immaculate white, with the cuffs turned up, revealing wrists carrying intricately worked bracelets. It is difficult to put an age on him. Fifty years? Forty years?

'Who are you?'

'My name is Jakar Singh.'

I shudder despite the tropical humidity. I have heard about him for so long, and now he is standing in front of me; the Marquis Avelus de Kersalaun's torturer. I recognise him from François Loutre's description. I am sure I have never met him...and yet...and yet...his face, especially his eyes, seem vaguely familiar.

'Have we met before?' I ask.

He sits on the bench opposite me. This movement opens the flaps of his waistcoat, revealing the richly decorated silver handle of the dagger thrust in his belt. He places his hands flat on the table. Beautiful hands with long, sensitive fingers.

'Four years ago. In the town where there is a bishop. In Brittany.'

He speaks slowly, looking for his words. His pronunciation is odd but his French is good.

'Vannes! At the door of the cathedral, in front of the Cohue market.'

'Yes, that's how they call it over there.'

I had only seen him for a moment but I had not forgotten that look.

'At the Mesquer church. Was that you too?'

'I often followed you at that time.'

'But...why?'

'We wanted to be sure of what you really knew.'

'What I knew?'

He smiles in a way I suddenly find very unpleasant.

'You play your part very well, Monsieur Dombourg, but it will do you no good. We know that your mother shared some secrets with you. We have a map, drawn and signed by you, showing where something is hidden. We have also read a letter written by Ship's Lieutenant Laforest-Dombourg, your father.'

‘It’s you who stole it?’

‘So you see it is a waste of time to try to tell us that you know nothing.’

‘What do you want from me?’

‘We want Suraj Mal’s war treasure.’

Vernon had guessed correctly. It really was all about treasure from India. The Marquis de Kersalaun, for a reason I still did not know, had entrusted it to my parents, and my father had built the hiding place under the stairs of our house at Port-Louis, to keep it safe. My mother must have taken it away, otherwise Flaharn would have found it. The sergeant at Port-Louis had made it clear that the hiding place was open and empty.

‘I don’t know the location of what you are looking for.’

‘Perhaps as yet you haven’t really looked for it, otherwise it would no doubt be lost to us. But we are convinced that you know enough to help us find it. And that is why you are going to help us.’

‘And even if that were the case, why would I do as you say?’

Instead of replying he takes out of his waistcoat a handkerchief that he unfolds on the table, smoothing it out to its four corners. For a moment I am speechless, my throat knotted, and I have to make a concerted effort not to cry. All I can see is this tiny object placed in the centre of the square of cloth: a little Saint Anne d’Auray forgiveness medallion.

‘What happened to my mother?’

‘He’s the one to tell you.’

‘Flaharn?’

‘Over there the sepoys call him Sher Sahib, because he has the strength, the patience and the cruelty of a lion. They are all afraid of him. You would do well to fear him too.’

‘Is that a threat?’

‘No, a deal. You help us find the treasure and we will tell you how to find your mother. If you refuse, then Sher Sahib will deal with you in such a way that you will end up telling him.’

They are threatening to torture me for something I don’t know. It is absurd! I grow angry.

‘You know what? In telling me all this you implicitly admit that you are guilty of several murders: that of my mother, that of my former governess and that of the Marquis de Kersalaun. I can denounce you and have you sent to the gallows.’

He laughs and shrugs his shoulders.

'You have no proof, and as for Kersalaun Sahib, you can do nothing against Flaharn since everything we did was covered by the general in chief.'

'You mean the Comte d'Estaing?'

'Yes, him. It's he who signed the orders to arrest the man you are talking about.'

'Is that what Flaharn told you?'

'He told me, *sans ambages*[81], as you say in French.'

'Well, I have good reason to think he lied to you.'

I explain how I had occasion to meet the Comte d'Estaing in person on the island of Grenada, and how he had clearly said that he had never heard of the Marquis de Kersalaun. I add that the arrest warrant was fake. Flaharn had forged the Comte d'Estaing's signature. I can easily prove it. Jakar pretends not to believe me, but I sense that I have unsettled him a little.

'Moreover,' I add, 'I have no idea what it is, your treasure!'

Instead of replying he takes from his waistcoat pocket a little key. I recognise it.

'You know what it is?'

Once again emotion clouds my eyes and I wipe them with the back of my hand.

'Yes, it is Vishnu's wheel.'

With his free hand he takes the key out of my pistol case and examines both keys, turning them in his fingers, then places them side by side on the table.

'They are identical. The craftsman who made these keys sold chests to the Europeans, telling them that their locks were unique. I should have told Flaharn not to trust him.'

'It was my father who ordered this case.'

He puts the key back into the lock of the box containing my pistols.

'That one, yes. The other was for Flaharn. Even though it was a little bigger, it has the same key. It's in that one that they put Suraj Mal's war treasure, at Chandernagore.'

I remember what my uncle had told me at Kermean, relaying what Kerscao had told him. Javahir Singh had become the Raja of Dig after

81 Translator's note: *sans ambages:* without beating about the bush.

the death of his guardian Suraj Mal, the previous Raja. Jamna, the Marquis de Kersalaun's wife, was Javahir's daughter. Kerscao had also said that Flaharn and his accomplice, Jakar, had been besieged in their capital and had negotiated their surrender very skilfully. They had not left empty-handed. Then, for reasons I do not know, they had lost the treasure and it had been entrusted to my parents by the Marquis de Kersalaun. Jamna, the wife of the Marquis, had certainly told her housekeeper la Fantig that fate had brought her father's treasure to her.

'In any case,' I say, 'this treasure doesn't belong to you.'

This seems to annoy him.

'The treasure belongs to the Jats. Suraj Mal entrusted the secret of the cache to Javahir Singh before his death. It was Flaharn who made me aware that Javahir was going to break his promise by giving our land to the English. I wanted to kill Javahir, but Flaharn had said that it would be better first to get him to say where the treasure was hidden. I went to see the Raja and told him that I knew that he was going to tell his secret to the foreigners, but not to me, his half-brother. He said I was mistaken, and told me where it was.'

'And you killed him!'

'It was Flaharn's decision, but I who did it. Yes, me, Jakar Singh. He had gone to watch the elephants fighting in the garden at Dig. He wasn't doing anything anymore, just amusing himself with his wives, drinking bhang[82] and watching elephant fights. He was no longer worthy of ruling the Jats. I went up behind him and lopped off his head with a single sabre blow. All those there knew why. They killed a water carrier and slashed his face, saying it was he who had killed the Raja.'

'And why did you do that?'

'Javahir Singh wanted to make peace with the foreigners. He was ready to sell Suraj Mal's inheritance in return for a vassal's income. The kingdom of the Jamna valley was founded on the courage of the Jats. The Rajas and all the Kshatriyas[83] should not forget they owe this debt. Suraj Mal had never forgotten.'

---

82 Translator's note: *bhang*: a traditional Indian edible preparation of cannabis, often infused into drinks such as lassi.

83 Translator's note: *Kshatriyas*: members of the second highest of the four traditional Indian castes, the warrior caste.

'Wasn't it just to steal the treasure?'

'I needed it to rebuild our army! But I did not have time. I don't know what happened. Things turned out differently. There was a revolt and we had to leave Dig. We went to Chandernagore, where Flaharn had the chest made. We put the treasure in it. And Kersalaun Sahib stole it from us with your father's help.'

'My father was not a thief!'

'He didn't exactly steal it, but it was the same thing.'

'What happened at Chandernagore?'

He hesitates.

'I went with Flaharn to see the French at Chandernagore. Flaharn wanted to leave by ship but it had not yet arrived. Flaharn became friends with the Governor and we were living in his house. While waiting for the ship Flaharn had the chest made by the same man who made this one…'

He places a finger on the case containing my pistols.

'The ship arrived in the river and stayed for a long time. Flaharn preferred to stay in the Governor's house, not wanting to meet the French sailors too soon.'

I can quite well imagine why Flaharn was not in a hurry to go aboard an India Company ship, given the Company's memories about him.

'We went aboard on the very last day. Kersalaun Sahib was aboard, the one the French call Avelus.'

'Avelus de Kersalaun,' I said.

'That's the one. Avelus was on the ship with the Princess Jamna. They had come while we were waiting in the Governor's house. We were very surprised, as nobody knew what had happened to them. And Avelus was a friend of the ship's captain.'

'That was my father.'

'Then Flaharn did a stupid thing. There was a long-standing hatred between him and Kersalaun Sahib for lots of reasons that would take too long to explain. They could not have lasted together on the same ship. He provoked Avelus, but the captain said there was to be no duelling aboard ship. He also told them not to be ashore for too long, as he would soon be leaving. I told Flaharn that I had seen Avelus fighting with a sabre and that he was very good, perhaps better than Flaharn. But Flaharn did not listen. He always thinks he is stronger than anyone. That is his failing. Kersalaun Sahib beat Flaharn. We even thought he had killed him. Avelus went back on board. When I saw that Flaharn was still alive I went for help. When I came back the ship was gone, our chest with it. He could have waited, don't you think?'

Why is he telling me all this? Flaharn has sent him to propose his 'deal', that I can well believe, but I would be surprised if Flaharn had told him to give me his life story. Did he feel the need to justify himself? I begin to wonder whether these two lawbreakers really see eye to eye.

'What did you do then?'

'Flaharn was cared for in the Governor's house and we waited for another ship. But that took a long time. The Governor said he would send an instruction to France to have Kersalaun Sahib put in prison along with his accomplice, your father.'

It is my turn to chuckle. I tell him that Flaharn had told the Governor that Kersalaun had murdered the Raja in order to take his daughter away, but I know that Flaharn had refused to take the memorandum that the Governor had proposed to him for supporting this accusation in France. This was on the pretext that he had no need for it in order see justice done. Jakar does not reply, but I am watching his reactions closely now, and once again I get the feeling that his self-assurance has been weakened.

'When you disembarked later, at L'Orient,' I continue, 'what did you do?'

'That's enough now! You are going to tell Flaharn where the chest is hidden. He will tell you everything you want to know, about that and your mother.'

'Why didn't he ask anything of me while we were at Brest? We were seeing each other every day. He could easily have done it!'

'At Brest he just wanted to get to know you and see what kind of person you were. He thought he would have lots of time later, at Saint-Malo, but things did not turn out as he had hoped. The situation is different now. He will meet you in town. You will take a room in a quiet inn where he will come to see you – the *Marmousets* inn, at the other end of town. At the end of the rue des Marmousets. It's easy to find, not far from the palace. The room has already been reserved.'

'The palace?'

'Yes, the government.'

'The Governor's palace?'

'That's it. You will wait for Flaharn there.'

'For how long?'

'You'll see.'

'But why did he not come straight here, with you?'

'He'll tell you why.'

'I would need permission!'

'It is all arranged. The one who took you to fight with him has spoken to your commander. Everything is in order.'

'The one who took me to fight with him?'

'Yes! The friend of the general that Flaharn has to obey.'

'The Vicomte de Noailles?'

'That's him! The Vicomte. When Flaharn heard that you could have been killed in battle he was angry.'

'How nice!'

This reminds me again of what the Vicomte de Noailles said when he came back on board *l'Amazone* at Martinique. Jakar was touchy and had been seen to get angry with Flaharn. They are accomplices, but perhaps all is not harmonious between them. When you start to commit murders to find a treasure and then don't find it, lots of things can happen. Clearly Flaharn has already lied to him several times. I put myself in Jakar's place. He would certainly have wished to get back to India as soon as possible. Instead, he finds himself aboard a ship going to the other side of the world. I think that there is perhaps a card to play here.

'What are you going to do with this treasure?'

'I want to mount a war to reconquer Suraj Mal's kingdom.'

'Why did you leave India then?'

'When there was this revolt at Dig, I thought all was lost. But Flaharn said that we could go to his country and buy arms from the French, then come back straight away. But Kersalaun Sahib robbed us at Chandernagore.'

The more I listen, the more I have the impression that Flaharn had always had it in mind to bring his booty back to France. He set Jakar against Javahir, pushing him to force Javahir to reveal his secret before killing him. Then he had negotiated the surrender of Dig without Jakar knowing. I start to think that this Jakar Singh has been hoodwinked right from the start. And given that he doesn't seem totally stupid, it is possible that he is starting to suspect this too.

'How did this revolt that you talk of arise?'

My question evokes a reaction. He purses his lips involuntarily. I have guessed right! I am sure he has already asked himself that question.

'I don't know. It happened suddenly. Flaharn had already negotiated our departure, so that we could carry off Suraj Mal's treasure.'

I am starting to understand what drives Jakar, but I play the innocent, to help get to the bottom of it.

'Are you going to share this treasure between the two of you? And if I help you, won't you let me have just a little share?'

'There is nothing to share. It no more belongs to you than to us. I told you, it's for buying rifles, cannons, for recruiting European soldiers and paying for a ship to transport them. That's what a war treasure is for, isn't it?'

I remember what la Fantig had told me at Kersalaun. If she was to be believed, the Princess Jamna had told her about a similar scheme.

'I think that the wife of the Marquis de Kersalaun was thinking of doing the same thing as you,' I said. 'Why did you kill them, her and Kersalaun Sahib, instead of joining forces with them? After all, you had fought together against the English, who are our enemies too. The King of France might even have helped you.'

He avoids my eyes.

'It was not possible. Kersalaun Sahib hated us, and his wife refused to trust me.'

'Given that you had murdered her father, that's understandable. It's a pity for you, as now you depend entirely on Flaharn. Do you still trust him?'

He is still trying to remain impassive, but a slight change in his look and demeanour make me think that I have touched a nerve.

'Do you really think he is going to give up his share to help you launch your little war?'

'I am a Kshatriya. He gave me his word of honour. I have killed many men for that. If he fails me, I kill him! And I won't hesitate to kill you too if I have to. I don't have to play games with you, as my cause is just.'

His voice has grown excited.

'Kshatriya?'

'It is a high rank for us and I am one of their most important. In my country even your Comte d'Estaing is nothing more than a beef-eating, wine-drinking firangi.'

I realise that this could open up some new possibilities.

'How does Flaharn treat you?'

'We are partners.'

‘Are you well thought of aboard *le Languedoc*? What position did you sign up for on the crew list?’

‘I am his partner.’

‘When you embarked at Chandernagore to come to France, you were a passenger with your own cabin, weren’t you?’

‘I was with Flaharn.’

‘While now, aboard *le Languedoc*, you are entitled to no more than a hammock in the ‘tween deck. You! A general! A Kshatriya, as you say, amongst common sailors!’

His long eyelashes flutter once more.

‘And Flaharn,’ I continued,’ has his own officer’s cabin beside the wheelhouse. Can you read French?’

‘I am a Kshatriya, but I am also literate. I know Sanskrit.’

‘Ask what is written besides your name in *le Languedoc’s* crew list. I suspect you are described as Flaharn’s valet!’

*

As he left, Jakar was careful to repeat that I had to go to the *Marmousets* inn. He had regained his aloof air, but his teeth were clenched and I thought that my malicious gossip had perhaps hit the mark.

Jakar had kept the second wheel-shaped key but left the little Saint Anne medallion with me. I was eleven years old when my mother had worn them in front of me for the last time, one December morning, in her room at Kermean. I had promised to make sure that that she was buried in our family chapel, along with her relatives. It was certain that Flaharn would never leave me in peace until I had told him where his treasure was hidden. On the other hand I could threaten to expose him. Jakar’s reaction when I had raised this proved that the two miscreants were not as sure of their impunity as they would like to think. I concluded that if I told them a credible lie, they could not verify anything before our return to France. Lots of things could happen between now and then. We were at war, after all. My situation was not quite so bad; I too had some cards to play.

If I had thought about it a little more deeply, I would have worked out that Flaharn would have foreseen this eventuality and that, like a good chess player, he would have prepared his moves a long time in advance. With him, the most dangerous pawn was not the one advancing first.

18

I spent the whole of Tuesday at the Fathers of Charity. Despite my reservations and the fear that Flaharn aroused in me, I wanted to find out what had happened to my mother, and so I decided to follow the bizarre instructions given to me by his messenger. I was now of the belief that my two adversaries were afraid of being denounced and I thought that this may put me in a stronger position for dealing with them. I did not believe my life was in danger, as they needed me. All the same, thoughts about the torture briefly mentioned by Jakar did occupy my mind a little. They had tortured Avelus de Kersalaun, who had resisted at first, but who had killed himself in the belief that he could not hold out forever. Everything that I had learned about the Marquis Avelus de Kersalaun showed him to be a man of exceptional calibre, whereas I was far from that. But he had found himself alone, forgotten, secretly jailed, whereas my situation was quite different. I was a member of the crew of a King's frigate whose captain would grow concerned if I disappeared for too long. All the same, this was not enough. I had to warn the Comte de Lapérouse. If there was no news from me after a day, he should look for me straight away. I would tell him about Flaharn as soon as I saw him.

As I was thinking about all this I had a surprise visit from the

Surgeon Le Choquet. He found me sitting on the veranda cleaning my pistols. When I stood up to welcome him he replied somewhat absent-mindedly to my greeting. Having looked at him closely, I asked what was on his mind.

'Does your shoulder hurt?' he began without ceremony.

'Not much,' I replied.

'Are you still feverish?'

'Not in the least. I feel fine.'

'And how are things here? Are you comfortable?'

'Good Lord yes! Things are excellent here! I've never before had so many comforts.'

The Surgeon Le Choquet raised his eyebrows and shook his head.

'I don't know what's going on,' he said. 'This morning the Comte de Lapérouse told me that he had had alarming news about the state of your health and that you are so poorly looked after here that you were considering renting a room in town at your own expense. He asked me to come and get you and to make a complaint to the Father Superior.'

'And do you know who told him that?'

'It was from the Vicomte de Noailles. The Comte d'Estaing held a party yesterday aboard *le Languedoc*; a hundred guests, the fleet dressed with flags, armed soldiers, the whole caboodle. Our commander met the Vicomte de Noailles there, who said he had received a note from you...'

Flaharn was behind this, for sure! He had a taste for forgery.

'It's a misunderstanding,' I said. 'I've not written anything to anybody. Did you come by carriage?'

'I borrowed one of the cabriolets put at our disposal by the Cap citizens.'

'May I ask a favour of you?'

'What is it?'

I could feel his mistrust.

'For reasons which I think I can guess, but which I'd rather not divulge at the moment, somebody has written the note you talk about as if it were from me. It's a serious business which threatens the honour of my family. I want to write a letter to the Comte de Lapérouse right now, explaining the position, and I would be grateful if you could take it to him. I would also ask you to deposit me in town. I'll show you where so that you can tell the Comte de Lapérouse where to find me if necessary, or if I am in danger.'

'Why don't you go and tell the Comte de Lapérouse all this yourself?'

It was a very good question, but it was exactly what I wanted to avoid. If I were to ask my commander's permission, he could always refuse. Whereas with a letter he would be faced with a *fait accompli* by the time he read it.

'You are not going to be duelling? In your state...'

'Not at all. Don't worry,' I said. 'I will explain everything in the letter, and moreover, you'll know where to find me quickly. I don't think I will be far from the port. You've no reason to be concerned.'

'You're going to leave the hospital, then?'

'Yes! And I'll leave with you. I'll get my things together and write a letter for the commander. Then I'll go and say my farewells to the Father Superior and thank him for the excellent treatment I have had here.'

The Surgeon Le Choquet made no objections. I thought that deep down he was relieved at not having to go and complain to the Father Superior. He waited patiently while I wrote my letter. It had to be short.

Sir

It is not I who wrote to the Vicomte de Noailles. The writer of this forgery is the Ship's Captain Flaharn. You may remember we spoke about him on our return to Brest last October. You told me that Captain Flaharn had made some serious allegations against my father. As you no doubt know, he is currently aboard le Languedoc. He learned of my presence at the hospital and sent his secretary to say he wanted to talk with me in a quiet place. I imagine that he decided to pass himself off as me, when writing to the Vicomte de Noailles, in order to make this easier.

In past times my father would have sailed from Chandernagore carrying an item, the nature of which I am ignorant, but which Captain Flaharn is demanding from me. The place chosen by Flaharn is the Marmousets Inn, in the rue des Marmousets, in town. The Surgeon Le Choquet has agreed to take me there. That will enable him to recognise the place. I have to tell you that I had to treat him firmly to agree to that, as he wanted to take me to see you first. I ask you to give him my apologies. I have accepted Captain Flaharn's proposal as I want to bring this business into the open as carefully as possible and I don't want him to continue slandering my father. However I do not trust

Flaharn. I know he is a violent man. That's why I have decided to keep you up to date on a daily basis. If a day should pass without you hearing from me, I would ask you to get somebody to look for me by coming to the Marmousets Inn at Cap-François.

I have the honour, Sir, to be your most humble and obedient servant.

I gave the letter unsealed to the Surgeon Le Choquet who, being a well-mannered man, put it in his pocket without reading it.

Our coachman knew the rue des Marmousets. It's easy to find one's way around Cap-François, as all the main roads are parallel, and intersected at right angles every fifty yards by secondary roads which are open to the sea and the cool trade-wind breeze. The *Marmousets* inn was on the other side of town, just before the slopes of the hills. It was a collection of buildings in a green square enclosed by palm trees and clumps of mimosas.

The innkeeper was expecting me. Flaharn had reserved a room for me in a small side-building set a little way away. My doorstep overlooked the bed of a dried up stream which was the natural edge of the town, and which ran down a little valley called the Ravine de la Belle Hôtesse. On the other side of this stream the slopes, covered in bushes and acacias, rose up to the summit of the hill, where there was a watchtower overlooking Picolet Point. The servant who showed us to the place explained that most of the time the stream was dry but that it became a torrent once there was a thunderstorm. The bed of the stream went down to the sea, reaching it near the circular battery at the artillery ground beside the fountain. I was ten minutes by foot away from the quayside where the ships' boats tied up to take on their water.

After the Surgeon Le Choquet had gone I settled in. The room was simply furnished but clean, including the bedding. The place had been very well chosen for our meeting. I loaded my two pistols and put them away on their case which I left on the night table. Then I waited.

A week passed – no Flaharn! No Jakar! I went every day to the quayside by the fountain and gave a note to the boatmen to take to *l'Amazone's* captain. I no longer knew what to think. And I began to grow bored, alone in my room, looking at the hillsides. I wondered if Flaharn had forgotten about me and I ended up frequenting the main room of the inn, where the waiting was less tiresome. The inn had its regulars, men and women, the housekeepers and shopkeepers who lived in the area, government employees and even the guards from the town prison, which was little more than two hundred yards away.

I cannot exactly recall the moment that my attention was taken by the manoeuvrings of a lady visitor who seemed to have an interest in my humble self, and to whom I was not indifferent either. She was always dressed in white: a skirt of light, very fine muslin, which by its transparency invited one to imagine the trim figure beneath; and over that a robe of the same cloth, which swirled up at the slightest breath of wind. She had long chestnut hair bound to her head with a silk scarf. She was certainly enough to spark the imagination of a lonely young man. I am not naturally forward with women, and at first I was content just to watch her surreptitiously. That filled my solitary waiting time. But as she often looked in my direction, our eyes finally met. The rest happened quite quickly, as is often the case. That day there was to be a big parade. The Comte d'Estaing was to review all of Saint-Domingue's troops and militias. This parade was to be followed by a Grand Ball at the Governor's palace. The beautiful Creole told me that she was married to an impotent old man who never left the house, and that she would really like to go to the parade and the ball with me. The parade ground and the Governor's palace were just five minutes from my lodgings. Only a saint could have resisted a proposal from such a pretty lady. To hell with Flaharn and his meetings!

The parade ground was bordered on all sides by double rows of trees which created the shady avenues where the troops were lined up. A big crowd had already arrived and surrounded the units' squads. Notable amongst them was the Voluntary Light Infantry of Saint-Domingue, which had just been formed by the Marquis de Rouvray, one of the island's rich landowners. Only the regiment's officers were white. All the soldiers were black freemen, whose drill was perfect. There were also colonial regiments from Cap-François and from Port au Prince, as well as several French regiments garrisoned on Saint-Domingue. The spectacle was enlivened even more by the presence of six squadrons of cavalry volunteers, sumptuously fitted out. Amongst them I recognised the two settlers who had kindly shown me their plantations on the day of my arrival at the Charity hospital. Seeing the tall figure of the Comte d'Estaing marching at the head of his troops, I thought to myself that the Governor of Saint-Domingue would soon see himself deprived of the best units in the garrison, just like the Governors of Martinique and Guadeloupe. And sure enough, at the Governor's palace, where we were then taken for the ball, the military men there talked of nothing, between their glasses of punch, but an imminent attack on Jamaica. There were lots of officers from the squadron there, and I made quite an impression on my comrades, with my beautiful Creole on my arm.

And what was bound to happen did happen: I found myself alone in my room at the inn with Betty. That was her name. I had already experienced the almost maternal indulgence of the girls at the *Dames de la Marine*, at Saint-Malo, but that was nothing compared to the fiery temperament of the beautiful Betty. She was like an erupting volcano! Apparently all the Creoles are like this. I think it may be something to do with the tropical heat.

The nightly thunderstorm rang out at midnight. Rain began to fall. We listened to it, lying side by side on our mattress, without clothes or sheets to cover us, tired from our exertions and savouring the freshness in the air after the torrid heat of the preceding hours. Before closing my eyes, I could hear water racing down the stream by my doorstep. When I awoke Betty was already up and dressed. She said she had to go home. She would come back and see me afterwards. She told me to go to sleep again while waiting for her. That way, she said with a smile, she would have the pleasure of waking me. She blew me a kiss with her fingertips as she left.

*

Cap-François, Friday 13th August, morning.

The door has scarcely closed when there is a knock. I think that Betty must have forgotten something but, instead of her pretty face, I am confronted by the jovial soldierly features of the Baron de Boismorau, commander of *l'Amazone's* infantry.

'Good Lord! My dear fellow! If the beautiful lady I have just seen is part of your treatment, I want to be a convalescent every single day! You look the picture of health, too!'

He has taken me by surprise and I am still lying on my back, everything exposed and still standing tall in honour of Betty. I don't know where to put myself.

'I understand!' continues the Baron. 'And I am sorry to have to tear you away from the delights of the Cap. The Comte de Lapérouse's orders! You must get up immediately. We are putting to sea and the frigate is already getting her anchors. Not a minute to lose!'

I jump from my bed and start to dress.

'Is the squadron leaving?' I ask.

'No. It leaves in two days' time to assemble the big convoy for France. But the Comte d'Estaing is sending *l'Amazone* ahead to give the fleet notice that it will be leaving. I went to see the innkeeper to find out which was your room. He said that as you are leaving earlier than arranged, he wouldn't repay your advance.'

I shrug. It's Flaharn who's paying.

'It doesn't matter,' I say.

I have finished dressing and I put my things in my bag. The case containing my two pistols seems very light. I open it and swear. There is only one.

'What's the matter?' asks the Baron.

'There's a pistol missing. I think that girl must have taken one!'

At that moment we hear a gunshot outside.

'Was it loaded?'

'My God, yes! We'd better go and see!'

I buckle my belt, throw my bag over my shoulder and rush out, followed by the lieutenant. We see a horse and cart going off down the road at a gallop. It turns off towards the town centre. Its wheels start thundering once they are on the cobbled road. The sun has risen. There are still one or two feet of water in the stream. I pull the Baron along the path which goes down to the stream, as that's where the sound of the shot seemed to have come from. A hundred yards further on we see a group gathered beside the path. A body is lying between the path and the watercourse. I immediately recognise the skirt and robe of white muslin, despite the red blood which has sullied them. As for the rest of her, poor Betty looked as one would after swallowing a large calibre bullet fired with the barrel in one's mouth.

'It's Betty,' I hear someone say. 'She was a loose woman. It was going to end badly, but she didn't deserve this.'

Another gunshot rings out. It seems to come from the slopes on the other side of the stream.

'He must have fired at Jean and Matthieu!' says one of the men besides Betty's body.

'What happened?' asks the Baron de Boismorau.

'We were coming up the path and we saw the girl coming down towards us. She was joined by a Naval man who came out from the rue Saint Louis and who spoke to her. Then suddenly he shot her, without warning, and ran off towards the *Marmousets*. But just then he saw Garcia's cart coming down in the other direction. We all started to shout. He changed direction and got away by crossing the stream. As he had thrown away his pistol I thought he was unarmed and sent my two blacks after him. They aren't armed. I hope he doesn't kill one of them!'

'What was this man like?' asks the Baron.

'He was dressed just like your friend here. In Navy uniform. I know them well. Same size, black hair in a pigtail, like him, without a wig. And hang on,' he added. 'Martin! Show these gentlemen the pistol that he threw away. A beautiful piece, isn't it? It will sure be of interest to the men from the constabulary.'

He shows us the pistol with its butt decorated with a tiger's head; a pistol I know only too well. We hear the sound of iron horseshoes and five cavalrymen in the blue uniform of the constabulary come out at a gallop from a street lower down.

'They've come quickly!' says one of the men. 'They've come from the other end of town. Garcia went in his cart to alert them.'

The two blacks called Jean and Matthieu appear on the other side of the stream. They stop besides a path a bit higher up the slope.

'He gone that way!' shouts one of them, pointing towards a valley going off to the left of the stream.

'He's heading for the Convent!' says the man who spoke to us, this time addressing the sergeant from the Constabulary.

The latter dismounts. He gets one of his men to dismount too, and orders the others across the stream.

'After him, quickly! And watch out, he seems to be armed!'

The three cavalrymen sent off by the sergeant get their pistols out of their saddle bags and urge their horses across the stream before heading up the slope to the path where Jean and Matthieu are waiting for them. At that moment, turning my head towards the group of buildings that comprise the *Marmousets*, I see a tall man who seems to have come out of the building where I had spent the night. He looks our way then turns around and disappears from view. He is wearing a light-coloured frock coat. I haven't seen him for two years, but I still recognise that imposing figure and relaxed walk.

'Excuse me, Sir,' says the sergeant, coming up to me. 'According to the main witness, the suspect looks just like you. Where were you at the time of the murder?'

From the moment of recognising my pistol, I am paralysed by the fear of being accused of a crime I did not commit. I don't quite know how to answer, and sense that I soon might start trembling in front of everybody. The Baron de Boismorau comes to my rescue.

'He was with me. What's more, you've been told that the culprit was firing on the other side of the stream which, as you see, has water in it. Look! He has dry shoes!'

'But hang on, sergeant!' interrupts the man who had spoken to us first and who seems to be the 'main witness'. 'We told you that Jean and Matthieu saw him go off on the path to the hills. It can't be this gentleman. And what about this! Here's the pistol that the murderer threw away when he fled. It's not a Navy issue pistol. It obviously can't belong to this officer.'

On hearing my pistol mentioned again, my legs start to shake and I feel myself go pale.

'Well that's certainly true,' says the sergeant. 'All the same, I'm going to have to ask you to accompany me to the guardroom as soon as I've finished here.'

'Impossible,' says the Baron de Boismorau. 'Our ship is weighing anchor right now and we have to get back on board immediately. It's the frigate *l'Amazone.* We don't have a minute to lose! In the service of the King!'

*

The sergeant finally agreed to let us go. The Baron pulled me by the arm and we raced down the road to the harbour. *L'Amazone's* boat was waiting for us by the fountain. The frigate already had her anchor up and down. The two boats and the ship's sloop towed her as far as the north passage. Our lovely ship was to stop in front of the Picolet fort in order to take on our troops. An hour later we were at sea.

I was not on watch and I spent a long time leaning on the after rail, watching the hills of Cap-François grow smaller astern on the line of the horizon. The Baron de Boismorau came up.

'Have you spoken to the Comte de Lapérouse?'

I was still completely stunned by what had happened to us. I was unable to drive out the horrible image of poor Betty's head. The bullet had entered by the mouth that I had kissed so devotedly only several hours before, and had exited by shattering the middle of the skull. Some fragments were still hanging down the sides like a straw hat dripping blood.

'I don't know what to say to him.'

'Well, what I think, you see, is that if I had not arrived to get you at the exact moment that the girl, still alive, came out of your room, I really would have believed you killed her. You were seen with her at the ball yesterday and we have all admired, on more than one occasion, your magnificent cavalry pistols. I don't know why that poor girl was killed, but it seems obvious that things had been thought out beforehand to make you look like the perpetrator. It was lucky that urgent orders made me come to fetch you. For the moment we are on active service, but sooner or later you are likely to be called before an inquiry. Be assured that I will be witness to your innocence if it comes to that, but in the meantime I think it would be wise for both of us go and tell the commander what happened. And if you know something you don't want to tell me about, I'd advise you to be open about it with him.'

I went to see the Comte de Lapérouse, together with the Baron de Boismorau, who repeated what he had just told me. The captain had read my letter but, like me, he could not see why Flaharn would have wanted Betty killed. If indeed it was him behind all this.

'We have no proof against him,' said the Comte de Lapérouse. 'The main thing is that the Baron de Boismorau is able to put you out of the reckoning with his testimony, if ever the business surfaces again. I would be surprised if that happened before the end of this campaign.'

We were at war, that was true, and the Comte de Lapérouse, remembering this, took the precaution of having the Baron de Boismorau write a detailed statement that was dated and signed, and countersigned by himself, and which was put away in the chest containing the ship's documents. One never knows. In the meantime I had to do my best to keep away from Flaharn.

On Saturday 21st August, the fleet arrived at the muster point in the Bahamas and sent off the convoy of eighty ships, bound for L'Orient. The Comte d'Estaing was left with twenty-two ships, nine frigates, two corvettes, two transports and four and a half thousand soldiers. As was his habit, he had raised eighteen hundred fresh troops at Cap-François, including the Marquis de Rouvray's black regiment, leaving in their place a thousand sick sailors and three hundred sick soldiers. Along the way we learned that our destination was not Jamaica but the American coast south of Charleston.

I had once again become absorbed in the routine of the sea, but I could not help thinking about how my escapade at the *Marmousets* had ended. Why had Betty been killed? I began to construct a hypothesis, but it was so horrible that I could not pursue it any more deeply. Had Flaharn arranged this murder solely to have me accused? But what was his reason? And what were the stakes that could push him to such cruelty? Jakar had talked of an Indian treasure. Was it so fabulous as to warrant this?

Lieutenant Guillemin had been mate on an India Company ship and the Surgeon Le Choquet had made several voyages to Pondicherry. I knew he was keen on studying civilisations. I asked both of them what was used as money in Hindustan.

'They have different currencies,' replied the Surgeon. 'But the Indian princes pay mainly in rupees, on which they can imprint their effigies, just like our kings.'

'Are these gold coins?'

'What we call a rupee and the Indians call *rupia* are silver. There are at least seventeen kinds of rupee in India, all of them of high quality. There are also gold coins, of course: the *ashrafi*, that the Europeans call the gold rupee; and the *hoon*, that we call the gold pagoda. I think the most generally liked currency is the piaster, which is silver.'

'We'd pay for our return cargoes with piasters,' added Lieutenant Guillemin. 'When we left L'Orient bound for the Indies, we always sent a ship to stop at Cadiz to buy them. Usually we paid six pounds for a piaster.'

'Did you buy a lot of them?' I asked.

'Once, at Cadiz, I had to load seventy thousand piasters. That's a sum of money!'

'They must have taken up a lot of room,' I said.

'We brought them aboard in barrels, using blocks and tackles. The problem isn't the volume, it's the weight. To give you an idea, three thousand silver piasters can fit in a pretty small chest, but it weighs as much as a man.'

I went back to my quarters to work out the figures. Three thousand piasters equalled eighteen thousand pounds. The cache hidden under our stairs in Port-Louis could doubtless hold three thousand piasters in a single chest, but how could my mother, all alone, have moved it, taking it to Kermean without anyone knowing? What if she managed it, or even did it twice in a row? Two times three thousand piasters were worth thirty-six thousand pounds, equal to about fifteen years' pay for a captain of the India Company. This was a not inconsiderable sum, but it didn't seem enough to justify the relentlessness that Flaharn had shown thus far.

The treasure could not be in piasters. What about gold louis? The same weight in louis, equivalent to the weight of two men, according to my calculations, would be made up of twenty-four and a half thousand coins. This would be worth almost six hundred thousand pounds. That was a big increase. But it wasn't enough for Jakar to conquer India. A single ship of the line cost more than a million pounds! And how could the Raja of Dig have been in possession of louis d'or? It was impossible. The Surgeon Le Choquet had told me that some of the Moghul's rupees were in gold, but they could not be worth more than louis, weight for weight.

My reasoning was correct, but something was missing. Something that I ought to have remembered, as I already had the answer. But, suffering as I was from an accumulation of stress and tiredness, I had simply forgotten it. I tried to recall everything I had learned about Flaharn since the discovery of the burned wooden club at Brest. Somebody had already told me what I wanted to know, and I had the feeling that it wasn't at Brest. It wasn't the Chevalier de Kermean either. I had heard it at Saint-Malo. It could only have come from Duval.

19

On the afternoon of Wednesday 1st September, being due west of Charleston, we found bottom in thirteen fathoms of water, and *le Languedoc* signalled us to anchor in our three columns. Half an hour later we had let go our anchor. According to all our calculations we were still nearly fifty nautical miles from the coast of South Carolina. It was one of the Comte d'Estaing's clever ruses: to stop out at sea in the belief that the enemy could not see him. He signalled for the commanders to come aboard. The weather was mild with a light breeze from the south.

When he returned, the Comte de Lapérouse told us that the Comte d'Estaing intended to attack Savannah, which English troops had taken from the Americans. This town in the north of Georgia was built besides a river of the same name, in the countryside about eighteen miles from the coast. Several of our captains, including Captains Lamotte-Picquet and de Suffren, had pointed out to the Comte d'Estaing that there was a bar at the mouth of the River Savannah with only sixteen feet of water at half-tide, and our ships drew too much to cross it. Moreover, there was not enough depth for us to anchor in a more sheltered spot close to the coast. We would have to anchor out at sea, in an exposed position, which worried many captains, as we were coming to the middle of the worst season of the year – that of equinoctial storms and hurricanes.

The Vice-Admiral of the Seas of Asia and America responded that we would not be staying long. It would be over in a week, and it had only taken us three days to take Grenada.

The Vicomte de Fontange, the major-general of the landing force, was sent to Charleston that evening aboard one of our two corvettes. Charleston was in American hands. The Vicomte was tasked with joining forces with General Lincoln, who commanded the Georgia and Carolina rebels. Vicomte de Fontange was also to examine the military situation and ask for shallow draft boats to take our troops to Savannah, along with experienced pilots for the coast and river.

During the evening the wind fell away completely. There was no longer the slightest breath, the air warmed up, dark clouds slowly covered the sky and a light swell from the north-east set up a slight chop against the hulls of the squadron. At ten o'clock it began to rain. It was still raining at midnight when I went off watch. In the early morning of 2nd September I was awoken by jolts and an unpleasant clanking sound mixed with gurgling. I was cold for the first time in months. I recognised the rhythmic sound of the pumps in action. I almost fell flat on my face when trying to get out of my hammock. The swell was forcing the deck up under my feet, making me bend at the knees before the decking eased away again. I could hear the frigate's planking and frames shuddering as she strained at her anchor. The rig was also suffering greatly. The Comte de Lapérouse called all hands to send down the t'gallant masts and the studding sail yards. Once this was done I stayed on the after deck with the other officers.

It was blowing a half-gale from the north-east. By midday it had grown stronger still. Huge green waves rose one after the other, unceasingly, leaving long trails of foam behind their crests, lifting up the ships and exposing their hulls as they rolled and tugged at their anchors before plunging brutally forward into the next hollow. Their bows were burying themselves in a boiling sea up to the level of the forward rail. The sound of halyards clattering, of spars banging together, the squealing of the over-stressed parrels could be heard right through the squadron amid the roaring of the wind. The Comte de Lapérouse ordered all the officers to take a noon sight with him.

'Look! My God! It's *le Fantasque!* And *le Sagittaire!*' suddenly shouted the Chevalier de la Jonquière, pointing astern to the middle of the squadron.

Two ships anchored close to us had slipped their cables. We could only see their masts working slowly through the long columns of ships at anchor. They were progressing one behind the other like two partners in crime, under jib and staysails. They made off seawards, passing between the other vessels, and quickly disappeared behind a rain squall.

Le Languedoc ran up a series of flags. It was Lieutenant Rétif's watch, and the Volunteer Laborde who was second to him got out his signal book and sheltered behind the binnacle to keep his paper dry.

'Gale...north-east...now,' decoded the young Volunteer with his south of France accent.

Lieutenant Guillemin, who was beside me, put his hand over his mouth to whisper to me that he would never have known.

'Stay...,' continued Laborde, 'at anchor. Putting...to sea... forbidden. Stay at anchor, putting to sea forbidden!'

Nobody commented, as we knew that the Comte de Lapérouse did not approve, but the officers exchanged worried looks.

'At least, for once, he is perfectly clear!' Lieutenant de Tromenec could not resist saying.

Our commander, impassive, seemed not to have heard him. With his octant still tucked under his arm, he finished off writing down the result of his sight in a little notebook. When he had finished he gave it, along with his pencil, to the officer of the watch.

'Lieutenant Rétif, get everybody's results and go down and calculate our position. I have already entered our longitude in the ship's log. And send me the bosun.'

He looked at the sea, then at the clouds rushing past above, and leaned over the compass rose.

L'Amazone's bosun was a Saint-Malo man called Duparc. The captain ordered him to attach a line and buoy to the anchor cable, marked so that we could recognise it. Half an hour later *l'Amazone* slipped her cable and headed to sea to ride out the bad weather. It was the first time I had seen the Comte de Lapérouse deliberately disobey an order.

The gale lasted four days, and half the ships cut their cables to ride out the storm. There were anchors lost that would never be found again, and those who had obeyed the Comte d'Estaing suffered the most damage, starting with *le Languedoc,* whose rudder was broken. In all, five ships had to repair or replace their rudders. There was also a number of masts, yards and sails carried away. On Monday 6th September the weather eased and the sun came out again. The Vicomte de Fontange returned with his corvette. The Americans had promised guides and pilots, but they were not there yet. The Comte d'Estaing decided to move the fleet to an anchorage closer to the coast, to blockade Savannah while we waited. We did not have occasion to see how he managed that without a rudder, as *l'Amazone* was ordered to cruise off Charleston, following a request from the Americans. We were to protect the arrival and departure of their merchant ships against an English frigate which since the start of the war had been cruising regularly along the ports of Georgia and Carolina.

At dawn on Friday 10th September 1779, we were hard on the wind in a strong north-easterly. The sea was beautiful, with a four- or five-foot swell from the north-east, and we could see the tower marking the main passage into Charleston bay. At that moment we caught sight of a distant sail to our east, sailing a parallel course to ours. We tacked to give chase to her, but she changed course to come to meet us, so effectively that by eight o'clock we were only a mile and a half apart. She was a frigate of war, with a battery of twenty-six guns, like us, but she seemed much smaller. She raised the English flag, backing that up with a cannon shot. We too raised the English flag but she was not fooled, wearing ship onto port tack and running downwind towards Savannah with all sail set. We set off in chase and could soon see that *l'Amazone* was gaining rapidly. By half past nine we were a cable and a half astern of her. She was called *Ariel* and was copper-bottomed, like us. The Comte de Lapérouse brought us alongside, just a pistol shot away, raised the King's flag and fired a shot. For more than an hour we fired fierce broadsides at each other. She only had 9-pounders against our 12-pound guns, but she used the English tactic of firing at our hull, while we attempted to dismast her. We did the job so well that by eleven o'clock, although we had a dozen killed and thirteen wounded, *Ariel* had become no more than a pontoon, with no choice but to strike her colours. We had a lot of trouble launching a boat, as the falls were all shot up and we didn't know where to fix the tackles. We headed south-west, towing our prize, who now had just three mast stumps and a short length of bowsprit. She had sailed from Savannah on the 29th August and was normally cruising off the entrance to Charleston. Her commander was very young. His name was Mackenzie[84] and he was a Post Captain and son of a Royal Navy Vice-Admiral. He had been on station at Savannah for three years and taken twenty-four prizes off the Georgia and Carolina coast. He was completely unaware of our arrival there. While inspecting *Ariel* as we took possession of her, I had the pleasant surprise of finding a charming young lady in the great cabin. It was the English captain's mistress. In this regard, at least, the gallant Captain Mackenzie had more luck than the Comte de Lapérouse.

We re-joined the fleet on Sunday 12th September. Our ships were anchored ten miles south-west of the mouth of the Savannah river, a mile and a half off a low green and yellow coastline edged with wide beaches of white sand. The ships were well spaced out, to give time to react should any anchors drag. Captain Mackenzie saw all this, from *l'Amazone's* quarterdeck, at the same time as us.

'My God!'

He couldn't get over it. He told us that even at the favourable time of year the English would never dare to anchor there. He predicted that at the first blow all our ships would end up ashore. We anchored in eight fathoms with our prize astern of us, four cables from *le César*, seventy-four guns, above which flew the pennant of the Comte de Brovès, the squadron commander. The Comte d'Estaing had gone off to supervise personally the infantry regiments. Most of the troops had been disembarked, but there still remained the artillery, powder and ammunition to be put ashore.

On 23rd September the disembarkation work recommenced. The Comte de Brovès had received urgent messages from the Comte d'Estaing and commandeered all the sloops available in the squadron. The Comte de Lapérouse still needed his sloop, and the whole ship's crew, in order to complete his repairs, but he agreed to provide *l'Amazone's* big boat, along with ten sailors under my command. He allowed me to choose my men from amongst the Lower Bretons aboard. Most of them had fished for sardines and were skilled at handling small boats under sail. They all understood French but I did my best to speak their language, which endeared me to them. We were

84 Translator's note: *Post Captain Mackenzie*: Thomas Mackenzie (1753 – 1813), later Rear-Admiral. He was subsequently cleared at court-martial for the loss of *Ariel* and continued on to a career dogged by various disappointments and controversies.

detailed to carry light artillery pieces which the Comte d'Estaing had commandeered at Saint-Domingue. These were 8-pound cannons on wheeled carriages, each weighing twelve hundred pounds, and 6-inch mortars weighing six hundred and fifty pounds. I was not sorry to have only a small boat, as if I had had a sloop we would have had to load Naval guns weighing twice as much. I went to fetch my cannons from two transports anchored off Wassaw, an island between Tybee to the north and Ossabaw to the south. From there we had to go to the end of a brackish watercourse, called Saint Augustine Creek, whose mouth was just to the north of Wassaw island, and deposit our cannons at a place called Thunderbolt. This spot had the advantage of being less than three miles from our troops' encampment.

It was blowing strongly from the north-east with a big swell left over from the bad weather of the previous days. From the transport ship to the river mouth we had the wind on the beam. The advantage of a ship's boat over a sloop is that its hull is better suited to sailing. I had shipped both masts. With cannons for ballast and the prevailing wind, we had entered the shelter of the creek while the bigger boats were still struggling in the middle of the estuary, against the tide, making leeway, soaked by the spray from the swells and by the rain.

I had the oars shipped to give support to the sails once we had entered the creek. We had to stay in the middle as the banks were marshy and thick with aquatic vegetation. We saw alligators lying in the sun on the banks, or more often, level with the surface of the water, floating like innocent tree trunks, with just their nostrils and eyes showing. Sometimes they were so close that we could hear them breathing.

Thunderbolt was a place comprised of two settlements. One was the Greenwich plantation, which belonged to a former captain of the English East India Company. These were the quarters chosen by the Comte d'Estaing to command his sea and land operations, though he spent most of his time under canvas close to Savannah. The second settlement was called Bonaventure and belonged to a Colonel Mullryne, a loyalist who had joined the garrison at Savannah, leaving his wife and daughters in charge of his house. The Comte d'Estaing had installed our field hospital there, which was already full of sick men.

The artillery was all ashore by the end of September, but we had been hearing cannon for several days. Maybe it was the English guns. We had no idea what was going on at Savannah.

Thanks to my Breton seamen, I was the only one to make all my passages under sail. In a good breeze or a half-gale, which often blew here, the boat behaved better under sail than oars. We made as much progress as the others against the current, but without tiring the crew. My sailors made fun of their Provençal shipmates as we overtook them. The Comte de Brovès noticed how quick we were and asked the Comte de Lapérouse to let me carry the daily reports and orders between Thunderbolt and *le César*. He gave me the use of his personal gig, and so I had fourteen Provençal boatmen to help me handle it. They did not all speak French, and I do not speak Provençal, but the bosun in charge of them acted as interpreter. His name was Perrin. He was quite blond, with curly hair and an intelligent face. He seemed no older than me, but the boatmen respected him. When I congratulated him on how shipshape his boat was, he answered proudly that he was from Saint-Tropez, the home, in his view, of the best sailors in the Kingdom. In fact, Provençal sailors are good to command, being in general more disciplined and less stubborn than their Breton counterparts. And they are more sober, or at least they don't get drunk. The Bretons are perhaps more sober overall, but they like nothing better than to drink to excess from time to time. And, if you don't keep an eye on them, they are likely to put aside their daily tot during the whole week, in order to drink the lot in one go on a Sunday. On the other hand, in difficult situations, where there is danger and the need to fight, I personally prefer to be with a crew of Bretons from Vannes or Cornouaille.

The Comte de Brovès was in command of the squadron in the absence of the Comte d'Estaing. I was carrying messages several times a day between *le César* and the Greenwich settlement, where I dealt with Ship's Lieutenant de Truguet, the Comte d'Estaing's liaison officer. The Comte de Brovès' gig was extremely elegant; clinker built, with a gilded rubbing strake and leather cushions on the after thwart. But above all she had fine lines and sailed well. She cut through the water easily when we had to row in the bends of the Saint Augustine Creek amongst the alligators. Whenever possible we spent the night aboard *le César*, but if the weather was threatening, which happened often enough, we stayed at Thunderbolt. This was because it was impossible to board the ships when they were being tossed around by the swell at their anchorage. To pick up the Comte de Brovès' packages when a sea was running I went under the big ship's poop, with the mizzen backed, the mainsail let right out and the helm down. A topman would throw a line down, along which the sacks were transferred. Even there our position was perilous. The huge stern frame would rise eight or nine feet above our heads and a moment later we were level with the windows of the great cabin.

Every day the Comte de Brovès gave me packages for the Comte d'Estaing but there was little for him in return. On the other hand, there was often something for the Comte de Lamotte-Picquet. I took them to *l'Annibal,* where I was welcomed like a family member when it was calm enough for me to go aboard. I chatted with Vernon and the other Marine Guards while the Comte de Lamotte-Picquet wrote his replies. Each time he asked me whether the Comte de Brovès was sending his reports to the Vice Admiral. I could only tell him that every day the Comte gave me a huge package addressed to the Comte d'Estaing, which I took to Thunderbolt, and that I in general had very little to take back to *le César.*

By virtue of the fact that I was circulating amongst our ships, I had a good idea of the state of affairs aboard the fleet, and it was not especially good. Our ships were scattered over an exposed anchorage, unable to go ashore or revictual, under the threat of a hurricane or an attack from Admiral Byron. They were a long distance from the shore, on account of the shallowness of the water, and widely spaced. Even the shortest journey entailed hours of tiring rowing. And when the sailors got back on board, usually soaked by the spray and incessant showers, they then had to take turns on the pumps for the whole night. More and more men were falling sick. Scurvy had appeared, with the Toulon squadron the most affected. Every day men were dying who could have been saved had we been able to take on fresh food and water. This was even harder to take with the coast permanently in view, so close but forbidden. In many ways I was privileged to be able to go ashore every day.

At noon one day, just after I had come ashore at Thunderbolt, I saw a rider on a chestnut horse passing on the road to Savannah. From a distance he looked like Jakar Singh, but I thought it was no doubt an American, as Jakar and Flaharn must have remained aboard *le Languedoc.* There was no reason for them to participate in the land operations. That's what I thought, anyway. When I had a packet to deliver to *le Languedoc*, it was not without a certain apprehension that I went aboard. *Le Languedoc's* commander was the Marquis de

Boulainvilliers, father of the Comte de Boulainvilliers, and the Comte d'Estaing's Flag Captain. He received me in the great cabin. I presented myself to the Marquis, telling him that I had hunted woodcock with the Comte de Boulainvilliers, at Brest.

'So you know my errant son? What's he up to?'

I replied as best I could, explaining that we had parted company in May and that I knew nothing about what had happened since. The Marquis was so pleased with these few words that he very kindly invited me to sit down. He threw the package I had brought onto the table and asked his secretary to look at it.

'Would you like a cup of tea while we wait for my secretary to look at the mail? That's all I drink. The ship's water is so stagnant that it tastes vile.'

'Will I have to take back your reply this evening?' I asked.

'Reply? Why? In any case, the Comte won't read it. But I have nothing to complain about. And, if we weren't in such a terrible location, I would be happy that he is ashore. Particularly as he has taken his piratical aide with him, the abominable Flaharn.'

'So Captain Flaharn is not on board?'

'Heaven forbid, no! He stayed aboard during the Grenada operation and his arrogance was unbearable. This time I insisted so much that for once the Comte listened. And it's true that Flaharn was not unhappy at escaping being cooped up here.'

The secretary brought back the correspondence and the Marquis broke off to read it. He shrugged and sighed from time to time, then handed it back to the secretary, telling him to 'do the necessary as usual'.

'This Flaharn is a menace!' he continued. 'Here's an example! We have two companies of grenadiers aboard as our garrison, from two different regiments, the Royal-la-Marine and the de Hainaut. Normally this would create a healthy competition between the units. Well, Flaharn has been trying to sow ill-feeling between the two. He has picked out the worst individuals from the de Hainaut regiment, amongst whom was a sub-lieutenant of low extraction. He has formed a sort of Pretorian Guard that makes out it is acting on behalf of the Comte d'Estaing, and has started terrorising my good sailors. Luckily most of the de Hainaut grenadiers are honest men, especially the sergeant whom the Comte had promoted to sub-lieutenant at Grenada. He is a man of great rectitude, that one! Flaharn is a skilled seaman, I admit that, but he spends the whole time flattering the Comte d'Estaing, who has ended up believing he can handle a ship better than all the captains of his squadron put together. Here's an example – our entry to Cap-Français harbour. The Comte was in charge of the manoeuvre and wishing to impress Flaharn he didn't want to reduce sail. He wanted to make a glorious entrance. Nobody saw it, but we scraped bottom three times in the entrance channel and eventually were heading straight for the sandbank in front of the quays. Poor Bonneval, on *l'Alcmène,* was all the time sending us signals to warn us. Flaharn was smirking on the quarterdeck. Finally we bore away at the last moment and wore ship. It was a pretty spectacle for the onlookers, but we were within a whisker of a catastrophe! And here's another thing! You had already left, on *l'Amazone*, so you can't know this. I made the mistake of telling the Comte d'Estaing that we would have to leave a hundred sick sailors at Saint-Domingue, as they would not survive another campaign. Flaharn told the Comte that he would take care of it. The night before we sailed he went with his team of grenadiers in several boats and forcibly removed a hundred sailors from the crews of the convoy about to return to France, able seamen who had already served their proper time in the King's service[85]. That's press-ganging, isn't it?'

85 Translator's note: '*...proper time in the King's service*': At that time all professional seamen in France were required to spend one year in every four serving on the King's ships.

20

On 8th October 1779, I arrived at Thunderbolt towards two in the afternoon. The weather was fine and we had spent the night on board. The trip ashore had been quick, as we had the flood tide with us into the bay. That day, the cannon fire at Savannah had been strangely silent since morning. Having told my Provençal men to wait for me, I set off towards the entrance to the Greenwich settlement, our troops' headquarters, where Ship's Lieutenant de Truguet usually gave me the packages for the squadron. I was stopped by a grenadier in a bearskin hat and a bayonet on his gun. He was wearing the uniform of the de Hainaut regiment, which I knew well from Grenada. This guard told me it was forbidden to go further as there was a council of war in progress between the Comte d'Estaing and the American generals. Everything they said was classified and it was forbidden to go near the house until they had finished. I gave my name, rank and business to the guard but he absolutely refused to listen to me. Somewhat disappointed I was about to turn and leave when a young black, dressed in the sort of livery usually worn by the domestics at Greenwich, came out of the house and headed for me, signalling as he came.

'Please, want you, Mister!'

He handed me a sealed letter, kept closed by just a dab of unstamped wax, on which I could see my name: *Monsieur Laforest-Dombourg, Marine Guard.*

'Cap'n to give that letter for you, Mister.'

'French Navy?' I asked him.

He pointed at my jacket.

'Same coat…Navy…like you, Mister.'

I thought that he must be referring to Ship's Lieutenant de Truguet and returned to the creek bank where my boat was moored, guarded by one of my sailors. I opened the letter I had just been given. It was a pencil sketch. An arrow showed where north was. I recognised the shape of a river. Above it was written: *SAVANNAH RIVER*. There were several long islands in the river course. Behind one of these islands was drawn a tiny ship, quite recognisable, with its three masts, yards and bowsprit. Underneath was written, in very small letters: *French frigate la Truite.* The town of Savannah, beside the river, was represented by a simple, unmarked rectangle. The English defensive perimeter was also marked, without any annotation except a square to the south-west: *Spring Hill.* Cross-hatching indicated the contours of the hill. Several tracks were marked and at the bottom, two rows of little triangles no doubt symbolised tents, as under them was written *French camp* and *American camp.* Between the French camp and Savannah, little rows of information were pencilled in, still in English: *17 guns, 5 guns, 12 guns, 9 mortars* and so on. A big arrow went from the French camp, followed the edge of the wood and curved round to *Spring Hill.* This arrow had *Estaing* written over it. Another, smaller arrow beside it was marked *Lincoln.* There was a little square marked *Jewish burial ground* and above that, an underlined annotation: *French reserve October 9th at dawn.* It was the 8th October! The drawing seemed to show our approach lines. There was no doubt about the precision of the sketch. It represented the plans under discussion at that moment inside the Greenwich estate house. If I had had any sense I would immediately have torn up the compromising document and thrown it in the river. But my curiosity got the better of me. I had spent so much time trying to guess what was going on around Savannah, sharing the frustration felt by most of the officers of the fleet.

'That's him, Lieutenant!'

I looked up from the piece of paper and saw the grenadier who had barred my way. Beside him was a sub-lieutenant from the same regiment, with grey hair knotted behind his neck and a triangular face with sunken black eyes beneath heavy eyebrows. He did not look young, but he was big and strong in appearance. I hurriedly slid the compromising piece of paper into my pocket.

'Please follow me, Sir.'

His voice was hoarse and unfriendly. All the same, I was not on my guard. I thought that the council of war at the headquarters must be finished and that I would be allowed in to collect the packages I had come for. I asked the bosun Perrin to wait until I came back and followed the sub-lieutenant. I noticed with surprise that the grenadier was following us with his bayonet drawn. Instead of heading for the entrance to the house, the sub-lieutenant lead us towards a group of outbuildings a fair way from the main house. We went into a big barn filled with carts and agricultural implements. Nine other grenadiers, also from the de Hainaut regiment, were waiting there for us.

'That's him!'

Several bayonets were immediately pointed at my chest.

The sub-lieutenant searched me quickly, pulling out my pistol, the only one I had left. It was loaded. He unhooked my sword and scabbard and put them under his arm. Then he searched my pockets and pulled out the sketch I had just hidden. He seemed to expect to find this, as he did not bother to look at it, apart from a brief glance. He slipped it into his jacket pocket.

'I arrest you for espionage and treason,' announced the officer.

Hearing that, the soldiers looked at me with hostility. I felt they were all ready to do me harm. The sub-lieutenant tied my hands behind my back and had me surrounded by four grenadiers, their rifles at the ready. The six others, also with their guns in hand, formed up in twos behind me, and our little troop set off behind the sub-lieutenant. He had put my pistol in his belt and was carrying my sword in its scabbard in one hand. This all seemed completely absurd to me, but I thought that for the moment it would do no good to fight back and shout. I was clearly the victim of a misunderstanding. The soldiers genuinely seemed to take me for an odious traitor. There was no point arguing with them; they could easily have despatched me on the spot. It was better to wait until I was before a superior officer. Then I could explain myself and have Ship's Lieutenant de Truguet contacted.

*

Thunderbolt, Georgia, Friday 8th October 1779.

Our little troop turns onto a straight wide avenue which leads from the house towards the exit from the property to the north-west. It is a sort of bridle path, lined with regularly spaced oak trees. Huge green and elegant plants, with leaves like fans, fill the spaces between the trees. We leave the plantation. The road continues along an embankment, two hundred yards long, across an arm of the marshes. On the other side of the marsh is another plantation with avenues bordered by oaks. We then pass through fields of indigo plants and arrive at a crossroads and the officer turns right along a wide straight track heading north-north-west.

We enter thick undergrowth. It is now more than a quarter of an hour since we left Thunderbolt. Big trees interweave their branches above the road. After another quarter of an hour the track emerges from under the cover and continues straight on across a field towards a little hill. Marshes stretch out to the north, to our right, and I can make out the Savannah river, glinting along their middle about half a mile away. My escort leaves the road and turns left onto a footpath running across a wide clearing. As we walk I can for a few moments make out, in an opening between the curve of the wood and the hill, to my right, a big slope at the end of which I can see a sort of dark barrier created from what look like tree trunks set vertically beside each other. There is a flag flying above it and it is not white. It must be the south-east bastion of the Savannah defences.

A military camp has been set up along the southern edge of the clearing, out of sight of the enemy positions. As we pass I recognise Monsieur de Rouvray's black regiment which I had seen on parade at Cap-Français. The soldiers are all lined up, their equipment at their feet. Their officers are inspecting them. I think of the arrows drawn on the sketch, showing an attack for tomorrow morning.

The footpath goes through a narrow strip of woodland and we get to another wide clearing, hidden from enemy view by a wooded crest. Our troops' tents have been pitched here. When I say tents, that's just for the officers. The soldiers sleep under big tarpaulins stretched between tree trunks or posts put in the ground. It is just enough to shelter them from the showers; all that is really required for this time of year in Georgia.

The sub-lieutenant and his little troop head towards an officer's tent pitched on its own by the edge of the wood. I notice a chestnut horse, saddled and harnessed, tethered in the trees. Five or six de Hainaut grenadiers are sitting to one side in the shade of a tarpaulin, cleaning their guns. A corporal gets up and comes to meet the sub-lieutenant, saluting with his open hand against his bearskin hat.

'The commander has not returned?' asks the officer.

'No, lieutenant, but his secretary is here.'

'Ah! Him! How is he?'

'It gets worse and worse. I think he is going crazy, lieutenant. He talks to his horse in his gibberish, as if the horse could understand!'

The officer looks annoyed.

'Have we had our company orders?'

'The Chevalier de Bonneval came, lieutenant. He has orders for you and told us to prepare for inspection. I told him that you had escorted the general to the meeting with the Americans.'

The corporal looks at me. He is obviously intrigued by my presence and the fact my hands are tied. The sub-lieutenant looks ill at ease.

'The Ship's Captain told me to arrest him. He said he is a traitor and a spy, and that the commander in chief had asked him to interrogate him on the quiet. He told me he had stolen tomorrow's plan of attack. And in fact I found something like that on him. What are we going to do with him? There's no guard room here, and he is an officer all the same. We can't put him in the Ship's Captain's tent either.'

I am about to protest when a man comes out of the tent and heads towards us. I recognise Jakar Singh. But he has changed completely! It looks as if he shaved his beard and moustache a few days ago and is letting them regrow haphazardly. His skin is yellow, and he would have looked unwell had he not tied a muslin turban around his head, in the manner of the Hindus.

'Bring the prisoner behind the tent,' says Jakar in his strange accent, 'and tie him to a tree while we wait. Your commander will see him shortly.'

The sturdy sub-lieutenant looks appalled.

'Our commander! He's just a sailor, and we are grenadiers! Bellerose,' he says to the corporal, 'take care of that and organise a guard rota. I've had enough of these shenanigans. I'm going to see what's going on at the company.'

Jakar has me taken behind the tent, out of sight of the clearing. He points out a young tree to the corporal who undoes my bindings and reties them round the trunk of the tree, leaving enough slack to enable me to sit down.

'You are wrong,' I say. 'I am not a traitor.'

'Don't take it out on me, Sir. I'm just obeying orders.'

'Leave us now!' says Jakar. He leans towards me. His eyes are bloodshot and his breath so strong you could light it with a taper.

'You have been drinking alcohol? You?'

He shakes his head in denial, but he is clearly embarrassed.

'And you have shaved your beard?'

'You know why? I had to pretend to be you.'

I think immediately of the naval officer who looked like me, seen by the witnesses to Betty's murder at Cap-Français.

'It was you who killed Betty?'

Jakar does not reply, but his crazed eyes and his silence speak volumes.

'The other day you told me you were what? A noble Kshatriya? I thought your religion forbade you to shed blood outside of war. How could you do something so unworthy?'

He rubs his face with his hands.

'It was Flaharn Sahib's idea. I agreed because my gaol is important enough to justify it. When we have retaken Dig, none of this will matter. But you must tell Flaharn Sahib what he wants to know and he will give you justice for your mother.'

I feel too much revulsion to be afraid.

'You still trust him?'

He does not reply.

'He has lied to you from the start. All he wants is the treasure. And he won't share it. Are you blind? It's so obvious!'

Jakar remains silent. He looks at the undergrowth around us then turns to me.

'Well then, I'm going to check on what you say. When he comes back tonight, he'll have you brought to him for interrogation. I will hide in the wood, close to the tent, so that I can listen. He doesn't yet know, but the soldiers will have gone. There will be no sentinels tonight. I can come close and hide outside, and hear what he says when I am not there. But I hope I am mistaken. You had better know that I am quite prepared to torture you the way I tortured Kersalaun Sahib.'

He turns as if to go.

'Wait!' I shout. 'What exactly is this treasure? Is it pagodas? Gold ones?'

He turns back, suddenly alarmed.

'You don't know what it is?'

'I might tell Captain Flaharn where it is if you tell me honestly.'

'It is precious stones.'

He stands in front of me, waiting for a reply. He seems truly afraid that I know nothing about it. Despite my situation I find it comic. I decide to reassure him, as he is my only recourse now.

'Very good! I know where your treasure is.'

He leaves me.

Of course! Diamonds! I at last remember that Duval, at Saint-Servan, had said something to this effect at the end of his story about the Sumatra expedition. They are difficult to sell, as there are only a few diamond traders, but it is the best way to convert a huge fortune into a small, easily transported size. And my dear mother could have taken a chest of diamonds out of its hiding place at Port-Louis and carried it amongst her luggage without anyone knowing, when we left the house. And I know now where she hid it when we got to Kermean. Everything now makes sense: her worried look during the journey, her relief at the burial of my grandmother, why she had insisted on watching over her mother's body for the whole night, all alone in the chapel, and the prescient words she had delivered to me once she had seen the letter from my father, shown to her by my uncle the Chevalier de Kermean. If only François Loutre's brother-in-law had been able to deliver the Marquis of Kersalaun's last message! She would have got rid of this awkward burden as soon as possible, handing it over to the authorities, or to my uncle, to pass on to the King. Maybe she would still be alive. I am now sure that my father had thought of this, which is why he had written the strange letter to the Chevalier de Kermean before leaving for Brest. Particularly if he knew, as the message from the Marquis de Kersalaun seemed to imply, that Kersalaun had delayed carrying out his plans on account of my father being unexpectedly commissioned to captain *la Fouine* to the Antilles. At that time my father would have been too scrupulous to have done anything with a secret that did not belong to him, and he would have been expecting to return from his voyage. And so, for want of anything better to do, he had written this coded letter, rather as one throws a message in a bottle into the sea.

*

The French camp outside Savannah, night of Friday 8Th October to Saturday 9th October 1779.

Time passes. I have managed to sit down, my back against the tree trunk I am attached to, my legs stretched out in front. My hat falls down over my eyes and I manage to get rid of it by shaking my head. It is dusk and getting darker. I am now in exactly the same situation as the Marquis de Kersalaun, forgotten in some obscure hole where nobody can do anything for me.

I doze in a sort of torpor until woken by a strong need to urinate. The darkness is complete except for the faint light at the edge of the wood. I have no way of knowing what time it is.

The front line is strangely silent. I regret allowing myself to be arrested so easily. At Thunderbolt, at least people knew who I was. My sailors would have defended me. But here I am hidden in a dense wood, behind an encampment where nobody knows me. The soldiers I saw passing in front of the bivouacs are busy preparing an attack in which they might lose their lives. They have more important things to do than listen to my cries for help. Despite the pressing need that is starting to torment me, I start to hope that I really have been forgotten. I dread the moment when somebody will come to undo my bonds.

I hear footsteps at the edge of the wood. Somebody is talking. My hands are damp and my hair stuck to my temples. My shirt is wringing wet. Candles are lit in the tent. And what I dreaded is coming. Three men approach in the dark, one carrying a lantern. I recognise the grenadiers in their bearskin hats. They are carrying rifles. The one carrying the lantern puts it on the ground beside me. It is the corporal called Bellerose.

'The commander Flaharn has just got back. He wants to see you, Sir.'

There is no hostility in is voice. He leans behind me and frees my hands. I stand up and shake my swollen wrists, then hurry into the wood to satisfy the urgent need which has gripped me for hours. The two grenadiers lift their rifles.

'Let him be, lads,' says the corporal quietly.

I pick up my hat and follow the corporal. He has not tied my hands again. I follow him into the tent. Inside, at the end, I can see a camp bed, a sea chest and a table, on which I recognise the compromising sketch of Savannah. My sword is lying on top of it. The rest of the furniture seems to have come from *le Languedoc*: a writing desk on which I notice my pistol, apparently still loaded, and two box seats. The one facing the entrance, on the other side of the writing desk, is taken by the fine figure of a man wearing a Ship's Captain's uniform. I cannot but admire his imposing presence, his flat stomach, his big highly-charged body and the regular features of his face. He is smoking a pipe as he waits for me. The smell of Holland tobacco, that I know only too well, floats in the air.

'Sit down then, Monsieur Dombourg,' says Flaharn in his hoarse voice, indicating the other seat with the stem of his pipe. 'Sorry to have kept you waiting but the meeting at headquarters went on for ever. I thought it would last all night. We're fine!' he adds, looking at the corporal. 'I would like to have a quiet chat with my guest. It is not for your ears. Move the guard ten paces away and stay with him to watch the door. Understood?'

'At your orders, Sir!' replies corporal Bellerose.

He seems afraid of Flaharn. And he hasn't even heard of the impaled Sumatrans! I don't blame him; I am scared too. How had I been ready to confront him, even just with words, at Saint-Domingue? I am absurdly happy that my hands are free but facing Flaharn I feel as powerless as if I had my hands tied and my feet too.

'Well, Monsieur Dombourg, how are you tonight? You will forgive me for having passed you off as a traitor to my fine grenadiers, but I had to find a pretext to get them to bring you to me, seeing as you no longer reply to my friendly invitations. What now?' he shouts, looking towards the tent door behind my back.

I recognise the voice of the sub-lieutenant who arrested me.

'Excuse me for interrupting, Sir, but we can't stay here much longer. Captain Bonneval has ordered me to collect all my men and rejoin the company. It seems he is about to launch an attack. I will have to take everybody.'

'I'll keep two sentries!'

'I am sorry, Sir. It's impossible. There's nothing else I can do. We're not on board ship, here. You have no say over my superiors. I have to obey them. Would you like me to wake your secretary?'

'No! It's a waste of time. I'll manage without him.'

The sub-lieutenant departs with his men, leaving us alone. Jakar was right. Flaharn does not look pleased.

'Those fools will all be dead tomorrow! The assault is nonsensical. You don't attack a well-defended enemy, who has cannons, unless you have superior numbers. He thinks he's still at Tappanoolee. I swear! But we are not facing a handful of Malays!'

I suppose he must be talking about the Sumatra business that Duval told me about at Saint-Malo, but mostly I am thinking about what Jakar said about the guards leaving. I hope fervently that he will come and eavesdrop as promised.

Flaharn takes my pistol off the writing desk and makes a show of examining it.

'A very fine gun! The King's police inspector at Cap-Français would be very happy if I took it to him...particularly if I told him it was yours!'

He carefully lays the pistol on the desk and puffs again at his pipe.

'What do you mean?' I ask.

'You don't understand, then? It's very simple. I now have so much damaging evidence against you that I can either choose to point the authorities in your direction or else, if I want, keep the proof to myself and guarantee your cooperation.'

'Damaging evidence against me?'

'My dear fellow, you are the presumed killer of the girl Betty Moreau. According to all the witness statements that have been collected, her murderer was a Naval officer, perhaps even a Marine Guard, and the police inspector already has a pistol identical to this one abandoned at the scene of the crime by the killer. It seems easy to work it out. Especially considering that you had spent the evening before the murder with her at the Governor's ball. You can rest assured that as yet they don't know who is the guilty one. All they know is that it was a Naval officer. This business could well have annoyed the Comte d'Estaing, but luckily for you I decided off my own bat to supervise the inquiry on the Navy side and liaise with the police inspector at Cap-Français. I promised to make inquiries on his behalf, which I have kept up, with the help of a few little gifts. I have only to say the word for you to be accused and arrested. But we are on a campaign. If I do nothing they will forget about you...possibly. It's your choice!'

'So you would force me to tell you what you want to know under threat of denouncement?'

'I am pleased you understand so quickly. I am forcing you to tell me, without lying, where my diamonds are hidden. I would also advise you to avoid the temptation, which I know you have already had, of sneaking to the Comte d'Estaing to make accusations against me. At the slightest sign of bad faith on your part it will be very easy for me to have you go through the scandal of a trial and, without doubt, execution or forced labour. Your name will be ruined. The Grand Corps of officers won't hesitate to cast you out to preserve their reputation. For them you will be a rotten branch that needs cutting away completely. I can just imagine how that would affect the Baron de Kermean and his son, that pretentious little fellow who thinks of himself as a grandmaster because he plays around with the Secret Cabinet and spends his time opening my mail! To avoid all that you will do as you are told!'

'You killed poor Betty just for that?'

'What do you expect? You can't make an omelette without breaking eggs! I had to sacrifice a little whore. It wasn't a great loss and has always been part of my plan. I started to think about it the first time I saw your pair of pistols, at Brest. I was at a dead end. Kersalaun and his wife had been so indelicate as to kill themselves rather than help me, your mother was dead before she could talk. Every avenue was blocked! There was only you, my last card. But to get you to tell me I had to steer you in the right direction. This risked compromising myself, I know.'

He takes a puff on his pipe. Through the smoke I see his grey eyes. They are as cold and unmoving as a snake's.

'The problem was to get you to tell me what I wanted to know without you telling tales about me. I intended to play out this little scene at Saint-Malo. I would have had you under my thumb, on board ship, under my orders and control, every day, amongst a hand-picked crew. I would have had all the time in the world to construct a convincing scenario. I would have thrown a nice woman to you. There's no lack of whores in Saint-Malo. And hot little rabbit that you are, I would wager you have already tasted them!'

If only he knew, I think to myself, despite my critical situation.

'I would just have asked her to seduce you, while we took care of the business with the pistols. But here, at Cap-Français, time was running out and I knew I was cutting things fine. No doubt I should have waited for a better opportunity. But I can tell you that when I saw that you were continually refusing my invitations, and when I learned that you had even met the Comte d'Estaing at Grenada, and that he liked you, that raised the stakes. I started to get worried, you see, as the Comte could easily have listened to you if you had the nasty idea of denouncing me. I had to act quickly. So I ordered Jakar to prime you by having you believe I would tell you about your mother. That worked, but I thought I would never find a girl as compliant and stupid as your Betty in time.'

'She was worth more than you!'

Flaharn laughs.

'She wanted to sleep with you from the moment she saw you, I'll give you that. The problem was your pistol. I needed it for my plan. At Saint-Malo we could have taken it from its case ourselves, but here it was impossible. The only answer was to have it sneaked out by the sacrificial goat herself. But she didn't want to do wrong by you. To get her to take it without you knowing, I had to tell her that I just wanted a drawing made of it by an armourer. It would just take an hour. I would have it brought back by one of my officers and she could give to you. If she had known what it was for! I had promised her a big reward, with which she hoped to buy you some bauble to surprise you and make you forgive her. She swallowed the whole lot!'

Brave Betty! I had hardly known her, but I know she liked me a lot.

'I would willingly have tried her before you...' he laughed contemptuously, '...but she didn't want to. I didn't want to force her as I needed her too much. Anyway, it's done! Now we are even. If you refuse to cooperate, or if you try to denounce me, I will hand you over to the police and, moreover, unlike you I have concrete proof to back up my accusations.'

I take a moment to think through what he has told me. I realise that he does not know that the Baron de Boismorau can prove my innocence. I take heart from that, a little prematurely.

'I didn't wait for her in my room,' I say. 'I came out beforehand. There are witnesses who saw me going down to the port.'

'Yes, it's true. I didn't foresee that you would leave so quickly. My initial idea was to send the archers to your room, so they could grab you still in bed, with its sticky sheets stained with fresh juices. I would have rescued you from that, with your cooperation as my reward. It's a pity. But after all, what did they see, these witnesses? They saw a Marine Guard fire a pistol and run off towards your room. And as far as I know you are a Marine Guard.'

'You are completely wrong,' I say. 'I have real witnesses, totally reliable, who can prove my innocence.'

He takes his pipe out of his mouth and stares at me with his pale grey eyes.

'Go on then! Witnesses? Tell me about it.'

He is still calm and sure of himself. I ought to go along with his game and allay his mistrust, playing the scared and submissive child, but I do the opposite. I can't help myself.

'Your plan was well arranged,' I say heatedly, 'but chance intervened. My commander had received the order to sail and sent an officer who saw Betty still alive and who was at my side from that moment on. He is ready to swear under oath that I did not kill that poor girl. He has already signed a statement to that effect. What's more, the Cap-Français people who witnessed the crime saw Jakar go off in the opposite direction from which I came. Jakar Singh had started to run in the direction of the *Marmousets*, but his path was barred by a cart coming in the other direction. He had to cross the stream to go up the hill. Your accusations won't stand up.'

Flaharn does not turn a hair.

'That fool Jakar made a mess of it, then? It's not possible! He kept quiet about it, anyway.'

'It wasn't his fault. He couldn't foresee that my commander was going to send an officer for me right at that moment.'

I think that if Jakar is listening, he will appreciate me defending him. Flaharn reflects for a moment.

'And who is he, this officer who will stand witness for you?'

His voice is still just as cold.

'So that you can submit him to the same treatment as François Loutre?' I say.

This time he cannot help raising an eyebrow.

'You killed the huntsman to stop him talking to me. I have the proof. I found the club you tried to burn in the fireplace of your room. Holly doesn't burn well, you know.'

Flaharn's face hardens, but he gets himself under control. I have the feeling, too late, that I ought not to have fired off all my ammunition so quickly.

'Ah well, too bad for you! You force me to use more direct methods. This is my proposition: you agree to tell me here and now exactly where your mother hid my treasure, and we will share it. Otherwise I will do away with you. Nobody knows where you are, and once I am back in France I will lay waste to Kermean to find my property.'

I am shocked. This diabolical man has already guessed that the diamonds are at Kermean! My consternation does not go unnoticed.

'Ha! I knew it! Your mother hid my chest at Kermean! I will get it in the end. No old man is going to stand in my way. If you agree to help me, things will go better for you. You will help your grandfather to avoid a lot of trouble, and you yourself will be rich.'

I don't believe a word he is saying. The tiger does not share its prey so easily. A minute ago, Flaharn has decided to kill me. I know too much about him for him to allow me to live. What is Jakar doing? He is my last chance. As long as he is listening! I think as hard as I can. I have to win some time.

'I didn't think these diamonds were for sharing. I thought they were solely for financing the reconquest of an Indian kingdom.'

If the Indian cannot hear me, I am done for.

'And who told you this nonsense?'

'Jakar Singh.'

Once again he sniggers contemptuously.

'Jakar! He still imagines that we will be off on a crusade to save the Jats. You see me ending my life by declaring war on the English? Just to defend the interests of some stupid peasants in the depths of Hindustan?'

'You won't even share it with him?'

'I needed Jakar and if he wants to claim his share, so be it! But for the rest, I can do without him...'

He stops suddenly and looks behind me. I turn my head and see Jakar at the door of the tent. And not before time!

'Without me you would be nothing, Flaharn!' Jakar's reddened eyes seem to be flaming and his voice is trembling. 'Remember when you arrived at Dig with your torn clothes. I was a general! It's me who took you to the Raja. It's me who helped you recruit your sepoys. It's me who gave you your first jaghir[86] and showed you how to raise taxes to make yourself rich. It's me you asked to kill Javahir Singh and his brother. I tortured Kersalaun Sahib for nothing. I have done all this dirty work for nothing! I have destroyed this life and all my lives to come!'

'What are you talking about, Jakar? You know I have no intention of stealing your share. We will split it, that's all. There'll easily be enough for both of us.'

'Split it? That is not what was agreed.'

'We will have to talk about it seriously,' replies Flaharn. 'In the meantime, take care of this boy.'

The Indian does not move. He stares at his accomplice.

'No! I trusted you. I was blind. It's him who opened my eyes. You've lied from the start. I think I will have to kill you. I've got nothing to lose now.'

Flaharn bursts out laughing.

'Come now, Master Jack, are you being serious? I could break you in two with my bare hands to punish you for your arrogance. But I'm a good fellow. You will have your share and do what you like with it. You can go to the devil and take your little war with you. And consider yourself lucky.'

The Indian gives a little roar, pulls out his dagger and throws himself at his accomplice. Flaharn has not foreseen this, his only weakness being to believe that nobody would dare take him on. All the same, he reacts very quickly. He catches the Indian's flying wrist in his right hand and pulls it down, squeezing hard. Jakar slowly bends his knees under the pressure and cries out in pain. I can hear the bones breaking in his wrist. Flaharn takes the knife from him. Jakar has lost!

They are no longer thinking about me. I jump out through the door of the tent and run off into the night as fast as my legs will carry me. In desperation I run straight towards the camp I had crossed that afternoon with my escort. I can no longer hear what is happening in the tent, as at that moment the artillery opens fire on Savannah.

*

86 Translator's note: *jaghir*: a grant of land under the jaghirdar feudal land system prevalent in India since the thirteenth century.

The sound of explosions ripped through the silence of the forest. The flashes from the firing enabled me to see the mass of men stopped at the edge of the wood. Getting closer, I could see that they were formed up into a column for advancing along the line of the wood to my left. They were virtually at a standstill, their progress slowed by the darkness. I was sure that Flaharn would come after me. I could already imagine him, hot on my heels with his strong and supple stride. Unarmed, I could do nothing against his strength. I was a gazelle trying to escape a tiger. I had the choice of either fleeing into the empty undergrowth to my right, or running the opposite way, to my left, and mixing with the soldiers of the vanguard. They would be advancing more quickly than the soldiers I could see, which would create more distance between myself and my pursuer. I chose the second option. I thought Flaharn would have less chance of finding me in the middle of a crowd of soldiers than in the empty undergrowth.

The troops started moving again, very slowly. I overtook them easily, going along their left side through the trees. The column stopped as we reached a clearing. I could see the outlines of a row of tents to my left. Combat companies were assembling in the dark. I could hear English being spoken; it was the American camp. A track led north towards Savannah, through a wood. The soldiers I was level with had jackets darker than the usual light grey of the other units. Getting closer I could see they were the red jackets of the de Dillon regiment. I overtook them by threading along the edge of the track until I caught up with a group of officers. They were gathered around the Comte d'Estaing, whom I recognised because of his height. I was unarmed, empty-handed, but for the moment that could not really be seen. On the other hand, my blue Navy jacket could draw attention to me, even at night, amongst these front-line regiments. I decided to follow the Comte, hoping that I would be taken for one of his staff officers.

The cannons grew quiet and the columns once more stopped on the track. Detachments moved forward. First to pass were grenadiers in bearskin hats. The Comte d'Estaing said encouraging words as they passed. They were to be the first wave of the assault. Amongst them I saw the well-built sub-lieutenant who had arrested me the day before. They were followed by soldiers carrying ladders. The Comte d'Estaing set off behind them and I followed in his footsteps. We stopped once more, at the edge of the wood. Soldiers were posted around us, under cover. It was still night but the horizon was lightening on our right. I could make out the uniforms of the men around me, and recognised the light infantry from the Saint-Domingue garrison. It was they who had brought the ladders. The Comte d'Estaing was talking with their colonel, the Vicomte de Bethisy. I had seen him at the Saint-Domingue Governor's ball. He was going to lead the vanguard. With them was Ship's Lieutenant de Truguet, whom I knew well. The Comte d'Estaing was constantly saying that we were behind schedule, that the other two columns were taking too long to get into position. The Americans weren't yet there either. The Ship's Lieutenant saw me and expressed his surprise. The Comte d'Estaing recognised me.

'Ah! It's the Vicomte de Noailles' Marine Guard. He's just like you, Truguet[87]. He couldn't bear to wait in reserve with the Vicomte.'

I said nothing. My plan had worked. I was out of Flaharn's reach.

Day came, gradually revealing the countryside. We were at the foot of a big slope which the English had burned and cleared of vegetation to give themselves a clear field of fire. About a hundred yards to our left the track went out into the open, beside a marsh from which a thick mist rolled over the solid ground, for the moment hiding the English defences we were about to attack. To the right there was a cemetery, a cemetery without crosses; the Jewish cemetery on the sketch. That's when I heard the sound of bagpipes coming through the mist ahead of us.

'The Scots!' said the Vicomte de Bethisy.

I was behind a small group made up of the Comte d'Estaing, the Vicomte de Bethisy and Ship's Lieutenant de Truguet, and I think I was the only one who could hear them talking. The soldiers around us were straining to hear the sound of the bagpipes. It was a perfect match for this scene of mist, marsh and cemetery. The soldiers looked at each other in silence. For them is was a song of death.

'Colonel Maitland's men! Prévost[88] has changed them during the night! He has put his best troops on Spring Hill!' said the Comte

87 Translator's note: *Truguet:* Ship's Lieutenant Laurent de Truguet won the Cross of Saint-Louis for his bravery at the Battle of Savannah and eventually became an Admiral of the French Navy.

88 Translator's note: *Prévost:* Major-General Augustine Prévost (1723 – 1786): Genevan-born British soldier who served in the Seven Years' War and the War of American Independence, and was in command of the English forces at Savannah.

d'Estaing in a low voice. 'It's the most strongly fortified point on his perimeter. According to our information there would only be militiamen here. That's why we decided to attack here. They've been forewarned. We're late. The others aren't here yet and we have lost the advantage of surprise. Do we abandon the attack?'

I think that the Comte d'Estaing was truly about to call off the assault at that moment. A salvo rang out, a long way to our right. We could still see nothing because of the mist. It came from the English lines.

'The diversion!' said the Vicomte de Bethisy.

'In that case, we go,' said the Comte. 'The wine is poured and we must drink it! Good luck, Bethisy! Look after yourself, Truguet!'

He drew his sword, stood up and marched five or six paces up the slope. He turned towards the soldiers watching him, all on their knees with the butts of their rifles on the ground.

'Forward, men! *Vive le Roi*!'

His shout rang out in the early morning air. Drums began to beat the charge. The soldiers stood up, they too shouting *Vive le Roi*! They threw themselves up the slope, the Vicomte de Bethisy at their head. The Comte let them pass then started up behind them. As for me, I followed him. Behind us, the troops of the line making up the largest part of our column came out of the wood and followed in our footsteps.

The mist was lifting. I could see the Spring Hill redoubt, four hundred yards in front of us, at the top of the slope. It was a defensive structure composed of tree trunks placed in the ground at the top of a mound. There were others, but the one we were about to attack was the highest. It rose forty feet above the flatter ground covered in cinders and brush that we were working our way up. At the base of the mound was a ditch which considerably increased the height to be climbed to get to the parapets. I could easily see the red coats of the enemy soldiers. For the moment they were happy to watch us coming. About fifty yards in front of their firing positions, the English had built an obstacle made up of spaced out stakes, planted vertically in the ground, between which they had jammed interlaced horizontal branches. It was not thick enough to provide protection against ordinary or large calibre rifle bullets, but you had to climb to get over it. The de Hainaut grenadiers had brought axes to open breaches in this obstacle. This was less dangerous than climbing over, right under the noses of the Scottish riflemen.

We heard the first shots fired as the grenadiers and light infantry reached the first obstacle. This was not general fire, but carefully aimed shots which were hitting their targets. The first artillery salvo was held back until the de Hainaut grenadiers started hacking at the obstacle with their axes. The cannons were loaded with grapeshot and at fifty yards the effect was startling. I saw grenadiers tossed into the air before falling to the ground like bloodied puppets. Those who had not been mown down got through the obstacle and started running to the bottom of the ditch at the foot of the redoubt. A new burst of artillery fire knocked most of them to the ground. The light infantrymen who followed them managed to get their ladders up, but they were pushed away. When the Comte and I reached the obstacle, the company of grenadiers was lying in the ditch, with the English shooting anyone who could still move. The soldiers following us had caught up and we were all gathered at the base of the barrier.

We were not shredded by the artillery, as it was directing its fire against the de Dillon regiment's column, a little way behind us to our right. The English cannons were aiming grapeshot at their flank, from a distance of two hundred yards. Their efficiency was total: our redcoats were falling in groups of ten. The Scottish riflemen, for their part, were still searching out targets anywhere on the slope. I had my hat taken off by a bullet. The Comte himself took one in the arm. He spun round under the shock, swearing, and I had to hold him up. He recovered himself, but could not pull himself up with one arm to cross the barrier, and asked me to help him. I sat astride the top of the obstacle and tried to pull him, but he was as big as Flaharn and far too heavy for me. I forced myself to think of nothing, gritting my teeth and half-closing my eyes. I heard a bullet hit the interwoven branches, just above my thigh. The rifleman who had me in his sights must have fired too quickly and missed, thank God!

The Comte gave up trying to get across and I fell back down to his side. Before jumping down from my perch I had the time to see that the ditch at the base of the redoubt was filled with bodies. They were a good number hanging from the barrier too. And the strip of ground beside the ditch was carpeted with human debris. Pieces of flesh stuck to fragments of bone had been thrown anything up to fifty yards from the bottom of the ditch by the grapeshot salvos fired at point-blank range.

The hell to my right had distracted me from the progress of our column to the left. They had made their assault by going along the edge of the marsh to attack the next redoubt, further north. They had found themselves hit from the side by the English cannons there and had gone into the marshes. They could only make slow progress, offering an easy target for the Scottish riflemen.

The de Dillon column, together with what was left of Bethisy's, moved towards our left flank. The Comte d'Estaing wanted to rally all the survivors on the firm ground here, to get them behind him for a desperate surge. He shouted, brandishing his sword in his good hand. But he was hit again, in the leg this time, and he collapsed. We were on the south-west flank of the redoubt. To our left I could see the marshland scattered with bodies, half sunken into two feet of muddy and reddened water.

The artillery was now concentrating its fire on the assault by the Americans, who had come up from behind the left column. They launched the next attack and were as fierce as our Irishmen. They managed to get their flags up to the parapet but were repulsed almost immediately. They also had a squadron of cavalry dragoons commanded by a Polish officer, who lead them into a totally insane charge to the north of the Spring Hill redoubt. Their impetus was broken by the English artillery as they reached the barrier.

For the moment the English artillery was leaving us alone but we were still targeted by their riflemen. Our situation was not in the least comfortable. I stopped two grenadiers and they helped me pull the Comte towards our lines. Further on I came across the Comte de Dillon and Ship's Lieutenant de Truguet. The Comte d'Estaing told de Dillon that he could order the retreat. Those still capable of walking gathered at the Jewish cemetery from where we had started the attack. The reserve force commanded by the Vicomte de Noailles was stationed on the north side of the gravestones. There were riflemen there from several different regiments. As soon as we had passed them they opened fire on the beginnings of an English counter-attack, turning the enemy back.

The shooting stopped and a deep silence hung over the slope. It was over. The whole thing had lasted less than an hour. I could hardly believe it. The images of the attack would stay with me for a long time. I felt like a man who had journeyed to the other side of life.

The Comte d'Estaing had lost consciousness. Medics carried him to his tent on a stretcher. Even the cannons had fallen silent. The Comte de Dillon negotiated a four-hour truce with General Prévost, who commanded the defence of Savannah, so that we could collect our dead and wounded. I went to the Comte's tent with Ship's Lieutenant de Truguet. The Lieutenant was accustomed to giving me the mail for the Comte de Brovès and asked me to wait while he wrote his reports. I replied that I would go as quickly as possible to Thunderbolt to make sure my boat was still there and that I would wait there for him to send the packages by messenger. The Lieutenant kindly asked me if I had breakfasted before the attack, but I told him that my stomach was still too knotted to swallow anything. I showed him the soles of my shoes, to which were stuck pieces of flesh, some with hair attached. Seeing this, he grimaced and said he felt the same. I thought about mentioning Flaharn but decided it was not the right moment.

21

I went the other way along the route I had taken in the dark a few hours earlier. Soon I saw Flaharn's tent by the edge of the wood. From a distance I could hear the anxious neighing of Jakar's horse, still tethered in the trees. There was not a soul in sight. I approached carefully along the edge of the wood, expecting the tall figure of Flaharn to leap out at any moment. But all was quiet. I carried on even more delicately, ready to run off as fast as I could at the slightest danger. The horse calmed down and watched me come close, breathing heavily through its nostrils and shaking its mane. I could see the whites of its big eyes. A deathly silence hung over the place. I had decided to turn back when a kind of groan made me jump. It came from the edge of the trees on the other side of the tent. I retreated then made a wide detour. Beyond the tent I found a man sitting on the ground, head on his chest, his back leaning against a fallen tree trunk. I recognised Jakar Singh by his turban. I called out to him as gently as I could, from a distance, and he raised his head. He signalled me to join him. This I did with the greatest apprehension, fearing yet another trap.

*

The French Camp at Savannah, Saturday 9th October 1779, morning.

At fifteen paces from Jakar I stop again to look at him. He seems to have changed his waistcoat. His muslin headgear is all awry, giving him a grotesque look. His face is waxy. He raises his left arm again to signal me to come closer.

'Where is he?' I ask, not daring to raise my voice.

'There…'

He gestures towards the tent.

'He's sleeping?'

Jakar smirked.

'He's dead.'

'You beat him?'

'Pistol. I killed him with the loaded pistol. The pistol with the tiger. He had forgotten it on the table. That was his last mistake.'

I move closer and lean over him. He is still in his silver-striped waistcoat. If it looks different it's because it is soaked with dried blood. I put out my hand to move the flap of his jacket but he stops me.

'No! If you pull I will start bleeding again. I don't have much time…I must speak to you.'

'It was Flaharn?'

'He struck me, a lot…with my dagger.'

'I will get you taken to the field hospital.'

'No good. I have…lost too much blood. I don't feel anything… which means I am going to die.'

'Would you like me to get you some water?'

I don't feel any particular pity for him. He is a murderer. But in the end he too is a victim of Flaharn.

'Listen to me. It is more important. Your mother…I promised her. I want to keep my promise…perhaps in my next life I will be less punished…My intentions were…noble…that's what you say…isn't it?'

Talking is making him short of breath. He has to speak in short phrases. His voice is weak and his eyes unusually bright, but I doubt this will last for long. I kneel down beside him to hear him better.

'Where is my mother?'

'After…but first the princess…I have to talk to you about the princess.'

'The princess? You mean the Marquise de Kersalaun?'

'Princess Jamna. I did not kill her. It wasn't me...we crossed the little sea...with the soldiers...'

'You crossed Brest harbour with the halberdiers, is that it?'

'Halberdiers...they were pigs! We went into Kersalaun Sahib's chateau. He had gone hunting. We surprised the princess in her bed... she wouldn't tell us anything. Flaharn said we would wait for Kersalaun. The pigs were circling her. She was almost naked, in her bed...and so beautiful...Flaharn gave her to his pigs...and I did nothing to defend her...we searched everywhere and found the plan you had drawn... Kersalaun came back on his horse after. He threw the body of the wolf by the well, took out his knife and put it on the well. Perhaps he wanted to skin it and cure it...We surrounded him then. He recognised Flaharn, who was holding the princess and laughing. He threw himself at him, at Flaharn Sahib...I was the only one who wasn't surprised...I have always known that Kersalaun Sahib is afraid of nothing. Flaharn pushed the princess towards the well to defend himself...That's when she saw the knife...We didn't have time to stop her...she plunged it in straight away, like this!'

He places his closed left fist against his heart and tries to put his right hand behind it, but the hand does not conform. It makes an awkward angle with his arm. Flaharn has broken his wrist.

'She killed herself?'

'She was a true...Kshatriya.'

He hiccups and coughs, chokes and spits, then with his left wipes away a dribble of bloody saliva hanging from his lower lip.

'After...Kersalaun would not talk. We searched everywhere. We took Kersalaun with us in the little boat.'

'You also took the wolf's remains.'

'Yes, Flaharn told the pigs they could not pillage but could take the wolf.'

'After you took the Marquis to the Brest prison,' I say, 'you tortured him and he hung himself in his cell.'

'So then...you know?'

'Why were you at my mother's house, at Port-Louis?'

'We found the drawing with your name on it. We thought it showed the hiding place for Suraj Mal's diamonds, but we didn't know exactly where. At the post office Flaharn had found a letter for Kersalaun. It was from L'Orient and sent by Madame Laforest-

Dombourg. Kersalaun Sahib had not had the time to pick it up…your mother wrote to say your father was dead, but that this did not change anything. She would respect her husband's promises. Flaharn tried to find out who this husband was. That's why we went to L'Orient. When Flaharn realised it was the former Captain at Chandernagore, who had sailed off with the chest of diamonds aboard…everything became clear…'

'Why did you hire a coach at Hennebont?'

'It was so as not to be seen by the soldiers at the main gate. In the house at Port-Louis we found your mother…and an old lady…we recognised the hiding place from your drawing. It was empty. Your mother had already taken the chest away and she wouldn't say where she had put it…Flaharn broke the old lady in two in front of your mother…to frighten her. He said that she would be as obedient as a lamb. He was wrong…as always. He always thinks others are cowards. I've told him! She fought. We were up on the landing, and as she was struggling she fell down the stairs. She slid across the flagstones at the bottom… headfirst into a cupboard with a glass front…a piece of broken glass…into her belly…like a sword…'

I remember the report of the sergeant who was the first to get to the scene. I know it by heart: '*A glass-fronted cupboard had its panes broken and there were copious traces of blood on the tiles.*' Even I had not paid enough attention to this detail. I well remember this piece of furniture: a cupboard with a curved glass front. It had always been upstairs, but must have been taken down for the house moving.

'We searched everywhere…We took…your mother. Flaharn wanted to look after her…so that he could question her again…She died in the carriage. She told me before she died…listen…this is what she said to me…that I would be punished in my future lives for as long as she was not buried at her home…that I had to tell you this, how to find her…'

My mother must have learned a little about Indian beliefs from my father. Even at the end she had thought about leaving me clues so that I could find this cursed treasure.

'Where did you bury her?'

'The ground was…frozen. We could not…dig. I put her body in a tree…up high.'

'A hollow tree, you mean?'

'Yes, in the middle of a wood…hollow higher up…the hole covered by branches...I threw her in the hole. And I covered her up, with branches...stones...leaves.'

'What kind of tree?'

'They were all the same, except for those three there.'

'Yes, but what sort of trees? Oaks?'

'Yes, but all the other trees around, trees with a black fruit, brown... with spines too, you call that...'

'Chestnut trees?'

'Yes, chestnut, that's how you say it. There were a lot of them.'

'The wood is a chestnut grove.'

'While I was doing that, Flaharn slit the coachman's throat. He threw him in the river...so as not to leave any traces. It was...his idea, from the start, he said he had been seen by soldiers at the town gate. But...I think he also took pleasure in it.'

Nicolas Dugoin! The forced labourer picked up by Flaharn at the end of his prison sentence. Flaharn had sacrificed a lot of people.

'How can I find this chestnut grove?'

'The bridge after... the town.'

'After Port-Louis?'

'No...the other town...further up the river.'

'Hennebont?'

'Something like that, yes.'

'The first bridge when coming out of Hennebont, but in which direction?'

'Going to Port...Louis. The bridge goes over a stream...beside the river. A little stream. The place close by is called...Parco...After the bridge the river turns to the right. You leave the main road to follow a smaller one...on the left side of the river...which turns...another stream...up...to the left...the chestnut grove.'

His chin has fallen to his chest. He won't last much longer. I quickly repeat what he has just told me.

'On the road to Port-Louis, coming from Hennebont, you come to the first bridge which crosses a stream which flows into the river. After this bridge you leave the road to take a path which goes to the right, following a curve in the river. You cross another stream and go up to the left and there is a chestnut grove there. Is it big? Are there lots of trees in this wood?'

'A lot...but there are three...big trees...together...in the middle.'

'Three oaks in the middle of the chestnuts?'

'Yes.'

'He is still looking at me, trying to talk. I see his lips moving.

'Gho...Ra...'

I think that he is in his death rattle, that this is the end. I get up but he tries to hold me back. I go down on one knee again and put my ear close to his mouth.

'Gho...Ra...my horse...set my horse...free.'

His head falls to his chest again. This final effort has drained him. His eyes glaze over. There is nothing to be done for him. I stand up and go to the tent. The huge body of Flaharn is lying in the middle, on the ground. My pistol, discharged, has fallen beside him. One of the seats has been overturned. The candles on the writing desk are completely burned down. I take my sword and the cursed sketch of the Savannah attack. But I leave the pistol, despite the cost to me. If the Cap-Français investigators do their job properly, it could become an unnecessary problem. Better to leave it near Betty's real killers, where it may perhaps be found. I am still so afraid of Flaharn Sahib that I don't look at him closely. I turn on my heels and leave as quickly as I can, buckling on my sword and going off without looking back. I return to the former Indian general Jakar Singh, but he is no longer alive. The chestnut horse tethered under the trees watches me constantly and I understand what Jakar meant. I go up to the animal, who snorts and pricks his ears. I stretch out my hand and place it on his shaking withers. He calms down and I untether him. He follows me obediently. What am I going to do with him?

*

Passing in front of the tent where the de Hainaut grenadiers corrupted by Flaharn were bivouacked, I came across the corporal, Bellerose. He was alone and was sorting out the soldiers' bags left there. He turned round when he heard me and recognised me.

'Ah, Lieutenant! Morot saw you on the battlefield this morning, with the general. He asked me to apologise to you and ask you to forgive him. It was commander Flaharn who told him to arrest you.'

'Morot?'

'Our sub-lieutenant.'

'Where is he?'

'He was taken to the field hospital but died on the way.'

'What are you doing here?'

'I was told to come back and make an inventory of my comrades' things. They're all dead. I was the only survivor of the group.'

'Captain Flaharn and his secretary had a fight,' I said. 'They are both dead, over there.'

I pointed to the tent.

'Another death or two makes no difference! And at least nobody will be sorry about those two. Don't worry, Lieutenant. I'll have them picked up. They'll be put in the common grave with the others.'

'That's good!' I replied. 'I don't know what to do with this horse.'

'The secretary called Jakar got it from the English colonel's plantation, where the hospital is.'

'Greenwich?'

'That's it.'

Returning to Greenwich I overtook the carts carrying the wounded. A temporary field hospital had been erected in the clearing where the black regiment from Cap-Français had been bivouacked. I took the horse back to Colonel Mullryne's plantation. I was pleasantly surprised to see that my boatmen had quietly waited for me at Greenwich. They seemed unsurprised to see me come back after such a long time, although it was less than twenty-four hours since I had left. This mystery was explained by my bosun. Perrin told me that a 'gigantic' Ship's Captain had told him the night before that I had been called to the camp at Savannah and that they would have to wait longer than foreseen. It was Flaharn's final deception.

I was immediately handed all the reports written by Ship's Lieutenant de Truguet. They had been brought to headquarters while I was listening to Jakar's last words. It was eleven in the morning. The tide would be ebbing for another three hours and I decided to leave straight away to make the most of it.

The truce was extended during the afternoon and our wounded were evacuated to the field hospital and then to Thunderbolt. The dead were buried in common graves. The English loaned us carts to carry our wounded. The Comte d'Estaing handed over command to the Comte de Dillon and came back to Thunderbolt that same day. General Lincoln, the Americans' commanding officer, asked the French to cover his withdrawal before they embarked. On the evening of 9th October the cannons started thundering once more.

It was not a hasty retreat. We had first to embark our artillery, then withdraw our troops in stages, to get them back on board the ships of the squadron. All this took about ten days.

I made no attempt to find out whether the disappearance of Flaharn and Jakar had aroused any comment in the fleet. Few people knew of my connection with them. I continued carrying the mail until Tuesday 19th October 1779. I then asked permission of the Comte de Brovès to rejoin *l'Amazone*, making the journey aboard the Comte de Lapérouse's boat. I have to say that whereas our land-based withdrawal was quite orderly, the same cannot be said for the re-embarkation aboard our ships. These were moored a long way out to sea, well scattered and a long distance from each other. And in general the elements were against us, with a lot of wind, a high sea and squalls. The sloops sometimes took a whole day to get to their ships. The bad weather forced many crews and their passengers to take shelter aboard ships other than their own, leading to a great confusion. This was made worse by the fact that the ships of the squadron were due to split up after leaving this coast. The Toulon squadron was to return to France, to Brest. The Comte de Lamotte-Picquet's division was to go to Martinique, and the Comte de Grasse's to Saint-Domingue. *L'Amazone* was not staying with the Comte de Lamotte-Picquet but was joining the squadron returning to Brest.

There were still a lot of preparations and repairs to be made before our final departure. We had too to move round the troops who had accidentally ended up on ships whose destination did not correspond with their own. On the 28th we were hit by another gale. In his usual way, the Comte d'Estaing ordered the ships to stay at anchor. It became impossible for the ships to communicate other than by flags, as the sea was too rough for us even to consider launching our boats. During the night, *le Languedoc* dragged and had to cut her cable so as not to fall back onto *le Robuste*. In those sea conditions that catastrophe would certainly have caused a lot of casualties. In theory we should have waited for the return of our Vice-Admiral, but we knew that he had neither a sloop nor an anchor, and so had no choice but to continue on to France. He had on board soldiers from the colonies who had not yet been able to transfer to the ships going to Saint-Domingue. These unfortunates would disembark in winter, at Brest, with nothing but their cotton uniforms.

At last, on 1st November, in a good breeze from the north-west and an easy sea, we left forever this exposed anchorage. Captain Mackenzie had sworn we would not last two or three days there, but we had held for a full two months. But at what price!

The temperatures became wintry as we approached Europe. On 1st December we had a gale from the south-south-west and a terrible sea. Our fleet commander had finally decided to make for Cadiz, the nearest port, as so many men were ill. Scurvy had started to appear at the beginning of December. This was inevitable, as the frigate had not been able to re-provision since leaving Cap-Français. During our long stay at the exposed anchorage off Savannah, all our ships had been concentrated on the maintenance of our troops on land.

On 12th December, at midday, we finally saw the towers of Cadiz to the south-east. The wind fell and we stopped moving. On the 13th, at eleven o'clock, we finally anchored in the Bay of Cadiz and disembarked our sick men. There were three hundred of them, and many would have died within the next few days if we had not managed to get into port in time.

We waited for our orders in the Bay of Cadiz, in the meantime caring for our crews and putting our ships back into order. Our captains wrote their reports. We were told we could add our personal mail to the despatches. I had a big package for Maria Kirwan. Having seen death from so close up at Savannah, I had started to think about her a lot. I had written to her almost every day of our return voyage, piling the letters one atop the other. However I did not want to surrender them at Cadiz. Instead, I wrote to Kermean. I wanted to tell my grandfather that I had at last discovered what had happened to my mother. I told him that she had died the day after the attack on our house at Port-Louis and that I knew where to find her. I promised to give him the full story once we were together again. I told him that my ship was awaiting orders in the Bay of Cadiz, and everybody thought we would be told to make for a port on the west coast of France. I intended to ask permission for leave of absence as soon as we arrived, so that I could find the remains of my mother and take them to Kermean.

Our orders came on 23rd January. Our sick had all recovered by then. That's how it is with this strange disease, the scurvy. One can die of it in three months, but you only need several weeks of clean air and fresh food to recover completely. We were ordered back to Brest.

The Comte de Lapérouse wanted to sail immediately, but the winds were in the west, confining us to port. The Bay of Cadiz was far from empty. On our arrival we had found at the anchorage twenty Spanish ships and four French ships waiting for favourable winds to go and attack Gibraltar. On the 18th January, what remained of Admiral don Juan de Langara's squadron arrived. It had been surprised two days earlier by Admiral Rodney and had been forced to flee towards Cadiz after losing the convoy it was escorting. The English had chased it and caught it up during the night. During the ensuing battle a Spanish ship, *Santo Domingo,* had exploded. There were no survivors. This had caused a great deal of grief in the Spanish Navy.

We also learned that a combined Franco-Spanish fleet of sixty-six ships, under the command of the Comte d'Orvilliers, had the previous summer gone up the Channel in order to support the landing of troops in England. This operation had failed, mainly because an outbreak of typhus had so weakened our squadrons that once they arrived off Portsmouth they were incapable of manoeuvring. The Comte's own son had died in his arms. And, to cap it all, our fleets were pitifully confined in Brest. It was being said in France that the responsibility for this catastrophe lay with the Spanish, as they had taken too long to rendezvous with the Comte d'Orvilliers off Cadiz. The Comte de Lapérouse was saddened by this news. Like all our officers, he had based all his patriotic hopes on this campaign. For my part I was surprised that the King had changed his mind by supporting an invasion that he had initially opposed. Perhaps he had finally ceded to the demands of his Ministers, counsellors, and maybe our Spanish allies. I remembered my conversation with the Chevalier de Kermean at Saint-Malo, during the winter of 1778. To disembark an invasion force on the other side of the Channel was a gamble almost impossible to pull off without a great deal of luck. Of course, I could not share these thoughts with anyone, and I was already sufficiently taken up with my own problems.

On Wednesday 9th February, the winds being in the east, we collected our final orders and sailed at eight in the morning, heading due west. At midday we took our departure, having raised the Saint Sebastian tower to the south-east. The next day we weathered Cape Saint Vincent, with a fine breeze from the south-east and a big swell from the west, the norm hereabouts. The Comte de Lapérouse laid a course to the north-north east, to sail up the coast. We had a fine sea and a north-east wind for the whole of our crossing of the Bay of Biscay, but adverse weather forced us away from Brest. On the 27th February we could make out the island of Groix, off the coast at L'Orient. By midday we were three miles from the high cliffs of Pen Men Point. We tacked back and forth in the tidal race, waiting for the half past three tide, and went through the west passage into L'Orient at the start of the flood. The Navy had wanted us to go to Brest, but the winds had decided otherwise, as if they wanted to bring me closer to my mother. I had tears in my eyes seeing once again these places that held such happy memories of my childhood: the Notre Dame de Larmor tower, which the ships of the India Company saluted with a cannon shot when leaving; the Errants rocks; the old ramparts of the citadel, their feet carpeted in seaweed, along the top of which my mother and I would go to watch my father's ship come in from India. We went into Port-Louis and picked up a coffin buoy in the harbour, between Saint-Michel island, the Kernevel battery and the citadel.

Monsieur de Thévenard, the Naval commander at L'Orient, sent news of our arrival to the Ministry, which decided that *l'Amazone* should stay there to be careened. Our orders said that we would leave for Brest shortly after the big equinoctial tides, with *l'Amazone* re-joining the Chevalier de Ternay's squadron. This squadron was preparing to escort an expeditionary force to America.

Together with these orders was a most unexpected piece of news, that the Comte de Lapérouse wanted to be the first to tell me. There was a round of promotions to Ship's Ensign with effect from 16th February and, although normally I would not qualify, I had been added to the list on the personal recommendation of the Comte d'Estaing. Most of those promoted to Ensign at the same time as I had distinguished themselves by their application to nautical science, and by having recited the complete Bézout to their examiners. As for me, I had earned this early advancement by dint of having sat astride the obstacle on the Spring Hill redoubt while under fire from Colonel Maitland's Highlanders. But few people knew this. Nevertheless I rushed to a master tailor to order a dress uniform and have an epaulette and gilded lapels put on my working uniform, now delightfully faded after six months of campaigning. All that remained was to do some book work to catch up with the other Ensigns. But, first, I had a filial duty to fulfil.

The Comte de Lapérouse had obtained a leave of absence until 20th March 1780 and I asked for leave for the same period.

While waiting for the answer from the Navy Office, I went to L'Orient to look at the archives kept in the former offices of the India Company. Flaharn and Jakar had arrived at L'Orient on board *le Gange,* under a Captain de Kerangal, from Chandernagore, on 14th December 1772. They had not wasted any time! On the 3rd January they went to Kersalaun with their gang of bandits. The Marquis de Kersalaun probably thought Flaharn was dead. His feelings were clear in the sad message he sent to my mother: '*he has returned like a devil vomited out of hell*'.

I was given leave and decided to go straight to Le Croisic by sea. The name Laforest-Dombourg was still well known in Port-Louis; all those years had still not erased the memory of my parents. The tragic fate of my mother had also touched people's hearts. When I went down to the port, with my new epaulette, I was treated like a local boy and had no trouble finding a coasting skipper happy to put me ashore at Le Croisic.

My return to Kermean was more moving than the previous one. My grandfather was alone in his manor house. He would soon be sixty-six, but he still carried his years well. I was surprised by the genuine pleasure he showed on seeing me. He also noticed the scar on my left cheek.

I told him in detail how I had taken up his inquiry into the disappearance of my mother and how I had finally resolved it. I told him almost everything: the Brest jail, François Loutre, Louis Duval, Jakar Singh...

After getting my letter from Cadiz, the Baron had had a coffin made. We set off on horseback, together with Ottmeyer and Jean Leguen, who were leading packhorses and a saddled horse for the Abbot of Kermean, who had asked to come with us. The Chevalier de Kermean was busy with his Court duties and my little sister was still at her convent.

I easily found the chestnut grove with the three oaks in the middle described by Jakar Singh. The tree in which my mother was resting was very old, with a wide trunk. Walking around it, it was not possible to see that it was hollow. I had to climb it and push away the curtain of branches at its top. Only then could I see the beginnings of a sort of pit filled with dead leaves, twigs and stones. I emptied the cavity with the help of Jean Leguen. My mother was there. Together with the remains of her clothes I found a blood-stained sheet. An unknown body usually arouses a revulsion that is hard to suppress. The memory of the pieces of human flesh stuck to the ground of Spring Hill had for a long time kept me awake. It is different for the remains of somebody dear to you. You do not see the exterior of the dead person; you see with the eyes of remembrance, feeling sadness, tenderness and love.

The day before my mother's burial, early in the morning, I went into the chapel with the Baron de Kermean. Using my seaman's skills, I rigged a hoist with blocks fixed to the beams of the vault, to enable us to lift the flagstone under which lay my grandmother. At her feet we found a hardwood chest reinforced with metal straps. My mother had hidden it there during that night in December 1772 when she had watched over the Baroness de Kermean. I took it out and placed it on the stone floor. Although it wasn't light I could lift it easily enough. I no longer had the key that my mother had once shown me. Flaharn must have kept it on him and I had had no wish to search his body. But I had the key for my pistol case. I tried it. The Wheel of Vishnu turned easily. The lock clicked quietly. Jakar Singh had not been wrong. When I lifted the lid of the chest, reflections, glinting like butterflies of light, leapt out into the semi darkness of the chapel. It was filled to the top with diamonds. There were diamonds of every quality, some very big, but all of great purity. They had been cut to perfection by the Dig jewellers. There was much more than the value of a ship of the line right there. You could have fitted out a whole squadron with that treasure!

A piece of paper had been placed in the chest. I recognised my mother's handwriting.

> *This is the treasure of the Raja of Dig. It rightly belongs to his daughter the Princess Jamna, who wishes to take it back to India to re-establish the fortunes of her family. If anything bad happens to me, warn the Marquis Avelus de Kersalaun. He lives on the River Camfrout.*

We remained silent for a while, not knowing what to say at the enormity of what we had just found.

'Laforest-Dombourg,' said my grandfather eventually, 'we are the last people alive to know about this treasure which has caused so many deaths. But what are we going to do with it?'

'It should go to the King, Sir,' I said. 'That was the last wish of the Marquis de Kersalaun.'

I told my grandfather the whole story that I had reconstructed during my investigations since the Chevalier de Kermean had shown me the letter written by my father in Brest harbour, before his final sailing.

'You must go to Versailles yourself to alert the King,' said the Baron. 'The Chevalier de Kermean will help you. But it must be done as discreetly as possible. In the meantime, we will once more entrust this chest to our dear Emilie to keep guard over.'

My beloved mother was buried where she had wished, in the manor chapel beside her own mother and her ancestors. The ceremony was simple. The Baron had added to the flagstone a plaque in commemoration of Ship's Lieutenant Laforest-Dombourg, Chevalier de Saint-Louis, lost at sea. One could have added that he was the grandson of a Micmac chief, but I had said nothing about this to my grandfather. That was my parents' secret, not mine.

The next morning I took a horse from the stable and rode alone to Roche-Bernard, where I posted the package containing all the letters I had written to Maria Kirwan.

LIST OF MAIN CHARACTERS

Real historical figures are indicated by an asterisk*.

THE LAFOREST-DOMBOURG/DE KERMEAN FAMILY

Pierre-Marie Laforest-Dombourg	a young orphan
Anne Laforest-Dombourg	his younger sister
Ship's Lieutenant Jean-François Laforest-Dombourg	his father, lost at sea 1771
Madame Emilie Laforest-Dombourg	his mother, murdered
Baron de Kermean	his maternal grandfather
Baroness de Kermean	his maternal grandmother
Chevalier Jean-Baptiste de Kermean	his elder maternal uncle
Father François de Kermean	his younger maternal uncle
Jean-Baptiste Laforest-Dombourg	his paternal grandfather
*Marquis de Becdelièvre	his Godfather and benefactor

FAMILY SERVANTS

Lénaïc de Lomalo	the Laforest-Dombourg family governess
Nicolas Ottmeyer	the Kermean head groom
Squire Pierre-Jean Henry	the Kermean estate steward
Mélanie	the Kermean estate cook

OFFICERS, ADMINISTRATORS AND POLITICAL FIGURES

*Antoine de Sartine, Comte d'Alby	Secretary of State for the Navy ex-Lieutenant-General of the Paris Police
*Chevalier de Ternay Squadron chief in the French Navy	Witness at Laforest-Dombourg's father's wedding
*Marc-Joseph Marion Dufresne also known as 'Macé'	India Company captain and explorer Witness at Laforest-Dombourg's father's wedding
*Comte de Lapérouse	Naval officer and explorer Witness at Laforest-Dombourg's father's wedding
*Charles-Henri, Comte d'Estaing	Served as both an Army General and Navy Admiral
*Louis Guillouet, Comte d'Orvilliers	Vice-Admiral charged with rebuilding the Navy At this time Navy Commander at Brest
*Marquis de Langeron	Army commander at Brest
*Chevalier de Monteil, Ship's Captain	Commander of the Brest Marine Guards
*Etienne Bézout	Mathematician and examiner who wrote the standard textbooks for Army and Navy cadets
Baron de Kilpinnec	Senior Cadet
Henri Vernon, Chevalier des Aulnes	Fellow-Cadet
Ship's Captain David Flaharn	Laforest-Dombourg's nemesis
*Jean-François Testanières	Governor of the Brest Prison
Ship's Lieutenant de Clesmeur	Section Leader at the Brest Marine Guards
*Comte du Chaffault	Navy Squadron chief then Vice-Admiral
*Marquis de Boulainvilliers	Ship's Captain
*Comte de Boulainvilliers	his son, Marine Guard
*Dr Benjamin Franklin	Polymath and first US Ambassador to France
*Caron de Beaumarchais	Playwright, inventor and speculator
*Chevalier de la Rozière	Military commander of Saint-Malo
*Comte de Broglie	Head of Louis XVI's secret service
*Chevalier de Fleurieu	Ship's Captain and Director of Ports and Arsenals
Fireship Captain Le Meur	Captain of the cutter *le Moucheron*

Frigate's Lieutenant de Kerlaziou	First lieutenant of *le Moucheron*
Monsieur Chollet	Second lieutenant of *le Moucheron*
*Colonel Dumouriez	Distinguished soldier and expert in coastal defence
*Chevalier de Drucourt	Military governor of Louisbourg
*Jacques Necker	Swiss banker and Finance Minister to Louis XVI
*Ship's Ensign Chevalier de la Jonquière	Second captain of *l'Amazone*
*Ship's Captain Taffanel de la Jonquière	His father
*Ship's Lieutenant Mengaud de la Hage	Captain of the frigate *la Gentille*
Lieutenant Frémont	Officer of the Auvergne regiment garrison aboard *l'Amazone*
*Ship's Lieutenant de Tromenec	First lieutenant of *l'Amazone*
Colonel de Guypair, (based on the Comte de Guibert)	Soldier, Academician and writer on military tactics
Baron de Boismorau	Commander of *l'Amazone's* infantry
*Ship's Lieutenant de Truguet	Comte d'Estaing's liaison officer aboard *le Languedoc*
*Vicomte de Noailles	Distinguished soldier and Lafayette's brother-in-law

OTHER CHARACTERS

Marquis Avelus de Kersalaun	Army Lieutenant-Colonel
Princess Jamna de Kersalaun	his wife
Konan Hurennek	his huntsman
Fantig Le Goff/la Fantig	his housekeeper
Nicolas Dugoin	ex-convict
Le Touze	Bosun's mate on *le Formidable* at the Battle of Quiberon Bay
Legouez	Head warder, North Hall, Brest
jail	
François Loutre	Huntsman to Marquis de Boulainvilliers, previously deputy warder, Brest jail
Louis Duval	Ex-merchant navy officer, go-between with Cornish agents

Madec	Nom de guerre of a French mercenary in India
Chapelain de Kerscao	Madec's envoy to the French Court
*Javahir Singh	Raja of Dig, assassinated
Jakar Singh	Indian general, guardian of Javahir Singh's Nephew, Flaharn's accomplice
*Suraj Mal	Javahir Singh's adoptive father
Vicomte de La Croix de Lormes	Father-in-Law of the Chevalier de Kermean
Captain Royer	Captain of the slaver *le Duc de Choiseul*
Monsieur Dubuys	Saint-Malo shipowner
Elizabeth de Malaga	Courtesan and spy
*Jean Régnier	Entrepreneur and shipowner from Granville, Normandy
*Silas Deane	American secret envoy to France
*Mademoiselle Eléonore Broudou	Comte de Lapérouse's fiancée

ABOUT THE AUTHOR

Eric Gautier is descended from a long line of Nantes and Lorient shipowners and was born and raised on the south coast of Brittany. He has been a lifelong recreational sailor and amateur student of French maritime history. He served in the French army alpine regiment for more than thirty years, retiring with the rank of colonel. A talented artist, he has also produced illustrated monographs on the traditional fishing boats of Brittany.

www.ingramcontent.com/pod-product-compliance
Lightning Source LLC
Chambersburg PA
CBHW041749010726
47507CB00009B/339
* 9 7 8 1 7 3 9 2 1 4 2 2 7 *